Midnight

THE SONJA BLUE COLLECTION

Nancy A. Collins

White Wolf Publishers

Midnight Blue: The Sonja Blue Collection
A White Wolf, Inc. Publication

Edited by: Susan Barrows, Robert Hatch and Liz Tornabene
Cover Art: Thom Ang
Cover Design: Michelle Prahler

For information address: White Wolf Publishers, 4598 Stonegate Industrial Boulevard, Stone Mountain, GA 30038.

Published by:
White Wolf Inc.
4598 Stonegate Industrial Blvd
Stone Mountain, Georgia 30083

Publisher: Stewart Wieck
Executive Editor: Staley Krause
Director of Sales: Michael Krause
Director of Marketing: Wes Harris
Marketing: Kim Shropshire
Art Director: Richard Thomas
Graphic Designer: Michelle Prahler

CONTENTS

Sunglasses After Dark

Moon.

Big white moon.

White as milk moon.

You're all I can see from my window, here in the dark. Your light falls silver and white across the walls of my cell. The night-tide surges strong in me. So strong I can feel the grip of their drugs loosen. They fancy themselves high priests. Their gods have names like Thorazine and Lithium and Shock Therapy. But their gods are new and weak and cannot hope to contain me much longer. For I am the handiwork of far more powerful, far more ancient deities. Very soon my blood will learn the secret of the inhibiting factors the white-coated shamans pump into my veins. And then things will be very different, my beautiful moon.

My big moon.

White as milk moon.

Red as blood moon.

the Danger Ward

> Millions of spiritual creatures walk the earth
> Unseen, both when we wake, and when we sleep.
>
> —Milton, *Paradise Lost*

Claude Hagerty's watch played "The Yellow Rose of Texas." Grumbling to himself, he stuck the dog-eared Louis L'Amour paperback in the top drawer of the desk and produced the keys to the Danger Ward from the depths of his orderly's whites. Three o'clock in the morning. Time for his rounds.

Claude had been an orderly for most of his adult life. He'd originally intended to go into pro football, but a bad knee injury in high school put an end to that career before it had the chance to begin. He later discovered that standing 6'3" and tipping the scales at 280 pounds had its distinct advantages in the healthcare field. However, even at the age of thirty-eight, with high school twenty years gone and his midsection devolved into flab, Claude Hagerty was still an impressive specimen.

He started work at Elysian Fields seven years ago, and as funny farms go, it was an okay job. It sure beat the hell out of the state hospital. Elysian Fields didn't waste time on charity cases. The hospital's clients were the sons and daughters, mothers and fathers of prestigious families. The sanitarium specialized in "dependency problems," but for those with relatives whose difficulties tended to be far more serious than a fondness for tranquilizers and vodka, there was the Danger Ward.

The reinforced steel door, painted a festive pastel for the benefit of the visitors, separated the nursing station from the rest of the ward. Claude rolled the barrier back enough to squeeze through. He remembered an old cartoon from his childhood, where a mouse ran in and out of the jaws of a sleeping cat. Funny how he always thought of that when he did his rounds

He walked past the dayroom, where the better-behaved inmates were allowed to watch television and play Ping-Pong during the afternoon. Most were so heavily medicated all they could do was sit and stare at the tube or out the windows. There was no attempt at rehabilitation in the Danger Ward, although no one came right out and said it. Just as no one mentioned the exact reasons why these people were locked up. That was what you paid for. All in all, Elysian Fields wasn't any different from any other private asylum. Except for her.

He grimaced involuntarily. Hell, this used to be an easy shift. Except for a patient having the odd nightmare now and then, there wasn't much for him to worry about. He could catch up on his reading, watch TV, even nap if he felt like it, without worrying about being disturbed.

That was before they dragged her in, six months ago. It had been during his shift; she was bound in a straitjacket and, God as his witness, a length of chain, with four strong men handling her. And still she lashed about, yowling like a wild thing. For a minute it looked as if she would get loose. Claude could still hear the sharp snap of the chain breaking. Then Dr. Wexler was there, syringe in hand, jabbing the needle through the canvas into the woman beneath. She collapsed immediately, motor nerves severed. Judging from the size of the dosage, she should have died. Claude was ordered to carry her into Room 7. That was the first time he touched her. It was enough.

That's when his job got tough. Since that night, his shift had yet to go by without one of the inmates waking up with the night horrors. They all claimed the woman in Room 7 walked into their dreams. They couldn't—or wouldn't—elaborate on the details. Claude described the dreams to Dr. Morial, the ward's on-call psychiatrist. Morial asked him if he liked his job. Claude let it drop.

Life was complicated enough without trying to figure out why a bunch of loonies should fixate on a fellow inmate they had never seen. Or how they could describe her so well. He wondered if the patients were as restless during the day. He didn't think so. *She* wasn't active during the day.

I hear the warder's heavy tread as he checks his charges one by one. It is night and the doctors have fled, leaving the patients alone with their dreams. It's been too long since I could think this clearly. It took me two months to crawl out of madness. Another three passed before my biosystem began to break down the narcotic cocktails they pump into me every day. Their drugs won't do them any good; with every night that passes my immunity grows stronger. My mind is my own again. It's been so long. Perhaps too long.

I fear irreparable damage was done while I was away. The Other has been doing . . . things. I'm not sure what, but I can feel the changes deep inside me. The Other has been free to move unchecked. I have to get out of here before something horrible occurs. I may have already done something. Possibly hurt someone. I can't remember, and I do not want to scan the Other's memory for clues. I'm still weak and could easily become lost in its personality. I cannot risk that. Not now.

The Other's been dream-walking, of that I'm certain. It hasn't gone unnoticed, although I should feel lucky they're only lunatics. No one believes them. No one wants to believe them. I've got to get out of here before I lose control. I haven't fought the Other this long in order to surrender in a madhouse. But I'm so tired. Too receptive. I can feel their dreams pressing in on me, like some great unseen weight. I've become a magnet for their nightmares. That worries me. I've never been able to do this before. What other changes have occurred during my lapse?

The guard is nearing the end of his rounds. I can hear his footsteps echoing in the hall and his ragged breathing. He's a big man. I can smell his sweat. I can taste his fear. He's checking on the inmate next door. It ll be my turn next. He always saves me for last. I guess it's because he's scared of me. I don't blame him. I'm scared of me, too.

Claude's frown deepened as he watched Malcolm whimper in his sleep. Even without medication, Malcolm usually enjoyed the slumber of a child. Now he writhed under the bedclothes, his face blanched and perspiring. His lips moved in feeble protest to some unknown command. He'd be waking up in a few minutes, screaming his lungs out, but Claude knew better than to try to shake the boy awake; the last time he'd tried it he'd damned near lost a finger. Malcolm liked to bite.

Locked in his dream, Malcolm moaned and knotted the sheets with blind fingers. The muscles in his clenched jaw jumped as his teeth ground together.

Claude shook his head and shut the observation plate set into the face of the metal door.

There was only one patient left to check. The one in Room 7. Claude wasn't even sure of her name. The charts and medication logs simply read "Blue, S." She was the last one on his rounds every night, simply because it took him that long to work up the nerve to look at her. Maybe it was different during the day. Perhaps in the sanity of daylight she was just another loony, but he doubted it.

The door to Room 7 was the same as the others, a cheerily painted piece of metal strong enough to withstand a two-ton battering ram. An observation silt, covered with heavy-gauge wire mesh and protected by a sliding metal plate, was set into the door at eye level, although Claude had to stoop a bit to look through it. The interior of Room 7 was radically different from the others on the ward. The other inmates had rooms that—except for the heavy padding on the walls, the narrow high-set windows, and the naked light bulbs locked in impenetrable cages of wire—could be mistaken for suites found in a typical Holiday Inn. Elysian Fields furnished the rooms with unbreakable fixtures and beds with matching designer sheets and restraining gear.

Room 7 was bare of everything but its occupant. There wasn't even a bed. She slept curled up on the padded floor, tucked into the far corner, where the shadows were deepest, like a hibernating animal. At least that's how Claude imagined it. He'd never seen her asleep.

Taking a deep breath, he flicked back the latch on the observation plate and slid it open. Yep, there she was.

Blue crouched in the middle of her cell, her face angled toward the high, narrow window set ten feet from the floor. She was naked except for the straitjacket, her bare legs folded under her as if she were at prayer.

It was hard to tell how old she was, but Claude guessed she couldn't be more than twenty-three. Her filthy hair hung about her face in rattails. None of the nurses wanted to touch her after what happened to Kalish. Not that Claude blamed them.

She knew he was watching, just as he'd known she'd be there, crouching like a spider in the middle of its web. He waited silently for her to acknowledge him, yet dreading it at the same time. It had become a ritual between them.

She turned her head in his direction. Claude's stomach tightened and there was a thundering in his ears. He felt as if he was barreling down a steep hill in a car without brakes. Her eyes locked on him with a predator's guile. She inclined her chin a fraction of an inch, signaling her awareness of his presence. Claude felt himself respond in kind, like a puppet on a string, and then he was hurrying back down the corridor.

In the darkness, Malcolm woke up screaming.

The scene opens on a vast auditorium, its floor jammed with row upon row of metal folding chairs. Wheelchairs clutter the aisles. Behind the raised stage hangs a mammoth banner bearing the likeness of a smiling man. His nose is strong and straight, the cheekbones high, and his wide, toothy grin does not extend to the hawklike eyes nestled beneath the bushy white eyebrows. His silvery mane would be the envy of an Old Testament patriarch.

The eternally smiling man is Zebulon "Zeb" Wheele: Man of God, Healer of the Sick, Speaker of Prophecy, and founder of the Wheeles of God Ministry. The superimposed electronic graphics explain, for those viewing at home, that this "healing event" has taken place in Dallas, Texas, three months previous.

The audience, most of whom are encumbered by canes and walkers, clap and sing hymns while awaiting their chance to be touched by the divine. Many study the huge portrait tapestry, comparing it to the reduced likenesses printed on the back of their programs. The air is heavy with sweat, hope, and anxiety.

Suddenly, the lights go down and a spotlight hits the stage The organ music swells and a figure strides from the wings. It is a woman in a gold lamé pantsuit, her hair shellacked into a Gordian knot. The applause is thunderous.

The woman is Sister Catherine, widow of the late Zebulon Wheele. It is she they have come to see.

Catherine Wheele accepts the welcome, smiling broadly and throwing kisses to the crowd. She takes the microphone from the podium and addresses the faithful.

"Hallelujah, brothers and sisters! Hallelujah! It gladdens my heart to know that the words and deeds of my late husband, the Reverend Zebulon Wheele, are still manifest in the healed flesh and joyful spirits of those who felt the power of Our Lord Jesus Christ through his loving hands! Every day I receive hundreds of letters from y'all out there, telling me how Zebulon changed your lives. The sick made well! The deaf to hear! The blind to see!

"But I also hear from those who say they are forlorn. They are afraid they'll never know the miracle of Jesus' divine mercy, that they'll never see salvation, because Zebulon was"—she struggles to suppress the hitch in her voice—"called to God. Are these poor souls doomed to live their lives in pain and torment, never to know the grace and forgiveness of Our Lord? Say no!"

"No!" Only a few voices respond.

"Is it? Say no!" Her voice becomes harsh and demanding.

"No," the coliseum answers.

"Is it? Say no!"

"*No!*" Two thousand voices—shrill and pure, baritone and falsetto, weak and strong—join together.

Catherine Wheele smiles. She is pleased. Once more she is a pleasant Sunday-school teacher.

"Do not fear, brothers and sisters! While it is true Brother Zebulon is no longer among you, Sister Catherine is here! As Elijah's mantle fell upon Elishah, so was Zebulon's gift passed on to me. At the time of my darling Zeb's tragic death, I received a vision! I saw Zebulon standing between two angels so beautiful it hurt to look at them. Zebulon said, 'Honey, I have to go now, but promise me you'll carry on my work. Promise me that.'

"I said, 'Zeb, I can't do the things you do. No one can!'

"But Zeb just smiled and said, 'As I leave all my earthly things to you, so do I bequeath my gifts! Have faith and the Lord shall see you through!' Can I get an amen on that?"

"Amen!"

"As it was written in First Corinthians, Chapter Twelve, I found myself blessed with the gifts of knowledge and healing! 'To one is given utterance of knowledge according to the same Spirit, to another gifts of healing!' I was overcome by the glory of Christ and I fell to the floor and stayed there all night, crying and praying and blessing my sweet savior. Now I am able to continue my husband's good works, and that's what y'all are here for, isn't it, brothers and sisters? Say yes!"

"*Yes.*"

"I shall not disappoint you, friends. I have mighty big shoes to fill"—she gestures to the banner draped behind her and its lesser brothers hanging from the coliseum's I-beams—"and for me to let you down would be the greatest sin I have ever committed."

The "healing event" then proceeds according to its own peculiar rituals and traditions. The choir sings. Sister Catherine exhorts the crowd to give generously to her crusade to build a Zebulon Wheele Memorial Chapel in his Arkansas hometown. Strapping young men work the crowd carrying large plastic trashcans in place of offering plates. A thirty-nine-year-old woman with "sugar diabetes" is brought from the audience and told to throw down her insulin. She obeys and Sister Catherine grinds the ampules into the floorboards with one deft twist of her high heel. The crowd roars amens. Sister Catherine reminds the congregation to give generously to the Zebulon Wheele Memorial Home for Unwed Mothers. An elderly man suffering from a heart condition is wheeled on stage. Sister Catherine places her hand inches from the man's forehead, then strikes him with the flat of her palm. The man begins to shriek and howl in ecstasy, his arms spinning like pinwheels. Sister Catherine grabs hold of the supplicant and pulls him to his feet. To the amusement of the crowd, the euphoric old man pushes her across the stage in the wheelchair. By the time they reach the speaker's podium, the old man's face is beet-red. Two young men in dark suits with narrow ties and narrower lapels emerge from the wings and hastily escort him into the darkness beyond the lights.

The congregation is well-pleased. They clap and shout and stamp their feet. "Hallelujah! Amen! Praise the Lord!" rebounds from the walls. Sister Catherine accepts their veneration, not a hair out of place, her hands held high. Her gold lamé pantsuit shimmers in the lights from the cameras. Tears of humility smear her makeup, leaving dark trails on her cheeks.

"His will be done! His will be done, brothers and sisters! As it was said in Matthew, Chapter Fifteen: 'Great crowds came to him, bringing with them the lame, the maimed, the blind, and the dumb, and he healed them so that they marveled when the dumb spoke, the maimed became whole, the lame walked, and the blind saw!' Praise God! Praise . . ." Sister Catherine falls abruptly silent, her eyes sweeping the auditorium. "Someone here is in dire need of healing. I can feel that need, calling out to God to ease the pain. I have healed others tonight, but this need is greater than all of those combined. Tell me, Lord. Tell me the name of this afflicted soul, so I might minister to his needs." Sister Catherine lowers her head, seeking divine counsel as she prays into the microphone.

The camera slowly pans the audience as they wait for God to speak to Catherine Wheele. Who will it be? Who will be called out to be healed? There are many worthy of attention. The ushers made sure they were seated in the front rows, where the camera could see them. The cameramen linger on particularly pathetic cases: an elderly woman so twisted by osteoporosis she sees nothing but her feet, a drooling microcephalic supported on either side by his parents, a once-pretty girl who fell from her boyfriend's motorcycle and slid twenty feet across an asphalt road facedown. The camera studies these deformities of accident and nature with the eye of a connoisseur.

Catherine Wheele's head snaps up. Her voice is tight with excitement. "Is there a George Belwether here tonight? George Belwether of 1005 Hawthorne?"

The crowd murmurs among itself as everyone turns in their seats to see who will rise and go to be healed. No one doubts there is a body to go along with the name and address. She always knows.

A fragile-looking man seated near the front stands up. The same young men who helped the old man with the heart condition, or their twins, move from the base of the pulpit and into the congregation. Flashes of gold at their wrists leave smears of light on the camera's retina. Their eyes are shielded from the klieg lights' glare by expensive designer sunglasses.

The man they escort from the audience is dying of cancer. He stands between the healthy young men, his flesh the color of bad meat. Chemotherapy has robbed him of his hair and most of his teeth; it is impossible to say if he is young or old. By the time they reach the podium, the man is visibly exhausted.

Sister Catherine rests one hand on his shoulder. Her manicured fingernails, lacquered until they shine like fresh blood, grip the man's ill-fitting suit.

"Brother, how long has the cancer afflicted you?" She thrusts the microphone into his face.

Belwether forces his eyes from the mammoth visage of Zebulon Wheele hanging from the ceiling. "Five years, Sister Catherine."

"And what did your doctors say?"

"It's inoperable. I only have a few months, maybe weeks . . ."

The crowd moans in sympathy, like the prompted gasps of surprise and envy heard on game shows.

"Have you tried everything, Brother George?"

Belwether's balding head bobs up and down. "Chemotherapy, laetrile, crystals, fire-walking, channeling . . ."

"But have you tried God, brother?" Her voice develops an admonishing edge. Once more the microphone is thrust into his trembling face.

"No, not until now . . . not until tonight!" Tears stream down the dying man's face. The camera moves in closer; his pallid features fill the screen. "Help me, Sister Catherine! I don't want to die . . . Please . . ." His hands, as thin and flaccid as an old woman's, clasp hers. His sobs threaten to knock him to the floor.

"Do you believe in the Lord God Jesus Christ's power to bring the dead to life, to make the blind see, the deaf hear, and the lame well again?"

Belwether presses his cheek against her fingers, his eyes welded shut by tears.

"IbelieveIbelieveIbelieve."

"And are you prepared, Brother George, to accept the Ultimate Healing?"

He nods, overcome by emotion. The congregation mutters knowingly.

Catherine Wheele motions for one of the stagehands to take charge of the microphone and her gold lamé jacket. The camera pulls back to get a better view of the miracle. She grasps the dying man's shoulders, forcing him to kneel before her, his back to the audience. The congregation holds its collective breath; the Ultimate Healing is the reason they attend services. Even in his heyday, Zebulon Wheele never attempted anything so grandiose and controversial.

After rolling back her sleeves, she raises her right hand above her head, splaying the fingers and rotating the palm so everyone can see it is empty. Her hand remains suspended, the muscles in the forearm twitching and jumping like live wires. Then her hand plunges downward, like an eagle diving to snatch its prey, and disappears into George Belwether.

The supplicant's mouth opens so wide the skin threatens to split and reveal the skull beneath. There is no sound. His head snaps backward until the crown nearly touches his spine. His eyes roll in their sockets and his tongue jerks uncontrollably. The audience cries out in horror.

It is impossible to tell if George Belwether is being eviscerated or having a powerful orgasm. The front of his torso is hidden from the lens of the camera, but it looks as if she is rummaging around in an empty gunnysack.

With a yell of triumph, Catherine Wheele removes her arm from the dying man's stomach. Her bare arm is slick with blood and bowel juices. The congregation comes to its feet, roaring their approval and shouting her name over and over. The thing she holds aloft is a grayish-black lump the size of a child's softball. It pulses and twitches in her grip. Belwether lies at her feet, showing no sign of movement. The young men reappear and drag him off stage. The rubber tips of his shoes leave skid marks on the stage's waxed surface.

A stagehand hurries on camera with a silver washbasin and a white towel. Another stagehand pins a lapel mike onto her vest so she can speak as she cleanses herself.

"See, brothers and sisters? See what belief in the Word of God can do for you? See what the power of Jesus Christ Our Lord is capable of if only you open up your hearts and accept His divine glory? Thus sayeth the Lord: 'He who Believeth in me shall not perish, but shall have Everlasting life!' and if y'all don't want to perish, brothers and sisters at home, send me your love offering and I shall protect you from the diseases of sin and Satan, just as my husband did before me. Send us your seed gifts, and remember, that which you give to the Lord shall be returned to you tenfold! So send us twenty dollars, or ten dollars, or whatever you can, brothers and sisters! Don't let doubt enter your mind. Act today! If you doubt, then you are lost to Jesus! Pick up your phone and give ol' Sister Catherine a call!"

An electronic superimposure comes on the screen, explaining how the check and money orders should be made out and what major credit cards are accepted, should the audience at home wish to call the toll-free Love Offering Hotline. Operators standing by.

"Jesus Christ," muttered Hagerty, thumbing the off button on the TV set. Sister Catherine and her congregation became the dwindling white dot in the middle of a cathode tube.

Hagerty wondered, not for the first time, what the hell was wrong with him. Here he was, spending his waking hours among psychotics, paranoid-schizophrenics, neurotics, and compulsive personalities of every possible persuasion, so why waste his time watching a bunch of religious kooks who'd escaped diagnosis and bought themselves a TV studio?

Claude massaged his eyes. Deep down part of him was fascinated by the sleazy geek-show theatrics and cheap tricks. In a lot of ways it was not unlike watching wrestling. But the truth was that he was watching in order to keep from falling asleep.

Moving from behind the nursing station, Hagerty unplugged the little portable black-and-white set and carried it back into the staff lounge. He hated watching television in the lounge—especially alone at night. The damned vending machines hummed and clicked constantly. Claude always had the feeling they were conspiring among themselves.

There was a long, well-padded sofa located just inside the door. How nice it'd be to take a nap. He shook his head to clear it. No way! He stuck a quarter in the coffee dispenser and selected black, straight up. As if to give credence to his suspicions concerning vending-machine malice, the paper cup dropped through the chute at an angle, and before he could act to correct it, the hot coffee sluiced out, splashing his crotch, the legs of his trousers, and the floor.

"Great! Just fuckin' great!"

After mopping up the spilled coffee and dabbing halfheartedly at his pants with a wad of wet toilet paper, Claude returned to his post. He was still sleepy.

Hagerty wasn't afraid of being discovered asleep on the job. He'd spent many shifts sacked out, his feet propped in an open drawer, but that was before the nightmares. That was the real problem.

He would be on the verge of drifting into deep sleep, where the senses ignore the outside world and react to signals generated by the mind. It always started there, for some reason. Hagerty's conscious mind, still striving for control, would realize he was starting to dream. Suddenly, he wasn't alone anymore. He couldn't see what it was that was sharing his dreams; it moved too fast, a hint of movement at the corner of his mind's eye, made of shadow and chaos. He could see its eyes, though, reflecting light like those of a cat caught in the headlights of a car. He wanted to tell it to leave, but he was too far into dreamtime to make a sound.

The shadow thing scurried through his brain, digging with the frantic energy of a burrowing rodent. When it finished ransacking his mind, it became very still, as if sensing Hagerty's awareness for the first time. And then it would smile.

Claude always woke up at that point, his limbs tingling as if from a mild electric shock.

Maybe he was going insane. All those years being exposed to crazy people were bound to have an effect, like water dripping on a stone, gradually eroding it away. His brain probably looked like the Grand Canyon.

He didn't feel insane, but that's how it starts; you're perfectly normal except for one little obsession, then—whammo!—you're wearing hats made out of aluminum foil so the men from Planet X can't see into your head and read your thoughts.

But he knew he wasn't crazy. There was something wrong with Blue, S. Something no one wanted to acknowledge, much less talk about. Kalish was proof of that.

Hagerty didn't like thinking about the last time he saw Kalish. And without meaning to, he began to doze.

He was at work. He wasn't supposed to be there. It was his night off. He'd been bowling with some friends. Out late. Left something at work. Couldn't remember what. Decided to stop by and check his locker. It was after midnight when he got to Elysian Fields.

Went to the locker room. Surprised to see Red Franklin going off-shift. Red was supposed to be filling in for him. Red said there'd been a change in the schedule. Archie Kalish ended up pulling Claude's shift.

The dream memory begins to speed up and slow down at the same time. Kalish. The damned fools put Kalish in charge! His heart began pumping faster. He didn't want to go to the Danger Ward. He knew what he'd find there. But his dream pulled him down the corridor of memory. Maybe if he was faster, this time things would be different. His movements were slow and clumsy, as if he were moving underwater. The elevator took an eternity to arrive, the doors opening in slow motion. Hagerty wanted to scream at it to hurry up.

He shoved his hand into his trouser pocket, searching for the key ring that would give him access to the Danger Ward. His arm went in up to the elbow. His pocket had been replaced by a black hole. He reached farther down until his shoulder was level with his hip. His fingertips brushed cold metal and he withdrew the keys. His fingers were numb from being in the black hole and he had to struggle to keep from dropping the keys. Fumbling, he finally located the circular key that fit into the recessed override lock that would take him to the Danger Ward.

The elevator groaned and began its sluggish movement upward. Hagerty cursed and pounded his fists against the walls, trying to hurry the damn thing along.

Kalish! The idiots left Kalish up there. Alone. Unsupervised. Hagerty had no love for the bastard. It was rumored he abused patients, like poor Mrs. Goldman. And the brain-dead teenager in Ward C. The one who'd smacked her head into a dashboard at 80 mph. The one who turned up pregnant.

The doors of the elevator opened like a wound. The Danger Ward was dark, the only light coming from the empty nursing station. Claude moved forward, his feet adhering to the floor with every step. His muscles strained until he thought they'd tear from their moorings. His clothes were plastered to his skin.

The gate was unlocked, but had somehow trebled its weight. Dozens of voices were raised in mindless sound. As he continued down the hall, he separated individual words and occasional sentences from the verbal chaos.

"Mamamamama. . ."

"Blood . . . see blood . . . on the walls . . . the halls full . . . flood of blood . . . "

"They're here! I can feel them! Make them stop, please . . .

"Go away, go away, I don't want you here, go away . . ."

"Get her out of me! Get her out!"

Time expanded. Every heartbeat was an hour. Every breath a week. He could see his arm stretching out, his hand reaching for the door handle of Room 7. It took a year for his fingers to lock around the knob. Two years for it to turn in his grip. It was unlocked. Of course.

The door swung open and Hagerty saw he was too late. He would always be too late.

It was dark in Room 7. Unfortunately, there was still enough light for him to see what was going on.

Kalish was sprawled on his back, arms and legs akimbo. His pants and underwear were snarled around his ankles. He still had his shoes on. His legs were pale and skinny. Kalish's penis lay cold and wet against his thigh like an albino slug. Hagerty couldn't see Kalish's face because the room's tenant was kneeling over the body, her head tucked between its right shoulder blade and neck.

Time snapped and Hagerty found himself speeding toward the woman in the straitjacket. Grabbing her by the shoulders, he pulled her off the corpse and held her at arm's length. He caught a glimpse of Kalish's face and the shredded mess where his throat should have been.

Claude pinned the struggling madwoman against a wall, making sure her feet cleared the floor. Her screams, twisted by memory and dreamtime, began to echo inside his head.

When he was a kid he used to spend his summers on his grandparents' farm in Mississippi. During one of his vacations a swamp cat went rogue and terrorized the community, killing chickens and neighborhood pets. When an itinerant field-worker was found badly mauled in a ditch outside of town, the farmers formed a hunting party and chased the panther into a canebrake. Rather than risk their prize coon dogs by sending them after the big cat, they decided to set the field ablaze. The panther was roasted alive, screaming its rage and pain like a demon in hell.

The crazy woman opened her mouth, and the burning panther's yell came out.

All he could see of her face, hidden by a filthy tangle of hair, were eyes that resembled twin bullet holes. His throat burned with bile, but he managed to keep his grip on her.

What now? He couldn't hold her until the day shift showed up. And if he let go, she'd be on him before he could make it to the door. His arms ached as if skewers pierced his biceps.

A white-sleeved arm snaked around his left shoulder. Light glittered off glass and sterile steel as the syringe punctured the straitjacket and the flesh underneath. The woman shrieked, then went limp. Claude stepped away and allowed her to drop to the floor. She looked like a mistreated rag doll.

Dr. Wexler pushed Hagerty aside, kneeling beside the straitjacketed patient. Her head lolled back and for one brief moment Claude found himself looking into the eyes of an animal with its leg in a trap. Then he saw the blood on her mouth. As he watched, her tongue wriggled between her bloodied lips and licked them clean, like a cat grooming itself after the hunt.

Wexler glanced up at him. "Good job . . . Hagerty, isn't it? Good job." As he stood, Wexler wiped the palms of his hands against his pant legs. "Of course, none of this happened."

Wexler wasn't really looking at him. Claude turned to see two young men in dark suits and sunglasses dragging Kalish's body from the room by its ankles.

Wexler cursed out loud. He was staring at the drugged madwoman in undisguised disbelief. "She's coming to."

A high-pitched whine came from the woman in the straitjacket. Rocking from side to side, she rolled onto her stomach. Using her head for a prop, she inched her knees forward, looking like a Muslim at prayers. She turned her face toward Wexler and growled. Her upside-down grin was enough to make Claude back away.

The heavy door slammed behind Hagerty. He felt very cold, despite the sweat running down his back. Something thudded against the door from the other side.

Time melted and he was sitting in an all-hours joint near his house, trying to blot out sounds and sights. An old man hawking newspapers moved from table to table, selling the morning edition. Hagerty bought one and read about Kalish's second, official death.

Local Man Found Burned To Death In Car

I am drowning in the dreams of madmen.

I can feel them pressing against my brain, a dozen insistent ghosts with empty eyes and prying fingers. For the first time since I've reclaimed my flesh, I realize the extent of the Other's evolution. If I had remained doped any longer it would have been too late. I would never have found my way back and everything would be lost. Now I have the ability to shape nightmares. It is a power I do not want or relish, but the Other loves it.

I do not have the strength or the knowledge to block their dreams. The Other knows I can't—I won't—let it surface long enough to control the problem. I'm being pulled down by the undertow.

A smiling young man with the face of a bible student and the eyes of a reptile puts out a cigarette on the naked crotch of a four-year-old boy whose screams are warped and swallowed by the vacuum of dreamtime . . . I am surrounded by twisted mountains and weirdly sculpted buttes; the earth is a cracked spiderweb of baked red clay, where animals and people are staked out on the desert's floor. Horses, pregnant women, men in business suits, dogs, old ladies—they're all doused in kerosene; a man stands in the middle and laughs as he clicks his Zippo over and over and over . . . Walking through an empty house, where the doors are ajar I can see things crouching in the dimness, waiting for me to make the mistake of entering, but I'm afraid to stay in the corridors because I know something will jump out and grab me if I don't hide . . . Tied to an iron bedstead, hands manacled above my head, there is a figure made of leather standing at the foot of the bed; the leather demon is covered with zippers and spikes. As it lifts a hand to caress my face, I see the scalpels growing from its knuckles . . . and I start to laugh because I know I'm in a dream, but it's not me who is laughing; it's the Other. I try to run away because the Other is coming and I need to escape the dreamtime before it gains full control, but I get lost . . . Explosions of lava . . . animals that speak . . . letters in wax melt into walls of blood . . . the sound of the Second Angel crying like a hungry child . . . cadavers smeared with quicklime and cinders . . . burning dogs hanging from lamp posts . . . I'm standing in a barren room, staring at a tall, thin man dressed in institutional pajamas. He looks pissed.

"Get out of my head, bitch."

I've got to get out of here. The Other is free.

How pathetic. Minor-league monsters strutting and performing in their private Grand Guignols. How fucking lame. You want fear? You want terror? You want to see what it's *really* like?

You used to know, before they caught you and threw you in this playpen. Now you have to dream about blood and pain instead of living it out. You're no longer free to actualize the perfection of your private hells on the flesh of your victims. But that's the way life is. Once you're caught, assholes, you're at the mercy of others. Welcome to your nightmares.

The leather demon moved to strike the woman manacled to the bedframe. Laughing was not allowed. Screaming and begging for mercy, yes, but laughing was strictly forbidden. It raised its bristling fist in anticipation of slicing through unresisting flesh. The woman shrugged, indifferent to the threat, and the manacles fell away like cheap plastic toys. The leather demon faltered, realizing for the first time that the course of the dream had been altered. The woman was on her feet, and her hands attacked the demon's shiny black leather shell.

The face mask was a mass of fetish zippers. She ignored them, digging her fingers into the top of its skull and pulling downward with the ease of a woman peeling an orange. The leather demon started to struggle as its head split open, the husk parting to reveal empty air. There was no blood, no flesh. It raised a groping hand to where its head should have been. The scalpels and bits of jagged metal grafted to its knuckles began to rust away, turning into oxidized flakes of corrosion. Its body jerked crazily as the dream thing died, spurting invisible blood.

The Other strolled into the next dreamscape. At first there was only fire, then the inferno lessened and she could see the things that were burning.

A wino dressed in rags and doused in kerosene rolled on the ground, clawing at the flames that ate his hair and skin. His face was a riot of heat blisters and broken capillaries. A dog, its tail alight, raced madly from place to place, howling in dumb, uncomprehending pain. A curtain of flame parted to reveal a family of Puerto Ricans crouching against the red earth. The parents had the children clustered around them, and although their mouths never opened, the Other could hear the wailing of frightened infants and violent coughing.

The Other found the dreamer squatting in the heart of the fire. He was dressed in white and there wasn't a drop of sweat marring his linen suit.

The Other smiled at him and laughed even louder when he recoiled. He tried to squirm away by shifting dreams, but the Other was too fast for him to escape her so easily. She clamped her hands around his wrists, pulling him to his feet. She felt him shiver in revulsion as she pressed her mouth to his.

The dreamer began to sweat. The first beads broke out on his forehead and upper lip. Within seconds he was soaked in perspiration, his lips cracking from dehydration. A wisp of smoke rose from his collar. His pant leg ignited with a polite cough. He struggled desperately to free himself. The Other shook her head as if admonishing an unruly child. His hair ignited with a dry crackle and blisters rose on his face with the speed of time-lapse photography.

By the time his eyes boiled in their sockets, the Other had grown bored and was looking for fresher game.

She walked into Malcolm's dream, trailing shreds of black leather and the acrid odor of smoke in her wake. She knew what she'd find Malcolm doing. He'd become her favorite over the past few weeks. Malcolm possessed a surprising wealth of fear and evil. More than enough to go around.

Malcolm was putting alligator clips on a nine-year-old girl's nipples. She was sitting upright, her girl-scout uniform hanging in tatters about her waist. He'd bound her hands behind her back with the badge sash and stuffed the beret in her mouth. Her face was made up like a *Vogue* model's.

The Other placed a hand on Malcolm's shoulder, easing herself into the rhythm of his dream.

Malcolm began to dwindle. He whimpered, trying to shield himself, and prayed he would wake up soon. The Other's laughter grew deeper as her features flowed into coarser, far more familiar contours. The Other towered over him like a mountain; its voice was thunder, shaking him to the marrow.

"Come on, Malcolm. Time to play with Daddy."

Claude was still in the after-hours joint, staring at Kalish's death notice. He was startled when a sixteen-year-old girl popped into existence in the chair opposite him.

"Are you awake?" was the first thing she asked him.

Taken aback, Claude had to think about it before answering. "No, I don't think so."

“Damn! Then I’m still dream-walking. I need to get back before she gains control.” The girl got to her feet and began to pace the confines of Hagerty’s dreamscape. She turned and stared hard at him. “You’re not one of the patients, are you?” It wasn’t a question.

“No, I work here . . . I mean, at Elysian Fields. Hell! Why should I bother explaining myself to a dream?”

“Am I?”

“What else could you be? You’re not that god-awful nightmare. At least I don’t think you are.”

The girl stopped smiling. “She’s been here? In your dreams?”

Claude felt his conscious mind starting to rebel. He didn’t want to dream anymore, but his subconscious was forcing the issue. The walls of the club began to melt. The girl drew her legs under herself and floated in midair, hands locked across her knees. There was something familiar about her, but Hagerty couldn’t place it.

“Pretend you never saw us. Pretend we never existed. Leave this place and go somewhere nice and peaceful, Claude Hagerty . . .”

“How do you know my name?”

“You created me, didn’t you? I’m your dream, aren’t I?”

She fell silent, as if listening to something far away. Hagerty thought she was beautiful. “I’m afraid I can’t stay. She’s in control now. And she’s decided it’s time to go.” The girl unwrapped herself and kicked upward, soaring through layers of dream with the ease of a championship swimmer.

Hagerty moved to follow, but his feet were mired in syrup. “Wait! Tell me who you are! Are you the woman in Room 7?”

She did not pause in her ascent, but her voice sounded as if she was standing beside him. Or in him.

“My name is Denise Thorne. Her name is Sonja Blue.”

Time to go.

She’d had enough of this place, with its endless drugs and intravenous feedings. Her defenses against the narcotics were complete. The madhouse was not without diversions, but they did not justify delaying her departure.

Time to go.

She stood up, tossing matted hair out of her eyes. She felt the drugs as her system purged the intruders from her bloodstream, reducing them to phantoms. Her mind was clear and her body her own. She could hear Malcolm as he wept in his sleep. She smiled and shrugged her shoulders once. Twice. The canvas fabric fell away, revealing naked white flesh. She lifted her arms, studying the scars studding the inner forearms. They had not bothered to trim her fingernails during her imprisonment. Good. She’d need them.

Moonlight limned her in silver and shadow, beckoning her to leave. She sank her nails into the padding of the wall and chuckled as it tore in her grasp. Lizardlike, she scaled the wall of her prison until she was level with the window. It was three inches thick, interwoven with wire mesh, designed to withstand repeated blows from a sledgehammer. It took four blows from her right fist for it to break, although every finger in her hand shattered on the third try. She pulled herself through the narrow window into the darkness, midwife to her own rebirth. Her ribs groaned then snapped as she forced herself through the opening, spearing her left lung. She spat a streamer of blood into the night air.

She clung to the brick face of the building, luxuriating in the feel of cold air rushing past her naked flesh. For the first time in months, she was alive. The wind caught her laughter, sending it across Elysian Fields' grounds. Behind her she could hear the Danger Ward's inmates shrieking and wailing as their nightmares dumped them back into the reality of their madness. Her right hand was beginning to burn, but she was used to pain. It would pass.

Sonja Blue began to crawl, headfirst, down the wall of the madhouse.

Claude Hagerty woke to find himself standing outside Room 7, the keys in his hands. He came to his senses with a startled intake of breath. A wave of disorientation struck him and he reached for the doorframe to steady himself. Looking down the corridor, he could see the security gate standing open.

Then he heard the patients. How could he have slept through that, much less sleepwalk?

The dream was still with him. He could see the young girl with the honey-blonde hair, dressed in clothes that were just coming back into style. He saw the sadness in her eyes and heard the weariness in her voice. What was it she had said?

She's decided it's time to go now.

Hagerty unlocked Room 7 and pushed the door open. He wasn't concerned about the patient escaping or worried about getting hurt. He already knew what he'd find.

The straitjacket lay on the floor like an empty snakeskin. He tracked the vertical rips in the canvas wall padding. Cotton ticking oozed from the rents. Cool air gusted into the room, dispelling the closeness. Even in the half-dark he could make out the jagged teeth of the broken safety glass lining the window. The blood drying on the wall was the color of shadow.

Affidavit of William "Billy" Burdette, Night Manager of Hit-n-Git #311

Burdette: Look, I told you guys this shit five times already. If you don't believe me, why don't you give me one of them lie-detector tests?

Officer Golson: It's for our files, Mr. Burdette. We have no reason to doubt your account of what happened. We just simply need to have it transcribed by a departmental steno, that's all. It'll save you from coming back downtown should we have any further questions . . .

Burdette: Oh . . . all right! So where do you want me to begin?

Officer Golson: Start from the beginning, Mr. Burdette.

Burdette: Huh? Oh, okay. Uh, my name is William Burdette, I work at the Hit-n-Git over on Claypool. I'm the night manager there and I work the graveyard shift—that's from eleven at night to seven in the morning—by myself. It's a rough part of town. Lots of street people and junkies. I've been held up a couple of times before this. This morning, I guess it was around 4 a.m.. I was in the back of the store, near the canned-food section, when she comes in. We've got one of them chimes that goes off when someone comes through the doors. So I look up and see this bag lady come in. I think, Oh, great! That's all I need is some old scuzz coming in and tracking up my store! So's I put up my mop and go behind the counter so I can keep an eye on things, right? But when I get up front I sees she's no bag lady. At least I don't think so. She's real young—early twenties, maybe—and she's wearing these grungy clothes that look like she took them off a wino or something.

Officer Golson: Could you describe what she was wearing in more detail, Mr. Burdette?

Burdette: Oh, sure. Let's see . . . Well, the shirt was a long-sleeved flannel jobbie, like they give out at the mission. It was three sizes too big for her and she had the sleeves rolled up over her elbows. That's how I seen them marks up and down her arms.

Officer Golson: Marks? You mean the type left by hypodermic needles?

Burdette: Yeah, I guess, so. I didn't get too good a look. And she was wearing a pair of tan workpants a size too big for her. They were seriously gross . . . smeared with mud and God knows what else. I noticed she weren't wearing no shoes. Her hair was hanging down in her face and it was real long and dirty, like it hadn't been washed in a month of Sundays. She was one fucked-up chick, I can tell you. I'm used to the junkies wandering in at all hours. But what was weird about this chick was what she didn't do. Most junkies usually head straight for the snacks and load up on Cheetos, Chocodiles, Suzy Qs, Popsicle Bombs . . . that kind of crap.

But this one went to the far aisle, where we got this carousel rack full of sunglasses, and started trying on shades. She had her back to me and hair in her face, so I never got a real good look at her head-on, but I watched her try on a few of them. She moved kind of jerky. Real weird. I knew she was going to try to steal some shades. Didn't have to be Sherlock to figure that one out. I was so busy watching her, I didn't notice the guy who walked in at, oh, I guess it must have been half-past.

I heard the door chime and glanced up, long enough to see it was some white guy. I was keeping an eye on the junkie when the next thing I know there's this sawed-off staring me right in the face. The white guy says, "Hand over what's in the register." I forgot all about the girl. All I could see is that damned shotgun. So's I open the till. I got forty bucks and some food stamps, and that's about it. I give it to the holdup man and he says, "That's all?" I know right then he's going to wipe me. I can hear it in his voice and see it in his eyes. He was going to blow me away because I didn't have enough money. I had this picture of my brains getting splattered all over the cigarette display and dripping off the funny-book rack.

Then I hear this . . . noise. Sounds like cats being boiled alive. For a minute I think the cops are coming. Then I realize it's coming from inside the store! I remembered the junkie was still there. I don't think the holdup guy even knew she was in the store. He turns around and shoots blind, blowing hell out of my Dr Pepper display. That's how I got this cut on my cheek, from flying Dr Pepper glass.

Anyways, the junkie chick runs at the dude like she's going to tackle him, and all I can think is that she's going to get us both killed. She's screaming her head off when she plows into him. Now you got to understand, this guy was big. An ex-jock or a biker or something. And she takes him out! Drives her left shoulder blade into his gut and grabs his gun hand at the same time and forces it back. That's when the second barrel went off, knocking that damn big hole in the ceiling. Damn thing went off inches from my head. Felt like someone up and hit me with a two-by-four! Guess that's when I blacked out, because the next thing I know there's a cop bending over me asking me if I'd been hurt. My ears were still ringing pretty bad and it took me a while before I could hear good enough to understand what people were asking me. I guess I was in shock or something, because I kept asking the paramedics about the girl. They didn't know what the fuck I was talking about.

When I got up off the floor, all I saw was a bunch of shattered Dr Pepper bottles. No dead girl. No blood. The stickup man's gun was on top of the counter, wrapped in a plastic bag. The cop that found me said it had been on the floor. I couldn't figure it out. Then I saw the doors.

You see, the store's got these swinging glass doors. During the day both of them are unlocked, but after midnight I lock one side so's I can keep better track of who's coming in and going out, see? Both them doors were hanging off their hinges and there was busted glass all over the parking lot! Locked like someone rode a motorcycle through them . . . from inside the store!

I don't know what the hell she was on, but judging from them doors, I'm glad I didn't get in her way. That's all I can tell you about what went on, save that I never saw her before and I hope I'll never see her again. I'm quitting this chicken-shit job.

Officer Golson: Mr. Burdette, what exactly was stolen from your store?

Burdette: Well, the money the holdup guy took from the till was scattered on the floor, near the gun. So the only thing I know for sure was taken from the store was a pair of sunglasses. The mirrored kind. And that's only because I saw her wearing them just before she plowed into the asshole.

Officer Golson: You're sure that's all that was stolen? A pair of mirrored sunglasses?

Burdette: You got it.

Irma Clesi opened the door to her apartment. She was dressed in a shapeless housecoat and fluffy houseshoes, her head lumpy with rollers.

Five-thirty in the god-damned morning! Every day for twelve years she woke up at five-thirty so she could fix that lazy slob's breakfast. And what thanks did she get for sending him off to the factory with something beside cold cereal in his gut? A kiss? A hug? A simple "Thanks, honey"? No fucking way. The bastard didn't even have the common decency to offer to take out the garbage.

Irma Clesi struggled down the front stairs, cursing her husband, Stan, under her breath, the shiny black bag bouncing against her thighs with each step. Metal cans and glass bottles clanked in the predawn quiet.

The trash cans for their apartment complex were set flush with the pavement, the lids opened by foot pedals. It was an old, uniquely urban form of trash collection. Irma wasn't sure how the garbage men got the cans out; Stan claimed they used special hooks to lift the aluminum containers out of their dens. Irma didn't really care, just as long as it kept the neighborhood dogs from scattering trash all over the sidewalk.

Irma's left houseshoe, a wad of pink synthetic cotton candy, slammed down on the pedal and the trash can's lid popped up. Irma caught the lip of the cover with her hand and opened it further, leaning over to drop the plastic bag full of coffee grounds, beer bottles, and chili cans into the hole in the sidewalk.

There was someone looking up at her from inside the trash can.

A man in his early thirties, his long hair bunched around his face, lay crumpled in the Clesis' rubbish bin. Whatever it was that killed him had stuffed his corpse into the garbage bin a couple of hours earlier, for now his limbs were stiffened into obtuse angles, like those of an abstract sculpture.

Irma dropped the lid and her bag of garbage. Her screams were short but explosive as she ran back to the safety of her apartment.

The neighborhood dogs, drawn by the aroma of chili, tore at the plastic bag, spilling garbage all over the sidewalk.

Claude Hagerty sat in his booth at the Cup 'n' Saucer, a greasy spoon specializing in the early breakfast trade. He'd been taking his breakfast there for twelve years and the waitresses knew him on sight. A plate with two eggs sunny-side-up, biscuits, and hash browns with country gravy appeared without his having to order.

The morning newspaper was unfolded before him, the updated edition having hit the stands just after he got off work. He stared at the front page while his eggs congealed, searching for traces of her passing. He found it on page three: Man Sought In Connection With Armed Robbery Found Dead In Trash Can.

Claude shut the newspaper, resting his brow on the heel of his palm. His stomach roiled and the sight of breakfast made him even queasier. He was back at Elysian Fields, listening to Dr. Wexler have hysterics.

Wexler was a tall, tanned, conventionally handsome man in his late fifties who looked like his dust jackets. Except when he was angry. And he'd been real angry at four o'clock in the morning. Angry enough to fire Claude for "not doing his job."

Tired as he was, Hagerty couldn't bring himself to go home and sleep. Something was eating at him. He couldn't help but feel that he'd been given a clue, but he was too stupid to recognize it. His dream had faded during the excitement and recriminations following Blue, S.'s escape, and his attempts to recall the details met with frustration. As he sat and stared at the columns of newsprint, Claude's vision blurred and his mind began to drift.

"Denise Thorne."

The voice sounded as if someone had spoken in his ear. Claude started awake with a muffled shout. Several of the Cup'n' Saucer's patrons stared at him. He pulled himself out of the booth and left a ten-dollar bill next to his untouched meal.

His mother, bless her, had tried her best to get him to use his brains and not just rely on his brawn. And, to a certain extent, she had succeeded. Claude was a voracious reader, and he was familiar with the public library.

He was the first one through the library doors. He'd had to wait an hour before they opened, but he used the time to read the newspaper from front to back, attempting to find further evidence of her activities. He'd even scrutinized the want ads and lost-dog notices. Except for the dead man stuffed in the trash, he could not find anything he could link to her. That made him feel a little better.

He checked in the subject catalog and found a single entry for Thorne, Denise. It was a nonfiction book called *The Vanishing Heiress*. When he had no luck locating it in the stacks, he asked one of the librarians where it might be. The woman checked her computer terminal and scowled.

"I'm sorry, sir. That book was checked out over six months ago and it's never been returned. People can be so thoughtless. The computer says it's an out-of-print book, so there's no chance of us being able to reorder it . . ."

"There aren't any other books on Denise Thorne?"

"No. That's the only one I've ever heard of."

Hagerty's hands curled into fists. It was all he could do to keep from smashing them against the countertop.

"However, you could check our newspaper morgue. Everything's on microfiche. I'm afraid I couldn't give you the exact date. Late 60's, early 70's. That's all I can recall."

"You know something about her?"

The librarian, an older woman, nodded. "I remember when it happened. I had a daughter the same age, so I guess that's why. Those things have a way of making you stop and thank God it wasn't you."

"What happened to her?"

The librarian shrugged. "No one knows."

Wexler was shaking. He moved to the wet bar and fixed himself a Scotch on the rocks, eyeing his surroundings with distaste.

He'd never liked the house. She'd bought it after her husband's death. It was a twenty-room mansion, decorated like a bordello and filled with icons of Zebulon Wheele.

Images of the deceased televangelist covered every wall; a tasteful if unexceptional portrait in oils hung alongside a picture composed of 125 varieties of pasta. A charcoal study commissioned from Andrew Wyeth was displayed next to a life-sized Zeb executed in Day-Glo colors on a black velvet background.

Catherine Wheele's personal study—the one she used to receive visitors—had to be the worst example of kitsch iconography in the entire house, and that was saying something. The walls were covered by murals depicting the life and career of Zebulon Wheele.

The "story" began with a cherubic, barefoot urchin in ragged overalls holding a bible to his narrow chest, his Keane-ish eyes cast heavenward. It ended with the silver-haired Zebulon, attired in his trademark powder-blue three-piece suit, mounting a celestial stairway. The Pearly Gates sat atop the stairs. Two robed, Aryan-looking men bedecked with halos stood on the steps, welcoming Zebulon with open arms. Zebulon was looking over his shoulder at the woman standing at the foot of the stairs. Although weeping, Catherine Wheele's likeness somehow kept its makeup dry.

Wexler remembered how feverishly she had spoken of Zebulon's "crusade" that night. He recalled how bright her eyes had been, the pupils large and unfocused. She'd spoken unceasingly of her late husband, the words blurring into one another to form a tapestry of sound, until she pushed him onto the love seat and fellated him. Wexler found himself staring at the same love seat and shuddered.

That was the first night he'd been in the house and the night he'd been made aware that one of her dummy companies controlled the board of directors at Elysian Fields. That was the night she'd told him she knew about the money he was embezzling from the hospital and how she was going to "overlook the whole thing" if he simply agreed to take on a special patient. No questions asked.

Raymond Wexler stared at the love seat and contemplated the unraveling of his life. He finished his drink and was starting on his second when she entered the room. He started guiltily, slopping liquor onto the polished surface of the bar.

"Raymond," she said frostily.

Abandoning his drink, Wexler tried to smile and look concerned at the same time. It didn't work. Catherine Wheele was not a woman who took bad news graciously.

She was dressed in a peach chiffon negligée, its décolletage and hem lined with ostrich feathers. Her wig showed signs of having been put on in a hurry. She wasn't wearing any makeup, and the feral intelligence he saw in her eyes disturbed him. Wexler realized that he'd never seen her real face before, even during their brief sexual tussles.

"You must have your reasons for waking me at this hour, Raymond." She walked toward her desk, her body moving like a ghost underneath the opaque chiffon. Wexler tried to recall what she looked like naked and failed. "You could have at least phoned . . ."

"She's escaped." He grimaced after he'd said it. He hadn't meant to blurt it out like that, but he was afraid she would look into his mind. Anything was better than that.

Her back stiffened but she did not turn to look at him. Wexler felt a sharp twinge in his forebrain, but could not tell if it was her doing or simply a nervous headache. She was studying the large framed photograph of Zebulon that rested on the corner of her desk. Zebulon was standing next to the governor, smiling into the camera as they pumped each other's arms. Catherine stood behind and to one side of her husband, watching him with coon-dog devotion.

"I see. Does anyone know?"

"She's killed someone already, Catherine. It's in the papers!"

"That's not what I asked."

Wexler was sweating. His skin felt cold. "The orderly on duty at the time, name of Hagerty. But I've already had him dismissed."

She swung around to face him. He knew it was going to be bad, but he hadn't expected it to be *this* bad. The rage gave her eyes a weird shine, like those of an animal. "I'm afraid that won't do, Raymond. I'll have my boys . . . take care of it."

Wexler opened his mouth to protest, but she closed the distance between them, pressing her body against his. Her perfume was overpowering. He could feel a cold pressure in his head as she reached inside. He wondered if she would tell him to stop breathing.

"I'm afraid you've failed me, Raymond. Failed me in a big way."

She lifted a hand to his face. Her fingertips stroked his cheek, then dipped beneath the surface of his skin. She traced the tilt of bone and sweep of muscle as if trailing her fingers through the waters of a still pond. The ripple that went through him in ever-increasing circles was pain. Wexler tried to scream, but nothing would come out of his distorted, gaping mouth.

When it was over, his face was unmarred, although fierce muscle contractions threatened to grind his teeth to chalk. Catherine Wheele's fingers were stained bright red.

Hagerty passed a hand over his eyes, gently massaging them in their sockets. After hours of searching the microfiche archives, scanning the front pages of the nation's major newspapers for a face he'd glimpsed in a dream, he'd finally found what he was looking for.

The face smiled at him from a news item dated 1969. Now he realized why she'd looked familiar.

Denise Thorne.

That Denise Thorne.

She was the daughter and only child of Jacob Thorne, founder of Thorne Industries. Her net worth was estimated between ten and fifteen million, making her one of the world's richest teenagers at the time of her disappearance. She'd been educated in exclusive schools and vacationed in exotic locales. Her entry into Vassar was assured. Then she vanished from the face of the earth.

Every year or so one of the news services would do an article on missing celebrities, and certain names were sure to pop up. Names like Judge Crater, Jimmy Hoffa, Ambrose Bierce, D. B. Cooper . . . and Denise Thorne.

Along with some school friends and a hired traveling companion, she had jetted to London in the summer of '69. They were rich young Americans out to sample the forbidden pleasures of "Swinging London." Three days after arriving at Heathrow, the group decided to investigate the discotheques in the Chelsea district. They may have been underage, but they were wealthy and that made all the difference.

Denise Thorne was last seen talking to an older, aristocratic-looking gentleman. When questioned later, her companions could not recall his name but were under the impression he was of the ruling class. No one saw either of them leave. That was August 3, 1969.

Kidnapping was a natural assumption, and suspicion automatically fell on the hired companion. As he read the news accounts—weeks condensed onto a single fiche—Hagerty could feel the mounting frustration as the authorities ran out of leads. After a week they dropped all lines of inquiry involving the companion and focused their suspicion on radical political groups—the IRA in particular. But the persistent absence of a ransom note or a statement claiming responsibility for the crime forced Scotland Yard to abandon that line of questioning as well.

By the end of 1969 the case was still open. Some optimistic souls speculated she had run off to India with a band of hippies. The general consensus, however, was that Denise Thorne was lying dead in a ditch or, more likely, moldering in a shallow grave out on some lonely moor. By New Year's day of 1970 she was old news and the papers had more than their fair share of new atrocities to report.

Hagerty sat in the dark and stared at the face of a girl missing and believed dead for over eighteen years. The face of his dream intruder. She had been a pretty girl, with a strong jawline and high cheekbones. She wore her hair in the fashion of the day: long, parted down the middle, and straight as a board. He tried to superimpose the features of Sonja Blue. His mind rebelled. She couldn't be the same woman. Denise Thorne—if she were alive today—would be close to thirty-five, and Sonja Blue couldn't be more than twenty-four.

Claude vaguely recalled the newspapers reporting the case when it first happened. He'd been nineteen at the time, and the bum knee that'd kept him from being a college draft pick had also kept him out of Vietnam. He'd been working nights at the state hospital when the Thorne disappearance made the papers, over eighteen years ago. So what was the connection?

Maybe if he rested his eyes he could think better.

The librarian shook his shoulder, waking Claude from the first decent sleep he'd enjoyed in over forty-eight hours.

"Sir . . . sir? I'm afraid you'll have to leave. The library closes in ten minutes."

Hagerty stumbled from the library and entered the parking lot, fumbling for his keys. He was suffering from the disorientation that accompanies sleeping while sitting upright; his mouth felt like a ball of damp cotton and his back ached from his hours in the chair. He had the car door open before he realized he was no longer alone.

There were two of them, dressed in conservative dark suits with narrow lapels and even narrower ties. Their hair was short and brushed away from their foreheads. They were wearing sunglasses after dark. They had come up from behind and were now flanking him. Hagerty felt his scalp tighten as he realized his was the only car left in the parking lot.

One of them spoke. It didn't matter which. "Claude Hagerty?"

Cops. That was it. They were police. They'd found out about the escape and were asking questions. Nothing to be worried about.

Smiling his relief, Hagerty turned to face them. "Yes? Can I be of some help?"

The air in his lungs escaped in one agonized gasp as a fist sank up to its wrist in his stomach. The blow knocked Claude against the car door, slamming it shut. His hands opened in reflex, dropping his car keys to the pavement.

The man who sucker-punched him withdrew his fist from Claude's gut. Light glinted dully off the brass knuckles. He drew back to deliver another blow, but Claude's instincts were in gear. He lashed out with his right arm, catching his attacker across the chin with a closed fist.

The stranger staggered backward, his sunglasses askew. Blood dribbled down his chin. The second man drew a blackjack from his coat pocket.

"Wexler didn't say nothing about no linebacker," growled the man with the blackjack.

The recognition was sharp, like a needle jabbed in a boil. The last time he had seen these men they were grasping the ankles of Archie Kalish. There was only a moment for Claude to realize that they meant to kill him, then the back of his head exploded.

Claude fell to the pavement. He did not see which one kicked him in the ribs or who dealt the blow to his kidneys.

The last thing he saw before he passed out was one of the identical strangers standing over him. The stranger was saying something, but Hagerty's ears were roaring too loud to make it out. The stranger gestured to his companion and Claude saw the streetlight reflecting off his cuff links. Cuff links shaped like little spoked wheels. Hagerty wanted to know where the man had gotten his cuff links, but they kicked him in the head before he could ask.

He came to in the train yards.

He was sprawled over the hood of a car. The engine's warmth was pleasant against his back. He wanted to go to sleep, but there was a horrible roaring in his head that actually shook the ground. Then he heard the train whistle.

Someone grabbed him by his shirtfront and hauled him upright. Hagerty screamed aloud. It felt as if his head had been sewn together with carpet thread and the sutures were ready to pop. The identical strangers, the ones who accosted him in the library's parking lot, were still there. They had removed their sunglasses, revealing eyes as cold and flat as those of sharks. Claude preferred the sunglasses. One of them had a split lip, which he kept fingering as he looked at Claude.

The other one was talking, asking him questions, but Claude's hearing kept fading in and out. He realized he was suffering from a mild concussion. When he didn't answer their questions, one of them held his arms while the other went to work on his stomach. When the man holding his arms let go, Hagerty collapsed on the ground.

"Who you workin' for, huh? You workin' for Thorne?"

The stranger with the split lip gathered twin handfuls of Hagerty's hair, lifting his head off the ground. The pain was immense and tears streamed from his eyes, but all he could do was stare in stupid fascination at the killer's spoked cuff links.

"Leave it, Frank. Look at him. We're not gonna get anywheres with him. Better just get it over with."

"She's not gonna like it. She'll want to know." Frank's voice took on the whine of a petulant child, but the other waved him quiet.

“What difference does it make as long as he’s dead? Here, help me with this bastard. The next train will be along in a few minutes. Christ, this fucker’s heavy.”

Panic gnawed through the gray cotton of the concussion. Claude wanted to scream, but his tongue had been transformed into a swollen wad of flesh blocking his throat. They were trying to pull him to his feet, one tugging on each arm. Frank was swearing.

Good. If you’re going to kill me, the least you can do is get a hernia.

Both men bent over Claude, sweat dripping from their brows and running their impassive masks. Hagerty was amazed by the purity of the hatred he felt for these killers. It swelled against his breastbone like a helium balloon. Fine. He would die hating.

The hands emerged from the darkness, moving like moths dancing in the night. They landed on the shoulders of the hit man who’d kicked Hagerty in the head. Hagerty found satisfaction in the look of fear that crossed his attacker’s face. The man let go of Hagerty’s arm and reached for the gun inside his jacket. He never made it.

The hands snapped upward, the left clamping over his ear and bottom jaw while the right grabbed his forehead and jerked. The sound of breaking vertebrae was like a gunshot.

Frank freed his gun and kept his grip on Claude. Adrenaline gave him the strength to pull Hagerty off the ground and splay him against the car. He kept his hand on Claude’s throat while he held his gun inches from the orderly’s face.

“Cute trick, whore! Real cute trick. Try anything else and I’ll blow your boyfriend’s brains all over the fuckin’ countryside, understand?” Frank shouted into the dark. His eyes jerked back and forth, but they kept straying to his companion sprawled in the dirt.

There was only laughter in response.

Frank turned and fired in the direction of the sound. The muzzle flashes revealed only gravel train beds and empty boxcars.

The hit man’s face was the color of clay. Dark crescents had appeared under his arms. He let go of Hagerty, who managed to stay upright by hugging the hood of the car. Frank wrapped both hands around the grip of his gun and fell into a wary shooter’s stance.

She landed on the roof of the car, hissing like a cat. Frank jerked around, his mouth a lipless line, and fired. The bullet struck her in the left shoulder, the impact spinning her backward. Hagerty heard her cry out, then the sound of her body striking the ground on the other side of the car.

Frank stood and blinked at where she had stood, then began to inch his way around the front of the car, his gun at ready. It was obvious he wasn’t worried about Hagerty sneaking up on him from behind or doing anything but falling down.

Frank cleared the hood of the car and stared at where her body should have been.

"Oh, shit."

Her fingers dug into the back of Frank's neck before he had time to realize she was behind him. Her grip was so tight it pinched the nerves, temporarily paralyzing him. She reached around with her free hand and squeezed the wrist on his gunhand. Delicate bones ground together and collapsed, splinters of bone spearing the pulse point. Frank screamed like a girl.

Hagerty wasn't surprised when Frank came flying over the hood of the car. Sonja Blue followed at her leisure, boot heels ringing against Detroit steel.

Frank wallowed in the dirt, clutching his ruined hand to his chest. It was black with congested blood and resembled an inflated surgeon's glove. The hit man's face was white with shock and his lip was bleeding again. He babbled to himself in a sibilant whisper, "Antichrist, Antichrist, Antichrist."

Sonja Blue bent over and grabbed a handful of suit, pulling him upright without any noticeable effort. "Now, is that any way to talk?"

Frank's only answer was a high-pitched, nasal whine.

She dragged him back to where Hagerty stood propped against the car. She glanced at him and Claude saw his own battered, bleeding face reflected in twin mirrors where her eyes should be. Still more sunglasses after dark.

"Tell your playmate good night, Mr. Hagerty." Placing her hand at the base of Frank's skull, she slammed his head against the hood of the car. It sounded like a watermelon dropped on a gong. Frank's body jerked spasmodically under her hands. Claude was reminded of the full-body immersions he had witnessed as a child at the Baptist church his grandparents attended, only there wasn't any water this time. Just a spray of brains and blood and bone.

But that's not what made him faint.

It was when she pulled her lips away from her teeth, revealing canines that belonged in the mouth of a wild animal, and tore open the throat of the ruined thing that had been Frank. That's when he fainted.

Hagerty's dreams were not empty.

He was wandering through a library with bookshelves as tall as skyscrapers. He could hear a train roaring down one of the aisles, its passage shaking the stacks.

He glimpsed movement ahead, where the bookshelves intersected. He didn't want to go any farther, but felt trapped in the book-lined maze.

Two men loitered on either side of the shelves, watching Claude as he approached. They wore dark suits with narrow lapels and narrower ties. They both wore sunglasses. Claude recognized them as the identical killers. Only they were no longer identical. One of them stood with his head propped against his left shoulder; when he shifted his weight to the other foot, the head lolled onto his chest so that he was staring at his feet. The other's hands resembled a cartoon animal's. His forehead was cracked open and the brains spilling out of the wound ruined the cut of his suit.

They moved in concert to block Claude's path.

"Get out of my way, assholes."

The mismatched killers turned sideways and disappeared. Claude kept moving.

Archie Kalish leaned against one of the bookshelves, smoking a cigarette. Or trying to. Most of the smoke escaped through the ragged hole in his throat. He grinned at Claude, as sleazy in death as he was in life.

"Hey, Hagerty! So what d'ya think? Some kinda piece, huh?"

Claude watched Kalish's larynx vibrate as he spoke. Claude kept walking. Kalish's laughter sounded like whistling.

Dr. Wexler was thumbing through a leather-bound volume of Freud. There was something wrong with his face. He did not offer to speak to Hagerty.

There was a door up ahead. An exit sign glowed over the threshold. Claude picked up his pace. He could see someone waiting for him by the door. A woman.

Denise Thorne looked very sad. Her long, straight hair was the color of raw honey. She was wearing a paisley miniskirt with a buckskin vest, the fringe longer than her dress. She was wearing white go-go boots and held a bouquet of flowers in her hands.

"I told you to get away while you still could," she said.

Claude felt it was important to speak to her. He stopped and tried to touch her shoulder.

Denise Thorne shook her head. "Too late."

Lozenges of mirrored glass dropped from her brow ridge, merging into the cheekbones and sealing away her eyes. Her hair writhed, drawing in on itself. Darkness welled from her scalp, radiating outward like ink in a water glass.

She opened her mouth, letting the lower jaw drop impossibly low, like a snake swallowing an egg. Her teeth were way too long and sharp to fit into a human mouth. Claude could hear the train coming. The whistle blasts sounded like a woman screaming.

And he woke up.

He was surrounded by white. At first he thought he was in a hospital, then his eyes focused and Claude found himself staring at egrets. The birds were frozen in a ritual dance on the translucent surface of a rice-paper screen.

There was a sound from the other side of the divider. The egrets folded in on themselves, allowing Sonja Blue to come forward and place a damp washcloth on Claude's brow.

Hagerty dug his elbows into the mattress, desperate to avoid the touch of the woman who'd saved his life. He wanted to scream, but all that came out was a stream of profanity.

"Stay the fuck away from me. Get your goddamn motherfucking hands off me!" His throat tightened as if the words meant to choke him.

To his surprise, she flinched.

"I should have expected this." She sounded tired.

A sledgehammer caught him between the eyes as he tried to sit up. He struggled to keep from fainting. He did not want to lose consciousness in the presence of this woman.

"Don't move so fast, you'll black out again." Her voice carried a note of concern. She stood at the foot of the cot and watched him with twin panes of polarized glass in place of eyes.

Hagerty cursed and dragged the washcloth off his forehead. He didn't want to look at her. Her very existence made his forebrain swell until it threatened to leak out his sinuses. It dawned on him that he was very thirsty.

She suddenly moved from out of his line of sight. Claude fought a surge of hysteria; as much as he hated having her around, at least he knew where she was. Careful of the malignant throbbing in his skull, he studied his surroundings.

He was in a warehouse loft; the ceiling loomed far above him and the room was poorly lit. He could barely make out the geometric shapes of the rafters overhead. He wondered how he might escape, but his mind refused to stay on the subject.

Sonja Blue returned with a Mason jar filled with water. Hagerty stared at the proffered glass but made no move to take it from her hand.

"Okay. If that's how you want it." She set the water on an upended orange crate next to the cot and stepped away.

Hagerty lifted the container with shaking hands, slopping water onto his bare chest.

"It's after ten p.m., you've been out for nearly two hours. Thought you might like to know." She crouched at the foot of the bed, hands dangling between her knees. Without wanting to, Claude found himself looking at her.

Her hair was shoulder-length and black as goddamn, as his grandpa used to say; styled in the bristling fashion made popular by music videos, it rose like the crest of an exotic jungle bird. She wore a battered black leather jacket a size too big for her over a sleeveless French-cut T-shirt of the same color. The jacket was going out at the elbows, and an attempt had been made to repair it with electrician's tape. The legs of her tight-fitting black leather pants were tucked into a pair of scuffed, low-heeled engineer boots. Her hands were encased in fingerless black leather gloves. And, of course, there were the mirror shades. Claude's dream tried to resurface, but it was quickly banished.

"You, uhhh, look different," was all he could come up with.

"I no longer look like a drugged-out madwoman, is that what you mean?" She laughed without smiling. "Yeah. I guess I do look different."

Claude heard himself speaking before he knew what he was saying. "What are you?"

She did not seem to take offense. She cocked her head to one side and regarded him with polarized eyes. "Do you really want to know?"

"Do I have a choice?"

She shrugged. "Not anymore."

She stood up. It was a simple, fluid motion, like the uncoiling of a snake. She moved across the floor of the loft to the opposite wall and drew back the heavy blackout curtains that covered the windows. The staccato glow of neon illuminated the room, revealing a maze of rice-paper screens. Sonja Blue leaned against the windowsill, arms folded. Claude sat upright, clutching the mattress with both hands until his knuckles ached.

"You must have an idea as to what I am. And it's not an escaped lunatic, is it, Mr. Hagerty?" She pushed the mirror shades onto her brow, exposing the eyes they hid. Hagerty began to shiver like a man with fever. She let the glasses drop back into place.

"Welcome to the Real World, Mr. Hagerty."

Can't push it too fast. I'll lose him if I force too much on him. I wanted it to go down quick and clean, damn it. Just go in there and take out those bozos and get him to safety. An impersonal kill, that's all I wanted. But I lost control! It couldn't resist playing with them. I've got to be careful. Ever since the escape, the Other's been strong. Too strong. It's just waiting for me to screw up. Looking for a chance to get out. I can't let my guard down. Not with him around. It's not his fault he was drawn into this. He's innocent.

Since when did that make any difference?

Shut up, damn you. Just shut up!

Hagerty wished he knew what was going on. As dangerous as Sonja Blue might be, that wasn't as disconcerting as his not knowing what part he was playing in this horror show. Was he the hero or the victim? And if Sonja Blue was the monster, why did she go out of her way to rescue him?

She was no longer in the loft, although he could not recall hearing her leave. He shuffled around his "prison" in his underpants, trying to decide what kind of movie he was in. If he could figure out the movie, then he stood a chance of surviving to see the credits. But only if he could figure out the rules. If it turned out to be one of those slasher films . . . The thought depressed him so badly he gave up on the analogy and focused on exploring the loft.

The room was subdivided into cubicles by a network of painted rice-paper screens. He walked among sock-eyed carp, grinning lion-dogs, grimacing dragons, prancing monkey lords, glowering no-tail cats, and stalking tigers, their presence oddly comforting. He moved from compartment to compartment, searching for clues to what was going on. What he found made his head hurt.

One cubicle contained a videoplayer and monitor. The extension cord hung from the rafters like an orange python. An unmarked cassette jutted from the mouth of the player. Claude nudged the cassette, and the machine obligingly swallowed it. For a moment Claude felt safe, involved in the mundane ritual of technology. Then the tape began to play on the monitor: a woman in a gold lamé pantsuit exhorted her audience to stand up and sway from side to side, hands held over their heads. The sound was off, but Claude knew what she was saying. He watched the mascara mingle with her tears and trickle down her cheeks. It looked like her face was melting. He hit the stop button and the monitor screen returned to the gray nothing of an empty channel.

Another cubicle contained a low, Japanese-style table. Three books rested on the table. One was a large, very old-looking tome with metal edges and leather binding. Claude did not recognize the language, but there were several pages of complex, overlapping illustrations that made his eyes throb when he tried to decipher them. The second was a slender, hardbound volume in German. The third looked to be far more accessible. Claude turned the book over in his hands, noting the brittle plastic binding protecting the dust jacket and the shelving code affixed to its spine. The title was *The Vanishing Heiress: The Strange Disappearance of Denise Thorne*. The book fell open to a page with two photographs on it.

The larger picture was a photoportrait of the Thornes in happier days: Jacob Thorne stood in the background, looking every inch the self-made captain of industry. His women were seated on a small divan in front of him, his hands resting on their shoulders. Shirley Thorne, a delicate woman with a gracious smile, held her daughter's hand in her lap. Claude was surprised rich people could look so normal.

The smaller picture was blurred, obviously blown up from a snapshot. It showed a slightly older Denise Thorne in a crowded nightclub. She was not looking at the photographer. She seemed distracted but otherwise enjoying herself. She held a champagne glass in one hand. The caption read: *Last known photo of Denise Thorne, taken by club photographer the night of her disappearance at the Apple Cart Discotheque, London, August 3, 1969*. A ballpoint circle hovered just over her shoulder. Inside it was the blurred outline of a man. The man remained a grainy, ill-defined blot even on close inspection. Scrawled in the margin, in the same blue ink as the circle, was the word "MORGAN."

Claude shut the book and replaced it on the table. For the first time since waking up, he noticed the dust coating everything. His hands were grimy with it and the soles of his bare feet itched. His hostess obviously had not yet found the time to catch up on her housekeeping.

The kitchen was located in a corner where the raw brick met the jutting angle of the roof. The only piece of furniture was a Salvation Army–issue dinette set. A pair of midget iceboxes, stacked one atop the other, sat on the rickety table. Claude tried the taps on the double-basin sink, only to be rewarded with the plumbing equivalent of an epileptic seizure and water the color of rust.

His stomach growled. He opened the top cooler and heard glass containers clink together. He reached inside, fingers closing around chill glass. Soft drinks, milk, anything would be welcome.

He stared at the pint container of blood for five seconds before dropping it. The bottle shattered, splattering his naked legs. Claude clamped his hands over his mouth and staggered into the tiny bathroom located off the kitchen.

He sounded like a cat sicking up a hair ball.

When he was through, he remained hunched over the sink, his palms against the cold enamel, and stared at his reflection in the medicine chest. Although the swelling was going down, it was surprising he'd woken up at all.

His right eye was covered by a bruise the color of a hybrid rose. His bottom lip looked like a piece of raw liver. A knot the size of a pigeon's egg hung over his left eyebrow, and it felt like his nose was broken. Again.

He let his hands stray to the Ace bandages wrapped around his chest. It hurt a bit when he moved too fast; otherwise his ribs seemed okay. He spat into the sink and studied his saliva for traces of blood, then tried the same experiment with his urine. He was damned lucky to have escaped without serious internal injuries. If you consider being held captive in your underwear by a vampire as being lucky . . .

Claude laughed in spite of himself. Funny how good that felt. He was surprised to discover he was no longer in mortal terror. He experienced a sense of relief, not unlike emptying his bladder after a long road trip. He decided that while he did not fear Sonja Blue, neither did he trust her. He'd learned the hard way never to rely on the semblance of sanity.

Back when he was younger and his hair longer, he'd come to trust a patient who, on the surface, seemed perfectly harmless. Then one day the patient turned into a screaming, hissing wild thing and pulled out a handful of Claude's hair by the roots. Now he wore his hair cropped close to his skull in order to camouflage the missing piece of scalp.

He remembered the hit man called Frank and the way she'd toyed with him before the kill. Hagerty had no love for the man, but he could not repress revulsion at the memory of his murder.

When he was fifteen, he'd found the family cat—a fat, good-natured old tom—"playing" with a mouse. The cat snapped the rodent's spine, leaving the creature alive but paralyzed. Then, gripping the mouse by the head, it repeatedly hurled the tiny rodent against the garage door. The crippled mouse squeaked each time it rebounded onto the pavement. This prompted the cat to swat the mouse again; *squeak*-thud. The rodent's eyes had gone white with pain and fear, its rib cage shuddering with every breath while blood leaked from its twitching nostrils. The cat continued its grisly game of handball for a minute or two more, then it grew bored and bit the mouse's head off. After that, Claude was never able to look at the old tomcat in quite the same way, just as he could not look at Sonja Blue without sensing the feline sadism lurking below her surface, waiting for a mouse.

"There you are. Made a mess, didn't you?"

He reacted as if she'd poked him with a cattle prod. She stood in the bathroom doorway, a grocery sack in one arm and a suit of clothes draped over the other. Claude was acutely aware of being dressed in nothing but a baggy pair of BVDs.

"Thought you might like some clothes. The ones you had on were covered in blood. Hope these fit." She shoved the clothes at him. "You can change in here while I clean up." The door closed in his face.

Getting dressed in the bathroom was like changing clothes in a broom closet. Claude stopped swearing after the third time he slammed his knee into the toilet tank. The dungarees fit him well enough, although his neck overflowed the collar of the flannel shirt and the cuffs ended an inch above his wrists.

He opened the door in time to see Sonja Blue wringing a mop in the kitchen sink. The water was the color of cranberry juice.

"What the hell are you looking at? Expect me to lick it up off the floor with my tongue?" she snapped.

Her feelings were hurt. Claude was taken aback by the realization. It occurred to him that he was a lousy, ungrateful house guest. He didn't know what to say, so he watched her mop the floor in guilty silence.

"I picked up something down at the corner superette. *Haute cuisine* it ain't, but it'll do for now." She didn't look up from her work, but motioned with a curt nod to the sack resting on the table.

Stepping over the pool of blood and tap water, Claude rummaged through the bag and produced a jar of peanut butter, a loaf of white bread, a quart of milk, and three cans of potted meat. He stared at the cartooned demon on the can of deviled ham and smiled.

The smile grew wider. He felt as if his lips were going to split.

"What's so funny?" Sonja Blue glanced at him as she wrung the mop for the last time. The water was now the color of pink lemonade.

Claude began to laugh. Tears squeezed from the corners of his eyes. His laughter carried the shrill edge of hysteria. He realized that if he lost control he would laugh until he blacked out. Which is what he did.

Alive. I'm only really alive when I'm on the prowl. Alone. Unobserved. I'm glad Hagerty is too unsteady to leave the loft. I could not track my prey with him queering the game.

The night is an origami rose, unfolding itself for those unafraid to look. As much as I hate them, my eyes allow me to know the half-glimpsed marvels and nightmares that fill this world. Sapphires among the rot.

My eyes are windows to hell, enabling me to spot those who Pretend. Their spoor hangs in the air, as obvious as street signs.

Over there, lounging in a doorway, sharing a cigarette with its unwitting prey, is a *vargr*. It rests its shoulder against the doorframe, holding a Marlboro between thumb and overlong index finger. I can see the animal in its eyes as it studies me with the detached speculation of a predator. But I am not interested in such beasts tonight.

I round the corner and enter the city's tenderloin district. The porn shops, titty bars, and adult cinemas are all very busy, like maggots in a corpse. I like downtown. It's my element.

Sensing my intrusion, a succubus glances up from her transaction. As she leans into the open passenger window of a nondescript rental car, she looks like all the other whores working the neighborhood. She lifts her head, tossing back a mane of copper curls, and scans the streets. Is she on the lookout for vice cops or other wayward children of Gehenna? The faltering neon of the Triple X Sinerama's marquee illuminates her true face as it shifts and roils beneath the carefully constructed facade. I do not meet her gaze and hurry away. Out of my league.

The Pretender population in America is nowhere near that of Europe, but immigration is picking up. Standing in line at the Pussy Kat Theater, its deformities masked by a shapeless raincoat, an ogre watches me with the eyes of a rabid rat. I make a note of him. Child-eaters are a rarity nowadays, but missing children aren't. The ogre's gaze follows me as I walk past. He knows I'm not human, but cannot identify my clan. That makes him nervous.

I smell roasting flesh and burning hair, and I nearly collide with the pyrotic before I see it. It sidesteps me, leaving a vapor trail in its wake. It wears the flesh of a middle-aged man in a business suit, his skin the color of a boiled lobster. His hair is ablaze and smoke billows from his ears and nostrils. The pyrotic is either very strong or has been in possession too long. Now it is looking for another body, male or female. It doesn't matter. Once elementals get a taste of being incarnate, they often end up addicted to the earthly plane. Kind of pathetic, really. No one pays any attention to the burning man as he hurries down the street.

Something catches the corner of my eye and I discover the reason for the Pretenders' uneasiness. It seems I am only partly to blame.

It sits on the bottom stoop of an old brownstone, rummaging through its shopping bags, muttering the litany of the out-patient.

To the humans it is just a bag lady, another bastard child of Reaganomics. But I see the seams in the costume and the stage makeup on its face. It is a *seraph*, come for a brief visit. The aura that surrounds the wrinkled, grime-caked face is blue fire. It looks up from the Macy's bag and stares at me. Its eyes are golden and have no whites or pupils. It smiles and speaks, but its language is beyond me. I am too base a creature to understand. All I hear are wind chimes. If I try to answer, all the *seraph* will hear is a cat being skinned alive.

The Other is frightened of it, just as the succubus and the ogre were afraid. *Seraphim* never interfere with Pretenders. But they could if they wanted to, and that is why the Pretenders are fearful of them. The Other digs its claws into my brain. If I do not leave it will try to gain control. It knows I cannot afford to let it do that. Not tonight. Not while I still have to find Chaz.

I turn and run from one of the nine billion faces of God.

She stood in the doorway of the bar, sucking in ragged gulps of air. Her heart rabbited in her chest and her hands trembled. That was close. Too damn close.

She could feel the Other raging just below the surface, and bile burned the back of her throat. For the first time since she'd ducked in to escape the *seraph*, Sonja noticed her surroundings.

The bar was located in the basement of one of the old brownstones fronting the street. A frosted pane of glass faced the stairwell. It didn't have a name, but she recognized it as one of Chaz's haunts. The drinks were cheap, the lights dim, and the clientele sleazy—Chaz's kind of place.

The front room was large and had a low ceiling. It stank of stale beer and decades of trapped cigarette smoke. The actual bar was against the far wall, situated under the only decent lighting in the joint. Clustered against the opposite wall were a handful of arcade video games, their cases covered with graffiti and cigarette burns. A Rockola jukebox strained the Ramones' "Pinhead" through failing speakers.

The tables and booths scattered throughout the room boasted three hookers, a ferret-eyed dealer, two glowering skinheads, and a couple of hard-core alcoholics. None of them was Chaz. She noticed a doorless passageway flanked by twin cigarette machines. Taped over the lintel was a yellowing sign that read: POOL.

Why not check it out? Maybe the little shit was back there, hustling the marks. She walked past the sentries posted by the tobacco company, aware of being watched by the people at the bar.

For a moment she thought she'd stumbled into a nest of minor demons. She'd expected to find a roomful of teenaged boys, but not ones with blue hair. She paused as her vision shifted spectrums, scanning the faces for traces of Pretender energies. Low-level demons were identifiable by the sworls of power marking their features, like the tattoos of Maori tribesmen. But every face she scanned was clean, at least of Pretender taint.

One of the blue-haired youths leaned across the scuffed green of the pool table, his back to her as he lined up his shot. He wore a black leather jacket garnished with loops of chrome chain at the shoulders. Emblazoned across the back of the jacket was the grimacing face of a bright-blue ape. Jesus, she had been away too long! These were members of the Blue Monkeys, one of the city's more volatile youth gangs. And she'd just walked, unawares, onto their turf.

The Blue Monkey made his shot and moved back to watch the break go down. His competition grunted and the others made rude noises. No one bothered to look up. She moved about the room, scanning the audience for a sign of Chaz. Unless he'd taken to dyeing his hair, her prey wasn't there. She turned to go.

A hand grasped her upper arm, just above the elbow. "Hey, baby. Looking for someone?"

The Blue Monkey was seventeen—maybe eighteen, if he pushed it—his indigo hair short and spiky. Despite the acne that pitted his cheeks like a spray of buckshot, he was moderately good-looking. He wore an Iron Maiden T-shirt under his club jacket.

She shook her head. "Just looking for . . . a friend who isn't here."

The Blue Monkey smiled in what he imagined was his best James Dean imitation. The gang members gathered around the pool table were watching them now. "You can forget that asshole, baby. Rafe's here."

She shook her head a second time, smiling wanly. "No, I don't think so." She slipped out of his grip and started for the door.

Sniggering laughter ran through the gang. Rafe flushed red all the way to his indigo roots.

The hand was on her arm again, only tighter this time. "Maybe you didn't hear me so good," Rafe ground the words out between clenched teeth. "I said I'm your friend now."

She felt her patience begin to melt. The Other strained on its leash. It sounded almost friendly this time.

C'mon! Let's settle this little fucker's hash. Just this once . . .

No! It was so tempting to give in, to indulge her dislike for these swaggering, no-necked little Hitlers. But once the jinn was out of the bottle, it took blood to get it back in. Better to leave now and avoid the risk, before things got any worse.

"I don't think yer her type, Rafe," jeered one of the gang. More snickers. Rafe's face was the color of a fire hydrant.

"I have to go now." She disengaged herself a second time.

"Whassamatter, whore? Ain't I good enough for ya?"

Rafe's eyes were no longer sane. She recognized the madness in them. Rafe was the Blue Monkeys' pet psychotic, their own personal whirling dervish. He might look like a teenage boy, but he was something far more dangerous, and the gang knew exactly what it took to set him off. They knew which responses were guaranteed to trigger his transformation into the living incarnation of the Tasmanian Devil from the old Bugs Bunny cartoons.

Rafe grabbed a fistful of her hair, moving so fast she could not dodge his attack. He jerked her off-balance, so her palms were planted against his chest for support. His breath reeked of dope and Jack Daniels.

That's it. I'm not gonna play pattycake with this jerk.

She levered herself backward, ignoring the tearing at her scalp. She'd endured far more pain in her past than the loss of some hair. Rafe was staring, mouth open, at the hank of hair he was left holding in his hand when she hit him. She still had the self-control to deliver the blow with the back of her hand, but it was enough to send Rafe sprawling into the arms of his tribe. Blood leaked from one nostril and his lower lip was split. His eyes rolled like an enraged mule's.

The Blue Monkeys clotted around her, blocking the exit. There were nine of them. His friends struggled to put Rafe back on his feet.

"You bitch," Rafe mumbled through rapidly swelling lips.

One of the older gang members chuckled. "Looks like we got us a gash that knows *jew*-jitsu!" He reached out to snag her mirrored sunglasses. "Bet you got trouble seein' with them fancy-ass shades on, bitch."

Her hand flashed up, fast as a cobra, and her fingers closed around his wrist before he could touch her. There was a sound of balsawood crunching and the Blue Monkey screamed like his namesake.

One of the gang tried to back away, but the others held him in place. "Fuck. Oh, fuck. It's her. The chick Chaz was talkin' about."

Rafe spat a wad of blood and phlegm on the floor. "Shaddup, you goddamn lit'l queer. Chaz was jackin' us, and you know it! This here's just some poon with fancy moves." His eyes were unfocused. "Clear off the table. We gonna have ourselves one wingding of a gangbang." Rafe glanced contemptuously at the Blue Monkey with the shattered wrist. The youth was whimpering, his lips white with shock as he cradled his arm against his chest. "Somebody shut that fuckin' whiner up."

The gang took up its war cry. The backroom sounded like the monkey house at feeding time. Rafe lurched forward, wrapping his arms around her waist. He intended to slam her onto the pool table and fuck the bitch until she bled.

Her knee pistoned up, smashing into his denimed crotch and rupturing his testicles; it was as if a napalm bomb had gone off in Rafe's jeans. He managed one high, thin scream before collapsing. The agony of his ruined *cojones* was so great he didn't even know she'd fractured his pelvis.

The Blue Monkeys watched as Rafe spasmed on the floor, clutching his groin, their ape yell fallen silent.

That was when the Other made its move.

"You fuckers think you're tough, huh? You think you're bad? You shitheads can't even handle a girl!"

Shut up. Shut up. It's bad enough without you provoking them. Let's go! Let's just walk out of here, damn you!

Two of them lunged at her, one from behind and one in front. The one behind grabbed her arms, pinning her elbows to her side. The Other laughed and stamped on his instep, breaking it in two places. The Blue Monkey yowled and let go of her arms. The Other grabbed her frontal assailant by the throat and crotch, lifting him off the floor.

No, stop. Please . . .

The Other tightened her grip on the boy's crotch. He made a bleating sound as she castrated him.

No. God, no. Stop . . .

She lifted the struggling youth over her head.

Don't!

The Other laughed as she hurled the boy against the wall. The sound his spine made as it snapped was delightful.

Someone swung a pool cue. She absorbed the blow across her back, although it cost her a couple of ribs. No big deal. Her laughter grew louder. The Other hadn't enjoyed herself so much in months.

A burly youth with a royal-blue mohawk grappled with her. She caught a glimpse of the knife seconds before he slid it between her ribs, puncturing her left lung. She wrapped her arms around the mohawked punk, pressing him to her breasts. They looked like a high-school couple slow-dancing at the prom. The Blue Monkey stared into her upturned face, expecting her to die. The Other grinned and belched a gout of blood into his face. The Blue Monkey began to panic. He backpedaled, desperate to break free of her embrace, but she refused to let go. His face was a blood-slick mask, his eyes bulging like a vaudeville minstrel's. The Other unsheathed her fangs.

Every synapse in the tough's brain overloaded and blew. "Get her offa me! Get her offa meeeee!"

Two of his friends grabbed the Other's shoulders and wrested her from her unwilling dance partner. They stared dumbly at the knife buried to the hilt in her chest. The Other plucked it out as if it were a bothersome thorn.

"Hey, lover! You forgot something." She flicked her wrist and the blade buried itself in the punk's Adam's apple.

"Wa-hoooo!"

The Other leapt atop the pool table, surveying the carnage: two dead, two crippled, one maimed. Not bad for starters.

One of the boys made for the door. No, no, no. Mustn't have that. Not while the party was still in full swing and she was having such a good time. She snatched up one of the cue balls on the pool table and lobbed it at the fleeing Blue Monkey. The crunch it made upon connecting with his skull was satisfying. The Blue Monkey staggered drunkenly for a step or two, the seepage from his head turning his hair purple.

Fun was fun, but the thrill was losing its edge. She'd better split before the cops finally decided to show up. Only three loose ends left. She hopped off the pool table and ducked a roundhouse from a Blue Monkey with a sterling-silver skull pinned to one earlobe. She punched his face and felt his jaw restructure itself. She let him fall without a second look.

The next-to-last Blue Monkey almost had the fire exit open. She let fly with an empty beer bottle. It struck the fleeing gang member in the right knee. The boy fell to the floor, clutching his shattered kneecap.

The last of the Blue Monkeys was smaller than the rest. Fifteen years old, at best. He was the one who'd mentioned Chaz. Figured. Chaz liked 'em young, rough, and stupid. She held the boy by his club jacket's lapels. The toes of his boots brushed the floorboards.

"Where is Chaz?"

"I . . . I . . ." The kid was terrified beyond speech. His eyes were as blank as her mirrored glasses.

She pushed against the wall of hysteria surrounding his mind. *(Tell me where he is.)* The boy's will folded like a Chinese fan.

"Don't know! Truth! Truth!"

"Now, that can't be true. Surely you know where he likes to hang out? You can tell me."

"Hell Hole! Look in Hell Hole. Don't hurt me."

"Hurt you? Now, why would I want to do that?"

The Other lowered the boy until his feet once more touched the floor but did not relinquish her hold. There was a gnawing pain in her chest from the knife wound, her scalp itched, and she was breathing like a bellows. It would take an hour for the damage to heal on its own, but she could boost the process with some blood. Not much. Just enough.

The littlest gang member stood trembling in her hands like a trapped rabbit. She had glimpsed his sins during their brief touching of minds. Gang rape. Hit-and-run. Mugging. Liquor-store robbery. Street-fighting. Quite impressive, for a squirt with parrish-blue hair.

It'd have to be fast. She could hear the sirens in the distance. Her fangs unsheathed, wet and hard. She pulled him to her in a lover's embrace. He had an erection.

They always did.

The Other watched the cop cars fishtail to a halt outside the bar with no name. She stood in the shadows of the alley across the street, arms folded. The bartender broke down and called the police when he heard the gang screaming. She'd slipped out through the fire exit before any of the patrons worked up the nerve to check out the pool room. *A wonderful establishment. I'll have to go there more often.*

The Other smiled as she walked away from the flashing lights and ambulance sirens. Marvelous workout. Simply marvelous. Just what she'd been needing. She hawked a piece of lung onto the pavement without breaking stride. Just the thing to take the edge off before she got her hands on Chaz's sweet little butt.

The Hell Hole was proud of being a dive.

A lot of time and money had gone into selecting the proper decadence for the club. That way its patrons wouldn't notice it was just another bar. It was a natural for Chaz.

The walls were festooned with rubbish salvaged from the city dump and places even less savory. Baby doll heads were affixed to the walls by nails driven through their eyes. The front end of a '58 Chevy jutted onto the dance floor, a moth-eaten moose head mounted in place of the hood ornament. Instead of glass eyes, golf balls graced the creature's sockets; sawdust dribbled from its nostrils, while a used jockstrap dangled from its antlers. Loops of Christmas-tree lights hung from the ceiling, none of them flashing in sequence.

Chaz sat at his table in the corner, staring at the centerpiece: a Barbie doll shoved headfirst into a Suzy Homemaker oven. Christ, the place was dead tonight. London had the States beat when it came to the clubs. Sometimes he wished he'd never left England. But things had been different then. His meal ticket was in danger of being nicked, and America seemed as good a place as any to escape to. . . .

Chaz frowned and took another swallow of gin. Wouldn't do to think about Sonja. He'd learned long ago to put people out of his mind. He erased them from his memory so well it was like they'd never existed. That was the best way. The only way. Attach yourself to 'em, become "indispensable," use 'em up then throw 'em away. He'd done it hundreds of times in the twenty years since he first hit the streets. You have to learn fast if you're on your own by age twelve and want to stay alive.

Then there was Sonja. Their relationship had lasted the longest. What had Sonja called it? Symbiotic, that was the word. Yeah. She needed him to lure her prey into the open. It'd been dangerous, but she paid him well. And the sweet rush of adrenaline and fright involved in the hunt got him higher than any street drug. He could have lived without her, sure. But it was so easy to keep hanging around. Hell of a lot easier than peeping into the heads of dope peddlers so he could be at the right place at the right time when a deal went down. Yeah, it was much easier being Sonja's Judas goat. Safer, too, providing he stayed out of her way during her "spells."

But, in the end, he'd committed a major sin, as listed in the Gospels According to Chaz. He'd become dependent on her. Now *that* was scary.

Bloody hell, where was everybody? He glanced at his Rolex. He'd agreed to meet that little shit and his blue-haired friends here, so where were they? If they didn't show up soon, he'd be forced to go looking for a party. Chaz hated that Muhammad-and-the-mountain jazz. He enjoyed being the focal point. Make 'em dependent on me, that's the way it should be.

Still, the little Yank had his points. Maybe he'd take him along to Rio. On second thought, Rio was full of beautiful boys with skin the color of café au lait. He could buy any number of dark-eyed Cariocas, so why bother importing a petulant, blue-haired punk? No, Rio would definitely be wasted on his pet Blue Monkey.

God, he hated this depressingly young country and its populace of bourgeois mall-crawlers. He just had to be patient. Come Carnival he'd be spending his days drinking espresso and eyeing the samba dancers as they paraded down the streets.

He'd dreamed of Brazil for years, ever since he saw the poster in the window of a West End travel agency. He was seventeen at the time and already well-versed in the language of exploitation. He was posing as houseboy for a withered old pouf while wringing him for whatever he could get. It wasn't a demanding job, really—the odd suck and fuck—mostly the old queen simply wanted a handsome boy following him around. They went to the theater a lot. That's how he happened to be walking past the travel agency.

The poster's layout consisted of two figures, male and female, photographed against an aerial view of Rio de Janeiro at night. Fireworks filled the sky like chrysanthemums made of colored fire. Both the man and the woman were the color of milk chocolate, with the dark eyes and exotic features of true Cariocas. The man wore skin-tight white satin pants that flared at the knee, the vents lined with red silk. His white satin shirt boasted the billowing, layered sleeves of the samba dancer and stopped just below his breastbone. Chaz admired the muscles that rippled across the dancer's exposed stomach. He wore a simple domino mask and the sunniest smile Chaz had ever seen. The samba dancer held a pair of brightly painted maracas in his slender hands.

The woman was also outfitted in white satin, her dusky skin in sharp contrast with her clothes. One beautifully naked leg was extended from the voluminous ruffles of her skirt. Her midriff was also bare, but far more subtle in its muscularity than the male's. A white halter concealed breasts the shape and color of chocolate kisses. Her head was covered by a carefully wound turban the color of snow, and she wore a mask identical to her partner's. But where the male samba dancer held maracas, she balanced a magnificently plumed parrot on her wrist.

Chaz stood and stared at the samba couple until his patron, having lost his temper, stormed off. There was a row later that night and within two weeks Chaz was back on the streets. The fact that the relationship was over didn't bother him, except that it meant he couldn't "visit" his beautiful dancers as often as he would have liked. After a time, the samba couple was replaced by a poster advertising package tours to Sorrento, but the smiling Cariocas were never far from his mind.

Sometimes he woke with the rhythm of steel drums echoing in his head and the smell of the Amazon rain forest clinging to his pillow. Now he was going to Rio. All he was doing was waiting for the right time to leave. For some reason, it hadn't felt right yet, and for Chaz that was important. He still had enough money to live—and do it well—in his precious Rio. A man with his savvy and unique abilities could do well for himself down there. Maybe he'd buy into a cocaine plantation. Or perhaps he'd found his own escort service, specializing in handsome, smooth-skinned Cariocas of both sexes. And, if his luck failed him, there were always the *turistas* . . .

He cast his thoughts outward and touched the minds of those in the bar. His talent was slight but he'd become its master years ago. He was proud of his skill. Better to be a dead-on shot with a .22 than a blind man armed with an assault rifle. Like that painted, holier-than-thou bitch. He groaned. Thinking about Sonja was bad enough, but he refused to let that whore preoccupy his thoughts. He returned his attention to his probes. At least it'd keep him from being bored.

Hmmmm . . . the manager, Rocky, was lounging near the door. Rocky didn't like him. Didn't like the crowd that Chaz attracted. Thought he was a dealer. Didn't want him hanging around, but business was real shitty.

Chaz was not upset by the manager's low opinion of him. You didn't remain sensitive if you were a telepath, otherwise you went psychotic or ended up with your head in the gas cooker. Like poor ole Mum; she couldn't handle knowing what the neighbors *really* thought. Silly cunt never learned how to screen herself.

Lise the barmaid's mind, however, was more to his liking. Where Rocky's thoughts were chunky, Lise's internal monologue was mental champagne. She was bored. Bit lonely. She knew he had money. Knew he had access to drugs.

She was debating whether she should let him pick her up. She thought he was a bit creepy, but the prospect of free drugs sparked a vague heat between her legs.

Chaz smiled into his drink.

"Hello, Chaz. Long time no see."

The hand on his shoulder pinned him to his seat.

Chaz's skin grayed and sweat jumped from his brow. "Sonja."

She smiled without revealing her teeth. "Sure is. Mind if I join you?"

"No. Of course not. Have a seat."

As she slid into the chair opposite him, the barmaid left her station to take the new customer's order.

"Get your friend anything, Chaz? Cocktail? Beer?" There was a trace of jealousy in her voice.

Sonja did not bother to look up at the barmaid. "We are not here, is that understood?"

The girl wobbled and blinked a few times, then left the table, rubbing her forehead with the heel of her palm and looking slightly confused.

"What did you do?" he hissed.

"Nothing serious. I just don't want our little discussion interrupted. After all, we haven't seen each other in such a *long* time. I take it your employers didn't see fit to tell you I'd escaped?"

"I don't have the slightest idea what you're talking about."

"Cut the bullshit, Chaz. You can't lie to me. Not that I don't know it, anyway. They must have paid you well; I can't see you slitting your throat for tuppence." She studied him for a second. "Jesus, you look like shit."

It was true. Nearly every dollar he'd earned had gone up his nose or in his arm. Back in London, during his peak, he'd been handsome. Some even called him beautiful. But his dissolution had brought out the rodent in his features. She marveled at the transformation; not even her own fall from grace had been so thorough.

Chaz lit one of his foul French cigarettes, his eyes searching the bar for some hope of escape.

"Where is it, Chaz?"

"What?"

Her voice was as sharp and cold as a surgeon's scalpel. "I don't have time for games, Chaz. I know you have it. You filched it from me when you kissed me. I thought, at first, that was why you shot me."

"Sonja—"

"I want what belongs to me, Chaz." She extended one hand and waited. It was an elegantly menacing gesture.

Chaz reached inside his breast pocket and withdrew a folded switchblade. The handle was six inches long and made of lacquered teak. A golden dragon winked its ruby eye in the dim light of the club. Chaz held it in his palm, admiring the gold leaf one last time, then handed it to its rightful owner.

She turned the weapon over with trembling hands, caressing it like a lover. She pressed the dragon's eye, and the blade leapt from its hiding place within the hilt. She turned it so the braided silver surface caught the light. In the erratic flashing from the Christmas lights the knife resembled a frozen flame.

"I'm surprised, Chaz. I thought you would have pawned it by now."

"I kept meaning to . . ." He stared at the silver blade, his eyes focused on something far away. "I dunno. Maybe I wanted a keepsake . . ."

"Something to remember me by. How sweet." She grinned and Chaz shuddered. "How much did you get for setting me up?"

"I don't know what the fuck you're going on about!"

"You were checking out Catherine Wheele for me, man. You told me to meet you at the playground at midnight. I went there, Chaz, but you weren't alone. You had Wheele and her goons with you. Your new friends. You didn't even tell me she was Real! You somehow forgot to mention that, mate. I woke up in an insane asylum. I hope you got your thirty pieces, Chaz."

"Look, Sonja, it's not what you think . . . I'm your mate, ain't I? I wouldn't do anything to hurt you. I'm glad you escaped. But I didn't have a choice. Honest! That Wheele slut, she sussed me out. She would have turned my brains inside out! She's powerful, Sonja! Too powerful for the likes of me. She was gonna burn my brain. What could I do, eh? What could I do? You believe me, don'tcha?" He reached across the table and took her hands in his. "C'mon now, luv. We're friends. We've been more'n friends. It could still be like that. Like the old days. You got away from that loony, right? We could go somewheres safe. Mexico. Brazil, maybe. What d'ya say, pet? Rio sounds nice, don't it?"

He looked into her face, searching for signs of her weakening. He'd played the game before. He'd gotten rather good at it, over the years, despite the lack of eye contact. He'd have to fuck her, but that was the easy part. He'd long since learned how to get it up and keep it up, regardless of his partner. It was sidestepping her wild, sadistic rages that was tricky.

"I'm sorry, Chaz." The Other smiled. "But Sonja isn't in right now. It's a good thing, too. She'd probably do something really stupid. Like forgive you."

Chaz tried to pull away, but it was too late, she'd already reversed the grip on his hands. "Let me go! Sonja, let go!"

Her voice was politely detached, like that of an airline stewardess. "How about if I broke one of your bones for every day I spent locked up in that stinking loony bin? That sound fair to you, Chaz? I was in there for six months. That averages out to one hundred and eighty days. Did you know there are two hundred and six bones in the human body, Chaz? That'll leave you with twenty-six unbroken bones. That's not too bad, is it, now?"

She tightened her grip. Chaz screamed as the bones in his left hand snapped like a bundle of dry twigs. "That's twenty-seven . . . ." His right hand crunched and became a mess of right angles. He yelled for someone—anyone—to help him. No one seemed to hear. ". . . and that's fifty-four. Only one hundred and twenty-six more to go. Oh, and don't bother yelling for help, Chaz. I told the manager we weren't to be disturbed. He was very obliging." She smiled, her fangs unsheathing like the claws of a cat.

Chaz's brain wrapped itself in shock, refusing to allow the pain in his ruined hands to escape past his wrists. He noted with detached fascination how the jagged ends of the finger bones pierced his flesh. His thinking was astonishingly clear now that his pain receptors were on hold. He was going to die, but it was up to him as to how horrible it would be.

"I'll tell you . . . who paid me."

"You don't need to. Wheele paid you. Really, Chaz, I thought you could do better—"

"Not Wheele, that bitch! She thought leaving me alive and whole was payment . . . enough. No, he paid me the ten thousand to shut up. Told me to leave the country. They think I'm in Brazil."

He had her hooked. She leaned across the table, her face inches from his own. He could see himself reflected in her shades. He didn't look good.

"Why didn't you leave, Chaz? Surely you must have known I'd come looking for you."

Chaz blinked. That was a genuine puzzler. One he'd asked himself every night for six months. He should have jumped the first flight to Rio de Janeiro the minute he'd received that nice flight bag full of twenty-dollar bills. But he'd gone against his nature. He knew, better than anyone, that nothing short of death—and maybe not even that—would keep her from tracking him down.

"Dunno. Maybe I had some unfinished business." The numb throbbing was starting to creep up his forearms. He had to hurry. His hands would be waking up soon. "He paid me the ten thousand . . . almost gone now. Should have gone to Rio. The coke's cheaper there. Could have sailed up the Amazon . . . learned how to chew the coca leaves, just like the Indians do." He smiled at the idea. Flocks of brilliantly colored macaws fluttered at the corners of his eyes.

"Who paid you, Chaz?"

"Sonja, my hands hurt . . ."

The Other was losing its patience. Chaz felt a shadow flicker through his forebrain, like a pig rooting for truffles. He wasn't so far gone she could invade him as easily as that. Besides, he had every intention of telling. But he had to do it right. He raised a barricade and the dark thing in his head hissed its displeasure. The shield would not hold for long, but it didn't have to.

"Who paid you, Chaz?"

"Jacob Thorne."

There was a heartbeat's worth of silence. Then the face below the sunglasses writhed. Chaz was pleased to see how deeply he had hurt her.

"Liar!"

She grabbed Chaz by the throat and dragged him from his seat. She shook him, determined to flail the truth out of his pale, wasted body. Chaz's head lolled backward, the weight of the skull no longer supported by the neck. The bastard was smiling.

Hustled again.

Lise finished cleaning the countertop and tossed the damp bar rag into the sink. God, what a slow night. The only customer in the joint was that Brit, Chaz. Lise still wasn't sure what to make of him. He was kind of creepy and he hung out with sleaze like the Blue Monkeys. She always felt like she was naked when he was around. But he was sort of good-looking, in a Keith Richards kind of way. And no American girl's completely immune to a British accent, even one by way of the council blocks. Besides, he tipped well and occasionally offered a little crystal meth if the service was good. She'd screwed guys for less than that.

Time to check up on him. He was bound to have finished his gin and tonic. She winced. Her head felt like it was about to split open. Probably her sinuses again. Oh, well, Chaz no doubt had something for a nasty headache.

As she approached the table, she noticed Chaz was slumped in his chair, hands folded in his lap. His chin was propped on his chest, a shock of dirty blond hair obscuring his face. Lise groaned aloud. The asshole was strung out. Rocky didn't like the customers nodding out before they settled their bar tabs, and he didn't like Chaz, straight or not.

"Hey, Chaz! Hey, man. You want Rocky to see you?" She grasped his shoulder, her hopes for a big tip and a free line of meth rapidly disintegrating. "C'mon, man, wake up!"

His head rolled forward, the eyes turned up so only the whites were visible. His mouth flopped open. Blood and saliva dribbled onto the floor.

Her screams were audible from the street.

He was walking through a featureless maze. There was no sky. Every turn led him down a corridor that looked the same as the last. Claude did not know where he was or how he got there.

He realized he was being led through the identical passageways. At his side walked a huge lion with a long black mane. The lion guided him as a seeing-eye dog would a blind man, except that it held Claude's right hand in its mouth. Claude could feel the gentle pressure of its jaws against the flesh of his palm. Although Claude was not afraid, he was somewhat perturbed to find his hand in the mouth of a lion. The beast showed no signs of harming him and it seemed to know the way. Still, it *was* a lion . . .

He awoke in darkness. What time was it? Three o'clock? Or had an entire day slipped past without his being aware of it? No. Only a couple of hours, he was certain. Something had woken him up. But what?

Somewhere in the dark, a door closed.

That was it. His enigmatic hostess had returned. He sat up in the narrow cot, fumbling with the orange crate that served as a nightstand. His hands closed on a plastic cylinder.

How considerate. After tucking him back into bed, the vampire left him a flashlight in case he had to find the john in the middle of the night. He bit back another fit of hysterical giggles and thumbed the flashlight on.

The beam wasn't very strong and did little to illuminate the blackness of the loft. The painted animals on the screens seemed to move in the weak light as if stalking him.

He found her leaning against a brick wall, her back to him. Claude noticed for the first time the rungs sunk into the brick face and the trapdoor set in the ceiling. He watched for a couple of minutes as the shoulders of her leather jacket hitched in short, sharp spasms before realizing what she was doing.

She's crying.

Claude stepped forward, lifting the flashlight so he could see her better. He felt awkward and intrusive, but he could not stop from trying to comfort her.

"Denise?"

She whirled about, startled by his presence. Claude heard himself cry out as if from somewhere far away. Her mouth was smeared with blood, but that wasn't the bad part. The bad part was she didn't have her sunglasses on.

The whites of her eyes swam with blood and were red as fresh wounds. There were no irises, just overexpanded pupils the size of shoe buttons. There was no humanity in them. They were the eyes of a wild thing.

She recoiled from the light, lifting a forearm to shield her horrible, flat eyes. The hiss that escaped her made Claude's testicles crawl.

"Don't look at me! Don't touch me! Don't talk to me! Just leave me *alone!*" She struck out blindly, knocking the flashlight from his hand.

Claude watched the beam of pale-yellow light as the flashlight cartwheeled through the darkness before shattering on the floor. He felt her jacket brush his elbow and then she was gone, swallowed by the labyrinth of rice paper.

Claude stood in the dark and massaged the fingers of his right hand. They were numb from where she'd knocked the flashlight out of his grip, but otherwise he was unharmed.

Somewhere in the loft, Sonja Blue wept dry tears of frustration.

RESURRECTION BLUES

This year I slept and woke with pain
I almost wished no more to wake.
—Lord Tennyson, *In Memoriam*

She lay silent and still, hands folded on her chest in mimicry of the dead. Her pulse slowed itself, her breathing becoming so shallow her chest did not rise and fall as she entered the sleep of the undead. But vampires are denied the luxury of dreams. They can only remember.

I do not remember *being* Denise Thorne.

I can recall events, dates, and names from the time before, but they are not my memories. They are dry facts, summoned from an impersonal computer file, snapshots from someone else's life.

Her dog's name was Woofer.

Her best friend in the third grade was Sarah Teagarden.

The chauffeur's name was Darren.

The names have faces and information attached to them, but the emotion is gone. I feel nothing for them.

Except for her parents.

I am amazed there is still a spark of emotion left for them. I'm not certain if this is anything to celebrate. That is where the pain comes from.

I remember her last hours vividly; I guess that's because they are the hours of my conception and lead directly to my birth in the backseat of a Rolls Royce. No human can claim such memories. Guess I'm one lucky bitch.

I remember the discotheque with the loud psychedelic music—the Apple Cart—and the pulsating amoebas on the wall and the bored-looking girls in miniskirts dancing in cages suspended from the ceiling. Really Swinging London, man.

Denise splurged on champagne cocktails. No society child is a stranger to alcohol, but she had yet to master it. Being treated like an adult and ogled by men was intoxicant enough. She was giddy. And careless. And stupid.

I do not recall the exact moment Morgan made himself known. He was just there, as if he'd been present all along. He was tall, distinguished, and looked early middle-aged. He was elegant and debonair and Cary Grant-ish, with streaks of silver at his temples and an impeccable Saville Row suit. He called himself Morgan. *Sir* Morgan. He was an aristocrat. The way he carried himself, the way he moved, his tone of voice, made it evident he was a man used to issuing commands and having them obeyed. He looked out of place in the club, but no one would have dared challenge his right to be there.

Sir Morgan plied her with champagne and produced an endless stream of urbane banter. Despite her millions, Denise was a teenage girl and, therefore, susceptible to romance and fantasy. She imagined herself the Poor Little Rich Girl with Morgan as her Prince Charming. Unaware of her fortune, he had picked her, out of all the older, more experienced women in the nightclub, to be his companion. Stupid little get.

A girl with savvy would have pegged Morgan for an upper-class rake with a taste for squab. She would have been wrong, but that was closer to the truth than the romantic sap sluicing through Denise's overheated imagination.

She could not take her eyes off him. Every time he looked at her, she was certain he saw all the things she kept secret inside herself. She wanted to fuck him real bad.

I'm certain he did not know who Denise Thorne really was. Careless of him. If he'd known, he would never have approached her. Had things gone as planned, the resulting headlines would have spoiled everything and eventually spelled not only his death, but the ruination of centuries of careful planning.

After succeeding in separating her from the herd, Morgan suggested a midnight ride through the streets of London. How romantic. Stupid! Stupid! Stupid!

The Rolls was the color of smoke. The chauffeur opening the door wore livery so black it didn't reflect light. The windows in the rear of the car were also heavily tinted. For privacy, he assured her. A bottle of champagne awaited them, nestled in a bucket full of ice. Denise felt like she was in a movie. All it needed was a soundtrack.

After her second glass of champagne things began to go wrong. The interior of the car rippled and warped. It was very warm and close. It hurt to breathe. She had trouble keeping her eyes from rolling like greased ball bearings.

But worst of all, Sir Morgan . . . changed.

He opened his mouth and his canines grew, extending a full inch. His tongue flicked over his teeth, wetting the razor-sharp points. His eyes seemed to shimmer. The pupils wavered, like candle flames caught in a draft, then narrowed into reptilelike slits. The whites surrounding his eyes looked like they were bleeding.

Denise screamed and threw herself against the car door. She clawed at the space where the handle should have been, then pummeled the wall of glass that separated her from the driver. The chauffeur glanced back at her and smiled, displaying sharp teeth. She dropped back against the upholstery, clutching her elbows. She was too frightened to scream. All she could do was shiver.

Morgan smirked and shook his head. "Silly girl."

She felt his will enter her, hot as pig iron. She started to cry as Morgan pulled her to him without using his hands. He reached into her head and ordered her to crawl across the backseat, and her body obeyed. She struggled against him the best she could, but Morgan was far too old and far too powerful to be denied by a sixteen-year-old girl. Her body was a marionette fashioned of meat, and Morgan the red-eyed puppet master.

Her prayers were incoherent by the time she reached his lap, her fingers numb as she opened his fly.

His penis was huge and marble-white. It was erect, yet empty of blood. It was cold in her mouth and felt dead, despite its pretense of life. Her facial muscles cramped and it felt as if her jaw would dislocate. Her fear turned into shame, then blazed into hate. She tried to force her teeth down onto the meat violating her throat, but her body refused to cooperate. She nearly choked on her own vomit when the glans of his penis struck her tonsils.

Morgan eventually grew bored with oral rape and retracted his control over her flesh. Denise collapsed in midstroke. Her throat was scalded by bile and her face ached. Her cheek lay pressed against the wool blend of Morgan's pant leg. His crotch was stained with her tears and saliva. She could hear the Rolls purr as it wound its way through the streets of London with no particular place to go.

Morgan flipped Denise onto her back. She was in shock, beyond reacting to what was done to her. She watched him shred her clothes with detached interest. His hands were cold. Dead man's hands.

He lifted one of her arms, turning it so the inner forearm was exposed.

He ran cool, dry lips over the pulse point in her elbow. He drove his fangs into her arm the instant he shoved himself between her legs.

Denise cried out once. Her scream was so shrill the dogs in the neighborhood the limo rolled through howled in sympathy.

The horror of what was being done to her broke through the shock barrier her mind had erected to protect itself. Everything that was Denise Thorne disappeared, raped into oblivion by her demon prince.

And I was born.

My first sensation was pain—pain as Morgan punctured my forearms with his blood kisses, pain as his ice-cold dick rammed into my blood-slick vagina. His jism burned like battery acid. He slammed against my bruised and bloodied crotch for a few more minutes after his orgasm before finally growing bored with the game.

I ceased to exist the moment he disengaged his dick. He was too busy buttoning up to notice I was alive.

I couldn't move. I was still weak from being born. I noted his clothes were covered with blood, mucus, and sperm. Morgan enjoyed a sloppy fuck.

The car rolled to a stop and the doors unlocked themselves. Morgan threw me into the gutter like a passing motorist tossing out a fast-food wrapper. I heard a bottle shatter under me, but I couldn't feel anything. I was dying.

Death's funny. It fans whatever spark of self-preservation is left in your carcass into an inferno. Somehow, I found the strength to pull myself onto the sidewalk. I dug my fingers into the cracks in the pavement and hauled myself along the concrete an inch at a time. The blood kept making me lose my grip.

Even though I was horribly bashed up, I kept thinking about how badly my teeth hurt. The pain in my upper jaw overwhelmed my other injuries.

I remember hearing a man yell, "Oi!" And I can remember the pavement vibrating under my belly as he ran toward me. But the very last thing I recall before sliding into my coma was a weird tingling in my fingertips, like bugs were crawling all over them. It wasn't bugs.

It was my fingerprints changing.

I woke up nine months later. But that's not the point. The thing is, I woke up empty.

I wasn't a complete tabula rasa; I knew that two plus two equaled four, I could still speak and understand English, and I knew all the words to "Strawberry Fields Forever." But as to *who* I was and where I came from, I drew a blank.

That didn't bother me, at first. When I came to, I was lying on my side in a hospital bed with tubes up my nose and an IV stuck in my arm. I woke up thinking, *I gotta get outta here*. I didn't know my name, or even how old I was, but I did know I couldn't stay in that place anymore. Time to leave.

I sat up for the first time in nine months, my joints cracking like dry timber. Pain bit into my calves and spine as I forced my muscles to flex and bend, but the pain seemed very far away. Numb fingers pulled at the tubes sunk into my nostrils. There was a brief sunspot of pain, then blood streamed from my nose. I ignored the warmth dripping off my upper lip and clawed at the needle sunk beneath the surface of my wrist. Another flash of cold light and the smell of saltwater flooded the room.

I fumbled with the protective railing for a couple of minutes. There was a click and the side collapsed. I felt a quick jolt of hurt in my crotch. I had just performed a rather crude decatheterization on myself.

I felt giddy and numb. Maybe I was dreaming of escape. I lowered myself to the floor and stared at my surroundings, wobbling on thin, uncertain legs like a newborn colt.

I was in a hospital ward. Beds were lined up to the left and right of me, each housing a silent, motionless mound of blankets and meat. I tottered toward the door, peering through the gloom at my wardmates. They lay curled in their beds like giant fetuses, umbilical cords emerging from their arms. It was night and the lights were off; but that made little difference to the sleepers. It was always night in that ward.

I passed through the door into a corridor. I hesitated on the threshold, blinking back tears. The light in the hall hurt my eyes, but I hunched my shoulders and continued to stagger along. I did not see a single doctor, nurse, or patient, but I could feel their presence nearby. I did not want to be discovered. I did not want to stay in that antiseptic, brightly lit place any longer. I rebounded off the door to the fire escape before I saw it. The fading letters on its surface read FIRE EXIT. I pulled on the handle with both hands, painfully aware of how weak I was.

A gust of cold air mixed with light rain struck my face. I stumbled onto the landing and sucked in a lungful of fresh air. Old cigarette butts littered the metal floor. The interns no doubt used it for quick smokes while on duty. I might be found out if I stayed too long.

I began the long climb down to street level, my body finally starting to wake up. The pain and discomfort were no longer ghost sensations. Blood and phlegm leaked from my nostrils, and my hands were stained orange by a mixture of blood and rusty metal. It was bitter cold and all I had on was a faded hospital johnny. My legs cramped violently and I was afraid I would overbalance and fall over the railing into the alley below.

After what felt like an hour, I reached the bottom of the fire escape. My legs trembled and I felt feverish. I was ten feet above street level and couldn't figure out how to work the mechanism that released the ladder. I rattled the escape ladder, tears of frustration running down my face. I was terrified of being caught.

I tried lowering myself to the sidewalk. My arms felt like they were being pulled from their sockets. Probably were. Everything went gray and my fingers slipped. Then I was lying on my back in the middle of some garbage cans. All I saw was a tiny strip of night sky sandwiched between two old buildings. It was drizzling and raindrops dripped on my face.

I got to my feet and stumbled away. I had no idea of where to go, but I knew I had to get away. London is an ancient city, full of crooked streets and dead-end mews. It's easy to get lost there. I don't know how long I wandered the back alleys, avoiding the lights and traffic, but it was dawn when I collapsed in the doorway.

It was late April, and it's bloody cold in London that time of year. I was wet to the skin and shivering. I ached horribly and was badly bruised from my fall. My bare feet bled, but I didn't care. I sat in a shallow doorway that faced the alley, shoulders hunched and knees drawn to my chest. I felt unconsciousness boiling up inside me, but I was afraid to close my eyes. I remembered the beds full of unborn sleepers, their eye sockets filled with shadow. I started trembling and could not stop.

Suddenly, there were hands on me, lifting me from my deathwatch.

"See Joe? There she is, just as I said . . ." The voice of a woman, shrill and sharp.

"Yeah, yer a reg'lar blood hound, Daphne. Here now, help me with her . . ." A man's voice, barely more than a bass rumble.

Faces swam into view: a thick-featured man with a broken nose and a pinch-faced woman wearing too much makeup bent over me. The pinch-faced woman clucked her tongue solicitously, sounding like a cockney hen. The big man wrapped his jacket around me and lifted me in his arms.

"Cor, look at th' state she's in! Looks more like a drowned rat," grumbled the man.

"But she's young, Joe," whined the woman. "You'll be makin' more than a bleedin' fiver off 'er, ducks."

"Awright! Awright! Here's yer bloody finder's fee! Now, sod off. I got business t' attend to."

I relaxed in the stranger's arms. I was warm and, for the moment, safe. I listened to his heart thump in his chest and the rasp of his breathing. I felt secure. My world had a focal point.

My savior's name was Joseph Lent. Joe was a pimp.

He was a big man in his early thirties. He resembled a Mick Jagger who'd gained fifty pounds and decided to play goalie for the Hammers. He wore his dirty blond hair long enough to touch his collar. He dressed flash—nicely tailored suits that could pass for Saville Row jobs. He used to laugh at how the "poncey bastards" who ran the shops sniffed while they waited on him.

"Like they was afraid of smellin' somethin' bad. Har! Har! Har!" He'd laugh and show his tooth—the gold bicuspid. That was always a bad sign. He'd laugh with his mouth but his eyes would never join in. Later on, he'd get drunk and use his fists.

Joe didn't know what to make of me, but he had his guesses. Shortly after I was strong enough to sit up and keep down a little soup, he laid down the law. He sat on the bed and stared at me with his dark eyes.

"I dunno what yer game is, but it don't take much to figure yer runnin' from somethin'. Or someone. Izzat it? You some kind of runaway?"

I blinked. I really didn't know what to say. His guesses concerning my origins were as valid as anything I could volunteer.

"You escape from a government scheme? Mebbe th' methadone clinic, eh? I seen th' scars on yer arms. Y'into smack? Coke? Morphine? Don't make me no never-mind, love. Whatever turns y'on, like they say. I've put a lot o' time in on you, girl. If y'works f'me, you can have anything yer heart desires. I'll protect ya. I'll see that th' bobbies never get a hold of y'again. Is it a deal, now? Yer Joe Lent's girl now, ain'tcha?"

Joe became my man. Not just any man. He was *the* Man. He was my father, brother, lover, boss, and personal terror. He schooled me for my role in life. He taught me how to walk, talk, dress, and tell vice plants from the regular tricks. I was a good student. I was desperate for an identity. Any identity. And Joe Lent was more than happy to define my world. He's the one who named me Sonja Blue: "Sounds exotic. Like one o' them long-legged Danish birds."

It was perfectly natural that I should walk the streets and proposition strange men and give my money to Joe. Didn't every woman? I was barely a year old. How was I to know any different?

My life revolved around Joe. I fixed his meals. I cleaned his flat. I turned tricks for him. I gave him my money. I had a name, a function in life, and I belonged to someone. I was happy. The only time I wasn't happy was when Joe beat me.

Pimps are an insecure lot. They live in fear of their meal tickets walking out on them for someone bigger and better. Joe was *real* insecure. He'd lost his last girl to the competition, and that hurt. That's why he carried the cane. The one with the bronze knob on the end shaped like an eagle's claw. The bobbies might not approve of him walking down the street with a cricket bat, but a cane . . . Well, that was gentlemanly. Style made all the difference.

Whenever Joe got bad drunk, he'd use his fists. He was good at slapping girls around. He knew how to beat the bloody daylights out of a woman without messing up her face or putting her out of business. And he knew how to do it so I'd lie on the floor, my nose gushing like a fire hydrant, and beg him to forgive me. And mean it, too.

Joe was my life, my love, my universe. If I lost him, where would I be? Who would I be?

Things went on like that for a year. We'd go through periods where Joe would alternately shower me with gifts, then beat me until it hurt to breathe. I always recovered quickly and rarely needed to see a doctor. The only time I had any problems with my health was when I developed anemia. I grew very pale and my eyes couldn't handle direct sunlight, so I took to wearing sunglasses.

When my appetite began to seriously dwindle, Joe dragged me to the aged quack who "fixed up" all the working girls in the district. Joe was terrified of losing me to disease or pregnancy. I was quite successful on the street; I attracted the odd fish out looking for a bit of kink. You could charge extra for that.

The old charlatan prescribed ox blood and milk to "strengthen my constitution." It actually worked. For a while.

Occasionally, Joe tried to get me to talk about my past. He entertained the notion that I was the daughter of a rich man and doubted the extent of my amnesia. His attempts at making me remember never worked. As far as I was concerned, Joe was my real family. For some reason, I never told him about the hospital and the roomful of empty sleepers. Perhaps I was afraid he'd try to take me back there.

I was two years old when it happened. Joe was drunk again. He'd gotten it into his head that I was trying to cheat him on his take and planning to walk out on him. He was out of his mind. I'd never seen him so angry. He didn't use his fists that night. He went after me with the cane, instead.

The first time the cane struck me, all the air went out of my lungs in one big *whoosh!* The second blow caught me in the pit of my stomach. I fell onto the floor. I couldn't draw in a second breath. It felt like I was drowning. The third stroke caught me on the right shoulder. I heard, rather than felt, the bronze eagle's claw break my collarbone. Then he started kicking, all the while calling me foul names and raving at the top of his lungs.

I tried crawling away, but he followed me. He wouldn't let me be. And, for the first time since he found me, I began to hate Joe. The hate surprised me with its strength. There was so much of it! It seemed to grow in direct proportion with the pain. I was so full of hate it threatened to pour out my mouth and nose. I was so astonished by my capacity for it I nearly forgot my beating.

Joe brought his cane across my back and I felt ribs snap. Suddenly, my hate changed. I felt it curdling and churning inside of me, transforming itself into a force I couldn't contain. I opened my mouth to scream, but all I could do was laugh. And laugh. And laugh.

I do not remember what happened after that.

I woke up on what was left of the bed.

Every muscle in my body ached. I had at least two broken ribs, a broken collarbone, and my left eye refused to open. There was blood in my mouth. I squinted through my rapidly swelling right eye, expecting to see Joe sitting in his favorite chair, the cane propped across the armrests. Joe was always serene and composed after a beating.

Joe wasn't in his chair.

In fact, the chair was a jumble of kindling.

Then I noticed the blood on the walls, and how high some of it was splattered. I felt dizzy and looked down at my hands. My fingers were digging into the mattress and I could see the mattress ticking through the huge rents in the bedclothes. My ears were ringing. I looked up again, afraid of what I might see.

I saw Joe.

He was sprawled in the corner like a big rag doll. He didn't move when I called his name.

I got to my feet, although I almost swooned when I stood up. My stomach was the color of a ripe eggplant and hurt with every step I took. I staggered over to where Joe lay.

There wasn't much left of him.

His arms and legs were bent funny, like a scarecrow's; then I noticed all the long bones had been snapped in two. The jagged edges stuck out through his clothes.

His head was a mass of hairy pudding attached to his neck. His eyes were pulp and his teeth lay scattered like mah-jongg tiles. Maybe it wasn't really Joe. The corpse could be anybody . . . Then I saw the gold bicuspid. I shivered and looked away.

There was a ragged hole just above his breastbone, as if someone had attempted a tracheotomy with a can opener. Then I noticed the rest of him.

His killer had torn off his trousers and shoved the cane up his ass. An inch or two of wood and the bronze eagle's claw protruded from between his buttocks. The eagle's claw was clotted with blood, hair, and brains. That meant

Joe was probably already dead when his killer rammed three and a half feet of mahogany up his rectum. At least, I hoped so.

I stumbled backward, clamping a hand over my mouth. My guts heaved, angering the bruises purpling my abdomen as I hobbled to the loo. My brain was starting to wake up; what if whoever killed Joe was still in the flat? Maybe it was the gang from the next district. Joe had a lot of enemies. That was his way. But no one hated him enough to do that kind of job on him. No one.

The bathroom was empty. I tried to make it to the toilet but got as far as the sink before throwing up. God, how it hurt. I forgot about Joe and clung to the washbasin. My knees tried to buckle but I forced myself to stand. I didn't like the idea of fainting with a dead man in the other room. I opened my eyes and found myself staring into the sink, at what I'd sicked up.

The sink was full of blood. But it wasn't my blood.

I began to shake. Sweat trickled down my back. It felt like a spider crawling down my spine. I was startled at how easy it was for me to identify the blood I'd puked as belonging to Joe. Blood has its own identity, just like fingerprints, voiceprints, or semen. It tasted of Joe.

I was right. Nobody hated Joe Lent enough to do such horrible things to him.

Except me.

I looked in the mirror and saw the blood smeared across my lips. I opened my mouth in dumb protest and saw, for the first time, my own fangs. They emerged from my gums hard and wet, stained with stolen blood. I cried out and pressed my hands over my mouth in an attempt to hide my shame.

I remembered.

I remembered who I was and where I'd come from and how I got there. I remembered what I was. I heard Morgan's dry farewell laugh as he tossed me from the car. I recalled the weird writhing in my fingertips just before I went into hibernation. I stared at my hands, fearful that they might turn into the claws of a monster. Suddenly, the room flexed and I watched as the whorls and lines on my fingers and palms melted. New ridges and patterns emerged, only to be swallowed by yet another set. I forced myself to look away and caught sight of my face in the mirror. No wonder they never found me. Even my face . . . I tried to scream but all that came out was a dry choking sound. My flesh halted its dance.

I think I went insane then, at least temporarily. The part of me that fancied itself human went on vacation. My memories are fuzzy, as if I were drunk the whole time. I came back to find myself on a small boat owned by an Irish fisherman sympathetic to the IRA. I told him I was in trouble because I'd killed an English soldier. That was good enough for him. Money was no problem. Joe Lent taught me well, and now I no longer had to share the wealth.

I entered France through Marseilles, one of Europe's most glamorous hellholes. I spent a few weeks trawling the narrow streets and open-air cafés of the Pigalle, earning my keep and learning the language. I also discovered what Joe had referred to as "the Etonian vice" was not limited to England. I was pursued more than once by prospective "protectors," but always managed to escape. I lived in mortal terror of losing control again and killing someone. The beatings my clients paid for . . . Well, that was different. I also feared remembering. I did my best to live in the present and limit the future to my next meal. However, my condition, once awakened, could not be ignored.

My eyes, already sensitive to strong light, now required protection in the dimmest surroundings. I could deal with that. The hunger was my biggest problem.

The hunger was a balloon in my belly; when the balloon was full, I functioned normally; I even felt good enough to fool myself into thinking I was human. But when the balloon was empty, the hunger was released, threatening to destroy me from the inside out. It felt like a massive meth overdose: my heart and pulse nearly shook me apart; my lungs were filled with cold lead and my guts full of bamboo splinters. Compared to the pain I've endured since then, the early stage of my addiction was a cakewalk.

I bought live rabbits and geese from the markets—a benefit of being stricken with vampirism on the Continent—and drained them as humanely as I knew how. The salty hotness of blood as it filled my mouth was appallingly delicious. A warm, pleasant feeling replaced the pain as I drank. But it was never really enough. Deep down, I knew I wanted something more than the blood of animals.

I left France within two months of my arrival. I was afraid of being picked up by Interpol. I did not fear being punished for Joe's death. I was terrified that Denise's parents would discover the truth. Better they should believe their daughter dead.

I drifted from city to city, using stolen passports to cross the borders. Finally, I got tired of fighting off pimps and signed up with a Norwegian brothel catering to the North Sea oil trade.

Bordellos servicing wildcatter rigs aren't posh joints; they resemble frontier cathouses from the turn of the century. They're loud, cheap, vulgar, and rowdy. Gangs of drunken, horny men constantly squabble over a handful of available women.

The launches came in with the men from the rigs on a regular basis. The usual crowd consisted of Swedes, Norwegians, Brits, and the occasional American, but they were all the same by the time they made it to our place—roaring drunk and ready to fuck. There were always twice as many tricks as girls and at least one john who didn't want to wait his turn. Brawls over girls were pretty common.

The madam was an old whore named Foucault. She liked to brag about how she'd "seen service on all fronts" during the Second World War. Maybe the First one, too. She knew the business and kept a bouncer on hand for when the brawls got out of control. Which proved to be almost every night.

The *Amphitryon* was a rig so isolated its crew managed shore leave only once a year. The men came in loud and rowdy, bragging about their dicks and their staying power. It looked like a typical workshift.

Madame Foucault greeted the "gentlemen" at the door and ordered a round of drinks on the house. She explained that since there were over twenty men and only twelve girls, there would be a slight delay in attending to their needs, but she promised that everyone would be "taken care of."

She ordered us to come out and model for the customers. The girls were decked out in their work lingerie, which was starting to show signs of wear and tear; the feather boas needed dry cleaning, the fishnet stockings sported badly patched ladders, and some of the Frederick's of Hollywood-style costumes fit a bit too snugly.

The men of the *Amphitryon* didn't give a damn. They argued among themselves as to who'd go first and who'd get which girl. One of them swaggered over to me and began to feel my tits. He reeked of peppermint schnapps.

"That one's mine," one of them slurred in Swedish.

"Hell she is," retorted the bigger man, fumbling with my bra straps.

I looked past the man attempting to undress me and stared at the Swede. He was smaller than his fellow and stood clenching his fists. There was anger in his face. The other man was built like a linebacker and it was clear he was used to being deferred to. The Swede wanted to kill the big man, but was afraid of being humiliated in front of the others.

Waves of hate emanated from the Swede. It felt as if I were standing in front of a heat lamp. I started to get excited, and the big drunk thought I was responding to his pawing.

"See? She likes a *real* man," he jeered.

The Swede's rage was exquisite. He stared directly at me and I felt a brief connection between us. Like the spark that detonates a keg of dynamite. He wanted to see the big man's blood. So did I.

The smaller man's face reddened and seemed to swell, as if trying to contain an internal explosion. His eyes glazed and he began to tremble. One of his companions touched his arm and the Swede bellowed like a bull and lunged at the big man.

The drunken giant was taken by surprise, stunned by the ferocity of the attack. The Swede slammed a fist into his tormentor's kidney. The big man's jaw dropped in mute pain. I stood, motionless, and watched the two of them writhe on the floor at my feet. The hatred radiating from the Swede was of tsunami proportions.

The Swede was astride the other man's back, delivering vicious punches to his head. Some of the victim's friends grabbed the Swede and pulled him off the prone figure. The Swede swore and struggled violently. They tried to calm him down, but the little Swede kept kicking and clawing, his curses degenerating into a wordless shrieking.

The bouncer, a muscular German, emerged from the backroom and immediately jumped to the wrong conclusion; he thought the men restraining the smaller man were responsible for the fight, so he grabbed one of the men holding the Swede. The big man was on his hands and knees, staring uncomprehendingly at the blood from his nose puddling on the sawdust-strewn floor. The Swede landed on his spine feet first, forcing the big man back into the floorboards. Then he began to throttle him from behind. The big man's back was broken and he was helpless to shake off his attacker.

The big man's face purpled. His tongue stuck out and his eyes looked like deviled eggs. Four men grappled with the crazed Swede in an attempt to dislodge him, but he refused to be budged.

By this time the men from the *Amphitryon* were either trying to pry the Swede off his victim or they were fighting the bouncer. The girls fled to the safety of their rooms. I didn't move a muscle; I was basking in the Swede's homicidal frenzy.

The riot was in full swing. The men arguing with the bouncer were now brawling among themselves. Furniture was trashed. Bottles were smashed. All I could hear was men swearing and women screaming. The smell of blood was sharp and brassy. I felt wonderful.

The Swede finally succeeded in killing his foe. The big man lay prostrate on the floor like a Muslim at prayers. However, this obvious conquest didn't appease the Swede's bloodlust. He grabbed a chair and renewed his attack on the corpse. He screamed and laughed at the same time. His mouth was fixed in a rictus grin and tears streamed down his face.

There was a loud noise and something warm splashed my face.

The Swede let go of the chair. He stood for a second, staring at the hole in his middle and the loops of shiny pink intestine dangling around his knees, before falling to the ground. The hate was gone; it was as if someone had thrown a switch, allowing me to move and think again. I looked at myself. I was covered in the Swede's blood. I had to fight to keep from licking my hands.

Madame Foucault held a smoking shotgun, her face unreadable. The fight was over as suddenly as it'd begun. Everyone gathered around and stared at the dead men.

Madame Foucault finally spoke. "He went crazy. That's all there is to it."

I felt her looking at me. I stared at the blood congealing on the floor. I left the next day.

I realized there was more to being a vampire than simply drinking blood. I had been one of the undead for nearly four years and I had yet to understand my powers and their corresponding weaknesses. My knowledge of vampirism was incomplete; it was shaped by popular fiction, old superstitions, and other faulty attempts to mythologize a reality imperfectly perceived. I was trying to divine my true nature in a funhouse mirror.

According to folklore, vampires have their own set of rules, just like cricket or Monopoly. Vampires drank blood and only came out at night. They couldn't stand daylight or the sight of crosses. They were repelled by garlic. Silver was anathema. Holy water had the same effect as battery acid. They could be killed by a stake through the heart. They could not enter a church. They never aged. They turned into bats and wolves. They had powerful hypnotic powers. They slept in coffins during the day.

I was confused by these rules and fearful of testing their validity. It had been over three years since my birth in the backseat of Sir Morgan's Rolls, but I had yet to make an attempt to explore my dark heritage.

Some things didn't need much in the way of proving. I didn't like going out in direct daylight; it made my skin itch and caused headaches that threatened to separate the lobes of my brain. However, I did not burst into flame or crumble to dust the moment I set foot outside. As long as I wore heavy clothing and sunglasses, I could function with only a minimum of discomfort.

The only noticeable effect garlic had on me was bad breath.

I did not experience revulsion or pain in the presence of crucifixes. However, visions of Christopher Lee, the flesh of his stigmatized forehead bubbling like molten cheese, kept me from touching one.

Silver did not bother me, whether in the form of crosses, flatware, or coin of the realm. As for the stake through the heart bit, well . . . I didn't consider it a feasible test.

I was still ageing, although my years of hard living did not show; there were girls in the business younger than myself who could have passed for my older sisters. My stamina was incredible; I was rarely sick and I healed quickly. Too quickly. I was strong, although nowhere near as powerful as I would become. I had nothing to fear from even the roughest trade.

I ventured into a church and was not seized by epileptic fits the moment I crossed the threshold. Half-expecting to be struck by lightning, I approached the altar. Old women, their heads covered with babushkas and dressed in widows' weeds, knelt at the prayer rail. A priest dressed in a long, flowing cassock moved about in the shadows, tending the votive candles flickering at the feet of wooden saints.

The baptismal font was built into the altar rail. The lid pivoted to expose a shallow silver basin. I stared at the holy water. I'd intended to immerse my hand, but my resolve faltered at the possibility of my flesh being stripped to the bone. I noticed the priest, standing by the image of St. Sebastian, was watching me.

I hurried from the church, the holy water untested.

I wasn't too hot on turning into a bat. Did I need a magic potion or a special incantation to trigger the metamorphosis? And if I did succeed in becoming a bat, how would I reverse the transformation? Cinema vampires changed by lifting their capes and flapping their arms, but that was too damn silly. Perhaps if I concentrated real hard . . .

My body felt as if it was covered with ants. I cried out and leapt to my feet, swatting my arms and legs. I was afraid to look in the mirror, but I knew my flesh was dancing again. I rode out the skin tremors, and when they'd finished, I was still human. At least physically.

The hypnotic powers I'd experienced firsthand, although none of the legends I'd ever heard mentioned vampires drawing sustenance from the emotions of others. Nor did they mention telepathy, as I was becoming increasingly aware of the thoughts of those around me.

At first it was a mental variant of white noise; thousands of different voices merged into a backwash of unintelligible gibberish. Occasionally a snatch of coherent thought would bob to the surface, but nothing more.

I thought I was going mad. Then I realized the voices in my head weren't telling me to kill small children or derail streetcars; they seemed preoccupied about what to have for dinner and who stood a chance of winning the football pools. The only time I had problems was when I got too close to drunkards, madmen, or the truly evil. Their thoughts came through all too clear.

By spring of 1974 I found myself in Switzerland. I was employed in a house operated by Frau Zobel. Brothel-keeping was something of a family tradition for her, stretching back to the Napoleonic era. While Frau Zobel did not pretend to like me, she realized the financial benefits of having an employee specializing in "fancy passions."

I enjoyed working for Frau Zobel. She ran a first-class house, discreetly located in a respectable Zurich neighborhood. The girls were clean and the clientele genteel. It was light-years removed from my apprenticeship under Joe Lent and my time with Madame Foucault. But despite her grand airs and left-handed pedigree—she claimed to be the illegitimate granddaughter of Napoleon III—Frau Zobel was made from the same stuff as old Foucault; tenpenny nails and boot leather.

I had no friends among the girls in Frau Zobel's stable. I'd made it a practice not to get friendly with anyone, for fear of being discovered. Not that I had to actively discourage anyone from making overtures. Most women dislike me on sight. Men, on the other hand, react in one of two ways: either they are uneasy while in my presence, or they want to involve me in a minor sex atrocity.

I didn't mind being tied up with clothesline or beaten with a bundle of birch twigs, but I rarely played the submissive role. I attracted those who wanted to be dominated and degraded, and I assumed the mantle of dominatrix without complaint. It wasn't a one-way relationship; I experienced a diluted version of the pleasure I'd received from the Swede's berserker rage. I thought I was keeping that part of me in check. Instead, I was nursing it.

One of my regular clients was Herr Wallach, a pudgy man in his late fifties whose particular fancy passion involved a block-and-tackle and ice water enemas. Herr Wallach was a tenured mathematical theoretician. He also belonged to an esoteric fellowship composed of thinkers, artists, and poets. At least that's how he described it. Every year the group held a party at the home of one of its members. The host for the 1975 party was Herr Esel, a professor of metaphysics. Wallach wanted me to be his guest. The prospect of attending what sounded like a dreadfully dull evening in the company of Herr Wallach was far from appealing. Then he showed me the evening gown he'd bought for the occasion. It was a strapless dress made of black velvet, stunning in its simplicity, complete with matching silk opera gloves. Wallach told me I could keep it after the party.

Funny how something as trivial as an evening gown changed my life.

Professor Esel's estate was located on the outskirts of Zurich. It was an old mansion, inherited from an ancestor who made his fortune with pikemen and timepieces.

Herr Wallach made a great show of introducing me to his associates. The only time he seemed self-conscious was when he realized I meant to wear my sunglasses during the party. We argued about it on the way over and he sulked for a little while. However, parading around with a beautiful girl on his arm restored his good spirits. There were a few raised eyebrows, but the Swiss are nothing if not polite.

Wallach introduced me to Professor Esel, a florid little man who resembled a burgomaster more than a metaphysicist.

"Ah, Herr Professor, I would like you to meet . . . a friend of mine, Fräulein Blau."

"Gut*en tag, Fräulein Blau.*" Esel bowed smartly. I received a mental image of myself tied naked to a canopied bed, surrounded by frisky dachshunds. Esel spoke to Wallach, although his eyes never left me. "You'll never guess who has shown up tonight, Stefan. Pangloss is here!"

Wallach was genuinely surprised. "*Nein!* You must be joking. After all this time? It must be ten years since he last attended one of our gatherings."

Esel shrugged. "See for yourself. He was in the music room, the last time I looked. The bastard hasn't changed at all."

"Come along, Sonja. You simply must meet Pangloss." Wallach led me away, unmindful of Professor Esel winking me *auf Wiedersehen*.

Pangloss was in the music room, seated on an antique sofa, flanked by two lovely women who listened to him avidly and laughed at his witticisms. There was a feverish gleam in their eyes as they followed his every movement. Their laughter was synchronized; it reminded me of the clockwork toys the Swiss are so adept at creating. They did not look away from Pangloss when Herr Wallach introduced me.

"Herr Doktor Pangloss, I would like you to meet Fräulein Blau."

Pangloss halted in mid-anecdote and gazed at Wallach. My first impression was of a man in his early fifties, his longish black hair randomly streaked with gray. He wore an evening suit and wire-rim glasses tinted dark green. He smiled frostily at Wallach, then focused his attention on me.

"I am delighted to make your acquaintance, Fräulein."

Wallach cried out as my fingers bit into the soft flesh of his upper arm. I was close to fainting, but I could not look away. Wearing Pangloss's clothes and seated between the twin automatons was a dead thing, resembling an unwrapped mummy, its flesh the color and texture of parchment. There was enough nose left to keep the wire-rims in place, and I caught a glimpse of banked embers deep within the sockets. A few strands of silvery hair clung to the yellowed, flaking scalp. The creature lifted a skeletal hand—its fingers capped by filthy, splintered talons—and fitted an ebony cigarette holder in its lipless mouth.

"What is the matter with your lovely companion, Wallach? It is Wallach, is it not?" rasped the dead thing. "She seems to have taken ill."

Flustered, Wallach hurried me onto the balcony. Pangloss followed. His lady friends, forgotten for the moment, blinked like mediums emerging from deep trance.

After seating me on a bench, Wallach babbled something about fresh air and scampered off in search of a glass of water. I caught the odor of dust and cobwebs and found Pangloss standing beside me. He no longer looked like an unraveled pharaoh. I wondered if I was going mad.

"Perhaps I can be of some assistance, Fräulein Blau. After all, I am a doctor . . ." He reached to feel my pulse, but his hand was bone and desiccated flesh. I recoiled.

His features flowed and hardened into a mask of normalcy. "I was right. You can see." He stepped closer. The smell of rot threatened to choke me. "Who's get are you? Who sent you here? Was it Linder? Answer me!"

I staggered to my feet; I did not want that dead thing near me.

"You dare?" Red fire flickered behind green glass and something cold stabbed my brain. I remembered Sir Morgan and how he raped Denise's mind before he raped her body.

Not again. Never again. I pushed back, desperate to force the intruder out of my mind, even if it meant my eyes popped out on their stalks. I felt Pangloss's frustration boil into rage, then I was alone in my head.

We stood facing each other, both of us shivering. Pangloss was furious, but I sensed uncertainty in him.

"How old are you?" he hissed. His image flickered like a failing fluorescent light. One moment he was a well-dressed bon vivant, the next an animated corpse. It was rather distracting.

I told him the truth. There was no point in lying. "I was born in 1969."

"Impossible! You could not possibly have such power!" He grabbed my wrist, forcing me to look him in the face. The flesh sloughed away, revealing a death's-head. "Don't lie to me. I don't know whose get you are, but you aren't going to count coup with me. You may have caught me off-guard that time, but I won't make the same mistake twice. Oh, you're strong, that's true, but you don't know what to with it, do you?"

"Ah, Herr Doktor! There you are. Herr Wallach mentioned you were looking after Fräulein Blau for him . . ."

Pangloss and I stared at the man framed in the french windows. He was a small, slender man in his sixties with a dapper little mustache. Hardly a knight in shining armor, but he'd do.

Pangloss dropped my wrist as if it were leprous. He bowed stiffly in my direction. "I am relieved to hear that you are no longer ill, Fräulein. Now, you must please excuse me. He pushed past my savior, who regarded him with a wry smile, and disappeared into the house.

"A most unusual man, the Herr Doktor, is he not?" the little man mused aloud. "Ah! But I have not introduced myself. How rude! I am Erich Ghilardi."

"Do you . . . know Doktor Pangloss?"

Ghilardi shrugged. "Let us say I know of him. I fear Herr Wallach will be returning with your drink soon, so I shall dispense with small talk. May I visit you at your place of employment, Fräulein? Ah, do not look so surprised! Your behavior this evening was most proper. It was no failure on your part, I assure you. Everyone in our little clique knows how Wallach locates his companions."

I smiled and handed him my card. He bowed neatly and slipped it into his breast pocket. "*Auf Wiedersehen*, Fräulein Blau."

I watched him leave. Such a polite old gentleman. It was hard to imagine him dangling from the chandelier or groveling on all fours with a rubber ball in his mouth.

Wallach frowned when he returned with my glass of water. "What was Ghilardi doing out here?"

"Simply making sure I was all right. Nothing you need to worry about."

Wallach continued to fret. 'I don't like him paying attention to you. He's disturbed, you know."

"No, I didn't know. Who is he?"

Wallach didn't approve of me asking about Ghilardi, but his love of gossip overcame his misgivings. "He's one of Europe's leading scholars on fantasy and the occult. Rather, he used to be. He wrote several volumes on the masters of the genre: Poe, Lovecraft, and the like. Then he went over the edge. In fact, ten years ago he suffered some form of fit while hosting our little event. Most unfortunate. After that, he started claiming werewolves and vampires were real, or some such trash. He even wrote a book about shadow races living in secret coexistence with humanity for thousands of years. Of course, the book was widely ridiculed when it was published. Made himself a complete laughingstock."

It was late when I returned to my room. I stripped down to my skin and sat in the dark, thinking about what had happened at the party.

I'd finally come face-to-face with one of my own. What had Morgan really looked like? The thought was enough to make me shudder.

I contemplated the cheval glass in the corner of my room. What about me? What did *I* really look like?

I'd dismissed the belief that vampires hated mirrors as an old wives' tale, like the inviolability of sacred ground. Maybe *I* was the ignorant one.

Perhaps vampires loathe mirrors not because of what they *don't* see, but because of what they *do*.

It was dawn before I mustered the courage to stand before the mirror. I was terrified of what might stare back at me, but too curious to remain ignorant. Although my reflection wasn't that of a withered hag, I was outlined in a faint nimbus of reddish light. It was strongest about my head and shoulders; I was reminded of the corona glimpsed during an eclipse. My reflection smiled at me. I put my hand to my mouth, but my mirror twin didn't. A long, pointed tongue, like that of a cat, emerged from my duplicate's lips.

"No!" I struck the cheval glass hard enough to make it spin. I backed away, watching the mirror as it flashed reversed images of the room. It came to a halt with its back to me, the mirror facing the wall. I left it that way.

Ghilardi came to visit me within a week of our encounter at Herr Esel's party.

I received him in the parlor and, after sampling the house wine, escorted him to my room. He had a black valise, like the ones doctors carry. I didn't think anything about it, since my clients tended to rely on props.

Once we were alone, I excused myself and ducked behind a screen to change. I told him to make himself comfortable; he nodded politely, glancing about the room nonchalantly. He looked at the inverted mirror for a long moment before moving to the bed. I tried to engage him in conversation, hoping to divine his kink.

"So, Herr Ghilardi, what is it you like?"

"Like?" He sounded distracted.

"*Ja.* What is it you would like me to do to you? Or you to me? Don't be shy, *Mein Herr*, there's nothing you could say that could possibly shock me."

"I see." He didn't sound convinced. "Fräulein Blau . . ."

"Sonja."

"Umm, very well, then. Sonja, I would like you to do nothing to me."

I stepped out from behind the screen. "Are you quite sure about that, Herr Ghilardi?"

Ghilardi was standing beside the bed; he was still fully clothed and had the black bag open. He opened his mouth to answer but nothing came out. My work clothes often affected the customers that way.

I was dressed in a black chamois Merry Widow corset that lifted and separated my breasts like jelly molds. My legs were sheathed in black nylons with seams up the back, held in place by a black lace garter belt. I walked toward him slowly so I wouldn't overbalance on my spike-heeled patent-leather pumps. I still had my shades on. Most of my clients didn't mind that I kept my eyes hidden while I serviced them. Those who demanded to see my eyes never returned.

"Lilith!" It was a gasp of recognition and repudiation.

Before I could tell him he could call me whatever he liked, Ghilardi thrust a hand into his valise and withdrew a silver flask.

"*Verdamt Nosferatu!*" he cried, and dashed its contents in my face.

I staggered backward, spitting out a mouthful of lukewarm water. My makeup was ruined.

Pressing his advantage, Ghilardi produced a large silver crucifix and slammed it against my forehead, knocking off my shades and throwing me off-balance. I landed solidly on my rump.

I clapped my hands over my face and screwed my eyes shut. I was vaguely aware of Ghilardi intoning the words to the Lord's Prayer in Latin. I was too dumbstruck to notice if the skin had been flayed from my skull.

I'd been found out! I'd been identified as a monster and was going to die like one, that was the important thing. I thought of Denise's parents; how it would hurt them to find out what had really happened to their child.

There were hands on my shoulders. "Forgive me. Forgive me, *bitte!* You must think me a crazy old man, *nicht wahr?* How can I explain why I did such a cruel, insane thing . . ." He pulled a neatly pressed linen handkerchief from his breast pocket and began to daub at my face. "Please, Fräulein. I'm sorry if I frightened you. Are you hurt? Let me see . . ."

I took my hands from my face, and to my surprise as much as Ghilardi's, I began to cry. It was the first time I'd done so since Joe Lent's death.

"I am *Nosferatu*. You're not mistaken."

"*Nein.*" His voice was soft, comforting. His hand strayed to my damp, unmarred forehead and patted it reassuringly. "You are not one of the Damned, child. Forgive me for thinking such foolishness."

A flare of anger sparked deep inside me. "What do *you* know about it, old man?" I tried to pull away from him, and when he would not let me go, I bared my fangs. He sucked in a sharp breath, but did not draw away.

"Let me see your eyes."

I complied. Even the dim light of my room was painful.

"How long have you been like this?"

"Since 1970. Maybe 1969."

"*Unmöglich!*" He seemed as astonished as Pangloss. He wiped away my tears and told me to blow my nose. "You are something very rare, Fräulein Blau. Maybe something that has never happened before." He handed me my shades, which I gratefully slipped back on. "But you are confused, aren't you? And you do not want to be *Nosferatu*, eh? Maybe we can work out an agreement between us, *ja?*" The old man smiled and rocked back on his heels. "How would you like to come live with me?"

Herr Ghilardi bought my contract from Frau Zobel and promptly installed me in his home, changing my life forever, if not for better.

He was independently wealthy. The Ghilardi fortune originated from a series of arranged marriages between minor Italian princes and the firstborn daughters of Swiss moneylenders. The family estate was located on the shores of Lake Geneva, far removed from city life and nosy neighbors.

The manor boasted a private library devoted to the fantastic, although Ghilardi's filing system was an anal-retentive's nightmare; leatherbound first editions sandwiched between garish paperbacks, while secondhand book-club volumes were thrust among rare folios.

I was surrounded by fictionalized reflections of my affliction. Ghilardi allowed me the freedom to examine whatever I wanted, but did not steer me in the direction of any one book.

I searched countless volumes for information, no matter how distorted, that might shed some light on my condition. I had access to Ariosto's *Orlando Furioso*, Rabelais' *Gargantua*, Walpole's *Castle of Otranto*, Beckford's *Vathek*, Radcliffe's *Mysteries of Udolpho*, Huysmans' *Là Bas*, and even the infamous

Malleus Maleficarum. I met with nothing but frustration. There were no fictional counterparts for the likes of Morgan and Pangloss—or myself; Rymer's Varney was a penny-dreadful scarecrow and Stoker's Dracula a pathetic Victorian sex fantasy.

I sifted through the works of Polidori, Poe, Le Fanu, Wilde, Macher, Hodgson, Lovecraft, and a score of others and came away with nothing. Whatever clues I succeeded in plucking from the morass were inevitably contradictory. It was six weeks after my arrival when he finally gave me the book.

Ghilardi was on the terrace, studying a storm building in the mountain tops. The lake had grown dark and choppy. When storms break on Lake Geneva, they are awesome testimony to nature's potency. Ghilardi liked to watch.

"Did you know, my dear, that it was on the shores of this very lake, while watching a storm, that Mary Shelley first conceived the idea for *Frankenstein?*" He did not take his eyes off the darkening clouds as he spoke, a brandy snifter cradled in one hand.

I did not answer. I had already learned to recognize his rhetorical questions.

"So, you did not find what it was you were searching for?" His eyes flickered sideways, regarding me carefully. "Then, perhaps, this might be of some assistance." He removed a slender hardbound volume from a nearby table and handed it to me.

The book was entitled *Die Rasse Vorgabe*. *The Pretending Race*. This was the book Wallach had mentioned at Esel's party. The one that had ruined Ghilardi's reputation, reducing him to the level of von Däniken, Churchward, and Berlitz. It became my bible, the revelation on which I built my world.

Humans insist on defining reality by their standards. They are poorly equipped to do so, since they are selectively deaf and blind in one eye. They are beings with an insatiable need to categorize the universe that surrounds them, but demand that the facts reveal a universe suited for human cultivation and exploitation. Things must remain status quo.

The Pretenders dwell in the cracks in mankind's perception of reality. To the untutored eye they are nothing to look at: beggars, cripples, prostitutes, anonymous strangers. Their faces are unremarkable, their demeanor bland. They aren't the type that like to draw attention to themselves. That is why Ghilardi referred to them as Pretenders; they pretend to be human, hiding their demonic *otherness* behind a mask of carefully constructed banality.

Only to the trained eye do the beasts stand revealed, their auras suffused with fearsome energy.

Ghilardi held the belief that mankind possesses a genetic trait for telekinesis, telepathy, clairvoyance, and all the other sixth-sense stuff. Aeons of civilization and trickery by Pretenders led to the gradual withering of these psionic powers, the extrasensory equivalent of an appendix. Ghilardi was convinced he held the key that would awaken these dormant powers in any human, be they sigma cum laude or a hod carrier.

According to Ghilardi, Pretenders are the creatures found in human myth and legend, twisted beyond recognition: vampires, werewolves, incubi and succubi, ogres, undines, and demons too numerous to mention. They escape detection by hiding in plain sight. The various species have only two things in common: they can pass for humans, and they prey on them.

Five years after the fact, I finally discovered how vampires—or what humans refer to as vampires—reproduce.

The bite of the vampire is not the factor that taints the victim; it's the saliva—in some cases, the sperm—that triggers the transformation. Once the victim dies, the corpse undergoes radical physical and genetic restructuring, readying itself for the new occupant. Once the transmutation is complete, a minor demon enters the host, but that is far from the end of the process.

The transition from the spiritual plane to the material world is traumatic. The newborn vampire enters the host body without a personality or past. It has no frame of reference, only raw instinct. The neonate monster uses as its template the only thing on hand: the brain of the victim. This is either a good or bad move, depending on how long the victim has been dead.

If the host is freshly dead—say, two or three days—the fledgling vampire resembles, for the most part, a normal human, complete with memories and intellect. However, if the resurrection takes too long, what arises is a shambling mockery, all but brain-dead. These hapless monstrosities are revenants, the idiot children of the vampire race. Humans call them zombies or ghouls. They are far more plentiful than the traditional vampire, but their stupidity ensures their inevitable destruction. Many are so slow-witted they forget to hide during the day and die their final death, burned to the bone by the sun's rays.

True vampires of power—like the fictional Count Dracula and his real-world counterpart, Sir Morgan—are rare. Even under ideal resurrection conditions vampires are born with imperfect brains. It takes decades for them to learn how to master their powers. Most end up killed, either by humans, or rival predators, or their own ignorance, long before they gain enough experience to lay claim to being a Noble, one of the vampiric ruling class.

Nobles are proud and arrogant. They are not afraid of being discovered; they flaunt their powers, often going out of their way to attract attention to themselves. They can control the minds of others, their strength and vitality are immense, they practice a form of astral projection, and, by human standards, they are practically immortal.

The most interesting difference between Nobles and their wet-mouthed country cousins is that they do not feed on blood alone. In fact, they prefer feasting on human emotion—the blacker the better. Nobles are skilled in summoning and manipulating the darker aspects of man's nature, cultivating it so it provides them with an excellent vintage. Ghilardi claimed that Nobles had been covertly involved with the Nazi death camps and the Stalinist pogroms.

It was easy to see why Ghilardi had been treated like a pariah dog by his peers. If I didn't know better myself, I would have dismissed the book as the ravings of a crank. Ghilardi claimed that the key to his discovery of the Real World was an ancient grimoire called the *Aegrisomnia* or, loosely translated, *Dreams of a Fevered Mind*.

I asked to see this so-called tome of forbidden lore, still uncertain whether Ghilardi might be a good-natured crackpot.

"It is a most wondrous book, the *Aegrisomnia*," he explained as he unlocked the display case. "I came across it while researching the folklore of the vampire. Most interesting. Shortly after I read it for the first time, I discovered I could . . . see things. That was ten years ago. I was hosting our little *klatsch* that year. When Herr Doktor Pangloss arrived I . . ." He fell silent, then glanced up at me. "I am told I had a collapse of some kind. I do not remember very much. But after that, Pangloss did not attend our parties for nearly a decade. That is when I began working on my book."

The *Aegrisomnia* was a large, rather awkwardly bound volume with metal hasps and an Arabesque lock. It looked like a medieval teenager's diary. The text was in Latin, although some passages looked to be Greek. There were alchemical tables, conjuring diagrams, and what Ghilardi claimed were non-Euclidean geometric formulas. Every other page was covered in complex, multilayered patterns that, at first glance, resembled a child's collection of Spirograph drawings. However, when I looked at it a second time, I detected words hidden amid the esoteric scribbles.

Although my Latin was rusty enough to inflict lockjaw, I managed to decipher the opening line: "Greetings. You have regained that which was lost." I had to rely on Ghilardi's translation of the "secret text," which detailed the habits of the various Pretender races.

There were discourses on the matriarchal structure of the *vargr*, treatises on the reproductive cycle of incubi and succubi, and essays on the diet of ogres. Ghilardi was convinced that the *Aegrisomnia* was a Rosetta Stone for viewing the Real World. In theory, once exposed to its wisdom, the readers' "inner sight" would awaken, allowing them to pierce the veil and see the Real World. Unfortunately, Ghilardi's attempts to prove the existence of the Real World were disastrous. Most of the hand-picked initiates saw nothing but meaningless scribbles. The last one started screaming and didn't stop until he was sedated. After that, Ghilardi kept his precious volume of forgotten lore under lock and key.

Once I accepted him as my mentor, Ghilardi outlined the details of our arrangement. He would provide me with shelter and an identity while I would permit him to observe my evolution into a Noble.

Ghilardi stated that I was a fluke, a freak even by Pretender standards. I was proof of man's tampering with the reproductive cycle of the vampire. Human technology had interfered in the natural order of things. Morgan had left me for dead in the gutter—and by all rights, I should have died—but new blood was forced into my veins, diluting, if not completely neutralizing, the virus polluting my flesh. The demon was trapped inside a living host, not a piece of dead meat. Most irregular. Since I never died and my brain was in perfect working order—well, almost—I was evolving into a Noble, a "king vampire," at an unheard-of pace. Ghilardi was thrilled by the prospect of documenting my progress. I was to be his proof that he wasn't a crazy old fool.

He also had other, far less academic plans for me. He'd spent his entire life steeped in the romance of the occult investigator. He fancied himself in the role of Professor Van Helsing, tracking down the scourge of humanity and driving a stake through its heart at cockcrow. But he was too old and infirm for such heroics. It wasn't until much later that I realized how insanely brave his attack on me at Frau Zobel's had been. Ghilardi had stepped into that room expecting to be killed, yet determined to play the role of fearless vampire hunter. Now he had the chance to vicariously experience the danger and adventure through his pupil.

I should never have allowed him to do it; it was stupid and foolhardy—neither of us had any idea of what the consequences might be. But I had come to trust Ghilardi as a wise man who knew what he was doing, and if he wanted to hypnotize me so he could talk to the demon trapped inside my psyche . . . well, who was I to tell him no?

It didn't take very long for him to put me in a trance. I felt as if I was sliding down the throat of a huge animal. I was surrounded by red darkness; part of me started to panic as I felt control of my body slip away. I realized I'd made a big mistake, but it was too late to do anything but fall. I thought I heard something begin to laugh. I regained consciousness thirty seconds later.

He kept insisting it wasn't my fault. That I wasn't responsible for what happened. Maybe he was right, maybe it *wasn't* me. But they were *my* hands. The bones are so brittle at that age—so fragile, like a bird—and broken arms don't heal as fast as they used to. I'm sorry; I'm so very, very sorry. Wherever you are, please forgive me. Forgive *us*.

From then on, the Other was my constant companion. It had always been there. At first it was too weak to assert itself, except during times of extreme stress, such as Joe Lent's beating. For years it had been my silent, parasitic partner, feeding on the emotions generated by my clients. Now it was my intangible Siamese twin, joined at the medulla oblongata, and I could no longer ignore its existence. I was unable to predict its behavior or, worse yet, safely control it.

My first outing as a vampire hunter was in Frankfurt, since Ghilardi deemed it wise to avoid a ruckus in our own backyard.

The neighborhood had been a ghetto before the Nazis emptied it. Then the Allies had bombed it until nothing remained but the cellars. Although rebuilt after the war, the neighborhood's soul never recovered. The nice new apartment buildings quickly withered, transforming the district into a slum. There was so much despair permeating the area the half-life would last for another thirty years. Perhaps that's what attracted him.

He was new; he still had grave dirt behind his ears. He wasn't experienced at Pretending; he'd forgotten the basics, such as breathing all the time. That's a problem among the recently resurrected: most of them suffer from massive brain damage. This one didn't look too zombed-out, although he was far from MENSA material.

I watched the derelict, fascinated and appalled. I'd never seen a revenant before. Morgan was as far removed from the thing huddled in the doorway as *Homo sapiens* is from *Homo erectus*. The human eye could see nothing but a starveling junkie, shirtless and barefoot, shivering on the doorstep of an abandoned building. He was just another street person, made invisible by poverty. How long? How long had I been walking among the dead?

The revenant wore the body of a white male in his mid-thirties; he stood in the shadows of the doorway, thin arms wrapped around a narrow, sunken chest that did not rise or fall. His clothing consisted of a pair of ill-fitting pants held up by a length of rope and an old greatcoat the color of smoke. The uninformed would have attributed the derelict's shivering to the cold, but I knew better. He was a junkie, but it wasn't smack he was hurting for.

Ghilardi wrinkled his nose in disgust. "*Mein Gott!* I can smell him from here."

I nodded, never taking my eyes off him. "Probably a bum to begin with. The district's full of them; they sleep in condemned buildings and in the piles of uncollected garbage in the alleys." I put one hand in my coat pocket, caressing the silver blade Ghilardi had presented to me in Geneva in anticipation of our first kill.

"Stay put, *verstadt?* I don't want you getting hurt."

Ghilardi said nothing, but we both glanced at his arm resting in its sling.

I walked across the street, aware of being watched from both sides. I prayed the old man would not try to interfere. If anything else happened to him . . . I suppressed the thought. I was going into battle and I needed to concentrate my attention on my prey . . . the enemy.

The revenant straightened as I drew near, his eyes gleaming hungrily. I spoke to him in German.

"You look like you're in a bad way, friend."

The undead thing nodded. He still wasn't breathing. Bad camouflage: the creature was seriously ignorant of the laws of supernatural selection.

"I can fix you up, if you can meet the price. You *do* have it, don't you?"

The revenant stuffed a pale hand into his pants pocket; the fist emerged bristling with deutsche marks. Following a dim memory from his previous existence, he rolled his victims after he finished draining them. He had no intrinsic understanding of money, except that it made good bait.

I smiled and nodded in the direction of the alleyway. The revenant complied, his movements insectile.

Once we were in the solitude of the alley, the revenant hissed; his pupils dilating rapidly until they swallowed the entire eye. He expected me to scream and try to escape. Instead, I grinned, baring fangs as sharp as his own. The growl percolating in his chest became a confused whine. This had never happened before, and the revenant was unsure as to how to proceed.

"C'mere, dead boy."

The derelict tried to flee; I grabbed a fistful of greasy hair and jerked him back into the alley. There was a wet tearing sound and I found myself holding a snarl of matted hair and dripping scalp. The revenant fell among the overflowing garbage cans, disturbing a small army of rats. He hurled one of the writhing bags of fur and teeth at me. I batted it aside with a swat of my hand. The undead thing leapt at me, shrieking like a tea kettle. His ragged nails raked my face, leaving wet trenches. I stumbled backward and instinctively tried to shield my face with my forearm.

The derelict grabbed my wrist in an attempt to throw me off-balance. I lunged forward, slamming him against the cold brick wall. Pressed belly-to-belly amid heaps of rubbish, we resembled low-rent lovers enjoying a sleazy tryst. I kept my left forearm wedged under the revenant's chin, forcing his fangs away from my face. The beast reeked of clotted blood and dried feces.

The thing whined piteously when he saw the knife, the blade forged to resemble a frozen silver flame. I realized I was grinning.

The blade went in easy, piercing skin and muscle like rotten sailcloth. The knife slid home between the fifth and sixth ribs, puncturing the heart as if I'd jabbed a pin into a toy balloon.

The revenant yowled and thrashed like a landed fish, but showed no signs of dying. Frightened for the first time since the fight began, I stabbed his chest three more times. Nothing. Obviously the old legend concerning impaling a vampire's heart was unreliable. I began plunging my knife into every organ I could think of, clinically, at first, but with increasing frenzy as I realized I was beginning to tire. The Other laughed at me as I stabbed the struggling revenant. She was amused by my ignorance.

Don't take it too badly. It's your first time, after all. The first time is always messy and clumsy. You've got to expect it to be bloody. But it leaves you with a taste for more.

"Get out of my *head*, damn you!" The knife buried itself in the revenant's neck, severing the spinal cord.

The screams stopped as if I'd pulled the plug on a stereo system. The derelict's eyes disappeared into their sockets, retracted by withering eye stalks. Repulsed, I stepped back and let the thing fall; his limbs curled inward, like the legs of a dead spider. I moved away quickly, clapping a hand over my nose and breathing through my mouth. It didn't help.

"*Mein Gött . . .*"

It was Ghilardi. He stood at the mouth of the alley, staring at the corpse as it continued its accelerated deterioration. The body bloated and grew black, its head resembling the release valve on an overinflated tire.

"How long have you—"

"Since he screamed. I was afraid for . . . Jesus!" Ghilardi's face was the color of oatmeal. The corpse exploded with a ripe gush of gas. Ghilardi vomited before he could finish his sentence. I grabbed his good elbow and hurried him onto the street.

Ghilardi was visibly shaken. The vampire-hunting fantasies of his youth were full of adventure and suspense. They never mentioned the stink of putrefaction and the taste of vomit.

I looked at my hands; they were trembling, but not out of fear.

It leaves you with a taste for more . . .

". . . you're hurt." I realized Ghilardi was speaking to me. "We'll have to see about those gashes on your face."

We halted beneath one of the remaining functional street lamps so he could examine my wounds.

"Gashes?" I replied dreamily. "What gashes?"

All that remained were four pencil-thin, rapidly paling lines of pink.

Ghilardi lost interest in vampire hunting after Frankfurt. I didn't. The mass of hate and frustration knotted in my guts was sated by my hunts. I wanted to feel Morgan's unlife squirting between my fingers, but was willing to settle for killing lesser beasts.

I talked myself into believing it was a safety valve that allowed me to keep the Other in check, that I was performing a public service. Idiot. I was doing it because I got off on it.

I traveled all over Europe—even going so far as to make raids into Czechoslovakia, Yugoslavia, and Poland—while Ghilardi stayed home and filled his notebooks with information relating to the care and feeding of a vampire.

Time begins to blur at this point. Ghilardi warned about that. Vampires can go to ground for years, not because they're superhumanly patient but simply because they have such a lousy sense of time. The years begin to run together. I can recall fragments . . .

1975: She looked so out of place, wandering among the burn-outs and old hippies. Her blond curls, starched pinafore, and patent-leather Mary Janes made her strangely archaic, like a child lost in time as well as space. She drifted in and out of the crowd, plucking at the sleeves of passersby.

It was very late for a child to be alone on the streets of Amsterdam, and the neighborhood was not one where mothers normally let their children roam unattended. I was lounging in front of a live-music club, waiting for the band to start playing. Several other patrons milled outside the front door, smoking their foul tobacco-and-hash cigarettes. Inside the club, locked inside a special kiosk, an elderly woman sold state-approved hashish, morphine, heroin, and clean syringes.

Most of the people clustered outside the bar were young. Many were dressed in faded denims sporting "Give Peace a Chance" and "Eco" patches. Amsterdam was a favorite spot for aging hippies fleeing the growing complacency of the '70s and the inevitability of their adulthood. The hippies looked stoned and bitter, as if perplexed by society passing them by. Judging by their accents, a good number of them were American. Amsterdam was also popular among draft-dodgers.

The little girl—surely no more than five or six—flitted from person to person, her small voice lost in the noise from the street. I couldn't hear what she was saying, but I had a good guess; "Please, won't someone take me home to my mother? I'm lost. I want to go home, but it's too dark and I'm scared. Please, won't someone take me home? I don't live too far away . . ."

A tall, thin hippie with long hair and a longer face stooped so he could listen to her. He straightened, toying with the hash cigarette he held in one hand. He glanced back at the doorway to the club, then down at the pale little face. He shrugged his bony shoulders and she slipped her tiny hand into his large one and started down the street.

I followed at a discreet distance, listening to the little girl as she chattered away about her mother, her brothers, and her kitten. The hippie nodded every so often, the scent of Turkish tobacco and hash marking his passage.

The neighborhood began to decline and soon the little girl was leading the hippie through one of the uglier districts in the city. The row houses were red brick and had once been pleasant, well-scrubbed homes, with pleasant, well-scrubbed families living in them. But that was before the Second World War. Something happened in that neighborhood during the Occupation—something nasty—and the neighborhood never recovered from the wound dealt it by the Nazis. I paused, fascinated by its similarity to the place in Frankfurt. It felt the same.

I shifted my vision, curious to see what marked this spot as a Bad Place.

The buildings shimmered, as if I was looking through a curtain made of rising heat, and I was standing on the same narrow cobblestone street. A large flag marked with a swastika fluttered over the doorway of the center house. The banner fluttered in a long-ago breeze as unsmiling men dressed in black leather topcoats escorted frightened men, women, and children into the house. The vision burst like a soap bubble, dispersing in time for me to see the little girl leading the slack-faced hippie across the same threshold.

I dashed across the street and up the flight of stone steps that led to the front door of what had been, thirty years ago, Gestapo headquarters.

The hippie must have been exceptionally stoned or too thoroughly tranced not to notice that the little girl's "home" was an abandoned building marked for demolition. I came to a halt in what was once the foyer.

Strips of yellowed wallpaper hung from the wall like soiled bandages. Broken glass and a decade's accumulation of filth gritted underneath my heels. There were discarded wine bottles and syringes scattered about, but the pungent aroma of human piss and vomit was missing; this wasn't squatter territory.

The first floor was a long central hallway flanked by two rooms on either side. At the end of the hallway was a rickety staircase that led to the second story.

I moved cautiously down the hall toward the stairs, glancing into each of the abandoned rooms. None of the rooms had doors. I felt a buzzing in my skull and the curtain of shimmering heat reappeared. The foyer changed; the wallpaper was no longer peeling and a thick carpet ran the length of the hall.

Everything looked very cheery, except for the Gestapo agents putting out cigarettes on a young man tied to a chair.

In the next room a pudgy man in a spotless white smock—like a kindly doctor sent from Central Casting—carefully adjusted the connections on the car battery attached to an older man's genitals. And in the third room a screaming woman was raped by a German shepherd while three Gestapo agents smoked cigarettes and laughed.

I staggered backward, my guts convulsing. One of the Gestapo men—a short, rat-faced man with wire-rim glasses—swiveled his head in my direction, scowling as if he'd seen something.

The buzzing stopped and I was back in the deserted hallway, shivering like a junkie. No wonder there weren't any signs of recent squatting; even the most insensitive *Lumpen* could feel the evil in this place! I fought to control my trembling. How many other slices of hell did the Nazis leave scattered across Europe?

I turned to look into the fourth, and final, room before ascending the stairs to the second story. The hippie lurched forward, one hand clamped against the wound in his neck, trying to staunch the flow of blood spurting from his jugular. His Hawkwind T-shirt was already muddied beyond reading, and his long, sad face was horribly white.

The hippie wobbled drunkenly for a second, his eyes empty of sanity. His mouth opened and shut like a landed fish. I could hear the high-pitched tittering of a child echoing through the empty house. The hippie pitched forward, collapsing in my arms. I let the body drop onto the bare boards. My hands were slick with his blood. My revulsion was heightened by the thrill sparked by the sight and smell of the red stuff.

The thing was upstairs. I mounted the staircase carefully, grimacing as the stairs groaned and creaked under my weight . . .

Something small with crimson eyes landed on my back, tearing at my throat with sharp nails and needle-like teeth. I tumbled down the stairs, the hell-child riding me like a demented jockey. Pain raked my shoulders and the back of my neck as the thing tore at me. I had a vision of the unholy creature chewing away at my neck, like a harbor rat on a rope, as I staggered to my feet.

I slammed against the walls, attempting to shake loose the thing clinging to me. Plaster fell from the ceiling in gritty clouds, mingling with my blood, but the child-beast held tight. Desperate to free myself, I did a running cartwheel down the hall and was successful in dislodging my attacker.

The child-vampire lay among a pile of discarded wine bottles and strips of wallpaper. She no longer resembled the golden-haired little girl who'd coerced the hapless young man into walking her home.

When I looked at the child-thing, I saw a hideously withered crone's face set atop tiny shoulders. Her mouth was toothless except for two sharp little fangs, and her eyes glowed like molten steel. The child-thing straightened her blood-soaked pinafore, and stared at me for a moment. Then the little girl was back, weeping and shivering and calling for her mother.

It was a good illusion. The urge to protect children is strongly ingrained in humans—especially the females. I wavered, suddenly overcome with the desire to lift this darling child in my arms and hug her . . .

Trick! It's a trick! The Other's voice was like ice water in my brain.

"I. . . . I was going to pick that thing up," I muttered aloud in astonishment.

Hissing her anger, the child-vampire sprang at me, fangs unsheathed. The beast was as fast as an ape, but I managed to catch the girl-harridan in midleap. My hands tightened around her wizened neck. There was no way I could get to my knife without exposing myself to another assault, and I was already weakened by blood loss.

The hateful thing twisted and writhed in my grasp, slashing my hands with her fangs and claws. Her eyes shone like a trapped rat's. A surge of hate and disgust swept over me, and I began to throttle the child. Her yowls and curses grew in volume and she kicked at me with her tiny Mary Janes. A reddish froth rimed her lips; a combination of her saliva and my blood.

It felt as if all of my willpower was being channeled down my arms and into my hands. The vampire-girl's struggles became more and more frenzied as her eyes started from their sockets. I glimpsed exposed muscle and finger bones gleaming wetly in the dim light, but I did not loosen my hold.

I didn't notice the buzzing at first, as my attacker's screeching served to camouflage it. But I had the feeling I was being watched . . .

There was someone standing in the doorway of the room the hippie had staggered from. It was a man in early middle age, his hair touched by silver at the temples. He was dressed in a German SS colonel's uniform, the stainless-steel skull on his hat glinting in the light. He stood holding a pair of black leather gloves in one hand, and it was evident from the look of mild surprise on his face that he could see me.

That face. I *knew* it. I knew it all too well.

It was Morgan.

The Nazi Morgan flickered, like the picture on an old television set, then disappeared.

I looked down at the vampire-child. She'd stopped struggling because her head had come off in my hands. The tiny body lay on the cold floor; a liquid with the same color and consistency as congealed spaghetti sauce oozed from her neck.

I stared at the little head I held in my hands. The child's face had returned.

God, ohGodno. I've gone mad and killed a child. I hallucinated the whole thing. I kidnapped some poor little girl and took her to this terrible place and I murdered her.

The little girl's smooth, baby-soft face turned the color of antique ivory and the skin cracked and peeled like parchment.

I dropped the vampire's head and kicked it like a soccer ball. It bounced once and came to rest against the corpse of the hippie in the Hawkwind T-shirt.

The old Gestapo headquarters did not offer any further glimpses of Morgan, although I stumbled across evidence of far more human monsters.

Although I searched the house from front door to attic, I could not bring myself to investigate the cellar. I took five steps into the darkness, then began to shiver uncontrollably. Whatever went on down there, thirty years ago, was unspeakable; it was the source of the evil that tainted the neighborhood like a ghostly cancer. I had no doubt that was where the vampire-child had nested during the day.

I fled the house, choking on bile and fear.

1976: It was the cemetery Morrison was buried in. It was also the same place Oscar Wilde, Balzac, Voltaire, Molière, Sarah Bernhardt, Victor Hugo, Edith Piaf, Max Ernst, and Gustav Doré, among others, happened to be interred. But as far as the teenagers were concerned, Jim Morrison was the only noteworthy occupant.

Père Lachaise was a fantastic necropolis located on the northeast side of Paris, off the Boulevard de Belleville. It was once the gardens attached to the villa of François d'Aix de Lachaise, confessor to Louis XIV; now it was home to over 20,000 monuments and 800,000 graves.

There were more famous dead people in Père Lachaise than live ones in New York City. Sublime masters of the written word lay next to petit-bourgeois shopkeepers. Infamous hedonists and adulterers rested alongside proper Christian ladies who would have been scandalized by their proximity to such sin while alive.

Like any great city, Père Lachaise attracted a steady stream of tourists and vandals. The tour guides were fond of recounting how a Victorian lady was so shocked by the rampant griffon guarding Oscar Wilde's tomb, she removed the offending organ with a hammer she just happened to have in her purse.

The French are pragmatic in regard to such acts; it's the price you pay for fame.

However, the vandalism perpetrated by the thousands of young pilgrims who flocked each year to the tomb of the Lizard King transcended mere desecration and approached true folk art.

Outside of a modest marble bust depicting the singer at his peak—the nose smashed by a recent incarnation of the Victorian castratrix—Morrison's grave was simple and not very big. The graffiti radiating from the doomed poet, however, was far from simple.

It had been added to over the years, layer by layer, in a thousand different hands and a dozen different languages, until it formed a dense, interlocking mural. Whether the medium was aerosol spray paint, felt-tipped marker, or pocket knife, the messages all boiled down to WE MISS YOU.

Once Morrison's plot could no longer contain the scrawled endearments, they began to spread onto the surrounding monuments, until the testimony of the fans' love for their fallen hero obliterated the inscription on the plaque marking the resting place of Abelard and Héloise.

There were always young pilgrims wandering through Père Lachaise, the majority of them tripping their brains out. Normally, vampires avoid such well-trafficked areas, preferring to haunt lonelier locations.

I was lured to Paris by the rumors circulating among the counterculture diehards that Morrison's ghost wandered Père Lachaise at night in search of groupies. While in a nearby bar I overheard a gang of teenage fans discussing "visiting Jim" that night. I followed them from a safe distance.

There were four pilgrims, three boys and a girl, full of wine and acid and exhilarated by the prospect of glimpsing their idol's ghost. Since they'd never seen Morrison in concert, this was as close as they'd ever get to actually meeting him in the flesh.

I followed them over the fence into the graveyard, watching as they wove through the field of tilting stones. It was obvious they had made the trip dozens of times; they threaded their way through the maze of marble and granite with the surefootedness of Sherpas.

Why not? This was their shrine and as much a part of their lives as the prayer wheels of Katmandu.

Of the four, the oldest couldn't have been more than fourteen at the time of their messiah's death. It was a chilly October night and they were outfitted in American jeans and sneakers; two of the boys wore leather jackets while the third shivered in a flannel shirt that was no protection against the autumnal wind. The girl wore a heavy denim jacket with an intricately embroidered slogan on the back that read NO ONE HERE GETS OUT ALIVE.

The boy in the flannel shirt carried a large wine bottle, which he stopped to drink from every few steps. His companions hissed at him to keep up. Looking cold and disgruntled, he hurried after them.

One of the boys in the leather jackets had a knapsack with him, which he proceeded to empty once they reached the grave site. He produced several candle stubs, two more bottles of wine, and several joints.

"Think we'll see him?" whispered the girl as she hugged her elbows for warmth.

The older boy nodded. "Sure. Philippe—you know, Jean-Michel's cousin?—he saw Jim just last week."

The boy in the flannel shirt snorted derisively, shifting from foot to foot in order to keep from freezing. "Philippe sees lots of things. He virtually lives off acid and Vichy water."

The girl's tone was colder than the wind knifing through the graveyard.

"I don't think you *want* to see him, Pierre. You're going to ruin *everything*."

Pierre looked wounded. It was painfully obvious that the only reason he was standing in the middle of a cemetery in the middle of the night, waiting for a ghost to put in an appearance, was because she was there. "Céleste . . ."

The boy who'd unloaded the knapsack arranged the candles into a lopsided circle atop the marble slab covering Morrison's grave. "Céleste is right," he said, touching each wick with his lighter. "If you don't want to see him, you *won't*. You can't think negative, Pierre, or you'll scare him away."

The candles flickered wildly in the wind gusting through the cemetery, throwing strange shadows on the disfigured bust situated at the head of the grave. The group uncorked the remaining wine bottles and huddled around the meager light. Soon the odor of marijuana mingled with the smell of lichen and dead leaves.

After a half-hour's vigil, Pierre stood up and kicked at the extinguished candles. "This is bullshit! I'm going to end up with pneumonia because Philippe Daigrepoit thought he saw something while he was tripping!"

The other members of the group shifted uneasily, but it was evident they had each come to similar conclusions.

"I don't know about you"—this was addressed to Céleste alone, although she was unaware of it—"but I'm going home to . . . Oh, my God!" The half-empty wine bottle slid from his numbed fingers, smashing onto the grave slab. Pierre stared down the narrow alley that wound between the tombs opposite the Morrison site.

His companions turned to see what he was staring at. Céleste gasped aloud and put her hands over her mouth.

"It's . . . it's him. It's Jim!"

From my hiding place among the monuments, I could see a slender masculine figure standing a hundred yards away, its skin as pale as moonlight. I felt a momentary shock of recognition as I stared at the face of the dead rock star. Was it possible? Was Morrison a Pretender?

The Lizard King, resplendent in jeans and a leather jacket, beckoned with one languid hand but did not come any closer. Despite the cold, he was bare-chested underneath the jacket.

"Céleste, he wants *you*," whispered the older boy. "He wants *you* to go with him." His voice contained awe and envy.

Céleste's eyes had the glaze of someone discovering her fondest fantasy brought to life. "Me . . . he wants *me* . . ." Her voice was dreamy and detached, as if she was talking in her sleep. She stepped forward, eager to embrace her one true love.

"Wait a minute, Céleste! Hey, are you going to stand there and let her go with that thing?" Pierre stared at his friends, then at Céleste. He sounded genuinely frightened and more than a little jealous. He grabbed her forearm, trying to force her to look at him. "Céleste! Céleste, listen to me. Don't go with him. You can't!'

"Let go of me, Pierre." Her gaze remained fixed on the Lizard King.

"No!"

"What are you worried about? It's only Jim. He won't hurt me."

"Céleste . . ."

She wrenched herself free of his grasp, hurrying toward the dead singer.

I moved from my place in the shadows, bowling over the leather-jacketed youths. I saw the Lizard King touch her cheek and take Céleste by the hand. He was going to lead her deep into the necropolis, where he could feast undisturbed. If he disappeared into the labyrinth of crypts and tombstones, I'd never find them in time.

I tackled the retreating vampire, knocking it free of Céleste. The thing thrashed violently underneath me, but couldn't break free of my hold. On closer inspection I could see the leather jacket and jeans he wore were filthy, the jacket moldering. Morrison's face snarled at me, but the vampire wasn't the dead singer resurrected.

Vampires are the chameleons of the Real World; they can remodel their faces into any semblance they choose. It's the supernatural equivalent of protective coloration. And this vampire had chosen the semblance that would ensure him good hunting. The vampire's features were exactly the same as those on the funerary bust—right down to the smashed nose. At a distance of a hundred yards, the illusion was good enough to attract prey; and by the time they were close enough to notice something was wrong, the vampire had them securely tranced.

The Lizard King hissed, exposing his fangs. I kept one hand clamped on his throat, pinning him to the ground, as I reached for my knife.

"Leave him *alone*. You're spoiling *everything!*" Céleste brought a memorial vase, filled with rank water and withered daffodils, crashing down on my head. I fell back, momentarily stunned.

"Jim! Oh, Jim, sweetheart! Are you all right?" She helped the vampire to his feet.

The Lizard King grinned at her, his eyes glowing and fangs unsheathed.

"*Nooooo!*" Her denial was thin and high-pitched, like a child refusing to go to bed.

The Lizard King grabbed her by the hair, pulling her closer to his mouth. Céleste struggled, her screams bursting from her like the cries of frightened birds.

Although blood from my head wound was trickling down behind my shades and dripping into my eyes, I got to my feet.

"Let her go, dead boy."

The Lizard King snarled again, tightening his grip on the girl. Céleste sobbed hysterically, too frightened to scream.

"Céleste! Merciful God . . ."

It was Pierre. The boy was still there, even though his companions had fled the minute the girl began to scream. The youth stood just beyond reach of the vampire. I could tell the young idiot was getting ready to jump the monster.

I stepped forward, hoping to draw the Lizard King's attention from the boy. It worked. The vampire snapped his head in my direction, baring his teeth like a cornered rat. I could hear the keeper's hounds baying close by. So did the vampire, his stolen face registering fear. There were too many witnesses. He'd have to abandon his catch. He propelled the hysterical girl into Pierre's arms. The boy did not bother to question his luck and ran in the direction he and his companions had come from, Céleste in tow.

The Lizard King turned and ran, but I was right after him. He sprinted through the graveyard like a broken field runner, but I managed to keep up with him. I caught him by the iron fence. He was clambering over the ancient iron spikes when I buried the knife to the hilt in the meat of his left calf.

I'd discovered that while *I* was impervious to silver, most Pretenders were hyper-allergic to it. The vampire screamed as silver penetrated flesh and muscle, but succeeded in boosting himself over the wrought-iron fence. I could tell the vampire's nervous system was already affected by the silver toxins in his bloodstream; he dragged a rapidly degenerating left leg as he plunged into a knot of late-night party-goers, bleating and waving his arms. Luckily, they thought he was just another geek visiting Jim Morrison's grave. I took my time killing the bastard when I caught up to him.

That was also the year I noticed I'd stopped aging . . . at least to human eyes. For some reason, my metabolism decided twenty-three was the ideal time of life, and stayed there. That was also the year I began buying black-market blood. After years of living off the blood of animals, the thirst upped the stakes.

1977: In Rome people walk the most chaotic streets in Europe, unaware that twenty-two feet below the soles of their shoes lies a kingdom that extends nearly six hundred miles, with an estimated population of six million.

I was seated at a sidewalk café, nursing a glass of red wine while I watched the evening crowds, when the messenger arrived.

He was a thin, pasty-faced young man with unhealthy purple blotches under his eyes. I divined by the flicker of his aura that he was a human sensitive. He was also quite mad.

"You are Blue?" His English was execrable, but I knew no Italian.

“What do you want?” I stared at the black halo crowning his head; the rays emanating from his skull snapped and fluttered like banners caught in a high wind. The sensitive’s eyes were wet and bright, the pupils oscillating to a secret beat. He was dressed far too warmly for a Roman spring. Not only was he a crazed esper, he was a junkie as well. What a combination!

“He says tell you come.” The sensitive’s eyelids twitched as he dry-washed his hands.

“Who told you?” I didn’t relish the idea of tapping into the junkie’s mind to get my information. God only knows what lay coiled behind those eyes.

“He say you know. Tell me say: Pangloss.”

The smell of old death came back to me. “Very well. I’ll go.”

The sensitive grinned, revealing crooked teeth. Was this pathetic creature Pangloss’s renfield?

I followed the sensitive through a series of twisting back streets that took us deep into the city’s oldest neighborhoods. I could feel myself being watched by scores of dark, suspicious eyes as we hurried through the narrow alleys. I glanced skyward. Although my view was hampered by a Jacob’s Ladder of laundry lines, I could see the moon of Islam hovering over Christendom’s city.

The sensitive led me to an ancient, crumbling villa with an overgrown garden. The ground floor was deserted of life and furniture but the door to its cellar stood open. The young man hurried down the stairs without bothering to see if I was following.

The basement had a dirt floor and smelled strongly of mildew. The only light came from a flickering candle jutting from a Chianti bottle perched atop a card table. The card table was situated against the far wall, alongside a small, narrow oaken door with old-fashioned hinges. Sitting behind the table was a huge figure dressed in the hooded robes of a monk.

The monk did not see us enter for his head was lowered, as if in prayer. The motion of his right arm, however, was far from sacred.

The sensitive snarled something in Italian and the monk pulled his hand free of his cassock. Pangloss’s messenger made a withering remark, then gestured first to me, then to the door.

The monk got to his feet, the peak of his hood brushing the low ceiling. I bit my tongue to keep from gasping aloud, my heart banging against my ribs like a hammer. Whatever his religious beliefs and vices might be, it was obvious the monk who stood guard in that empty cellar was not human.

The ogre’s lambent eyes glowered from under beetling brows, his nose wide and flat like a gorilla’s. His jaw jutted strangely, as if the lower mandible did not match the rest of his skull. The skin was coarse and large-pored, with a grayish complexion that made him look like he needed a good dusting. He was massively built, his hands large enough to conceal a cured ham in each palm. I could tell he was bald underneath the hood he wore, and I caught a brief glimpse of pointed ears set flush against his head. The folds of his vestments camouflaged his twisted physique, although it accentuated the unnatural width of his shoulders.

The ogre studied me warily, then spoke to the sensitive, his voice a bass rumble that sounded like rocks being ground together; I saw rows of sharp, inward curving teeth, like little Saracen blades, set in pink gums. While they were occupied, I looked at the book the ogre had left open on the table. It was a volume of nursery rhymes, lavishly illustrated with pictures of plump, apple-cheeked children dressed in sailor suits and pinafores jumping candlesticks, fetching pails of water, and going to bed with one shoe on. My gorge began to rise and I quickly averted my gaze. The ogre fondness for veal is well-known, but it seemed this one liked playing with his food.

The ogre monk produced an antique key fashioned of iron and unlocked the worm-scored door. The sensitive had to stoop in order to cross the threshold and I nearly banged my head on the lintel. The ogre grunted noncommittally and locked the door behind us.

I found myself in a narrow, sloping passageway lit by a string of low-wattage bulbs attached to the roof of the tunnel.

Most of the catacombs are located near the Appian Way, in what had once been the farthest reaches of the city. I was not aware of such extensive catacombs in that particular section of Rome.

We passed row upon row of *loculi*, the narrow shelf graves cut in the soft stone that house the bones of the poor. The surrounding rock formations were porous and there was little moisture found in the catacombs, the end result being that even the oldest bodies were surprisingly well-preserved. The dead, dressed in the remains of their winding-sheets, watched with empty sockets as we traveled deeper into their realm.

After walking for a half-hour and descending three levels, the corridor emptied into a *cubiculum*, one of the larger and more elaborate burial chambers reserved for the wealthy dead.

I stepped into the vaulted chamber, staring at its grisly decor. The *cubiculum* had been turned into a shrine of some kind, although I had a hard time imagining who might be so desperate as to seek solace in such a place.

The far wall was studded, from floor to ceiling, with human skulls embedded in its mortar. The skulls—all of them missing their lower mandibles—were stacked one atop another. The heads of adult males rested, upper plate to crown, alongside those of women and the unfinished craniums of infants.

The skulls surrounded a reliquary recessed into the wall. The reliquary's interior was composed of thousands upon thousands of painted tibia, finger, and toe bones fitted into a gruesome mosaic. Although the colors had faded over the centuries, I could still make out the figures of a man and a woman, one hand lifted in greeting while the other hid their genitals. A withered, mummified arm—whole from the shoulder—rested in the shrine, apparently fixed to the shelf by a large metal bolt in its palm. I was uncertain whether the relic was an obscure saint or an unlucky pilgrim.

Chandeliers made from bones and wire hung from the ceilings. Candles burned in upside-down skulls, casting warped shadows throughout the burial vault. The walls that weren't dedicated to the skull shrine were pocketed with larger versions of the shelf graves the poor had been unceremoniously dumped in, resembling bizarre multiple built-in bunk beds.

Mummified monks and priests, dressed in the rotting clerical garb of some long-forgotten religious order, stood eternal vigilance alongside their patrons' tombs; suspended by hooks set into the walls, their ancient skeletons were held together by wire and petrified ligaments. I was reminded of a brace of marionettes dangling from their strings.

Some of the dead holy men clutched the rusted remains of swords, while others fingered rosaries. I wondered if they were there to keep the occupants of the catacombs from being molested or escaping. Most of the dead sentinels possessed enough skin to cover their bones, although it was as stiff and yellow as parchment. Some seemed to laugh, others to cry, their black tongues exposed between toothless jaws. The ones who still had their faces were the worst; their lips twisted into parodies of a kiss.

One of the dead things stepped forward and fit an ebony cigarette holder between his grinning jaws. "Miss Blue. Delighted you could make it."

My vision wavered and the walking corpse became Dr. Pangloss, international scholar and *bon vivant*. Although he was dressed in the latest Italian fashion, his eyes obscured by Mastroianni-style sunglasses, he looked perfectly at home among the inhabitants of the catacombs.

The sensitive blurted something in Italian, his manner anxious. He dry-washed his hands, watching Pangloss expectantly.

"Yes, I can see that she's here," the vampire snapped in English. He said something more in Italian, then reached inside his breast pocket, producing a small packet of white powder.

The sensitive snatched the heroin from the vampire's hand, scurrying into the shadows.

"You must forgive Cesare," apologized Pangloss. "He is a telepath with no control over what he receives. Imagine having a radio in your head that you are helpless to turn off. He depends on me to provide him with the means to escape the voices, the poor lad."

"How humanitarian."

Pangloss arched an eyebrow. "Yes, isn't it." He brushed past me to perch on the edge of a sarcophagus. "This place"—he indicated our surroundings with a languid wave of the hand—"was forgotten by the Christians after the eighth century, *anno domini*, and has yet to be rediscovered by the human world. Pretenders, however, never forget. These catacombs are held sacred by the Pretending races. It is one of the few locations where we can meet without fear of vendetta. It is a neutral territory, so to speak. You need not fear violence from me while we are here. I trust I can expect the same from you?"

I nodded. Even though Pangloss was a monster that preyed on the weak and helpless, I had no reason to doubt his manners.

"Were you surprised to hear from me? Do say yes, it would flatter me so."

"Yes. I admit I was surprised. How did you know where I would be?"

"Do you think I would waltz away from our last encounter without bothering to keep myself informed as to your whereabouts? I know many things about you, my dear. I know you've taken up with that deluded old fool, and I know all about your 'hunting trips.' Who are you warring against?"

"What makes you think—"

"You must be warring against someone. Who is your brood master?"

"I don't have any idea what you're talking about."

"Surely you're not that ignorant! Who is responsible for you?"

"He called himself Sir Morgan."

Pangloss's mocking smile diminished. "You're operating under Morgan's orders?"

"His orders!" I didn't bother to restrain my burst of derisive laughter. "I'm looking to kill the motherfucker!"

Pangloss looked genuinely perplexed. He toyed with his cigarette holder and stared at his shoes. His voice was distant and detached, as if he was thinking aloud. "Morgan . . . I should have pegged you as one of his gets. All that anger and hate boiling away inside . . . I'm surprised. He must be getting forgetful in his old age. Foolish of him, really. Seeding a specimen like you . . ." He saw the confused look on my face, and the sardonic smile returned.

"What you must understand, my dear, is that we vampires are a prolific race. Like the Greek gods of Olympus, where falls our seed there is life. Or unlife. Every human we drain will rise again. Every schoolboy knows that. And since it wouldn't do to have too many undead running loose, we take matters into our own hands." He pantomimed wringing the neck of a chicken. "Most of us take birth control very seriously. That is not to say I don't have a brood of my own. You're looking confused again. Don't you know anything about . . . No, I guess you wouldn't.

“Anyway, every Noble has a brood, those vampires who owe their existence to him. You see, when Morgan took your blood he left some of himself behind— remaking you in his own image, shall we say? However, it is the strength of *your* will that decides if you will become a Noble. And we are usually very careful in our choice of prey. It wouldn’t do to pick a victim who possesses a powerful will.”

“Who needs the competition?”

“Correct! You do catch on quickly. The size and quality of a Noble’s brood determines his or her social status. Don’t look so surprised, child. Our lives are long. What else is there to fill them besides intrigue?

“There are periodic outbreaks of brood war, where rival nobles command their gets to attack one another in an attempt to rise in the social ranks. That is why we prefer to prey on humans with weak wills; they make compliant gets.”

“Are you saying Morgan is my father?”

“In a way, yes. That is why I thought you were under orders. But I can see that you are something of a rogue, by our standards. It takes a vampire decades, if not centuries, to break free of his brood master and start thinking for himself. I’ve only had it happen to me once before. You see, my dear, Morgan was once one of my gets. I guess you could say I’m your grandfather.”

“I’d rather not.”

“Sarcasm suits you, my dear. Try to cultivate it. But this does put a new face on things. You see, your little ‘hunting trips’ have not gone unnoticed. I have remained silent up to now because it suited my purpose. You have, unwittingly, kindled a brood war between two highly placed nobles. Each has accused the other of participating in hostilities without a formal declaration of war. If things go any further, the entire pecking order will be restructured.”

“And you want me to stop?”

“Nonsense, my dear! What made you think such a thing? No, feel free to continue what you’re doing. By all means, be my guest! You see, my charming young one, by Noble standards I am quite puny. I don’t even have a real title. I abhor blatant game-playing. I find it so debasing. No, I prefer biding my time, waiting for those brash fools above me to tear each other apart. My betters underestimate me, simply because I prefer to feast on lighter fare.

“I possess a discerning palate, my dear. I find rage, pain, and fear far too overpowering. They lack subtlety. Where’s the finesse in leeching off a Ku Klux Klan rally? While these emotions are, unquestionably, very potent, they lack focus. That is why I prefer the petty jealousies and backbiting found among art movements and intellectual societies. Shattered friendships, bitter denouements, ruined marriages, stormy personal relationships . . . Ahhh!” He smiled knowingly, like a chef reciting the ingredients for a prize-winning recipe.

"I've sampled them all, mind you, and I must say that the best still remains a toss-up between the modernists and the *fin-de-siècle* school. On one hand you had Pound, Picasso, Modigliani, and Stein, but then there's Beardsley and Wilde. Although I must admit the Pre-Raphaelites were a tasty lot—Rossetti in particular, although his sister had her good points." Pangloss smacked his lips and rubbed his palms together, as if he was a wine connoisseur discussing his favorite vintage. "But I digress. When I sent Cesare looking for you, I'd originally planned to discover which Noble you were working for and plan my strategies accordingly. But now that I know that you're a free agent, I can offer you something far more profitable; I am willing to take you on as my pupil, seeing how grossly ignorant you are of the basic facts of unlife. You'll never learn anything from Ghilardi, that doddering old fool. You need me, my dear, if you wish to survive for long in the Real World."

"I have the *Aegrisomnia*."

Pangloss snorted. "Ah, yes, Ghilardi's holy writ. While it may prove useful now and again, I'm sure you've noticed that it's far from complete. Ghilardi knows nothing of its true origins. Its author was a brilliant fellow by the name of Palinurus. Lived in the thirteenth century, if I remember correctly. He composed the original text and illustrations while afflicted with a strange fever of the brain, dying a few days after its completion. Come now, do you suppose we'd allow something like that to fall into Ghilardi's hands if it were of any *real* use? It suits our purposes that he be ridiculed as a member of the lunatic fringe. We have long believed the best hiding place is directly under the human nose.

"There is so much I could show you, if only you'd put aside this irrational hatred of our species. You deny what you *are* by destroying that which is like you. It's a futile gesture, my dear. You seem to think that being human is something exalted, something to be proud of. As the years pass, you'll see them for what they really are: myopic little beasts intent on destroying their world. Why, if it weren't for us, the human race would have nuked itself out of existence nearly thirty years ago."

"You mean the fleas are keeping the dog alive?"

"If that's how you choose to see it. Humans are little more than cattle in a mad race to the slaughterhouse, and they don't care whom they stampede along with them! Must we stand by and watch as they destroy both their world and the Real one?"

"You make it sound so noble and self-effacing. I thought you enjoyed human pain and suffering?"

"That is true, in most cases. But where is the percentage in killing off the entire human race, just for the sake of a good dinner? Don't be naive. There is no atrocity mankind has perpetrated on itself that was the direct result of a Pretender command. In fact, up until this century we have remained fairly

The Book Bin

215 SW 4th St.
Corvallis, OR 97333
(541) 752-0040

Transaction #:00661643
Station:Register 3, 30007 Clerk:JOSEPH C.
Thursday, December 14 2017 3:38 PM

SALES:

1@ 8.25 414600-0101	8.25
Midnight Blue: The Sonia Blue Collection	
SUBTOTAL	8.25
GRAND TOTAL	8.25
TENDER:	
Cash	10.25
TOTAL TENDER	10.25
CASH CHANGE	$2.00

Merchandise may be returned with the receipt up to January 15th, 2018 for in-store credit only. Returns are subject to the Manager's discretion.

00661643

The Book Bin

215 SW 4th St
Corvallis, OR 97333
(541) 752-0040

Transaction # 00661643
Station Register 3, 30007 Clerk JOSEPH C.
Thursday, December 14 2017 3:38 PM

SALES:
1@ 8.25 4114600 0101 8.25
Midnight Blue: The Sonja Blue Collection

SUBTOTAL 8.25

GRAND TOTAL 8.25

TENDER:
Cash 10.25

TOTAL TENDER 10.25

CASH CHANGE $2.00

Merchandise may be returned with the receipt up to January 15th, 2018 for in-store credit only. Returns are subject to the Manager's discretion.

00661643

passive. It wasn't until humans stumbled across a means of destroying themselves en masse and forever that we felt compelled to intervene."

"I'm having difficulty picturing you as a protector of the human race."

Pangloss shrugged. " 'Husbander' would be a better word. Would a farmer stand idly by and watch his herd die of hoof-and-mouth? No! It is in *our* best interests that the human race continue. Of course, that doesn't mean their future will be a pleasant one. You're avoiding answering my proposal. Will you join me?"

"And what do you expect from me in exchange for learning at your feet?"

"What you're already doing."

"Except that I leave your gets alone."

"Precisely. Think about it, my dear. I'm offering you a chance for a title. You could become a *marchesa*, perhaps even a duchess!"

"You might as well bribe me with Monopoly money."

A look of incomprehension flickered across Pangloss's face. It was unnatural for a Noble to turn down a chance at advancing in social position. "Extraordinary," he murmured. "I can lead you to Morgan."

My heart jumped at the idea and I began to sweat. It was tempting . . . very tempting. There was nothing I wanted more than the opportunity to tear Morgan to shreds with my bare hands. And Pangloss was offering to take me to him. If . . .

The Other was eager to accept his invitation. *You'd be among your own kind. You wouldn't have to worry about being on the outside, of being a freak. You would be accepted for what you are.*

I looked at Pangloss, dressed in his fancy silk shirt and fashionable trousers. I looked at his finely manicured hands and carefully coiffured hair. I looked at him and saw a wizened, mummified dead man with no lips and skin the color of rancid tallow.

Among your own kind . . .

"Go to hell."

"My child, most of my closest friends are from there." Pangloss sighed. "I'd hoped you would be cooperative, but I can see there is too much of Morgan in you. Very well. I'll have Cesare escort you back the way you came." He called for the sensitive. "Cesare!" There was no response. "Cesare!" Pangloss's shout rattled the bones of the forgotten dead.

Cursing under his breath, Pangloss brushed past me to investigate the corner where his flunky had crawled to do his fix.

Cesare squatted on his haunches, propped against one of the lower death shelves. The candle and spoon he'd used to cook his fix lay at his feet, along with a spilled flask of mineral water. The candle had burned itself out, snuffed by a pool of its own wax. The bottom of the spoon was black with carbon from the flame. The rubber tubing was still knotted above the youth's elbow, the empty syringe dangling from his forearm by its needle. Vomit dripped slowly from the corner of his mouth.

"I'm afraid that was a little too pure for the poor boy. Humans are so fragile." Pangloss sounded like a housewife trying to estimate the correct patent medicine dosage for the family pet.

I turned away from the tableau; the sight of a fresh corpse among the ancient dead was oddly disconcerting. There would be no more voices for Cesare. A chill worked its way through my body; the youth had died while Pangloss discoursed on Pretender sociology. Had he known all along that the heroin he'd given his servant was uncut? The more I thought about it, the more I wanted to be free of the subterranean maze of vaults and dead things.

"Bother. I guess this means I must escort you back myself," sniffed Pangloss, heading toward one of the narrow passageways that opened onto the *cubiculum*.

"Wait! What about him?" I pointed to Cesare's body, crouched in a rough semblance of devotion.

Pangloss glanced around the burial chamber, then shrugged. "He's in good company."

The passageway was close and dark and smelled of dust and cobwebs. Pangloss walked just ahead of me, keeping up a constant chatter about the foibles and vices of famous dead people. I found being in such close quarters with the leering vampire unpleasant, but I was dependent on him to lead me out of the catacombs.

After we had been walking for some time, Pangloss stopped and turned to face me, his tone conversational.

"Do you remember when I told you that the catacombs are sacred neutral ground? Well, we're no longer within its jurisdiction."

The low-wattage bulbs strung along the ceiling suddenly surged, burning at three times their strength before bursting in a chain reaction of *pops!*

Pangloss was on top of me, his fingers closing around my neck like steel bands. I could see his eyes, glowing like a rat's, in the pitch black as I drove my knife into the good doctor's chest. Pangloss howled as the silver blade sank deep into his flesh and the surrounding dead trembled at the sound. I slashed again, but Pangloss was gone.

I got to my feet, panting and shuddering like a winded racehorse. There was blood on my shoulder. I'd been bitten. I heard something that sounded like a cat in heat, shrieking and cursing from one of the myriad galleries that extended from the main corridor. I must have wounded Pangloss more than I thought. Holding my knife at the ready, I proceeded through the catacombs, following the lightbulb shards. I felt like Hansel or Gretel, following the trail of bread crusts after the evil stepmother left them in the woods to starve. I thought about the ogre waiting on the other side of the door and began to giggle.

I was alternately freezing and sweating; my joints ached horribly and my head felt like it was coming apart at the seams. Had Pangloss infected me with some kind of poison? I remembered what he'd said about vampires injecting part of themselves into their victims. Maybe the Morgan inside of me was battling with Pangloss for possession. I had a vision of them locked in mortal combat: deep within my stomach, aristocratic jet-setter versus effete intellectual.

I don't know how long I wandered the catacombs in a delirious stupor, but I managed to stay in the right passageway. I stared at the heavy door for several minutes before recognizing it as the end of my journey. The hinges were on the outside and there was no handle on the inside, only a keyhole.

Beyond caring whether the ogre heard me, I used my knife to pick the lock from my side of the door. It wasn't very difficult; the door was very old and the locking mechanism crude by today's standards.

I opened the door slowly, knowing at any minute the ogre would reach out and snare me by my hair. I experienced a vivid image of myself being held aloft by my ankles and lowered, headfirst, into the creature's waiting jaws. I shook off the vision and peeked into the basement, only to find it empty. The ogre's place beside the door stood deserted.

Relieved, but still cautious, I pushed open the door and entered the basement. Judging by the light angling through the windows set at ground level, it was late afternoon. I hurried up the stairs, unmindful of their creaks and groans. I had to get out of there before the ogre came back.

I was on the deserted first floor, at the foot of the crumbling remains of a curved staircase, when I caught sight of the open door at the top of the stairs. It had been closed when Cesare first escorted me through the old villa. Even though I was weakened by fever and my bones felt like they had been hollowed out and filled with lead, something in me had to investigate the room at the top of the stairs.

I was being dragged up the stairs by a force I was helpless to resist or comprehend, like the toy skaters that pirouette atop their mirror lakes. I did not want to see what was in the room. I wanted to escape the villa and its monstrous guard, but I mounted the stairs one by one, my eyes focused on the half-open door.

Back when the villa was alive, the room had been a nursery. It was light and airy and I could still make out the fairy-tale characters that decorated the molding near the ceiling. There was no furniture except for a soiled mattress in one corner covered with filthy blankets. The room smelled like a lion's cage. There were urine stains on the wall at the height of a man's head.

There were toys scattered throughout the nursery, some new, others antique, all of them broken. An Edwardian rocking horse, its back broken and saddle askew, stared at me from the gathering shadows.

I crossed the threshold, stepping across a battalion of painted lead soldiers bent into clothespins. The walls near the ogre's bed were decorated with illustrations torn from children's books. My foot nudged something. It was a large Raggedy Ann doll, its red yarn hair askew and missing one shoe-button eye. Stuffing dribbled from the gaping hole between its candy-striped legs. Grunting in disgust, I turned to leave the monster's boudoir when I stumbled. I looked down and saw what looked to be the dislocated arm of a baby doll. Then I saw the knob of bone that had once fit into the shoulder socket. No. Not a doll.

I vomited loudly and copiously, ridding myself of Pangloss's contagion. I was so centered on my purging I didn't hear the monster come home. There was something like a cross between a panther's snarl and the shriek of a bat from downstairs, then the villa began to shake as the ogre stormed up the stairs.

The door flew open, smashing into the wall so hard it sagged on its hinges. The ogre filled the threshold, his monk's hood pushed back to reveal his hideous, inhuman face. He glared at me, his gorilloid nostrils flaring, and a dim flicker of recognition sparked deep within his eyes. Then he charged, hands outstretched, bellowing at the top of his lungs.

I sidestepped five hundred pounds of enraged ogre as he crashed into the nursery wall hard enough to shake the house. Rotting plaster fell from the ceiling and a huge crack marked where he'd collided with the wall. The ogre spat out a curved tooth, ignoring the trickle of blood seeping from his nose.

There was no way I could go toe to toe with such a monster. I wasn't even sure if ogres *had* weak spots. My back was to a double casement that faced the back of the house. Without bothering to see where I might be landing, I smashed through the windows and plummeted into the unknown.

I came to in a nearby alley with a broken arm and some busted ribs. I'd landed in the overgrown garden attached to the villa and somehow succeeded in scaling the wall before the ogre located me. I still felt like shit and it took several days to fully recover from the effects of Pangloss's bite. At one time I distinctly heard him talking to me inside my head, telling me to join him. But it might have been an auditory hallucination.

I returned to Geneva, but I could not bring myself to tell Ghilardi of my encounter with Pangloss and the revelations he'd made. It would have ruined his book.

1978: Ghilardi suffered a massive stroke while trying to find a publisher for his new work. I curtailed my hunting expeditions and remained in Geneva. When I first met Ghilardi, his eyes were blue fire, the color of sapphires held to the light. After the stroke they started to fade, growing paler every day. It was hard to watch him die like that, knowing the vitality he'd once had, but I was equally curious. I had never participated in a natural death before.

He died June 2, 1978. I was with him when it happened. By that time his eyes were so pale a blue they were without color, like those of a child fresh from the womb. The left side of his face was slack and his left hand a useless snarl of meat and bone.

"Sssonja . . ." he slurred. He seemed more alert than usual that day. "Do you see it?"

I scanned the bedroom on all levels; and as far as I could see, we were alone. "See what, Erich?" I turned around in time to watch his eyes close. I didn't need to touch him to know he was dead. I sat there for a long moment, my sense of loss so overwhelming it couldn't register as an emotion, and stared at what was left of my friend and tutor.

I was named Ghilardi's principal heir and executor of his will. I inherited the house, the grounds, the family fortune, and a professionally forged set of documents that provided Sonja Blue with a recorded past.

I also inherited Ghilardi's notebooks and the typewritten manuscript concerning his greatest discovery: me. This was the book that would lay to rest the idea that Erich Ghilardi was a kook. I burned every last page in the central hall's marble fireplace.

After I'd consigned Ghilardi's reputation to the flames, I drove my Jaguar to Geneva. After wandering the streets for several hours, I found myself standing on the shores of Lake Geneva. I stared at the same lake on which Jean-Jacques went boating with his beloved dullard, Marie-Thérèse, and where, fifty years later, a poet's wife gave birth to a monster.

I was certain I would not find my answers in Europe. I rang Ghilardi's solicitors and liquidated my entire inheritance, except for two books, and bought a one-way ticket to the Orient.

I went to Japan, hoping its saffron-robed holy men and black-garbed assassin priests might know more of the Real World than the scientists and occult investigators of the West.

While waiting for the bullet train that would take me into Tokyo from the airport, I noticed a young girl dressed in the drab uniform the Nippon educational system had copied from German private schools earlier in the century. She looked to be no more than twelve or thirteen, although the roundness of her face made her seem even younger.

She was chewing gum and paging through a comic book the size of a telephone directory. I glimpsed a woman, naked except for strategic shadows, cowering before a hulking giant. The giant was covered with scars and tattoos. A poisonous snake with dripping fangs was wrapped around the monster's erect penis; rather, it was wrapped around where the giant's erect penis *would* have been, if the censors hadn't airbrushed it out.

The schoolgirl extruded a bubble the color of flesh, flipped the page, and continued reading. The giant pressed his thumbs into his protesting victim's eyes. I realized that finding answers here would not be as easy as I'd thought.

I soon discovered that coming to Japan had been a mistake. I stalked the human beehives of Tokyo, frustrated in my search for Pretenders. Everyone in the city wore a mask; it is a part of their culture. Pretending to be something they're not is second nature to the Japanese. Their thoughts formed an impenetrable wall I was neither skilled enough nor ready to understand. I felt even more alienated than I had in Europe.

Still, it wasn't a complete loss on my part. I was in a mammoth downtown Tokyo department store; it was a busy afternoon and it seemed as if the entire country had picked that day to come and shop. Despite the crowds, I was able to maintain suitable personal space. I was unsure whether their reluctance to come too close had to do with my being *gaijin* or Pretender.

Either way, I followed the path of least resistance, allowing myself to be buoyed along in the general direction of the shoppers. The Japanese equivalent of canned music blared from hidden speakers, mixing with the roar of a thousand alien voices.

I found myself standing near a bank of elevators. There were two young Japanese girls, dressed in feminine versions of the department store uniform, posted outside the lifts. Both wore spotless white gloves and spoke in artificial falsetto voices, like cartoon mice. The elevator girls smiled fixedly, bowing to the customers with machinelike precision, and made what looked like ritual hand gestures. Their arms rocked back and forth, like metronomes, indicating which lifts went to which departments. I watched the puppet women as they repeated their robotic gestures over and over for an endless stream of shoppers, their smiles never faltering. I was suddenly overcome by the need to cry. Strange. I didn't weep at Ghilardi's death.

I was surprised to see a small, bowed man with the wrinkled face of a sacred ape looking up at me. At first I thought I was being accosted by some exotic variation of Pretender. Then I realized I was looking at a *very* old man.

"You come away from this," he said in English. "No place for you." He gestured with a crooked finger and began threading his way through the dense packing of consumers. Intrigued, I followed him. The old man's aura was roseate, but I could not divine if he was of Pretender origin.

The bent old man led me to a traditional Japanese house, sequestered from the bustle of the street by ancient stone walls. He showed me his garden, with its intricate patterns raked in the sand, and shared tea with me.

His name was Hokusai, and he was a descendant of Shinto wizards and samurai swordsmiths. He had been trained in the art of "seeing beyond" by his grandfather, and was adept at identifying people and places of power.

"You shine very strong. Maybe too strong. And sometime there is darkness at the edge of the bright." He frowned, unable to fully explain himself in English.

I suspected that even if I spoke fluent Japanese he would still have trouble finding the right words. "Why did you ask me to follow you here?"

"I watch you watch elevator girls. The dark was eating the bright."

I nodded that I understood and the wrinkled monkey face beamed happily. For the first time since Ghilardi's death, I found myself at ease in another's presence.

The old gentleman told me that, as a child, his grandfather filled him with stories of the elemental spirits that had once ruled the island kingdom before the days of the first emperor. The old wizard had been adamant that the spirits would return within his grandson's lifetime and wished that Hokusai be trained in recognizing their signs. Now it seemed his grandfather's predictions had come true.

I was humbled by the old man's hospitality and what I knew to be uncharacteristic openness to a foreigner. I didn't have the heart to tell him he was sharing tea with a monster. It was Hokusai who reforged the silver dagger Ghilardi had given me years ago, transforming it into a handsomely mounted switchblade. The handle was fashioned of teak and the inlaid dragon adorning it from gold leaf. The small ruby that was the dragon's eye also served as the triggering stud. Hokusai refused payment, claiming that he owed it to the ghost of his grandfather.

I left Japan after a month's stay. My next port of call was Hong Kong. I never saw or heard from Hokusai again.

What occurred in Hong Kong was bound to happen, eventually. I'd succeeded in forestalling the inevitable for years. Hong Kong is so alien a place for Westerners, even inhuman ones, that it's easy to forget your past and your future. There is only now in Hong Kong and that is, in itself, timeless.

I found myself in one of the city's huge open-air bazaars, if you consider a street jammed with fish peddlers open air. The noise was terrific, hundreds of voices yelling, haggling, and arguing in as many dialects. Street urchins of indeterminate sex and age waved chintzy, mass-produced gewgaws in my face, shrilling "Yankee! Cheap! You buy!" After my failure in Tokyo, I limited my mind scan to random samplings of the crowd. Then I saw him.

He was an elderly priest, dressed in the saffron robes of a Buddhist monk, a neat smear of red on his shaven brow. Though he hobbled with the aid of a gnarled stick, his power was evident to those who could see. The monk paused in his journey and glanced in my direction. His placid, moon-round face was replaced by the features of a fox. I tried to go after him but a group of housewives, haggling over the price of snake, blocked my path. By the time I reached the spot I'd last seen him, the monk was nowhere to be found.

"You look somebody?"

It was a long-haired, seedy Chinese male in his late twenties who'd spoken. He lounged against a nearby doorway, arms folded across his chest. He wore a pair of much-mended American jeans and a faded T-shirt bearing the logo BRUCE LEE LIVES.

"Yes. There was a monk here just a second ago. Did you see where he went?"

The man nodded. "I see. I know priest. Show you where he go. Ten dollar."

Too eager to be cautious, I shoved a note in his hand. He smiled broadly, revealing crooked teeth the color of wild rice. He led me through a series of narrow streets that took us away from the main thoroughfares, emptying into a squalid, dimly lit alley.

"Priest live here. Very holy man. Very poor," explained my guide.

I was dubious of his claim, and I knew what was going to happen, but I couldn't risk the chance that he was telling me the truth. I took a hesitant step into the alley. "Are you sure this is where—"

I never finished the sentence. There was a sharp blow on the back of my skull and the pavement tilted up to greet me. Stupid. My guide's hands were on me, searching my pockets with the speed and skill of a professional mugger. He found the switchblade and paused to admire the craftsmanship. His thumb brushed the tiny ruby dragon's eye and the knife revealed itself. He knelt and pressed the tip of the switchblade against the hollow of my throat, teasing a drop of blood from my skin.

"Good knife. You got money, Yankee? Dollar? Traveler check? What you got for me? Huh? What you got?"

He didn't like my answer.

My right hand clamped around his throat and I saw his eyes bulge inside their epicanthic folds. He forgot about slicing my throat and tried to pull my hand away from his windpipe. I felt his larynx turn to pulp. I got back on my feet, keeping my erstwhile guide at arm's length. Normally, I would have snapped his neck and let it go at that, but I was in a foul mood. I had come close—so close—to finding what I was looking for, only to have this geek throw me off the scent.

My attacker was turning colors, his tongue so swollen he'd bitten halfway through it. He made a noise like mice trapped in a shoe box. Vaguely curious, I looked inside his head to see what his thoughts might be, now that he faced death.

I found an open sewer. My guide was a nasty piece of work, as humans go. He'd spent several years in Vietnam buying children orphaned by the war and selling them to brothels in Hong Kong, Tokyo, Seoul and Manila. When that no longer proved profitable, he sold junk to the Yankee GIs until the South Vietnamese bureaucracy chased him out of Saigon for failure to pay bribes on time. Now he lured Anglos into dark alleyways under pretenses of sightseeing or sex, murdering for the contents of their wallets or a wristwatch. It was safer and easier than dealing with the Yakuza or the Triad, and he had a low overhead.

I withdrew, disgusted by my victim's lack of humanity.

Who's the monster, Sonja? You or him?

I flinched. I wasn't used to the Other speaking directly to me. The strangling man at the end of my arm looked like a perverse hand puppet. Spittle, blood, and foam flecked the corners of his mouth. His tongue was the size and color of a black pudding

"Monster" is such an unfair word, don't you agree?

I was aware of the hunger building inside of me. A cold sweat broke across my brow and I began to tremble.

What makes the word "human" so damned wonderful? You're always mourning your humanity, denying yourself the power and privilege that are yours by right for fear of becoming inhuman. You fight to keep from doing what is natural for you, simply because you pride yourself on being human. What is being human? Is it being like him? Why don't you put him to some use, eh? You'll be doing society a favor . . .

I was standing on the mountaintop with Satan whispering in my ear. And I was weak.

He was so close to death when I took him there was no real fear left in him, only resignation. The flesh of his throat was unwashed and tasted of sweat and dirt. The faint odor of ginger clung to him.

I trembled as if caught in the heat of erotic passion. His skin was taut and soft under my lips as I felt his weakened pulse throb against the points of my fangs, inviting penetration.

"No. I can't do this, even if he is murdering scum. I didn't come all this way. . . not for *this*."

Didn't you? You knew what his intentions were the moment you saw the alley. You knew but you went ahead. Why? Hasn't it been leading up to this ever since you first tasted human blood and found it good?

"No! I can buy blood on the black market. Not like this . . ."

Ah, yes. The blood in the bottles. Sterilized for your protection. How fucking bland. You really do disappoint me, Sonja . . . Or do you?

The hunger was a dark bubble in my gut. I could *smell* the bastard's blood waiting for me on the other side of his skin. I couldn't do it. I *wouldn't* do it. But I did.

The man jerked as my fangs entered the warmth of his jugular. It was so sweet. I realized how bland and characterless the bottled blood really was. The Other was right: nothing can compare to the taste of blood stolen fresh from the vein. It was the difference between beer and a fine champagne. It felt so natural to have hot, fresh human blood squirting into my mouth. I drank like a woman rescued from the desert, afraid of wasting a single drop.

Wave after wave of pleasure washed over me. I had been a prostitute for five years, but that was the first time I experienced orgasm.

By the time I was finished, my would-be murderer was very pale and very dead. I left him in the nameless alley, along with my humanity.

More disturbed than enlightened by my sojourns in the East, I decided to visit the scene of the crime: London. It seemed the logical place to start if I was going to track down Morgan. It was 1979, ten years after Denise Thorne's mysterious disappearance and my secret birth.

Things were very different from the last time I was in town; the punk music scene was building up the PR to jump the Atlantic. The hippie sentiments of peace and love had curdled into bitterness and resentment. Yet, in their own way, some things were the same.

The Apple Cart Discotheque had mutated over the past decade and turned into Fugg's. Fat tarts in cheap wigs and cheaper makeup did the bump-and-grind down a runway for the edification of a handful of hard-core rummies. The dancers chewed gum and made crude fuck-motions with their hips. The men scattered up and down the runway looked about as aroused as dead newts.

I crossed to the bar, my memory decorating the dive with phantom go-go girls and jet-setters in paisley-print shirts.

The bartender gave me a sour look. "Ain't hirin'. Business is bleedin' awful."

"I'm not looking for a job. Do you know a man called Morgan? Claims to be a peer." I handed him a fiver.

The bartender shrugged. "Mebbe. Think that's what he calls hisself. Used to, rather. Ain't been around in a while."

"How long?"

"Year. Mebbe two. Suits me if th' bleeder never shows his face again. Every time he comes 'round, one of me best girls ups and quits. Never fails. They go packin' off with him without givin' proper notice and I never see hide nor hair of 'em again." He shook his head. "Just can't figure it. What would a toff like him want with birds like that? Me, I met the wife at a church social."

Everywhere I went, the story was the same: yes, they knew Morgan, no, they couldn't say when he might show up again and could care less if he did.

Morgan kept to a schedule, at least in London, and I was unlucky enough to have returned during his off-season. I realized it might be another ten years before he made the circuit again, since time means little to Pretenders. The idea of waiting chafed. I wanted to have my revenge while I could still *feel* it.

I consoled myself by cleansing London and its neighboring districts of undead.

Clearing out the revenants was easy enough, although the vampires—the ones with enough skill and brains to pass for human—proved to be a different matter. Most of them posed as nondescript shopgirls and junior bank clerks—no one you'd look at twice. Although I had no trouble locating them, they usually succeeded in giving me the slip.

I was in a small pub near the East End when I spotted a pale young woman nursing a pint at one of the back tables. She was dressed dowdily and was rather unremarkable in appearance. Just another lower-middle-class working girl out for her weekly glass of stout. But there was something odd about the way she brought the glass to her lips and how the amount of ale stayed the same. I shifted my vision to see what she looked like in the Real World.

An ancient crone was seated where the girl had been, her face wrinkled hideously. When she noticed me watching her, she put down her drink and left the pub. I hurried after her. The hag moved faster than I'd expected and was already a block ahead of me. I saw her dodge into one of the mews that riddled the district. I followed, switchblade in hand and eager for confrontation. Instead, I found nothing. Not a trace. But how did she know?

"That you were goin' t' kill her? Have y' tried lookin' in th' mirror lately, pet? You got 'big-time predator' writ all over!"

He emerged from the fog, dressed in a silk suit the color of reptiles, a foul-smelling French cigarette hanging from his lower lip. I grabbed him by his narrow lapels. He looked a bit nonplussed, but there was no fear in his voice.

"Here now! Don't go wrinklin' th' material, luv."

"Who are you? How'd you—"

"Know what you were thinkin'? It's me job, ducks."

Something dark and fast with sharp edges scampered through my mind. I grunted and let go of him.

He carefully rearranged his clothing. "I'm human, don't you worry. As if that bleedin' means anything. I know some things. I know yer not human, but y' ain't one of *them*, either."

"You . . . you can see them? You see the Real World?"

"If that's what y'call it . . . Yeah, I see shit. Used t'think mum was balmy, rattlin' on about th' old lady down th' row bein' a werewolf. Until I started seein' things, too." He grinned, revealing National Health teeth.

I didn't like standing in the open discussing the Real World, and I especially didn't like the leering youth who'd come out of nowhere, claiming to know my secrets. The Other whispered that there was a quick and bloody solution to my problem.

Fear flickered across his face, only to be replaced by a crafty grin. "Yer lookin' t' kill them beasties, ain'tcha? I mean, th' very sight of 'em makes you want to heave, right? But y' got way too much mojo, luv. They can spot y' half a mile off. See?" He produced a small pocket mirror from inside his jacket and held it so I could glimpse my reflection. I'd avoided looking in mirrors ever since the night my reflection had taken a life of its own. I realized it'd been a mistake.

I was surrounded by a crimson nimbus that strobed and pulsed with my heartbeat. I looked like an Eastern Orthodox saint. "That's why th' minute you show yer lovely face, they split. What you need is a Judas goat, see? Someone t' lure 'em away and set it up so you could snuff 'em easy, eh?"

"Go on. What would you get out of this? Besides money?"

He grinned and I was suddenly aware that he was an extraordinarily handsome man. "Y' got a good head f' business, luv. First rate. Let's just say I'm in th' market for a wee bit of protection. There's this bloke—couple of them, really—that's hot for me. Think I burned 'em on a business deal. They're wrong, of course."

"Of course," I echoed, retracing my steps out of the mews. My companion fell in beside me, still talking.

"I've checked y' out. Yer good. Real good. So what d' ya say, luv?"

"My name is not luv."

"Fair enough, luv. So what's it gonna be? We gotta deal?"

"What's your name?"

He came to a stop and scowled, his eyes fixed on something in the fog.

"Bloody hell!" He turned to flee back into the mews. The toughs emerged from the fog, as swift and silent as sharks. They were husky skinheads, dressed in the tatters of American denim jackets and leather pants. Their wrists bristled with chrome-studded black leather.

"Y'ain't gettin' away from us this time, y' lit'l soddin' queer," growled one of the skinheads as he snagged a handful of lizard-green jacket. "Stig, take care of th' bird."

"Like hell you will!" I grabbed the one called Stig, twisting his arm in a way it was not meant to go. His scream revealed him to be younger than he looked.

The first punk was pounding my newfound partner's head into the pavement. Since he didn't have any hair, I grabbed his ears. One of them came off in my hand; just don't make 'em like they used to, I guess.

Blood leaked from the sensitive's nostrils and his left eye was swollen shut. I lifted him in a fireman's carry and headed for my digs at a dead run. I could hear the shrill cry of a bobby's whistle from somewhere close by.

"Now, as I was saying before we were so rudely interrupted, what's your name?"

"Geoffrey Chastain . . . Look, call me Chaz, okay?"

The seven years I spent in the company of Chaz, waiting for Morgan to resurface, were . . . educational. I got to know every lowlife dive and sleazy after-hours club in the kingdoms, associating with the trashiest bastards ever to draw the dole. Don't get me wrong; I learned a lot from Chaz.

Although his telepathic abilities weren't up to Pretender standards, he'd mastered them to an amazing degree. He knew how to dampen his reception so he wouldn't be "on" twenty-four hours a day, and claimed that half the schizophrenics walking around complaining of "voices" in their heads were sensitives unable to turn down the volume. He also knew how to shield himself from other sensitives. Bright boy. A complete and utter prick, but still a bright boy. He was my only friend.

I hadn't realized how much I missed having someone to talk to, someone I didn't have to Pretend with. Chaz was my friend and confidant—and, at times, my lover.

He peddled dope on the side—"I *know* what you need" was his favorite come-on with the junkies—without fear of reprisals from disgruntled customers or rival dealers. Word on the street had it that Chaz was under the protection of someone—or something—mean enough to shit plutonium.

He relied on me to save his ass whenever he got in trouble, which proved to be a regular occurrence. In '83 he nearly got us both killed, thanks to his involvement with a Scottish gangster named Edward "Thick Eddie" Magruder.

Thick Eddie was famous for his brutality and intolerance of betrayal. Chaz had skimmed several hundred quids-worth of cocaine during a deal he'd set up for the mob boss, and Thick Eddie wasn't about to let Chaz go around bragging about it.

Thick Eddie sent the prerequisite goons around to rough up Chaz. They were large, squarish men dressed in cheap suits. I had no intention of letting Chaz be hurt, but I'd grown somewhat weary of his reliance on me. Chaz's tendency toward self-destruction showed in his taste for rough trade and the habit of making enemies of the wrong people. So I took my time before rescuing my Judas goat from Magruder's agents.

Since Magruder had a legitimate grievance, I let his men off easy with a broken arm apiece. Magruder didn't see it that way and within twenty-four hours there were two more chunks in cheap suits coming around Chaz's digs, only this time they were armed.

One of the hit men ended up in the hospital with a fractured skull, two broken arms, and a ruptured spleen. The second was dumped in front of Magruder's "legitimate" business, which happened to be wholesale carpeting. I should say the Other dumped the body there, for she was the one who killed him.

I remember nothing of my second confrontation with Thick Eddie's men, beyond one of the squarish men pulling his gun on me. I regained my senses hours later, only to find myself miles from where I last remembered being, soaked in blood and aching from broken bones and internal injuries. My right shoulder throbbed fiercely, meaning I'd taken a bullet.

I found Chaz at my flat. He'd fled his own digs when Thick Eddie's men jumped us the night before. We both knew Magruder wasn't the type who'd take kindly to having his employees murdered. I suggested that Chaz give

Thick Eddie restitution for the cocaine he'd stolen. Chaz wasn't thrilled with the idea, but finally agreed to do it under the condition that I accompany him.

Using underworld channels, Chaz sent his proposal to Thick Eddie, stating that he would meet him if he came alone. Magruder refused to meet anyone, including his own mother, alone, so Chaz grudgingly agreed to the presence of a "personal bodyguard."

The rendezvous point was an old warehouse facing the Thames. The place stank of dead fish and less wholesome flotsam. Magruder was already there by the time we arrived. He sat on an old shipping crate, smoking a smelly cigar and reading the evening paper. The headline read BOY TRAPPED IN REFRIGERATOR EATS OWN FOOT.

Thick Eddie glanced over the top of the paper at us, chewing his cigar speculatively. "I dinna believe th' lads a' first, when they told me 'twas a lassie. Me lads are brave 'uns. Not th' kind t' run scared an' tell wild tales, they are." Magruder fixed his eyes on me. "Then, things 'tain't always what they seem, eh? Me gran, she were allus sayin' that."

Of all the people in the United Kingdom he could choose from, Chaz would have to pick a Pretender crime boss to piss off! Actually, Thick Eddie was only part Pretender. Although his ogrish heritage was evident in his heavyset frame and coarse features, he was, essentially, human.

"Why didn't you tell me Magruder was part ogre?" I hissed into Chaz's ear.

"I didn't know! I've never seen him in person before." For once I had no reason not to believe Chaz's excuse.

Chaz cleared his throat and stepped forward. "I, uh, got yer money right here, Eddie." He hoisted a small overnight bag as proof. "I hope yer'll, uh, see fit t' let bygones be, uh, bygones, eh? It were all a misunderstandin'."

Thick Eddie stared at the proffered bag, his heavy-lidded eyes resembling those of a basking lizard. "Yew know I make more'n that every hour, lad. 'Tain't th' money that's important. Nay, 'tis th' principle o' th' thing. If I let yew go now, every punk in London'll be thinkin' he can pull a fast'un on Eddie Magruder. That's why I decided t' call in some help." Magruder motioned with his cigar, and a chunk of shadow separated itself from the darkness of the warehouse. "I'd like yew t' meet me cousin, Jo'die."

The ogre towered over his mongrel kinsman. Despite the differences in their heights and builds, there was a marked family resemblance. The ogre growled something in his native tongue and Magruder lifted an eyebrow.

"Aye, now? It seems Jo'die finds yer lady friend a wee bit familiar."

The ogre pushed the brim of his hat back with a taloned finger the size of a small sausage, his brow furrowed by unaccustomed brainwork. It was the ogre monk.

"Fuck this!" shrilled Chaz, hurling the bag of money at Magruder and fleeing in the direction of the exit.

The ogre roared like a lion and bounded after Chaz. It only took three strides of his long, oaklike legs for Jordie to catch up.

Chaz shrieked as the ogre grabbed him by the back of the neck, dangling him like a puppy.

"I'd see aboot that, if I were yew, lass," suggested Thick Eddie as he bent to retrieve the bag Chaz had abandoned. "Jo'die may just be a wee bit peckish right now."

Cursing the ogre and the northern climes that produced such changeling bastards as Thick Eddie Magruder, I sprinted to Chaz's rescue.

Jordie had reversed his grip and was now holding Chaz by his ankles. I slammed into the ogre just as he began to lift his apelike arms. Ogres like to eat their prey headfirst. I don't know why, they just do. Jordie let go of Chaz and swatted me with a hand the size of a telephone directory. Chaz didn't waste any time getting to his feet and leaving me alone with Magruder's cousin. Jordie, seeing his prey making its getaway, moved to follow.

"Jordie!" The ogre's huge, hairless head swung toward me, momentarily distracted from its victim. "Remember me, Jordie? In Rome? At the villa?"

I could almost hear the cogs turning in the bullet-shaped head as his brows furrowed and unfurrowed. Comprehension dawned in his orangish-brown eyes, and his lips pulled back to expose a mouthful of knives.

I leapt to meet his charge, moving inside his reach in order to drive my knife deep into his side. The blade tore through the ogre's outer garments. However, it slid along the monster's ribs as if his skin were made of rubber. Not even a scratch!

Jordie bellowed his hunting cry, his throat sacs swelling like a howler monkey's. He locked me in a simian embrace, and began to squeeze. His brutish face was inches from mine as he crushed my bones. Black sunbursts filled my eyesight as the ogre laughed, exhaling a fetid breath that was like standing downwind of a slaughterhouse on a hot August day.

I was still clutching my knife, although my arm was pinned to my side. I squirmed frantically in his grip, trying to work my knife hand free. This seemed to amuse and excite the ogre, and he licked my face with a long, rasplike tongue. I received an explicit mental image of myself being ravaged, then devoured. He was still trying to decide whether to kill me before or after the rape.

I voiced my disgust with ogrish courting techniques by wrenching my arm free and driving my switchblade to the hilt in his right ear. It slid in beautifully, like they were made for each other.

The ogre yowled, dropping me in favor of clawing at the weapon embedded in his brain. I assessed my damage: only a few broken ribs and a dislocated shoulder. Jordie crashed about, flailing his arms and squealing like a frightened sow before finally collapsing face forward, his cries halted in midsqueal. Blood seeped from his nose, mouth, and ear. I retrieved my blade, making sure to give it an extra twist, just in case, and hurried away before Thick Eddie came looking for his kin.

Luckily, Eddie Magruder didn't have time to send for any more of his family. For reasons unknown, his car mysteriously exploded two days after our "business transaction" in the warehouse. The wholesale carpeting business can be very cutthroat at times.

That's funny. I'm having trouble visualizing Chaz. The face is there, but it's blurred, like an old movie that's jumped its sprockets. Everything's jerky . . .

I remember the last vampire I killed in London. Chaz went to a gay bar in one of the seedier districts. There were always plenty of vampires to be found in the bars, not to mention *vargr* and incubi. True predators, they found those living on the periphery of human society the perfect victims: homosexuals, prostitutes, junkies, and the homeless make up the Pretenders' staple diet.

Chaz had picked up a handsome young man dressed in exquisitely pressed chinos with neatly rolled cuffs and a tight-fitting white T-shirt. Chaz led the vampire into an abandoned house; the place was partially demolished and there was a gaping hole where the first-floor ceiling should have been. I crouched upstairs, watching my Judas goat as he lured the sacrificial victim deeper into the trap.

I jumped, savoring the split second of free-fall before I crashed on top of the startled vampire. I pinned him to the floor, straddling his chest.

He was a strong one, and as vicious as a rutting tiger. I managed to stick him once, twice. Then he rolled over and I saw his face for the first time. I froze, the knife poised for the killing thrust.

Chaz was shrilling, "Kill him! Kill him! Fer Chrissakes, kill him!" But I couldn't. I was paralyzed. I *knew* the bastard!

The vampire writhed under me, spitting and clawing like a rabid cat, but I couldn't drive the blade home. The last time I'd seen him, he'd been behind the wheel of a Rolls Royce the color of smoke, dressed in the livery of a chauffeur.

"Where is he? Where is he?" I didn't recognize the voice as my own. I tasted bile and blood rising in my throat. My rage bordered on euphoria.

"Where is he? I know you're one of his gets. I saw you with him!"

The vampire twisted his head from side to side, babbling incoherently. My paralysis ended and I smashed my fist into his mouth. I didn't feel his fangs as they shredded my knuckles. His blood was thick and dark, like dirty motor oil. All I could see was his demonic leer as Denise beat on the glass partition in the back of the Rolls. I brought the switchblade across his face, laying his handsome features open to the bone.

The vampire chauffeur screamed and put his hands to his ruined face, pushing me off his chest.

Chaz was shouting at me to stop him before he escaped as the vampire staggered toward the front door.

Blind in one eye, he tumbled down the front steps and landed on the street. There were viscous smears on the steps and his white shirt was the color of old ketchup. The vampire got to his feet, clinging to a nearby streetlight for support. He looked like a music-hall drunk.

I charged out of the building, Chaz on my heels. I had every intention of dragging the thing back inside and finishing my interrogation, even if it meant skinning him layer by layer.

The knife had sliced away the vampire's upper lip and left cheek, exposing his teeth and upper jaw. He looked like he was leering at me again. Maybe that's what made me lose control.

The vampire raised his hand in a feeble attempt to deflect the next blow and said, "No . . ."

Perhaps he was trying to tell me he didn't know Morgan's whereabouts. Maybe not. I'm no longer sure. I was beyond caring. I was in the backseat of a Rolls Royce with a chauffeur whose grin was impossibly sharp. The switchblade impaled his right eye, burying itself in the spongy softness of the frontal lobes, severing left brain from right. I made sure to twist the knife.

The vampire slid off the blade and lay sprawled in the gutter under the streetlight. I felt as if I was emerging from heavy sedation. I was vaguely aware I was standing on a London sidewalk with a rapidly bloating corpse at my feet. Blanched faces watched me from behind the curtains of a dozen windows.

Chaz tugged on my sleeve, his voice urgent. "C'mon, Sonja! What's wrong with you? Cor, y' really fucked it this time!"

That's how I returned to the land of my birth. The last time I was in America I'd been a pampered rich kid with her whole life laid out for her like a party frock draped across the foot of her bed. Now I wasn't even me anymore.

Socialite, hooker, vampire hunter, and vampire—no one could accuse me of leading a dull life.

Chaz came along at the last minute. Turned out to be a mistake. The scuzziest down-and-out dive on Skid Row was too wholesome for him. No sense of history.

All he did was bitch about how much he missed the clubs in Soho. He was the one who brought Catherine Wheele to my attention.

Shit! What's wrong? Everything's jumping and rolling like the picture on a cheap TV set. The weird part is that it's so familiar . . . like it's *supposed* to do that. I can't even *think* about Catherine Wheele without the signal trying to scramble.

We control the horizontal. We control the vertical.

Like fuck you do! What's going on here? Damnit, if this is your doing . . .

Me? Why should I keep you from continuing your boring little monologue? I've only heard it every sleep for the past six months. "Poor pitiful me, I've become a big bad monster." Give me a break! No, as much as I'd love to change channels, I'm not the one behind your technical difficulties. You gotta dig deeper.

Deeper?

Just tell your story. You'll find out.

Chaz showed me the article in a cheesy supermarket tabloid he'd brought home. It had Sister Catherine Wheele, dressed in a red-white-and-blue spangled jumpsuit, holding a microphone. Her makeup was running. A smaller photo was cropped and inserted into the lower right-hand corner. The photo was of Shirley Thorne, wife of industrialist Jacob Thorne and mother of missing heiress Denise Thorne.

The article claimed Mrs. Thorne was funneling a small fortune into the Wheele ministry in an attempt to contact her long-lost daughter.

I sent Chaz to scout out Wheele, to see if there was any truth to the rumors behind her being a wild talent. He was gone a long time. It's getting hard to think.

Tell the story.

Meet me . . . He was going to meet me at the playground after midnight. He was standing by the basketball goal. Why is this so *difficult?* I walked up behind him. He turned. He was smiling. As usual. Before I could question him about Wheele, he kissed me. Didn't say a word, just kissed me. And fired point-blank into my gut. Knocked . . . knocked me down. He ran away, didn't look back. Smart boy, knew better than to hang around. There was a flechette lodged in my belly. Tranquilizer of some kind . . .

Hands. Hands all over me. Set me up. Little shit. Set me up. But he didn't tell them the truth. Not the whole truth. The pain and rage made it so hard to keep control, the Other emerged. Men were screaming. Blood in me and on me. Someone chanting "Antichrist" like a mantra. And then . . . then . . .

Aw, don't tell me you're not going to finish this exciting episode.

Can't. Nothing but static, white noise, hurts when I try to remember . . .

What a wimp! You're real good at slam-dunking bad-ass bikers into trash cans, but come the first aversion barrier and you're whining like a goddamn baby!

What are you blathering about?

Look, bright girl, you've been running the same damn autobiographical saga every sleep for the past six months and you never get past the first barrier. Never. I've let you slide because . . . well, because it suited me. But it's time for you to finish the story, Sonja.

No.

You don't have much to say about it.

No. You're lying. There's nothing there. You can't fool me into looking.

Whatever you say, luv.

The barrier is gone and white-hot static fills my head and I try to yell and tell it to stop, but the noiseless noise fills my mouth and nostrils. I'm drowning in emptiness.

Something clicks inside my skull. I feel as if a searchlight has been trained on my brain. Something's in there. Something big and powerful and mean. Fingers of laser light probe the contours of my frontal lobes. I can't move. I can't think. I can't breathe. The intruder isn't a nimble sneak thief like Chaz, but a vandal intent on ransacking everything, unmindful of the damage. My memory is ruptured and the past spills out, filling my head with a thousand simultaneous emotions. I imagine synapses burning, fuses blowing. The creature in my head hits bottom, but that's not good enough for it. It worries at the capstone separating my mind from that of the Other's. I can feel it tugging inside my skull, like pliers on a bad tooth. Then all hell breaks loose.

I can't! I can't! Don't make me, please, don't make me.

Don't make you do what?

Look. Don't make me. Can't make me. She won't let me.

Who won't let you?

She won't!

What are you so scared of? What could possibly frighten you so badly you'd rather go mad than look at it? What is it Sonja?

Shut up! Shut up! I won't look. I refuse to listen to you.

Who erected that barrier, Sonja? Was it Wheele? No, Catherine Wheele is expert at knocking down walls, but I doubt if she knows the first thing about building them. No, Sonja, I think you know who built that wall. It was Denise, wasn't it?

Denise is dead.

Is she? Why won't you look?

Liar. Liar. Liar.

What is Denise afraid of? Finish the story, Sonja. What is Denise afraid of?

You.

Me?

She's afraid you're not what Ghilardi thought you were. That he was wrong. That you're *not* a demon from hell. That there's no Other and no Sonja Blue, only Denise.

Now, was that so bad? The last time you wimped out and went nuts rather than consider that possibility. And look where it got you! You and your humanity hang-up! You provided Wheele with a loaded pistol and invited her to fire it point-blank!

Is it true?

Hmmmm?

Is it true that you and I aren't real? That we're just parts of Denise Thorne's imagination?

You got me. Even if I did know, would you believe me if I told you?

But if it *is* true, then I don't exist. Neither do you. Doesn't that bother you?

Maybe. We're still here, aren't we?

But . . .

Time to wake up.

Claude bent over the motionless body on the futon. He'd found her earlier that afternoon, fully dressed, right down to her ubiquitous sunglasses. At first she didn't seem to be breathing and her pulse was abnormally slow. Was she asleep or languishing in a coma?

He'd spent the rest of the day crouched beside the pallet, watching his captor for signs of life. He'd dosed off once or twice, only to be awakened by vivid images of a man being beaten to death with a cane and a moldering, sharp-toothed thing wearing tinted glasses. He tried reading the old, leather-bound book in order to pass the time, but the text was indecipherable and half the pages were covered with baroque geometric patterns. The only other book in the loft was a slender volume in German, so Claude leafed through *The Vanishing*, staring at the photos of Denise Thorne.

The funny thing was—at least Claude thought it was funny—that he could have escaped. But he'd decided not to. There was too much he didn't know, and like it or not, Sonja Blue was the only way he'd ever find any of the answers.

The shadows in the loft had lengthened into early evening when the muscles in her arms, legs, and face began to contract and relax. He was reminded of the dead frog he'd hooked up to a dry-cell battery back in high-school biology class.

Her abdomen hitched sharply as her lungs shifted back into gear. The fingers of her hands, folded flat over her rib cage, stretched themselves backward, the joints crackling like dry leaves.

"Are you, all right? I thought you were sick or something."

The first thing she thought as she surfaced was, *I'm going to kill that bitch.* But what she said was, "Yeah. I feel fine."

THE REAL WORLD

Catherine Wheele stood at the bedroom window and watched the night arrive. She wore the peach-colored negligee from the day before, her wig resting atop a Styrofoam skull on the night table. She fingered a strand of her real hair as she sipped her highball.

She remembered the day Zeb informed her that the wives of prophets and power brokers didn't have hair the color of mice. The wig had been Zeb's idea, like so many other things. He claimed the congregation wouldn't sit still for a dye job, but a wig . . . Hell, their mamas wore wigs. And he'd been right. As always . . .

Well, almost always.

She watched her ghost image in the window. Without her wig and makeup she looked a lot like her mother. The thought made her scowl; that made the resemblance all the more telling. Now she looked *exactly* like her mother.

She didn't like thinking about her family. Whenever she let her mind wander back to North Carolina, it triggered the things lurking at the corners of her eyes.

The flickering shadows had been there as far back as she cared to remember. But now . . . now they seemed to have mass and substance and definite shapes and sizes and recognizable features. She wondered about her sanity; maybe she was going mad. What worried her was the possibility she *wasn't* losing her mind.

A sodden groan emerged from the heart-shaped bed dominating her boudoir. She glanced at a pile of bedclothes the color of cotton candy. The shadows capering at the edges of her vision turned into mist.

Wexler. She'd almost forgotten about him.

The bedclothes stirred fitfully, then were still. She snorted derisively as she finished her drink. Wexler! What a disappointment. How could she have deluded herself into thinking he was worthy as a consort?

Oh, he was adequate enough between the sheets. But he lacked Zeb's savvy and Ezra's selfless devotion. She needed those a hell of a lot more than she needed his spurting member. How could she have been so blind as to trust him with something as delicate and potentially dangerous as the Blue woman? Ezra would have seen through Wexler's media-celeb glamour within seconds. But Ezra was dead by the time she'd been forced to coopt Wexler and his sanitarium into her plans. He'd been killed—murdered!—by the same abomination Wexler, the damned fool, allowed to escape. She projected a splinter of anger at the bed, smiling as Wexler whimpered like a drowsy child.

She returned her attention to the nightfall outside her window. The photosensitive burglar lights, set flush in the ground and nesting in the branches of the trees, switched on one by one as the shadows lengthened.

She watched her employees, dressed in their identical dark suits and narrow ties, as they patrolled the perimeters of the estate. Most of them were her own elite guards, the ones Ezra had dubbed "Wheelers." They were loyal to her, and she'd made sure their devotion contained the proper synthesis of religious awe and pit-bull savagery. They'd gladly lie, cheat, steal, or murder for her—and often did.

Ezra hadn't approved of her method of conditioning the Wheelers. Poor old-fashioned, possessive Ezra.

"If it wasn't necessary when Zebulon was alive, why is it so damned important now?"

"A lot of things weren't necessary when Zeb was alive. Paying them isn't enough, Ezra. I want to make damned sure no one turns Judas and gives state's evidence. Is that clear, Ezra? It's to protect the ministry!"

He didn't really believe what she'd told him, but he never forbade it. Would she have stopped if he'd really put his foot down? No. Although she'd loved Ezra, he'd never been capable of inspiring fear like Zeb.

One of the guards patrolling the garden terrace below halted, having spotted her in the window. Who—or what—was he associating her with? She tried to place the Wheeler and his pet obsession. So many of them were fixated on their mothers . . . Ah, yes, Dennings. His heart's desire had been Sophia Loren, circa 1962. She moved away from the window. Dennings shivered as if seized by a sudden chill, then continued on his rounds.

Spurring unquestioning loyalty among her Wheelers was absurdly simple. All it involved was tapping into the right fantasy and constructing the proper illusion. She called her personal form of conditioning "Heart's Desire." And the best time for brainwashing was during sex.

She enjoyed the looks on their faces as they humped famous movie stars, heads of state, or professional athletes, although nothing could compare to the horrified pleasure-guilt of those who found themselves erupting inside their mothers.

The Oedipal desire was, by far, the most common, although there could be nasty backlashes if not handled carefully. Like the boy who'd put his thumbs in his eyes. That had been most unfortunate. But most of her "recruits" were men of questionable moral fiber to begin with, and being a motherfucker was nothing new to them.

Her Wheelers served her without question or qualm, eager for a replay of their ultimate fantasy. While she had no intention of ever permitting an encore, she encouraged the belief that repeat performances were possible. Her punishments, however, proved to be far more frequent.

She moved to her combination wet bar and vanity table, pouring herself another Wild Turkey from the commemorative Elvis decanter. A larger-than-life oil portrait of her late husband grinned down at her from over the bar.

She'd come into the world squalling white trash, the daughter of Jeremiah and Hannah Skaggs and the third of eight children. She wasn't Catherine back then. Her mama had named her Kathy-Mae, and she was just another snot-nosed, scabby-kneed, malnourished yard ape destined to grow up hard and ignorant in the Carolina hills.

Jeremiah Skaggs worked at the sawmill, when he could get the work. Papa liked to get a belly full of liquor and Jesus, and when he was like that, he wasn't very careful.

"God looks after His children," he used to say. God must have been looking the other way when Papa lost his left pinkie, then the first joint on his right pointer. The sawmill boss refused to hire him again after he buzzed his left ring finger up to the second knuckle. Papa accused him of being a communist devil-worshiper.

Mama took in laundry. Catherine could not remember her mother smiling or laughing. Mama's voice, when she bothered to speak, was a nasal whine, like the droning of a giant mosquito. She was ten years younger than Papa, although you couldn't tell it by looking at her. Both her parents seemed ancient, their faces seamed and pitted by years of deprivation. They looked like the apple dolls Granny Teasdale sold to the Yankee tourists during the summer.

Her childhood consisted of dirt, hunger, backbreaking labor, and fear. Violence, in the form of her father's drunken tirades, was a daily occurrence—like breakfast and dinner, only far more reliable.

She didn't have much to do with her siblings, but she thought it was because she was her mother's first girl child, and the only one she'd named herself. Papa had been on a bender when she'd delivered. He'd been scandalized when he found out she hadn't picked a biblical name.

She never played games with her brothers and sisters, preferring the company of an imaginary friend called Sally. When she was involved in her make-believe games, pretending she was rich and living in a big house with running water and electricity, was the closest she ever came to experiencing childhood.

When Papa found out she was holding conversations with an invisible friend, he hit the ceiling and her as well. She was possessed and needed the devil beat out of her or she'd be sentenced to eternal damnation. Papa took her to a backwoods preacher called Deacon Jonas so she could be saved proper.

Deacon Jonas was a big fat man with white hair and a lumpy red nose the size of a potato. He listened to Papa describe her relationship with Sally, nodding and grunting and looking at Kathy-Mae with watery eyes. He told Papa that he wanted to pray over her and that Papa would have to wait outside until it was done.

After Papa had left, Deacon Jonas opened his pants and showed Kathy-Mae his thing. Even though she was only six, Kathy-Mae had already seen several of them and was not particularly scared or impressed by the deacon's. The deacon buttoned himself back up, then said the Lord's Prayer.

Sally stopped coming to visit her, and after a while, Kathy-Mae forgot about her imaginary friend. There was too much work to be done for her to waste time on such foolishness. She helped her mother take care of the house and look after the little ones, who tended to blur into an amorphous, nameless face with dull eyes and an upper lip caked with dirt and dried snot.

Her life in the Skaggs household had never been great, but things started to get really bad after she turned twelve. When she'd started her monthlies, she noticed Mama looking at her funny. Papa was doing it too, but in a different way. He looked at her the same way Deacon Jonas had when he'd prayed over her, only not so timid.

Sometimes he'd come home liquored up and Mama would meet him on the porch and they'd get to arguing and then he'd use his fists. He'd be too exhausted after he finished beating her to do more than sleep it off, so Mama'd get in bed with Kathy-Mae. They both knew it wouldn't be long before Papa got what he wanted, but it was a ritual Mama felt obliged to perform.

Maybe that's why she confessed. Perhaps she thought it would take the edge off what was to follow.

Mama told Papa that he wasn't Kathy-Mae's real father.

Thirteen years ago, when Mama was young and only had two children, a stranger came to the house. Papa was working at the sawmill and Mama was in the dooryard, scrubbing clothes in the big washtub, when the stranger walked up from nowhere and asked for a drink of water. He didn't look like anyone in particular, just another raggedy man wandering the countryside, looking for a handout. But his eyes . . . The next thing Mama knew she had her skirts up and the raggedy man was humping her on the front porch in broad daylight. She couldn't remember if she'd agreed to it or not. In fact, she couldn't remember if the stranger was short or tall, fat or thin, dark or fair. It didn't take him very long, even by Papa's standards, and as soon as he'd finished, he was gone. Not even a "thankee kindly, ma'am." Mama passed it off as a particularly vivid dream . . . until she saw her newborn daughter. Kathy-Mae had her daddy's eyes.

Papa repaid Mama for cuckolding him with two black eyes and a busted lip before turning his attention to Kathy-Mae. Kathy-Mae tried to run, which only made him madder. The sight of blood geysering from her nose excited Papa to something more than physical abuse. He dragged her out to the toolshed behind the house and raped her on the rough plank floor until her buttocks were full of splinters. He left her huddled atop a pile of old burlap sacks, her eyes swollen and crotch bleeding. He informed her, through the locked door, that he didn't want her "polluting" his *real* children and that he meant to keep her in the toolshed for the rest of her life. Or until he got tired of her.

At first she couldn't think. Her brain was a lump of cold, insensate clay. She hoped it would stay like that forever, but knew it was too good to last. Although ravenously hungry, she managed to cry herself to sleep.

She had a strange dream that night.

She dreamed Sally came back to visit her. She couldn't see Sally very clearly, but she could hear her voice inside her head.

"Do you want out of here? I can take you away from the pain and the bad things. If you agree to that, it's a bargain. I'll always be here and you'll never be able to leave me. Do you want that?"

"Yes."

Sally rushed forward, her arms open to embrace Kathy-Mae, and for one brief moment she could see Sally clearly. She tried to cry out, to renege on her bargain, but it was too late. Sally's arms closed about her shoulders and she seemed to sink into her, like a snowflake melting on her tongue, then Sally was gone. Or was she?

She dreamed she could see inside the house, even though she was locked in the shed. She saw Mama and Papa sleeping side by side in the old wrought-iron bed. Mama had the littlest one in the bed with her, cradled in the warm hollow between her right arm and breast. Somehow, she knew it was Sally who was showing her these things. Kathy-Mae dreamed Sally told her Mama to get out of bed. Mama got out of bed. Then she dreamed Sally told Mama to go to the kitchen and fetch the butcher knife. It was a big, ugly, and very sharp piece of cutlery.

Sally told Mama to slit Papa's throat. Since he was full of squeeze and exhausted by his earlier activities, it was pretty easy. The blood escaping his throat formed a sodden halo around his head.

Sally told Mama to go and visit each of the sleeping children and make sure their dreams never ended. The baby was the only one who woke up; it whimpered as Mama slit its tiny throat from ear from ear. Mama had butchering piglets down to an art.

In her dream, Sally told Mama to unlock the shed. Funny how real it seemed, not at all like a proper dream. Kathy-Mae could feel the dew on the grass as she walked alongside her mother. Sally was walking on the other side, but Kathy-Mae couldn't really focus on her. Shadows seemed to crowd the corners of her eyes, obscuring her view. It was a dream, wasn't it?

Mama looked funny in the moonlight. She wore her old flannel nightgown, but the blood made it look different. She still clutched the dripping butcher knife in one hand. Her eyes were blank and glassy, but her cheeks were wet with tears and nervous tics twisted her features into a rictus grin. That scared Kathy-Mae, but not enough to make her stop dreaming.

Sally climbed into the bed of Papa's pick'em-up truck and handed the can of gasoline to Kathy-Mae's mother. No words passed between them. In Kathy-Mae's dream, Mama knew what to do.

The gasoline fumes made Mama's eyes water even more as she doused her nuptial bed. Then Mama got back into bed and lay down beside her butchered husband. She cuddled the dead baby to her breast as she struck the match.

Kathy-Mae experienced only the slightest twinge of guilt as she watched her home go up in flames. After all, it was only a dream, wasn't it? Not even a nightmare, really. Besides, Sally was the one responsible, not her.

When she woke that morning, she found herself shivering on the front lawn. The three-room shack that had served as the Skaggs' home was a jumble of charred timber and smoking brick. Kathy-Mae knew she should scream or cry, but there was nothing inside her. At least nothing that was sad.

The nearest neighbors were the Wellmans, three miles up the road. She figured she could work up some passable tears by the time she got there.

Despite her claim that she'd never leave, Kathy-Mae could not find any evidence of Sally's presence. She *did* feel kind of different, as if there was something glowing in her belly, sometimes. Kathy-Mae didn't think it was Sally. During the months following the fire, Kathy-Mae gradually forgot Sally's oath and convinced herself that the reason she alone had escaped the horrible blaze that had claimed her family was that she'd chosen to sleep on the porch that night.

Being an orphan wasn't too different from the life she'd known before her family was destroyed. The state put her in a succession of foster homes, where she was mistreated and malnourished, until she ran away for good at the age of fourteen. She doubted her "parents" would bother to inform the state, since that meant they'd stop receiving maintenance checks.

She hooked up with a passing carnival and, since she could pass for sixteen and lie about being eighteen, ended up working one of the shill booths during the day and dancing the hoochie-coo at night. Sometimes she sat in for the Gypsy Witch, reading the fortunes of popcorn-munching, goggle-eyed fish. That's how she met Zebulon.

He called himself Zebbo the Great and dressed like a third-rate Mandrake the Magician, right down to the patent-leather hair and pencil mustache. Kathy-Mae thought he was the most debonair man she'd ever seen outside the movies.

Everyday she watched him from her place behind the Hit-the-Cats booth, too terrified to even talk to him. She was afraid she'd come across as a crude, unschooled hick, so she kept her adoration to herself. She didn't have to suffer unrequited love for long, since Zebbo the Great could read minds.

Oh, he was nowhere as powerful as she would eventually become, or even as facile as that sleazy Brit. Zebulon had a gift, and that gift happened to be low-wattage psychic receptivity. If someone thought about something fairly simple—like a color or a face card—Zebbo the Great could pick up that thought with minimum effort. Telephone numbers, street addresses, and the like were beyond his limited retrieval methods.

Kathy-Mae was astonished and incredibly flattered when Zebbo the Great started paying attention to her. Zebbo was as dashing and romantic a figure to be found on the midway, and he could be relied on to say things like "your love called to me with the voice of angels. We were meant for each other."

She was fifteen, Zebulon thirty-two, when they got married.

They hadn't been married two days before Zebulon started talking about her gift and all the things they could do together.

Kathy-Mae wasn't too sure about whether her gift was real or not, since it was tied to Sally and her dream and she didn't like thinking about *that* at all. Zebulon was insistent. She knew the power was still inside her, that it hadn't gone away, but she was afraid of it. What if it got away from her and she ended up hurting Zebulon? She tried to explain her fears to her husband, but he couldn't understand her hesitancy. She'd never been able to bring herself to tell him about what happened the night her family died. Maybe if she'd broken down and told him, maybe things would have worked out differently. Knowing Zebulon, probably not.

Zeb finally coerced his bride into serving as a "psychic transmitter" in his act. The marks filled out index cards, listing their addresses and the names and ages of their next of kin, then handed them to Catherine—Zebulon renamed her on their honeymoon —who "broadcast" the information to her blindfolded husband on stage. On the occasions when she attempted to dip into the minds of the audience for additional, unsolicited information, she unwittingly triggered epileptic fits or temporary paralysis among the rubes. Zebulon insisted she stick to the note cards.

Their act was successful, but Zebulon wanted more than top billing at the state fair's sideshow. In 1960, two years into their marriage, he hit on the idea of becoming an evangelist.

"Honey, this racket's perfect for us! All we need is a tent, some folding chairs, a podium, and a secondhand pickup truck. We'll have flocks of suckers lined up, practically begging us to take their money! What do you say, sweetie? You think it's okay?"

Of course it was okay. Anything Zeb wanted was okay.

The early days were the hardest. There was hardly enough money to feed them, much less pay for the gasoline to get them from town to town. When it was hot and the tent was full of sweaty, reeking crackers and Zebulon's voice boomed on about damnation and the sins of the flesh, Catherine thought she could see Papa sitting in the audience, his eyes full of whiskey and the Lord and his throat a ragged, blood-caked mess. Sometimes Mama was there, cradling a butchered infant to her blackened breast as she rocked in time to the gospel music. That's when Catherine took to drinking.

Zebulon disapproved at first, although he never went so far as to actually forbid it. Maybe he was afraid she'd cut off his "pipeline to the Lord."

During their second year on the hallelujah trail, Catherine became pregnant. Zebulon was less than thrilled. A baby meant added distractions and hassles. Catherine was convinced that once it was born, Zebulon would change his mind. The miscarriage occurred in her second trimester, triggered by stress and drinking. Zebulon refused to take her to a hospital. It wouldn't look right for a miracle man to have to take his wife to an emergency room. Instead, he fed her handfuls of aspirin and wrapped her belly in warm towels.

After their third year as the Wheeles of God, things began to change. Zebulon's reputation grew, thanks to his ability to "call out" the faithful. Believers flocked to their tent shows, eager to witness even the tattiest of miracles. Professional debunkers would occasionally sit in on the services and observe Catherine as she distributed "healing cards" among the congregation, telling them to write down their specific "prayer needs," as well as names and addresses. She enjoyed the look of confusion on the unbelievers' faces when she did not take the cards backstage or make hand signals to her husband while he was on stage.

Zebulon's healing gift, however, was a product of his years as a stage magician. His greatest success was a variation of the old man-who-grows carny trick. In order to heal someone with a short leg, all he had to do was find an appropriate mark with loose shoes, place his hand beneath the mark's feet when they sat down, and twist his hand so that the shoe on the farthest foot was pulled slightly off and the shoe on the nearer foot was pressed tightly against the sole. Then, by reversing the twist, the farther shoe was pushed on against that sole, giving the appearance that the two shoes—and, more important, the feet inside them—were the same length. The marks hobbled away, convinced they were cured, and the love offerings doubled with each show.

Catherine was amazed at how little was needed for the faithful to justify their belief in Zebulon's claim that he was a conduit to God. Most of the time there was no need for sleight of hand or carny scams. Zebulon simply bullied them into thinking they were healed. The people who attended their revivals weren't humans; they were sheep. Sheep to be herded in and fleeced as quickly and as efficiently as possible. By the time the Wheeles of God came back through town again, everyone would have forgotten how they'd kept their arthritis but lost their savings.

The radio ministry came in '64, just in time for Zebulon to rant over the air about the Communist/Jewish conspiracy orchestrating Kennedy's assassination and allowing four long-haired, homosexual foreigners to pollute America's youth.

Their first real church—with solid wood floors and walls made of something besides canvas—materialized in '66. This gave Zebulon a bit more respectability among the evangelical crowd and enabled him to ally himself with a loose coalition of fundamentalist churches somewhere to the right of hard-shell Baptists and Seventh-Day Adventists. Zebulon was forty and Catherine twenty-three when they bought their first Coupe de Ville.

The years became an endless succession of radio appearances, revival tours—held inside air-conditioned public auditoriums instead of tents—and incoming checks and money orders made out to their home ministry. Zebulon already had hopes of expanding into television and broadening the church's power base.

During those years Catherine's understanding of her powers grew. Zebulon didn't approve of her using her gift outside the routine, and she knew better than to displease him. Zebulon's wrath was frightening and his healer's hands could be cruel. So her drinking grew heavier in order to keep the power inside her damped. It didn't work too well.

If she looked at the sheep too long, she could see what was wrong with them: lungs the color of soot and sticky as fresh asphalt, tumors buried deep inside the folds of the brain like malignant pearls, cancer creeping like kudzu, bones twisted by arthritis into abstract sculpture . . . Well, at least her parents no longer made appearances during services.

Her feeling for Zebulon had always involved awe and fear; he was an emotional man, prone to acts of extreme temper, although he learned to control it in front of the cameras. As the years passed, the love she'd once felt for him was replaced by respect for his canniness. Although Zeb never got beyond eighth grade, he had an innate understanding of the best way to bilk a sucker.

Since his acceptance as a messiah figure, he'd revised his past so it would better fit God's gift to a suffering world. He'd received his calling as a barefoot, dirty-faced boy in rural Arkansas. No mention was made of his years on the carny circuit as Zebbo the Great. He'd somehow grown a war record, acquiring two Purple Hearts and a Bronze Star, even though he was only fifteen when World War Two was declared. He also managed to squeeze some missionary work in an obscure China province into his résumé. Catherine's past also underwent radical fictionalization: she'd somehow become the eldest daughter of one of the oldest and most respected Tidewater families.

Their life-style was far from ascetic; by the mid-'70s there were no fewer than six cars in the Wheeles' personal possession, the most humble being the Coupe de Ville. Catherine owned five fur coats, and Zeb's wardrobe boasted dozens of expensive silk suits, although he always made sure he was photographed in the powder-blue three-piece polyester outfit that had become his trademark.

Their last sexual act, as man and wife, occurred sometime in 1971. Although she knew he was sating his carnal desires with a succession of sweet young things culled from the secretarial pool, Catherine wasn't concerned about losing her husband. By her parents' standards, their marriage was perfect.

In 1973 Zebulon introduced Ezra into the entourage. Ezra was everything Zebulon wasn't: formally educated, from a good family, and adept at handling the business needs of a rapidly growing television ministry. He became her lover a year later.

It was Ezra who talked her into trying to control and fully exploit her powers. She openly confided in him, revealing the secret of Zebulon's "gift of knowledge" in blatant disregard of her husband's orders.

Acting under Ezra's advice, Catherine tried dipping into the minds of the audience for the first time since the carnival days. She discovered that if she pushed too hard, she ran the risk of triggering convulsions. Skimming the upper layers of conscious thought proved fairly easy, as long as the sheep had their attention focused on Zebulon. The names of doctors, medicines, and hospitals were quickly snagged and broadcast to Zebulon for use in the act.

When Zebulon realized what she was doing, he was very upset.

"I told you to stick to the script! No freelancing. You want to blow it for us now? After we've come so far and have so much to lose?" He raised his hand, and, out of habit, Catherine cringed, but her voice remained defiant.

"What are you making such a fuss about? Nothing went wrong, did it? Hell, the arena's full of old geezers with heart problems, so what's so unusual about one or two of them having fits? Most of them think they're experiencing some kind of religious ecstasy, for Pete's sake! *You're* the one that comes off looking like God's gift to backwoods hicks, so what are you bitchin' about?"

The hand wavered but did not fall. For the first time in their relationship, something akin to uncertainty flickered in Zebulon's eyes. Uncertainty . . . and fear.

That's when she felt the balance of power first shift in her direction. It wasn't long before things began to change between the two of them . . . and inside them as well.

The truce between the Wheeles was uneasy. Zeb didn't like being reminded that without his wife he'd still be doing a bottom-of-the-barrel mentalist act in some godforsaken carny. And he especially didn't like the idea of Catherine using her gift whenever and however she liked.

Catherine reveled in his fear. It made her feel good. So good, in fact, she almost didn't mind it when her parents reappeared, although she was dismayed by the fact they'd brought the rest of the family with them.

Zebulon's miraculous new ability to divine the nature of a supplicant's illness simply by looking at them drew more and more followers. Their television ratings soared. The other televangelists considered the Wheeles beneath their dignity and dismissed them as "tasteless." Zebulon said they were jealous of his ratings share.

Catherine's drinking problem reached chronic proportions. Ezra begged her to stop, but she couldn't. He didn't understand. The alcohol kept the things at the edge of her vision safely blurred. After a couple of years, the sexual side of her relationship with Ezra sputtered out, although he remained devoted to her. Bored, she began seducing the hired hands and, by accident, discovered the process she later developed into Heart's Desire.

His name was Joe. She couldn't remember his last name, not that it mattered. He was Joe, and that was enough. He was one of Ezra's underlings, handpicked by her former lover as a suitable proxy. Everyone in the organization knew that Ezra served as her panderer and that spending a few hours in "private meditation" with Mrs. Wheele often proved financially rewarding.

Nothing seemed out of the ordinary that night. They engaged in ritual small talk while enjoying a drink together. Joe knew what was expected of him; he was to play the adoring servant, confessing his long-denied passion to the lady of the house. The seduction occurred with clockwork precision.

He was in the saddle, grunting and sweating his way through a workmanlike act of coitus, when something inside Catherine's head reached out on its own volition and snared Joe's mind. His eyes glazed and his face went slack, yet his pelvis picked up its rocking-horse pace and his grunts became rougher. A weird moan escaped him as orgasm took him. After a few seconds the glassiness left his eyes, to be replaced by an expression of extreme revulsion.

Joe pulled himself from her, his face twisted into a horrified grimace, and stumbled into the bathroom, where he was noisily sick. More intrigued than offended by her partner's attitude, Catherine peeked into his mind.

(I could have sworn she was Carolyn . . . just for a minute, that's all. That Carolyn's eyes were looking at me while I . . .) Another spasm of nausea overcame him and she lost the thread of his thought.

Later that evening she ordered Ezra to bring her Joe's personnel file. In it she discovered that Joe's younger sister had been named Carolyn and that she'd died of leukemia at the age of thirteen. Understanding and exploiting this newly discovered power soon became her favorite hobby.

She and Zebulon seldom spoke anymore, outside of their folksy scripted banter in front of the cameras. Catherine had become so adept at maintaining the facade of the constantly cheerful, sloppily sentimental, and unswervingly loyal country preacher's wife that crying and laughing on cue was instinctual behavior for her.

Zebulon was a great believer in playing every angle, but the Heavenly Contact scam was a big mistake. If his congregation had ever gotten wind of what he was doing, it would have ruined the ministry for good. Zebulon's sense of self-preservation was very acute, but on this occasion his greed was stronger.

Since he'd been raised ignorant of the Gospel, he had no idea how the faithful might react to the news that their beloved minister was holding seances, a form of witchcraft condemned in the Bible.

Although he might have been foolhardy, he certainly wasn't stupid. The Heavenly Contacts were never mentioned, much less discussed, in the computer-generated "personal letters" to his followers. Only select members of the Wheeles' Hub Brotherhood—those who'd donated over five thousand dollars at one time—were extended the offer of relaying personal messages to their dearly departed through the powers of the Reverend Wheele. All Catherine had to do was lift enough personal data from the minds of those present to convince the sheep that Zebulon was in touch with the correct spirit.

Zebulon decided to put an end to the Heavenly Contacts when Catherine started producing ectoplasm during a contact with the ten-year-old daughter of a well-to-do furniture-store owner. Zebulon leapt out of his chair, turning over the table, and the ectoplasm disappeared. At first she thought he was actually concerned for her personal safety, then she realized he resented her stealing the show. After all, *he* was supposed to be the pipeline to Heaven.

They had a big fight over whether to discontinue the Contacts, and to her surprise Zebulon agreed to back down. It was a good thing, too, because the Contacts scam ended up netting them their biggest sucker ever.

Shirley Thorne, the wife of the millionaire industrialist, contacted the Wheeles and begged them to conduct a Contact for her. She was desperate to find out if her missing daughter was among the divine choir. She'd hired dozens of psychics, parapsychologists, spiritualists, and mediums over the years, scouring the afterlife for hints concerning the whereabouts of her only child, and had yet to come up with a suitable answer. She'd heard positive things about the Contacts and was willing to pay whatever they asked.

Mrs. Thorne soon became the Wheeles' sole Contact patron. Catherine discovered it was fairly easy to sculpt the greenish-white ectoplasm she exuded into a crude semblance of the lost heiress. In fact, the hardest thing she had to do was keep from laughing out loud whenever Mrs. Thorne, weeping and babbling endearments, tried to touch the weird puppet bobbing over the tabletop.

Mr. Thorne was not pleased by his wife's insistence on pumping money into what he considered a two-bit scam, and he was especially outraged to find his wife's name associated with the Wheeles in the pages of supermarket tabloids. Despite his opinion of the Wheeles, he never threatened to expose them.

Zebulon was sixty, Catherine forty-four; they'd been married twenty-eight years. They had a house in Palm Springs, a mansion in Beverly Hills, and a holiday bungalow in Belize. They owned two dozen automobiles, not counting the Coupe de Ville. They had their own mobile video unit and a state-of-the-art television studio. Zebulon's voice was heard on over one hundred radio stations in the continental United States and the syndicated *Wheeles of God Show* was seen by an estimated 2.5 million viewers every week. Their ministry boasted 150 paid employees. Zebulon was in constant demand as a lecturer at conservative Christian rallies, and there were numerous photographs of him in the company of politicians, movie stars, ex-presidents, and dictators adorning his office.

They had it all, with no end in sight for the foreseeable future. So it came as something of a surprise when her husband told her he wanted a divorce.

"Are you crazy? Do you honestly think the rubes who watch our show instead of going to church are going to stand for you divorcing me? The ratings—not to mention the love offerings—would fall through the floor! And why *now*, for the love of Pete? We haven't lived as husband and wife for close to fifteen years. What's the rush?"

"I'm in love, Kathy-Mae. For the first time in my life."

She winced when he said that. She'd always suspected Zebulon's interest in her had more to do with her gift than her self, but that didn't mean she enjoyed having it rubbed in her face. She also disliked it when he called her by her real name. It usually meant trouble.

"What is it? Have you knocked up another one of your precious little secretaries? Which one is it this time?"

Zeb's face paled. "What are you going to do?"

She folded her arms, looking at him with new interest. "If I didn't know better, Zeb, I'd swear you were serious about this one. It sure as hell never bothered you when I fixed up the others with that quack in Tijuana."

"That was different, Kathy-Mae. I'm not as young as I used to be. A man wants to leave something of himself behind. It's only natural."

"You didn't feel that way when I had the miscarriage." Her voice was very still. She remembered the contractions she'd suffered in the back of the old converted school bus that had been their home during their early days on the road, and how he'd refused to take her to the hospital. "You said it'd be in the way. Hold us back."

"Things have changed, Kathy-Mae."

"You're damn *right* they've changed! You're Zebulon Wheele, God's gift to modern man! Champion of the Lord's will and hero to thousands of ignorant shitkickers all over this grand nation! You're no more free to run off and marry some little slut you've been screwing between the filing cabinets than the president is to take a shit on the White House lawn!"

Zebulon's anger overcame his fear. He grabbed her by the wrist and pulled her to him. He was madder than she'd ever seen him. She felt a sick thrill of lust build inside her. It was their first unrehearsed physical contact in years.

"You're a goddamn *freak*. You don't belong with decent folk! You've got no heart, no love in you! You're some kind of monster pretending at being human. I'm not letting you spoil this for me!"

"You're right, Zeb. I don't belong with decent people. I belong with *you*. Who is she, Zeb? Tell me now and I'll forget all about this and we can get back to business." She was surprised how calm and in-charge she sounded.

Zebulon's answer was a stinging backhanded blow to her left cheek. She tasted the blood pooling in her mouth. Okay, I gave him his chance. It's not my fault.

She could have read his mind any time during their relationship, but something always made her hang back. Perhaps it was simple fear of what he'd do if he found out. Or maybe she didn't want to know what he really thought about her.

She hoped he wouldn't fight it. She'd never gone into the mind of anyone who knew what was being done to them. His awareness might complicate things and only make it harder on himself.

She was surrounded by memories; some were fresh while others badly faded: Zebulon shaking hands with a local politician, Zebulon eating at a cheap lunch counter outside of Topeka in 1953, Zebulon consummating their marriage, a dim glimpse of breast and nipple as seen by a nursing infant, a pretty girl smiling and placing his trembling hand on the gentle swelling of her bared belly . . . *That one. Follow that one!*

The fool tried to block her attempt to trace the memory to its source. It was a noble gesture, but a vain one.

It had been a near thing, she had to give him that. Just as she'd accessed the girl's name and address, she'd felt the pressure building. Zebulon had triggered a massive cerebral hemorrhage. She'd never been "inside" during a blowout and she wasn't eager to find out what would happen should she get caught in the explosion. She had withdrawn halfway when the artery burst, pumping blood into the surrounding brain tissue.

Zebulon's memory banks emptied themselves simultaneously, disgorging the mass of stored conversations, old television shows, bank-account numbers, quotes from the bible, excerpts from Houdini's handbooks, and snippets of popular song that comprised Zebulon Wheele's past. A thousand voices, sounding as if they were being replayed on countless tape recorders, each set on different speeds, washed over her. Catherine panicked, terrified of being drowned in the minutiae of her husband's life. As the initial flood of information receded, she realized one by one, the voices were dying out.

Zebulon's memory had bled itself dry. The silence that followed resembled the hiss of blank magnetic tape.

When she regained possession of her physical self, she found Zebulon sprawled on the floor, barely alive. She called Ezra, explaining that Zebulon had suffered "some kind of fit" when his girlfriend called him on the phone and demanded that he divorce Catherine and marry her instead. Ezra was properly shocked and called an ambulance.

Zebulon died in the hospital three days later, never having regained consciousness. Ezra issued a press release citing the televangelist's collapse as the result of too much praying. The death of Mary Beth Mullins, whose car's brakes failed while attempting to merge onto the Interstate, was mentioned briefly on page twelve.

When she looked into the gilt-edged coffin and saw Zebulon's lifeless body, Catherine experienced the giddy mixture of satisfaction and joy she'd known when she'd realized her parents were dead. She was free! Free to shape the ministry in her image. Oh, she'd play the game and be the grief-stricken widow. But once her period of mourning was over, she'd make them forget all about Zebulon Wheele.

Unencumbered by her husband's jealousy, she gave the sheep exactly what they wanted: bigger and better miracles.

The Ultimate Healing was the most daring step ever taken by a television preacher. The legitimate press accused her of bringing the carny into the church, and even her staunchest supporters in the field of checkout counter journalism balked at her psychic surgery stunts.

It didn't matter to her what outsiders did or didn't think about the Ultimate Healing. She made sure to use a ringer and fake blood when professional debunkers were in the audience. As long as the faithful were convinced she was performing first-class miracles and the professional media dismissed her as a hustler, everything was fine.

She picked terminal cases without immediate family or close friends. The ones who were going to die anyway. Who would notice—or even care—if they died shortly after being healed? That simply meant the supplicant's faith had failed and the disease returned. The blame lay with the patient, not the healer.

One or two of her patients actually survived the Ultimate Healing, although most died within a few hours, if not seconds, of being dragged off stage. Already weakened by the ravages of cancer and radiation treatment, most could not withstand the shock of having an unsterilized hand thrust inside their bodies. Then there was the time she'd gone in to remove a tumor and ended up yanking out the guy's gall bladder. But that wasn't her fault. She wasn't a doctor.

The knowledge that Zebulon would never have allowed such an exhibition pleased her. It was too dangerous, too controversial. And most damning of all, it smacked of the geek show.

Step right this way, ladies and gentlemen! Step this way and for the price of twenty-five cents, a mere quarter of a dollar, you can see the Amazing Geek bite the heads off live chickens and snakes! See him put needles in his tongue! Is he man or is he beast? Hurry! Hurry! Hurry!

The Ultimate Healing was tasteless, grotesque, and insulting. The sheep loved it. Within six weeks of the first public demonstration, she'd reclaimed the ten television stations who'd dropped *The Wheeles of God Hour* upon Zeb's death and added seven more.

The only thing ruining her happiness was Zebulon monitoring her sermons. He sat right in the front row, dressed in the powder-blue polyester suit he'd been buried in, his arms folded and legs crossed. The left side of his face drooped, like a mask made from wax and kept too close to an open flame. He looked awful when he smiled. And if that wasn't bad enough, he'd taken to sitting with her family. The members of the congregation seated near the front were blissfully unaware of the ghosts balanced in their laps. Sometimes Zebulon would lean over and say something to Papa, who would nod his head very gingerly, for Mama had done a good job and he was afraid of it coming off. She was glad she couldn't hear what they were talking about.

As annoying as Zebulon's persistent haunting might be, he was only a shadow and she had nothing to fear from him. No, her real problems stemmed from that damned *thing*. She should have known there'd be trouble when she first saw the Brit. What was his name? Chastain.

Just thinking of that leering little bastard was enough to make her uneasy. She'd always imagined she was unique, not counting Zebulon and his paltry gift. Then this swaggering jerk walks in and throws everything out of balance. The irritating part was that while he possessed barely a tenth of her power, he succeeded in outfoxing her.

He sat slumped in the chair opposite her, toying with the paperweight as he spoke.

"Gotta deal f' you, yer holiness. Once-inna-lifetime chance, y'might say. There's this bird I work for—schizzy as hell—says she's Denise Thorne. Yeah, I thought that might snap yer garters."

"Denise Thorne is dead."

"Mebbe. Mebbe not. How are you t' know? Talk to her anytime recent, have you? Y' can fool th' old ladies with that load of bollocks, Wheele, but not me. I know what y' are better'n you do."

She tried to grab him then, reaching out to ensnare him with her mind. To her surprise, he darted away. She made another attempt to trap him, only to have him slip past her again. And again. He seemed to be always just out of reach. She felt like a grizzly bear fishing for minnows. She could overpower him, as she had Zeb, but there was a good chance she'd fuse his synapses and end up with nothing.

"Tsk-tsk! So much horsepower and all y' got is a learner's permit," sneered Chastain. "Now, are y' gonna cut me a deal or are we gonna run 'round Robin Hood's barn again?"

Her cheeks reddened. It was as if she were back at the Hit-the-Cats booth, and she didn't like that at all.

"Ten thousand American, that's all I'm askin'. Not much f' the whereabouts of a millionaire's long-lost daughter, innit? I'll lead y' right to her. No prob. What y' do with her once y' got her . . . Well, that's yer problem, eh?"

Ezra was against it from the start. He was convinced Chastain was lying. "Forget him, Catherine. He's just out for a quick buck." But she knew he was telling the truth. There was no way she could possibly explain that to Ezra in a way he'd understand, so she didn't try. He didn't like it, but he did as he was told when she ordered him to pay off the Brit. Ezra was right, of, course, but he never got the chance to say "I told you so."

They were sitting in the car, watching as Chastain met the woman at the playground. She couldn't see what was going on too clearly, but it looked to her as if Chastain kissed the woman. The woman staggered backward, clutching her stomach, and Chastain was gone, swallowed by the shadows. Ezra signaled for the man in the second car to join him and they spilled onto the abandoned playground, leaving her to watch from the safety of the Lincoln.

The woman was on one knee, arms wrapped around her gut. The tranquilizer should have knocked her out within seconds, but she was still moving. Ezra was the first one to reach her. He knelt beside her, trying to make identification. It was the last thing he did.

The thing thrust its fingers into his sad brown eyes, puncturing them like overripe grapes, then slammed the flat of her palm into the bridge of his nose, sending slivers of bone and cartilage into his brain. Ezra died instantly. Catherine knew this because she heard his brain shut off as neatly as if someone had pulled the plug on a radio.

The Wheelers were doing their best to keep her contained, although it was clear they wouldn't be able to hold her much longer.

Catherine was in shock. Ezra. Ezra was dead. No, not dead. Murdered. The shock became first grief, then anger. She was startled by the immensity of the hate in her. She had not felt such raw emotion since the night her father raped her. Not since the night Sally came to her and changed her life forever.

She grabbed Sonja Blue and squeezed. The contents of the vampire's mind squirted out like toothpaste. There was too much for her to assimilate fully, but she discovered that this creature had indeed once been Denise Thorne.

There was also a lot of confusing, meaningless garbage about "Pretending people," someone called Sir Morgan, and a lot of conversations in foreign languages. There was also a lot of sexual deviation. She ignored the parts that did not directly pertain to the Thornes.

Blue went into a coma before her memory had the chance to completely empty itself. Catherine had her secured and transported back to the mansion. She had originally planned using psionic interrogation on her, but that strategy was junked the moment Blue regained consciousness; when she wasn't hissing and growling like a rabid animal, she was laughing at the top of her lungs.

When Thorne dismissed the photographs as fakes, she had the videotape made. It was then she made the mistake of putting Wexler in charge.

She shuddered, surprised by the force of her memories. She'd tried to forget the past and banish the phantoms that flickered at the corners of her eyes. The liquor usually helped, but sometimes the shadows refused to be ignored. Like tonight.

Zebulon sat on the edge of the bed, watching her with a horrible, lopsided smile skewed across his face. Her father puttered around the wet bar, pawing bottles with fingers made of smoke. Her mother, a barbecued baby at her breast, studied the array of cosmetics cluttering the vanity table. The rest of the Skaggs children were clustered around their mother, staring dully at their surroundings.

"Go away, damn you," she slurred at her dead husband. "I've made you into a goddamn saint. Ain't that enough?" She hurled the highball glass at Zebulon. It passed through his forehead and smashed against the wall.

Wexler peered out from beneath the bedclothes, eyes white with fear.

There was a knock on the door and a masculine voice. "Mrs. Wheele? It's Gerald, ma'am. You all right in there?"

The room was full of dead people and stank of gin, jism, dried blood, and soot. Her head was full of nitroglycerine and Tabasco sauce. She placed her cupped hands against her temples, blinking her eyes.

"It's okay, Gerald. I'm fine. Just fine."

"I'm not sure about this..."

"Look, you're the one bitching about how much you hate being left behind when I go out. If you want to get out of here, you gotta leave my way." Sonja Blue stood with her hands on her hips, scowling at him impatiently.

"Maybe if I tried it one more time . . ."

She sighed and lifted her shoulders in a see-if-I-care-if-you-break-your-neck shrug. "Go ahead. Knock yourself out."

That was exactly what he was afraid he would do. Claude craned his neck, counting the metal rungs leading to the trapdoor set in the ceiling. Thirty. It was the third time he'd counted them, and there were still thirty. He'd hoped that a few would disappear at each recount, but their number refused to decrease.

He grabbed the bottom rung; it was cold to the touch and lightly coated with rust, making it rough against the flesh of his palm. He clutched the second rung with his other hand, using upper-body strength to pull himself along. His right foot groped blindly for purchase on the lower rung he'd just cleared. So far, so good. His head felt like a balloon full of dirty water, and his heart was beating hard enough to shake his ribcage. He could do it. Sure. No prob. All the way to the top. Yeah. He managed two more rungs before his body rebelled.

"Hagerty! Get down from there before you bust your skull."

Sonja's voice cut through the cotton stuffed between his ears, and for one moment he thought he was back in junior-high gym class and Coach Morrison was yelling at him again. Startled, he lowered himself to the floor. His sinuses ached and his shoulders felt as if he'd been attacked with a broom handle.

Sonja Blue positioned herself before the rung ladder. "Hold on tight around my neck, okay?"

"I don't know. Are you sure?"

"Just do it."

Hagerty looped his arms over her shoulders and around her neck. He felt more than a little silly. Here he was, a grown man riding piggyback on a girl four inches shorter and at least a hundred pounds lighter than himself.

Sonja Blue climbed the ladder as if she had a ten-pound sack of potatoes strapped to her back. Claude glanced down at the hardwood floor as it quickly receded beneath his shoes. Vertigo squirted bile through his esophagus and he tightened his grip. Sonja pushed open the trapdoor, and a rush of chill, heavy-industry-tinged air struck Claude in the face. It felt wonderful.

They emerged onto the roof of an old building located in what Claude recognized as the city's warehouse district. It was early evening, judging from the stars overhead, and the area abandoned except for winos and junkies clustered around the down-and-out dives fronting the main traffic artery. Claude collapsed onto the tarpaper covering the roof, staring up at the night sky. His head still ached and his clothes were too thin for the night air, but he didn't care. He'd escaped the monster's lair, if not the monster.

He glanced at Sonja Blue as she peered over the ledge into the alley below. Could she hear what he was thinking all the time? Probably not, or she'd have let him dash his brains out on the floor.

He'd panicked when she first suggested that he hold on to her. Talking to her was one thing, but actual, prolonged physical contact . . . He'd rather have a tarantula set loose in his shorts. But it hadn't been *that* bad.

"So what do we do now? Use the fire escape?"

She shook her head. "That's not how I operate. Never know who, or what, might be watching. Never let 'em see where you go to ground. That's rule number one. Besides, there's no fire escape on this rat trap."

"Oh. Then how . . . ?"

"Don't ask. Just hold tight, savvy?"

Claude did as he was told. He was sweating despite the cool air.

She took three steps in the direction of the nearest building and jumped. Claude glimpsed empty space beneath his toes and, below that, a darkened alleyway full of garbage cans and broken bottles. He was jarred loose by the landing impact before his brain had time to register what had happened. He lay sprawled across the roof of the neighboring building, and after a couple of minutes his heart resumed its beating.

"Jesus! You could have at least *warned* me!"

"Told you to hold tight, didn't I?" She helped him to his feet, dusting off his clothes.

"Okay, what now? Do we rappel down the side of the building?"

"You're free to do as you like. You can go home, if that's what you want, but I suspect Wheele's got her zombies watching your place. I can give you enough money to get out of town and start somewhere else. I'll make sure you get away safely."

"What about you?"

She shrugged and smiled without showing her teeth. "I've got payback to attend to."

Yes, I bet you do, he thought. "I think I'll take you up on that offer to get out of town."

"No problem. I need to take care of a little business first, though."

"What kind of business?"

"Gotta go see someone I used to know."

After what had happened to him in the past twenty-four hours, Claude was actually relieved to find himself in one of the worst neighborhoods in town. The menacing shadows and derelict storefronts seemed to exude a folksy charm. His surroundings may have been dangerous, but at least they were normal.

He walked a step or two behind Sonja Blue, who strode down the street with her hands jammed into the pockets of her leather jacket. She looked preoccupied, so he didn't offer any small talk.

Without saying a word, she swerved and headed down a dimly lit alley a platoon of marines would have had second thoughts about entering. Claude hung back for a second, warily eyeing the foul-smelling passage. Sonja did not miss a step, her boot heels measuring out a steady *tap-tap-tap* as she continued on her way. To her this was just another shortcut, nothing to be worried about. Claude hurried after her, breathing through his mouth in an attempt to keep the alley's pungent aroma from overpowering him. It didn't work too well.

It was so dark he nearly stumbled and fell when he collided against her. She lifted a hand for silence and he closed his mouth before he could ask her why she'd stopped. She stood perfectly still, her hands clear of her pockets. She held something in her right hand that Claude couldn't make out. She tilted her head to one side, like a robin listening for earthworms.

Claude felt fear enter his bloodstream. His heart went into overdrive and his ears strained to catch the faintest sound. They weren't alone; he was certain of that, although he'd seen and heard nothing.

There was the sound of an empty bottle rolling across pavement and the scrape of a garbage can being pushed aside. Sonja shifted in the direction the noises originated from. Claude realized she'd placed herself between him and whatever it was in the darkness.

There was a low hissing sound, like the laughter of snakes, before they emerged from the blackness. Claude heard Sonja swear under her breath.

He couldn't see what the problem might be. All that blocked their path were two winos, one black and one white.

The black wino stood a little over six feet tall, although his badly stooped shoulders made his exact height impossible to guess. He was incredibly thin and his head resembled a burnt-out light bulb. He was dressed in filthy castoffs and his feet were bare. His companion was shorter, older, and hairier, with a snarled white mane the color of dirty ivory and a discolored beard that looked like it belonged on a goat.

"Look what we got here, brother," wheezed the stoop-shouldered black, pointing a spidery finger at Claude and Sonja. "We got ourselves a trespasser."

"Tresssspassser," agreed the goaty wino. Claude recognized him as the source of the snake laughter.

"If you wanna come this way, sister"—the stooped Negro smiled, revealing pointed teeth—"you gots to pay a toll. Ain't that right, brother?"

The goat wino grinned, exposing equally sharp fangs. "Yessss. Toll."

"Cute. Since when do your kind work together?" Despite her tone of voice, Sonja did not relax her stance. Claude felt an overpowering need to piss his pants.

The black vampire looked confused. "Don't know what you mean, sister. Old Ned an' me's been together forever. We was partners before. Saw no reason to end such a bee-yoo-ti-ful friendship, eh, Old Ned?" The vampire regarded the bearded revenant with something close to affection.

"Friennndssss," echoed Old Ned.

"Don't see how you can kick, sister. By the looks of him, there's more than enough to go 'round."

Claude made a choking sound and took a step backward. Sonja quickly repositioned herself. Old Ned was trying to outflank them. There was the efficient *click!* of a spring-loaded mechanism, and Claude saw the glint of twisted silver in her hand.

The stoop-shouldered vampire shook his head sadly. "I was hoping you'd be more friendly, sister. Open to nee-go-she-ay-shun. Guess you'll have to learn to share the hard way."

"Sissterrrr."

Claude screamed when the goat-faced old man slammed into him, but no sound came out. It was like his worst nightmares made real. He fell amidst a collection of garbage cans and overflowing plastic trash bags. A squealing rat wriggled out from under him. Hagerty's reflexes were the only thing that kept the revenant from burying his fangs in his throat; Claude grabbed Old Ned's thin neck and squeezed as hard as he could. The beast's face was inches from his own. Saliva dripped onto Claude's cheeks and eyelids. The undead bum stank of soured wine, dried feces, and rotten meat. Claude did not want to go through eternity with that stench in his nostrils.

A hand emerged from the darkness and grabbed a fistful of Old Ned's greasy hair, yanking him free of Claude. Hagerty rolled out from under the struggling revenant in time to see the silver blade slice the air.

The body stood upright for a few seconds, the hands clawing at the spurting stump where a head had been, before toppling into the surrounding garbage.

Sonja Blue held the severed head aloft like a demented Diogenes, studying it with mild distaste. Old Ned's eyes flicked back and forth, as if looking for direction from his companion. The mouth continued its ineffectual biting motions for a few more seconds until the brain registered its final death. Claude was reminded of rattlesnakes, how they're capable of delivering a deathblow even after decapitation. Then he blew his lunch all over the alley.

"Damn revenants. Bad as gila monsters," Sonja muttered in the same tone of voice used by homeowners to complain about termites. "Still, that's the first time I've seen 'em work together like that. Revenant and vampire, that is. Pretenders are loners by nature. Unless one of them's a Noble, it's almost unheard of for them to team up. Good thing, too, or the human race would be confined to cattle pens by now." She tossed Old Ned's head, which was beginning to resemble a cross between an overripe cantaloupe and a deflated basketball, into a handy dumpster.

The stoop-shouldered vampire lay sprawled in the garbage, his head twisted at a weird angle. Claude stared at it in sick fascination. "It's still alive," he marveled, staring at the crippled vampire. Its fingers wriggled like the legs of a dying spider.

"So it is." Sonja drove her switchblade into the base of the vampire's neck just as he spoke his final words. Claude could not hear what he said but he could see his lips move.

"I ain't your damn sister," hissed Sonja Blue as she straightened. She aimed a kick toward the dead thing's head, but it had already degenerated into foul-smelling sludge.

Claude leaned against the alley mouth. He was bathed in sweat, his heart felt like it'd been put through a juicer, and his mouth tasted like he'd just gargled with battery acid.

"You okay?"

"Yeah. Sure."

Jacob Thorne was a workaholic. A lot of men at his age and station in life had their vices; some drank too much, others were addicted to various white powders, while still others involved themselves in illicit love affairs with women young enough to be their granddaughters. Thorne's vice was being wrapped up in his work. That's why his household was located atop Thorne Tower.

There were smaller homes salted across three continents, but Thorne never really felt comfortable at the villa on the Côte d'Azur or in the chalet in Colorado. What he liked about the tower penthouse was that he could lock himself in his office and be immersed in the very heart of his empire, concentrating on mergers, takeovers, insider trading, and the like while his wife went quietly mad.

Thorne lay in bed, listening to his wife mutter as she slept. She was taking more and more Valium, but it didn't blot out the dreams. Shirley had always been delicate. That was part of what had attracted Thorne to her, forty years ago. She'd been the eldest daughter of a respected banking family, while he was an audacious young upstart, the son of Swedish parents who'd had their name "Americanized" from Thorensen to Thorne by the officials at Ellis Island. It was just like the Hollywood versions of the American Dream said it would be.

Shirley was four years Thorne's senior—which, at the time, was almost as shocking as her choice in husbands—and it was five years before she conceived.

Unhappy with the way his thoughts were going and unable to sleep, Thorne eased himself out of bed and glowered at the digital clock on the night table. Eleven o'clock. *I must be turning into an old man,* he mused sourly. Since he couldn't sleep, he put on his robe and slippers and headed downstairs to his office. Maybe an hour or two of paperwork would take the edge off and allow him to sleep.

Shirley's pregnancy had been difficult, resulting in a dangerously premature baby and the doctor warning that any more attempts might prove fatal. Thorne could still recall Denise's earliest days. He remembered the feeling of frustration when he realized that no matter how much money he had, he was as powerless as some poor shmuck of a charity-ward father.

He didn't sleep the first week of his daughter's life. All of his time had been split between the board room and peering through the plate-glass window at the maternity ward, watching his newborn child in her incubator. She looked so tiny, as pink and fragile as a little bird, that Thorne was overwhelmed by a desire to protect her and make sure nothing bad ever happened to her. He watched the nurses' every move, fearful they might prick his baby while changing her diapers.

When Denise was finally allowed to come home, Thorne scandalized his in-laws by refusing to hire a nurse for their grandchild. For the first six months of his daughter's life he changed diapers, walked the floor, and administered three o'clock feedings, just like any other father would. He was proud of that. So was Shirley.

Thorne cherished those memories, but he resented them as well, for they made the past two decades all the more empty. He had come to grips with Denise's disappearance from his life by submerging himself in his work. His wife, however, did not have that option.

Thorne had watched his wife grow more and more obsessed with attempting to locate their daughter. After the private investigators had run dry, she began frequenting psychics, dowsers, spiritualists, and other sleazy con artists. By the time he'd decided it was time to step in and try to get professional help, it was too late. The Wheeles had their hooks in her. He'd hoped the faith healer's sudden death would set her free, but he hadn't counted on the widow. She was a thousand times worse than her slime-ball husband ever thought of being.

Thorne opened the door to his private office. He was letting himself get upset. There was no point in worrying about that witch and her threats right now. He smiled to himself as he glimpsed the reassuring outlines of his office, familiar even in the dark. His hand brushed the light plate inside the door and the room jumped out of the shadows.

There was a man sitting in his chair.

Thorne shook his head in order to clear it. The man remained seated in Thorne's green leather chair behind the mahogany desk. The man was large, resembling a football player gone to seed, and his hair was cut short. He looked to be in his late thirties, his blocky chin covered in a dark stubble flecked with gray. He had also been the recipient of a recent beating.

"Who are you and how the *hell* did you get in here?" Thorne stepped into the room, too outraged by the intrusion to be frightened. It was the same instinct that had helped him amass several million dollars over the years. He was suddenly aware of the reek of garbage permeating the room.

"He's with me, Mr. Thorne. I was gambling that you would keep the access code on the private elevators as a sort of keep-the-home-fires-burning gesture."

Thorne turned to see a woman, dressed in a black leather jacket and mirrored sunglasses, step out from behind the door. He went pale, grabbing the edge of the desk in order to steady himself.

"Oh, God . . . no . . ."

Sonja Blue smiled, revealing her fangs. "Hello, Mr. Thorne."

The big man with the bruised face got up, grasped Thorne by the elbows, and eased him into the vacated chair.

"You better fix Mr. Thorne a brandy and soda, Claude. I think he needs one in a bad way. I'll close the door. I'd hate to have our little reunion spoiled. If I remember correctly, the bar's next to the bookshelf."

Thorne stared at Sonja with open fear and disgust. "She . . . she said you'd never get out."

"Who? You mean Wheele?" Her face was unreadable, but there was something in her voice that made Claude look up from his place behind the bar.

"Why? Why couldn't you stay away? After all this time . . . I used to pray someone could prove you were dead. That way I could get it over with. Grieve and be done with it. That's a horrible thing to pray for, isn't it? Proof of your only child's death? I had my prayer answered, all right." His mouth twisted into a bitter smile. "My daughter's dead."

"Then why did you agree to put me away if I'm not your daughter?"

"She threatened to tell my wife about you. I couldn't allow that."

"But you said I'm *not* your daughter."

Thorne shuddered, refusing to look at her. "No, but you're *hers*. I buried my Denise years ago. My wife's Denise is another story." Thorne let his head drop into his hands. He looked like a tired old man instead of a self-made business tycoon.

Sonja stepped closer, one hand extended toward him. "Father . . ." Her voice contained a hint of Denise.

Thorne snapped back to attention, glaring at her from beneath steel-gray brows. "Don't call me that! *Never* call me that!"

Claude set the brandy and soda on the desk, staring at Thorne in fascination. At first he'd seemed like just another old duffer in his pajamas, but now that the initial shock was wearing off, he was turning into the fabled Jacob Thorne. The old guy was tough as a rhino. Claude was amazed how much alike he and Sonja were.

Thorne's hands trembled but his voice remained steady. "First there was Wheele, threatening to reveal the truth to my wife. Then that degenerate Englishman coming around, hinting that he'd leave the country if I made it worth his while. I didn't believe Wheele at first, naturally. It was just a lot of psychotic hogwash . . . or so I thought. She showed me pictures, but pictures can be faked. Besides, you don't look like Denise. Oh, there's some resemblance, but not enough to convince me. Then she sent me the videotape."

"Do you still have it?"

He nodded wearily. "God only knows why I kept it. It's a hideous, blasphemous thing."

"Could I possibly see it?"

The tape went from magnetic static to picture without any preface. The picture rolled a bit, then automatically straightened itself. The scene resolved itself into a blurred medium long shot of a figure trussed in a straitjacket and a length of chain. As the camera pulled back, it became evident the scene was shot from above. Claude recognized the video-Sonja's prison as a racquetball court. He remembered Elysian Fields' racquetball court for the better-behaved patients.

There was no sound to go along with the picture, but it didn't matter. There was a crude power to the silent, slightly out-of-focus events not unlike the hard-core stag films he'd seen as a teenager in Mike Goddard's garage.

The video-Sonja shrieked and howled soundlessly, slamming herself against the hard white walls. Blood dribbled from her nostrils and the corners of her mouth. She looked drunk. She didn't have her glasses on. Claude realized the graininess of the picture was due to infrared light.

Something fluttered at the corner of the camera's field of vision. A chicken. Someone had thrown a live chicken from the observation deck. It hit the polished wood floor like a bag of suet. The injured fowl flapped about in a feeble attempt to escape the video-Sonja. After she drained the chicken she calmed down. There was a jerky cut, as if the camera had been shut off. The digital readout in the left-hand corner of the screen stated a half-hour had elapsed. This time they threw an alley-wise tomcat into the makeshift geek pit. The video-Sonja ended up with some nasty facial scratches, but it didn't seem to slow her down. An hour later a large dog went sailing off the observation deck. The poor mutt's legs shattered on impact and the video-Sonja's ministrations seemed almost merciful. Two hours after that they threw the wino in.

Claude hadn't expected a human sacrifice. He'd imagined they would continue to work their way through the domestic animal kingdom, hurling innocent sheep, goats, and pigs to their deaths, one after another. He glanced at Sonja Blue as she watched herself murder a man, courtesy of the miracle of videotape.

The wino lay sprawled on the floor of the racquetball court, his legs hopelessly smashed. He looked like every other street person over the age of thirty, with a tangled beard, crooked teeth, and an unwashed face rendered featureless by hardship.

He struggled to raise himself on one elbow. The video-Sonja jumped him like a hungry spider. It was a fierce, bloody transaction, but Claude could not look away. He felt the same uneasy thrill of guilt, excitement, and disgust that had overtaken him when he'd witnessed his first sex act in the Goddards' garage. After the wino's thrashing faded into twitching, the video-Sonja rocked back on her heels and laughed. The camera shut off, leaving the room awash in the hiss of blank tape.

“You aren’t my daughter.” Thorne’s voice was that of a man suffering a deep wound without anesthetic. “You’re some kind of freak, an aberration of God and nature. You might have her memories, but you aren’t her. You *can’t* be her. I won’t let you be her.”

Sonja Blue said nothing. She stared at the blank television screen, her back to Thorne.

“What do you want from me? Money? Do you want money to go away?”

She shook her head and turned to face him. “No, Mr. Thorne, I don’t want your money. I want protection for Mr. Hagerty.” She gestured to Claude. “He was my keeper while I was incarcerated. Wheele ordered his death under the mistaken belief that he was working for you. As you can see, they almost succeeded. Mr. Hagerty is an innocent bystander and I do not wish to see him harmed.”

Thorne glanced at Claude. “What do you expect me to do about it?”

“Tell Wheele to back off or you’ll ruin her.”

Thorne made a snorting noise.

“You’re very good at bluffing, Mr. Thorne. Just pretend she’s attempting a takeover. Even if you don’t pull it off, it’ll give me time to make sure he gets out of town safely.”

“What are you going to do?”

Sonja hesitated, uncertain as to whether she could trust him. “Whatever I do—believe me—I’ll keep Mrs. Thorne’s name out of it.”

“Jake? What’s going on down here?”

Shirley Thorne stood in the threshold, one hand on the doorknob, the other touching the door frame. She blinked at the strangers standing in her husband’s office.

“Shirley, go back to bed. It’s nothing.” Thorne was trying to sound casual, but his face was that of a man trapped in his worst recurring nightmare.

“What are these people doing here at this time of night?”

“Please, dear, just go back to bed. It’s nothing that concerns you.”

Sonja stepped back, trying to pull the shadows around herself. The movement attracted Mrs. Thorne’s attention. She peered at the girl dressed in denim and black leather, her eyes hazed by tranquilizers. Claude could feel the dread radiating from both father and daughter.

This was the stuff Claude’s mother, bless her, had lived for, whether in the form of trashy novels, sudsy afternoon TV shows, or tearjerker movies. Claude bit back a hysterical giggle. He was trapped in an episode of *The Edge of Tomorrow,* directed by Wes Craven.

Mrs. Thorne gave a strangled cry of recognition and rushed to embrace her daughter. She buried her face in Sonja’s shoulder, her tears rolling off the leather jacket. Sonja’s arms moved to encircle the old woman but halted before they actually touched her shoulders. Claude could see the effort it took to keep from returning her mother's hug.

Claude was painfully aware of Denise's presence permeating the room, like the moan of a tuning fork resonating inside the ear.

"You've come back. Praise the Lord! You've come back to me. Just like she said you would! You've come back. Everyone told me to give up, that you were dead, lost to me, but I never believed them. Never. Never. I knew you weren't dead! I would have felt it if you were really gone. You were always there . . . always."

It was hard, so very hard to deny her. Sonja felt something breaking inside. Her heart was full of shards. She was afraid to speak, afraid that her voice would be replaced by the sound of breaking glass. But she had to speak. There was no way back into the bosom of her family. She'd known that the day she killed Joe Lent. But there had always been the faint hope that she would be forgiven her trespasses and accepted by her family. Now it was time to pull the fantasy out by its roots.

She ached to fall into her mother's arms and weep for the years lost to her, but that was impossible. She knew what she had to do, even though it pained her more than Thorne's denial.

"I'm afraid you're mistaken, Mrs. Thorne."

Shirley Thorne looked into Sonja Blue's eyes, perplexed by the twin reflections of her own face. It was easy to slip into her mind, even though Sonja was repulsed by this most intimate of intrusions.

Sonja dropped through the layers of Shirley Thorne's consciousness, shocked by the other woman's proximity to true insanity. Her mind was an unlanced boil, filled with years of accumulated grief and anguish. At the core of the infection was a human figure.

The nucleus of Shirley Thorne's malaise was Denise. A Denise with features wiped clean of human imperfection or vice. An umbilical cord, as thick and black as a snake, emerged from Denise's belly, fastening her to Mrs. Thorne's unconscious. The Denise of Shirley Thorne's obsession smiled beatifically, glowing like an Orthodox saint, untouched by the corruption it generated.

Left unattended, Shirley Thorne would retreat deeper and deeper into her self-inflicted wound, content to spend the rest of her days in the company of her canonized ghost-child.

Saint Denise stared at the intruder in her realm with the passive eyes of a caged doe. There was no sentience in their depths. Wherever Denise Thorne went when she surrendered her flesh to Sonja Blue, she wasn't gestating in her mother's head. The ghost Denise was a parasite, a cherished memory turned malignant.

Shirley Thorne had spent two decades denying herself the catharsis of mourning the loss of her only child. She'd refused her husband's solution, preferring to embrace hope. But unrewarded faith can curdle, and in time her optimism gave way to desperation and, finally, delusion.

Sonja knew what she had to do, but she was uncertain whether her actions would heal Denise's mother or drive her over the edge.

She was back in her own flesh. A second, perhaps two, of real time had elapsed. "Mrs. Thorne, I'm not your daughter. Your daughter's *dead*." Her words were quiet but firm, just like the push she gave her mother's mind.

She was inside the older woman's head, dressed in black leather and a surgeon's mask. In her hand gleamed a switch-scalpel. The malignant umbilical cord pulsed and writhed and the Denise tumor bobbed lazily like a balloon on the end of its string.

Was this murder? Suicide? Or was it closer to abortion? If so, the mother's life was at stake. There could be no hesitation this time. The scalpel sliced through the fake Denise's lifeline. A look of confusion crossed the clone's blank face as it began to dwindle.

Shirley Thorne stared at the strange woman with mirrors for eyes. She opened her mouth, prepared to deny her daughter's death, but something stopped her. There was a white-hot needle in her head. Something convulsed inside her brain and she thought she heard Denise's voice crying out to her, "*Mommmmmeeeee.*"

For the first time since 1969, she knew her child was dead. With that realization came a rush of relief and an overpowering sense of loss. The emotions clashed and raged inside her like powerful rivers, and she began to cry. The sobs racked her frail body, threatening to knock her to the floor. The girl with the mirror eyes reached out to steady her, but Mrs. Thorne shrank from her touch.

"Don't you touch her!" Thorne was angry and frightened. "Get away from her! You've done enough damage already." He hurried to his wife's side, placing himself between mother and child. Mrs. Thorne clutched his arm, her tears splashing on his hands.

"Jake, Jake, our baby's gone. She's dead, Jake. Denise is dead."

Thorne's sinus cavity ached with unshed tears, but he refused to weep in front of the thing that wore his daughter's skin. "Get out," he hissed. "*Now!*"

Sonja Blue left without looking back, her bruised companion in tow. If she had permitted herself one last look at Denise's parents, she would have seen Thorne reach for the phone.

Claude did not offer any words of sympathy. It was obvious Sonja did not want to talk. Not that he could blame her. He fell into his own private reverie.

He felt increasingly unreal and he wasn't certain if that disturbed him or not. For the better part of two decades his life had revolved around a pattern and, in time, the pattern had come to describe his life.

Due to his work, he'd found himself increasingly on the outside of normal existence. He worked when others slept and slept when most people were at work. He spent his waking hours either isolated or in the presence of lunatics. He had few friends and even fewer lovers. At the age of thirty-eight he could talk of leaving everything he owned and everyone he knew without real regret. There was nothing to tie him to the city except his job, and now he didn't even have that.

Funny, only three days ago he was just another slob, trapped in a dead-end job with nothing to his credit except a high-school diploma and a library card. Now he was privy to secrets theologians would kill for, conspiring and conspired against, and permitted the frankest of looks at the private lives of the rich and famous. It was enough to make his head spin. Or was that the cognac? He'd helped himself to a quick, appreciative swig from Thorne's stock. He doubted any of the principals at the family reunion had noticed or cared.

Maybe this was a dream, after all. The mixture of horror, melodrama, and insanity seemed appropriate to fantasy. But if it *was* a dream, it was a particularly vivid one. He could even smell the exhaust fumes, hot as dragon's breath, from the dark sedan that was headed toward them.

She'd been too preoccupied to see the danger until it was almost on her. She was thinking of Thorne and how he'd looked like a scared old man, when the dark sedan jumped the curb and headed right for her.

She planted her right hand on the hood of the car, vaulting onto its roof before she had time to realize what she'd done. Her landing was not smooth and she tumbled off the roof, bashing her left shoulder as she bounced off the trunk.

Where was Hagerty?

She got to her feet, scanning the pavement, fearful that his benign bulk might be wedged under the front wheels of the sedan. No, the orderly had leapt clear of the vehicle, although not as gracefully as she had. Hagerty sat half in the gutter, looking somewhat dazed. His nose was bleeding again. For some reason that scared her.

The doors on the sedan opened, disgorging lookalike young men outfitted in suits, ties, and sunglasses. Hagerty began to laugh. He didn't offer any resistance when two men thrust their guns in his face and pulled him toward the car.

Claude was flattered. All this fuss over an ex-jock gone to middle-aged flab and male-pattern baldness! Who'd a' thunk it?

“Stay away from him! Keep your hands to yourself!” The Wheelers paused in their abduction, their fear made obvious by their body language if not their faces. The Other wanted to break bones and rupture soft tissues. Sonja felt the familiar surge of adrenaline that signaled the loss of her self-control. She stepped toward the knot of faceless men; she could almost taste their blood on her lips.

The bullets punched holes in her abdomen, their hollow heads exploding on impact and sending shrapnel through her guts. She'd been hurt hundreds of times before, but not like this. *Never* like this. She collapsed face-first on the street, her torso a mass of blood and exposed intestine. She caught the scent of ruptured bowel and it took her a moment to recognize the stink as being her own.

In all the previous woundings the pain had been sharp but brief. After all, what was pain but the animal flesh reacting out of instinct? But the agony she now felt was unrelenting and quadrupled with every breath, like sunlight reflected in a house of mirrors. Her spinal cord must have been damaged by one of the dum-dum fragments.

The spinal cord—that flexible cable of nerves and tissues—was the vampire's Achilles' heel. Once damaged it could never be regenerated—the same for the brain perched atop it in its box of bone. Sever a vampire's spinal cord and it died. Crush it and the creature was paralyzed and soon died of starvation. It was one of the few physical frailties they shared with their prey.

The car sped off, Claude in the backseat. She found some irony in the fact that she was sprawled in the gutter, exiting the world as she had first entered it, two decades past. It was as if the past twenty years had been the dream of a dying girl. She laughed, but all that came out of her mouth was a lungful of dark blood frothed with oxygen.

As she died, she began to hallucinate.

Or maybe not.

Ghilardi bent over her, his face pinched with concern. Sonja recognized him by his aura more than his physical appearance. He'd been dead for several years and his spirit was hardly the type to confine itself to the structures of aged flesh. He shimmered bluish-white, like the sky on a bright summer's day, and his blurred features were younger than those she'd known. But then, no one ever pictures themself as being old.

“Sonja?”

She'd expected his voice to be as ephemeral as his form, but it was the same as it'd ever been. There was no static on the line. He wasn't talking long-distance. That meant she was close. Closer than she'd ever been before, even in the London gutter.

"I've so much to tell you, Sonja! I was such a fool about so many things! The flesh deluded me, misled me. Everyone finds that out, once they're rid of it. Most do, that is. Some never surrender the illusions of the flesh and refuse to free themselves of its limitations. But I had it all wrong. The *Aegrisomnia* isn't a key to lost powers—I mean, it *is* a key, but not to the doors of human perception. It was written by a Pretender *for* Pretenders. It was intended for Pretender changelings who were ignorant of their birthright and thought they were humans—the ultimate pretense! I had some Pretender blood in me; not much, but enough to be sensitive to the Real World. It was easier for me to claim my powers were inherent in all humans rather than to contemplate an ogre or an incubus in the family tree."

This was all very interesting, but Sonja could not see why her mentor had intruded on her last moments with such late news.

"There's so much to learn and forget once you're free of the business of living. But, you can't die, Sonja. Not *yet*. Much depends on you."

Wheele? Was she that dangerous?

Ghilardi caught her thought and dismissed it. "Wheele is nothing. A fluke. The bastard product of a backwoods incubus. A Pretender unaware she is pretending and armed with more power than she knows what to do with. No, grander and far more horrible things await you."

"Death has made you oblique, old man," she whispered, but Ghilardi was gone. In his place was Chaz.

Unlike Ghilardi, who had problems regaining human form, Chaz's apparition was a perfect replica of his physical self, right down to the collar buttons. The only flaw in the illusion was that he happened to be composed of violet fog instead of flesh.

Chaz leaned forward, studying her with the detached interest he'd give an ant farm. A ghostly French-cut dangled from his lips, phantom smoke curling about and through his head. Chaz and the cigarette smoke shared the same consistency.

"Bummer, innit?" His lips pulled back into a mocking smile. "Spend six months in a loony bin and not three days out when—hey, presto!—yer lying in th' gutter with yer guts in yer hands. Yeah, yer knackered awright. But don't worry about bein' alone, pet. Me an' Joe—you *do* remember Joe, dontcha? *Sure* y'do! —me an' him's waitin' for you, luv. We want t' show you a good time, eh? Joe's been waitin' longer'n me, so he's got seniority. Kinda like a shop steward. But I can wait. I got time, right, luv?" He reached out with insubstantial fingers to caress her. Moth wings brushed against her bloodied cheek.

"Get away from her, hyena!" It was Ghilaldi's voice. "Vile, idiot thing! Wasted in life, useless in death."

Chaz's body dispersed like a cloud caught in a high wind, and Ghilardi's oscillating blueness was back.

"Sonja, I've brought you some help. Sonja?"

Her eyesight had dwindled to monochrome tunnel vision. She felt like she was peering at a Sony Watchman through a cardboard tube, but she recognized the smiling bag lady bent over her.

I'm hallucinating. None of this is real. She hadn't been certain until the appearance of the golden-eyed hag. It was all an illusion, a dream before dying.

The *seraph* trilled crystalline bird song and thrust a gleaming hand into Sonja's guts and there was no more contemplating the nature of reality and illusion.

The maître d's scorn was palpable. The very idea that she would set foot in his restaurant outfitted in jeans and a leather jacket filled him with cold contempt.

"Mademoiselle has been waiting for you," he said stiffly. "Please follow me." The head waiter turned his back on her with military precision and marched into the main dining room. Sonja followed, staring at the pristine tablecloths and untouched place settings of fine china and expensive crystal. Although the room seemed to be deserted, she could hear the low murmur of polite conversation going on around her.

The maître d' led her to a table located directly under a large crystal chandelier, which swayed and jingled to itself. Denise Thorne sat at the table, dressed in a paisley miniskirt, white midcalf go-go boots, a fringed buckskin vest, and a shapeless, wide-brimmed hat. The maître d' did not seem to think *her* wardrobe inappropriate.

"Thank you, André." Denise smiled, and the waiter retired with a formal bow. Denise turned her attention to her guest. "Please, won't you sit down?"

"Am I dead?"

"What makes you think I could answer that question?"

"Because *you're* dead."

"So you keep insisting. But you wear my flesh and have my memories."

"But I'm not you. I'm not Denise."

"So who are you, then? A ghost? A reincarnated soul? A demon?"

"I . . . I don't know."

"But you know you aren't me. How can you be so sure?"

"Because you're there and I'm here."

"Very scientific."

"Okay! So I don't know who I am, or even what. Does it really matter anymore? Your father denies me and your mother thinks you're dead."

"They're your parents, too."

Sonja shook her head. "My father was a rapist. My mother was a London gutter."

"And the Other? Is it your Siamese twin or an unwelcome lodger? Or is it you?"

"Look, I've been through this already. Maybe things aren't as clear-cut as Ghilardi made them out to be. I've known that since Pangloss tried to bribe me into joining forces with him. But I'm not the Other and I'm not Denise Thorne."

"You saw what the Other was like when it was fully ascendant, when your personality refused to function. Was that the Other you're familiar with?"

"Look, what are you trying to get me to admit to? That I'm a figment of Denise Thorne's imagination? That the Other is my id and not a separate entity? Okay, I'll admit those are possibilities, but I don't know if it's *true*. Maybe I'm a synthesis of Denise and Morgan's egos. Hell, I don't even know if you're Denise."

"That's right. You don't." Denise lifted a wineglass to her lips. A drop of wine fell from its rim, staining the tablecloth bright red.

Sonja pounced, digging her fingers into Denise's placid face. The skin came away with a thick, syrupy sound and Sonja stared at the woman smiling at her.

"Time to unmask," said the woman with mirrored eyes. "No more pretending."

"Hey, Moe! Gotta fresh'un for ya!"

Brock looked up from his egg-salad sandwich as the attendant, a grinning black man, trundled another gurney into the morgue's basement.

"Great. Just great. Can't a guy finish his break without being interrupted by a corpse?"

"Hey, you knew th' job was dangerous when you took it," chided the attendant. He thrust a clipboard at Brock. "You wanna sign for this mama?"

Moe Brock quickly scribbled his initials and the corresponding time of arrival while trying to juggle the uneaten portion of his sandwich and a cup of coffee. "A woman, huh?"

"Yeah. Real looker, too. If you like 'em ventilated. The ME said he'd be in to give her a checkup within an hour. Catch ya later, Moe."

"Yeah. See ya." Brock took a quick swallow from his thermos and scanned the ME's street report: unidentified Caucasian female, age approximately twenty-five. Great, another shooting.

"C'mon, honey," he sighed. "Let's get you situated. It's not your fault you screwed up my break, right?"

The morgue dated back before the Depression and showed its age. The walls were covered in white porcelain tiles, except for the patches where squares had been pried away by bored municipal employees, exposing the fossilized epoxy. What wasn't tile was stainless steel. The place echoed like Mammoth Cave, amplifying the squeaking of the gurney's wheels to an unpleasant degree.

Brock maneuvered the gurney into the small, well-lit autopsy room located off the storage facilities. A large stainless-steel table, complete with drains and a microphone dangling from an overhead boom, dominated the available space.

He swiftly transferred his charge to the autopsy table and began the morbidly intimate act of undressing a dead stranger. Every article of clothing had to be tagged, bagged, and recorded in case further examination was required by the forensic boys. Once that was taken care of, it was up to the medical examiner to continue the stripping.

The ME would crack her skull and lay bare the folds and creases of her brain, open her ribcage like a venetian blind, juggle her liver and lights, and explore the cold cradle of her womb for signs of violation or stillborn offspring. Then, and only then, would she be handed back to Brock. After her secrets had been revealed, he would deftly mend the wounds made by murderer and coroner alike, so her loved ones would be able to identify her.

They called him the Tailor. Never to his face, but he knew that's what they called him. He didn't mind. He'd inherited his dexterity with needle and thread from his maternal grandfather, who'd spent his life working in the Garment District. Let them call him whatever they liked. He was good at his job. The last guy they had doing it left the poor bastards looking like escapees from a Frankenstein movie.

He glanced at the corpse's face. Yeah, she was a looker, all right. At least she'd missed getting a slug in the skull. God, he hated those! Three bullets at close to point-blank range. Whoever did it ruined a perfectly good leather jacket, not to mention the woman inside it. He hoped he could finish before the rigor mortis set in. Funny thing, though, she still had her sunglasses on.

The jacket slid off easily enough, and he saw the flesh of her inner arms. Junkie. That explained it. Dope deal gone wrong. He folded the jacket carefully. He'd had one just like it, back in college, and it'd taken him years to break it in just right.

He reached for the mirrored sunglasses that covered the dead woman's eyes. One of the lenses was cracked but still intact. He wondered what color her eyes were.

The body twitched, but it didn't surprise Brock. In the ten years he'd spent prepping and stitching the dead, he'd seen plenty of twitching cadavers. Some jerked like poorly manipulated marionettes. He'd even seen one sit up. It was just the delayed response of the muscles, like the dead frogs and dry-cell batteries back in high-school biology class.

The dead woman's cold hand clamped around his right wrist. Dark lights, like those left by flashbulbs, swam before his eyes. He watched dumbly as the cadaver's abdomen hitched sharply. Once. Twice. For some reason he saw himself sitting behind the wheel of his old Chevy, cursing the motor. The dead woman coughed and a lungful of black blood gushed forth. Brock felt his egg-salad sandwich struggling to freedom.

He tried to pull away, but the corpse wouldn't let go. So he screamed. It echoed and re-echoed in his ears. The dead woman relinquished her hold in favor of sitting up and Moe Brock fled through the swinging doors of the morgue.

Sonja Blue sat up on the autopsy table, her hands laced gingerly over her stomach. She wasn't sure what the *seraph* had done to her, but it'd worked. And not too soon, either. She shuddered at the thought of regaining consciousness as the coroner's electric bone-saw bit into her skull.

Miraculous resurrection or not, she felt like shit. Her head was full of burning water the color of midnight. Another coughing spasm shook her as she slid off the table. The room tilted under her feet.

No! Not now! Not here! People will be down here in a few minutes.

She caught sight of her folded jacket and groaned when she saw the bullet holes. *Oh, well, maybe if I use some more electrician's tape . . .*

She staggered out of the morgue and headed down the corridor leading to the loading dock where the mortuaries came to pick up the dearly departed. Luckily, she'd come to in that particular morgue before and was familiar with the layout, so there wasn't any problem escaping.

She was vaguely aware of a terrible pain in her gut, but that no longer mattered. What mattered was the anger. The anger fed on the pain, creating a hatred crystalline in its purity. The rage in her unfurled like an exotic, night-blooming orchid. And there was power in the hate.

She felt its siren call, beckoning her to relinquish control and surrender to its acid embrace. In the past she'd always panicked, disturbed by the visions it conjured, and refuted its source. She'd allowed it to run riot, and when it was sated, she'd blamed the Other for its excesses. Now, for the first time since she'd been remade in Sir Morgan's image, she did not deny herself the pleasure of exulting in her fury.

She embraced the hate as part of her, as natural as breathing or pissing. She felt the power as it coursed through her, teasing her with serpent tongues and electric sparks. She looked down at her hands and saw they were sheathed in a roiling red-black plasma.

She moved through the night streets, unseen but not unfelt. Her passage was marked by a shock wave that affected those around her like skiffs caught in the wake of a battle cruiser.

A mother slapped her child, then slapped it harder when it began to cry.

A small boy pinched his infant sister hard enough to raise a bruise on her defenseless flesh.

A bored housewife glanced at the cutlery rack, then back at her husband, sprawled before the blaring television set.

A thin young man with horn-rims and hair cut so close his scalp gleamed through the stubble pulled down the shade in his bedroom before opening the dresser drawer where the two deer rifles, five handguns, and five hundred rounds of ammo were stashed.

Wrapped in each other's arms, amid tangled sheets and sweaty afterglow, two lovers began to quarrel.

The family dog growled, its ears laid flat against its skull, then drew the blood from the master's hand.

Sonja Blue was aware of her handiwork on a level alien to humans. She was with each of them, in some fashion, when they reacted to her goad.

A dozen outbursts occurred with every step she took. Some reacted with petty tirades. Others were far more brutal. She did not create the resentment and frustration locked inside these incidental strangers; she merely permitted its expression. Pangloss had been right: the seeds of self-destruction lurked within every mind she touched. Humans hungered for extinction, be it their own or their enemies'. She felt herself growing stronger with every outbreak, as she incorporated their rage into her own.

Part of her was repulsed by the careless sowing of discord and struggled to make itself heard over the bloodlust singing in her veins. She moved through the city, touching off a thousand domestic quarrels, barroom brawls, backroom altercations, and rapes. She heard the police sirens and the strident squawking of ambulances as they responded to the epidemic of shootings and stabbings. Good. That would give her the cover she needed. She nimbly dodged a police car, its lights flashing and siren cranked to full volume, as it rounded the corner.

She laughed, and it seemed as if the sky trembled.

“Claude? Claude? Claude?”

Although distorted by echo, the name sounded familiar. Maybe it was his. He tried to open his eyes and see who was calling, but the lids were epoxied shut. Who’d want to do a dumb thing like that? He moved to rub the glue from his eyes, but his arms refused to respond properly. He felt as if he were moving underwater.

“Claude?”

The lassitude began to seep away, to be replaced by a sense of well-being that was almost frightening. When he tried to remember why he was happy, his head began to swell and his eyeballs throbbed in their sockets.

Why think? Just accept.

The words felt good in his head, even if they weren’t his own. Seemed like good advice. Why fight it? He settled back in the comfortable leather armchair, determined to follow the not-voice’s suggestion. He turned his attention to his surroundings. He was in a sumptuously appointed apartment, dressed in a quilted smoking jacket. He tried to bring the room and its furnishings into sharper focus, but a lancet of pain jabbed his frontal lobes.

Just accept, warned the friendly not-voice.

“I’m so glad everything’s been taken care of, aren’t you? Now we can be alone.”

Someone was speaking to him. A woman. No, not a woman, a girl. But where was she? He was wary of looking around, fearful that the pain would return.

Denise was sitting on the bed. Claude couldn’t remember seeing her there before. She looked just like she had in his dream. She was smiling timidly, her cheeks flushed.

“My parents are so happy you found me. My father will repay you handsomely.” She smiled at him and the room flickered. Denise was dressed in a long, flowing gown with a golden diadem perched atop her head. “Half a kingdom is a just reward for the return of a lost princess.” The diadem disappeared, although the gown stayed. It was virgin white, her cleavage frothy with lace and satin ribbons. Claude ached to touch it.

Denise left the bed and came to Claude. He couldn’t move or talk or think. All he could do was stare at the beautiful creature nesting in his lap. The dress rearranged itself into a bridal gown, complete with veil. Claude brushed his fingers against lace and mother-of-pearl buttons. Real. It was all real.

Of course it’s real. Just accept.

But what about Sonja Blue? She’s Sonja Blue, isn’t she?

The Denise on his lap shuddered. “I’m so glad you got rid of that nasty woman. The one who went around saying she was me. As if that wasn’t the silliest thing anyone ever heard of! Why, she didn't even look like me!" Denise leaned forward and kissed his cheek, causing him to forget he hadn't mentioned Sonja Blue out loud.

It had been a long time since he'd last had sex. He was uncomfortably aware of how hard his cock was getting. He was afraid of insulting Denise by prodding her. But she was so close, so warm. He inhaled, savoring her scent. He was surprised by the fragrance of tea rose that clung to her. His aunt smelled of roses. It was hardly the perfume he associated with a blushing nymphet princess.

Denise's flesh became transparent, revealing the skull underneath the skin. The virgin expanse of the bridal gown was mottled with fungus, as if it'd been underground for a long time. The lidless eyes goggled at him from their bared orbits.

The scream wouldn't come out; it sat in his chest like a dead weight.

"What's wrong, Claude? Were you thinking about that horrible woman?" Denise was once again wrapped in flesh and unsoiled satin. "You know how it affects you, and when you're upset, I'm upset. You don't want to see me upset, do you?"

"No . . . no, of course not."

"Very well, then. I don't want you to think about that horrible woman anymore, understand?"

He nodded, the skull face with its peeled-grape eyes already fading from his memory.

The bridal gown was gone. In its place was a sheer white negligée. Although the exact details of her body were obscured by the chiffon, Claude could tell she was nude underneath it. His breathing was ragged and his brow slick with sweat. His fingers trembled as he stroked her hair.

He'd given up wanting things a long time ago. Life had cheated him of everything he'd ever hoped for; athletic scholarship, professional-football career, a decent job. There was no point in wishing for things he'd never have. All it led to was frustration and disappointment. He wanted Denise. He'd wanted her from the moment he saw her in his dream, but that was impossible. Denise was a shadow. His desire for her made as much sense as that old movie he saw, where the cop fell in love with a portrait of a murdered woman.

The not-voice was right. There could be no room for doubt. So what if Denise Thorne didn't really exist? And even if she did, she'd be closer to thirty-five than seventeen. Big deal. She was real and alive and young *right now,* and that was all that mattered. For some reason he'd been granted his heart's desire, and he'd be a fool if he let it go to waste.

He stood up, cradling Denise in his arms. She pillowed her head on his shoulder, the soft fragrance of her hair all around him. He was pleasantly surprised by the strength in his limbs. There was no more throbbing in his head or aching muscles, as if his decision had been rewarded by the erasure of pain.

Denise was like a drug, insinuating herself into his bloodstream with every breath. He felt strangely invigorated, as if every cell were supercharged. He wanted to lose himself in her flesh and never return to reality.

They lay side-by-side atop the mattress. Claude was hesitant at first, but the way she wiggled against him dispelled his fear of offending her. Denise teased him with quick, birdlike kisses until his breath came in gasps and his heartbeat matched the throbbing in his crotch.

They were naked but he had no memory of undressing. Not that it bothered him. He'd always hated that part, with its gradual unveiling of physical imperfections. Denise's naked body seemed to give off a warm, diffuse glow that kept him from paying true attention to the details of her flesh, just like the pinup back in his locker.

He entered her, holding his breath lest she break. He needn't have worried. She gasped and moved her hips to meet him, clutching at his buttocks with sharp fingernails. Denise wriggled under him like a wild thing, hissing and moaning with every stroke.

He was afraid he'd erupt upon insertion—it had been a long time—but after the first few thrusts he relaxed, confident he would go the distance.

Denise clung to him, her legs wrapped around his hips. Her cries and whispers devolved into moans and shuddering gasps that seemed, at times, to come from someone else. Claude ignored it. He was riding a sleek dolphin, his arms and legs wrapped around its madly gyrating form as it porpoised through the waves. It was frightening and exhilarating and he never wanted it to end. He felt the urgency that heralds orgasm and strove to contain it. He didn't want the ride to end. He opened his eyes, hungry for the sight of Denise's face.

She didn't have eyes anymore. Lozenges of mirrored glass returned Claude's stare. Her long, blond hair writhed like a sea anemone as it rearranged itself.

"No!"

Too late. The darkness was already staining her hair the color of bibles. She smiled, revealing her fangs, but that didn't scare him. What scared him was the fact he was still hard. He should have lost his erection the moment he realized what was under him; it should have deflated like a toy balloon, but it was still stiff. He tried to push himself off her, but Sonja pulled him back down.

"This is what you wanted all along, wasn't it?" she leered. She moved her hips against his. They were Siamese twins, joined at the groin by a traitorous piece of meat.

"Kiss me, Claude. Kiss me . . ." She laced her arms around his neck and tried to drag his face toward her waiting mouth. Her fangs were the color of aged ivory. Claude couldn't decide whether he was going to vomit or orgasm.

Sonja looked genuinely surprised when he clamped his hands around her throat. His fingers tightened their hold as he brutally thrust himself between her legs. She struggled under him as he strove to squeeze life from her lungs while injecting it into her womb. Her legs flailed and her fingernails sliced into his face, but he refused to stop. He wondered if her head would come off in his hands.

Trick! Trick! Should have known! It was too good to be real! Bitch! Trying to turn me into a fucking Renfield. I'll kill you for this.

Sonja Blue's face disappeared as if someone had changed the channels on a television set. Claude stared at the naked, middle-aged woman thrashing beneath him. Despite the smeared makeup, crooked wig, and bulging eyes, she looked familiar.

Perplexed, Claude loosened his grip on her throat. Before he had time to understand what the hell was going on, he was seized by his own orgasm. He didn't feel it when she reached inside his skull and squeezed his brain.

Catherine Wheele experienced a moment of sheer claustrophobic terror when the dead man collapsed on top of her.

She felt as if she were buried alive under the corpse's bulk, the smell of sweat and jism smothering her senses. She wriggled free, an ululating whine escaping her lips.

Her lungs were full of broken glass and razor blades. She touched her throat gingerly—it was already the size and coloration of a ripe eggplant. She stared at Claude's body. *I should have killed him the minute I saw him. That's what Ezra would have done. But, no, I had to try to make him one of my own. Just in case Thorne got any bright ideas about getting rid of me.*

There was no way she could hurt him enough for what he'd done to her. No one, but *no one* treated her like that! She opened her mouth and tried to curse the dead man beside her, but there was only pain and an incoherent gargling.

Her hands flew to her throat, prodding the swollen flesh with shaking fingers. No! He couldn't have! She began to tremble. Her eyes filled with tears. *Nononono . . .* Her fear gave way to rage and she threw herself on Claude's rapidly cooling body, pummeling it until she raised post-mortem bruises. Exhausted, she lay sprawled on the rumpled bed, her vision swimming with tears, as the last of Claude's seed trickled down her thigh.

What had gone wrong? She'd provided the appropriate scenario, the proper stimulation and illusion. So what went wrong? She'd been in control, just like always. . .

But that wasn't completely true, was it?

How did you like it, Kathy-Mae? Did you enjoy your first orgasm?

She clamped her hands over her ears. She refused to open her eyes. She recognized the voice and was fearful of what might be sitting on the corner of her bed, watching her. She prayed it would go away.

But I can't go away, Kathy-Mae. I'm always here. I'm always with you, like I said I would.

Why are you here? Why now, after all these years?

Things are moving. Changing. I came to warn you. You will be having visitors. In fact, one of them is already at the gate.

Catherine knew she was gone before she opened her eyes. Or was she? Sally was right, though. She could feel her visitor approaching. It was time to receive her guest.

Sonja Blue stood outside the gates of Catherine Wheele's mansion, studying the brightly lit driveway and the phalanx of armed guards patrolling the green space around the house. Either Wheele was a practicing paranoid or she was expected.

She slipped over the top of the wall, oblivious to the pieces of broken bottle embedded in the mortar. Such precautions were good for deterring paparazzi and other celebrity-watchers, but not someone back from the dead.

Wheele chose her sanctum well. The mansion was located in an exclusive suburb situated beyond the zone of shopping malls and fast-food strips that separated the city from its satellite communities. A crushed shell drive, flanked by crape myrtles, curved toward the front of the house. During the day the estate could pass for yet another stronghold of privilege. But at night . . . Well, that was a different matter. The manicured lawn shimmered in the light from the floods mounted in the trees, turning the identical guards into sharply defined silhouettes.

What should it be? Full frontal assault or a sneak approach? What the hell . . . Why waste time on subtlety?

The driveway crunched beneath her boots. *C'mon, bitch, let me see you try to stop me this time. C'mon, whatcha waitin' for, an engraved invitation?*

The floodlights sputtered and flickered like cheap Christmas lights. She could feel the rage-joy creeping along her scalp, sending sparks from her fingertips. No lights. The darkness boiling in her belly was the antithesis of sight and sound and life. Light would not be tolerated—or exist—in her presence.

She scented the dog before she saw it. Seventy pounds of German shepherd bounded out of the shrubbery, aimed for her throat. She caught it in midair, holding it by the scruff of its neck like she would a pup. Its death was swift.

"Shaitan? Shaitan, what is it, boy?"

The Wheeler stood on the edge of the light, peering into the darkness, his Uzi at ready. He glanced about uneasily when the floods began to stutter.

"Shaitan? Answer me, boy!"

The dog's corpse struck the Wheeler full in the face, knocking him to the ground. The short, staccato burst from his Uzi shredded the bushes and shot out one of the faltering spotlights mounted in a nearby crape myrtle.

The dazed Wheeler pushed the carcass off his chest. His nose was bleeding and he could taste blood at the back of his throat. Dogs were barking and he could hear the others running in his direction. Someone was bending over him. He looked up and saw twin reflections of his bloodied face. God, he looked stupid.

They found him dangling from the smooth, twisted branches of a crape myrtle; his entrails spilled and looped into a hangman's noose. Some of the guards—the ones yet to undergo Heart's Desire conditioning—decided that it was time to desert when they saw him hanging from the tree like a depraved Christmas ornament. Bilking old ladies of their life savings and roughing up investigative journalists was one thing. This was something else *entirely*. They seemed honestly surprised when their fellow Wheelers opened fire, splashing their insides all over the front lawn.

The dogs began to howl and snarl, straining on their leashes and snapping at one another's flanks. One of the animals, a Doberman, sniffed at the splattered remains of the disloyal guards. Another dog, a German shepherd, nosed the red mess; the Doberman sank his fangs into the other dog's shoulder. Within seconds the dogs were engaged in a fierce melee, tearing at one another's throats and testicles.

When one of the Wheelers made the mistake of trying to drag his dog free of the tangle and lost three fingers, the others opened fire on the animals, raking them with their automatic weapons. The growls of combat became yelps as the hounds forgot about fighting among themselves and tried to flee the barrage.

When the smoke cleared, there were four dead German shepherds and three dead Dobermans on the lawn. A fourth Dobie—the one who'd started the fight—was still alive, although a bullet was lodged in its spine. The animal lay among its kennel mates, whining piteously as it tried to get back on its feet. One of the Wheelers finished it off with a short burst from his Uzi.

The four Wheelers stood and stared at the collection of dead men and animals heaped about them. The lights flickered, dimmed, flared briefly, then went out.

"We have to get back to the house. We're useless out here without the lights."

"What about Dennings?" whispered the one with the maimed hand, his face pale from shock.

The others looked to their eviscerated partner dangling from the crape myrtle.

"Shouldn't we, you know, cut him down or something?"

"Fuck that. Dennings's not going anywhere."

"Yeah, but—"

"But what?"

"Where's his gun?"

The Uzi fire ripped through them as if they were plastic bags full of foam rubber and strawberry jelly. Sonja marveled at the chaos chattering away in her hands. *No wonder they're so fond of these things*. She kept firing until the clip jammed, then she tossed the gun away. The site resembled an abattoir more than an exclusive suburban front lawn.

The porch light flared, doubling its intensity, the moment she touched the steps. There was a sharp *pop!* and a shower of frosted glass fell from above.

She passed a large mirror set in a gaudy mock-rococo frame. Blank-eyed, baby-fat cherubs smiled at her amid a welter of gilt grapevines. She paused to stare at her reflection.

She was Shiva. She was Kali. She was all that is dark and terrible in nature, adored and scorned, worshipped and reviled. She was sheathed in a transparent caul of darkness the color of a fresh bruise. The caul rippled and roiled like a jellyfish and, while she watched, extruded a tendril that groped blindly in the air as if scenting prey. She knew that it was seeking, and the knowledge neither thrilled nor dismayed her.

She felt no guilt or remorse; the evil that radiated from her wasn't the evil incarnate conjured forth by centuries of theologians in an attempt to shift the blame. It was human evil, nothing more. Granted, it had been recycled and refined until it was the psychic equivalent of rocket fuel, but its source was mortal, not diabolic.

Nobles could live for years on such stored power before requiring a recharge. But Sonja was an unfinished vessel. She couldn't properly synthesize the emotions she drained from others. She was in danger of overloading and spontaneously combusting. She had to release the charge before that happened. But no matter how she did it, it would still prove dangerous.

She remembered the rumors of how the Nazi camps, the Stalinist purges, and the Khmer Rouge re-education farms were the side effects of similar blow-offs. Nothing happens in the Real World that is not mirrored in the half-life of human existence, and part of her was still unwilling to unleash evil on the innocent.

She extended her fangs and grimaced at the mirror. *That's better. There's no point in pretending anymore, right? Where are you, bitch? Come out and fight face to face, like a real monster.*

(I'm in the study. Third door on your left.)

Sonja started, the mirror and its reflection forgotten. The voice had been loud and clear, as if Wheele had been at her elbow. So she was ready, huh? Good. She felt like a Viking berserker, stoned on bloodshed and the inevitability of death. She noticed that she was sweating heavily and that her hands trembled. Fire on the outside and fire on the inside. It would be so simple to surrender to the anger that frothed and foamed in her and charge into battle, screaming like a hell-bound soul . . .

She had to be careful and use her brain. The last time she'd surrendered to mindless savagery it'd come close to costing her what sanity she had left. Still, the temptation was strong. The power filled her until she felt like a balloon made out of skin, stretched to capacity. What would happen to her—and those around her—should she explode?

The lights were off in the study, although it made little difference to her. It might have been high noon with the drapes open.

Catherine Wheele sat perched on the edge of the huge oak desk that dominated the room. She was dressed in a silver lamé pantsuit with a pink cravat knotted around her neck. Her aura shimmered like heat rising from the sidewalk on a summer's day. The hate that emanated from her was nearly enough to make Sonja swoon.

(You've caused me no end of trouble. I should have killed you right away, like Thorne suggested.)

Sonja flinched. She had to be careful and keep herself screened. Wheele had been inside her head and knew how to twist the knife for maximum effect. They were within easy striking distance of each other, not that it mattered. The attack, when it came, would not be on a physical level.

"Why didn't you? Kill me, that is. Why keep me around? Was it just simple greed?"

Wheele looked uncomfortable and plucked absently at the scarf knotted under her chin.

"Or was it something else? Was it because we have something in common?"

Wheele stiffened, her eyes slicing into Sonja like scalpels. Her voice detonated in Sonja's head. (Shut up! Silence, Abomination!)

Sonja clutched her head, her vision momentarily dimmed by the thunder inside her skull. *If she does that again, my brains are going to leak out my ears, vampire or not. But, what the hell . . .*

"Yeah, not all the monkeys are in the zoo, are they? And maybe all the monsters aren't locked up, safe and sound."

Another bolt of white-hot pain surged through her and she narrowly missed biting her tongue in two.

"I'm not drugged and disoriented this time, Wheele. You've got power—I'll admit that—but you don't have knowledge." She smiled bitterly, hearing an echo of Pangloss's infernal wisdom. "What have you chosen to do with your abilities? You bilk sick and deluded humans into giving you their money and—if you're careless—their lives. How pathetic! It's like using a laser to engrave postcards."

Wheele did not move to repudiate her harangue, but her thoughts bristled with anger and embarrassment.

"Why don't you speak?" she asked, exposing her teeth. She grinned even wider at the sight of Wheele's blanched face. "And where's Hagerty? The orderly your zombies snatched. Where is he?"

Wheele's answering smile was unpleasant.

(Why, he's right here. . . waiting for you.)

She gestured to the oversized swivel chair behind the desk. Sonja touched the chair, causing it to turn toward her. She knew what was waiting for her. She did not want to see, but she could not bring herself to look away. Wheele's voice became white noise.

(Too much . . . bastard . . . crushed larynx . . . easy to reach inside his head and *squeeeeze* the aneurysm. It burst like an overripe tomato. Did him a favor, really. It could have ruptured anytime, anywhere; he could have been driving a car when it happened, could have ended up crashing into a school bus or something . . .)

Claude was sprawled, nude, in the chair. His flesh possessed a bluish tinge, the blood having settled in his buttocks and legs. He looked horribly vulnerable, his face slackened and his privates shriveled by death.

Sonja closed his eyes, her fingers lingering on the cool surface of his brow.

(He watched over you and you tried to return the favor. But you failed.)

Sonja jerked her head in Wheele's direction. Wheele's face was replaced by a lump of shimmering white light that seemed to grow with every heartbeat. Sonja felt her own energy coalesce itself into a protective hood, like that of a cobra.

Long, snakelike tendrils emerged from the force field surrounding Catherine Wheele. She resembled a Gorgon transfixing her prey. The creepers hovered in the air for a second, then snapped like whips at Sonja's head, sinking their barbs into the bruise-colored glow.

The castle was very old. It sat on top of a foreboding mountaintop, looking down into a cheerless ravine, at the bottom of which wound a gray ribbon of cold alpine water. It was storming around the castle, its dark corridors erratically lit by sheets of lightning. All the rooms were full of heavy, ornate furniture covered with sheets. The huge portraits on the walls were coated with dust three inches thick. Cobwebs hung from every corner like tattered mosquito netting, fluttering lazily in the breeze.

The vampire killer stood in the main hall, holding the carpetbag that contained the tools of her trade. The peasant coach driver had deposited her at the foot of the road leading to the castle, then driven away as fast as he could, leaving her to walk the rest of the way. Now it was twilight. Soon it would be dark. She had to find the monster and stake it in its lair before it was too late. Hundreds had suffered the beast's leprous touch. The time had come to put an end to its unholy reign of terror.

The vampire killer made her way to the dungeons, where legend had it the family crypts were located. The lightning seared the darkening sky, throwing everything into stark shadow. She made her way down the winding stair, one hand holding aloft a kerosene lantern, the other gripping her bag.

The dungeons were dark and smelled of mold and damp earth. She could hear the rats as they scurried away from the lamplight. Clusters of bats, hanging from the stone arches like bananas, chittered and squeaked as she passed.

She came to an imposing wrought-iron gate, locked and bound with heavy chain. Beyond it lay the ancestral vaults, where the monster slumbered during the day and from which it traveled each night to sate its unnatural lusts and spread its loathsome contagion among the weak and the innocent. Setting aside the lamp, she opened her carpetbag and produced a mallet and chisel. She worked the chisel's point into the lock and began hammering. After the fifth stroke the lock broke and the gates swung inward on rusty hinges.

There wasn't much time left. The vampire killer had to hurry if she was going to catch the beast asleep in its coffin. The burial vault was a huge subterranean room with numerous stone sarcophagi scattered throughout. Which one was the vampire's resting place? And how could she lift the heavy marble lid in time? She fought the panic blossoming inside her as she moved from grave to grave, lantern held high.

There! There it was! The only sarcophagus missing its sealing slab. The light from her lantern reflected off the dark, highly polished wood of the casket. There was an emblem, made of gold, fastened to the top of the coffin. It showed a large bat, wings unfurled and jaws agape, clutching a woman and a man in its taloned feet. The vampire killer was uncertain whether the tiny humans were terrified or ecstatic.

She shook herself free of the languor the golden bat seemed to radiate. Clutching a silver crucifix, a wooden stake, and her trusty mallet, the vampire killer threw back the lid of the casket, steeling herself for the evil that lay within.

"Sur-prissssse," cried the vampire, popping up from its coffin like a grinning jack-in-the-box and slamming a pie into the vampire killer's face.

The vampire killer stumbled backward, her vision obscured by pie crust and Boston crème filling. She clawed at the muck clogging her nostrils and eyes, sputtering her rage.

"You must really think I'm stupid," laughed Sonja Blue as she climbed out of the casket. "Did you really think I'd be taken in with these third-rate illusions?" She dug her fingers into the surface of the sarcophagus. It broke off in her hand with a dry crackling sound and she shoved it under Wheele's nose. It was Styrofoam spray-painted to resemble marble. "And look at this." She waved a fistful of gauzy cobweb in her face. "Spun sugar!"

Sonja snatched up Wheele's carpetbag, scattering its contents across the dungeon floor. "I can't believe you were actually inside my head and didn't learn a damned thing!" She pointed at the garlic, rosary, and flask of holy water, shaking her head in amazement. "Ghilardi was right: you *are* a fuck-up."

She grabbed Wheele by the collar, jerking her to her feet. "You picked the wrong woman to fuck with, preacher. You let something out that should never have been free."

Wheele stared at the sweat pouring from the vampire's brow. She looked like a woman in the grips of malarial fever, radiating heat like an old-fashioned stove.

Let it go, the Other whispered. *Set me free. It's the right thing to do. Can't you feel it?*

She *could* feel it, that was what worried her. The overload was affecting her dream self as well as her physical form. She was racked by alternating waves of freezing cold and boiling heat. She thought she could smell circuits burning, deep in her head.

Set me, free. Set me free or we both die.

"No."

There was a noise, like a hundred angry voices shouting, and the villagers burst into the crypt, holding aloft burning torches and waving pitchforks and scythes in a menacing manner.

"Kill the vampire!"

"Death to the monster!"

The vampire dropped the vampire killer, hissing her anger at the intrusion. She made to escape, but the village priest moved to block her path, holding aloft the crucifix from the church. The vampire shrank from the upraised cross, lifting her arms to shield herself from its glory.

"Catch it!"

"Kill it!"

"Murderer! Fiend!"

Rough hands grabbed the snarling, impotent vampire, pinning her to the wall. The ruddy faces parted to allow the vampire killer access.

"Permit me." The vampire killer held aloft a sword. As the peasants looked on, the sword's blade miraculously burst into blue flame. The villagers gasped in awe, but did not lessen their hold on the captive vampire.

The vampire hissed, thrashing wildly in an attempt to free herself, but it was no use.

Wheele placed the tip of the burning sword above the vampire's heart and pushed the blade home.

The vampire screamed, arching her back as the sword pierced her heart. Wheele wrapped both hands around the hilt of the sword and pushed it in deeper, until the vampire's body was transfixed by the blade. Blood seeped from the corner of the vampire's eyes. The vampire was laughing.

"Oh, puh-leeze, Miz Wheele, don't strike me with that terrible swift sword." The voice was and wasn't Sonja Blue's.

"Now you've done it," sighed the vampire, wrenching the sword from her chest. The torch-bearing peasants wavered, then winked out like holograms. "Now you've *really* done it."

Catherine Wheele was once more in her own body, although she couldn't remember disengaging. Blue must have been responsible for jettisoning her. She hadn't expected the vampire to be so strong. She'd planned to spear Blue's unprotected psyche as easily as she would gig a frog. For the first time in her life, Wheele was facing an adversary as powerful as herself.

Blue was the center of an energy field that wobbled and warped about her like a malignant soap bubble. Catherine's eyes were focused on Blue—her arms now upraised, as if in ecstatic communion with the darkness she generated.

She knew she should try to flee, but she couldn't move. She watched in dumb fascination as Sonja Blue's head expanded until it assumed the proportions of a Macy's Parade balloon. The sunglasses that shielded her mutated eyes dissolved, revealing bottomless pits and the purplish-black nebulae that swirled in their depths. Blue-green sparks danced from the vampire's fingertips, tracing alien designs in the ozone-heavy air.

Catherine Wheele experienced a response to the vampire's evil that went beyond the sex urge. For one brief moment, the doors of Catherine Wheele's perception were thrown open. The Pretender in her emerged from its hiding place. The part of herself that considered itself Catherine Wheele cringed at the sight of its demonic counterpart. The Pretender was smooth-bodied, its skin the color of cinnamon. It had two pairs of breasts, one above the other, with tiny eyes, like those of mice, in place of nipples. Despite its monstrous otherness, the Pretender exuded a horrible familiarity, and she felt an urge to name the beast, but her larynx could no longer form words.

Catherine wrenched herself free of the vision before she could see the thing writhing in the folds of the succubus's labia. Blue still stood in the middle of the bubble, her eyes rolled back and a beatific smile on her face.

(To hell with this. I'm going to blow her fucking head off.)

Catherine opened the top drawer of her desk, careful not to brush against Claude's cold flesh. The Luger was there, primed and ready. The gun had originally belonged to Zebulon. While working the carny it had become something of a necessity. Later on, he used it as proof of his stint in the army ("Took it off a dead Kraut") and his support of All-American values whenever the NRA came around. Catherine was glad she'd ignored Ezra's pleas for her to dispose of it.

She flicked off the safety and aimed at Sonja's head. She wasn't sure what killed vampires, but *nothing* could survive having its brains splattered across the room.

The pistol kicked in her hand and she saw the bullet emerging from the barrel of the gun. Everything seemed to be going much too slow; it was as if she'd fired while underwater.

She saw the nose of the bullet touch the skin of the bubble surrounding her enemy. She saw the skin dimple slightly, then bend slowly inward. She had a vision of herself lighting a match while sticking her head inside a gas oven.

Wexler knew it was time to abandon ship when he heard the machine guns on the front lawn. He didn't have to look out the window to know the score.

His body ached and his head felt like it was full of barroom sawdust. He passed and repassed the vanity table's mirror as he got dressed, each time trying not to look at what she'd done to him.

The grimace disappeared after the first hour, but the facial tics that skewed his features into a death's-head grin occurred every ten minutes. He glimpsed the raw scratches left by her nails crisscrossing his back, shoulders, and the flat of his belly. His dick was swollen and red, but sexual arousal had nothing to do with it. His penis hadn't felt so maltreated since the day, back in sixth grade, he'd jerked off twelve times in a row.

How long had she been in control? Hours? Days? The fact that she'd used him for her puppeteer experiment was reason enough to chuck it all. To hell with Elysian Fields! He'd welcome being shunned by his peers if it meant he'd be safe from that painted *thing*.

He found himself experiencing a delayed memory, mercifully blurred and missing its soundtrack. He watched himself service Wheele as if he were a spectator at a cheesy live-sex show, only there was no sense of excitement. His prick was hard—as rigid as it'd ever been—but there was no pleasure involved.

Wexler nearly retched on the shame flooding him. He'd been turned into a living dildo. He struggled into his pants, relieved to find his keys still in the pockets. His BMW was parked on the turnaround in front of the house. If he were lucky, he might escape while the two horrors fought it out downstairs, just like in the old monster movies he'd watched as a child.

He'd empty his bank account and take the first plane out of the country—it didn't matter where: Rangoon, Mexico City, Düsseldorf, even a malaria-ridden pesthole would be preferable to another night in Catherine Wheele's arms.

He eased down the heavily carpeted stairway, his Gucci shoes in one hand and the keys to his car in the other. Everything was so quiet. No, wait! He thought he heard the murmur of a woman's voice coming from the study, although he didn't recognize the speaker.

Wexler's testicles tried to crawl up into his belly, and his face twisted itself into a grotesque parody of a leer. The effect was devastating, transforming one of the country's leading popular psychologists into the stereotypical dirty old man—wink-wink, nudge-nudge. He'd have to lay low, anyway, until the facial tics went away. He doubted he'd sell many books looking like a refugee from an old Batman comic, even on *Donahue*.

The grass was wet with dew and other things, but he couldn't afford to be squeamish. He hurried toward his car. His luck had held out, after all. He wanted to laugh, but was afraid it'd set off another spasm.

Made it. I made it. Home free.

The shock wave slammed into him like a fist, knocking him to the ground.

He was in the middle of a firestorm whose flames did not burn flesh and bone but seared the mind. He felt something reach into him with knitting-needle fingers, exposing the soft, wiggling things at the bottom of his soul. The something had vermilion eyes and a gaping mouth outlined in blood.

There was a brief spasm of pain in his chest that mirrored that in his head. Wexler dropped alongside his BMW, felled by an exploding ventricle.

Wexler was the first, but not the only, victim of the blast to die of acute cardiac arrest that morning.

Coroners and emergency-room personnel claim that the hours between two and five in the morning are when most humans decide to enter or depart this world.

After a hard day shuffling papers and wending their way through the barbed wire of office politics, the victims go to bed, and during deepest sleep, where the dreams are never recalled, their hearts malfunction. Some wake up long enough to know what's happening to them; others don't. It's a perfectly natural phenomenon.

When the authorities got together with their files and maps in an attempt to discern a pattern in the madness and death that marked that night, their data resembled the concentric circles that mark an atomic bomb blast.

Two miles out: Dogs howled like lost things while neighborhood cats cried like abused babies. Children awoke in tears, screaming that a "red-eyed woman" hovered over their beds.

One mile out: Four epileptics suffered grand-mal seizures, including one previously undiagnosed case. Mrs. Darren McClintock, a widow and chronic insomniac, claimed she saw the outline of a woman, doused in blood, standing on her back patio.

Half-mile out: Nine recorded cardiac arrests were phoned in, four of them instantly fatal. Three of the attacks involved individuals not known to be suffering heart ailments. The surviving patients, when interviewed, complained of a vivid nightmare involving a "woman with red-glass eyes."

Three blocks out: Two suicides reported, both involving victims described as "perfectly normal" by family and friends. Mr. Jackson Marx, age thirty-eight, got out of bed without waking his wife, then retired to his study, where he blew the top of his head off with a handgun he'd purchased the year before as a precaution against burglars. Cynthia Anne "Cissy" Fife, age eighteen, was last seen watching the *Late Late Show* in her room. Her exact time of death is uncertain. She was found by her parents at eight the next morning. She used her manicuring kit to open her veins while in the tub.

One block out: Noel Landry, age thirty-four, fell asleep in front of the television at eleven P.M. His wife, Elizabeth, knowing he'd wake up on his own accord once the station went off the air, retired for the night. Landry woke as expected but took the shotgun from the hall closet with him when he went upstairs. He shot his wife and their two children (ages six and four) before placing the barrel in his mouth.

Ground zero . . .

She'd been unsure as to what would happen when the charge was purged, but Sonja never expected *this*.

Catherine Wheele stood with her arms splayed outward, like a small child playing Frankenstein. A greenish material seeped from the televangelist's nostrils, mouth, eyes, and fingertips. The muck possessed a faint luminescence, like a cheap glow-in-the-dark Halloween mask. Sonja recognized the viscous glop as ectoplasm, although in quantities unprecedented in the annals of paranormal history.

Wheele literally dripped the stuff, like one of those grotesque toy monsters that squirt slime from every possible orifice when squeezed.

The ectoplasm writhed and bubbled, sculpted by invisible hands into humanoid shape. Sonja stepped back, wary of the phantoms emerging from the goo.

There was a ragged, hawk-faced man in overalls and a woman with hollows where her eyes should have been. The woman held a half-formed infant to her breast. An amorphous clump of slack-faced, empty- eyed children—joined like paper dolls—drifted in the phantom mother's wake.

There were ghostly senior citizens, walkers growing out of their hands, and cancer victims that could almost pass for living, save for the luster of their skin.

The entourage was dominated by the spectral image of a tall, well-groomed man with the manners of a fox. His three-piece suit merged with his flesh and his hands sprouted growths that resembled a bible and a microphone. Sonja recognized the man as being Zebulon Wheele, Catherine's late husband.

The final figure to emerge from the supernatural plasma was massive. She belatedly recognized Claude's blurred features. Sonja moved deeper into shadow, uncomfortable with the idea of brushing against the dead man.

There was a weird quiet, like the hush in the eye of a hurricane. The room was bathed in the strange greenish light given off by the assembled ghosts. Their odor was a cloying mixture of woodsmoke, burned pork, white lightning, and decaying roses.

Wheele blinked as if she'd emerged from a deep sleep. She seemed baffled by the witch light permeating the room. When she saw the blurred faces of those surrounding her, her sanity disintegrated.

The Claude-thing grabbed her, pinning her arms. She emerged from her state of shock, struggling fiercely to free herself, but it was no good. All she did was unseat her wig.

A weird chuttering—like the sound of high-speed helicopter blades—emerged from the mouths of the dead. They were laughing.

Zebulon Wheele separated himself from the others crowding around his widow. The dead evangelist gestured broadly, pointing to his wife. His lips moved, voicing a warped imitation of human speech. He sounded like a badly out-of-synch foreign film.

Sonja wasn't adept enough—or dead enough—to understand what he was saying, but she got the drift. So did Wheele, judging from the look on her face.

As if to drive his point home, the shade of Zebulon Wheele thrust his bible hand into Catherine's face and disappeared, absorbed through the pores in her skin.

The faith healer's body convulsed, then went limp. The Claude-thing let her drop. The other ghosts crowded around the fallen televangelist, watching as she twitched and shuddered on the floor.

Catherine Wheele lifted her head and grinned at the dead. It was Catherine's mouth, but not her smile. Her gaze fell on Sonja, but it was not Catherine looking at her. Wheele was wobbly on her feet, suddenly unfamiliar with high heels. She moved like a drunkard, her eyes and lips twitching like a poorly operated ventriloquist's dummy. Zebulon had been dead little over a year. That's not very long, as the dead estimate time, but it was enough time to forget the complexities of flesh.

His fellow dead pressed against Catherine Wheele, their faces expectant. The eagerness in their expressions made her skin crawl.

Catherine Wheele's mouth opened and from her ruined larynx came a sound that might have been a word.

"Tak."

She gestured with a perfectly manicured hand, the fingers writhing.

"Taik."

The hand became a claw.

"Take," gargled the almost voice. The claw disappeared into Catherine Wheele's abdomen.

The hand reemerged a second later, slick with blood and clutching a length of pink intestine.

"Take," growled Zebulon. "This is my body."

Pale hands closed on the proffered intestine, stringing like a ghastly party streamer. The warped corpse laughter swelled as the Skaggs children grabbed their sister's entrails and began to twirl around her as if in a perverse May dance.

Wheele's hands dug deep into the wonders of her flesh, offering up the choicest morsels to the wraiths clustered around her.

Papa Skaggs snatched at his daughter's liver, his radiant fingers probing the cirrhosis scars. Mama Skaggs, having received her child's kidneys, unleashed a pungent shower of blood and renal fluid on the Persian carpet.

Claude was made a present of her uterus, while George Belwether received a lung. Mrs. Barker, who'd thrown away her insulin at Catherine's behest, was presented with a bladder. Mr. Winkler, who'd poured his nitroglycerine tablets down the drain, ended up with a matching set of breasts. And still they thronged about her, eager to participate in communion.

Sonja watched as Catherine Wheele dispensed chunks of her body like an indulgent grandmother handing out Halloween candy.

When the last of the phantoms had received its due, Wheele turned and stared at Sonja with empty sockets, the eyes having been parceled out long ago. She stood there, waiting for Sonja to come and take her pound of flesh. Sonja wondered how much of the faith healer was actually left inside the shell that stood before her. Surely there wasn't much: Zebulon had been doling out fistfuls of gray matter at the end. She looked at the army of ghosts as they milled about the room, each fondling its own souvenir. She shook her head and stepped toward the door. Her desire for revenge had disappeared, leaving a heaviness in the pit of her stomach.

Wheele resembled a hideous scarecrow robbed of its stuffing. Her skin hung like an emptied sack. Zebulon's essence oozed from the empty sockets like a cheapjack jinni attired in otherworldly polyester. He hovered near the ceiling, scowling at what remained of his wife.

The hollow woman tottered, bereft of the supernatural energy that had sustained the illusion of life. She raised scarlet fingers to her blind face, the lower jaw dropping in a parody of a scream. There was no sound since she no longer possessed larynx or lungs.

How much did he leave? Just enough to know what had been done to her, that's all.

Catherine Wheele collapsed like a dynamited building, toppling into herself. The ghosts flickered, their faces dripping as they began to melt. Sonja Blue watched as Zebulon Wheele, Claude, and the Skaggs clan ran together like candle wax. Within seconds the room was ankle-deep in viridescent muck. The ectoplasm's phosphorescence was already waning, and within an hour the stuff would be indistinguishable from fungus.

Sonja stared at the carcass sprawled amid its own viscera. Wheele's body was unmarked, except for the mutilation to the head. The medical examiner was going to have a hell of a time explaining this one as suicide.

Wexler lay on his back in the grass, one hand clutching the embroidered polo player over his heart. His feet were bare and a pair of shoes lay in the grass alongside him, the expensive leather ruined by the dew. His face was pulled into a crude parody of the classical Greek comedy mask. He reminded Sonja of the nameless hobo thrown into the racquetball court.

She shifted her burden as she bent to retrieve the keys to the BMW. Wexler refused to let go. She brought her boot heel down on his hand. The sound of breaking fingers brought a smile to her face.

She had to hurry. The cops would be there soon. She glanced over her shoulder at the mansion. She could detect a glimmer of the fire in the downstairs windows.

She unlocked the trunk, placing Claude's body inside. She'd made an improvised shroud from one of the drapes in the study. She'd used the other to start the fire.

It would be better, in the long run, that no questions be asked as to the exact nature of Wheele's demise. Mysterious deaths were one thing, inexplicable deaths another.

Sonja paused once more before sliding behind the wheel of Wexler's car. It was almost dawn and the morning air was redolent with the smell of death.

✸

The TV anchorman, his hair styled and face unmarred by frown lines or crow's feet, smiled into camera number one.

". . . and congratulations to the zoo's newest proud parents!"

The smile dimmed, but did not fully disappear, and the anchorman lowered his voice to indicate the next item was serious.

"The city's police and fire departments continue to be baffled by what is being called Mad Night. Early this morning, during the hours between midnight and dawn, the city and its surrounding suburbs were plagued by an unprecedented number of violent domestic disturbances, suicide attempts, rapes, street fights, and outbreaks of arson. At least fifteen people are known dead and forty-five reported injured during the early-morning chaos.

"In a related news item, authorities are investigating what is being described as a 'Guyana-like spectacle' at the estate of controversial televangelist Catherine Wheele. The carnage was discovered early this morning when the city fire department responded to a three-alarm fire at Wheele's exclusive Jonquil Lane address. Details are as yet unclear, but Mrs. Wheele is believed to have perished in the blaze. Also listed among the dead is noted pop psychologist and lecturer Dr. Adam Wexler, author of the best-selling *Sharing, Caring, and Swearing*.

"Well, so how's the weekend shaping up, Skip?"

"Looks like a doozy, Fred, with almost no chance of rain."

EPILOGUE

Children begin by loving their parents. After a time they judge them. Rarely, if ever, do they forgive them.

—Oscar Wilde

Sonja Blue stood among the monuments and watched them put Claude Hagerty in the ground.

It was drizzling and the rain served to muffle the words spoken over the casket. The coffin rested above the open grave on a machine that would lower the loved one into the cavity with the press of a button. Besides the sad-faced minister reciting the burial prayer, the only other mourners were an elderly woman Sonja guessed was an aunt and a couple of former co-workers.

Sonja quietly studied the old woman clutching a damp bouquet of Kleenex. She kept shredding and reshredding them as she stared at her nephew's casket.

Would his aunt appreciate the fact that she'd climbed the fire escape to Claude's apartment, all the way to the fifth floor, his corpse slung over her shoulder? That she'd tucked him in bed? No, probably not. She turned the collar up on her jacket and squared her shoulders against the rain.

Perhaps she'd done him a greater disservice in death than she had in life. If she'd left him among the smoking ruins of Wheele's mansion, at least he'd have had a decent crowd for his send-off. Atrocity victims are always popular. But that would have led to questions about exactly what a lowly orderly was doing at the home of a famous religious leader, and Sonja could not allow that.

"Ms. Blue?"

She'd been so involved in her thoughts she didn't hear him until he was at her elbow. She turned, a bit too swiftly, and glared at the little man in the dark suit. A taller, younger man in chauffeur's livery stood behind him, holding an umbrella.

The little man in the dark suit faltered, his eye contact sliding across her polished lenses. He coughed into his fist.

"Ahem, Ms. Blue, my name is Ottershaw. I represent the interests of my employer, Mr. Jacob Thorne. I have been instructed by Mr. Thorne to give this to you"—he produced a business envelope from his breast pocket— "and to inform you that, while he greatly appreciates the efforts you have taken on his behalf, he hopes you understand that he wishes to never see you again."

Ottershaw handed her the envelope and, having relayed his message, turned and walked toward a limo parked on the narrow road that wound through the cemetery, the chauffeur following him.

Sonja slit the seal on the envelope with her switchblade. It contained a cashier's check drawn on the family bank. She stared at the zeroes for a while, then at the limousine.

The windows were tinted black, but she could make out two figures huddled on the backseat. Ottershaw . . . and Thorne.

He's as guilty as Wheele. He told her to kill you. And you know he's the one who told Wheele where you were you were after you left his apartment. He probably even ordered Claude's death.

"Yeah, I know that."

Is that it? Are you going to stand here and let him get away with it?

The chauffeur started the car and the limousine pulled away, Thorne's profile a darker blur behind the glass.

Claude's funeral was over and none of the mourners stuck around to see him lowered into eternity. A cemetery worker operating a small earth-mover scooped fresh dirt into the hole.

Sonja stuffed the envelope into the pocket of her jacket and began walking toward the gates of the graveyard, threading her way through the field of the dead.

"What do you expect me to do?" she asked the Other. "He's our father."

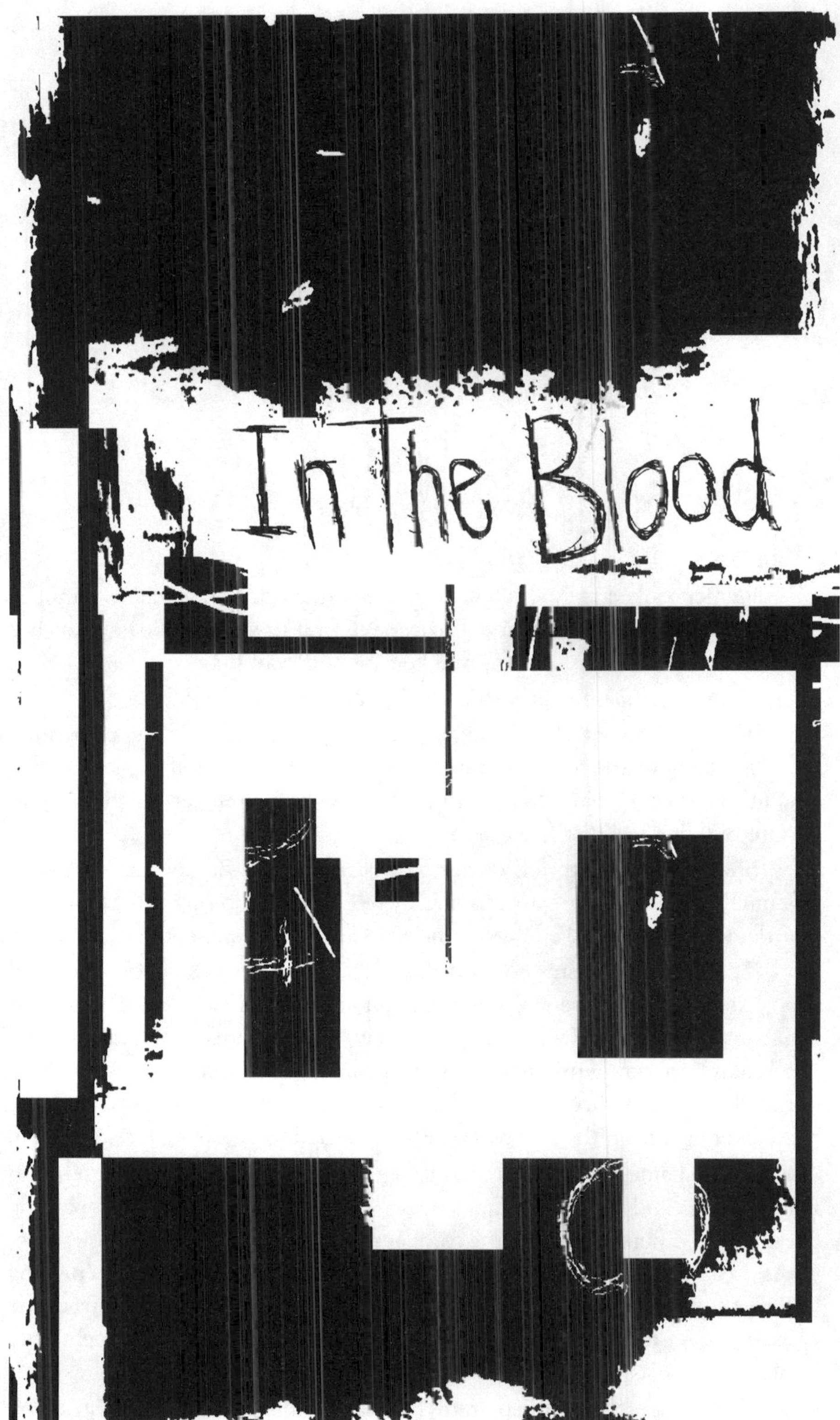
In The Blood

Where is she?

Palmer looked at his watch for the fifteenth time in as many minutes. She was late. Again. He wanted to believe that it wasn't deliberate on her part, but the truth was Loli enjoyed keeping him waiting.

No, not waiting; twisting in the wind on the end of a meat-hook.

The woman knew she had him: heart, soul, and gonads. Palmer recognized Loli as bad news the moment she sashayed into his office, but the knowledge hadn't kept him from falling hard and messy, like a jumper on the Empire State Building.

She'd hired him to follow her husband, a well-to-do contractor named Samuel Quine, trying to get some dirt on him for a nice, juicy divorce settlement. It didn't take long. Quine was seeing someone on the sly, all right.

They met at a motor court at the edge of town twice a week. It was all very discreet and proper, in a suburban middle-class kind of way. Palmer was all too familiar with the pattern; he'd spent a good chunk of his professional life taking incriminating photos of unfaithful husbands and wives sneaking in and out of hot-sheet joints. What he couldn't understand was why Quine needed to get it on the side when he was married to a woman as sexy as Loli.

Before Palmer could finish that thought, he was dazzled by the high beams from Loli's candy-apple red Trans Am as it pulled into the deserted parking lot, Bon Jovi pumping out of the speaker system. Palmer grimaced. Loli's taste was dreadful. Except for him, of course. She shut off the engine, returning the lot to shadows and silence. There was still enough illumination from the distant street lights for him to see her slide out from behind the wheel of her car.

She was dressed all in red, from the ribbon wrapped around her ash-blond ponytail to the skintight red leather stiletto-heeled knee boots that matched her miniskirt. Her fingernails and lips glistened as if she'd painted them with fresh blood.

Palmer's anxiety and aggravation transformed itself into pure lust. It was like being high on a wondrous drug that made rational thought and common sense not only irrelevant, but impossible. He wondered if this was how male praying mantises felt during the mating dance.

"You got it?" Her voice was honey and whisky poured over crystal-clear ice. She raised her cornflower-blue eyes to his dark brown ones.

He nodded dumbly, his tongue turned into a useless wad of dry cotton. Palmer handed her a manila envelope full of pictures of Sam Quine and his mistress leaving their trysting place, information detailing the days and times they kept their rendezvous, and the name they registered under.

Loli quickly scanned his notes, her mouth set into a predatory smirk. Palmer was startled by the cruelty he saw in her eyes, then shamed by having felt revulsion. But he couldn't help feeling he'd been allowed an unintentional glimpse of the woman Sam Quine was married to.

"Loli, we need to talk."

"I'd like to stay and chat awhile, Bill. I really would. But there's something I need to attend to." She opened the carmine designer purse that hung from her shapely, white shoulder as she spoke.

"Loli, it's about us . . ."

"Now, where did I put that thing? Oh, *here* it is!"

"When will I get to see you again?"

Loli turned to face him, pulling a Smith & Wesson .38 out of the tangled mess of cosmetics and half-read romance novels in her purse. "I guess you'll see me in hell," she replied, leveling the gun at his chest.

Palmer stared in mute horror at the piece of blue steel pointed at his heart. He recognized the weapon as his own, supposedly locked in the desk at the office. He disliked guns, but his clients expected it of him. Damn Bogart.

"But, Loli . . . I *love* you!"

Her painted lips pulled back into a grin that seemed to spread until it bisected her face. "That's sweet of you, Bill. I love you, too."

And then she shot him.

William Palmer woke in a puddle of sweat. Had he screamed? He listened to the other inmates in the prison, but all he heard were the usual snores and farts. He uncoiled his rigid shoulder and leg muscles. He'd recently taken to sleeping with his arms crossed, corpse-style, across his chest. The prison psychologist had made a big deal out of that.

Palmer sat up, dabbing at the sweat rolling off his brow with the edge of the bed sheet. His hands trembled and he wanted a smoke *real* bad. Hell, he'd even settle for one of those shitty big house cigarettes, made from Bugler tobacco and a page from the New Testament. Regular cancer sticks like Camels and Winstons were hard to get under these circumstances, much less his preferred brand: Shermans Queen-Size Cigaretellos.

That dream. That goddamned dream.

How long was it going to keep on? He'd been having the same dream—or variations on the theme—ever since he'd come out of the coma six weeks ago and been informed of Loli's perfidy. The dreams varied widely, but they were essentially all the same: they involved him, Loli, and his gun. Each dream ended with Loli opening fire. Sometimes the dreams were nonsensical, the way dreams normally are; he and Loli riding a merry-go-round in the middle of a forest when Loli pulls out the gun and shoots him. Others were so realistic he didn't know it was a dream until he was jerked back into consciousness by the sound of the gun: he and Loli naked in bed, screwing away, and she pulls the gun out from under the pillow . . . Palmer squeezed his eyes shut, deliberately blocking the image. That one had been bad. Worse than the one tonight.

None of the dream-shootings were the real one, though. He guessed he should be grateful for small favors. It was bad enough remembering what had happened in the motel room without being condemned to relive it every night. His right hand absently massaged the scar on his chest that marked Loli's parting gift.

She'd called late, babbling that she needed his help and protection. She'd decided to confront Quine at the motel but things had gone wrong. They got into a fight and she was locked in the bathroom—although she'd somehow succeeded in dragging the phone in after her. Quine had gone crazy, threatening to kill her. She was scared; Palmer didn't realize what a violent temper Quine had, how brutal he could be.

She'd pushed the right buttons; Palmer was in his car and on his way to the motor court before the receiver hit the cradle.

The door was unlocked when he got there. He wasn't too worried about Loli's husband. Quine was in his late fifties and heavier than Palmer, but not in the best of shape. Palmer knew how to handle himself in a fight. However, he was unprepared for the sight of Sam Quine sprawled naked across the motel room's double bed, his brains splashed across the headboard and nightstand.

Palmer heard the bathroom door click open behind him. He turned in time to see Loli at the threshold, stark naked and holding a recently fired .38. *His* .38.

"Loli, what the fu—"

And she'd fired.

Three weeks passed before he was able to stay conscious long enough to understand what was being said to and about him. Sometimes he wished he could return to the painless gray of twilight sleep and never come out. Anything would be better than the truth.

Loli was dead.

The whole thing was like a bad Mickey Spillane novel. It was typical of Loli, though. The cops kept commenting on the half-baked nature of the scheme. Did she really think no one would question her version of what happened? Didn't she know that forensics could read the splatter pattern left by her husband's exploding head and triangulate the trajectory of the fatal bullet? Did she really think the police were *that* stupid? There was no way she could have pulled it off. It didn't make any sense unless you knew her. Or thought you did.

Loli had never been one to concern herself with consensual reality. If she said her husband was a brute, a cheat, and a liar, then it was true. That she refused to have sex with him for two years was unrelated to his infidelity. He was the one in the wrong, the one to be punished.

If she told the police that she and her husband had gone to a certain motel to celebrate their reconciliation, and while they were there, her jilted lover broke in on them, blowing her husband's gray matter all over the wallpaper, then that's what happened. It never occurred to her that she would be suspected as well.

When the police began asking her questions, suggesting that she and Palmer had conspired to murder Quine, it proved too much for her. That Palmer had survived the bullet she'd pumped into him was another contingency she had been unprepared for. She kept insisting that she'd wrested the gun from Palmer and shot him in self-defense, but the police suspected Palmer's wounding had more to do with a falling-out between illicit lovers.

Frightened and confused upon finding herself, possibly for the first time in her life, in a situation where her sex appeal could not free her from the consequences of her actions, Loli panicked.

A fifth of Everclear and a bottle of sleeping pills provided an escape route from justice, but not before she penned a venomous farewell note, implicating Palmer in Quine's death, and mailed it to the district attorney: "It was all his idea. I didn't want to go along with it."

What she *really* meant was that it was all his fault for not dying. If he'd died like she'd planned everything would have gone off the way it was supposed to. Funny how he was finally becoming adept at understanding Loli, now that it was too late to do him any good.

As soon as the doctors proclaimed him fit, he would be brought before the judge for bail designation. As far as the district attorney's office was concerned, it was a clear-cut case of conspiracy to commit murder; it didn't matter who actually pulled the trigger. His public defense attorney told him there wasn't much hope of making bail.

Palmer craned his head so he could catch a glimpse of the sky through the heavily secured window over his bed. It was still dark out. He remembered his mother insisting, during the periodic hard times the family roller coasted through, how "it's always darkest before the dawn." His mother was a good woman, bless her, but incapable of making a statement that wasn't cobbled together from clichés.

His father had been a great one for clichés as well. His one real effort at handing paternal wisdom to his only son had come in the form of a nose-to-nose yelling match when he'd told the fifteen-year-old Palmer: "*Boy, if you don't get your head outta your ass, you're gonna find yourself up shit creek without a paddle!*"

Thanks, Dad.

"Palmer? Somebody here to see you."

Word had come through that morning that the doctors had okayed his transferal to the prison. He was to be placed with the rest of the prisoners the next day. This had not come as welcome news.

"Is it my lawyer?"

"Beats me. The guy says he wants to talk to you." The orderly jerked his head toward the single door leading to the recovery ward. A man Palmer had never seen before was standing at the check-in desk, an expensive attaché case in one hand. "You wanna see him?" There was no privacy in the prison infirmary, but the patient-inmates had the freedom to turn away visitors if they chose.

Palmer looked at the stranger for a moment. "Yeah, send him over."

Moments later the stranger with the attaché case stood at the foot of Palmer's bed. He was a middle-aged man dressed in an expensive, if drab, silk suit. His skin was pallid, even by today's melanoma-conscious standards. He looked like a man who spent a lot of time indoors.

"Mr. Palmer? Mr. William Palmer?"

"Yeah, that's me. Who're you?"

The stranger's mouth smiled, but his eyes did not join in. "My name is Renfield. And I believe I can be of some service to you, Mr. Palmer."

"That so? You a lawyer?" Palmer motioned him to a metal folding chair next to the bed. Renfield lowered himself into the seat; his movements were so rigid and stylized that he reminded Palmer of an animated mannequin.

Renfield's mouth curled into another simulated smile. "Not exactly. I am a representative for a third party who has an . . . interest . . . in your case."

"Look, Mac, I don't know what it is you're getting at. Say what you have to say and get it over with, okay?"

"You are innocent, are you not? Of the crime they accuse you of, I mean. You did not murder, nor did you conspire to murder, Samuel Quine. Is that right?"

"You got it." Palmer wished he had a smoke. This pasty-faced suit was making him nervous.

"Would you care for a cigarette, Mr. Palmer?" Renfield leaned forward, pulling a pack from his breast pocket. Palmer was surprised to see a flat, red-and-white case of Shermans Queen-Size Cigaretellos in the man's pale hand.

"Yeah, don't mind if I do." He eagerly accepted one of the thin, unfiltered brown cigarettes.

"Go ahead, take the pack."

"Uh, thanks." He stared at the cigarettes, then back at Renfield's blandly smiling face. "How did you know I smoke this brand?"

"There is a *lot* we know about you, Mr. Palmer."

Palmer looked up from his cupped palms as he lit the Sherman. "We?"

"Meaning my employer."

"Exactly who *is* this guy interested in my well being?"

"That is not important—for now. What is important is that he can—and will, providing you agree to work for him—clear you of all charges with the district attorney. He can also get your private investigator's license reinstated."

"What is this? Some kind of joke? If so, it's not a real knee-slapper."

"Joke?" Renfield's brow creased. "I never joke, Mr. Palmer."

"I should have guessed. Okay, let me rephrase what I just said. What's going on? Who sent you and what exactly am I to him that he's willing to pull those kind of strings? You're not Mafia, are you?

Again the smile. Palmer felt a sudden urge to grab the drab little bastard and shake him by his lapels. "I assure you, Mr. Palmer, my employer has no need of such petty power brokers. All I need to know is whether you are amiable to certain terms of employment in exchange for your freedom."

Palmer shrugged. "If your boss can spring me like you said, I'll walk on my hands all the way to Timbuktu, if that's what he wants."

"I doubt that will be necessary. Then you accept my employer's offer?"

"That's what I said, didn't I?"

Renfield nodded and closed his eyes. "It is done." It sounded like a verbal signal. Palmer wondered if the creep was wired for sound. Renfield stood up, straightening the creases in his suit. "You will be hearing from us shortly. Good day, Mr. Palmer."

"Yeah. Sure. Hang loose, dude."

Palmer lay back in the bed, arms folded behind his head, puffing thoughtfully on his cigarette. Who the hell was this Renfield geek? He didn't like the whey-faced bastard, but if he was telling the truth . . . Well, it wouldn't be the first time he had shaken hands with the Devil.

He glanced at the pack of Shermans resting atop the bedside table.

There is a lot *we know about you*, Mr. *Palmer.*

Twenty-four hours after his initial meeting with Renfield, Palmer was standing on the street outside the Criminal Justice Building, blinking at the late afternoon sun. It had been over two months since he'd last been outside. He was still a bit weak from the gunshot wound that had creased his heart, but, all in all, he felt pretty damn good. Freedom was an amazing tonic.

I'll be damned. The little wonk said he could do it, and whatever else he might be, he sure as hell isn't a liar.

Palmer hefted the plain canvas tote bag the prison quartermaster had given him before jettisoning him back onto the streets. Inside were what few possessions he could call his own, salvaged from his apartment by his erstwhile public defender before the landlord changed the lock. Hardly the most auspicious of new beginnings.

Palmer glanced at his wristwatch. He'd received a note from Renfield just prior to his release telling him to wait on the corner, but for what? He'd been waiting fifteen minutes already. . . .

A stretch limo, black and shiny as a scarab, pulled up to the curb, its windows polarized against prying eyes. The rear passenger door opened and Renfield leaned halfway out, motioning for him to climb in.

"You seem surprised, Mr. Palmer."

"Dazed is more like it. How did you do it?"

"Do what?"

"Pull that trick with the D.A.'s office? They said something about Loli's diary turning up."

Renfield shrugged. "My employer is not without . . . connections, Mr. Palmer. Besides, what does it matter, so long as you are cleared?"

Palmer wanted to press the issue, but there was something in the way Renfield smiled that made him keep silent. Renfield may have saved him from a jail house welcome-wagon party, but that didn't mean he had to like the guy. In fact, Palmer felt uncomfortable sitting next to him. He couldn't help himself; there was something inherently loathsome about Renfield that he couldn't quite peg.

"Where are we going?"

"We are going to meet my employer. He is as interested in seeing you face-to-face as you are in meeting him. You should relax, Mr. Palmer; it will be some time before we reach our destination." Renfield leaned forward and opened the liquor cabinet built into the back of the front seat. "Help yourself."

A hour later the limo coasted to a halt. The time had passed in silence, except for the occasional rattle of ice as Palmer replenished his bourbon-and-coke. Renfield drank nothing but bottled mineral water, and that sparingly.

The driver moved from behind the wheel of the car and opened the door for Renfield. Palmer slid after him, feeling a bit more tipsy than he'd realized.

It was dark outside the car—early evening out in the country. At least to Palmer it looked like the country. They were at the end of a long, crushed gravel drive, standing outside a spacious ranch-style house with handsomely manicured lawns and artfully concealed exterior lights. No doubt there was a nice big redwood deck and a hot tub out back. He followed Renfield up the front walk.

Before they reached the porch, one of the shadows detached itself from the shrubbery and blocked their path.

The shadow was a damn big son of a bitch armed with an automatic weapon that looked like a child's toy in his massive hands. He towered over Renfield and Palmer, his shoulders wide enough to block out the sky. Palmer guessed him to be close to seven feet tall, if not an inch or two over. And the bastard was *ugly*, too. The giant's long, horse-like face was made even more unattractive by a complete lack of facial hair, including eyebrows and eyelashes. The guard said something to Renfield in a register so low it was close to subvocal.

"It's all right, Keif. He's been cleared."

The guard didn't take his eyes off Palmer as he made a strangely delicate motion with his free hand that was either sign language or his pantomiming breaking a twig.

Renfield shook his head. "No, that won't be necessary. Like I said, it's been arranged. Now get on with your job. We must not keep the doctor waiting."

The guard nodded and returned to his post. Palmer could feel the giant's eyes on his back as they entered the house.

The living room was right out of a prime-time soap, with a high ceiling, tastefully arranged Danish furniture, and a handful of modern paintings scattered along the walls. It was obvious no one spent any time living there.

"This way." Renfield led Palmer down a narrow hallway to the back of the house. He stopped outside a door at the end of the corridor and rapped lightly.

"Bring him in, Renfield."

The room behind the door was lined with books and smelled of old leather and moldering paper. Seated behind an antique roll-top desk was a handsome man in his middle years, his dark hair touched with silver at the temples. Despite the dim wattage cast by the Tiffany lamp set atop the desk, the older man wore a pair of green-tinted aviator shades.

"Ah, Mr. Palmer! Pleased to make your acquaintance at last!" He rose from the antique swivel chair and extended his hand to the detective. He was dressed in crisp, white cotton pants, a white cotton shirt, loosened at the collar with the sleeves rolled up past the elbows, and a pair of old-fashioned red leather suspenders. Palmer was reminded of Spencer Tracy in *Inherit the Wind*.

Palmer winced at the strength behind the older man's cool, dry grip. "I'm told I have you to thank for arranging my freedom, Mister . . . ?"

"It's Doctor. Dr. Pangloss. Pleased to be of some service." He grinned, revealing pristine bridgework that made Palmer's nicotine-stained teeth look like a demilitarized zone.

"Uh, yeah . . ."

Pangloss motioned for Palmer to seat himself, then nodded to Renfield, who was still standing at the door. "That'll be all for now, Renfield. Have the cook prepare a tray for Mr. Palmer."

Renfield nodded and retreated, leaving them alone.

"You must forgive me for not dining with you." Pangloss smiled. "I've already eaten. May I offer you a drink?" He pulled a bottle of bourbon, its seal intact, from one of the desk's pigeonholes. Palmer recognized it as one of his favorite brands, when he could afford it. "Oh, and help yourself to the cigarettes," Pangloss added, nodding to a Chinese lacquer box resting on the table next to Palmer's chair.

The cigarette case was, like practically everything else in the room, an antique. A Chinese dragon, looped around itself, adorned the lid. Inside were Shermans Queen-Size Cigaretellos.

Palmer lit his Shermans with a Fabergé cigarette lighter, admiring how the light from the Tiffany lamp played across the jeweled platinum scrollwork. "Look, Dr. Pangloss, it's not that I'm ungrateful for what you've done . . . but what the hell is going on? I mean, who are you, and what am I to *you* that you would go so far as to spring me out of jail?"

Pangloss flashed his teeth as he handed the detective the highball glass, but it was impossible to tell if the smile extended to his eyes. "You've got a legitimate right to know, and I respect your forthrightness, Mr. Palmer. I really do. I appreciate men willing to speak their minds. The fact of the matter is, I am in dire need of your services."

"That's flattering, Doc, but there are hundreds of perfectly good private investigators in this country. Some I'll even admit are better than me. I'm hardly Sam Spade, especially in light of the shit both you and I know I've recently been through."

"You underestimate yourself, Mr. Palmer. Or may I call you Bill?"

"Call me Palmer. Everyone else does."

"Very well—*Palmer*. You have tracked down missing people before, have you not?"

"Yeah, sure. I've traced a couple of skips and runaways. Most P.I.s have, sometime or another—it's part of the job. Why?"

"Because there is someone I want you to find for me. A girl. It's very important that she be located. I'm willing to pay you what it's worth."

Palmer sipped at the bourbon. It had been a long time since he'd been able to afford liquor this good.

"Keep on talking, Doc. I'm listening."

"It won't be easy, I'm afraid. She doesn't want to be found and has been highly successful at avoiding my . . . field operatives. She recognizes them on sight and does her best to . . . avoid them." Pangloss's handsome face grew dark. "She's a wild woman, Palmer—crafty, shrewd, fiercely independent, and more than a little crazy. She is also very dangerous. I'll tell you that right now, just to make sure you don't develop cold feet later on."

"This 'wild woman' you want me to find—exactly what is your relationship to her?"

"She's my granddaughter."

Palmer doubted that was the truth. Pangloss certainly didn't look old enough to have a grandchild capable of helling around; but you never can tell, what with plastic surgery nowadays. And while Pangloss hadn't exactly told the truth, Palmer had the feeling he wasn't lying, either.

"I'll pay you a thousand dollars a day, plus expenses. I trust that is satisfactory?"

Palmer nearly choked on the bourbon. "Uh, it'll do."

"There will also be a twenty-thousand-dollar bonus should you find her and successfully deliver this letter." Pangloss pulled a legal-sized envelope from one of the desk's pigeonholes. It was expensive cream stationery, stiff and heavy, and bore an old-fashioned wax seal on the back: a dragon looped around itself.

"Can I ask a question? A purely hypothetical one, that is."

"Go ahead."

"What would you do if I decided not to take the case?"

"That assumes you have a choice in the matter, Mr. Palmer. I prefer keeping the fiction of free will intact, don't you? I find my employees work much better when they believe they have some say in what they can and cannot do."

Palmer stared at Pangloss's pleasantly smiling face, the expensive liquor suddenly bitter in his mouth.

Pangloss slid a companionable arm over Palmer's shoulder, walking him to the door. For the first time Palmer noticed how long the other man's fingernails were. "I have confidence in you, Palmer. I'm sure you'll be a great asset to our team. Now that you're here, why don't you make yourself at home? I've had the guest room specially prepared for your arrival, and I'll see to it that my cook gets your dinner to you. If there's anything you need, don't hesitate to ask."

"There's just one thing . . ."

"Yes?" Although Pangloss was still smiling, Palmer was certain the eyes behind the tinted aviator shades were watching him intently.

"What's the name of this girl you're looking for?"

"How thoughtless of me! Her name is Sonja Blue."

Pangloss opened the door. Palmer wasn't surprised to see Renfield standing on the other side of the threshold.

"Renfield will see you to your room. Oh, and Mr. Palmer?" Palmer glanced over his shoulder; Pangloss was grinning at him, showing way too many teeth. "Pleasant dreams."

"Will there be anything else, sir?"

Palmer stared blankly at the bellhop for a double heartbeat before answering. "Uh, no. No, I don't think so." He stuffed a couple of dollars into an outstretched white glove. The bellboy grimaced as if Palmer had just hacked a gob into his hand.

Well, he wasn't going to let some college student's wounded sense of self-worth sour the pleasure of having his very own suite at the Hilton.

Palmer shrugged out of his jacket and plopped down on the couch in the sitting room. He rang up room service and ordered a New York Strip and a couple bottles of imported beer, all courtesy of the good Dr. Pangloss. He wasn't sure what his employer was a doctor *of*, but it sure paid well.

While he waited on his food to arrive, Palmer thumbed through notes scribbled during his time as Pangloss's "houseguest."

1. Is Sonja Blue really Pangloss's grand-d?
2. Is S.B. into illicit drugs? Prostitution?
3. Is Pangloss?
4. What the hell am I doing here?

So far he'd failed to turn up answers to any of those questions, although placing a jet flight between himself and his "employer" made #4 seem less pressing than when he first wrote it.

He glanced at the stiff, cream-colored envelope jutting out of the breast pocket of his jacket. No doubt the letter would give him some answers, but that wasn't how the game was played. At least not when he was on the field.

Still, for a man supposedly desperate to locate his grandchild, Pangloss had been stingy with personal information concerning the girl. After some questioning, Palmer had finally learned that she might be traced through a boyfriend, if that was the proper word to use, named Geoffrey Chastain, better known as "Chaz."

From what little Palmer had pieced together, this Chastain was an expatriate Brit with a taste for hard drugs and unsavory sex partners. Your basic low-life hustler. Palmer scrounged a pencil from his hip pocket and added to his notes.

5. Is Chastain S.B.'s lover? Connection/Pimp?
6. Pangloss sure S.B. no longer in area, but thinks it good a place as any to start.

Palmer looked at the photograph of the elusive Chaz that Pangloss presented him with before he left the estate. Odd that Pangloss should have a picture of the bad-ass boyfriend but not a single snapshot of his own granddaughter. It looked like a passport photo; either that or a mug shot. The man glowering at him from the other side of the camera was in his late twenties, his hair combed in a rebellious rooster tail. There was still a hint of masculine beauty in the shape of his cheekbones and the tilt of his eyes, but what physical attractiveness Geoffrey Chastain had once possessed had been eaten away by his addictions; the drug hunger was obvious even in a photo. Still, it was easy to see how a young, impressionable girl might become fascinated with such a sleazeball.

Room service brought him his steak and beer. He always prepared himself for a night on the prowl by eating his fill of red meat. It put him in the proper mood for the hunt.

"You know this guy?"

It was roughly the four hundredth and fifty-seventh time Palmer had asked that question that night. His feet were tired and his bladder ached from too many beers.

The man with the anarchy symbol chalked across the back of his black raincoat glanced first at Palmer then the snapshot. He took a swig from his beer and shook his head.

"Sorry. Can't help ya."

A slightly built youth seated on the opposite side of the man in the anarchist coat craned his head over his companion's shoulder, looking mildly curious.

"How about you? You know this guy?"

"He don't know him, either," snapped the man in the raincoat. "He don't know nobody I don't know, do ya?" This he addressed to the boy seated next to him. It didn't sound like a question.

The boy cringed, smiling nervously at this friend. "Course not, Nick. I don't know nobody."

"Fuckin' A."

Palmer cursed under his breath and headed for the men's room. This wasn't the first time he'd run into such aggressive ignorance. He'd come close to getting somewhere at least twice, only to have the parties in question suddenly clam up on him.

As he relieved himself at the urinal, he heard the rest room door open and close behind him.

"Hey, mister?"

Palmer glimpsed enough out of the corner of his eye to recognize Nick's boyfriend.

"What is it, kid?"

"I know that guy. The one in the picture."

"Do you now?"

"Yeah. Chaz. He's from England."

"How come your friend didn't want you talking to me?"

"Nick? Oh, he's just jealous, that's all." The boy giggled. "He and Chaz crossed swords a couple of times, so to speak. Chaz muscled in on a couple of his boyfriends."

Palmer shook off and made himself presentable before turning to face the boy. The kid couldn't be more than seventeen, his strawberry blonde hair cut short in front with a long, braided rat-tail at the base of his neck. He wore a pair of designer jeans and a Psychic TV T-shirt.

"What's your name, kid?"

"Terry."

"Look, Terry, can you tell me where I could possibly find this Chaz? I'll make it worth your while . . ." He produced a twenty from his pocket, holding it tight between his knuckles. It was obvious the boy was interested, but his eyes flickered away whenever Palmer tried to look him in the face. "Is this Chaz a friend of yours? Are you afraid you'll get him in trouble?"

Terry snorted. "Chaz? A friend? I always thought he was a creep! Always looking at me like he knew what was going on inside my head. Besides, no one's seen him in almost a year. Not since what happened to the Blue Monkeys."

"The Blue Monkeys?"

"Yeah. This gang Chaz used to hang with. Bunch of real hard-asses. Used to dye their hair blue. He was friends with 'em . . . but they only hung with him on account of the blow he always had on him."

"Where can I find these Blue Monkeys?" Palmer handed Terry the folded bill.

"You can't."

"What do you mean?"

"They're dead."

"Dead?"

"Well, not *all* of them, but enough got killed off to deep-six the gang."

"What happened?"

"No one's real sure; it got hushed up pretty quick. But there was this gang war, or something, in the back of some bar. Those that weren't killed got crippled up bad. I . . . wait a minute. Jimmy!"

"Jimmy?"

"That was the kid Chaz was seeing. He was the only one that didn't get trashed."

"Where can I find this Jimmy?"

Terry grinned and stuck out his hand, looking like a kid asking his father for this week's allowance. "That's worth more'n a twenty, dude."

Palmer grumbled and produced another bill. Terry's hands moved so fast he couldn't tell which pocket the money disappeared into.

"His name's Jimmy Eichorn. He lives with his mom somewhere over on Thirty-Ninth."

"You're learning quick, kid."

Terry shrugged his narrow shoulders as he turned to leave. "Nick's stingy when it comes to buying nice things."

"Mrs. Eichorn?"

The woman peering at him from the other side of the burglar chain scowled, as if deciding whether she should answer.

"Mrs. Eichorn, my name is Palmer . . ."

"Whatcha want? You from th' Welfare Department? If so, it's too late for a business visit!"

It had taken him a couple of hours to find the right house. Terry's instructions had been off by a few blocks. It was long past Palmer's supper time and his scar was giving him trouble. He'd been forced to climb five narrow, badly lit flights of stairs, the smell of human piss and old garbage pungent enough to make his gorge hitch. He felt his temper start to flare.

"Mrs. Eichorn, do I *look* like a fuckin' caseworker?"

Where Mrs. Eichorn was concerned, there was no such thing as a rhetorical question. He could feel her taking in his shaved temples and narrow goatee, lingering on his wavy, gray-shot hair, combed straight up; a holdover from the days, more than a decade gone, when he used to slam-dance down at Club Lies.

"I'd like to talk to Jimmy, Mrs. Eichorn. Is he in?"

Mrs. Eichorn blinked. "Yeah, he's here. He's always here. Whatcha want with my Jimmy?"

Palmer slid a crisp twenty through the crack in the door. "It's important, ma'am."

Jimmy's mother hesitated then closed the door, taking the twenty with her. A second later the door reopened, allowing Palmer a better view of both her and the apartment.

Mrs. Eichorn was an unsmiling woman with pale, washed-out hair that had once been blonde. Her skin was pasty and her eyes so light a shade of blue they seemed to lack any color at all. Deep lines creased the corners of her mouth. The only color evident on her face was a purplish-red lipstick smeared on her mouth. She wore a much-washed yellow waitress's uniform with the name "Alice" stitched across the bosom in red thread. The few items of furniture in the living room looked as worn and over-used as their owner.

"Whatcha want with my Jimmy?" She pulled a filtered cigarette from her apron pocket and clamped it between purple-red lips. Palmer wrinkled his nose in distaste. Funny how other people's smoking got on his nerves. "You better hurry it up, whatever it is. I gotta leave for work in a few minutes."

"Mrs. Eichorn, was your son a member of a youth gang called the Blue Monkeys?"

The look she gave him was hard enough to cut glass. "You a cop?"

"No, ma'am, I'm a private investigator. I'm not familiar with what happened. I heard there was a gang war—"

Mrs. Eichorn snorted smoke from her nostrils. "You believe that shit?" She gave him another look, this one not quite as hard as the last. "You're not from around here, are ya? Shoulda figured when you asked if Jimmy was in. Not that it matters. People forget things, get the stories wrong, make up stuff because they like the way it sounds. You know how it is."

"There wasn't a fight?"

"Massacre is a better word for it. I'm just thankful my boy was spared, that's all. The rest of those sleazebags you could've flushed and no one would've cared. But Jimmy . . . he was new to the gang. They hadn't had time to mess him up yet, least not much." The creases at the corners of her mouth deepened.

"Can I talk to him?"

"You can try."

She led him down a narrow, unlit hall and opened a door with a Metallica poster tacked to it. It was dark in the small room, although enough illumination spilled through the window facing the street to allow Palmer a quick glimpse of a narrow child's bed in one corner and heavy metal posters plastered on the cracked and peeling walls.

Jimmy Eichorn sat in a wheelchair, staring at the world beyond the windowsill.

"I left the room the way he had it." Mrs. Eichorn's voice dropped into a lower, softer register, as if she was in church. "I think it makes him happy." She went and stood beside her son's wheelchair, one hand absently stroking the back of his head. "The blue's almost grown out. I hated it when he dyed it. He always had such pretty hair, don't you think so?"

Jimmy's hair was the same mousy non-color as his mother's. Palmer grunted something non-committal. The boy slumped in the wheelchair looked to be sixteen years old, although his slack features made him seem even younger. He was dressed in a pair of pajamas, a blanket draped over his lap. Jimmy ignored the adults standing to either side of him, his attention fixed on the street below.

"Jimmy? Jimmy, look at me, sweetheart. This nice man wants to ask you a question."

Jimmy took his eyes away from the lamppost across the street and tilted his head in order to stare at his mother. After a couple of seconds his lips pulled into a smile, drool wetting his chin. He reached up and clasped his mother's hand. Mrs. Eichorn smiled indulgently and brushed the hair out of his eyes.

"Jimmy?"

The boy's eyes flickered toward the window then shifted to Palmer. They were the eyes of a preschooler; wide and clear and uncertain of strangers.

"Jimmy, I need your help."

"Go ahead, darling. It's all right." Mrs. Eichorn squeezed Jimmy's hand.

Palmer pulled the photo of Chaz out of his jacket and held it up so the boy could see it. "Do you know where I can find this man, Jimmy? Do you know where Chaz is?"

A muscle in Jimmy's face jerked. Palmer couldn't tell if the boy had shook his head "no" or suffered a muscle spasm. Before he could press the issue, Jimmy gave a weird, high-pitched squeal and began to twitch.

Palmer stepped back in disgust as the boy voided his bowels. Jimmy's eyes rolled in their sockets and then glazed, staring at some unknown fixed point.

"Get out! Go on, get out!" snapped Mrs. Eichorn.

"But—"

"Just get out! I can't deal with him with you in the room!"

Jimmy clawed at his own throat, as if trying to pull an invisible attacker from his windpipe. Palmer glimpsed what looked like puncture marks in the shadow of the boy's chin. He stood awkwardly in the Eichorn's drab front room, listening to the mother soothe her imbecile son. Palmer looked at his hands and noticed they were shaking.

"He was such a happy baby."

Mrs. Eichorn stood slumped against the doorway, lighting another cigarette. Her hands were trembling as well.

"He used to laugh like nobody's business," she continued. "His daddy thought the world of him, because of that laugh. It made him stay around a couple of years longer than he would have if Jimmy had cried like most babies, I guess. When he ran off in '79, Jimmy was just five. Things changed. I . . . I was just fifteen when Jimmy was born. What did I know about bringing a kid up by myself?" She looked at the cigarette in her hand then glanced at Palmer, as if daring him to say otherwise. He suddenly realized this hopeless, washed-out woman was seven years his junior.

"It's not my fault he got like this . . . someone *did* that to him." Her voice tightened and she looked away. "He wouldn't be like that if he hadn't been with the gang that night. I asked him not to go—to break it off. But he wouldn't do it. He said being a Blue Monkey was important to him. More important than anything. You know what they made him do to be a part of their goddamn special gang? They made him suck their . . . their *things!* I couldn't believe he still wanted to have anything to do with them after what they made him do, but he was *proud* of being a Blue Monkey." She shook her head in disgust. "I told him that night I didn't want him hanging around that bar with those scum. I told him that if he went there he better not come home. He cursed me out! His own mama! And he went anyway." Her eyes were bright with unshed tears, but her cheeks remained dry. "I guess we're both paying for our sins, huh?"

Palmer couldn't bring himself to look at her. "Mrs. Eichorn . . . I'm sorry, I didn't realize my questioning your son would . . . *upset* him."

She shrugged. "No way you *could* know. It's funny what sets him off sometimes. But you didn't have to ask him, though. I could have told you where to find Chaz."

"You know Chaz?"

"Yeah, I *knew* him. He's dead. Died the same night the Blue Monkeys got into trouble. Jimmy brought him here once or twice. I figured him for a dealer. I told Jimmy I didn't like the kind of trash he hung out with, so he stopped bringing Chaz over. Rumor had it Chaz got himself bumped off."

"You mean it was a hit?"

"That's what it looked like, at least. I wouldn't have been surprised. Chaz was the kind of jerk who'd cross the wrong people just for kicks."

"Mrs. Eichorn, this is *real* important: did Jimmy ever mention if Chaz had a girlfriend?"

"Not that I recall. But, then, Jimmy and I didn't exactly talk a lot by then."

"I don't want to delay you any more than I already have, Mrs. Eichorn. I appreciate everything you've been able to tell me." Palmer slipped a couple of fifty-dollar bills into her apron pocket as he left.

"You know something?" she said, opening the door for him. "It's funny, in a way, but I can't bring myself to really hate whoever it was that did those things. In a way, I got what I wanted. I got my little boy back. Don't you think that's funny?"

Palmer simply nodded and hurried away. On the third landing he paused long enough to sneak a pain pill. By the time he reached the street, his ribs no longer felt like they were being cracked open with a lobster mallet. He did not look up to see if Jimmy was watching over him.

That night he dreamed he was in a wheelchair, being pushed down a long, poorly lit corridor. The wheelchair needed to be oiled and squeaked whenever it moved. Everything seemed so vivid, so *real*, Palmer thought he was back in the prison infirmary. Then he remembered he'd been released. Confused, he twisted around to find out who was propelling the wheelchair.

Loli smiled back at him, looking both sexy and menacing in her starched white nurse's uniform. Palmer was acutely aware of the erection tenting his hospital johnny.

"Did you miss me, darling?" asked Loli, her lips painted the color of fresh blood.

"Yes. Very much." He hated to admit it, but he *did* miss her, no matter what she'd done to him. It made him feel stupid, powerless, and degraded, but his dick was hard enough to cut diamonds.

"I missed you, too. But I won't *this* time!"

Loli halted the wheelchair at the top of a flight of stairs that seemed to stretch, Escher-like, into another dimension. Palmer's head began to swim. He tried to stand up, but his arms and legs were strapped to the wheelchair.

He twisted his head around, hoping to catch another glimpse of Loli. Instead, he found himself staring down the bore of his gun. He knew he was dreaming and knew what would happen next. He also remembered an old wives' tale—or was it a disputed scientific fact?—that if you dreamed you were killed, you'd die in your sleep. Surely even an imaginary Loli couldn't miss at *this* range.

Palmer threw himself headfirst down the warped, endlessly replicating stairwell. Miraculously, the wheelchair remained upright as he caromed through gothic arches and past half-glimpsed crumbling facades. He could hear Loli shrieking obscenities from the top of the stair, along with the sound of receding gunfire. He wasn't sure where he was going, but at least it was away from Loli, with her bleeding mouth and punishing .38.

For a brief, giddy moment, Palmer knew what it was like to be free. Then he saw the massive brick wall blocking his way. And in front of the wall, standing in a policeman's firing stance, both hands wrapped around the handle of the gun, was Loli.

"Fooled you!"

When he woke up, he realized he'd wet the bed.

Palmer looked at the rows upon rows of cold marble and granite, then back at the map the caretaker had given him at the gate. According to what information there was, Geoffrey Chastain, better known as "Chaz," was buried in Sector E-7. Most of the headstones in the area were newer models, some even looked machine made. The names and dates were still sharply defined and easy to read; it would be several years before the wind and the rain rendered the inscriptions as vague as those found on the older stones.

It was early February and frost crunched under his heels as he made his way amongst the stones. Palmer was cold despite his anorak, and his mood had not been helped by the nightmare that had jerked him awake, sweating and shivering, at four that morning. He'd been unable—unwilling?—to go back to sleep, his scar throbbing like a bad cigarette burn.

He rechecked what little information he'd been able to get from the cemetery caretaker's files as he trudged along. Chastain's plot had been paid for anonymously—in cash. The only point of interest was that the deceased had originally been interred in Potter's Field, then dug up and replanted in a proper grave, complete with headstone, a month later. Palmer was certain Sonja Blue was behind Chaz's change of address. But why? Was it out of guilt? Sense of duty? Love?

He literally stumbled across Chaz's grave by accident. His feet had become entangled in the faded remains of a funeral wreath, and to keep from falling, he had leaned against a nearby tombstone. When he'd finally freed himself, he saw he was resting his butt on Geoffrey Chastain's monument.

Palmer stepped back and stared at the nondescript granite marker: Geoffrey Alan Chastain 1961–1989. There was no other information, sentiment, or religious symbol to be found on its chill face, except for a stonemason's mark at the bottom.

Palmer cursed himself, the self-deprecations rising from his lips in puffs of mist. What had he expected to find out here in the first place? The missing heiress's forwarding address chiseled into her dead lover's tombstone?

Then he saw the flowers. At first he thought they were part of the same wreath he'd originally tripped over, then he realized they were wrapped differently. He bent and lifted the bouquet from its resting place atop Chaz's grave. What he thought were long-dead flowers were relatively fresh roses the color of midnight. Palmer handled the bouquet gingerly, since the bundled stems were full of thorns.

Black roses. With the florist's name and telephone number stenciled onto the ribbon binding them together. Palmer smiled as he pulled the ribbon free, wincing as a thorn bit into the meat of his thumb.

He stared at the bead of blood—as shiny and red as a freshly polished ruby—for a long second before bringing it to his mouth. As he sucked, he glanced up and saw a gaunt young man dressed in a unseasonably light jacket watching him from a few yards away, a lit cigarette dangling from his lips. Palmer caught the odor of burning clove on the crisp morning breeze. When Palmer looked again, the man was gone, although the scent of his French cigarette still hung in the air.

Palmer was sure he'd seen the stranger's face before. Was it possible he was being followed? Pocketing the florist's ribbon, he turned and hurried back the way he'd come. He wondered where the man could have gone so quickly. He also wondered how the stranger could stand hanging around a graveyard on an overcast February morning in nothing warmer than a silk jacket. He stopped and turned to look back in the direction of Chaz's grave. He reached into his anorak and pulled out the snapshot that Pangloss had given him.

Impossible. He could feel the sweat trickling down his back. His scar tightened. It was the lack of sleep doing it to him. And the dreams. Even though it was a perfectly rational explanation, it didn't make him feel any better. He had to do something about the dreams before they drove him completely out of his mind. But not now. It would have to wait until after the case was out of the way.

"Yeah, that's ours, awright," said the florist, studying the length of faded yellow ribbon Palmer handed him.

"I was wondering if you might be able to help me find out who placed the order."

"Look, fella, we sell a *lot* of flowers . . ."

"Black roses?"

The florist pulled his bifocals down a fraction of an inch and squinted at Palmer. "Black roses, you say?"

Palmer nodded. He was on the trail, he knew it. He could feel the familiar, almost electrical, thrill of connections being made, invisible machinery dropping into gear. "A dozen of them. Delivered to the Rolling Lawns Cemetery."

The florist moved to a filing cabinet. "Deceased's name?"

"Chastain."

The florist grunted and pulled a manila folder from one of the drawers. "Yeah, I remember filling that order. Customers usually don't order roses for grave decorations. Mother's Day, St. Valentine's Day, anniversaries, birthdays, sure. And black roses, at that—specially this time of year."

"I take it they're expensive."

"You could say that." He tapped the order form. "Says here it was a phone order. Long distance. Paid for it with a credit card."

"Could I see?"

"I don't know . . . My partner wouldn't like me letting strangers look at our files."

"Uh, I understand. Say, how much for one of those thingies over there?" He pointed at a large floral display shaped like a horseshoe, GOOD LUCK spelled along its rim in white carnations.

"That runs around seventy-five, a hundred bucks, depending on where you want it delivered."

CARNIVAL

During a carnival men put on masks over their masks
—Xaiver Forneret

When Palmer informed Pangloss of his destination, the good doctor assured him Renfield would see to airline tickets and accommodations. Palmer knew that flights into New Orleans during Carnival were booked solid weeks in advance, not to mention the hotels, and mentioned it to his employer. Pangloss laughed and said there was nothing to worry about; he kept an apartment in the French Quarter, away from the serious tourist cruising areas, but still close to the action. He'd call the housekeeper and have the place aired out in anticipation of Palmer's arrival.

He arrived late Sunday evening. The city was swarming with drunken, raucous merrymakers. Still, he had not expected Renfield to answer the door.

"You're here," was all the pale man said in way of greeting, stepping back into the hallway to allow Palmer entrance.

"Doc didn't say anything about sending you to keep tabs on me."

If Renfield noticed the barb, he ignored it. He pointed to the staircase, curled inside the house like a chambered nautilus. "Your room is on the second floor. Third door to the right."

"I thought Doc said he only kept an apartment here."

Renfield shrugged. "In a way. He owns the entire building."

Palmer frowned at the stack of junk mail piled haphazardly on the antique sideboard inside the foyer. Most of it seemed to be addressed to "Occupant" or "Current Resident." Renfield cleared his throat and lead Palmer upstairs. As they made their way to the landing, Palmer could tell by the echoes that the downstairs was empty.

Palmer's quarters were quite spacious, consisting of a bed-sitter, a sizable bathroom complete with a cast-iron tub with lion's feet, and a kitchenette furnished with a stocked refrigerator and a microwave oven. There was also a wide-screen color TV, a video deck, a stereo system, and a wet bar. The apartment also came with two of the wrought iron balconies the city was famous for.

The bedroom balcony offered a view of the patio and what, a century and a half ago, had been the slaves' quarters. It was too dark for Palmer to see much, since the patio below was unlit, but a faint reek of vegetable decay rose from the garden beneath his window.

The balcony fronting the sitting room was better, as it overlooked the street, empty now except for the occasional passing mule buggy and cruising taxi. As he stood savoring his Shermans in the pleasant evening breeze, Palmer could hear Bourbon Street—its roar blurred and muted, but still distinct in the otherwise quiet neighborhood. Every now and again a drunken celebrant would shriek with laughter, the echoes losing themselves amongst the ancient buildings.

Palmer experienced a slight twinge of unreality, as if he was dreaming and aware of dreaming at the same time. When he had left for New Orleans that morning, there was still frost on the ground, and in certain alleys where the shadows rarely part, there were still hard crusts of snow and ice to be found. Now he was standing in his shirt sleeves, taking in the fragrant subtropical night air while listening to the sounds of Carnival.

He contemplated going out and joining the party, but jet lag claimed him instead. He fell asleep splayed across the massive four-poster, wisps of mosquito netting fluttering in the breeze from the open French windows.

He dreamed that he woke up. In his dream, he lay in bed for a few seconds, trying to place where he was and what he was doing there. When he remembered, he sat up, rubbing his eyes. It was still dark outside; a pale sliver of moonlight fell through the open windows. There was a table and chair near the foot of the bed. Palmer's dream-self was aware that someone—or something—was seated in the chair, watching him. At first he thought it was Loli—he could see enough to tell his visitor was female—and he instinctively put his hand to the scar over his heart. The puckered skin remained cool to the touch.

Whoever this dream-intruder was, at least it wasn't *her*.

Palmer wanted to stand up and walk toward the mysterious woman, but he couldn't move.

Who are you?

The dream-woman did not answer but instead got to her feet. She stood in deep shadow, fingering the length of netting draped across the footboard. A spear of moonlight struck her face, but all Palmer could see was his own perplexed frown, reflected in miniature.

Who are you?

The shadow-woman smiled, revealing teeth too white and sharp to belong in a human mouth. *That's funny, I was going to ask you the same thing.*

It was her. The one he'd traveled so far to find. Palmer had never seen her photo, much less heard her voice, but he was certain that the woman standing at the foot of his bed was Sonja Blue. Before he could ask her another question, her attention was drawn to the balcony.

Here? No, not here. But close. On its way.

She sprinted for the French windows. Palmer opened his mouth to shout a warning that they were two stories up, but nothing came out. He felt slightly embarrassed for trying to warn a dream about breaking its legs. When she reached the open windows, she seemed to expand and elongate at the same time, stretching like a spaceship achieving light-speed, then shot headfirst into the early morning sky.

Palmer was suddenly aware that he was cold and sweating and shaking like a malaria victim. His scar began to burn like a hot wire pressed against his chest.

Loli popped up from behind the footboard like a malignant jack-in-the-box, the .38 leveled at his heart.

"Surrr-prizzze!"

He was unable to control himself this time and woke screaming, his fingers clawing at the scar.

There was no listing for Indigo Imports in either the New Orleans Yellow or White Pages. Palmer hadn't expected one, but you never could tell. Still, if you wanted a credit card, you had to have a phone. It was a fact of life. It was probably an unlisted number, but there was always the chance she relied on a message service to relay her calls. And those *were* listed.

After three hours and eighty-six answering services, he called Telephones Answered, Inc. and asked to speak to the head of Indigo Imports.

"I'm sorry, sir, but this is her answering service. Would you like to leave a message?"

He had her. He fought to keep his voice from betraying his excitement. "Yes. Tell her William Palmer called. It's very important that she contact me. She can reach me at 465-9212," he said, reading the number off Pangloss's phone.

"Very, good, sir. I'll make sure she gets the message."

Palmer replaced the phone in its cradle. Sightseeing would have to wait.

The call came at six that evening. He'd fallen into a light drowse, helped by a couple of shots of expensive bourbon he'd found in the wet bar, and nearly fell off the couch attempting to answer the phone before the second ring.

"Hello?"

There was silence on the other end of the line, then a woman's voice. "Mr. Palmer?"

"This is Palmer."

"What do you want of me, Mr. Palmer?"

"I'm a private investigator, Ms. Blue. I was hired by your grandfather, Dr. Pangloss, to find you."

"You work for him?" There was both suspicion and curiosity in her voice.

"In a fashion. Let's say I owe him a favor. All I know is that I'm supposed to deliver a letter to you. Please, I'd like to arrange a meeting with you, if it's at all possible."

"You will be alone." It wasn't a question.

"Of course. You set the time and place; whatever you're comfortable with."

"Very well. Tuesday night at eleven. The Devil's Playground, on the corner of Decatur and Governor Nicholls."

The severed connection droned in his ear like an angry hornet. Palmer's hands were shaking, his shirt glued to his back. It was the same woman. The one from his dream. He'd recognized the voice. He blinked and massaged his brow with the flat of his palm. Christ, what was going *on?* Was it the acid he'd consumed back in the seventies? If so, it had picked one hell of a time to treat him to a flashback.

Still, so many things had changed since he'd awakened from the coma. Sometimes it felt as if he'd spent the past thirty-eight years stumbling around in a sleepwalker's daze and was only now fully awake. Other times it seemed as if he was on the verge of complete and utter mental collapse.

He'd never considered himself an ordinary schmuck, but before his "accident" he'd never experienced much in the way of nightmares. Not since he was a kid, anyway. He'd had some doozies back then. His parents had disapproved of his discussing the dreams, so he'd stopped.

His father insisted that talking about "things that ain't real and never will be" was pointless and only lead to confusion and, in some strange logic that only his parents seemed to grasp, insanity.

Whenever Palmer pressed the point, his father would threaten him with Uncle Willy.

"You keep fretting about stuff that ain't real, you're gonna end up just like

Uncle Willy! He was always worrying about the things he saw in his dreams. Where'd it get him? In the State Hospital, that's where! You're gonna end up sharing a cell with him if you don't lay off this shit!"

Palmer smiled wryly as he reached for the bourbon. *Better shove over, Uncle Willy. Look's like you're going to have company.*

✸

Palmer let the crowd push him along Bourbon Street. It was slow going and intensely claustrophobic, but in spite of the overcrowding, the noise, and the reek of curbside garbage, he was enjoying himself.

It was Mardi Gras and he'd spent the day wandering the narrow streets of the French Quarter, marveling at the costumes and sampling the various local alcoholic beverages. Carnival revelers on the balconies overhead tossed beads and other trinkets at the crowd below. Occasionally a drunken tourist would bare a tit or a backside, causing a brief firestorm of camera flashes from the photographers in the crowd and a shower of hurled plastic beads. The whole thing was silly, trivial, bawdy, and dumb. Palmer thought it was great.

He broke free of the press of body on body at the next intersection and headed toward Jackson Square to watch the costumers promenade past the Saint Louis Basilica. He was amused by a band of masquers dressed as frogs heckling the handful of extremist Fundamentalists protesting the merrymaking by handing out their own bogus religious tracts. Palmer was so impressed he offered to pay for some of their literature.

"Don't bother," the young man grinned from inside the gaping cloth mouth of a frog's head. "We just do it to piss these jerks off. In fact, more people offer *us* money than them, and that *really* gets their goat! They've been out here for the last few years, being a major pain in the butt. There's not nearly as many of them this time, though. I guess their funding got the triple whammy, what with the PTL scandal, ole Jimmy gettin' caught out on Airline Highway, and that weird Catherine Wheele cult-massacre last year. Thanks anyway, mister! Happy Mardi Gras! Remember: Frog Croaked For Your Sins!" The frog priest laughed, hopping after his departing flock.

"You weren't offering that man money, were you, sir?" Palmer looked down at the florid-faced woman in the "Christ Is The Answer Crusade" T-shirt. Her eyes were so over-magnified by her coke-bottle glasses they seemed to hover in front of her face. "They do the Devil's work, mocking the Lord's word and deed! They shall burn in hell on Judgment Day! Jesus loves you, even if you *are* a sinner! If you confess your sin now, and kneel with me and pray for deliverance of your soul, it may not be too late for you . . ."

Palmer shook his head, too overwhelmed by the woman's conviction and madness to say anything. It wasn't until he'd disentangled himself that he realized she'd slipped a tract into his pocket. The title dripped red ink like slime and read: *Are You Ready For The End-Times ?*

Judging from the crude illustration beneath the question, no one was: terrified "sinners" in tattered rags ran from flying insects the size of dachshunds; haggard derelicts tried to slake their thirst at drinking fountains gushing blood; a busty MTV-style Whore of Babylon lolled on the back of a seven-headed Beast, while in the background a 900-foot tall Jesus beamed beatifically at the hundreds of souls zipping skyward from a tangle of wrecked and abandoned cars on the interchange.

Disgusted, Palmer hurled the offending tract to the ground and hurried away in search of a beer.

He passed the next few hours drinking concoctions with so much grenadine in them the back of his throat puckered. Darkness came, and as if upon clandestine agreement, the families vanished from the area, leaving only the hard-core to bid farewell to the flesh.

A shrill, almost hysterical, sense of abandon tinged the masquers' celebrations. Drunken horseplay turned into open brawls. Palmer could not tell the difference between screams and laughter. The eyes of the revelers gleamed from behind their borrowed faces, as if compelled to cram as much as possible into the few hours remaining to them before returning to their real lives.

The *need* Palmer glimpsed in their bleary, unfocused stares was both repellent and fascinating. It was as if he was surrounded by thousands of empty people desperately trying to fill themselves. He was overwhelmed by an image of himself being attacked by the screaming, laughing, empty people, devouring his soul as easily as a lion cleans the marrow from a broken bone.

Gasping, he pushed past a group of masquers dressed as cockroaches and stumbled inside one of the all-hours tourist traps that lined the street. He leaned against a postcard rack and shivered like a drunk with the d.t.'s. There was still an hour to go before he could consider his job done. He'd better lay off the booze if he wanted to be in any condition to talk with the elusive Ms. Blue. Or if he meant to steer clear of the nuthouse, for that matter.

He could still remember the day the men in the white suits took Uncle Willy away, screaming at the top of his lungs about the worms crawling out of his skin. His father had been quite upset. People on TV didn't have members of their family carted away. At least not on *Leave It To Beaver* and *Father Knows Best*. It happened on the soaps his mom liked to watch all the time, though.

"You awright, mister?"

He jerked his head up and stared at the man behind the cash register.

The shopkeeper was the overall shape and size of a small foothill, dressed in khaki pants and a "I Saw the Pope" T-shirt. He chewed on an unlit cigar, eyeing Palmer warily.

"You ain't gonna be sick, are ya? If yer gonna puke, do it outside, fer th' love'a Gawd! I awready cleaned up after three people awready t'night! Jesus!"

"I'm okay, thanks. It was a just a little . . crowded . . . out there."

"Yeah, ain't that the truth! I'll be glad when ever'body goes home so's I can get some sleep. I—Hey, is that some friend of yours?" He pointed at the busy street on the other side of the glass.

Palmer spun around, the hairs on the back of his neck erect. A well-fed tourist couple stood and stared at a "life-like" plastic turd stapled to the brim of a synthetic baseball cap which bore the legend "Shithead."

"You mean *them?*"

"No, it was some guy in a suit. You know, dressed like them queers down at the art galleries. He was smokin' a cigarette and wavin' at ya, like he was tryin' t'getcher attention."

"It must have been a case of mistaken identity. I don't know anybody in town."

The shopkeeper grunted and returned to thumbing through his porno magazine. Tourists is tourists.

Palmer stared out into the street. He hadn't lied. He *didn't* know anybody in New Orleans. So why did he feel as if someone had just walked over his grave?

The Devil's Playground was a block off the historic French Market, and the odor of discarded produce was strong on the night wind, mixing with the ever-present reek of beer and urine that seemed to hang over the district during Carnival.

The bar's windows were covered by painted flames. A fiberglass statue of a grinning Mephistopheles, resplendent in his skin-tight red jumpsuit and neat goatee, stood next to the door. The grinning devil held aloft a pitchfork in his right hand, his left fist firmly planted on one hip; the Prince of Lies' jaunty demeanor was far more reminiscent of Errol Flynn as Robin Hood than Goethe's demon.

Palmer pushed his way inside, ignoring the looks from a couple of young men sheathed in black leather and chrome chains lounging near the door. The place was packed, the buzz of a half-hundred voices lost under the crash and thunder of over-amplified rock music. He scanned the cramped quarters for sign of his quarry. He made a try for the bar, brushing against a tall, heavyset woman.

The woman turned, smiling good-naturedly if drunkenly. Her face was heavily made up, chunky costume jewelry dripping from her fingers and ears.

"Hey there, handsome. You look lonesome." Her voice was husky, her breath redolent of whiskey. She reached up with one beringed hand and patted her hair.

"Oh, I'm looking for someone, actually."

The woman's smile grew wider. "Aren't we all, sugar?" She leaned closer and Palmer glimpsed a hint of five o'clock shadow under the makeup. She placed a large, knobby-knuckled hand on his sleeve. "Maybe I can help you find what you're looking for."

Palmer shrugged. "You might. I'm supposed to be meeting someone here. A woman."

The transvestite removed her hand from his arm. "I see." Interest drained from her voice as she returned her gaze to the mirror behind the bar, readjusting her wig.

"Maybe you know her. She lives somewhere around here. Her name's Sonja Blue."

The transvestite jerked her head in his direction so hard she unseated her wig. Palmer glimpsed thinning hair the color of wheat straw.

"The Blue woman? You're meeting the Blue woman? Here?!" All pretense of imitating a woman's voice ended. The transvestite stared at Palmer as if he'd just announced he had an armed nuclear device strapped to his back.

Palmer was suddenly aware that everyone else in the bar was staring at him. The music continued to thump and growl like a caged animal, but no one spoke. Palmer felt his armpits dampen.

"Get out! Get *out* of here! We've got enough trouble as it is without you bringing *her* here!" The bartender, a muscular fellow naked except for a leather jockstrap, a ram's horn headdress, and a tattoo of a rampant dragon on his chest, gestured angrily at the door.

"But—"

A dozen pairs of hands grabbed him, lifting him bodily over their heads. Palmer recalled how he used to stage-dive at the hard-core concerts, leaping onto the stage for a brief moment of stolen glamour before jumping back into the seething dance floor. He didn't try to fight them and allowed himself to be roughly passed over the heads of the bar's patrons and dumped, unceremoniously, back onto the street. He straightened his rumpled clothes as best he could, glancing back at the doorway. The two young men dressed in leather and chrome blocked the entrance.

"Fuck this shit." Palmer was in no position to take on two guys ten years his junior. Not if he wanted to keep what was left of his teeth. He shoved his hands in his pockets and stalked off around the corner.

He paused halfway down the block, lighting a cigarette with trembling hands.

"Palmer?"

He spun around so fast he burned himself with his lighter.

She was dressed in a pair of faded, much-worn blue jeans, a "Cramps 1990 Tour" T-shirt, a ragged leather jacket a size too big for her, scuffed engineer boots, and sunglasses. Even though he could not see her eyes, Palmer was aware of being watched.

"Sonja?"

"You are Pangloss's agent?"

He shrugged. "You could say that."

"Were you followed?"

"No.

Her lips twisted into something like a smile. "You seem sure of yourself."

"I'm good at what I do."

"No doubt. You spoke of a letter from my . . . grandfather."

Palmer reached into his jacket and withdrew the letter. "Funny, the Doc doesn't look old enough to have a granddaughter your age."

"He's very well preserved. It's a family trait. I'll take that letter now, if you don't mind." She extended a pale, narrow hand toward him.

Palmer handed over the sealed envelope, his fingers accidentally brushing against hers.

There was a sound like a flashcube going off in the back of his skull and his fingertips tingled. He saw Sonja Blue jerk her head as if she'd received a sudden electrical shock. The street disappeared and Palmer found himself in a strange room.

He saw a pool table surrounded by splintered pool cues, scattered cue balls . . . and broken boys. The smell of blood and fear was strong. The fear smell's primal intensity was erotic; the greatest aphrodisiac he'd ever known, and most of it radiated from the frightened boy clutched in his hands. The youth's hair was the color of a Maxfield Parrish sky, his face that of an errant choirboy. There were brief, blurred glimpses of rape, robbery, looting, each involving the same baby-faced miscreant. . . . An orgasm shuddered through Palmer's nervous system as a hot gush of thick, salty blood filled his mouth.

Sonja Blue jerked her hand away from his, growling like a mountain lion. She turned and ran, disappearing into the darkness before Palmer had a chance to reorient himself. He felt dizzy, as if he'd just stepped off the Tilt-A-Whirl at the State Fair. He could still taste the boy's blood. The thought made him moan, and bile burned the back of his throat. He didn't want to think about it. Not now, not ever. He especially didn't want to think about how he'd recognized the blue-haired boy's face as belonging to Jimmy Eichorn.

All he wanted to do was get back to the apartment, phone Pangloss, and tell him he'd fulfilled his part of the bargain. He'd collect his bonus and go somewhere nice and sunny. Mexico sounded good. He'd retire to Mexico and sell stuffed frogs playing mariachi instruments to the *turistas*. That sounded *real* good.

He started back toward Pangloss's house. It was almost midnight and Bourbon street was jammed with party-goers determined to wring the few remaining minutes of pleasure out of Carnival. The noise and excitement was almost enough to make him forget what had just happened.

At first he thought the tugging on his sleeve was the wind. Then it spoke his name.

Palmer turned and stared into the pale, smiling face of a man in his late twenties, dressed in an expensive, loose-fitting suit. The stranger lifted a smoldering French cigarette to his thin lips, his eyes strangely sunken in the fluorescent and neon glare from a nearby live-sex show sign.

There was something familiar about his arrogant, smirking features—then Palmer recognized him.

He took an involuntary step backward, his scalp tightening as his heart began to race. The street noise faded into an indistinct rumble, as if he was under water. He prayed he wasn't having a stroke, although that would at least explain the things happening to him.

"You're *dead*!" It sounded like an accusation.

Geoffrey Chastain, known to friends and enemies as Chaz, shrugged. "Is that a crime? I've been tryin' to get yer bleedin' attention all bloody night! Coo! Yer a dense bugger!"

Palmer noticed that parts of Chaz were semitransparent. The dead man drew another lung full of smoke from his phantom cigarette, causing his midsection to swirl. Palmer wondered if he'd still be toking on his beloved Shermans a year after his own death.

"Look, there's not much time left. Mardi Gras night's one of th' few times th' friggin' spirits of th' dead can corporalize 'n mingle with th' livin'. As it 'tis, it's damn near Ash Wednesday. I know we dead men ain't supposed to be tellin' tales, but I was ne'er one for th' rules. So take some advice from one who knows, eh? Get th' hell outta town while yer able. Fuck gettin' yer money from Pangloss. Just get on th' next bleedin' bus outta town and don't look back! Fergit y' ever laid eyes on her!"

"Who—?"

"Who th' bloody fuck y' think I mean? Sonja soddin' Blue! The Bloofer

Lady herself! She's death, boyo! Death on two legs! Pure 'n simple. Not that she can help it, mind you. It's just her way. But knowin' that won't help you none when the time comes. An' it will. Look, mate—I was a real pisser when I was like you. Alive, that is. Bein' dead's changed how I see things. It innit pretty, lookin' back an' seein' meself for th' bastard I was. But it ain't bad, really. Actually, I prefer it to how things was when I was flesh 'n blood. So mebbe how she did me weren't so bad. Mebbe."

Palmer's stomach knotted tighter. "Are you saying she—"

"Snuffed me? Aye, that she did. Ain't you th' bright student? She killed me, awright. Just like she did th' lads with th' blue hair. She was feelin' her oats that night. Not that I should blame her for it—but I still do. I guess I haven't been knackered long enough t' forgive her fer that. But I don't hate th' lass, if that's what yer gettin' at. Like I said, bein' dead changed how I look at things. I used t' think I hated her, back when I was alive. Now I see that I loved her, that was me problem. Me! *Lovin'* someone! It scared me so bad I got to hatin' her fer it. That's why I did her th' way I did. That's why she did *me* th' way she did. Love. Funny how death makes things so much clearer, innit?"

"Then why are you warning me, if you're so ambivalent?" Palmer's fear had abated in the face of this mundane, chain-smoking specter. He was starting to feel more aggravated than frightened.

"Shall we say you 'n me, we're kindred spirits?" Chaz's smirk widened. "That bullet did more'n punch a hole in yer skin, ducks. It woke up somethin'. Jump-started it, as it were. Yer what they call a 'sensitive.' How else y'fancy ol' Pangloss found you, eh? You might have been unconscious th' whole time you was in hospital, but part of you was broadcastin' like a bloody short-wave radio! They like usin' sensitives like you—an' me. We make handy servants, don't you know? So far you've only had a taste of what it's like—'avin' th' world turn itself inside-out like a bloomin' magician's sack, an' you bein' th' only one noticin'. But get used t' it, mate. Yer'll ne'er get t' like it, but yer'll get *used* t'it, if it don't drive you mad first. Like it did me mum. An' yer Uncle Willy."

"Wait a second! What do you *mean?*"

"Sorry, luv. Seems me time's run out." The bell in the basilica's tower rang, marking the transition from excess to penance. Chaz grinned as he stepped into the street.

"What do you mean? Who are *they*?"

Second stroke. Third stroke.

The ghost laughed and shook his insubstantial head. "Yer not goin' t' leave it be, are you? Yer in love with her already! You don't even know it, yet, but I can see it in th' folds of yer brain, mate!"

Fourth stroke. Fifth stroke.

"Why are you telling me these things? *Why?*"

"Because y'put flowers on me grave, *that's* why! Th'dead are a sentimental lot."

Sixth stroke. Seventh stroke.

Halfway up the block uniformed policemen appeared astride horses, riding four abreast, bullhorns held in their hands. Behind them Palmer glimpsed the huge street-sweeping machines, brushes spinning in anticipation of flushing the gutters clean of accumulated filth, human and otherwise.

Eighth stroke. Ninth stroke.

Chaz shimmered with every toll of the bell, like a reflection in a bestirred pool. Palmer tried to push past the throng of revelers, desperate to win one last answer from the smiling ghost.

"MARDI GRAS IS OVER! EVERYONE GO HOME!" bellowed the police as they moved forward, forcing the people milling in the street either onto the sidewalks or into the bars.

"MARDI GRAS IS OVER! EVERYONE GO HOME!"

The sanitation trucks blasted their horns to punctuate the mounted officers' commandment.

Tenth stroke. Eleventh stroke.

A huge, heavy hand closed on Palmer's shoulder, pinning him so he could not move. He looked up and stared into the brutish features of the man he'd seen skulking in Pangloss's shrubbery.

"Renfield say come now."

"MARDI GRAS IS OVER!"

Twelfth stroke. Midnight arrived, ushering in Lent.

Chaz wavered like a hologram projected onto smoke. Palmer watched as one of New Orleans' finest rode through the dead man. He expected the horse, at least, to react to the ghost, but all it did was flare its nostrils, toss its mane, and leave a pile of dung in its wake.

"Renfield say you come *now*."

The gorilla tightened his grip on Palmer, causing him to cry out in pain. This made the gorilla smile; something Palmer definitely wished he hadn't seen.

He had a funny feeling he was soon going to find out exactly who "*they*" were.

Sonja Blue watched as the police and sanitation workers brought Carnival to an end. She knew that the hard-core partying would continue well until dawn, but from now on it would have to be indoors, not on the streets. The harlequin's mask had been exchanged for the sackcloth of the penitent. She lifted her gaze from the streets, watching the spirits of the dead spiral upward like bats leaving a cave. Neither variety of tourist would be staying to take communion.

She frowned and pulled the envelope from her pocket, turning it over and over as if by handling it she could divine its contents. Pangloss. Had it been a decade since they last met? Like most Pretenders, her time sense was distorted. It was becoming more and more difficult for her to distinguish months from years.

She ran her fingers over the wax seal, her mood darkening as she recalled Pangloss's treachery below the streets of Rome.

The seal cracked easily, falling in three separate pieces at her feet. The letter was on expensive stationery that felt like silk and smelled of cologne. The penmanship was exquisitely baroque. No doubt the good doctor favored an old-fashioned quill pen.

My Dear,

Please forgive the method in which this letter was delivered. I have attempted to contact you on numerous occasions, through various menials, but you are a difficult woman to communicate with. I do not hold such rash disposal of my minions against you. In many ways, I find your gift for carnage reassuring. It has been far too long since we last spoke, and I fear that the conditions of our previous meeting may have influenced you to view me in an unfavorable light. I have followed your antics with great interest since we last met. I must admit I found your handling of the Catherine Wheele situation gauche but effective. You have a natural talent for atrocity, my dear. It needs refining, but I believe you have it in you to produce a tableau on the level of Baron Luxor's Jonestown, Lord Marudes' Stockton Elementary School Massacre, or even Marchessa Nuit's classic McDonald's McMassacre! But I am not writing simply to compliment your style. There is much I must tell you, my dear, and it concerns one who I know you are interested in. I speak of your maker and my former student, Lord Mauride's Stocton Elementary School Slaughter, or even Morgan. You can contact me through the human, Palmer.

Sonja looked at her left hand. The hand the private investigator had touched. She hadn't recognized the human as a sensitive at first—it was obvious he was unaware of his own talent—so she'd been unshielded. She'd received a barrage of sensory images, the most vivid being that of a scarlet-clad nymph with a smoking gun, before breaking contact. The exchange had been unexpected and unwelcome, but she had gleaned enough information from the jumble to discern that William Palmer was exactly what he thought he was: a free agent.

She knew where Palmer was staying—she made it a point to be familiar with the city's nests—and wondered if it was time for her to get in touch with the "family."

Renfield sat in an antique chair, his pallid bureaucrat's features breaking into something like a smile at the sight of Palmer in the company of the gorilla.

"Excellent. I assume you fulfilled your part of the bargain, Mr. Palmer. You did succeed in delivering the letter?"

"Yeah, I delivered your fucking letter! What the hell are you trying to pull, Renfield?" Palmer tried to jerk free of the gorilla and heard the seams in his jacket tear.

"Pull?" Renfield smiled again. Palmer wished he'd stop. "Mr. Palmer, if you continue struggling, I'll have Keif pull your right arm off and beat you with it."

Palmer didn't doubt Keif could do it and ceased trying to break free. He glanced around the room—empty except for the chair and Renfield—and wondered if the louvered shutters were nailed shut. If they weren't, he might stand a chance of escape, providing his guard let go of his shoulder, and he didn't break every bone in his body jumping from the third-floor balcony onto the patio below.

"I wouldn't recommend trying such heroics, Mr. Palmer," Renfield said, smiling and crossing and recrossing his legs like a bored personnel manager at a job interview. "The shutters are, indeed, nailed in place. Oh, don't look so surprised! Of course I can read your mind, such as it is. It's an open book—

although short story would better describe it. You may let go of him, Keif." The vise clamping Palmer's shoulder disappeared. "I can handle our friend from here on. Go and watch the door."

Keif grunted, pausing on the threshold to give Palmer a final, hungry look.

"Go on! Go on! Do as I say!" snapped Renfield, waving at the goon as if shooing a bothersome child out of the kitchen. "You'll get your share, as always!"

Palmer swung toward Renfield, fists balled. "Look here, you mealy-mouthed bastard! What the hell do you think you're doing? If I don't get some answers I'm gonna—"

"You're going to die, Mr. Palmer."

Fire coursed through Palmer's veins, turning his blood to slag. His intestines boiled in their own juices as his bones powdered into ash. His eyeballs exploded and dribbled down his cheeks like egg yolks. He tried to scream, but his lungs were full of burning water.

The fire disappeared as quickly as it descended. Palmer lay on the bare floor, knees drawn up under his chin. He could taste blood in his mouth. Had he bitten his tongue?

"Wha—What did you do to—?"

"You died, Mr. Palmer. And you will continue to die until I decide otherwise. Honestly, I can't understand what it is the Doctor sees in you. True, you have *some* talent," he sniffed, "but all this other mental and emotional baggage—empathy, sympathy, the ability to love—it's simply not worth the effort of deprogramming!"

Cold shot through Palmer, spearing his nervous system with a million icicles. His lungs filled with ice crystals and his urine turned to slush in his bladder. He whimpered as his toes and fingers turned black and fell off.

"I have no intention of letting you survive this little ordeal." Renfield was back, only this time his head was wreathed in a strange glow the color of a fresh bruise. Funny how Palmer hadn't noticed that before. "I've worked too long to allow some upstart to turn the Doctor against me!" Renfield's wan features were flushed now. He was drunk on emotions long held in check, his eyes bright and feral as a starved coyote's.

Renfield abandoned his chair, dropping to his knees beside Palmer. "You think I don't notice how he favors you? How he looks at you? He promised me power and life eternal! He said he loved me! *Needed* me! *Me*, not you!" There were tears in the other man's eyes. "He lied to me! But he won't have you. I won't let you take my place! I'll tell him you couldn't handle the deprogramming—it won't be a lie, really—and I gave you to the ogre for disposal. No one will know! Not even the Doctor!"

The louvered shutters shattered inward as Sonja Blue made her entrance, leather-clad arms lifted to shield her face. She hit the bare floor and rolled, distracting Renfield away from his victim.

Palmer felt the numbness in his limbs vanish as Renfield faced the intruder. The reverse-negative halo surrounding his head pulsed, snapping a whip-like tendril in Sonja Blue's direction.

Sonja made a motion with her left hand, as if flicking away a worrisome insect. "You'll have to do better than that!" She laughed.

Renfield looked confused, then frightened. "Keif! Get in here! Keif!"

Palmer got to his feet, surprised to find the recent agonies he'd undergone had left his flesh unscathed. He could hear the gorilla fumbling with the lock. Sonja grabbed Renfield by his lapels, pulling him so close they were literally nose-to-nose. A spiky crown of reddish-black light seemed to radiate from the woman's head, flickering in and out of Palmer's vision like a defective neon sign.

"Where's Pangloss?"

"Do you honestly think I'd tell *you?*" Renfield sneered.

"You've got a point." She let go of his jacket. Renfield smiled hesitantly, straightening his lapels. She moved so fast Palmer almost didn't see it; grabbing Renfield's chin and forcing his head up and back at an unnatural angle. The door banged inward, sagging on its hinges. Keif had grown frustrated with opening the door.

The gorilla squeezed through the doorway, his piggy little eyes moving from Palmer to Sonja before settling on Renfield's corpse. Sonja stepped forward, motioning for Palmer to get behind her. He saw she held an open switchblade in one hand.

"Jesus Christ, woman, there's no way you can go up against that goon—"

She waved him silent, never taking her eyes off the hulking figure filling the doorway. "Keep quiet! I know what I'm doing!"

Keif rumbled deep in his throat and stepped forward, sniffing the air like a hunting dog. Keif glanced at them suspiciously, his nostrils flaring, but did not offer to attack. His attention was fixed on Renfield's carcass. Saliva dripped from his lower lip in thick ropes. Keif emitted a loud sniffing sound, like that of a hog at a trough, and pounced on the corpse. Palmer heard fabric rip as the giant tore at the dead man's clothes.

Sonja motioned Palmer toward the door. She moved to follow, never taking her eyes off the drooling goon.

"What's he *doing?*" Palmer hissed.

"You don't want to know. Let's get out of here while he's preoccupied. Ogres aren't very bright to begin with, and when they're hungry they tend to let their bellies override their brains. We're lucky this one hadn't had dinner yet."

Palmer sat on the penthouse patio, a glass of bourbon in his hand, while everything he'd assumed was real disintegrated.

Palmer prided himself on his ability to adapt to adverse conditions. He'd learned how to cope when his family kicked him out of the house at the age of seventeen. He'd survived three hellish months on an Alabama work gang, back when having long hair was a criminal offense. He'd watched friends unwilling to admit they were no longer as young and invulnerable as they used to be succumb to overdoses and disease. There was no percentage in denying change. Evolve Or Die. He should have it tattooed on his forehead.

He took another swallow of his drink, glancing over the rim at his savior. She sat on the edge of the parapet, scanning the surrounding rooftops. Palmer was uncertain as to whether he trusted the mirror-eyed woman, but did not see he had any choice.

"Is Pangloss really your grandfather?"

She shrugged but did not turn to face him. "Some would say so. But if you mean is he my *biological* grandfather, no, he is not."

"I didn't think so. He's nowhere near old enough to have a grandchild your age."

"Pangloss is at least fifteen hundred years old, Mr. Palmer."

"So I'm lousy at guessing ages."

"You seem rather . . . calm . . . considering what's just happened."

"After talking to the dead, discovering I possess psychic powers, and being brain-raped by a crazed telepath, being told my employer is a vampire is rather anticlimatic."

Sonja glanced at him. "You spoke with the dead?"

"Actually, it was more the other way around. It was your old boyfriend."

"Chaz?"

He nodded, watching her face for a reaction. If the news affected her in any way, it did not show.

"And what did he have to say?"

"That I should avoid you like the plague and get the hell out of Dodge."

"Death has given him some smarts."

"He said you killed him."

"The dead don't lie. But they don't speak the truth, either. Yes, I killed him. Does it matter?"

"It did to him."

"Chaz was my . . . partner. He was like you—a sensitive. He was a small-time hustler when I met him. We clicked. It was good—for a while. Then there was trouble. Chaz ended up selling me out. He betrayed me with a kiss. He always did have a flair for irony. I spent six months in a madhouse because of him. I do not expect loyalty from humans, but I do not countenance treachery. His death was not just, but it was fair. I have been a murderer for a very long time, Mr. Palmer. Killing is a habit of mine. It is only proper that I tell you this."

"There was a boy . . ." He felt his throat tighten at the taste of Jimmy Eichorn's blood, but continued anyway. "A boy with blue hair you did something to."

"The Blue Monkeys? Yes, I remember. I take it the boy is still alive?"

"If you want to call it that."

She shrugged. "He possessed information. And I was in need of . . . well, let us say I was in need and leave it at that."

"He was only fifteen—"

"—and already guilty of gang rape, hit-and-run driving, and second-degree murder. Do not waste your sympathy on him, Mr. Palmer. Like I said: what I do is not just, but it *is* fair."

Sonja Blue showed Palmer to a small attic room. A narrow bed was placed where the slope of the roof met the wall.

"It's not much. Then again, I normally don't entertain guests. You'll be safe here. It's another four hours until dawn. I'll be outside guarding the door. Once the sun comes up you shouldn't have to worry about Pangloss's pet ogre."

"*Ogre?*"

"What do you think the lunk chowing down on dear departed Renfield was? The tooth fairy? They're big and dumb and have some seriously nasty habits, as you might have guessed, but they're pretty much helpless without a handler. Left to themselves, they'll spend their time eating children and wandering around raping and looting villages. They could get away with shit like that back during the Dark Ages, but it tends to attract notice nowadays. So most of them end up signing on as muscle with various vampire or *vargr* bigshots. That way their employers can dispose of the empties without calling too much attention to themselves. That's what Renfield had planned for you, if you haven't figured it out by now."

"But *why* did he do what he did?"

A flicker of sympathy softened her features. "There's no shame in admitting what happened to you. Renfield may not have not raped you physically, but the result was the same."

"Yeah, well—" Palmer looked away. He did not know what to say. He doubted he ever would.

"As to *why* Renfield hurt you—he was trying to twist you."

"Come again?"

"In order for you to be of any use to Pangloss, or any vampire, for that matter, he has to make sure you're twisted to suit his needs. That involves a complete and utter destruction of superego and restructuring of the ego. The sensitive's needs and desires must revolve around his master. He must be willing to live—and die—for his master. Sometimes this emotional dependence is reinforced with drugs, or sex. Inclinations to evil are fostered while any vestige of human emotion, except those required by the master, are systematically destroyed. While this may take some time, the initial programming is usually done within a matter of minutes, assuming the attacker is a skilled psionic. If the programming is pushed too hard, too fast, death occurs.

"Obviously, Renfield had orders to twist you, to add you to Pangloss's stable, so to speak. But he was jealous and rebelled. You're lucky he wanted to kill you, or you'd be Pangloss's slave right now."

"Yeah. Lucky."

Sonja Blue squatted on her haunches, listening to Palmer's breathing with half an ear. She doubted the ogre had the brains to come looking for them, but she'd learned the hard way never to underestimate the good doctor. She plucked Pangloss's letter from inside her jacket, flattening the paper against the attic floorboards.

There is much I must tell you, my dear, and it concerns one whom I know you are interested in.

Morgan.

Her hands balled themselves into tight fists and she exhaled a nervous, shaky breath. She had spent the better part of twenty years—her entire unlife—searching for the vampire that had raped a teenaged girl, tainted her blood, and turned her into something that called itself Sonja Blue. Now Pangloss, the vampire responsible for Morgan's own creation, was tempting her with information concerning his whereabouts. It wasn't the first time he'd tried it. The last time had been under the streets of Rome, in a catacomb held sacred to the shadow races that manipulated mankind. She had been too proud to agree to Pangloss's "business proposition." She was lucky to have escaped.

What was Pangloss planning this time? It was not in his nature to volunteer information. He wanted—or needed—something from her, that much was certain.

You can contact me through the human, Palmer.

It was obvious that Pangloss meant to lure her closer by using the human investigator, then putting him into thrall once his usefulness was at an end. Pangloss was astute enough to realize she would never allow a twisted sensitive or a Pretender within sniffing distance and allow it to live to tell about it. So what was she to do with Palmer? Part of her, that which she thought of as the Other, *knew* what it wanted to do with him, but she refused to listen to its counsel.

✷

Palmer moaned in his sleep, shifting uneasily on the narrow bed. Renfield's pasty face, as wide and pale as the moon, filled his dreams. The dead man's eyes were as flat and black as buttons, his lips thin and blue. Palmer could hear Renfield's voice even though the satellite-sized face's mouth remained caught in a rictus grin.

Like me. Like me. She's going to make you like me. Lap dog. Lap dog. Lap, dog, lap!

Palmer sat up suddenly, the sweat running into his eyes. His mouth was dry, his head aching as if the lobes of his brain were dividing like amoebas. He stared at the circular window set near the peak of the roof. He got up and swiveled the window open on its pivot, inhaling a deep breath of Mississippi River-saturated air. Somewhere on the river, a barge sounded a long, mournful note.

"Will-yummmm?"

No. It couldn't be. He leaned his forehead against the windowsill, trying to find some comfort in the peeling paint pressing against his skin. He was awake. He *knew* it.

"William? Why won't you look at me, baby? Aren't you glad to see me, honey?"

Palmer bit his lip as the familiar burning tore at his chest. His scar throbbed and pulsed as if he'd been branded with a red-hot coat hanger. He wouldn't look at her. She wasn't real. She was a dream. He was awake. He opened his eyes, scanning the world outside the window for proof.

New Orleans was on fire.

The city was wrapped in sheets of flame, yet no one seemed to notice. Burning children ran up and down the streets, smoke and laughter billowing from their lobster-red mouths. Women dressed in crackling aprons swept their stoops clean of ash. Business executives dressed in smoldering Brooks Brothers suits paused to check the melted slag strapped to their wrists before hurrying on their way, smoking attaché cases clenched in their roasted hands. On the balcony opposite Palmer's window two lovers embraced, oblivious to the blisters rising on their naked flesh, while the wrought iron bower softened and dripped like licorice left in the sun.

The pain spasmed through his chest, forcing an involuntary cry from his lips. There was no use in denying her. She was going to have her way, no matter how hard he tried to stop her. Groaning, Palmer turned to face Loli.

The smell of the *marui* started Sonja from her brooding. She'd scented it before, but had been uncertain then as to its intentions. The reek of ectoplasm was strong. Then she heard Palmer's stifled cry.

She kicked the door open, growling at the sight of the ill-formed creature crouched atop the sleeping man, its claws buried in his chest. The *marui* screeched in alarm and spread its membranous wings. Her fingers closed on its slippery flanks and the creature's high-pitched squealing became ultrasonic.

"Holy shit!"

Palmer was awake, staring in confusion at the combatants wrestling beside his bed.

"Don't just sit there gawking! Help me!"

"How?"

"Grab its neck!"

Palmer took one look at the *marui's* barbed teeth and shook his head. "Like hell I will!"

"Just *do* it, damn you!"

Palmer grimaced as his hands closed on the *marui's* telescoped neck. Its flesh was chill and rubbery, as if the wildly struggling beast was composed of phlegm. With its biting end under control, Sonja was able to pin the creature to the floor.

"What in the name of hell is this thing?"

"This, Mr. Palmer, is your nightmare."

The beast, weakened by the scuffle, no longer tried to escape. It lay crumpled like a damaged kite, mewling to itself. Palmer stared at the *marui's* twisted, almost human musculature and tattered, bat-like wings. The nightmare creature's neck looked like a loop of umbilical cord; its bald, old man's head dominated by large, fox-like ears and bristling barbed teeth. Just looking at the thing made his scar tighten.

"They're called *marui*," she explained, resting her foot on the brute's neck. "They're also called night-elves, *maere*, and *le rudge-pula*, depending on the part of the world you happen to be in. They batten onto sleepers, manipulating dreams in order to feed on the fear and anxiety born of nightmares. Judging by its size, this one's been feasting on you for some time. They only take on corporeal form while they feed."

"You mean this thing's a nightmare?"

"Bad dreams exist for their own reasons; *marui* simply benefit from the negative energy released by nightmares. But they're not what you'd call smart." She applied pressure on the *marui's* neck, smiling as it wailed in distress. "My guess is that Pangloss sicced this little darling on you, hoping to make Renfield's job easier when the time came. Isn't that so, Rover?" She applied more pressure to the *marui's* throat. The creature squealed.

"Will-yummm, help meee."

Palmer brought his heel down on the *marui's* skull, grinding it into a sticky paste. The *marui* shuddered once and began to dissolve, the ectoplasm evaporating like dry ice.

✷

"I trust you slept well."

Palmer put down his mug of chicory coffee and turned to stare at the vampire standing in the kitchen door. She was dressed in a green silk kimono embroidered with tiny butterflies the color of smoke. Her hair was hidden by a clean white towel piled atop her head turban-style. She was still wearing mirrored sunglasses. It had never occurred to Palmer that the undead took showers.

"Never slept better." It was the truth. For the first time in weeks, Palmer's sleep was free of the recurring nightmares. When he awoke late that afternoon, he felt genuinely refreshed and rejuvenated.

"I trust you kept yourself entertained while I was . . . indisposed." Sonja opened the refrigerator and removed one of the bottles of dark red liquid. Palmer had stumbled across them earlier and guessed their significance. "I'm afraid I don't have much in the way of houseguests." She cracked the seal and brought the bottle to her lips, then caught sight of Palmer's face. "Oh,

I'm sorry—I've forgotten my manners." She put the blood aside, apologetically.

"There's nothing you have to apologize for. After all, it's your house. I'm just a guest. I have no right to judge."

Sonja tilted her head to one side, regarding him with her one-way gaze. "You're quite adaptable . . . for a human."

Palmer coughed into his fist. "There's something I need to say. Look, it's pretty obvious that I'm at something of a disadvantage right now. Discovering everything I've ever known is wrong is unnerving enough, but to also find out everything I've ever been paranoid about is true. . . ." He spread his hands in an expressive shrug. "I need help. Big time."

"So?"

"Well, I'd like to make a business proposition. Call it a modest proposal. I need help with this ham radio set in my skull, right? You need help with Pangloss, right? How about we team up—just for a little while? You could teach me how to use what I got, and I could . . . do whatever it is you need me to do."

"Mr. Palmer, do you have any idea what you're getting yourself into?"

"No. I'll admit that up front. But I know that if I don't get help, I'm going to go mad. I can't handle walking around with other people's thoughts and fears and craziness going through my head." He could feel his hands tremble as he spoke, but he refused to look at them. "Look, I can't lie to you. You scare me, lady. But it's like my Uncle Willy used to say; better the devil you know."

When she laughed he saw her fangs. Even though he knew it was going to be okay, it still frightened him.

Compared to the day before, the French Quarter was practically deserted. Bourbon Street was open for business, as usual, but the barkers were, for once, uninterested in luring the handful of tourists wandering the neon and garbage-strewn strip into their dens of iniquity.

Local merchants swept the remaining debris of plastic cups and busted liquor bottles outside their shops into the gutter with powerful pistol-grip hoses. The overall mood was a mixture of exhaustion and relief, as if the city was recovering from a malaria attack.

Palmer trailed after his new employer, trying to ignore the stares that followed them down the narrow streets. Sonja Blue moved swiftly and purposefully through the clustered shadows, her hands jammed into the pockets of her leather jacket. She seemed preoccupied, but Palmer had no doubt that she was very much aware of the looks aimed at her.

The fear and loathing that radiated from the hustlers, pushers, and other Quarter habitués was strong enough to make Palmer's skin crawl. It felt as if someone had liberated an ant farm in his underwear. He ran through the mental exercises for blocking ambient emotions Sonja had taught him before they left the house that evening, and the horde of invisible ants disappeared.

"It appears you're not well-liked around here."

She shot him a glance over her shoulder. "Get used to it. Most humans have an instinctual dislike of Pretenders—and sensitives, for that matter."

Palmer recalled his own immediate, gut-level reaction to Renfield and winced.

"You've used that word before: Pretenders. What does it mean?"

"Ever read Lovecraft?"

"Back in high school. Why?"

"Remember that stuff about Cthulhu, the Elder Gods and the Old Ones? How mankind is only a recent development, as far as the earth is concerned, and that hideous giant outer space monsters used to rule the world back before the dinosaurs, and how giant ugly nameless horrors are just sitting around on their tentacles, waiting for when the time is ripe to take over the world?"

"Yeah."

"Well, it's kind of like that."

"I don't think I want to know any more."

"Too late for that. But showing's easier than telling. I can *tell* you anything I want. Whether it's true or not—well, that's up to you to decide. But when you *see* something, can actually smell its breath and body odor, well, that's a different thing entirely. Humans call it witnessing."

"Where are we going?" Palmer was starting to feel itchy again, but it had nothing to do with telepathic intrusion.

"Do you believe in hell?"

Palmer blinked, taken aback by the change in subject matter. "If you mean the Christian hell, where people are tortured by guys with pitchforks and pointy ears—no, I don't believe in that."

"Me neither. But I *do* believe in demons. And that's where we're going: to make a deal with a devil."

"You mean Satan?"

"Are you kidding? He's way too expensive. Doesn't deal for anything less than souls. No, the guy I go to is reasonably priced."

Palmer decided it might be better if he stopped asking questions.

The Monastery was a small, dark bar that had, in a fit of perversity, decided on an ecclesiastical decor. The booths lining the wall had once been pews; fragments of stained glass, salvaged from various desanctified churches, had been soldered together to create a disjointed jigsaw collage on display in the skylight. Plaster saints and icons in varying states of decay were scattered about; a Black Madonna and Child, whether darkened by exposure to too many votive candles or Vatican II's attempt at "modernizing" its appeal, stared at the Monastery's denizen's with flat, robin's egg-blue eyes from its perch over the liquor supply. A battered Rockola jukebox played scratchy Rolling Stones records.

With its cheap prices, slovenly service and haphazard attitude toward hygiene, it was obvious that the Monastery did not cater to the hordes of Visa-packing tourists the Quarter thrived on. A prostitute sat at the bar, sipping a sloe gin fizz while the bartender cleaned a highball glass with a grimy rag. Both watched Palmer and Sonja Blue intently as they entered.

"What if the guy you're looking for isn't here?" Palmer whispered hopefully.

"He's here, all right. He's *always* here."

Sonja's connection was seated in the back booth, where the shadows were the deepest. Sonja's lips curled into a thin, cold smile. "Hello, Malfeis."

The demon returned her smile, licking his lips with a forked tongue. "Ah, Sonja! Please, call me Mal! There is no need to stand on formalities."

Palmer frowned. Whatever he'd been expecting, it definitely wasn't been a teenaged boy dressed in faded denims and a "Surf or Die" T-shirt. A skateboard, its belly painted to depict an eyeball wreathed in Day-Glo flames, leaned against the converted pew.

"Kid, are you old enough to be in this place?"

Malfeis lifted an upswept eyebrow in amusement. "Who's the renfield, Sonja?"

"My name's *not* Renfield." Palmer fought the urge to grab the snot-nosed little skatepunk by his rat-tail. "What'd you mean by that?"

Sonja waved Palmer silent. "I'll explain later. After I get through with business. Wait for me at the bar."

"But—"

"I *said* wait at the bar." Her voice was as hard and cold as steel, and as unyielding. She waited until Palmer left before sliding into the booth.

"Quite a change from the last time, Mal." Six months ago Malfeis had worn the body of a young black male wreathed in coils of gold chain.

The demon shrugged, smiling slyly. "I like to keep up to date. I've always been something of a fashion plate. So, what brings you back into my clutches, sweet thing?"

"I think you know that already."

"Do I?"

"Don't play cute with me, Mal. I don't have the time or the patience right now. I need to know what Pangloss has up his sleeve." She pulled the letter Palmer had delivered to her out of her jacket, sliding it across the table.

Mal tapped the folded paper with an overly long fingernail and grunted. "Easy enough. What's in it for me?"

Sonja produced a black ceramic vessel the size of an unguent jar from her pocket and held it up so the demon could get a good look.

"Got it in from Kathmandu just last week. The powdered skull of a man who killed six Tibetan holy men, then murdered and raped three missionaries. It's good shit, man, as pure as you'll find it."

Mal's cat-like eyes seemed to fill with a strange fire. His fingers drummed nervously against the table top. "Gimme a taste."

Sonja carefully unscrewed the lid and dispensed a pinch of a fine, chalky yellow powder into Mal's outstretched palm. The demon daubed a forefinger in the pulverized skull and popped it his mouth.

"So? What's the verdict?"

Mal nodded, appreciatively. "Yow! Mama, buy me some of that!"

"Deal?"

"Done."

Sonja pushed the jar over to Malfeis's side of the table. The demon brought out a gold-plated razor blade and a flat piece of volcanic glass, quickly arranging himself a generous line of powdered skull. Oblivious to his surroundings, Malfeis lowered his head to the table and inhaled the line with both nostrils, snuffling like a bloodhound. He jerked his head up when he was finished, blowing out his cheeks and shaking himself like a winded stallion. His eyes were too big and the pupils slitted unnaturally, but otherwise he still looked human.

"Cold-blooded! True righteous shit!" He grinned, showing a mouthful of shark teeth.

"Glad it meets your approval. Now, about Pangloss . . ."

"No problem!" Mal picked up the letter and tapped one edge between his eyebrows. His eyes rolled up in their sockets, exposing green-tinged whites. A strange, basso profundo gargle rumbled from deep inside his narrow, hairless chest, but no one in the bar seemed to notice. After a second or two Mal reconnected, his eyes dropping back down like the symbols on a slot machine.

"There's not much available information concerning Pangloss, outside of his recent attempts to make contact with you. That much seems up front. There does seem to be a bit of a buzz concerning Morgan, though."

"Really? Were you able to find out what?"

"Sorry, that requires First Hierarchy clearance. I don't have the necessary power to access that information for you, at least not in detail. I *can* tell that whatever it is Morgan is doing, it's generating a great deal of speculation amongst the First and Second Hierarchies. Whether that means they approve of what he's doing is impossible to say."

"Don't you have some connections? I thought your uncle was a Second Hierarch."

"Uncle Oeillet? Yeah, but he's not exactly what you'd call a big wheel. I mean, he's in charge of tempting people to break their vows of poverty, for crying out loud! His star's been on the decline since the Reformation. In fact, most of the Second Hierarchs are pretty redundant, since they were originally conscripted to tempt holy men back during the Dark Ages. Still, a direct hookup with any of them rates a blood sacrifice. At least three quarts. I wish I could cut you a better deal on that, babe, but them's the rules."

Palmer glowered first at the highball in his hand then back at Sonja, still talking with the fresh-faced punk with the funny-looking eyes. The Black Madonna stared down at him from her place above the half-empty liquor bottles. The Black Baby Jesus looked like a doll someone had dropped down a coal chute, its chubby uplifted arms ending in misshapen fists since the fingers had rotted off.

"Hey, mister. You looking for someone?"

It was the prostitute at the end of the bar, the one he'd noticed when they entered. He shook his head without looking up from his drink. "Thanks, but no thanks."

"Are you *sure* you aren't looking for someone?"

There was something in her voice that made him look up, and what he saw was enough to push him to the brink.

He could feel insanity yawning like a snake eager to swallow him whole, right down to his Shermans and public library card. All he had to do was let go of the bar and let it suck him deep into its guts, never to be seen or heard from again.

The woman seated at the end of the bar was Loli. And this time he knew he wasn't dreaming. She smiled seductively and moved closer to him. She smelled of sloe gin fizzes and something Palmer recognized but could not name. Her fingers were cold and dry against his exposed flesh, but Palmer was beyond shivering. At her touch, his penis became erect. It was so hard it hurt, forcing tears from the corners of his eyes.

"I've been waiting for a man like you," she cooed into his ear. "I've waited such a *long* time!"

Palmer wanted to cry out, but his mouth had been sealed from the inside. His dick throbbed as if someone had slipped a piano wire tourniquet around its base and was slowly cutting off the circulation.

"Come on, baby. I got a place we can go and be alone." Loli hooked her arm in Palmer's, pulling him free of the bar. She was at least a head shorter than him, but she was strong. Too strong. "When we're alone, I'll fuck your brains out!" The way she laughed made it sound as if the joke was on him.

Palmer didn't want to go with her, but it was as if he was being pulled along by a wire fastened to the end of his dick. Every time he tried to fight it, the invisible tourniquet tightened its hold on his member. They were almost out the door before Palmer felt a second, equally female hand close on his right elbow.

"He's *mine*, you skaggy hell-bitch!" Sonja Blue yanked Palmer in her direction, but the succubus still held firmly to his left arm. The demon-whore hissed like a cat, digging her nails into Palmer's upper arm. He tried to scream, but his mouth was still pasted shut.

Palmer pictured himself being ripped apart like a wishbone as the vampire and the succubus fought over him. Then Sonja produced a switchblade and neatly severed the demon-Loli's hand at the wrist. Momentarily confused by this new development, Loli's grip on Palmer weakened enough for Sonja to wrench him free. Once away from the succubus's physical control, his overinflated sex organ rapidly shrank. It was the first time in his life he'd been relieved at losing an erection.

He stared as Loli picked up her severed hand and tried to stick it back on. To his surprise, the graft took.

"Loli . . . ?" It was the first time he'd had the power to speak since the trouble started.

"She's not Loli, Palmer. Take my hand. See as *I* see." Before Palmer could protest, she grabbed his right hand and squeezed.

The thing that had bewitched and tried to kidnap him had three pairs of floppy tits, arms as long and hairy as an ape's, crooked legs and a six-inch-long sheathed clitoris dangling between her shanks. Tiny horns grew from the creature's sloping forehead. The succubus hissed, her lipless mouth hinged like a piranha's. She stepped forward, growling a challenge to the mirror-eyed intruder that had dared steal her evening's repast.

"Jamara!"

The voice was as loud as thunder and so deep the speaker sounded as if he was at the bottom of a well. The succubus cringed, automatically turning her flank in submission.

Palmer turned and saw the boy called Malfeis rise from his booth in the back. But now he was no longer a boy. The demon stood well over six feet tall, although the curvature of his spine made him stoop. The demon was covered in coarse, brick-red hair, like that of an orangutan, except for his twin-pronged penis. His features were porcine, complete with curving boar's tusks. His feet were cloven.

Malfeis shouldered Sonja and Palmer aside, jabbering in a language that consisted largely of squeals and grunts. He reached behind Jamara and grabbed the succubus's tail, twisting it viciously. Jamara yelped and tried to break free of the demon's grip. Mal propelled the protesting succubus out the door and onto the street. When he turned back around he was a skatepunk again.

"I'm sorry about that. New girl. Actually, she's family. I promised one of my sisters I'd break her in, but I'm afraid it's just not working out."

Palmer shifted in his seat and tried to ride out the nicotine fit.

The flight was under six hours and therefore, according to FAA regulations, smoke-free. Palmer could feel the pack of Shermans calling out to him from inside his breast pocket, nestled against his heart like the picture of a loved one.

Sonja Blue sat beside him, mirrored shades in place, nonchalantly paging through an in-flight magazine. His companion was an up-to-date vampire; no crates packed with native earth for her. She believed in traveling first class.

"We should arrive at the airport within the next two hours. Pangloss said he'd have his car there to meet us. I have no reason not to believe him," she said without looking up from an article on Fun-Filled Florida Family Vacations.

Palmer nodded without saying anything. Personally, he considered Sonja's decision to meet with Pangloss something close to suicidal. At first he thought she'd used a devious form of mind control so he'd agree to come along, like she'd used on the security guards at the airport. The ones who'd demanded that she take the switchblade out of her pocket.

"What switchblade, officers?" she asked, holding up the ornately decorated knife. Her voice had been steady, without a tremor of fear.

"We're terribly sorry, ma'am. Our mistake. Have a nice flight," the security guards said, in unison, doing everything but tugging their forelocks as they backed away.

Palmer wanted to believe that his decision to become involved had been shaped by forces outside himself, that he had no say in what was happening around him, but that would be lying to himself. Like it or not, he needed her.

Disgruntled by where his thoughts were taking him, Palmer glanced at the night sky on the other side of the window and immediately wished he hadn't.

There were *things* sitting on the wing of the airplane.

At first he mistook them for children, although he had no idea what kids would be doing clinging to the aluminum skin of a DC-10, fifty-thousand feet in the air. Then one of the frail figures stood up, unfurling its bat-like wings as it embraced the jet stream, and shot up and away.

No, not children. At least not *human* ones.

There were at least six of the grayish-white creatures crawling up and down the length of the wing, their arms twice as long as their bodies. Their skulls were long and bullet-shaped, the bodies devoid of hair. As Palmer watched the things scuttle along, bellies pressed against the plane's vibrating skin, one by one they surrendered themselves to the winds. He was reminded of children taking turns on a tire swing.

One of the winged things caught some turbulence and struck the side of the plane near Palmer's window. He grimaced, expecting to hear a juicy thump as the creature hit, but there was no sound and no one else seemed to notice, not even Sonja. The thing peeled itself from the fuselage, peering through the window at Palmer.

The eyes were huge, lidless orbs the color of rancid butter that hovered over a tube-like proboscis that hung from the middle of its face. A long, worm-like tongue whipped out of the thing's snout, tasting the reinforced plexiglass that separated it from Palmer. Satisfied that it couldn't get in, the creature began climbing back to the wing.

Palmer could feel cold sweat running down his brow. He tugged on Sonja's sleeve, gesturing to the window. "Am I seeing things?"

Sonja looked up from her magazine and leaned forward, peering into the dark on the other side of the window.

"There's nothing to worry about. They're real."

"Great." He pulled the plastic shade down with trembling fingers. "That's all I need right now."

Sonja shrugged. "They're just *afreeti*, that's all. Nothing to get upset about. They're a form of elemental. They like hitching rides on airplanes. They're harmless, unless you get a couple of warring tribes arguing over who gets to go first. The few humans who've seen them—or had the misfortune to be in a disputed plane—usually mistake them for gremlins."

Palmer wished he could light up. It was a lot easier to tell himself that this was all part of the rich and varied pageant of life if he could soothe his jangling nerves with a double lungful of nicotine.

Sonja was watching him from behind her reflective lenses. She leaned toward him, resting her hand atop his.

"Look, I know what you're going through is tough right now. But, believe me, you get used to it. I remember the first time I started 'seeing things.' I thought I was going nuts! And I didn't have someone to walk me through it, not at first. I didn't know when I saw something if it was real or if I was hallucinating. You've got to watch out for that. The seeing things that *aren't* there bit, I mean. It's some kind of defense mechanism the human brain sets up to protect itself. Most real psychics end up schizophrenic. Only two percent of all active sensitives manage to stay out of the funny farm."

Palmer found himself staring at her hand as it lay atop his own. This was the first time she'd touched him, outside of saving his bewitched butt from the succubus, since their initial, accidental contact two nights ago. He was expecting her touch to be cold and clammy, like that of a corpse, but it wasn't. Actually, it was kind of nice. Suddenly the taste of Jimmy Eichorn's blood flooded his mouth.

He jerked his hand away from hers and stood up stiffly, trying to control the tightness in his throat. "Uh, yeah. Excuse me a minute, would you? I gotta go to the john."

Palmer screwed his mouth into a bitter grin as he made his way toward the first-class cabin's toilet. *Christ, as if my world isn't complicated enough, I got a goddamned punkette vampire putting the moves on me!* He shook his head in amazement. *Well, I guess it could be worse. I could have the IRS after me.*

Palmer tried the toilet door, found it locked, then noticed the Occupied sign. Sighing, he folded his arms and glanced back down the aisle, idly scanning the handful of passengers who could afford to fly first class domestic flights.

His gaze momentarily settled on a heavyset man in a rumpled business suit rooting through the contents of an attaché case. Wisps of smoke wreathed the businessman's frowning face.

What *the fuck? I thought this was a non-smoking flight! How come none of these tight-assed little bimbos haven't ragged his ass? This guy on the board of directors?* As Palmer stared harder at the florid-faced man, the smoke surrounding his head shifted and roiled, as if coming into sharper definition. Palmer's heart beat faster as he saw the shape crouched on the businessman's right shoulder. It looked like a squirrel monkey sketched by a skywriter and left to the mercies of a strong breeze.

Palmer quickly looked away, uncertain as to what it meant but certain a cigarette would help him deal with it, whatever it was. The rest room door opened and Palmer dived into its solitude without waiting for the previous occupant to completely clear the threshold. His hands were shaking as he slammed the bolt home and pressed his back against the door. Inches from his knees stood the undersized, uncomfortable airline toilet, its stainless steel bowl beaded with droplets of sky-blue disinfectant.

The equally tiny hand basin bruised his hip as he searched his pockets for a lighter. He glanced up at the smoke detector above his head and scowled.

The make such a big deal about how we shouldn't tamper with these damn things, so that probably means they're pretty easy to fuck up. Still, the last thing I need is to have the bloody thing go off while I'm messing with it. Then all I get for my trouble is a snootfull of CO_2 *and a five-hundred dollar fine slapped on me.* Palmer looked at the packet of Shermans liberated from his breast pocket, then back up at the plastic disc dangling over his head like an electronic Sword of Damocles.

Fuck it.

He stuck the cigaretello in his mouth and reached up to disconnect the smoke detector, giving himself a leg-up on the edge of the toilet seat. As he did so, he found himself staring into the shatter-proof mirror mounted over the sink.

Palmer snorted in self-derision. It was just like trying to cop a smoke in the boy's room at Mater Delarosa Junior High back in Akron. His hair was threaded with gray and he wore a tailored black trench coat instead of a school jacket, but essentially there wasn't that much difference between the between-the fourteen-year-old Palmer who'd been suspended for smoking behind the gym and the thirty-nine-year-old preparing to hamstring the smoke detector. Except for the smoke-monkey perched on the adult Palmer s shoulder like Long John Silver's parrot.

"*Yaaah!*"

Palmer screamed the moment he saw the apparition, losing his balance and plunging one foot into the toilet. The fear he'd experienced at the sight of the smudged gray thing crouched on his shoulder was replaced by the far more practical terror of accidentally being sucked out through the toilet's little trapdoor. Swearing viciously, Palmer yanked himself free, falling against the door with a thump.

"Sir? Sir! Are you all right? Are you hurt? Can you hear me?" It was one of the stewardesses, sounding both solicitous and suspicious.

"I'm all right! Just had an . . . accident, that's all!" Palmer glowered at the dye staining his lower leg. Luckily, his pants and shoes were dark enough to hide the discoloration. He avoided looking in the mirror as he exited the cramped confines of the toilet, smiling sheepishly at the flight attendants grouped outside.

"Please take your seat, sir. We're preparing to make our approach to San Francisco International."

"What in the name of hell is wrong with you?"

"Huh! What?!" Palmer flinched as Sonja snapped at him. He'd paused to light his cigarette the moment they were free of the jet's confines, only to find himself staring at a grotesquely thin woman—with a huge smoke-monkey the size of a gorilla riding her back—dragging her luggage through the terminal.

The woman seemed oblivious to the Gargantua straddling her narrow shoulders. A filtered Pall-Mall was clamped between her cranberry-red lips.

I've heard of Gorillas in the Mist, *but this is the first time I've seen a gorilla made of mist!* Palmer bit back a laugh he knew would sound too high-pitched and brittle to be mistaken for sane. He dropped the match cupped in one hand before it had a chance to burn him.

Sonja shook her head in disgust. "Come on, damn it! You'd think you'd never seen a tobacco demon before!"

Pangloss's chauffeur was waiting for them at the exit gate, holding a neatly printed cardboard placard that read *S. Blue*. They were shown to a stretch limo with tinted glass and a fully stocked bar in the back. Sonja hesitated a moment before climbing into the back seat.

"Something wrong, ma'am?" The driver's voice was as smooth and cold as glass.

"No, I was just remembering a limousine drive I took a long time ago."

The moment the door slammed shut behind them, Palmer popped one of his foul-smelling cigarettes into his mouth and opened the liquor cabinet. His hands were shaking.

"What's wrong?"

Palmer snorted, expelling a cloud of smoke. "What's *right?* That bastard tried to turn my brains into guacamole dip, and here we are riding in the back of his fuckin' limo! We're walking into a *trap*, for Christ's sake! It might as well have T-R-A-P spelled out in flashing neon letters!"

Sonja sighed and looked out the window. "Don't worry about Pangloss. I can handle him. He's not going to bother you. He got what he wanted. Adding you to his stable was a bonus—a little lag*niappe*."

"You sound real sure of yourself."

"Pangloss is crafty. I don't doubt he's got his own reasons for bringing me into this. But I don't care what they are. The only thing I'm interested in is Morgan."

"That's another thing: who *is* this guy Morgan and why do you want his head on a spike?"

She glanced at him, the corner of her mouth lifted into a bitter smile. "Ever hear of Thorne Industrials?"

"Yeah, sure. Old Jacob Thorne's one of the last 'bootstrap' millionaires, like Getty and Carnegie."

"Do you recall a kidnapping involving Thorne's daughter? Her name was Denise."

Palmer frowned and nodded: "Now that you mention it—didn't she disappear sometime during the sixties?"

"No ransom demands were ever made and she was listed as missing. It was a long time back. Over twenty years. Long before they started putting pictures on the back of milk cartons. . . ." Her voice was wistful.

"But what does that have to do with you?"

"In 1969, while on a vacation to London, Denise Thorne met a man who went by the name of Morgan. *Lord* Morgan. The title turned out to be real enough, but Morgan wasn't a man. He coerced Denise Thorne into taking a moonlight drive in his chauffeured limousine. It was all very romantic. Once they were alone, he raped her and drank her blood. He then threw her from the back of the moving car, leaving her for dead. By sheer luck, she was found and taken to the hospital, where she remained in a coma for nine months. Then I woke up."

"You're Denise Thorne." Palmer stared at her, cigarette smoldering, forgotten, between his fingers.

Sonja shrugged. "That is open to debate. But something in me *used* to be Denise Thorne. Perhaps still is." She returned her gaze to the window, staring at the dim outline of Candlestick Park as the limo sped along Highway 101. "There are a lot of things I do not know. But I *do* know one thing: I will send Morgan to hell, even if I have to take him there myself."

Pangloss's hideaway was in one of the older downtown skyscrapers. Dwarfed by Bauhaus-spawned megaliths like the Transamerica Pyramid, the Dobbs Building dwelt in perpetual shadow.

The limo slid into the underground parking garage, depositing its riders before an old-fashioned elevator shaft secured by sliding metal gates. The driver spoke into a hand-mike attached to the radio, and the elevator car descended into view.

Sonja Blue stepped out of the car, signaling for Palmer to follow. The elevator door opened and the protective gates folded back. The elevator operator, an old man in an ill-fitting uniform, gestured for them to enter. The interior of the car smelled of old leather and cigars.

Minutes later the car halted at the penthouse and the doors opened—to reveal the hulking figure of an ogre blocking the way.

The ogre's massive jaw jutted forward, flaring his ape-like nostrils. Palmer recognized him; the last time he'd seen him, he was chomping away on Renfield's left leg like a drumstick.

Palmer rolled his eyes. "I *told* you this was a bad idea."

The ogre's lips peeled back in a rictus grin, revealing teeth better suited for a shark's mouth.

"Keif! Heel! Heel, damn you!"

The ogre moved aside, permitting a narrow-shouldered man in a nondescript suit and tortoiseshell spectacles, a clipboard clutched to his chest, to step forward.

"I'm Doctor Pangloss's assistant. He's in the gymnasium right now. If you'd like to wait . . ."

"I'd like to see him. Now."

The assistant scowled at his clipboard. "I'm afraid that's not possible."

Sonja Blue stepped forward, pushing her face into his. "*Now.*"

The assistant's pale face grew even pastier. "Yes. Of course. Permit me to show you the way."

The gymnasium was larger than most of the apartments Palmer had lived in. Parallel bars and other acrobatic equipment were scattered about, while a state-of-the-art Nautilus machine crouched in one corner like a chromium spider. But what held their attention were the two men, dressed in the mesh faceguards and starched white tunics of professional fencers, dueling with sabers in the middle of the room.

As they watched, one of the duelists drove his weapon through his opponent's chest, neatly skewering the tunic's red heart. The wounded fencer, still clutching his saber, staggered backward, staring at the length of cold steel jutting from his breastbone. A dry chuckle emerged from inside the victor's visor as he turned to leave.

The moment his foe's back was turned, the wounded swordsman swung his blade, neatly decapitating his adversary in mid-stride. The head, still encased in the protective face guard, bounced a couple of times before rolling to a stop near Sonja's right foot.

Pangloss removed his own visor and tossed it aside, motioning for his assistant to pull the saber free of his chest. For the first time Palmer was able to see his erstwhile employer's eyes; they were the color of garnets, bisected by a narrow, reptilian pupil.

"I'm glad that's over and done with! What a bore! Always going on about those scars he got at Heidelberg. Why, I remember when Heidelberg was no more than a wide spot in the road!" He winced as the sword was removed. Blood the color and consistency of transmission fluid spurted briefly from the wound. "Ah! That's much better—it was starting to itch."

"Is there anything else I can do for you, Doctor?"

"That will be all, Renfield. I will see to our guest myself."

"Very good, sir. I'll have Kief dispose of Herr Gruenwald."

Palmer watched the pinch-faced young man exit the room, then swung to face Pangloss. "You called him Renfield!"

"What of it?" replied the vampire as he unfastened the buckles of his tunic.

"Renfield's dead! I saw him die!"

Pangloss sighed and his pupils flexed. "My dear Mr. Palmer, the world is *full* of renfields! Just like it's full of letter openers and paper clips. You don't christen each and every paper clip you use with its own name, do you? The operative our charming Ms. Blue terminated was one of my renfields. Just as you are one of hers."

Palmer felt his face color. "Hold it, buddy, I don't like what you're implying—!"

Sonja raised her hand for silence. "Stop baiting him, Pangloss. You lost out. You should have known something like that would happen when you sent a loose cannon to twist him."

"I prefer the term 'reprogram.' It sounds so much more up-to-date. Don't you agree?"

Sonja snorted and folded her arms across her chest. "I didn't come here to play word games, *herr doktor*."

Pangloss clucked his tongue in disapproval. "The years have not improved your etiquette, my dear. You're just as blunt as ever. I guess that's what comes of being American." He shrugged free of the bloodstained tunic, revealing a hairless chest as pale as milk and covered with the faint traces of hundreds of crisscrossing scars.

The newest wound, the one piercing his heart, was already puckering into pink scar tissue. Palmer thought the vampire's exposed torso looked like a braille road map. Without realizing it, he touched his own chest, tracing his near-fatal flaw. He wondered for a moment if Sonja's flesh was equally scarred, then hastily pushed the thought aside.

Pangloss strode across the room and removed a green silk dressing gown from a peg near the door. "You still cling to certain human conceits, such as the ludicrous idea that time is valuable. You're far too impatient, my dear! When will you realize that time is the one thing you have plenty of? Then again, I forget how young you are. You are indeed a prodigy, my dear. But, in many ways, you are a backward child. Come, let us retire to more amenable surroundings."

As they left the gymnasium, Palmer glanced over his shoulder and saw the ogre, Kief, enter from another door. As he watched, the ogre picked up the severed head of the ill-fated Herr Gruenwald from its resting place on the floor. The ogre shucked the head free of the fencing mask and grinned, revealing hideous teeth, and lifted the dead man's skull to its mouth. Palmer looked away, but he could still hear. It sounded just like someone biting into a big, crisp apple.

Marble art deco nymphs flanked the hearth while a panther carved from a single piece of obsidian crouched on the mantelpiece. There was a fire burning behind the ornate iron screen, but Palmer couldn't feel it. Perhaps it was just the notorious San Francisco Bay damp getting to him, but he doubted it.

Pangloss stood at the picture window, his back to his guests. The fog was heavy, obscuring what little view was available at two in the morning. The swirling gray mist reminded Palmer of the tobacco demons he'd seen earlier, so he returned his gaze to the fireplace.

"You said you know where Morgan is."

Pangloss glanced back over his shoulder. "I do."

"Well?"

"I would rather speak to you in private. Shall we retire to the patio?" Pangloss gestured to the sliding glass door that opened onto a rooftop garden.

Sonja glanced at Palmer, then nodded her assent. She followed the elder vampire onto the fog-enshrouded terrace. The sea air was sharp in her nostrils, reminding her of blood. The Other's voice stirred inside her head, admonishing her for having subsisted for so long on nothing but bottled plasma. She tried to ignore it; this was neither the time nor the place for the Other's yammering to put her off guard. Pangloss was dangerous. She'd learned that the hard way over a decade ago.

Pangloss stood with his hands clasped behind his back, staring into the fog bank. "You've changed, my dear. Matured. I noticed it the moment I laid eyes on you. You're not as angry as you used to be."

"Me used to be angry young man, me hidin' me head in the sand."

"Beg pardon?"

"Let's just say I've discovered how to work within the system since the last time we met. I've learned to . . . focus myself. Enough idle chatter, Pangloss. Now, about Morgan."

Pangloss turned to face her, and for a brief moment she was looking at an unwrapped mummy with red coals banked deep in its empty orbits. The vampire reached into the voluminous pockets of its dressing gown and retrieved an ivory cigarette holder with dry twig fingers. The first time she'd glimpsed Pangloss's true self she'd come close to screaming. But now, fifteen years later, his desiccated appearance seemed almost normal.

"Ah, yes . . . Morgan. It always comes back to Morgan, doesn't it?" His voice was melancholy. "He was my greatest mistake, just as you are his.

However, in my case I created him with full knowledge of what I was doing. Or so I thought." Pangloss frowned and his features were once more those of a handsome man in his early middle-age. "It can be lonely for beings such as you and I. I'm certain you've discovered this for yourself by now. Alliances with humans are, by their very nature, destined to be brief.

"Speaking of which, I congratulate you on claiming Palmer as your renfield. He's much better spoken than that piece of trash you picked up in London. Tell me, does he still imagine himself the captain of his own will?"

"That's none of your damn business!"

Pangloss held up a hand in supplication. "You're quite right, my dear! That was rude of me! Now, where was I? Ah, yes. When I was younger—younger than I am now—I longed for companionship. At the time, I fancied myself quite ancient—I was seven or eight hundred years old, which means it must have been either the eleventh or twelfth century. I was the same age as Morgan is now, if that means anything.

"I had grown bored and wished to have an equal as a companion. Since I was forced to recruit from serfs and peasants, with the occasional yeoman thrown in, the basic templates were far from the first quality. Most of my broodlings were unsuited for any intellectual pursuits beyond hunting down their next meal. Then I met Morgan.

"At that point, I was working for the Church as a gelder. The choir masters sent their most promising sopranos to me for alteration into *castrati*. I was renowned for having a low mortality rate, at least by the standards of the day. It was a good cover, allowing me access to the Byzantine jealousies and in-fighting created when human sexuality is subverted. I fed well at the Vatican's expense for the better part of twenty years. But Morgan's arrival changed all that.

"He was only twelve when I first saw him, but I knew I had found what I had been searching for. He was the fifth son of a nobleman and had been forced into joining the Church. The original intention was for him to become a priest, but his excellent singing voice had drawn the attention of the choirmaster. Instead of castrating the boy, I took him with me when I abandoned my identity.

"It was the closest I had come to experiencing genuine passion since my resurrection.

"Morgan accepted me for what I was. His intellect was astounding, and he proved himself an apt pupil. We traveled Europe in the guise of uncle and nephew for several years. He longed to be transfigured, but I withheld my benediction until I was certain he was seasoned enough to survive the change intact. When he was thirty, I remade him in my image.

"My faith in his innate superiority was justified. Within ten years of his resurrection, Morgan had evolved beyond the crude revenant stage. I was proud of him! For two centuries he was my constant companion. I was his brood-master, but I never abused my status. I allowed him far more liberty than I've granted any of my by-blows, before or since. In the end it cost me dearly.

"Morgan turned against me. I'd underestimated the strength of his will. And his guile. He came close to killing me—just as you did." Pangloss opened his robe and pointed at a long, ragged scar in the middle of his chest. Although she knew the wound had to be at least ten years old, it still looked fresh. "I nearly died from that silver blade of yours. It still hurts, even now."

"If you're expecting me to feel guilty, forget it."

"I know better than to expect pity from you, or from any of our ilk."

"So why are you telling me this?"

Pangloss's smile was bitter. "When you love someone as much as I loved Morgan, and find that emotion betrayed . . . You see, my dear, I hate him as much as you do. And for far better reasons. It is in my interest that Morgan's plan be foiled."

"Plan?"

The elder vampire chuckled, shaking his head in admiration. "The fool's ambition is boundless, if nothing else. He is plotting on revolutionizing Pretender society, although I'm uncertain as to how he expects to do so. Something about creating an army of silver-immune vampires."

"Don't you know anything else?"

"He's screened himself quite well. It took me five years to trace him to this city."

"Here? You mean he's *here?* In San Francisco?" Sonja felt her stomach knot. She'd been hunting for so long, traveling the world in search of the vampire who had made her into something beyond human. To be told that she was in the same city with him, after twenty years . . .

"He's operating under deep cover. Has been for well over a decade. I don't know what name—or face—he's wearing, but I have succeeded in tracking down the name of someone who does. His name is Russell Howard, a human real estate agent. He knows who—and what—Morgan is. I suggest you start your inquiry with him."

"Why me? Why are you telling me this? If what Morgan is planning on doing will disrupt the nature of things in the Real World, why aren't the other vampire nobles taking an interest in what's going on?"

Pangloss grimaced as if he'd sipped tainted blood. "The ruling class—those known as the Combine—are convinced his efforts are folly, that he's gone mad. It happens sometimes—vampiric senile dementia. But they don't know Morgan as I do. They are too preoccupied with their own blood-feuds and atrocity exhibitions. I can understand Morgan's disgust with their narrow-mindedness, but what he's proposing . . . It's too dangerous. For both the humans *and* the Real World! What is required is a free agent, such as yourself. You're unorthodox, but no one can deny your effectiveness. And what better weapon to turn against Morgan than one of his own making?"

"Flattery will get you nowhere, *herr doktor*. I still don't see why you haven't intervened if Morgan's scheme is so damned hazardous to your health. Unless you're afraid of him."

The vampire's smile faltered.

"I know you're scared of Morgan, just as I know you're scared of me. You've been frightened of me since you first saw me. Why is that, *Herr* Pangloss?"

Sonja removed her mirrored glasses. "What is it you see when you look at me?"

There was loathing in the old vampire's wine-red gaze, but he did not avert his eyes. "I don't know. And that's what scares me."

Pangloss's driver dropped them off at their hotel a couple of blocks from the famed dragon gates of Chinatown. The place catered largely to students and Asian businessmen, so it was both inexpensive and clean. As they exited the back of the limousine, a homeless person shuffled forward, gesturing and muttering unintelligibly.

The old man, dressed in several layers of cast-off clothing, his feet wrapped in old newspaper like dead fish, looked no different than others of his kind. He smelled of piss and cheap wine and reminded Palmer of a cross between his Uncle Willy and a pigeon. Yet Sonja seemed genuinely startled by the old man and hurried past him into the lobby. Perplexed by this unaccustomed display of fear, Palmer glanced back at the ragged figure as it returned to the fog-shrouded doorway it had shambled from. In the diffused light from the street lamp, the old man's eyes glinted gold.

By the time he reached the front desk in the lobby, Sonja was once more in control of herself. The night clerk, an elderly Chinese gentleman who moved with the grace of a *tai chi* master, did not seem terribly surprised by their unconventional appearances. After all, it was San Francisco.

Sonja asked for and received connecting single rooms. Palmer would have preferred separate floors, but said nothing.

After he'd stowed his suitcase in the shallow closet behind the door, there was a light rapping on the connecting door. He opened it halfway.

"What is it?"

"We need to talk."

Palmer glanced at his wristwatch. It was close to four in the morning and here she was, wanting to talk. He'd once fancied himself a night owl, but now he realized his previous estimation of his nocturnal stamina had been naive.

"About this Morgan guy?"

"That, and what Pangloss told me."

Palmer grunted. "Okay. But let me get cleaned up first, okay? I feel like a pile of dirty laundry."

"You got a point there."

"I know. That's why my mama made me wear a hat."

She laughed, and Palmer liked the sound of it. That disturbed him.

Twenty minutes later, after toweling his bristling mane dry and slipping into a clean pair of jeans and a loose-fitting sweater, Palmer knocked on the door between their rooms.

"Sonja?"

No answer.

He knocked a little louder, and this time the door swung open on its hinge.

"Uh, Sonja?"

Palmer stepped over the threshold, squinting into the darkness. From what little he could see, Sonja's room was identical to his, only reversed. Not yet adapted to the gloom, he jarred his hip against the dresser bureau opposite the double bed. Cursing under his breath, Palmer looked up, expecting to see his grimacing face reflected in the mirror. Instead, he found himself staring at a blanket. He touched the bed linen draped over the upright mirror.

Vampires cast no reflection.

It was one of the rules he remembered from the movies of his childhood. The films his father had condemned as junk and Palmer had consumed with uncritical eagerness and a sense of wonder so sincere it bordered on epiphany.

For a brief moment he could see his old room, circa 1965, in all its preadolescent glory. He could smell the chemical stink of airplane glue as the Aurora models of Hollywood monsters dried on his desk. He could glimpse the stacks of *Famous Monsters of Filmland* and well-thumbed *Dr. Strange* comic books stashed in the back of his closet. The flashback was so sharp, so immediate, Palmer had to steady himself. His hand dropped to the top of the dresser and touched something smooth and cold. His fingers closed on the object before he realized what he'd done.

She left her glasses.

It felt weird, standing there holding her sunglasses. They were so much a part of her, it was like he'd stumbled across her severed ear, like in that movie.

"Don't turn around."

Her voice was at his shoulder. She'd come up right behind him without his being aware of it. Sweat broke out on his brow and upper lip. He wondered what her eyes looked like. He recalled Pangloss's reptilian, red-rimmed pupils and how they'd flexed, and fought to repress a shudder.

Sonja's bare arm reached around and plucked the glasses from his grip. He could hear the quick rustle of material as she pulled on her robe.

"Okay, it's safe to look now."

Palmer turned around just as she switched on the lamp next to the bed. The vampire sat with her back against the headboard, her legs curled under her like a cat. She was wearing the same kimono he'd seen in New Orleans. Her hair, still damp from the shower, was plastered against her milk-pale forehead like feathers. She was beautiful and she scared him.

"Sorry I walked in on you like that. I knocked . . ."

"Forget about it." She motioned for him to be seated in the room's only chair.

"Uh, you said you wanted to talk?" Unsure of what else he could do, he lit a Shermans.

Palmer alternately blew smoke rings and frowned while she told him what Pangloss had said about Morgan being somewhere in the city and his connection with the real estate agent.

"So, do you think we can trust Pangloss?"

"Trust him? No. But I believe him."

"So. What's all this happy crappy about the Real World and Pretenders?"

"I think you already have some idea as to that."

"Yeah, well, sure—but I'm new to this. I don't know the rules, or even if there are any."

Sonja sighed and looked into the far corner, as if watching something. She was still staring absently at the shadows when she spoke. "Humans think they know what reality is, what life's about. They think they know because they can think. 'I think therefore I know.' Their attitude is 'I'm at the top of the food chain, so I get to decide what's real and what's not.'

"What they don't want to be simply doesn't exist. Except, perhaps, in their dreams. Or nightmares. So they end up watching the shadows on the wall of the cave, thinking that's how the world *really* is. They never look at the things throwing the shadows. Or, if they do look, they don't *see* them. Most humans are both separated from and yet a part of the Real World. Pretenders are, well, they're the ultimate predators. It's a generic term, really. It just means they're capable of passing for human. Like vampires, ogres, succubi, incubi and *vargr* . . ."

"The what?"

"Werewolves," she explained. "And then there are the *seraphim*, like the old man on the curb."

Palmer remembered the way the homeless person's eyes had seemed to burn like newly minted gold coins. "Are these Sara Lees, or what have you, dangerous?"

"Hard to say exactly wh*at* they are. One saved my life once. Take that for what you will."

There was a lull in the conversation and Palmer was suddenly, uncomfortably aware he was sitting in a hotel room with a good-looking, half-naked woman.

"Look, it's late and I'm not really used to staying up all night and sleeping all day." He moved to leave, but Sonja reached out and took his hand in hers.

"You don't have to leave."

Palmer wanted to go. He wanted to slam the door between his room and hers and barricade it with furniture. But part of him also wanted to stay. He looked down at her and saw his worried, embarrassed face reflected in her shades.

Jesus, do I really look that fucking neurotic? No wonder Loli nailed me as a sucker.

"I'm sorry if I frighten you. I don't mean to. But sometimes it's so hard to control . . ." She smiled then; it was as sad and delicate a gesture as he'd ever seen. "It's just that I get so lonely. And sometimes I need to be reminded what it's like . . ." She looked away and dropped his hand. She didn't have to finish the sentence because Palmer could hear it in his head. He wasn't sure if it was telepathy or simple empathy.

And sometimes I need to be reminded what it's like to be human.

"Look, Sonja, it's not that I don't—"

"Go." She refused to look at him. "Just go."

Palmer obeyed, uncertain as to what he wanted. Within ten minutes he was in his bed and sound asleep. He didn't hear her leave.

Sonja Blue left the hotel dressed in her faded jeans and leather jacket. She struck out toward Chinatown, scaling the steep hill with strong, purposeful strides. It would be another hour or so before dawn; still plenty of time for hunting.

She passed the dragon gate that marked the district's entrance; the shaggy-browed creatures with their trailing mustaches reminded her of the dragon decorating the hilt of her switchblade.

Grant Avenue was deserted, although she knew that by five o'clock the local merchants would start arriving to prepare their shops for another business day. Soon the narrow sidewalks would be crowded with wooden bins filled with exotic oriental vegetables, golden-skinned ducks dangling in the storefronts. The businesses hawking cheap electronic gadgets and knickknacks from the Far East would not open their doors until well after dawn, but Sonja would have finished her hunt long before then.

You should have made him do it. After all, he owes it to you. You saved his life.

She grimaced and tried to ignore the Other's words. She knew all too well what would happen if she weakened and let it have its way. She paused, sniffing the chill morning air. She could hear the distant thrumming of the cable car track and, fainter still, the ringing of church bells.

Every doorway she passed sheltered a lumpy form, wrapped in discarded clothing and old trash. One housed a family of four; the weary parents squatting on the lower steps while their children slept on a pallet of folded cardboard. The woman watched her pass with tired, fearful eyes.

She paused and sniffed again. The scent was strong. She was close. Very close. She ducked into a narrow alley. The walkway was littered with aluminum trash cans filled with garbage. Apparently the Soon Luck restaurant didn't believe in separating their bottles and cans. The odor was nearly overpowering enough to mask the scent she'd been following. But not quite.

The *vargr* rose from its hiding place amongst the jumbled garbage containers, growling a warning at the intruder who had dared to interrupt its meal. The werewolf stood almost six feet tall, although its curved spine and crooked legs made it seem even taller. The pointed, vulpine snout curled into a menacing snarl, exposing sharp teeth stained with fresh blood and flecked with flesh and gristle. Sonja spied the savaged remains of a bag lady—a real one this time—at its taloned feet. The beast's russet pelt bristled, raising hackles along its back. The *vargr's* thin, pointed penis slid from its furred pouch in ritual challenge.

Sonja Blue hissed unsheathing her fangs. The werewolf looked confused.

"C'mon, Rin-Tin-Tin! Whassamatter, furball? You too lapdog to take on someone your own size?" She knew she was being foolhardy. She'd only tangled with one or two *vargr* before. They were as dangerous as the more advanced vampires, although they lacked psychic powers. Physically, though, they were incredibly powerful and close to immortal. She wondered what the hell she was trying to prove to herself.

The werewolf stepped forward, tossing aside the fifty-gallon garbage cans as if they were ninepins. The beast reeked like a wet dog. Sonja palmed the switchblade and pressed the ruby stud in the dragon's eye. The *vargr* halted at the sight of the silver knife.

Sonja launched herself at the hesitant werewolf, knocking it to the ground. The *vargr* gave a yelp of surprise. The two opponents wrestled on the filthy bricks, knocking over even more garbage cans. Startled rats scurried for cover, their meals interrupted, while the werewolf and the vampire battled.

Sonja, already bleeding from a score of cuts from the beast-man's talons, cried out as the *vargr* sank its teeth into her shoulder, worrying her like a dog's chew toy. She stabbed blindly at her attacker and was rewarded by a yowl of pain and the smell of bile. She pulled herself free and staggered away from the wounded *vargr*. The bite on her shoulder had weakened her more than she realized.

Just before she fainted she saw the *vargr* hurrying down the alleyway. He was on the verge of reverting to his human persona, and the way he was hunched over told her he was trying to keep his intestines from spilling out.

When she opened her eyes again it was to find a strange man kneeling over her. She'd passed out propped against the alley wall. Her glasses were still on and the man could not see she was awake.

He reached into her jacket and removed her wallet. The man seemed pleased by the amount of money in the bill folder. He chuckled to himself. It was obvious he thought she was dead. He leaned forward again, in search of more loot.

She'd lost a lot of blood. She needed blood to heal. The man looked genuinely surprised when the dead woman grabbed his shirt front, pulling him closer. Then there was only fear.

Russell Howard was a self-satisfied man. He was only thirty-seven, but already well on his way to becoming a multimillionaire. Seven years ago he was a struggling real estate agent, handling third- and fourth-rate rental properties on the wrong side of Army.

Now he had a Lamborghini with its very own phone and fax machine. His office took up half of the fifteenth floor of a spanking-new high rise in the Embarcadero; his clients were some of the wealthiest in the Bay Area, if not the state; and his name and face often graced the *Chronicle's* society pages. Yes, Russell Howard was on his way to big things.

Thanks to his oh-so-silent partner.

Howard didn't like to think too much about his partner. It tended to make his palms sweat and his brain itch. Sometimes it even gave him nightmares. But if there was anything he'd learned from life, it was that money solved everything; and even if his problems didn't exactly disappear, at least they left him alone.

Howard sat in his wing-backed swivel chair and watched the shadows lengthen as the sun set. He'd just finished a late afternoon conference with a client and was contemplating calling his wife and telling her he'd be home late. He did not know the elevator was on its way to the fifteenth floor, carrying two visitors. And even if he had been aware of it, he would not have cared.

He occasionally read Dr. Seuss books to his three-year-old, Kristin, before she went to bed. Right now her favorite was *Yertle the Turtle*. The symbolism was lost on him.

The secretary looked up from her word processor to see two strangers, a man and a woman, enter the reception area. She frowned and glanced down at the calendar on her desk. It showed no more appointments scheduled for that day.

"May I help you?"

The man spoke first. "We're here to see Mr. Howard."

"Do you have an appointment?" she asked, her voice dripping icicles as she eyed his outlandish haircut.

"No. But he'll see us anyway." This from the woman in the leather jacket and mirrored glasses.

"I'm afraid that's not possible. Mr. Howard is a very busy man and—"

"It's time to go home."

The secretary stared dumbly at the woman in sunglasses for a heartbeat, then got up and switched off the word processor, snugged a plastic cover over the electric typewriter, retrieved her purse from its place in the filing cabinet, and marched out the door.

The sound of the outer door slamming shut brought Russell Howard from his office. He stared in surprise at the two strangers for a second before looking for his secretary.

"Where's Patricia?"

"She had to go home. Something came up all of a sudden. Besides, it's late. You work her too hard."

Howard was uncertain whether to be frightened or offended by the strange man and woman. They looked like they belonged on MTV or the back of an album cover instead of his reception area. The man seemed to be in his late thirties, dressed in faded jeans, a dark bulky sweater, and a black raincoat. His hair, while relatively short, was wiry and stood straight up from his head like he'd received a jolt of electricity. A profusion of gray frosted his temples and his chin was bisected by a narrow width of beard that made him look like a punk pharaoh.

The woman was much younger, wearing reflective sunglasses, tight-fitting jeans, steel-tipped boots, and a battered leather jacket over a Dead Kennedys T-shirt. Her dark, unruly hair made her look like an exotic bird.

"Who are you people? What do you want?"

The woman stepped forward. There was something familiar in the way she moved, but he couldn't place it. "My name is Sonja Blue, Mr. Howard. My . . . associate is Mr. Palmer. As to what we want—all we want is information, Mr. Howard. Information I have reason to believe you can provide." She motioned to the filing cabinets lining the wall. "Check 'em out."

Palmer nodded and began rifling Howard's files as if he worked there.

Howard's face had gone the color of a ripe tomato. "You can't do that! I'm calling the police!"

Sonja Blue clucked her tongue reproachfully. "Now, that's not a very nice thing to do, is it?" She took another step closer to the realtor. He could see his own outraged features, twisted and twinned, reflected in her glasses. Menace oozed from her like an expensive French perfume. "Why don't you tell me where Morgan is, Mr. Howard?"

Howard's heart iced over. Now he knew why she'd seemed so familiar; it was the way she handled herself, the way she talked, her mannerisms those of a creature impervious to threats and accustomed to power. Just like his partner.

He made a strange gargling noise that sounded like a deaf-mute's attempt at speech. He tried to slam the door on her, but she moved too fast for him. He stumbled backward into his spacious office with its muted pastel color schemes and trendy halogen light fixtures, his eyes riveted on the woman as she advanced on him. He could not look away from her. He remembered stories he'd heard as a child of snakes hypnotizing birds into their open jaws. When she grabbed him, it was with the speed and precision of a cobra striking.

She jerked him forward by his yellow silk power-tie and thrust her pale, ice-maiden's face into his own. He saw himself in her glasses again; this time his skin oozed beads of sweat like tiny pearls of mercury. She smiled, revealing canines as white as new bone and sharper than hypodermics. Howard moaned.

"I see Pangloss wasn't lying about your connection with Morgan. Most encouraging." Sonja Blue yanked harder on Howard's tie. He was suddenly aware that his feet had nearly cleared the floor and that he could no longer breathe.

Sonja dragged the strangling realtor around the desk and dumped him unceremoniously in his chair. Howard gasped and coughed and tried to free his neck of the power-tie cum garrote. The Windsor knot he'd done that morning was now the size of a small pea and could not be budged. The realization that he would have to destroy the eighty-dollar tie in order to get it off was enough to make him forget his predicament.

Sonja Blue walked back around the desk—an impressive walnut job the size of a pool table—and came to rest in one of the chairs he reserved for clients. This apparent resumption of the power structure Howard was familiar with triggered something instinctual in him: He automatically sat upright, attempted to straighten his ruined tie, and put on his best angry tycoon face.

"Now see here, whoever you are! I won't stand for this! How dare you come into my office and threaten me in such a manner!" He reached for the multiline telephone on his right. "I'm calling security right this minute!"

"Touch that phone, and I will tear your fingers, one by one, from your hands. Is that understood?"

Howard blanched and let the receiver drop back into its cradle. "What do you want?"

"I've already told you. I want Morgan's address and the name he's using." When Howard remained silent, she sighed and crossed her legs. "Mr. Howard, you know what I am. You know what I am capable of. I *could* pop your memory open like a raw cauliflower and get my information *that* way. However, such measures are drastic and not necessarily effective. It would also lower your IQ by more than a hundred points, and I have serious doubts as to you escaping unimpaired."

"I can't tell you anything."

"You mean you *won't*."

Howard pulled a monogrammed linen handkerchief from his breast pocket and mopped his forehead, his hands shaking. "He'll kill me."

"So will I, Mr. Howard, if you don't tell me what I want to know."

"Look, I haven't done anything—

"You traffic with monsters, Mr. Howard. Four hundred years ago you would have ended up in the hands of the Inquisition, your feet stuffed into iron boots full of molten lead. I am far more reasonable than Torquemada. If not as patient. Tell me what your connection is to Morgan."

"It's nothing important."

Sonja sighed again. "Mr. Howard, Lord Morgan would not bother to become involved with a dreary little human such as yourself unless you serve some purpose useful to him."

Howard shifted his weight on his buttocks, unhappy with his situation. "Look, he gives me money, okay? He's what's called a silent partner. He gives me money, I buy and manage properties for him. Nothing illegal about that."

"Indeed."

"I also find places for him to stay. He moves around a lot, okay? Never stays anywhere more than six months. There's nothing wrong with that, is there?"

"No. Nothing at all." It was obvious from her voice that she was thinking. Howard didn't want to know about what.

"Sonja?"

Palmer stood in the doorway, holding aloft a fat manila file folder. When Howard saw it he felt his guts knot into a sheepshank. Sonja took the file and began flipping through the documents inside, occasionally lifting her head to study Howard with her impassive, mirrored gaze. It did not take more than the most cursory of glances to realize that the properties in question were in the worst sectors of Oakland. Howard patted his forehead with the damp handkerchief.

"Well." Sonja closed the folder and handed it back to Palmer, returning her full attention to Howard. "Things are starting to make sense. Those are the 'properties' you purchased and manage for your partner?"

Howard nodded weakly. "Look, I can explain—"

"I'm sure you can. But you needn't bother. I understand all too well. Not all vampires are bloodsuckers. Only the more primitive species feed in that manner. Vampires as old and as powerful as Lord Morgan require far more refined sustenance. They feed on human despair, hate, fear, anger, frustration, greed, cruelty, madness . . . And what better breeding ground than some festering hellhole of a slum; where rats bite babies, old women are murdered for their social security checks, pregnant women smoke crack, children are abused, women are raped and beaten by both strangers and the men they love?" She smacked her lips and patted her belly in a broad parody of hunger. "That's good eating!"

Palmer snorted in disgust. "Fuckin' traitor!"

Sonja nodded in agreement and leaned forward, fixing Howard with her unseen stare. "Do you know what humans such as yourself are called? By the Pretending races, I mean, not your own species. No? You, Mr. Howard, are a bellwether. Some would prefer the term judas goat. Bellwethers willingly lead their fellow humans onto the killing floor in exchange for a reward from the butchers. Bellwethers like to think themselves immune. But all that means is that, once their usefulness is at an end, they are the last of the sheep to die."

"He—he's staying in a place near the Marina. Where they're rebuilding from the quake."

It did not surprise her that Morgan would make his nest close to a scene of destruction and suffering. The psychic aftereffects of a catastrophe would be as invigorating as sea air for such a creature.

"And his name?"

"I'm getting to that. He goes by the name of Caron. Dr. Joad Caron."

Palmer and Sonja exchanged glances. "*Doctor?*"

"Yeah, he's a shrink."

"Jesus H. Christ!" Palmer turned around and walked out of the room. He had enough of Russell Howard to last him several lifetimes.

Howard decided it was time for him to make his move. The woman was preoccupied, staring off into space. He slowly reached for the drawer where he kept his gun. If he was lucky, he could get the drop both on her and the middle-aged punk in the front office. He'd learned enough about what the bitch called Pretenders to know that a bullet in the brain killed them as dead as humans.

It would look funny to the cops, but he could claim they were hopped-up crack addicts he'd surprised in the act of ransacking his office. Yeah, that would wash. If there was too much of a fuss, Morgan could pull a few strings—or whatever the hell it was he pulled—and quiet things down. Like he had during the Harvey Milk fiasco.

He felt the cool metal grip of the chrome-plated pistol as his fingers wrapped around it. Yeah, it would be easy. Easy as shooting clay pigeons.

Sonja Blue leapt onto the desk, snarling like a leopard freed from its cage. It happened so fast it seemed as if she'd materialized out of thin air; one second she was sitting in a chair three feet away, the next she was squatting in front of him like a desktop gargoyle. She crouched on her haunches, her arms bent and hands splayed across the expensive walnut finish. Her head was thrust forward, reminding Howard of an attack dog straining on its leash. The crest on her head bristled like a wolf's hackle. Howard wet himself.

She jerked the gun out of his unresisting hand, studying it with mild distaste. A .22 automatic. She barked a humorless laugh as she turned the toy-like weapon over in her hands. "You'd have to do better than that, buddy. I've metabolized more .22 slugs than Carter's has Little Liver Pills!" She hopped off the desk, leaving deep scratches in the six layers of lacquered finish. After a moment's contemplation, she tossed the gun back to its owner.

Howard was too surprised to do more than ham-handedly catch it. He stared at the gun, then back at her. He set the weapon aside. He realized there was no way, even at such close range, he would be able to shoot her and still live.

"You're holding out on me, Howard."

The realtor shook his head vigorously in denial. "I swear I've told you everything I know about Morgan. What else do you want?"

"The truth."

"I *told* you the truth!"

"Not all of it. You told me what identity Morgan is operating under, yes, and where I can find him. But not where his lair is."

"Lair?"

"Yes, lair. Lions have them. Bank robbers have them. Every king vampire has one. It is a place where they can retreat to, without fear of attack."

"Look, I told you he lives in the Marina area, somewhere off Fillmore . . ."

Sonja shook her head. "He moves every six months or so—you said so yourself. This place you mentioned is a nest, nothing more. I want to know where he can be found when he goes to ground."

"I told you everything—"

"Pick up the gun, Mr. Howard."

The crisp, surgical steel civility was back in her voice. Without wanting to, Howard picked up the discarded .22 by its muzzle.

"Place your left hand on top of the desk, Mr. Howard. That's right. Now spread your fingers. Yes, like that. Now wider."

Howard stared in horrified silence as his left hand did as it was told.

"Now, hit your left hand with the butt of the gun. Hard."

Howard emitted a strangled cry of pain and terror as the butt of the automatic smashed into the middle of his hand. His fingers writhed, but he still could not move his left hand no matter how hard he tried.

"Again."

Another powerful, hammerlike blow. Howard felt something like a green twig break in the middle of his palm. He tasted blood and realized he'd bitten through his lower lip.

"Where is Morgan's lair?"

Howard whimpered.

This time the pistol smashed the knuckle of his index finger. Howard wondered if he would pass out before every finger on his left hand splintered. He was afraid he wouldn't.

"If you do not tell me what I want to know, Mr. Howard, I will make you pistol-whip your right hand with what remains of your left one. Then, if you're still being uncooperative, I will have you start on your left hand all over again."

"Ghost Trap."

"Beg pardon?"

"Ghost Trap!"

The vampire looked genuinely puzzled.

"It's the name of a house, somewhere out in the Sonoma Valley. Supposed to be haunted or something. Some crazy millionaire built it back before the Depression." Howard's face was the same shade of yellow as his tie. Sweat dripped from the end of his nose in greasy drops. "That's all I know about it. I swear." Tears leaked from the corners of the realtor's eyes. "Jesus, isn't that enough? Please go away. Go away and leave me alone."

"Very well. I see no reason to prolong our visit. But remember, Mr. Howard—you cannot shake hands with the Devil and not get sulfur on your sleeve." With that, she turned and disappeared into the reception area. A second later he heard the door to the outer office shut.

Howard slumped forward, cradling his head in his good hand. He was shivering and sweating and stank of fear and urine. Part of him wanted to leap up and chase after the intruders, pistol blazing. But then he remembered the hissing, needle-toothed face thrust into his own slack, well-fed one, and his heart beat so fast it seemed to stand still.

He found himself glancing at his Rolex. Only fifteen minutes had elapsed since the moment he first saw the strangers in his reception room. Fifteen minutes. One quarter of an hour. That was all it had taken to ruin the last seven years of his life. Howard picked up the automatic by the grip this time, although it was sticky with his blood.

Morgan would find out. He had no doubt about that. Although Howard was without religion or faith, he knew there was a Devil. He knew it with a certainty rare amongst even the most devout ecclesiastics. And no matter how fearsome and cruel the creature that called itself Sonja Blue had been, he knew Morgan would be a thousand times worse.

"Don't you think we were a little hard on that guy?" Palmer asked as they waited for the elevator.

Sonja angled her head in his direction, but because of the glasses, Palmer was uncertain as to whether she was looking at him or down the hall.

She shrugged. "He is a bellwether. A traitor to the species."

"Yeah, but maybe he didn't really know what Morgan was."

"Oh, he knew. He knew all too well. Just as the president knows what's held in check within the walls of the Pentagon. He simply found it advantageous to pretend otherwise. He does not even have a renfield's excuse of having been twisted against his will."

The elevator arrived empty. As Palmer stepped into the car he heard a muffled report from the direction of Russell Howard's office. He looked at Sonja, who shrugged yet again.

"No matter how far up a sheep climbs, it will never get beyond the killing floor."

"Are you sure this is the right address?"

Sonja nodded. "It's the only 'Dr. J. Caron' listed in the phone book. What's the matter? You weren't expecting a gothic castle with gargoyles and a moat, were you?"

"No, but I thought it'd look, you know, *different* somehow."

Sonja gazed at the building across the street from the rental car. She didn't want to admit it, but she'd been expecting something different, too. The surrounding houses reflected the Mediterranean revival architecture popular in the 1920s; the low, pastel-colored single-family dwellings lining the curving streets hardly looked like the kind of neighborhood to shelter a lord of the undead.

In the gathering dusk healthy-looking men and women, outfitted in expensive jogging clothes with Walkman earphones clamped to their heads, shared the streets with people walking their dogs. A few blocks over, newer, no doubt even more expensive, buildings were being erected on the site of property damaged by the '89 quake. She had a hard time picturing Morgan strolling down to the corner grocery for a six-pack of Calistoga Water and a package of squid-ink pasta.

"Wait a minute! Someone's coming out. Is that him?"

Sonja stared at the middle-aged man standing silhouetted on the front porch. He was dressed in a charcoal gray suit cinched by old-fashioned leather suspenders. The suit jacket hung over one forearm. His hair was graying at the temples and pulled into a brief ponytail, his eyes shaded by lightly tinted aviator glasses.

She closed her eyes and pictured him as he'd appeared twenty years ago: a debonair, jet-set English playboy bent on a wild weekend in Swinging

London. His strong, Cary Grant-like features rippled, revealing glowing eyes and sharp fangs. She could hear the sound of his laughter as he forced her to take his cold member into her mouth. She pulled herself free of the memory before she relived the agony of simultaneous penetration.

She was shivering and her breathing had grown ragged. Palmer stared at her.

"You all right?"

"It's him." She was surprised how hard it was for her to even speak. She felt strangely feverish. She'd spent the better part of two decades looking for this creature, and all she could do was stare at him. Now was her chance. She could leap out of the car and nail him before he had time to reach the Ferrari parked in the drive. But all she did was shiver and gasp like a malaria victim. It felt as if her marrow had been replaced with lead.

Morgan got into his sports car and pulled out into traffic. If he glanced in their direction, neither Sonja nor Palmer noticed it. The minute the Ferrari disappeared around the corner, the lassitude gripping Sonja loosened.

"Do you need to go to the hospital? You looked like you were going into shock."

She shook her head angrily, more to clear herself of the paralysis than to deny she needed help. "I'm okay now . . . I was afraid something like that would happen."

"What do you mean?"

"Morgan created me. Part of me—the vampiric self—was made in his image. I'm a member of his brood. The minute I saw him, I wanted to kill him. And I couldn't *move!* It was like someone had thrown a switch, shutting off my nervous system."

"You mean you were hypnotized?"

"It was more like my self-preservation instinct had been triggered. Some part of my brain considered killing Morgan the same as killing myself."

"Are you saying you can't lift a hand against this guy?"

"No!" Her denial was harsher and louder than it needed to be. She winced and fought to regain control of her temper. "It's a matter of will. That's how Morgan broke free of his own creator, Pangloss. He proved himself to have the stronger will."

"What about you?"

She shrugged. "I'll find that one out the hard way. Okay, since we're here and we know the monster of the house is out, what do you say to a little visit?"

Palmer sighed and pulled a leather wallet from his raincoat pocket. He flipped it open, displaying his collection of lock twirls.

Sonja grinned. "I like a man who's prepared."

It only took a few seconds for Palmer to pick the lock on the front door. He hesitated before opening it, gesturing to the sticker affixed to one of the windowpanes set into the door face.

Warning! This house protected by Phelegethon Home Security Systems!

"We'll just have to chance it. I'm betting Morgan wouldn't want the police showing up to check out a call."

"Whatever you say, boss."

Palmer crossed the threshold, wincing in anticipation. Silence.

Sonja moved cautiously into the vampire's nest, her head swiveling like a radar dish.

"He's not much on interior decorating, is he?" Palmer whispered.

The living room was devoid of furniture. The floor was covered by an off-white wall-to-wall carpet. To his left, Palmer glimpsed an equally barren dining nook.

"This isn't where he lives; it's just a nest. It's convenient for maintaining his identity. Kind of the vampiric equivalent of a place in the city. Most nobles have nests scattered all over the world, mostly in major metropolitan areas; places were the neighbors wouldn't consider an absentee owner unusual."

"Jesus, this place gives me the creeps."

Sonja held up her hand for silence. She sniffed the air and frowned. "Do you smell something?"

"Now that you mention it, smells like one of the neighbors is having a barbecue." His stomach rumbled in response to the aroma.

She moved down the hall and stopped in front of a closed bedroom door. The smell of cooking meat was stronger than before. She turned the knob and stepped inside.

The gloom was illuminated by a small color television set atop a plastic milk crate. Opposite the flickering television was an easy chair. Sitting in the chair was a middle-aged man dressed in a rumpled suit. The reek of roast pork filled the otherwise empty room.

The man watching the TV slowly turned his head toward the visitors. Palmer was aghast at the lobster-red color of the man's skin. He looked as if he'd been boiled alive. The man opened his blackened lips and let his jaw drop.

Sonja was suddenly backpedaling, trying to escape into the hallway. Palmer stared in horror at the smoke and steam leaking from the boiled man's ears and nostrils. He almost looked funny like one of those old Tex Avery cartoons.

A gout of flame leapt from the boiled man's throat, striking the wall a foot from Palmer's head, some of it splashing onto his shoulder. Palmer was too surprised to cry out, although he could smell his hair crisping.

Sonja grabbed him by the arm and jerked him out of the room. The pyrotic was getting to its feet, preparing to vomit another ball of fire. She slammed the door and hurriedly doffed her leather jacket, tossing it over Palmer's shoulder and forearm, smothering the flames. Satisfied the fire was out, she dragged Palmer in the direction of the front door.

Palmer looked back in time to see the boiled man lumber into the hall after them. He moved as if unused to arms and legs. He also seemed to be sweating bullets. Then Palmer realized that the man was dripping fat like a hot candle. The odor of frying bacon was omnipresent.

"We're *leaving*! Okay? We're leaving!" Sonja shouted at the melting man.

The pyrotic halted its clumsy advance and stared at them with the opaque eyes of a baked fish. It was still staring when they closed the door.

"I *said* I'm sorry, okay? How was I to know he had a fuckin' pyrotic as a home security system?"

They were back at their hotel, Sonja applying the last of the salve to Palmer's burns.

"I knew I shouldn't have let you talk me into this shit! I *knew* it! But do I listen to myself? Now I nearly get myself flash-fried by an escapee from a carnival sideshow!" Palmer winced as Sonja wrapped the gauze bandage around his upper arm. His right shoulder blade throbbed in time to his pulse.

"C'mon, it's not *that* bad. You've suffered worse." She nodded to the scar crossing his heart.

"You could have gotten us killed!"

"I could have gotten *you* killed. And for that I deserve the rebuke. I guess I was trying to prove something to myself: that I wasn't scared of the bastard. I was careless and stupid and you got hurt. I didn't want that to happen."

"You and me both."

Sonja finished dressing his wounds in silence. Palmer tried to find the strength to ignore the touch of her hands. At first the pain and fear had been enough to fuel his anger, but now it was fading. He wanted to stay mad at her. Being mad at her was a lot safer than liking her. He suddenly realized she'd said something to him. She was seated cross-legged on the floor, looking up at him as he perched on the corner of the bed.

"What was that? I didn't quite catch it."

"I said I keep forgetting you can't regenerate. I have to keep reminding myself how *frail* humans are."

Palmer allowed himself a smile. "I've been called a lot of things in my time, but 'frail' wasn't one of them. You keep saying 'human' like it's a brand name. Don't you still consider yourself, at least some part of you, to be like us? You're not like Pangloss. There's still something *alive* in you."

"Are you trying to flatter me? Don't answer that!" She smiled and leaned her chin into her palm. "You know, most vampires would consider being favorably compared to humans a gross insult. Humans are no more than *milch cows*—reliable producers of the two things vampires need to survive: blood and negative energy."

"What about you? Are you insulted?"

She smiled again. "No. Because I'm not a vampire."

"Huh?"

"Oh, I've got all the traditional vampiric qualities: fangs, a taste for the 'forbidden vintage,' nocturnal habits, the powers of hypnosis, and all that jazz. But I'm not a true vampire. I never died, you see. I'm a freak—a species of one."

Palmer didn't know what to make of this confession. He'd assumed Sonja's shunning of the daylight was because she would burst into flames and turn into a charred mummy. It hadn't occurred to him that she might sleep all day because she'd been up all night.

"You must be lonely."

She tilted her head, studying him from behind unreadable mirrored lenses. "Do you like me?"

His cheeks colored and he became interested in counting the dots in the acoustical tile. "Well, uh, it's just that I . . . "

"I understand." Her smile disappeared and Palmer heard his own words echoing inside his head. You must be *lonely*. Right on. Way to go, Mr. Milch Cow.

"What I *meant* to say is: *Of course* I like you." He was surprised to hear himself speak those words. He was even more surprised when he realized he was telling the truth. "You saved my life."

"Only because you were in danger on account of me. If it wasn't for me, you wouldn't be involved in this mess. You might not even have had your psychic powers activated. You'd be—"

"Stuck in the State Pen, getting my teeth knocked out and my asshole stretched, with no hope of parole until the next millennium. Believe me, as weird and as dangerous as this shit is, I could be a lot worse off." Palmer leaned over and touched her chin, tilting it upward. He didn't know *why* he did it it just seemed like the thing to do. Just like it seemed natural to pull her into his arms. He felt himself growing hard and that, too, seemed natural. It had been months since he'd last had sex. With Loli.

He tried to shut the thought from his mind, but it wouldn't go away.

Everything had seemed right and natural *then*, too. It had all seemed like some kind of beautiful, happy accident. He'd become so cynical it had made him naive. And Loli played him for the fool. From the very beginning she'd been in charge, manipulating him like a puppet on a string until he was no longer his own man. It had been a trap from the beginning, baited with honey and hot meat. And he'd never once suspected it until he'd faced the butcher on the killing floor. And the butcher had Loli's face.

Palmer made a strangling noise and pushed Sonja away from him. He pressed himself against the headboard, staring at her with wide, horrorstricken eyes. His penis went limper than cold pasta. "You're doing this! You're making this happen! It's not me, it's *you!*"

Sonja's face crumpled, and for a moment it looked as if she was going to cry. Then her features hardened and the left corner of her mouth curled into a humorless sneer. Her voice sounded ragged, as if her lungs were full of ice and razor blades.

"You fuckin' idiot! You're so damn neurotic, you don't even know what you really want, do you? You think I'm *making* you do this? Okay, I'll *make* you!"

Palmer tried to cry out as her will poured into him, seizing his brain in an invisible vise. All he could manage was a groan. His whole body felt numb, as if he'd been given a massive dose of novocaine. Although he could not feel any discomfort, the lack of sensation was worse than actual pain.

"Are you scared stiff yet? No? Then I'll have to see about that."

Palmer whimpered as his penis stirred. The numbness made it feel like it was a hundred miles away. He was vaguely aware of movement, but nothing else. The next stage was familiar. The last time he'd known such pain had been in New Orleans, when he'd narrowly escaped the "charms" of the succubus. His penis felt like an overinflated balloon on the verge of bursting. He gasped and struggled to keep his eyes from bugging out of their orbits.

"I could keep you like this for hours. Days, if I so choose. Of course, your bladder and testicles would rupture long before then. And even if you escaped being killed by your own sperm and piss, the blood vessels in your penis would be ruined for good. Assuming gangrene didn't set in and the doctors aren't forced to amputate, you'd be impotent for life." Sonja shook her head. "I don't understand what she sees in you. She must have a real weakness for fucked-up wimps; jerks with a taste for destructive relationships. *You* know what I mean, don't you?" She leaned forward, thrusting her face into Palmer's own. "Or do you need reminding?"

Her hair stood on end, waving like strands of seaweed. Palmer stared as Sonja's hair grew before his eyes, doubling, then tripling its length. As he watched, the hair turned from dark to light, becoming a raw honey blonde. Then her face rearranged itself, her flesh rippling, like a reflection in a disturbed pool. Then he heard a wet, squelching sound as the bones restructured. Her lips swelled, her chin becoming baby-doll round, her cheekbones sliding into place with a grinding sound.

Loli smiled down at him, her eyes screened by twin reflective mirrors.

"Hi, baby. Did you miss me?"

Palmer screamed.

He was free of the paralysis, his erection was gone, and he shivered like a half-drowned cat. Sonja stood in the far corner, her back to the wall, staring at the bed. Her face was her own again. She wrapped her arms around her stomach, as if she was struggling to keep from vomiting—or keep something from escaping.

"Get out!" She sounded as if she was in pain.

The sight of Sonja hugging herself, rapping the back of her head against the wall as if keeping time to unheard music, was almost enough to make Palmer forget what had just happened. Almost.

"Get out of here before I hurt you, damn it!"

Palmer couldn't tell if she was pleading or threatening him. He hurried into his room, slamming and locking the door behind him. He couldn't be sure, but he thought he could hear her talking to someone—or *thing*—and that she was being answered. Then he heard furniture being trashed.

Palmer retreated to the bathroom. He needed to take a shower. He wanted the hot water to turn his flesh the same boiled-lobster red as that of the pyrotic. Maybe if he could scrub off a layer or two of skin he'd feel clean again.

He sat on the toilet, smoking a Shermans with shaking hands, and watched the steam turn the mirror opaque. It almost obscured the tobacco demon squatting on his shoulder.

He closed his eyes, the roar of the water in his ears, and heard Chaz's ghost whispering its warning again.

Yer in love with her already! You don't even know it yet, but I can see it in th' folds of yer brain.

And the horrible thing was, it was true.

GHOST TRAP

A savage place! As holy and enchanted As e'er beneath a waning moon was haunted.
—Coleridge, *Kubla Khan*

She found him drinking espresso in a dark, smoky coffeebar across the street from the hotel. The sun was going down and she had her shades on. He glanced up from his drink, shrugged, and motioned for her to take a seat.

He expected her to say she was sorry or try to explain herself in some way. He'd played the scene before, but from the other side. He'd expected hesitant, incoherent emotional histrionics. Instead, she touched the top of his right hand with the index finger of her left hand.

Palmer gasped as her mind flowed into his. It was as unlike the brutal intrusion of the night before as a lover's caress from a molester's groping. There were no words, only sensations. The intimacy was both thrilling and intimidating. The temptation to let go, to lose himself in telepathic rapport, was strong. But so was his sense of self.

She recognized his fear of being subsumed and respected it, breaking the contact voluntarily.

He couldn't tell if she was looking at him or not, so he coughed into his fist and sipped his espresso before speaking. "No harm done."

She nodded and motioned to the paperback book at his elbow. "What's that?"

Palmer flipped the book over so that the cover was visible. "I found out what—and where—Ghost Trap is."

Sonja picked up the book and read the title aloud.

"The Architect's Guide to Haunted Houses?"

"I found it at a B. Dalton's, of all places. Check out page 113."

Sonja opened the book and began to read:

Northern California has long demonstrated an allure for the eccentric, the artistic, and the wealthy. One of the strangest transplanted Californians to combine these elements was the architect-millionaire Creighton Seward (1870–1930). Seward, heir to an industrialist fortune, has been lost amongst the shadows cast by Frank Lloyd Wright. That all but a handful of his buildings have been destroyed in the sixty years since his death has helped condemn him to obscurity. Yet none can deny that Seward's genius was very real. As was the tragedy that consumed him.

After spending the better part of a decade designing competent but uninspired skyscrapers and palaces-away-from-palace for America's upper class in the Great Lakes area, in 1907 Seward took a sabbatical to Europe, taking his family with him. What truly happened on that tiny Mediterranean island will never be known. That Seward was found roaming its shores, delirious and naked except for his wife's blood, is certain.

The official report was that a disgruntled servant had murdered the entire household, including the children, while they slept. The only reason Seward survived was that he'd been awakened by the killer hacking his wife apart and overpowered him, smashing the fiend's skull open with the very ax used to dispatch his hapless family.

However, rumor persisted that the ax-murderer was none other than Seward himself, although no one could provide motivation for such a heinous act on his part. That Seward spent three years in a private asylum following his ordeal did not help the gossip. In 1910, Seward resumed his career. Whatever he might have seen—or done—that night in 1907 changed him forever, as is evident in his work.

Previously a mediocre architect, Seward's new designs foreshadowed the work of Gaudi and Salvador Dalí. Seward only took on three commissions in the five years between his return to public life and his subsequent self-imposed seclusion, but each is a masterwork. Unfortunately, none of these structures remain standing, largely due to the so-called "Seward Curse."

While each of these buildings (two private homes in Minnesota and the old Zorn Publications skyscraper in New York) were incredible works of art and widely praised by the literati of the time, they proved to be uninhabitable. On the few occasions Seward would speak of his later work, he insisted that he had discovered, through the use of non-euclidian geometry and quantum physics, a way of creating lines and angles that would pierce the space-time continuum. Whether this was so, or simply the ravings of a brilliant but sadly unhinged mind, can never be verified. However, it was soon discovered that those who intended to live or work within these edifices were often stricken with vertigo and a nameless dread that led them to flee the buildings. (It is believed that these incidents later provided the fantasy writer H.P. Lovecraft with the inspiration for his short story "The Dreams in the Witch-House.") *In 1916, shortly before the Zorn Building, with its magnificent chromium gargoyles and eye-twisting zeppelin mooring spire, was scheduled for demolition, Creighton Seward disappeared from the public eye and would not resurface until his apparent suicide in 1930.*

It was later discovered that Seward had "disappeared" into the hills of Northern California's Sonoma Valley, where he set about creating a personal testament to guilt and madness: the infamous Ghost Trap Manor. Using a previously existing three-story mansion as its core, Seward had carpenters constantly working on a twisting maze of weirdly shaped and cunningly designed rooms and corridors that would, by the time of the architect's death, cover acres of land and tower over six stories high. The mansion was completed in 1925 and the workmen departed, each paid handsomely to keep secret the location—and nature—of Creighton Seward's final masterpiece.

It is uncertain whether Seward spent the last five years of his life in complete isolation, or if he shared the house with servants. When his nephew and heir, Pierce Seward, had the rambling house searched for signs of his uncle in 1930, it took the searchers three days to locate the body.

The exact manner of Seward's demise is unknown, although he is believed to have starved to death. Many of those who originally searched the house later complained of experiencing attacks of vertigo and extreme nausea.

Notes found amongst Seward's personal effects hinted at the architect's intended use for his unconventional home. Seward apparently suffered from the delusion that the ghosts of his slain family were haunting him. Consumed by guilt and fear, he devised a house that would effectively "confuse" the pursuing spirits and keep them from finding him: thus explaining Ghost Trap's bewildering number of blind staircases, doorways that open onto brick walls, and windows set into ceilings.

Apparently Seward himself lived in the original "normal" rooms that served as the nucleus for the sprawling mansion. Why the architect would wander into the maze of "ghost rooms" without provisions or a map is not certain. For lack of a better verdict, the coroner listed his death as a suicide.

For over fifty years Ghost Trap remained shuttered and sealed against the elements as part of the Seward estate. Then, in 1982, it was sold to a San

Francisco real estate agent and land developer acting for an unnamed third party. Ghost Trap remains closed to the public, although whether anyone currently walks its halls is unknown.

*

On the page opposite the text was a partial schematic of the house's floor plan. Sonja stared at it for a moment before realizing what she was looking at.

"I'll be damned!"

"I don't doubt it. What's up?"

She pointed at the diagram. "Can't you see? Look at that!"

Palmer frowned at the jumble of lines and curves. "So? It looks like a kid went crazy with a Spirograph. Big deal."

"You're seeing it with human eyes. Look again. Look *harder*."

Palmer shrugged and looked at the drawing again, this time focusing his attention on it. To his dismay the lines *writhed*, as if they had suddenly taken on three-dimensional life.

"Shit!"

"It's *Pretender* script! A form of—I don't know, call it a magic formula or glyph!"

"Are you saying this Seward guy was a werewolf or a vampire or something?"

"It's possible. Although I suspect he wasn't full-blooded, whatever he was. Probably wasn't even aware of his heritage. There are plenty of half-bloods and changelings out there, ignorant of their true nature and powers until something happens, later in life, to trigger it. They can be as dangerous as a purebred Pretender, given the right circumstances. Catherine Wheele, for example."

Palmer tried to keep his jaw from dropping. "I always wondered about her! Did you have anything to do with the fire?"

Sonja's manner stiffened. "That's old business."

Palmer let it drop.

"Like I was saying, Seward didn't design a trap for unwanted ghosts—he created the physical equivalent of a psychic jamming station!"

"Come again?"

"This entire house is a protective charm! No wonder Morgan is using it as his lair! It's probably the only place on earth he can relax without fear of being attacked, at least on a psychic level. No wonder the networks don't have any information on him. He's practically invisible!"

"Is this a good thing or a bad thing?"

"Hard to say. Obviously it's worked to Morgan's advantage. From what little information there is to go by, I'd say we're going to need a countercharm just to get inside the door."

"So how do we go about getting one of these 'countercharms?' Open a box of breakfast cereal?"

"It won't be that easy, I'm afraid. Before we left New Orleans, I checked with Malfeis to see if there was a reliable alchemist in the San Francisco area."

"You mean they're not listed in the Triple-A Guide?"

"Funny, Palmer. Remind me to laugh. You don't have to go if you don't want to."

"Did I say I wouldn't? Where do we have to go this time?"

"Chinatown."

He knew they were in for trouble the moment Sonja ducked into the alleyway. Since he had no choice, he followed her into the narrow, foul-smelling back street. It was dark and they had long left the Caucasian tourists on Grant Avenue behind them. He realized his basic instincts had been correct when he heard the sound of boot leather on concrete.

There were three of them blocking the way. Palmer was pained by how young they were. The oldest of the group was barely nineteen. The Chinese youths wore their hair short and choppy, and Palmer sensed the aggression rolling off them in crackling waves.

The tallest of the trio, stainless steel *shuriken* decorating the front of his leather jacket, stepped forward. His eyes were fixed on Palmer. "This is Black Dragon territory. No dogs or round-eyes allowed."

Sonja's fingers brushed against Palmer's bunched fist, touching his mind with her own. *Let me handle this*.

She moved to intercept the gang leader, speaking in Cantonese. "We're looking for Li Lijing. We meant no disrespect."

The youth scowled. His challenge had been aimed at Palmer; he had not expected the woman to know the tongue of his ancestors. "Li Lijing? The apothecary?"

"Yeah, Loo, maybe the geezer needs a fix of powdered rhino horn so he can get it up!" A slender boy with bristling, raven-back hair giggled.

"All we want is to speak with the *kitsune*."

"*Kitsune?* You're talking Japanese trash, white girl!" sneered the boy. "What's the matter, can't you tell the difference between Chinese and Japanese?"

"Round-eyes can't tell the difference between shit and tuna fish!" The third Black Dragon laughed, and yanked a *nunchaku* from the waistband of his jeans. "Only way they learn the difference is if you *beat* it into them!"

Palmer couldn't tell what the trio were saying; but he didn't like the way they were laughing or the way the one with acne let his *nunchaku* drop to the length of their chain.

"Loo! Hong! Kenny! Is this how you greet people looking for my shop? No wonder my business has been so poor!"

The youths jumped at the sound of the old man's voice, looking more like children surprised at a naughty deed than dangerous street toughs. An ancient Chinese gentleman stood at the top of the stair leading to a basement shop, leaning on an ornately carved cane.

"Go play hoodlum somewhere else! I will not have you harassing paying customers! Have I made myself clear?" The old man poked Loo in the ribs with the end of his cane. The boy looked embarrassed but did not protest the treatment.

"Yes, Uncle."

"Go now before I change my mind about paying you for the work you did for me!" The old man watched the leather-jacketed youths retreat and made a sour face. "Youth today! No respect! You must forgive Loo, my friends. He works for me, opening and sorting boxes of herbs from the old country. He is a good boy, but his brain is too often filled with foolish Western nonsense—no offense."

"None taken. I assume I am speaking to the honorable Li Lijing?"

The old man nodded, smiling cryptically. "And you are the one they call the Blue Woman. Malfeis told me I might expect a visit from you. That is why I was eavesdropping. Loo is a silly boy, but I have a fondness for him. It would pain me to dig a grave for one so young. Ah! It is rude of me to keep you chattering on my doorstep! Please, come inside and make yourself comfortable."

The apothecary's basement workshop was dark and close, the ceiling a foot over their heads. Various kinds of herbs and spices hung from the rafters, filling the space with an exotic aroma. Palmer noticed a stuffed Chinese crocodile suspended from the rafters and a bewildering collection of subhuman skulls in an open cupboard—one of which boasted a cyclopean eye socket and a large horn growing from its forehead.

"Permit me to light another lamp," Li Lijing said as he busied himself with an antique hurricane lamp. "You and I certainly do not need it, my dear, but your companion might benefit from some additional illumination." Li Lijing turned to face Palmer, a sharp smile on his long, black velvet snout. "Is that not so?"

Without meaning to, Palmer let out a startled yelp and stepped back from the humanoid fox.

"You're a werewolf!"

Li Lijing looked pained and shook his pointed ears in disgust. "Hardly! I am *kitsune*, not *vargr!* Would you compare a panda to a grizzly bear? An Arabian stallion to a Clydesdale? A samurai to a priest?"

"Forgive my companion, Li Lijing. He is new to the Real World and has yet to meet a *kitsune*, much less a *vargr*. He meant no offense."

The *kitsune* snorted as he hobbled through the shop, the staff he carried helping to balance him on his crooked legs. "I have come to expect such ignorance from humans. Still, it is a sore spot with me. But I can not find it in myself to dislike their species. I have lived long amongst humankind. Why, I even took a couple as wives!" He made a barking sound that Palmer recognized as laughter. "I will tell you a secret! Loo is not my nephew, but actually my great-grandson! Not that he knows this. As far as he is concerned, I am merely a good friend of the family who arranged for his father to escape the mainland. He calls me uncle out of respect, but is ignorant of his blood. I favor the boy, as he reminds me of his grandfather—my son—who was lost to me during the invasion of Manchuria. Ah, but I must be old and foolish to succumb to such sentimentality, yes?"

Li Lijing sat down behind a low teak desk carved with scenes of *kei-lun*, the Chinese unicorn, frolicking in the perfumed gardens of K'Un Lun, the City of Heaven. "Now, what is it I can do for you, my dear?"

"I need a counter-charm."

"I see." The *kitsune* pushed aside a scroll of rice paper and his collection of bamboo calligraphy brushes and picked up an abacus. "What kind of spell are you interested in negating? Protection? Ensorcellment? Bedevilment? Containment? There is a difference in the prices, you know . . ."

Sonja motioned for Palmer to hand the alchemist the book. "You tell me. I'm sure I'm nowhere as adept at reading conjuration patterns as you are, Honorable One."

Li Lijing accepted the compliment by fluttering his pointed ears. "You do me great honor. Now, as to this particular charm . . ." He pondered the drawing for a long moment, scratching his muzzle in contemplation. "This is a protective ward of immense potency. You were wise to consult me. Anyone—Pretender or human—trying to violate these lines of power would be risking their sanity, if not their very lives!"

"Can you do it?"

"Of course I can do it! Did I say otherwise? It's just that the preparation of the proper counter-charm will not be without some expense . . . or danger."

"I'm willing to pay what it's worth."

The *kitsune* smiled as if he'd just been handed the key to the henhouse. "Malfeis didn't lie, for once. You *are* a class act!" The alchemist barked another laugh and returned to his estimating, the abacus beads rattling like hailstones on a tin roof. "Let's see, I can have the appropriate counter-charm ready within the week—

"Twenty-four hours."

Li Lijing looked down his long black nose at her. "That's extra, you know."

Sonja shrugged.

The abacus beads were flying now. "Very well. I'll have Loo deliver it to your hotel once it's ready. However, I would advise that you, not your companion, be the one to use it. Frankly, a charm of this magnitude has no business being handled by humans. No offense. Now, as to the settling of my bill—"

"Sonja? You awake?"

Palmer glanced into the rearview mirror as she sat up in the back seat of the rental car. In the bright sunshine she looked pale and unhealthy, out of her element. She grimaced and smacked her lips as if trying to rid her palate of an offensive aftertaste.

"Daylight: phooey."

"I thought you said you weren't allergic to sunlight."

"I'm not. But I *am* nocturnal. Being awake during the day is . . . unnatural. Believe me, if I was allergic, you'd know it! Vampires exposed to direct sunlight develop a speedy case of skin cancer bordering on leprosy: noses falling off every which way, ears dropping like leaves. Hardly a sight for the weak of heart—or stomach."

"Ugh. Sounds like it."

"What is it you wanted? Or did you disturb my beauty sleep just to see if I'd dissolve à la Christopher Lee in *Horror of Dracula?*"

Palmer blushed and returned his attention to the highway. "No, it's just—well, I wanted to see the charm Li Lijing gave you."

Sonja sighed. "You heard what he said about humans handling it."

"Look, I'm not interested in *using* the damn thing, I just want to look at it. Is that okay?"

"I can't see what harm it could do. Besides, it might do you good to realize what kind of explosive we're playing with here."

"It's that powerful?"

"You'll see. Why don't you pull over at the next rest station? The last thing I need is to have you plow the car into the back of a semi by mistake."

"I never slam into the back of trucks by *mistake!*"

A few minutes later, Palmer pulled the car into a roadside rest area thoughtfully provided by the California Highway Commission. He killed the engine and turned around in the front seat, facing Sonja.

"Okay, let's see this powerful juju."

Sonja pulled a package wrapped in blue tissue paper out from under the seat and handed it to the detective. "Remember, you asked for it!"

Palmer wrinkled his nose at the strong spices. The tissue paper crackled under his fingers. Frowning, he unwrapped the talisman.

When he saw what it was, he instinctively tossed the thing away from him as if it was a poisonous spider. He felt a bitter surge of vomit scald the back of his throat, but he could not look away from the withered, severed hand nestled in the blue tissue paper like a perverse corsage.

"It's *horrible!*"

"It's a Hand of Glory. Lijing assures me that it is especially potent."

"It's got *six fingers!*"

"Yes, that's the secret of its power. It once belonged to one of the hereditary Mayan priest-kings. There was one particular royal family that was so inbred they all had six fingers and toes. They were known as *Chan Balam*, the Jaguar Lords. It was considered a sign of divinity."

Palmer swallowed the burning knot in his throat and watched an elderly man in tan slacks and a cream-colored windbreaker lead a miniature schnauzer toward a grassy stretch marked "Pet-Path." He suppressed the urge to get out of the car and sprint for the nearest parked car. Unfortunately, he knew he was more likely to get another hole in his chest from his fellow motorists than a free ride back to normalcy, so he remained seated.

"For crying out loud, are you going to leave it lying out where everyone can see it? Why don't you just mount it on the dashboard?"

The idea of touching the Hand of Glory was repugnant beyond belief, but she was right. If anyone got a good look at what was on the front seat, they'd have every CHIPS officer north of Los Angeles breathing down their necks. Grimacing in distaste, Palmer picked up the severed hand.

He was somewhere warmer, where the screeching of macaws and the screams of howler monkeys echoed from the lush green canopy outside his door. A naked brown child sat framed in the doorway, playing with a baby spider monkey on a leash. The child's forehead was oddly shaped, sloping backward. At first Palmer thought the boy was retarded, then the child smiled and turned his face toward him. The child's eyes were dark and sparkled with a natural wit. Confused, Palmer scanned the room he found himself in, frowning at the detailed charcoal renderings of Mayan dignitaries offering sacrifices to the gods decorating the white-washed stone walls. Above his head handwoven nets full of museum-quality Pre-Columbian pottery hung from brightly painted, ornate wooden rafters.

The naked child laughed at his pet's antics, lifting a six-fingered hand to his mouth. Palmer glanced down at his own nude body and saw he was seated, cross-legged, on a stone bench carved in the likeness of a jaguar. His breath was coming heavier now, but it had nothing to do with the oppressive humidity. Palmer stood up and walked to the doorway.

He was wobbly on his feet and had to steady himself by placing one hand against the wall. His hand had six fingers. He brought his other hand to his face and felt the stingray barb piercing his lower lip and the ritual scars on his cheeks. His gaze dropped to his borrowed body's exposed genitals. He knew he should be alarmed by the sight of a second stingray barb skewering his penis, but Palmer felt strangely disconnected from the mutilations done to his flesh.

The child looked up at Palmer from his place on the stoop and smiled. The baby spider monkey squatted on the boy's shoulder, chattering to itself as it searched its master's hair for vermin. Suddenly William Palmer, never married and an avowed enemy of small children, knew how it felt to be a husband and a father.

Somewhere, in the jungle, a jaguar screamed.

"Palmer! Palmer, are you all right? Answer me, damn it!" Sonja was in the front seat of the rental car, shaking him by the shoulders. She actually looked scared. Palmer wondered if he should feel honored or worried. "Damn it, Palmer! Say something! Don't make me come in there and get you!"

"Sonja?"

"You're back. Good. I don't like dream-walking under these circumstances. What happened?"

"I don't know—one minute I was here in the car with you, the next I was in a jungle in Central America. What's that awful taste in my mouth?"

"Blood." Sonja pulled a linen handkerchief from her pants pocket and offered it to the dazed detective. "You had some kind of seizure; blood started running out of your nose. You also probably bit the side of your mouth, if not your tongue. Now, what's this about you being in Central America?"

Palmer shook his head in disbelief as he dabbed at the corner of his mouth. "It was weird. It wasn't like a dream. It was more like being there. Or *remembering* being there. I was sitting in a stone house and I could hear the birds and monkeys outside, just like in the Tarzan movies. There was a boy . . ." Palmer frowned as he tried to recall more of his vision, but it was already fading.

"Palmer, do you believe in reincarnation?"

"I never really gave it much thought, to tell you the truth. Just like I never gave much thought to vampires and werewolves." His smile wavered and Sonja saw the fear in his eyes. "It's true, then?"

"To a point. There is such a thing as reincarnation. But not every human being is reincarnated. I don't know how it works—nobody does for sure, unless it's the *seraphim*, and they're not talking. But there are a number of humans who are pre-born. The Pretenders call them old souls. Most never know who—or what—they were before, and that's as it should be. But every now and again, they get a glimpse of their previous incarnations. Various random incidents can cue a buried memory. Or, as in your case, you can accidentally make contact with the physical remains of your previous self."

Palmer hunched forward, resting his forehead against the steering wheel. "Holy—!"

"You spoke while you were—away. Are you aware of that?"

"No. What did I say?"

"You said the word 'Tohil.' Does that mean anything to you?"

He closed his eyes and the sound of macaws calling to one another from jungle perches filled his ears. "Yes. Yes, it does. It was my son's name."

✹

"So that's Ghost Trap. The guy who built it really *was* crazy!"

Palmer was perched atop a nearby hill overlooking the infamous manor house, squinting through binoculars at the valley below. Not that he needed them to see Creighton Seward's fevered brainchild; the rambling mansion filled the small dell to overflowing.

Sonja pointed to the center of the grandiose concoction of towers, turrets, and flying buttresses. "You can still make out the original house in the middle. It looks like a spider squatting in the middle of a web. See anything?"

Palmer shook his head and lowered the binoculars. "Sealed up like a fuckin' drum. All the shutters are closed. I spotted what looks like an old stable off to one side—Morgan's sports car's in it. Our boy's here. No doubt about it."

"I never thought he wasn't. I can *feel* him."

"Looking at that house is making my head hurt." Palmer massaged the bridge of his nose. "I can't imagine anyone actually *living* in that monstrosity!"

Sonja scowled down at Ghost Trap. Morgan could be anywhere inside its labyrinth-like belly. She glanced up at the afternoon sky, careful not to look directly at the sun. It had taken them three hours, following narrow asphalt roads that twisted through the hills surrounding the Sonoma Valley like black snakes, before they located the isolated area that separated Ghost Trap from the rest of the world. There were still several hours to go before it got dark and Morgan would stir from his daily coma.

Still, in a place like Ghost Trap, where daylight rarely pierced its heart, Morgan might possibly be up and about. She was loathe to mention it to Palmer, but she was in bad need of recharging. It kind of scared her. She used to be able to function perfectly well during the day, but right now she felt like she'd just come off a week-long drunk. The temptation to crawl in the trunk of the car and enjoy a quick nap was strong.

"Put a sock in it," she muttered to the Other as it whined for the seven hundredth and fifty-second time that the sunlight was making it sick.

"Huh?" Palmer looked up from his binoculars.

"I wasn't talking to you."

"Uh . . . right. Whatever you say."

"I'm going down there."

"When?"

"Now."

Palmer sucked on his lower lip. "You figure it's safe?"

She barked a humorless laugh. "It's *never* going to be safe! Still, I think I stand a better chance during the day. Hopefully, he won't be expecting anything. And if Lijing's talisman does what it's supposed to"—she hefted the Hand of Glory before stuffing it into her leather jacket—"he won't know I've breached his defense before it's too late to do him any good. What about you? You packing?"

Palmer pulled a loaded .38 Special out of his waistband and held it up so she could see. "Figure this'll do the job?"

"Honey, you shoot *anything* in the brain, human or not, with that damn thing, you'll kill it!"

He nodded and returned her smile. Sonja gave him a thumbs-up signal and began walking. Palmer watched as she moved into the trees and made her way down the rugged hillside. When he could no longer see her, he focused his binoculars back on Ghost Trap.

He quickly scanned the windows and turrets for signs of movement, having already learned that if he let his eyes linger too long on any particular architectural detail it made his eyes water and his head hurt.

His attention was caught by a fleeting glimpse of a pale, moon-like face glowering from a fifth-floor window. Swearing as he fiddled with the binoculars' field of focus for a closer view, Palmer's heart thumped at 4/4 beat. But by the time he could refocus, the face was gone, the window once more shuttered. Or had it ever been open in the first place? Perhaps it had been an illusion created from staring too long at the weird house. And if not, whose face had he seen at the window? It sure wasn't Morgan's. He contemplated hurrying after Sonja and telling her what he'd seen.

Before he could get to his feet, he saw a shadow emerge from the tree line just beyond the east side of the mansion's ruined gardens and flit through the tangled rosebushes. He watched, awed by the woman's supernatural grace as she deftly avoided empty goldfish ponds and crumbling statuary and made her way to what had once been the coal cellar.

He smiled when he saw her yank the heavy-duty padlock off the cellar doors and whispered under his breath, "That's m'girl!"

Then she was gone, swallowed by Ghost Trap. Whatever dangers lay hidden within the mansion's sprawl, she would have to face them alone. And maybe, if he was lucky, she would never come out.

Sonja took a deep breath and paused to orient herself. The moment she entered the confines of the mansion she'd been hit with a surge of nausea. The empty coal cellar tilted under her feet, as if the ground was made of india rubber. Something in her jacket twitched.

She removed the Hand of Glory Li Lijing had given her. The six-fingered hand was now clenched into a fist. Hoping that was a good sign, she returned it to her pocket. She took a cautious step toward the stairs leading to the rest of the house, then another. The nausea was gone, although she was unable to shake the feeling of disorientation.

The first floor was dark, the bare wooden boards furry with dust. As she walked through the series of oddly shaped interconnected rooms, it became obvious that they had never been furnished. Some had never even been plastered and painted, the wooden slats giving the smaller rooms an austere, almost monkish flavor.

Sonja was impressed by the demented genius of Ghost Trap's creator. Even to her mutated senses, the building was disturbing. She found her eyes drawn to lines that both originated and intersected beyond the field of normal vision. She doubted an unprepared human could withstand more than an hour's sustained exposure to Ghost Trap's peculiar brand of architectural design without losing consciousness or going mad. The weirdly angled doorways and out-of-kilter rooms reminded her of the starkly rendered expressionist scenery from The *Cabinet of Dr. Caligari*.

The second floor was much like the first, as was the third. The house was indeed as huge and maze-like as she'd feared. She could feel Morgan's presence, hidden somewhere within the massive sprawl of zigzagging walls and staggered staircases; but whether the vampire lord was hiding in the attic, the basement, or the room next door was impossible for her to divine. All she could hope for was that if Morgan was conscious of her intrusion, he was equally helpless in pinpointing her exact location.

Judging from the thickness of the dust coating the floorboards and banisters, she doubted that the section of Ghost Trap she found herself in had seen any visitors—human or Pretender—since the day Creighton Seward's body was recovered, sixty years ago.

As she left a sitting room with faded, green patterned wallpaper and an upside-down fireplace made from Italian marble, she glimpsed something pale out of the corner of her eye. Turning to confront the apparition, she stared at a little girl no more than five or six.

Sonja knew the child to be dead because she could see through her. The ghost-child wore old-fashioned clothes and held a porcelain doll in her chubby arms. Both the girl and the doll had golden hair that fell to their shoulders in ringlets. The face of the china doll was marred by a hairline fracture that ran from its brow to the bridge of its nose.

"Hello, little girl."

The phantom child smiled and lifted a hand still chubby with baby fat and waved hello in return.

"Little girl, do you know how I can get to the middle of the house?"

The ghost shook her head "no." Sonja wished the tiny specter would speak, but knew that the dead often lost the ability to communicate coherently with the living after a few years. The use of dumb-show might be aggravating, but at least it was reliable.

"Is there anyone around who *does* know?"

The little girl smiled again, this time nodding "yes." She turned and signaled for Sonja to follow her. Sonja tried not to look at the brains spilling from the back of the child's smashed skull.

The ghostly child flickered from room to room like a pale but playful moth while Sonja followed. Finally the phantom entered a long, narrow room paneled in darkly stained walnut with bronze satyr faces studding the walls. On closer inspection, Sonja saw old-fashioned gas jets protruding from the grotesquely leering mouths. Suddenly there was an icy draft, as if someone had thrown open the door of a massive freezer, and the thirteen gas jets burst into flame, filling the room with the odor of blood, perfume, and butane.

The tiny ghost child hurried over to where her mother stood revealed, dressed in a high-collared morning glory skirt, her hair—the same golden hue as her daughter—puffed at the sides and pulled into a knot atop her head. Even with the left side of her face reduced to pulp, the eye hanging from its stalk onto the ruined cheek, it was obvious she had once been a stunningly beautiful woman.

The ghost-child tugged at her mother's skirts and pointed at Sonja. Her lips moved but all Sonja heard was a skewed, half-speed garble.

"Mrs. Seward . . . "

The dead woman looked up, surprised at being recognized. The undamaged side of her face frowned.

"Mrs. Seward, I need your help in finding my way to the center . . ." Sonja stepped forward, one hand outstretched.

Mrs. Seward looked down at her daughter, then at Sonja. As she opened her mouth, the flames issuing from the gas jets intensified. The ghost-woman, now looking more terrified than terrible, motioned for her child to leave. The little girl obeyed, rolling herself into a ball of witch-fire and bouncing from the room.

There was a distant whistling sound, as that of air being sliced by an axe, followed by a hollow booming. Whatever was creating the noise was making its way toward the room Sonja occupied with the late Mrs. Seward.

The ghost gestured for Sonja to follow, and moved to one of the walnut panels set into the wall. Her long, bell-like skirt left the thick fur of dust on the floor undisturbed. Mrs. Seward pointed to the molding where the plaster met the paneling and passed through the wall. It took Sonja a few seconds to locate the hidden catch that opened the secret door. The booming sound had grown considerably closer as she closed the panel behind her.

Mrs. Seward was waiting for her, glowing in the gloom of the secret passage like a night-light. Sonja followed her spirit guide through the narrow passageway to a cramped circular staircase that pierced Ghost Trap's various levels. Mrs. Seward motioned for her to go downstairs.

"How many levels? One? Two?"

The dead woman held up two transparent fingers and mimicked opening a door. Sonja nodded to show that she understood and began her downward climb. After a couple of steps she paused and looked back at the ghost-woman.

"You *are* trapped in this place, aren't you? You and the children!"

The ghost nodded, nearly dislodging her dangling eye.

"How can you be freed?"

The ghost hastily traced letters in mid-air. The ectoplasm hung suspended for a few seconds before wavering and losing shape, like a message left by a haphazard skywriter:

Diztroe Tarappe

The dead were notoriously bad spellers.

Before Sonja could ask anything else, Mrs. Seward disappeared. Sonja shrugged and resumed her descent into the bowels of Ghost Trap.

On the second level she found a narrow oak doorway at the base of the stairs. She could tell the door opened inward, but other than that had no idea where it might lead or what might be on the other side.

Taking a deep breath and hoping it didn't open onto a room full of hungry ogres, Sonja grasped the handle and yanked the portal open.

She found herself faced not by tigers, but with a lady.

The woman was seated in a tastefully upholstered easy chair, reading a thick paperback romance novel, her slippered feet resting on an ottoman. The room seemed very cozy, in a Victorian kind of way. Somewhere nearby a grandfather clock measured out the afternoon. A small, cheery fire crackled away in the fireplace. The woman had yet to notice the intruder standing in her sitting room.

Sonja frowned and moved further into the room, allowing the secret door to silently close behind her. She was wondering if the petite black woman was another ghost, albeit a bit more opaque than the last, when the woman looked up from her book and smiled at her. Her eyes were the color of claret. Sonja's right hand closed on the switchblade in her pocket.

"Hello," said the woman, putting aside her romance novel. "I'm sorry, I didn't hear you come in. Are you one of our Father's servants?"

Sonja adjusted her vision, scanning the woman to see her true appearance and strength. To her surprise, the black woman did not reveal herself to be a wizened crone or rotting corpse. She remained exactly what she looked like: a young African-American woman in her early twenties. Sonja hesitated pressing the ruby eye on her switchblade

"Is something wrong? Should I call Dr. Howell?" The pregnant woman reached for a cellular phone resting on the table next to an array of medication vials.

Before she had a chance to touch the receiver, Sonja wrapped one hand in her dark, abundant braids, yanking the woman's head back, exposing her café au lait throat. The point of her switchblade pressed against the pregnant woman's pulse.

"Who are you?" Sonja's words hissed like live steam.

"I'm Anise." She spoke loudly and slowly, as if communicating with an emotionally disturbed child. She was trying not to sound frightened, but Sonja saw how her hands clutched at her swollen belly. "What are you doing? You're hurting me . . ."

"Where is Morgan?"

"Our Father?"

Sonja cranked another length of braid around her fist, yanking Anise onto her tiptoes. "He's not *my* father, bitch! Answer me, damn you, or I'll go in and *take* what I want to know! Who else is in this fuckin' spook-house?"

Anise's eyes flickered, tracking something behind Sonja's shoulder.

The thought that there might be two of them entered Sonja's head the same time the fireplace poker came down on her skull.

Of course there are two of them, you pathetic ninny! The Other shrieked delightedly as the pain and rage sparked and fed on one another. *There has to be two of them! And baby makes three. Vampires that breed together bleed together.*

The Other wanted out. It wanted out *bad*. The Other wanted to twist the head off the bloat-bellied bitch. The Other wanted to gouge the eyes out of the asshole with the poker. The Other wanted to yank the little unborn shit out of its mother's womb and snap its head between her teeth like a terrier worrying a rat.

"No. I'm not letting you out. Not yet. Save it. Save it for Morgan."

As Sonja struggled to keep the Other under control, another blow fell across her shoulders, knocking her to the floor. She felt ribs crack and blood fill her mouth.

"Fell, stop it! I said *stop!*"

Anise grappled with her mate for control of the poker. The male was tall and thin, his features pale and finely chiseled. His hair was the color of raw pine, hanging to his shoulders in long silken tresses. His rubescent eyes were dilated, like those of a panther scenting its prey. Sonja knew that wild, cruel look all too well.

"I told you they hated us! They're all crazy with jealousy because our Father loves us more than them!"

"No, Fell! She's not a renfield. Look at her. *Look!*"

Fell grudgingly turned his gaze on Sonja. The poker in his hand wavered.

Sonja grinned crookedly, spitting out a mouthful of blood. "The little lady's right. you know—I'm not a renfield." She was up and moving before Fell had a chance to react, kicking the weapon out of his hand and catching it in midair.

Anise screamed as Sonja slammed the fire tool's butt into Fell's abdomen, knocking him to the floor. Sonja pinned him by firmly planting her boot on his throat. She reversed the poker, gently pressing its point between his eyes.

"Anyone moves, I'll ram the damn thing through his brain."

"Anise! Go get help!" Fell hissed, trying not to move.

"I'm not leaving you!"

"Do what I say, Anise!"

Tears trickled down Anise's cheeks as she shook her head no.

"You can cry." Sonja moved the poker away from Fell's forehead, but kept a firm boot planted on his Adam's apple. There was awe and envy in her voice.

"Of course I can cry!" Anise wiped at the tears with the flat of her palm. "Everyone can cry."

"No. Not everyone. Have you ever seen Morgan cry?"

Anise stared at her as if Sonja had started speaking in tongues. "What do you mean by that?"

"It doesn't matter. What matters is Morgan. I want to know where the bastard is holed up."

"Our Father?"

"Stop calling him that!"

Fell and Anise stared at her as if she'd told them not to call the sky blue or the grass green.

Sonja cursed and stepped away from Fell, motioning for him to join his mate. "Get up!"

Fell looked toward Anise, then back at his attacker, as if expecting a trick.

"I said, *get up!*" Sonja snarled, kicking him in the rump. This time he did as he was told, hurrying to where Anise stood. Fell wrapped his arms protectively around his wife, glowering at Sonja with unalloyed hatred.

"Well, if this ain't a fine little family reunion, eh?" she chuckled and twisted the poker into a pretzel. "I guess Big Daddy never told you you had an older sister. Not surprising, though. I doubt he knows I even exist."

"Can my wife sit down?" Acid dripped from Fell's words.

Sonja shrugged. She watched Fell help his pregnant wife ease into her easy chair. Sonja noticed that their auras were nearly identical, although the female's seemed the more robust of the two. She idly wondered if that had something to do with the mutant life form inside her.

On closer inspection, she saw that while the energy sheaths surrounding the two were similar to her own, they were definitely weaker. She had learned a long time ago how to guess the relative ages of various Pretenders by their auras. Anise and Fell were still quite young, by Pretender standards.

That explained a lot of things. If her own early development was anything to go by, they were still "mute"—incapable of telepathic communication.

"I'll give the bastard credit—he doesn't plan small."

"I take it you're referring to our Father."

Sonja grimaced. "Why don't you come off that 'our Father' bit, blondie, before you piss me off so bad I forget I'm trying to be nice and rip out your fuckin' tongue?"

"Nice? You call brutalizing my wife and attacking me *nice?*"

"So I'm lacking in some social graces."

Anise reached up and took her husband's hand in hers, her eyes fixed on Sonja. Despite their reddish hue, they could still pass for those of a human. "You seem to know a lot about our Father—Morgan, as you call him. I have never seen a creature such as you—outside of Fell and myself. Not even our Father, the few times He has favored us with His presence, is like us. You say you are our sister. How can that be so?"

"You talk about Morgan as if he's some kind of god."

"He is our Creator. He is our Father." Anise smiled up at her husband, who squeezed her hand in return. Sonja felt a sudden, sharp pain of envy. "From His Essence were we conceived, and in His Image were we shaped. We came into being within moments of one another and have been conscious of no other life, no other love."

Sonja fell silent, eyeing Anise speculatively. In 1970 she herself had emerged from a nine-month coma and discovered her long-term memory blank. She'd been desperate for an identity, any identity, to fill the void inside her. It wasn't long before she fell into the hands of a cruel, street-wise pimp named Joe Lent. Lent had been more than willing to shape her in his image and prescribe the limits of her world.

In the months between her initial awakening and the brutal beating that triggered the Other's emergence and resulted in the bloody murder of her erstwhile benefactor, Sonja had seen Lent in much the same light Anise and Fell viewed Morgan. And why not? Lent had given her life form and meaning. She had needed him the same way an empty pitcher needs water. But that innocence had ended with Lent's murder and the restoration of her memory. Her life had been a living hell ever since.

Sonja knelt before Anise and stared into the other woman's face. Fell tensed but Anise did not flinch or draw away when Sonja touched her chin.

"I'm sorry," she whispered to Anise, "but it's time for childhood to end."

Sonja's eyelids twitched as she downloaded into Anise's mind. The pregnant woman jumped as if she'd received a jolt of electricity, her eyes rolling back in their sockets. Her jaws snapped shut, an exposed fang slicing open her lower lip. The biggest problem with physically kick-starting another person's memory was the risk of triggering defensive shock. If Sonja wasn't careful, Anise might retreat into catatonia rather than deal with her memories.

"Anise! What did you *do* to her?"

Sonja was conscious of Fell's hands on her person, but she was too busy to shrug him off. All she needed was to give a little *push* . . .

You're no longer Sonja. Now you re Anise. Only you're not really Anise. You're Lakisha Washington. You grew up on Fourteenth Street in East Oakland, a part of the city so vile, dirty, violent, and hopeless that the police consider it an unofficial freefire zone. Your mother is a junkie who sells herself for drugs. Your father is a nameless white man who happened to have the right amount of money and lust. Your mother leaves you alone in your crib, screaming and squalling in fear of the rats, while she goes to meet her dealer The neighbors break in and rescue you after six hours.

You live with your grandmother after that. Your mother fades from your life, until her death from an overdose on your seventh birthday is meaningless—the death of a casual friend of your grandmother.

Despite the odds you thrive in an environment as hostile to innocence as the surface of Venus. You do well in school, striving to prove yourself, better yourself. You want to escape so bad you can taste it. You manage to avoid the other pitfalls that ensnare many of your friends and classmates: drugs, teenage pregnancy, alcoholism, dropping out. You want more of life than drudging for minimum wage at the corner Kentucky Fried Chicken outlet.

Your determination to succeed inspires respect and contempt amongst those trapped. You get a reputation for being a "nice" girl, one that's going places, but too smart and self-possessed to attract the opposite sex. You graduate valedictorian with an out-of-state scholarship. For the first time in your young life you escape the bone-grinding, soul-numbing poverty you were born in but never succumbed to.

Your grandmother dies in a charity hospital during your sophomore year. Despite your grief you're relieved; it means you'll never have to go back to Fourteenth Street ever again. You work as hard in college as you did in high school, landing a degree in Business. To your delight you're recruited by a prestigious financial firm stationed in San Francisco. You return to California, but this time you're on the right side of the Bay. You have a nice apartment in the Twin Peaks district, overlooking the city. From your balcony you can glimpse the place of your birth, on those rare occasions you look in its direction.

Separated from you by time and a large body of water, it looks deceptively serene. But never inviting. You are happy. Everything you've set out to accomplish, to prove to yourself and others, has been attained beyond your wildest dreams. You're respected at work, you're making more money than most Americans your age, white or black, male or female, and everything is looking up.

No one knows you're the bastard daughter of a whore who died with a syringe angling from her arm, stuffed between a couple of garbage cans like a broken doll for the trash collectors to find. There's no reason for them to know, and no way they ever will.

That's when the dreams start. The bad ones. About the things in the dark with the red glowing eyes and the razor-sharp teeth, watching you as you lie helpless in your bed. The dreams get so bad they intrude on your work. So you do what any other self-respecting young urban professional would do: You get yourself a shrink.

Dr. Joad Caron comes very highly recommended; many of his clients number amongst San Francisco's political and financial elite. He is handsome, sympathetic, understanding. The kind of psychiatrist a young woman can open her soul to without fear. Dr. Caron tells you there is nothing wrong with turning your back on the squalor and unhappiness of your past; that you need not feel guilty because you are now a part of the system that exploits your friends in the old neighborhood. You owe nothing to anyone, except yourself. Soon the dreams go away. But your dependence on Dr. Caron grows. Your will seems to dissolve when you are in his presence. But this does not frighten or worry you. Instead, you feel at peace.

One day Dr. Caron invites you to a weekend retreat hosted at his "place in the Valley." You are one of ten patients, five women and five men, who find themselves in Caron's strange, rambling mansion. All of you are single and live alone. All of you are either orphaned or estranged from your parents. All of you are people no one will miss. But you don't know that until the experiments begin.

Dr. Joad introduces a form of drug therapy, created by himself and a quiet, moon-faced man known as Dr. Howell. Each participant is given various dosages, injected intravenously. Dr. Caron mutters something about finding a "worthy vessel." Then all hell breaks loose.

Three subjects die of convulsions within minutes of injection. Two suffer massive coronaries. Another two blind themselves by plunging their thumbs into their eyes. One patient, screaming like a wounded animal, leaps onto the blinded subjects and tears at them with his bare teeth. You do none of these things—you go to sleep. A long, long sleep filled with dreams of a sterile environment full of hypodermic syringes and intravenous drips.

And when you awake, you are no longer Lakisha Washington. You are Anise, because your Father tells you that is your name. Which is as it should be. And your Father, knowing you are lonely and need companionship, gives you a mate: Fell. He is beautiful and you love him, as your Father commands. Which is as it should be.

"Damn you, get your hands off her!"

Fell's fist smashed into Sonja's face, knocking her away from Anise and sending her glasses flying across the room. Sonja lay dazed on the floor, blood seeping from her broken nose, as Lakisha/Anise's persona receded and her own identity reasserted itself.

Anise sat staring at her hands as if she'd never seen them before. She trembled like a malaria victim and would not look at Fell.

"What did you do to her?" Fell delivered a vicious kick to Sonja's side. She took the blow without complaint. She deserved the pain. "Answer me! What did you *do?*" He cocked his leg for another kick.

"Leave her alone, Fell."

"My glasses—"

Anise nodded. "Help her find her glasses, Fell."

"Anise, what's gotten into you?"

"Do as I *say*, Fell!" The acid in her voice caused him to flinch. He did as he was told, retrieving Sonja's mirrored sunglasses.

Sonja sat huddled on the floor, her upper lip smeared with blood. As Fell neared, she lifted her head and glowered at him. Fell's stomach knotted at the sight of her raw eyes and over-large pupils.

"Get used to it, kid," she hissed, snatching the glasses out of his hand. Fell wondered what she meant.

"I don't know if I should thank you for what you did, but I remember now." Anise sat with her hands resting on the swell of her stomach, her gaze fixed on Sonja. "I remember it *all.*"

"Self-knowledge is the hardest. I know what you must be feeling . . . thinking."

Anise nodded slowly. "It wasn't all one way. I picked up some of your memories as well."

"What are you two talking about, Anise?"

The pregnant woman leaned forward, ignoring her mate as if he was not there.

"What does he want from us?"

Sonja pointed at the other woman's midsection.

"The baby?"

"That's more than just a baby you're carrying around, honey. It's his ticket to godhood."

Anise frowned. "I don't understand . . ."

"Whenever vampires attack humans, they infect them with a kind of virus. The virus generates drastic mutations in the human's biochemistry and physical structure. It reshapes half of the host's chromosomes so they resemble the vampire's. It's not unlike human conception, except that the fetus is an adult corpse. Because part of the new vampire is the same as its Maker, there is a certain . . . biological fealty. Obedience to the Maker is in the blood."

Anise slumped back in the chair. "Then it's hopeless to try and fight him."

"No, it's *not!* Morgan can only dominate you if you don't fight him! How do you think Morgan came into being? He was Made, just like I described. But he had the force of will to break away from his Maker, to assert his personality over that of his creator. You can do it, too, Anise. For the sake of your child, you've *got* to!" Sonja was not a hundred percent certain what she'd just said was true, but she was unwilling to accept biochemical predestination, whether natural or supernatural.

"It all keeps coming back to my baby. Why?"

"Vampires like Morgan are incapable of live birth. They can't breed true. Most vampires are severely flawed because . . . well, they have to use dead meat. Their brains are screwed to the max. Only a handful are resurrected without some form of brain damage. It takes a new vampire a *long* time to develop into something as powerful as Morgan: decades, possibly centuries. Think what it would mean to Morgan to have a *living* vampire, one capable of perfectly replicating itself, bearing *his* chromosomal structure.

"Within the time it takes for a *single* king vampire to germinate, he'd have an entire *army* of obedient myrmidons, each immune to silver and capable of movement during the day! And not a single one of them possessing bothersome memories of having once been human. No wonder the renfields hate you. You're threatening to make them redundant! Morgan's out to make himself a god-emperor, Anise! And you're providing him with his first high priest."

"Anise, that's bullshit and you know it! Our Father would never do anything like—"

"Shut up, Fell! Just *shut up!*" hissed Anise, baring her fangs. Rebuffed, Fell bit his lower lip and looked away. Anise returned her attention to Sonja. "What do you want me to do?"

Sonja surprised herself by saying, "Come with me."

"Leave? You want me to leave?"

"Not leave. Escape!"

"Where could we go?"

"There's a *world* out there, Anise! I could find somewhere safe for you to have the baby. If not here, then in Central or South America."

"But Morgan . . ."

"Let *me* worry about Morgan, okay? So, what's the verdict? Are you with me?"

"I—yes. I'm with you." With a grunt Anise hoisted herself out of the chair.

"Anise! Darling, what's gotten into you? You've never acted toward me this way before! What did that crazy woman *do* to you?"

"She woke me up, Fell! I'm not a sleepwalker anymore. I'm finally doing something for myself that's *my* idea!"

"You're *not* going through with this!" He grabbed her upper arm. "I positively forbid it!"

Anise jerked her arm free of her husband's grasp. "Back off, asshole!"

Fell looked like a pole-axed young animal; left alive but forever altered. Sonja almost expected to see him stagger and fall.

"Come on, if we're going to leave, it better be now." Sonja motioned to the secret doorway she'd entered through.

"No, there's another way out. One that leads directly to the outside. I'm not supposed to know about it."

"Good. If we leave now, we should still have another hour or two of sunlight in our favor." Sonja shot a sharp look at Fell. "How about you? Are you coming with us?"

Fell opened his mouth as if to speak, then shook his head.

"I should kill you, you know."

He lifted his chin and squared his shoulders. "So why don't you?"

She didn't answer him. She was still puzzling over his question when Anise led her out of the parlor and into the hallway.

The heart of Ghost Trap, compared to its protective outer layers, was a large, comfortable, late-Victorian mansion decorated with antiques. As far as Sonja could tell, they were on the ground floor. It hardly looked like a vampire lord's sanctum sanctorum.

Anise motioned to a small, narrow door set into the side of a staircase.

"This leads to an underground tunnel that connects the main house with what used to be the stables. It's how Morgan and the renfields get in and out."

"What are you doing out of your room?"

Anise gasped and Sonja melted into the shadows. A stern-faced woman with the characteristic wan complexion and pinched face of a renfield glowered disapprovingly at Anise from the foot of the stairs.

"I was bored. I wanted to take a walk."

The renfield stepped forward. "You know you're not allowed to roam the house unsupervised! Did Dr. Howell tell you to do this?" There was an edge in her voice suggesting she would like nothing better than to accuse the good doctor of malpractice.

"No one told me to do anything! I decided to go for a walk on my own."

The renfield blinked and frowned as if Anise had suddenly started speaking in Swahili. "No one decides things for themselves. Who were you talking to?"

"I wasn't talking to anyone, just myself."

"You're a lying little shit." The renfield's lips peeled back, displaying a set of tobacco-stained teeth.

Anise struck the renfield with her open hand. The blow knocked the woman to the floor. The human supported herself on one forearm, the right side of her face already swelling. She fixed hate-filled eyes on Anise and spat a mouthful of blood and loose teeth.

"I don't care if you *are* his prize broodmare. I'll burn your brain for that!"

"I don't think so."

The renfield jerked her head in the direction of Sonja's voice just in time to catch a steel-tipped boot under the chin. She fell back against the worn Oriental carpet, her neck broken.

Anise stared at the dead woman. "You killed her!"

"Had to be done. Couldn't risk her raising the alarm."

Anise stared at her own hand, still smeared with the dead renfield's blood, then at Sonja.

"C'mon. We're wasting time!" Sonja shouldered the renfield's body and opened the door leading to the tunnel.

"You're taking her with us?" Anise looked genuinely repulsed.

"I've got to stash this stiff *somewhere*, don't I? We can't leave Little Miss Sunshine here lying around for the housekeeper to stumble over."

Anise followed Sonja into the space under the stairs. They wedged the renfield's corpse into a corner then descended a short, wooden stairway leading to a dark, brick-lined tunnel. The place smelled of damp earth, spiders, and rat piss. Neither woman was bothered by the lack of light as they hurried along. At the end of the tunnel was a series of iron rungs leading to an overhead trapdoor. Sunlight filtered around the cracks, illuminating fungus spores dancing lazily in the air.

"Okay, up you go, young mother."

Anise placed one hand on the bottom rung, looked up at the dim sunlight, then back at Sonja. "What about Fell?"

"He had his chance."

"He doesn't understand, Sonja! It all happened so fast. He's still unaware of what's really going on. He's scared of you. Maybe if I tried talking to him maybe then he'd listen."

"Anise . . ."

"I didn't ask for this!" Her voice was both angry and frightened. She sounded like a child trying to control her sense of grief and betrayal. "All I wanted was to be free of the nightmares! To get rid of the red-eyed things in the dark! Now I wake up from the dream and find myself still in the nightmare. Everything is upside down and crazy. I'm pregnant and I don't . . . I don't like men, Sonja."

"I know." Her voice was soft, conciliatory.

"But, still, Fell's the father of my child. I owe him something!"

"Anise, if you go back there, your chances of escape range from slim to none. How are you going to get away? You're not going to get very far on foot."

"Honey, you can't grow up East Oakland without learning how to boost a car."

Sonja contemplated knocking the pregnant woman unconscious and dragging her back to the car, but cast it aside. "Okay. Go back and get him. We'll arrange to rendezvous later this evening. There's a town nearby called El Pajaro. I'll be checked into the motel there. Look for a rented Ford Escort. But I promise, Anise, if you fall back under Morgan's control, I'll have no alternative than to kill both you *and* your baby. Is that clear?"

Anise nodded. "It's been over one hundred and twenty-five years since the Emancipation Proclamation. I have no intention to bring a child of mine into the world as a slave."

"I better be going, then." Sonja paused, then flung her arms around Anise's shoulders, dragging her into a hasty embrace.

Anise returned the hug and whispered, "God's speed, sister."

Anise watched Sonja climb into the sunlight then turned back into the darkness. She wanted to cry, but her eyes remained frustratingly dry.

14

THE PINK MOTEL

> No woman can call herself free who does not own or control her body. No woman can call herself free until she can choose consciously whether she will or will not be a mother.
>
> —Margaret Sanger

Palmer was well into his second pack of Shermans when Sonja reemerged from the undergrowth. He was surprised to find himself glad to see her.

He got up from where he'd been squatting in the shade, the binoculars' eyepieces capped. He had stopped studying Ghost Trap shortly after Sonja entered the building; he didn't like the reverberations the house kicked up in his hindbrain. He grinned a welcome to his partner.

"It's about time you got back! I was starting to get worried. There's only an hour or two before it gets dark. So, did you score? Did you off the bastard?"

"Get in the car."

"You *did* kill him, didn't you? I mean, we're not going to have to worry about some heavyweight bogeyman coming down on our asses, are we?"

"We'll talk about it later, Palmer."

His smile faltered. "You didn't do it."

"I *said* we'll talk about it later!"

Palmer ground out his smoldering cigarette with a sharp twist of his heel. "I should have known," he muttered as he crawled behind the wheel. "I should have fuckin' *known*."

The Pink Motel provided the only lodging in El Pajaro, a tiny hamlet of three thousand souls. Palmer scowled at the sign fronting the parking lot—a Tinkerbell clone hovered over the garish tubing spelling out the motel's name. The glowing end of the neon fairy's magic wand dotted the *i* in the word *pink*.

He looked up as Sonja returned from the registration desk, sliding into the passenger seat next to him. She held up a piece of pink plastic with a key dangling from its end.

"Room Twenty. I told him we were a honeymooning couple and didn't want to bother the other guests."

"No problem there," Palmer commented dryly, scanning the empty gravel parking lot. He put the car into gear and drove to the end of the twenty-unit motor court. The exterior of the long, L-shaped building was an aged pink stucco the color of well-chewed bubble gum.

The inside of the room was no better. The walls were a pale bisque, while the carpet looked, and felt, like dirty cotton candy.

"It's like I'm in the belly of a huge snake." Palmer groaned, eyeing the worn chenille spread covering the queen-sized mattress.

Sonja grunted and stared at the picture hanging over the bed; it was a cheap flea market print of a Keane waif with over-huge eyes and a tiny mouth set into a simpering pout. Snorting in disgust, Sonja yanked the offending artwork off the wall and sailed it into a corner. She flopped heavily onto the bed. The box springs squealed in protest.

Palmer was surprised by how tired she looked. In the week since their lives had merged, Palmer had come to think of her as preternaturally energetic. She was definitely the most intense woman he'd ever known. The sight of her sprawled across the bed sparked a vague lust in him.

"I feel so old sometimes." Sonja lifted a hand to her brow, slowly rubbing her forehead. "So horribly, horribly old. And I'm not even forty yet." Her laugh was dry. "I wonder how the truly ancient ones feel? Vampires like Pangloss. They must be so very tired. I've heard that when they grow weary of continuing, they simply go to sleep. A hibernation that lasts for years, decades. Sleep: the stepchild of Death." Her voice had a smoky, far-away feel to it. Palmer wondered if she was aware she was speaking aloud.

He sat next to her on the bed and stared at the worn carpet between his shoes. "Sonja—what happened in that house?"

"I discovered I'm not alone."

"What?"

In a soft, weary voice she told him about Anise and Fell and Morgan's plan to breed his own race of designer-gene vampires.

"And you left them there? Alive?"

"You don't understand, Palmer . . ."

"You're damn right I don't understand! Why didn't you kill them?"

"I couldn't."

"Wouldn't, you mean!"

"No. *Couldn't.*" Sonja removed her sunglasses, exposing her eyes to him for the first time. "I don't fully understand it myself. I used to think I could reclaim what I once was by killing what I'd become. It didn't work. Maybe it's time for me to build instead of destroy. I've been lonely, Palmer. So terribly lonely."

Palmer forced himself to look into her eyes. She silently stiffened, squaring her shoulders in preparation for rejection. The pupils were huge, dilated to maximize even the feeblest light source. They were the eyes of a hybrid, neither human or vampire. At first he was repulsed by how raw and inhuman they'd looked; but now he could see a perverse beauty in them. Even without touching her mind, he knew how much of herself she'd exposed to him simply by removing her glasses.

He kissed her without really knowing why, yet confident the action was genuinely his. His hands slipped under her shirt, his fingers tracing old wounds. She arched her back and moaned in pleasure. The way she stretched her lithe, tight body reminded him of the panthers at the zoo—so beautiful and so deadly with their predator's grace.

Her flesh was pale, marked by numerous scars. He closed his eyes and ran his hands over her naked torso. He had expected to be repulsed by the sensation, but found himself fascinated by the complex designs. It was like reading braille; each scar a story bonded forever to her flesh.

She helped him out of his clothes, her fingers tracing the scar over his heart. Palmer felt a tremor of apprehension in the back of his mind, as memories of Loli's betrayal surfaced then disappeared.

She closed about him like a velvet fist. Her arms and legs wrapped about his, holding him fast. He knew he could not break free of her embrace, but he felt no urge to escape. If she had wanted to force this upon him, she could have done it long ago.

Her mind reached out and touched his, teasing it from its cage of bone. She laughed, a telepathic bird-song echoing inside his head, as she urged him to surrender both body and mind to passion.

As he shucked his skin, the jungle surged behind his eyelids. He saw a beautiful woman with intricate ritual designs scratched into her cheeks and brow smiling at him. The smell of burning copal filled his nostrils. Then he was free of his flesh, their minds twining together like mating snakes.

He could not see her, but he knew Sonja was there, both within and outside him. It was a delicious feeling, one that transcended the human physical vocabulary. It went beyond any sensations he'd ever derived from sex or drugs or any other form of carnal gratification. He experienced the raw essence of orgasm, cut free of biological imperative—the promised reward of the faithful of Islam: the thousand-year climax. Or at least ten minutes' worth.

Suddenly he was back in his body, rutting like a bull in heat. Sonja convulsed under him, thrusting her pelvis against his with bruising urgency. His shoulders stung and something warm trickled over his bare skin. The sight and smell of his blood dripping from her fingernails stoked his lust even higher. Sonja arched her back, her muscles as taut as bowstrings, and yowled like a cat; her lips pulled back in a rictus grin as she bared her fangs. Palmer groaned as her contractions milked him dry.

He lay atop her, sweat and blood drying on his back, and smoothed the hair away from her face. There were no words. None were needed. He studied the tilt of her cheekbones and the shape of her nose in the failing daylight filtering through the rose-colored curtains. As he drifted into sleep, it occurred to him that this was the first time he hadn't needed a smoke after sex.

The room was in deep shadow and someone was banging on the door. Sonja moved with the speed and agility of an animal, untangling herself from their lover's embrace. She moved so fast he didn't even see her slip her glasses back on.

Palmer yanked on his pants and moved to answer the door, minus his shirt and shoes. He glimpsed Sonja out of the corner of his eye, moving along the baseboard like a tiger preparing to pounce. The sight of her muscles coiling and uncoiling underneath her moon-pale skin inspired a brief rush of lust in him.

He opened the door the width of the safety chain and peered out at a small-boned African-American woman shivering in the dark. Now that the sun was down, the air had a bite to it.

"Whattayawant?"

The woman tossed back her braids and looked him directly in the face. Her pupils were inhumanly large. The eyes of a hybrid. "I need to see Sonja."

"It's okay, Palmer. Let her in." Sonja was standing at his elbow. She'd moved so quietly he wasn't aware she was behind him until she spoke.

Palmer opened the door and Anise hurried in. She wore the same loose cotton dress she'd had on earlier that afternoon, only now there were dark, tulip-shaped stains on its front.

Sonja motioned for Palmer to keep watch at the window before pulling on her Circle Jerks T-shirt. "Where's Fell?"

Anise shook her head, causing her braids to sway. "It went bad. Real bad! Worse than I thought it would. I'm lucky I got away at all." She started pacing back and forth; the way she waddled and wrung her hands while she spoke made Sonja think of a worried penguin.

"What happened?"

"I went back and tried to talk to him, like I said I would. It was impossible! It was like his ears were sealed with wax. I told him that I didn't love him—that it was impossible for me to care for him. I wasn't going to be Morgan's brood bitch anymore! He tried to keep me from leaving. I ended up hitting him with one of the fire tools. There was a lot of blood. I tied him up and stuffed him in one of the closets. While I was busy doing that, I was surprised by one of Morgan's renfields. I . . ." She grimaced in distaste. "I killed him with my bare hands."

"How do you feel about that?"

Anise stopped her pacing and took a deep breath. "It was easy. Too easy."

"And?"

"It felt good." She shuddered. "Sweet Jesus, what am I turning into? What did that bastard *do* to me?"

Sonja did not answer. She looked at Anise's face and wondered what she could possibly say to make the fear go away, yet also curious as to how long it would be before Anise's version of the Other would make itself known. Or was it already active, ready for more murder and mayhem?

It had been so long since Sonja had last imagined herself truly human. Sometimes her life as Denise Thorne seemed little more than a pleasant, if vivid, dream. She imagined how must it be for Anise to wake up and find herself not only married to a man she didn't love and pregnant against her will, but no longer human, and was humbled by her sister's underlying strength.

"Think you're up to a three-hour drive to San Francisco?"

"What choice do I have? We sure as hell can't stay here! Morgan no doubt already has his dogs out looking for me. I'm ready when you—uh-oh."

"What do you mean 'uh-oh'?"

Anise grimaced. "I think I spoke too soon."

Palmer turned away from the window. He looked like he'd just swallowed a lemon. "Does she mean what I *think* she means?"

Anise emitted a groan as her water broke.

"I'm afraid so," sighed Sonja.

The first contraction doubled Palmer over.

He was coming from the bathroom with an armload of towels when it hit, crashing against him like a wave. The phantom pain radiating from his pelvis caused him to stagger and nearly drop what he was carrying.

"Screen yourself! She's broadcasting!" hissed Sonja, snatching the towels from his numb fingers.

"Now you tell me." Palmer groaned as he tried to force the pain back long enough to erect a mental barrier.

Anise gave a strangled cry and dug her fingers deep into the mattress, shredding the bedclothes like rotten silk. Palmer felt her pain press against his shield like a heavy, insistent hand, but, remarkably, the barricade held.

"This is not good. Not good at all." Sonja brushed a stray lock of hair from her face, leaving a smear of Anise's blood on her brow. "She's broadcasting like a damn communications satellite! Of all the times for her psychic powers to decide to kick in! Morgan's renfields will be able to zero in on our location soon, if they haven't done so already."

"Is there any way we could get her in the car and back to San Francisco?"

Sonja sighed and jerked a thumb over her shoulder. "What do *you* think?"

Anise lay on her back, gripping the metal bedstead with bloodless hands. A lamp situated on the dresser, its light muted by a towel thrown over the shade, provided the room's only illumination.

There was something primeval in the way Anise lay, sweating and grunting, with her dress pushed up and her legs spread open. All they needed was a shaman shaking a medicine rattle and dancing around the room in a ceremonial headdress to complete the scene.

"How long until the baby comes?"

"I don't know. Minutes. Hours. It's hard enough to tell with a normal pregnancy, much less something like this."

"Great."

"You got the gun?"

Palmer nodded to the .38, still in its holster, hanging from the back of a chair.

"Better put it back on."

"Sonja? Sonja, where are you?"

"I'm here, babe. I'm not going anywhere." Sonja moved back to the bed, mopping the sweat from Anise's face with a damp washcloth. "How you doing, kid?" Sonja took Anise's hand and clasped it in her own.

"It hurts, Sonja. A lot."

"So the Bible tells me so. That's only natural, Anise."

"No, that's not it—not all of it, anyway. There's something else." She grimaced as another spasm racked her body. "It's like passing a broken bottle. I—" She gave a brief cry and slammed her head against the pillows, squeezing her eyes shut. "Sweet Mother of Christ, what did I ever do to be punished like this? What?"

It was as if an invisible fist was squeezing her stomach. Just as she thought the pain would continue into infinity, the baby's head emerged from between her thighs.

Sonja moved to help the infant free itself, then stopped. The baby's head was bulbous, its eyes as black and flat as those of an insect. It had a flat nose with slits instead of nostrils and a tube-like mouth made of gristle, lined with tiny, lamprey-like teeth. It whipped its tiny, powerful shoulders back and forth until it finally freed one arm.

Five tiny fingers, complete with curved talons, hooked into the gore-stained bedclothes, giving it the leverage to drag the rest of it free of the birth canal. The newborn vampire child lay exhausted on the filthy sheet like a large maggot, glistening with birth fluids

Palmer stared at the thing on the bed and wiped his mouth with the back of his hand. Sonja moved to cut the umbilical with her switchblade. The creature lifted its oversized head on a surprisingly steady neck, regarding her warily with its flat black eyes.

"Easy. . . easy, now. . ." she muttered under her breath, as if addressing a skittish, potentially dangerous animal.

"Sonja? Sonja? What's wrong with the baby? Why can't I hear it crying? Why isn't it crying, Sonja?"

Swallowing her reluctance at touching the thing, Sonja severed the umbilical, quickly tying off the end. As she worked, she noticed that the infant was completely smooth between the legs, lacking even an anus.

"Sonja? Why don't you answer me?" Anise struggled into a sitting position. Sonja maneuvered herself between mother and child.

"You don't want to see it, Anise! Please, believe me!"

"What's wrong? Is it dead?"

"No, it's not dead. It's—well, it's not a baby."

"What do, you *mean* it's not a baby?"

"Anise—"

"Woman, let me see my child!"

Sonja sighed and turned to pick up the creature and hand it over to its mother. But it wasn't there anymore.

"Shit, Palmer! I thought you were watching it!"

"You didn't tell me to! Hell, the thing just got born! How was I to know it'd go walk about?"

"Where'd the little bastard go?" Sonja stepped away from the bed, scanning the shadows along the baseboard.

There was a blur of motion at the comer of Palmer's eye. He contemplated taking his gun out of its holster but quickly discarded the idea.

It's just a baby, for chrissakes! A really seriously ugly, mutant vampire baby, yeah. But it still wouldn't be cool to blow it away. It's just a baby.

Something small darted out from under the bureau and latched onto Palmer's right calf. He screeched as its ring of lamprey teeth began chewing its way to the meat beneath his pants leg.

Swearing and hopping on his free leg to keep his balance, Palmer tried to shake the hell-baby loose. On his second kick, he sent the creature sailing halfway across the room. The infant landed on its back and squealed like a suckling pig pulled from its mother's nipple.

Palmer risked a glance at his calf—his pants leg was shredded and blood oozed from dozens of tiny punctures in his skin. He looked like he'd been attacked with a needle-studded ping-pong paddle, but was otherwise unharmed.

The hell-baby flailed the air with its chubby arms and legs like a tipped turtle desperate to right itself.

"That's quite enough of that!" Sonja said sternly, snatching the shrieking infant off the dirty floor. She frowned at Palmer's leg. "You better see to that before infection sets in."

"What about *that?*" he retorted, jabbing a finger at the baby.

"Don't worry. I'll handle it." She held the tiny struggling mutant like a live rattlesnake, her fingers clamped behind the holes where its ears should have been, and presented it to its mother.

"I can take care of it, if it's what you want." Sonja's voice was flat and without emotion. She could have been offering to take out the garbage.

"No. It's my child. It's my responsibility."

Anise stretched out her arms to accept the wriggling infant. She fought to keep the repugnance she felt toward her own flesh and blood from showing on her face, but it was difficult. The mutant stopped its angry thrashing the moment Anise touched it, regarding its mother with unreadable, bottomless eyes. The gristle that formed its mouth puckered and unpuckered rapidly. It wanted to nurse.

"It's not its fault," she said sadly. "This was how it was born. It can't be anything else." She laughed. It was a hollow sound. "You know, I actually was considering having a child before all this happened. Not anytime soon—but sometime, when I could afford it. Maybe make a trip to the friendly neighborhood artificial inseminator." Her lips twisted themselves into a bitter parody of a smile. "I never thought I'd end up with . . . with . . ." She swallowed and took a deep breath. "Like I said—it's my responsibility."

She snapped the baby's neck like a green twig. It didn't even have time to cry. Anise stared at its tiny, motionless body and ran a trembling hand over its bulging brow.

"Poor little thing. It didn't ask for any of this." She suddenly grimaced and the mutant baby's corpse slipped from her arms and landed on the floor with a dull thud.

"Anise, what's wrong?"

"The contractions. They've started again. I—Oh Lord, not again! I can't go through this again!" Anise grabbed Sonja's shoulder as she pushed, digging her fingernails deep into the other woman's skin. "Ah! Oh, Jesus! Make it stop!" She drew a shaky breath through her teeth. "Whatever the first one did trying to get out—it screwed me up real bad, Sonja! I mean it! I don't know if I can—" A third contraction turned her words into a swallowed scream.

"Don't worry, Anise. Everything will be all right. I'm not going to let anything happen to you, understand?" Sonja untangled herself from Anise's grip and resumed her place at the foot of the bed.

Anise's second child came into the world wrapped in a caul. Sonja split the thick membrane shrouding the infant, relieved to see what looked to be a normal, human baby face underneath. She gave its tiny flanks a small pinch and was rewarded with a healthy, indignant wail. She swiftly severed the umbilical cord and wrapped the newborn in a clean towel. She smiled and held it out to its mother.

Anise turned her head away, pressing her face into the pillow. "I don't want to see it."

"It's all right—you can look."

Anise hesitated for a second, then cautiously lifted her head. Sonja was frightened by how drawn and sick she looked. She peered cautiously at the child wrapped inside the impromptu swaddling.

It was still as red as a piece of raw meat, but she could tell the child shared her coloration. It squalled like a Siamese cat in heat and had the face of a miniaturized prize-fighter.

"She's *beautiful*!"

"Yes, she is, isn't she?" Sonja whispered, placing the tiny bundle in her mother's arms.

While Anise was preoccupied with the baby, Sonja scooped its dead twin off the floor and wrapped it in one of the discarded, blood-caked towels. It would have to be burned later on. It wouldn't do to leave something like that for the housekeeping staff to find the next day.

She stared absently at the blood smearing her hands, then licked her fingers. She knew she was pushing her own tolerance dangerously far. She needed to feed, and her surroundings weren't helping much. The room reeked of blood.

Palmer limped out of the bathroom. He'd ripped open his right pants leg from the knee down and wrapped his calf with strips torn from his undershirt.

"How's the leg?"

"It's been better."

Sonja found herself staring at the crimson seeping through the makeshift bandage and quickly looked away.

What was I thinking? This is a man I think I might actually love! And I was imagining what his blood would taste like! I was actually picturing slicing open the artery in his leg and drinking from it! Sick! Sick! Sick! Can't you let me have any happiness?

The Other laughed, but no one else heard.

"Sonja?" Anise was looking at her funny.

"Uh, sorry. I guess I was busy—thinking."

"I said, how do you like Lethe?"

"Lethe?"

"I think that's what I'll name her. I like the way it sounds, don't you? It's from Baudelaire. A name is the least I can give her before I die."

"Anise, listen to me. I know you've experienced massive internal damage, but you're not going to die. I know this, because I've suffered a hell of a lot worse in the past. You'll regenerate, but you're gonna need blood. If you don't feed soon, your body will start cannibalizing itself. Do you know what that means?"

"You're saying I'm going to have to kill someone if I want to stay alive."

"Basically."

"I can't do that, Sonja! I don't care what that bastard did to me—I refuse to be a monster."

"Look, you won't have to do anything. I'll hunt for you. There are plenty of transients, people no one will ever miss. Drunks, hitchhikers, bums . . ."

"My God, Sonja! You sound just like him!"

"I'm not going to let you die!" Sonja was surprised she was shouting. "I won't *let you!*"

Lethe started at the noise and began to cry again. Anise did not look at Sonja as she spoke, but instead addressed her words to the newborn baby at her side, smoothing the few wispy strands of hair on her daughter's brow.

"I can't do it, Sonja. I can't take the step beyond. I don't have your. . . courage. I had enough to break free of Morgan, but not enough to deal with continuing my life by killing others. Not that I'm condemning you for it. But I can't live knowing I'm responsible for another human's death, no matter how worthless that person may be."

"That's what you're saying now. I felt the same way, myself, years ago. But later, once you get used to it, you'll see things differently."

"I know. That's what I'm afraid of! Please, Sonja. Don't try to talk me out of this. I know what I'm doing."

"But what about Lethe? What about her?"

Anise smiled sadly and kissed her daughter on the forehead. "I hope she can forgive me for not being there while she grows up. But if there's one thing she needs more than anything else right now, it's protection. I promised myself no child of mine would be born a slave, and I mean to keep that promise! That's why I'm trusting you to protect her, Sonja. You and poor Mr. Palmer over there."

"Anise, I'm the last person on earth you should put your faith in. I'm a murderer and worse a hundred times over. Every day I fight to keep the demon inside me from taking over, and a lot of times I *can't!* You might as well hire Typhoid Mary as a baby-sitter."

"You judge yourself too harshly, sister. Here, take the child. Leave now. Morgan will be here soon. I can feel him calling to me."

Sonja cocked her head as if listening to distant music. Yes, she could feel him too, now. She could take him. She was sure of it. But she was equally sure Morgan had at least two renfields with him. What about Palmer? He could handle himself in a fire-fight, but what about his ability to handle a combined psychic assault? And should either one of them fall to Morgan's forces, where would that leave Anise's baby? She couldn't protect them both at the same time.

Sonja bent and kissed her on the cheek.

"Good-bye, Anise."

“My name is Lakisha. Anise was just a dream. And not even mine.”

“You better give me the baby now.”

Anise hesitated for a long moment, staring at her daughter as if committing to memory every detail of her face. She suddenly closed her eyes and thrust the infant away from her. “Here! Take her! Take her before I change my mind!”

“Is there anything you want before we go?”

“Leave me the gun.”

Palmer looked sharply at Sonja.

“Give it to her.”

Lakisha smiled weakly as she accepted the .38. It wasn’t much of a trade-off, her child for the gun, but it’d do.

Sonja paused on the threshold, cradling Lethe against her worn leather jacket.

“Look after my baby, Sonja.”

“Like she was my own.”

"There's the car, milord. She must be inside the motel room," observed the chauffeur.

"A brilliant deduction, as usual, Renfield," Morgan sighed from the back seat of the Rolls.

He peered over the top of his tinted aviator glasses at the Ferrari parked outside Room 20 of the Pink Motel. The automobile was his, although the paperwork and owner's registration in the glove compartment claimed that the legal owner was one Dr. Joad Caron. The vanity plates agreed. But since Morgan was also the good doctor, whatever belonged to Joad Caron belonged to him. Including his patients.

Morgan glanced at the human seated beside him. The renfield was an ethnic Chinese whose ancestors had served as the imperial court's seers for six generations. They had deliberately interbred, cultivating some of the finest human psionic talents Morgan had run across in his travels. What was equally impressive was the line's reputation for relative sanity and stability, something rare amongst the more powerful wild talents. Morgan acknowledged his servant's special status by addressing him as something beside the generic renfield.

"Wretched Fly: scan."

The sensitive nodded silently, tilting his head to one side, like a robin listening for worms.

"She's there. Alone."

Morgan scowled. "Are you sure? Not that I doubt your abilities, my friend. I don't like to be caught unawares, that's all. Something our mischievous Ms. Blue seems to be quite adept at."

"She is alone. And in pain."

Morgan weighed the information carefully. It was possible Anise's would-be savior had abandoned her after all, although Morgan was curious as to why his enemy would leave the breeder alive.

Fell had informed him of how Anise had babbled on about "free will" and "the right to choose" before beaning him with the ash shovel. The speed and ardor of Anise's conversion bothered Morgan. He'd picked her as a breeder because of her keen psychological need to be assimilated by the dominant class structure. His programming should have held. That this rogue could have penetrated his defenses and undone so much work in so short a period of time troubled him. That his enemy had claimed to be one of his own by-blows disturbed Morgan even more.

Over the years there had been rumors circulating amongst the Nobility of a strange creature stalking various revenants, vampires, and their attendant renfields. A predator that preyed on predators. The stories amongst the brood masters credited the maverick Pretender with immense strength, the ability to walk in daylight, and an unheard-of immunity to silver.

Some thought their antagonist the product of human technology, created to destroy the Pretender race. Morgan imagined the stories to be the result of a group of pathetic, senile ancients made paranoid by centuries of intrigue and counter-plots. Morgan had been amused by their need to create a bogeyman.

Still, it had given him the idea to create his own race of hybrid vampires. With his specially-bred *homo desmodus* under his control, he would soon have the likes of Baron Luxor and Marchessa Nuit kowtowing before him, pledging fealty for all eternity. Or however long Morgan saw fit for them to continue.

But now his dreams of glory were collapsing, undermined by a creature he'd imagined mythical. Morgan savored irony, but not at his own expense.

"Signal the others," he said, straightening the cuffs of his Saville Row silk suit.

Wretched Fly nodded, silently relaying his master's commands to the occupants of the second car.

The doors of the accompanying Mercedes popped open, and two figures climbed out. One was a renfield. The other had once been a particularly obnoxious insurance salesman who had tried to pressure what he thought was Dr. Caron into buying a policy. Now his body housed a fire elemental. The renfield gave the pyrotic a wide berth, wary of the fierce heat it radiated.

Morgan climbed out of the Rolls, followed closely by Wretched Fly. The gravel crunched under his handmade Italian shoes as he crossed the parking lot to Room 20. The door was unlocked. Not that it mattered.

Anise lay curled atop sheets befouled with blood and the fluids of childbirth. Her pallor was grayish and her eyes sunken in their orbits. She clutched a bloodstained bundle to her breast. She cringed at the sight of

Morgan standing in the doorway, flanked by his most trusted—and powerful—renfields.

"You disappoint me, my child."

She closed her eyes, trying to subvert the conditioned responses his physical presence triggered in her. But simply shutting off the visual cues wasn't enough. He was all over her: in her mind, in her nostrils, in her taste buds. He was everywhere and everything. He was unavoidable and undeniable.

"I'm not your child!" She tried to make her voice hard, but the words came out sounding more petulant than angry.

Morgan's lips pulled into a thin, cruel smile. "If I am not your father, who is? God? Satan? A honky from Watsonville out for cheap pussy? Is this how you show your gratitude? By running away and killing my servants? Is this how a daughter repays her father for all the things he's done for her?"

"Done *to* her, you mean!" Her lower lip was trembling, but the hate in her eyes remained undimmed.

"Come now, my child! This isn't the way I want things between us! You're mixed-up, confused you don't know *what* to believe, do you? Your friend abandoned you, didn't she? Left you alone and helpless. She talked about freedom and free will, didn't she? Those are nice, pretty-sounding words, aren't they? But they're just words: simple-minded phrases deluded humans use to coerce themselves into believing themselves masters of their destiny. They are meaningless!" He opened his arms wide. "Come home with me, Anise, and all things will be forgiven."

Anise felt her defenses start to melt. She still hated Morgan, but part of her wanted to rush into his strong, protective arms. Thinking on her own and deciding for herself was exhausting, even frightening. Things would be so much better if she refuted the pretense of free will and let Morgan take control. It would be so easy to say yes and surrender, to become like him . . .

No! That's what he wants! That's what he's betting on! Stay angry! Stay angry! Don't let him win! Be strong, woman! If not for yourself, for Lethe!

"You can't fool me anymore, Morgan. I can see you for what you really are. I'm not going back!"

The pyrotic, its skin the color of barbecued meat, wandered over to the corner of the room where an old black-and-white Zenith television sat bolted atop a pedestal. The pyrotic's eyes resembled hard-boiled eggs, but this did not seem to impinge on its ability to navigate. It punched the television's "on" button and stepped back. *The Beverly Hillbillies* theme song blared from the TV's speakers at full volume.

"Come and listen to my story 'bout a man named Jed,

A poor mountaineer barely kept his fam'ly fed . . ."

Morgan spun around, his face livid. "Turn that shit off! Renfield! Get that damned elemental away from that accursed idiot box!"

The pyrotic showed its displeasure by making a noise like live steam escaping a radiator. The renfield grunted and moved to turn off the television. There was a loud crack and the side of the renfield's head disappeared.

Morgan spun to face Anise, his ears ringing from the gunshot. The muzzle of a .38 was leveled directly between his eyes.

"Put the gun down, Anise."

"My name's Lakisha!"

Morgan pretended not to hear her. "I said put down the gun, *Anise*."

She fired the gun a second time, but her hand was shaking too hard; the slug struck Morgan in the shoulder instead of the head.

"Nice try, Anise. But no cigar."

"I told you my name's Lakisha, asshole!" she hissed, and shoved the gun in her mouth and pulled the trigger. Her head opened like a cracked piñata, spraying the wall with the raw material of memory. Morgan stared for a long moment at the mess dripping from the walls as if divining omens.

Wretched Fly removed the bloodstained bundle from the bed and held it out to his master for inspection. Morgan grimaced at the sight of the mutant baby's hideous puckered mouth and skeleton-like nose and snatched the offending corpse from Wretched Fly, shaking it like a rag doll.

"This is Howell's doing! He promised that the child would be able to pass for human! The bastard lied to me! Lied! I'll make that junkie *pay* for this!" He hurled the dead baby back at its mother, turning his back on the tableau in disgust. "Torch it!"

The pyrotic stepped forward. Its mouth dropped open and a gout of liquid flame leapt free, consuming the bed and its lifeless occupants. The smell of burning mattress and roasting meat filled the room.

Morgan stepped outside Room 20, scowling at the night sky without seeing it. His mouth tasted of ash. There was only one thing that could wash away the bitterness of failure—the blood of his enemy.

"Hey, you! Keep your hands where I can see 'em!"

An elderly man armed with a double-barreled shotgun hurried across the parking lot from the motel's office. His bathrobe flapped open, exposing faded pajama bottoms and a stained T-shirt.

"What in hell's going on here? I heard gunshots! Where's the Smiths?"

"Smiths?" Morgan raised an eyebrow in amusement.

"You know who I'm talking about—the young couple that rented Number 20. You better answer me, fellah, or I'm liable to blow a hole in you! I ain't one to be fucked with!"

"Indeed."

Wretched Fly and the pyrotic stepped out of the motel room to stand beside Morgan. The motel manager frowned and took an automatic step backward. His eyes widened as he caught sight of the flames reflected in the windows.

"You crazy bastards set fire to my motel!"

Morgan, bored with the confrontation, turned his back on the man. "Take care of him," he yawned, waving a languid hand at his servants.

"Where you think you're going, asshole?" The manager's voice wavered as he fought to control his anger. He stepped forward, shouldering the shotgun. "You're staying put until the state police get here!"

The pyrotic belched and a fireball the size of a ripe cabbage struck the old man in the chest. He dropped his weapon and clawed at the flames eating his clothes and skin, spreading it to his hands and upper arms.

Screaming like an angry blue jay, the old man threw himself to the ground and rolled in the dirt and gravel, spreading the fire to his pajama pants and hair. During his final, conscious moments, he tried to drag himself back the way he came, his ears filled with the sound of his own flesh hissing and crackling like bacon fat in a frying pan.

He succeeded in crawling nearly six feet before he was completely consumed.

The pyrotic squatted next to the smoldering remains and inhaled the blue-white flames back into his nose and open mouth. The intense heat had reduced the old man's skull to the size of an orange. Wretched Fly signaled impatiently for the elemental to get back in the Mercedes.

Morgan slid behind the wheel of the Ferrari, sneering at Anise's crude hot-wiring job. Within seconds he was speeding down the highway, the Rolls and Mercedes following in his wake. The night was young and there was much to done.

"What the hell are we gonna do with a *baby*, for crying out loud? I don't know the first thing about what they eat or nothing!"

Lethe, nestled in an impromptu bassinet made from clean towels and an open bureau drawer, waved her arms and kicked her legs as if semaphoring her agreement with Palmer's statement.

"Well, here's where you're gonna *learn*. I went down to the all-night drug store on the next street and picked up this crap," Sonja explained, tossing a box of disposable Pampers at him like a medicine ball.

"You think I'm taking care of *that*, you're crazy!"

"You can't stick the kid in a tube-sock and hose her off once a week! I bought enough canned formula to last her a few days, plus a couple of bottles and a pacifier. You can cook her formula on this hot plate . . ."

"The hotel rules say no cooking in the rooms!"

"The old gent behind the desk didn't bat an eye when we came back from our 'winery tour' with a newborn baby. What makes you think the management is going to notice a lousy hot plate? Look, we promised Anise we'd take care of her . . ."

Palmer held his hands up, palms outward, and shook his head from side to side. "*You* promised, not me! I'll fight fuckin' ugly monsters for you, babe. I'll even allow myself to be involved in breaking and entering and murder charges. But I am *not* changing diapers!"

"Palmer!"

"Just because I fucked you doesn't mean I want to start a family, especially like this. Besides, how do you know she won't turn into something like the first one?"

"She's just a baby!"

"If she's just a baby, what is it with her eyes?"

Lethe gurgled and kicked and waved her arms even more. Sonja plucked at her ward's makeshift blankets. She'd had little experience with children, especially ones so young, but she was certain Lethe was unusually active for a baby not even a day old. She'd be damned if she was going to mention that to Palmer. He was spooked enough as it was. Lethe peeked out of her swaddling with golden, pupil-less eyes and gave Sonja a toothless grin.

"So, okay, her eyes are screwed up! Is that a fuckin' crime?"

"No, but you weren't the one her evil twin tried to turn into Gerber's strained beef!"

"I'm not asking you to take her to raise, damn it! I'm just asking you to baby-sit. If we're going to be on a jet to Yucatan within the next twelve hours, I've got to check with a few of my . . . connections. And I sure as hell can't do it dragging around a papoose!"

"Okay, I'll do it. But just this once!"

"Great! I'll try to be quick about it. Everything you need for fixing her bottle should be in the bags. Just read the labels on the can—they're pretty self-explanatory."

Palmer grimaced at Sonja's back, then turned his disapproving gaze onto Lethe.

"Sure, you're cute *now*. But if you try anything funny, you're going out the fuckin' window. You got that, munchkin?"

Lethe cooed and yawned, exposing soft pink gums.

"Yeah, well, don't you forget it."

The pay phone stood on the corner of Guerrero and Twenty-First Street, opposite a television repair shop with dusty windows full of half-assembled or partially demolished Philcos and Zeniths. The black-and-chrome face of the phone was covered with graffiti, the coin box had been forced, and a yellow adhesive strip bearing the legend Out of Order was plastered over the coin slot.

Sonja scanned the corner: Across the street a couple of young men dressed in bomber jackets and tight-fitting leather pants strolled arm in arm, walking their Pomeranian, while an intense-looking middle-aged man with heavy eyebrows ducked into an espresso bar. Somewhere a police siren wailed, throwing echoes against the hills.

Satisfied the area was clean, she sauntered from her watching place inside a doorway and picked up the dead receiver. The plastic was cold and hard in her hand. Sonja placed the earpiece to her head and casually stabbed the pay phone's push buttons. There was stone silence, then the sound of a receiver half a country away being lifted off its hook.

"Yeah?" A heavy, almost liquid voice.

"I want to talk to Malfeis."

The voice on the other end slurped. "Yeah. Sure. Who should I say is calling?"

"The Blue Woman."

"Sonja! Chicky-baby! Sorry 'bout the slug. Breakin' in a nephew—what can I say? So, what can I do for you, sweet thing?"

"Got tired of being a skatepunk already, Mal?"

"Hey, what can I say? I like innovation as much as the next guy, but a classic's a classic!"

"Mal, I need help . . ."

"Help?"

"Mal, I'm between your cousin and the deep blue sea! I've put my foot in it big time! I need magic, man!"

"What about Li Lijing?"

"He's just an alchemist, Mal. I'm talking *serious* mojo!"

"Uh, look, sweetie, I wish I could help you out, but—"

"*But* what?!"

"I don't know *what* you did out there, cupcake, but Morgan's stock's falling like a lead turd in the Mariana Trench! And a lot of the big boys in the First Hierarchy aren't exactly overjoyed, if you catch my drift. I'm in deep with the family over this, Sonja. I'm not supposed to give you the time of day, much less tell you where to score."

"Mal! Damn you, you know I'm good for it! I can get you Ed Gein's brain—pureed. How about Mengele's jawbone? The *real* one, not that fake they dug up in South America. C'mon, man! I'm not shitting you—I *gotta* score!"

"Okay. Tell you what—since you've been such a good customer in the past, I'm gonna help you out. But just this once, *capisce?* I don t want it getting around I'm a soft touch."

"Thanks, Mal! I owe you!"

"More than you realize. Awright, here's what I want you to do. There's this bar south of Market called the Shadow Box. Go there and wait for my operative. He should be there in the hour."

"What's he look like?"

"Don't worry—you'll know him when you see him."

It was after midnight and things were just getting heated up at the Shadow Box.

A disc jockey in a neon-encrusted sound booth generated a thundering, synth-heavy mixture of euro-pop, retro-disco, and acidhouse. Klieg lights hanging from the rafters threw elongated shadows of the dancers onto the stark white walls. Sonja noted the dancers' stylized movements, striking high fashion poses, and how they centered their attention more on their own shadows than on their partners. It was times like these she was embarrassed at ever having been human.

"Talk about dancing with yourself" she muttered in disgust.

A gaggle of stylishly coifed and painted future executives squeezed their way past, jostling her in their hurry to reach the dance floor. Sonja briefly contemplated hamstringing one of them, but pushed the thought aside. She couldn't risk calling attention to herself.

Bars and nightclubs always brought out the worst in her. She suspected it had something to do with the volatile emotions generated in such places that stimulated the Other, exciting it to mayhem. Even now she could feel the Other's silent, ominous presence just under the surface of her ego, like a shark patrolling its territory. She reflected on how Mal *could* have picked a rendezvous site a little less crowded, but beggars don't exactly get a choice in such matters.

The music got faster and louder, the shadows on the walls jerking and prancing like Burmese puppets. Sonja consulted her wristwatch. Mal had said her contact would arrive within the hour.

She felt it then: a spiky, adrenaline-charged surge of anger and excitement, as cold and bracing as vodka straight from the freezer. The hairs on the back of her neck bristled.

The emotion wasn't hers, however. It was being broadcast—unintentionally—by someone in the bar.

Someone *really* pissed off.

Sonja turned to scan the interior of the club. Within the last few minutes the number of people entering the bar had doubled. The Shadow Box was a solid wall of young men and women; dancing, drinking, and talking over the music blaring from the speakers.

She shifted spectrums, searching for telltale Pretender aureole. All she came up with was the comparatively weak flickering of human consciousness, augmented by drugs or hormones.

The second jolt of hate struck her, and she gasped as if caught in the grip of an intense orgasm. The Other moaned in pleasure and Sonja bit her lip, hoping the pain and blood would sidetrack it long enough for her to regain control.

Emotions as dark and powerful as hate provided vampires with as much nourishment as a seven-course dinner and a high that made crack look like baby aspirin. Her hair crackled with static electricity as she metabolized the charge.

She had to get out of here. Fuck Mal's mojoworker. She had to get away from this place, crammed full of empty-eyed foodtubes: She hadn't fed since she'd taken down the pickpocket in Chinatown, and it was making her weak, susceptible to the Other's inner voice. She had to leave or something really *bad* was going to happen.

Sonja pushed away from the bar and began shouldering her way to the exit. She bumped against a tall man with half his head shaved and a diamond stud in his left nostril, sloshing beer on his leather pants.

"Hey, bitch! Watch it!" The man with the pierced nose grabbed her elbow. She went rigid and snarled, the sound rumbling from her ribcage like the growl of a big cat. He let go.

That was close. Too close.

She took a deep, shuddery breath and resumed pushing her way through the massed bodies. Before she'd gone ten feet, a second hand clamped her shoulder. The hate that flowed into her was so strong it was as if she'd been stuck with a syringe full of one hundred percent pure China White.

She didn't resist as her attacker spun her around to face him.

She smiled crookedly. "The bastard set me up, didn't he? I'm gonna cut his stash with the bones of martyrs next time! I'd damn him to hell if it wasn't redundant."

Fell bared his fangs in ritual challenge. "I don't know what you're babbling about, whore, and I don't care! You killed Anise and my baby and I mean to even the score!"

"You always talk like a fucking cliché, Fell?"

He moved fast, even by her standards, slamming his fist into her jaw. Sonja's head snapped back, blood filling her mouth. The crowd surrounding them was too densely packed for her to be able to stagger back more than two or three steps.

Sonja spat out a few broken teeth and wiped her chin with the back of her hand. "Okay. Okay. I deserved that and I took it. But I *didn't* kill Anise, Fell! You've got to believe me, no matter what that bastard told you—"

Fell threw a second punch, but this time she was ready for it and caught his fist and held it. Fell grimaced and tried to pull free.

"I'm *trying* to be nice here, but you're not making it easy for me. I don't want to hurt you, kid—"

Fell swore and moved to strike her with his other fist, but she was ready for that, too. Fell tried to jerk free, but she tightened her grip even further.

"Let me go, murderer!"

"Why should I?"

The hate churning in Fell flowed into her like smoke into a bottle. The charge was so powerful that the hair on her head lifted like the crest of a cockatoo. She laughed, and blue-white sparks flew from the tip of her tongue. Her voice sounded like she'd swallowed ground glass. It was the voice of the Other.

"You don't get it, do you? You don't even have a fuckin' clue! How Morgan thought he was going to create a super-race using a lap dog like you for stud is beyond me! Go ahead, lover boy! Keep hating! Hate me as hard as you can! It only makes me stronger!"

Her grin disappeared as she let go of his hands and grabbed Fell by his shirt front, yanking him toward her so their noses touched. The hate he'd been radiating turned to fear. Delicious.

"You wanna play with *me*, you gotta play hardball, sucker! You got that?"

A clutch of secretaries out for a night on the town screamed as Fell crashlanded onto their table, sending broken glass and spilled beer flying. Fell, blood streaming from his nose, shook his head, trying to clear it of the ringing.

Sonja grabbed Fell by his long yellow hair and yanked him to his feet. He tried to pull away, but she refused to let go.

"I'm gonna make you a man if it *kills* you!" she hissed. She pointed at the people on the dance floor, entranced by deafening, rhythms and their own shadows. "See that? You're no better than they are! You're fighting your own shadow, not your real enemy!"

"Liar!" Fell yanked free, leaving her holding a handful of hair. "You do nothing but lie and destroy things! You turned Anise against me! You ruined everything I cared about!" He delivered a karate kick to her gut, sending her flying backward into the bar.

She grabbed a chrome-plated bar stool and hurled it at Fell. The people closest to the two combatants tried to move back, but those near the door, deafened by the music and unaware of what was transpiring, would not let them escape.

Snarling his defiance, Fell snatched a nearby human, lifted him over his head, and threw him at his opponent. Sonja ducked as the screaming man crashed into the mirror behind the bar.

The bartender yelled something and disappeared behind the counter. Sonja vaulted the bar just as he resurfaced with a shotgun. She snatched the gun from him before he had time to close the breach.

"I'd suggest you get your ass home," she growled, snapping the shotgun closed with a flip of her wrist. The bartender turned and fled into the stockroom.

Sonja swung the weapon at Fell as he began to climb over the bar. He froze at the sight of the double-ought pointed at his chest.

"Even a full-fledged vampire would have problems surviving a blast from this distance, much less a pantywaist like yourself! Whattaya think, pretty boy? Wanna chance it?"

Fell eased back, his eyes never leaving the shotgun.

"Yeah. That's what I thought." Sonja hopped onto the counter. "But before we take care of business, I think I ought to clear the field of interference!"

She could see them now, standing near the exit. Two renfields—one negro, the other oriental. They were the ones responsible for crowding the bar and cloaking Fell from her scans. Fell was nowhere near self-aware enough for such psionic sleight-of-hand. They were creating a veil, blinding the crowds nearest the door to the fact there was a brawl going on. They were setting up a killing box, all right. But for who?

She caught the negro renfield with the first round, spraying his brains across some slumming yuppies. The second round missed the oriental and struck an investment banker from Pacific Heights standing next to him. The renfield shrieked and clamped his hands over his eyes as the dead man's skull fragments flew like shrapnel.

The veil lifted. Suddenly people were screaming and shouting and knocking over tables and trampling each other in a wild scramble for the exit. Their panic made her giddy, as if she'd inhaled nitrous oxide. She only had a moment to enjoy the rush before Fell was on her.

His face was contorted into a mask of animal rage. He was not advanced enough to tap into the emotions that swirled about them, but he definitely had a contact high. He pounced like a young lion bringing down its first kill, bearing her to the floor. His strong hands locked around her throat.

He was going to squeeze until the lies and evil spurted from her ears like dirty water. He was going to rip off her head and shit down her neck. He was going to snap her arms off at the shoulders and beat her with them. He was going to make her pay.

Sonja snarled and shoved her knee into Fell's groin. He gasped and let go of her throat, toppling onto his side, clutching himself. Sonja staggered to her feet and grabbed him by the scruff of the neck, holding him aloft like a kitten. She slammed him against the wall, pushing his head back by pinning his throat with her left forearm.

She took a second to assess his wounds. He looked bad. His eyes were nearly obscured by flesh the color of eggplant, his nose was broken, and his swollen, drooping lower lip made him look like a mule. No doubt his cellular regeneration was slower than her own.

"Just—just wait until our Father comes!" he gasped through bleeding lips.

"You dumb bastard! You stupid, mindless meatpuppet! You don't understand, do you? He set us *both* up! You don't stand a snowball's chance against me, and he *knows* it! He sent you here to die, Fell! You were supposed to distract me until the renfields could work up a serious enough whammy to take me out."

"You're lying!"

"Look, jerkwad, I don't have the time or the patience to do this right. I *ought* to kill you, but since you're Lethe's father—"

"Lethe?" Fell blinked in confusion.

She reached into a pocket and withdrew her switchblade. "What's your name?"

Fell looked at her as if she had asked him who was buried in Grant's tomb. "Fell."

"Wrong." She flicked the knife and neatly cut off his left ear. Fell screamed and tried to escape, but it was hopeless; her grip was unbreakable. "Okay, I'm asking you *again*. What's your name?"

"It's *Fell*, damn it! You know that! What's the matter with—" His protest dissolved into another scream as the switchblade sliced open his left nostril.

"No, no! You're not *listening!* I said what's *your* name?"

"What do you *want* me to say? It's Fell! It's *always* been Fell!"

"I'm only gonna ask you one more time, pretty boy, then it's for real, understand?" she sighed, cutting away his right eyebrow. "What is your *name?*"

"I *told* you it's—" His eyes widened and his mouth slackened, as if he'd just remembered something important. "Oh. Oh, my God. It's Tim. My name is Tim."

Sonja sighed and allowed him to slump to the floor, hiding his mutilated face behind bloodstained hands. His shoulders shook as he tried to cry. She could hear sirens coming closer.

"C'mon, kid." Her voice softened as she patted the top of his head. "C'mon, we can't stay. The cops will be here soon."

Fell shrank from her touch, regarding her fearfully. "Aren't you going to kill me?"

"No. Look, I'm sorry about hurting you like that, but it was the only way I could get you to come out. Now, let's go! There's someone you need to meet."

"Who?"

"Your daughter."

Palmer leaned against the headboard of the bed, cradling Lethe in the corner of his left arm while holding her bottle in his right. He was amazed something so tiny could possess such an appetite. He didn't look up at the sound of the hotel room door being unlocked.

"That you, Sonja?"

"Yeah, it's me.

"You know, you were right about her, Sonja. She's not like the other one! She's got such tiny fingers! And each one has a perfect little fingernail . . ."

"Uh, Palmer? We got company."

Palmer stared at the young man standing next to Sonja. One side of his face looked like someone had used a tenderizer on it. There was blood crusted on his nose and right brow. He shifted uneasily, like a schoolboy brought before the principal.

"Palmer, this is Fell. Lethe's father.

"Is—is that her?" Fell's voice was almost a whisper.

Sonja nodded. "Sure is."

Fell took a hesitant step forward. "Can I hold her?"

"I don't see why not," Sonja said. "After all, she's your daughter."

Fell moved to take the baby. Palmer frowned and tightened his hold on Lethe, pressing her tightly against his chest.

"It's okay, Palmer. Fell's his own man now."

Grudgingly, Palmer surrendered Lethe to her father's embrace. Fell's bruised lips pulled into a smile at the sight of his daughter's face.

"She's beautiful! She looks so very much like Anise." Fell's voice began to shake. He sat on the end of the bed, the baby in his lap gurgling and cooing contentedly. "This is happening too fast. There's too much to think, too much I'm remembering!"

Sonja knelt beside Fell, placing a hand on his shoulder. "Start from the beginning. Who are you *really?*"

"My name is—was?—Timothy Sorrell. I was a sophomore at Berkeley. English Major. I'm from Indiana, originally. My parents and older sister were killed in a car crash when I was ten.

"I got passed around a lot by my relatives. They were good people, but they didn't know what to make of me, so they left me to my own devices. I was a morbid child. Fascinated and terrified by death at the same time. I really got into stuff like vampires, ghouls—the undead. By the time I went to college, I dressed in black all the time and spent most of my money on occult literature.

"My first few months at Berkeley were okay. I even met people who didn't think I was all that weird! But during my sophomore year I started having these . . . dreams."

"What kind of dreams?"

"Bad ones. Full of blood and walking dead things. When I was younger I used to dream I was a vampire, but these were different. In the old dreams, I played Christopher Lee or Frank Langella, seducing nubile young women. But these newer dreams . . . They were different.

"Sometimes I'd see myself and I looked like a rotting corpse. My victims weren't beautiful women but old bag ladies and scuzzy-looking whores—they screamed and tried to get away instead of surrendering, so I hurt them even more for trying to escape. It wasn't at all like in the movies!

"But what scared me the most was the feeling of *pleasure* I got from watching them scream and die. I'd always been considered eccentric, but this was the first time I was honestly worried about my own sanity. That's when I decided to seek professional help.

"Dr. Caron was highly recommended." Fell laughed, the sound dry and brittle. "He seemed to understand what I was going through. Soon after I began seeing him the nightmares returned to the old familiar erotic dreams. He told me I should not feel ashamed for being . . . well, dissatisfied with my station in life. After a few sessions, he invited me to partake in a special experimental therapy session at his estate in the Sonoma Valley. I think you know the rest."

Sonja nodded. "He picked people who wouldn't be readily missed and displayed certain . . . tendencies he could work to his advantage. Of the ten he handpicked, you and Anise were the only ones to survive, am I right?"

Fell nodded, looking down at his daughter, who was innocently playing with one of his blood-smeared fingers. "It was horrible—I can still hear the screams, even now. But, in a weird way, it wasn't all bad.

"I remember thinking how beautiful Anise was back . . . back when we were human. I knew I didn't stand a chance with a woman like that. I was kind of surprised she was even in the group. She seemed so *together.* I was happy for the first time in my life—or after it. I know now that Anise never really cared for me—that, unconsciously, she was only doing Morgan's bidding. But Morgan didn't have to *make* me love her! That's why losing her hurt so much. It was *real* love, not pretend!

"When Morgan told me that you'd killed both her and the baby, I went mad. I wanted to avenge myself and prove to Morgan that I was worthy to be his son." His laugh was bitter. "So what do I do now?"

"You come with us to Yucatan. Raise your child in peace."

"How can I? *Look* at me! I'm not human!"

"Neither am I. Nor is your child. Fell, you don't *have* to go through this alone. I know what you're feeling! I can teach you how to master your powers! That's a luxury I never had. I learned things on the streets, the hard way. There's still plenty of things I don't know or understand, but maybe, together, that'll change. But I *can* tell you that the next stage of your development will be dangerous, and if you're not careful, it will cost you your soul."

"You mean I still *have* one?"

"You're not truly undead, Fell. You never died. Just like I never did. Usually it takes years for a vampire to reclaim the intellect and memory he had before his resurrection. Some never do. The only difference between the two of us was that I was a fluke, while you were deliberately created.

"I'm not sure how, but Morgan succeeded in altering your genetic structure into that of a vampire's without killing you. Right now you're still more human than vampire—that's why you were able to impregnate Anise—but soon the vampiric side of your personality is going to emerge. And, believe me, you're going to need advice on learning how to control it. There's no going back to what you were, Fell. Adapt or die, those are your only choices."

"What about Morgan? He's not going to simply let us go."

"I'm well aware of that. I promised Anise I'd protect her baby from Morgan. There's only one way I can do that, and that's kill him."

There was still enough of the old programming clinging to Fell's synapses to make her words sound blasphemous. "Do you think you can really do that?"

"There's no way around it, Fell! As long as Morgan continues, we'll be constantly looking over our shoulders. We'll never know a moment of peace without wondering when he'll make his next move. We won't be safe and, more to the point, neither will Lethe. It's got to be done."

"When?"

"How about tonight?"

Palmer jumped up, making "time-out" gestures with his hands. "Now wait a minute! What happens if *you* end up getting killed instead of Morgan? What then?"

"If I'm not back at dawn, take Fell and Lethe to the airport. There are one-way tickets to Mérida waiting for you at the Taca International desk. Once you've arrived in Yucatan, check into the Smoking Gods Hotel. The manager there is holding an envelope that, essentially, transfers Indigo Imports—and all its assets—over to you. It's the best I could do on such short notice."

Palmer frowned. "You had this already planned, didn't you?"

She shrugged. "I told you I'd take care of things, didn't I? You were planning on retiring from the private detective racket, anyway. Now you can relax and sell stuffed toad mariachi bands and Day of the Dead tableaux to trendy Manhattan boutiques, just like you always dreamed."

"I'm going with you."

Sonja glanced down at Fell, still holding his newborn daughter in his arms. "Are you sure about that?"

"The bastard used me! He preyed on my weaknesses and exploited me! If I don't deserve to help kill him, who does?"

Sonja nodded. "We'll take the car. I'm betting he won't expect us to move against him so quickly. In fact, it's likely he thinks I've killed you by now."

"What about me?" asked Palmer.

"I need you to look after Lethe and make sure our luggage is ready. If you don't hear from us come dawn, take a cab to the airport and do what I told you."

"But—"

Sonja took Palmer's hands into her own and squeezed them gently. He felt her voice inside him, whispering in his brain.

I have to do this, Palmer. You can't stop me from going. We both know that. But please try to understand why.

Palmer struggled to answer her on the same plane and was surprised to "hear" his own disembodied voice echoing inside his head.

I understand. At least in part. I need you. Please come back.

You're going to do just fine, whether I'm with you or not.

That's not what I meant.

Oh.

She smiled, and it was as if she was sixteen and human again. Palmer turned to retrieve Lethe from her father. The poor bastard looked like a mile of bad road.

"Don't worry. I'll take good care of your baby." Palmer smiled, doing his best to reassure Fell. "I used to have a kid, myself, a long time ago."

*

Palmer didn't like what was happening at all, but there wasn't much he could do about it. When it came down to battling powerful six-hundred-year-old vampire lords, twenty-five years of street-smarts weren't much help.

Still, a part of him chafed at being ordered to mind the baby and pack the bags. Not that he resented looking after Lethe. If anything, he was astonished by how easily the golden-eyed infant had managed to override his ambivalence toward children.

He put Lethe back in her makeshift cradle and tossed an open suitcase on the bed. He didn't envy Sonja and Fell their task, but part of him wished he could be with them. After all, he'd been in on the case since the beginning, and it was only natural for him to want to be there when it ended—no matter what the outcome.

Sonja was right, though. Lethe was their biggest concern. Since she was unable to protect herself, it was up to him to make sure she didn't fall into Morgan's hands. The very thought of the bastard turning the child into one of his drones made Palmer so mad he felt giddy.

There was a knock on his room's door, interrupting his train of thought. Palmer paused at the threshold connecting his and Sonja s rooms. It couldn't be maid service, not at one in the morning. There was second knock, this one heavy enough to rattle the doorjamb.

Palmer pulled his backup gun, a Luger, free of its case on the bed. Checking the breech, he stepped into the other room, closing the connecting door behind him.

"Who is it?" he barked.

The hinges on the door bulged inward as the doorknob turned sharply left then right. There was the sound of metal and wood grinding together, and the door flew open, its lock snapped. It hung from its hinges like a broken bird's wing.

The ogre had to duck his head under the lintel to enter the room. Dressed in a trench coat over a black turtleneck sweater and corduroy jeans, Keif looked like a young, upwardly mobile linebacker on the go. He emitted a rank odor of bull-ape aggression that made Palmer's testes crawl.

"Pangloss say you come now."

"He promised to leave me alone! I—I'm Sonja's renfield now!"

The ogre chuckled, exposing a mouthful of yellow, serrated teeth. "She leave. Gone play with Morgan. She not coming back. Pangloss say he got dibs."

Palmer pointed the Luger at the ogre. "Back off, Kong! I don't care if the Pope himself wants an audience! I'm not going anywhere with you!"

Keif growled and advanced. Palmer fired. The bullet struck the thick ridge of the ogre's brow and slid across his bald pate like a pad of butter on a hot skillet. Except for a thin red line bisecting his skull, Keif showed no ill effect from being shot in the head at close to point-blank range.

"That sting," the ogre grunted, cuffing Palmer with the back of his hand.

It was like meeting the business end of a weighted Louisville Slugger. Palmer sailed across the double bed, landing on a small table in the corner that collapsed under his weight.

Palmer struggled to sit up, his vision swimming from the blow. He cringed at the sight of the ogre lumbering closer, displaying his fearsome shark's grin. Then, to his amazement, the giant halted.

Keif tilted his head and sniffed the air with wide, gorilla-like nostrils. He beamed an idiotic smile, a rope of thick saliva dangling from his lower jaw. The ogre's behavior was gruesomely familiar.

"Baby. Keif smell *baby*." A gray, forked tongue snapped out of the ogre's gaping mouth, licking cracked lips. His eyes narrowed as he regarded Palmer. "You got baby round here?"

"No! I mean, of course not. What would I be doing with a baby? You must be smelling the Joneses down the hall. They've got plenty of babies—at least three or four! Nice big, fat, juicy babies. There are no babies here though! No, sir!"

The ogre didn't seem convinced. "Baby smell *strong*." He snuffled again, casting for scent like a bloodhound. "*Real* strong!"

Lethe began to cry.

The ogre grinned in triumph. "Keif right! You got baby!

"Leave her alone, damn you!"

But it was too late. Keif was already heading toward the connecting door, following the infant's thin, kitten-like wail. Palmer pulled himself to his feet and staggered after the ogre, trying to ignore the pain in his head. The door connecting his and Sonja's rooms now stood wide open, yanked off its hinges.

Gasping for breath, Palmer stared in horror at the sight of the ogre holding the crying baby upside-down by her ankles like a live chicken.

"I said leave her *alone!* I'll go peacefully if you just leave her alone!"

The ogre didn't seem to hear him. "Yum-yum! Babies good eatin'!" Keif tilted his head back and dropped his jaw, lifting the frightened infant at arm's length, lowering her into his gaping maw

Suddenly Palmer smells copal burning and he is back in the jungle. He is walking along the narrow path that runs from his people's village to the natural spring that provides them with their drinking and cooking water. His young son, Tohil, is several lengths ahead of him. Tohil laughs and tosses rocks and sticks at the monkeys and birds in the nearby trees. He turns to wave at Palmer with his small six-fingered hand. Palmer envies the boy his spirit and energy. He has no doubt that Tohil will grow up to be a fine ballplayer. Before he finishes the thought, the green parts and jaguar leaps from its hiding place and grabs the startled boy. Palmer sees the jaguar's sharp fangs sink into his son's shoulder, sees the blood leap from his son's skin. Palmer hurls his spear at the great cat, but it is deflected by a branch. Tohil screams his father's name as he is pulled from the path into the jungle. Palmer runs to where the jaguar ambushed his only son, but all he finds are bloodstains, bright as rubies, splashed across the broad leaves. The men from the village search for Tohil the rest of the day, but the boy is never seen again.

"*NO!*"

Grief and rage pulsed through Palmer. He seized the anger coursing through him and channeled it outward, and it was as if he'd suddenly discovered a third arm, invisible to him until that moment. Palmer *squeezed* the ogre's skull just as it was about to drop Lethe, headfirst, into its razor-toothed mouth.

The ogre grunted as if stricken by a gastric attack. It staggered drunkenly, thick black blood trickling from its nostrils and ears. Keif gave a bullfrog-like croak and let go of the squalling baby, pointed a trembling finger at Palmer, and took an unsteady step in the detective's direction.

"You . . ."

A pink fluid seeped from around the ogre's eyes. A froth of blood and mucus dripped from the corners of his mouth. Palmer took a step away from the advancing child-eater.

"Did . . . this . . ."

Jesus, what does it take to kill one of these bastards? A direct nuclear strike?

Keif collapsed onto the floor, his brains reduced to a jellied consommé seeping from his eyes and ears.

Lethe was still crying. Palmer stepped over the fallen giant and checked on the child. Luckily, when Keif dropped her he'd been standing over the bed. The minute Palmer picked her up, Lethe's wails died down to whimpers.

"There, there, sweetheart. Bad monster's gone now."

Or was it? If Pangloss was still hot for his bod, he was sure to send other operatives once Keif didn't show up with the goods. He couldn't stay here, that was certain. Even if the management had overlooked the hot plate in the room, Palmer doubted they were willing to ignore gun shots, a screaming baby, and an undeniably dead motherfucker.

Palmer reclaimed his Luger, wrapped Lethe as warmly as he could, and put on his coat. It looked like his only option was to take a cab out to the airport, sans baggage, and wait things out there.

With Lethe tucked inside the front of his raincoat, Palmer felt like a pistol-packing kangaroo. He could just imagine what some of his old cronies would have to say about *this*. He hurried to the stairway exit just as the elevator dawn the hall pinged open. He didn't look to see who—or what—got out.

Four flights later Palmer strolled through the lobby, trying his best to look nonchalant while gasping for breath like a landed trout. The wizened oriental seated behind the registration glanced up from a Cantonese newspaper, shrugged, and resumed his reading.

Once outside, the panic Palmer had been suppressing since the ogre had appeared in his room finally kicked in. He hurried through the shadowy streets, no longer sure of what he thought he was doing or where he was going. The plans he'd made back in the hotel seemed far away and to belong to someone else.

He'd become so distraught, he didn't realize he'd gotten lost until he turned a corner and found himself at the end of a blind alley.

Palmer stared at the peeling movie posters and graffiti scrawls for a long moment before seeing them. His heart was beating way too fast and his breathing sounded ragged. He wanted a smoke real bad, but he'd left his Shermans back at the hotel room.

Lethe, curled inside his coat, was a ball of warmth pressed against his belly. Feeling her there reassured him and helped him swallow the fear rising inside him. Behind him, a bottle skittered across pavement and broke.

There were several of them blocking the entrance to the alley, huddled together like mounds of ambulatory garbage. Palmer felt the tension drain as he realized he was looking at street-people and not Pangloss's hirelings. Lethe stirred against him and gave out a kittenish mew.

One of the street-persons, a man dressed in filthy castoffs with newspapers swaddling his feet, shuffled forward. To Palmer's surprise, the vagrant responded to Lethe's call with his own, slightly deeper version. The others grouped behind him grew excited and muttered amongst themselves.

Palmer took a tentative step forward. "Uh, look, I know this sounds weird, but can anyone here tell me where I am?"

An old woman, her hair the color and consistency of a dirty string mop, sidled closer to him. She wore several layers of sweaters over a dingy, printed housedress. She smiled, displaying bare gums and golden pupil-less eyes that glowed in the dark.

"Shit!" Palmer jumped back from the old woman, his skin tingling as if he'd just received a mild electric shock. Although he'd never really seen them, he knew these were what Sonja had referred to as "   ."

The *seraph* with its feet wrapped in newspapers made a reassuring hand gesture, then it spoke. From cracked, filth-caked lips rushed a mixture of crystal chimes, bird song, silver bells, and crashing tide. The beauty of the *seraph*'s language brought tears to Palmer's eyes. And even though he could not make out a single word, he understood perfectly.

Nodding his assent, Palmer unbuttoned his coat and held Lethe so the assembled *seraphim* could see her. They grew agitated and crowded in closer so that they could touch her dusky baby flesh with their callused, dirty hands. Lethe did not seem to mind and responded to their strange, ethereal language with her own, babyish version.

The sweater woman made a sound like a dolphin and began spinning in place, like a bedraggled whirling dervish. Soon the others joined in her dance. Palmer watched in dumb fascination as blue-white sparks leapt from the twirling *seraph*'s outstretched hands and hair. Within seconds the ragged street-people had been transformed into pure light, spinning around him like luminous dust devils.

Palmer was so dazzled by the beauty of what was happening, he was caught off guard when one of the light-beings danced forward and plucked Lethe from his hands.

"Hey! What do you think you're doing!? Give me back my baby!"

Lethe giggled and clapped her hands as she was lifted high into the air on a pillow of colored lights. The other *seraphim* joined in, transforming themselves from electric-blue tornadoes to rainbow-colored clouds.

One of the *seraphim* twined about Palmer's shoulders, whispering to him in its strange non-language.

He need not fear for the child. She would be returned to him when it was safe. Palmer tried to snare the bright intelligence with his own mind, but it was like trying to trap quicksilver in his bare hands. The *seraph* eeled its way free of his grasp, more amused than insulted by such a clumsy attempt at interrogation.

Lethe bobbed in the night air, smiling down at Palmer like an infant saint taken up by angels. Within moments she had drifted away from view, like a balloon caught in a jet stream.

Palmer knew he had nothing to fear from the *seraphim*. If anything, Lethe was safer with them than with him. Now he was free to follow Sonja. Provided he could find ready transportation.

As he left the alley he scooped up a loose brick, hefting it experimentally. It'd been a long time since he'd boosted a car without his tools. Not since the Sex Pistols' American Tour, at least.

THE TIGER'S CAGE

Fell sat beside Sonja while she drove, his posture rigid. In his faded denims and loose-fitting cotton shirt, he could almost pass for a college boy. Provided you ignored the bruises and dried blood on his face.

"I'm sorry I did those things to you, kid."

Fell started, blinking rapidly. "Huh? Oh. Don't worry about it. I understand what you were trying to do." His hand strayed to where his ear had been. "Besides, it'll all grow back, won't it?"

"In time. Your regenerative powers at this stage aren't so advanced that you'll recover overnight, though."

"How long, then?"

"I'd give it a couple of days. Maybe a week."

Fell grunted and glanced at his warped reflection in the windshield. "What about my eyes? When will my eyes be like yours?"

Sonja shrugged, trying to pretend it didn't matter. "Hard to say. It took mine several years to mutate. Maybe yours never will. Maybe it's different with different people. Who knows?" Sonja cleared her throat. "Uh, there's a few things I need to know about Morgan's setup at the house, if you don't mind talking about it.

"Sure. Go ahead."

"Anise mentioned someone called Dr. Howell. Who is he? Another vampire?"

Fell looked back down at his hands. Without his realizing it, they had become fists. "No. He's not a vampire. He's human."

"A renfield?"

"I've never given it much thought before, really. But, no, he's not a renfield. I guess he's just a normal human. If you could call Doc Howell normal." Fell snorted. "He's Morgan's pet mad scientist, although they don't get along too well—and Howell openly *loathes* the renfields."

"Interesting. If that's the case, what hold does Morgan have on him?"

Fell smirked and held up his left arm and pantomimed sinking a hypodermic needle into his bent elbow with his right hand. "The Doc's a stone junkie. Morgan provides him with all the heroin, morphine, and opium he can handle. And then some."

"And this guy's a scientist?"

"That's what he keeps saying. He's some kind of hotshot geneticist. Occasionally he'd get hopped up and start ranting about how *he* was our true father, not Morgan! I always thought it was just crazy talk. We got a lot of that from the renfields, whenever they'd bother to talk to us at all."

"How many servants does Morgan have at Ghost Trap?"

Fell frowned. "I'm not sure. I never saw them together at one time. They avoided us as much as possible. There might be as many as six. Plus Wretched Fly."

"Wretched Fly?"

"Yeah, Morgan's top renfield. He was at the disco."

"The oriental?"

"Yeah, that's him."

"Well, I took out one at Ghost Trap this afternoon and one at the bar, and Anise said she'd killed one while escaping. That depletes his backup by half," mused Sonja, ticking off the kills on the fingers of her right hand. "Does he have any mercs?"

"What?"

"Muscle for hire. Various species of Pretender make their way by hiring themselves out to vampires as powerful and well connected as Morgan. I know he's got a pyrotic on the payroll. Did you see any ogres? *Vargr?* Skindancers?"

"Whozits?"

"Boy, he sure did his best to keep you ignorant, didn't he?"

Fell flushed. "Anise and I were restricted to a suite of rooms on the ground floor for most of our lives. The first few months we were kept in a sterile environment, and only Morgan and Doc Howell were allowed in. Most of the time we stayed in our rooms, except for when we were escorted to and from Doc's laboratory on the second floor.

"We were only allowed outside once—it was during the day, and we were under heavy supervision by the renfields. Dr. Howell was there, too—taking notes. I guess they wanted to see if we'd turn into crispy critters when exposed to the sun."

"Weren't you even a little bit curious as to what was really going on?"

Fell's face reddened even deeper. "No, not really. At least I wasn't. I know that's a horrible thing to admit to, but it's the truth. Anise was a *little* more inquisitive than I was, and that didn't become part of her behavior until after she became pregnant. Until yesterday afternoon, it had never occurred to me that the life I was living was in any way . . . unusual. After all, I didn't have anything to compare it to, did I?" Fell shook his head, amazed at his own naïveté.

"But what *really* makes me sick is that a part of me, deep down, *liked* Morgan running my life for me. And what's worse, I enjoyed what I had become! I was never any good at sports back when I was Tim Sorrell, Super-Geek. I never did real well with the girls. I was a gold-plated wimp if ever there was one. Although I didn't consciously remember any of that stuff, it was still buried inside me.

"There's a fully outfitted gymnasium on the second floor we were allowed to use. I can bench-press eight hundred pounds. *Me!* Scrawny little 'Dracula Weirdo' Sorrell!" He flexed his biceps, parodying a Charles Atlas-style bodybuilder.

For a fleeting moment he was what he had once been: a bright, sensitive nineteen-year-old boy, standing on the threshold of manhood. Then the smile disappeared and he was staring at his hands again.

"Morgan used to talk about 'the cattle' and how easy it is to control them. Sometimes he'd bring in humans from outside . . . I don't know who they were. Transients, I guess. And he'd let me . . ." He closed his eyes, trying to blot the image from his memory. "I'd *play* with them." His voice shook, the words burning his tongue. "Sometimes there was sex. Man. Woman. It didn't matter. And then after . . ."

"Fell, you don't have to tell me this."

"But I *have* to! I *have* to tell someone!" His voice was high and tight, like a frightened girl's. "My god, Sonja, if I can't tell *you*, who *can* I tell it to?"

She pursed her mouth into a thin line and nodded. "Go on."

Fell took a shuddering breath, anxiously knotting and unknotting his fingers in his lap. "After the sex was over, I'd bite them on their arms and legs and groin . . . Like I was kissing them, only they were screaming and bleeding instead of moaning with pleasure. And it wasn't because I was hungry, either! Morgan provided us with all the bottled blood we could ever need. I did it because . . . because it felt *good!* It was better than sex or drugs or anything else. It made me feel *alive!* It was like my nightmares, only I wasn't scared of the things I was doing anymore.

"Morgan would stay in the room and watch me do these things. I pray to God he was controlling me, making me do those horrible things. Because if he wasn't, *I* did them!"

"What happened was in the past. You've regained your conscience, and with it self-autonomy. Whatever you may have done while under Morgan's influence, it's over and done with. It's up to you to realize that and accept it, Tim."

"Don't call me that. I'm not Tim anymore, not where it really counts. I don't know who—or what—I am. Part of me remembers what it was like to be Tim Sorrell. I can still recall all the times the bigger, more popular kids made fun of him, called him names. I can remember the hatred he felt for them. I can remember his parents, and how he felt about them, but it's not the same as when I *was* Tim. But I'm not what Morgan wanted me to be, either. When I think of things I did before I regained my sense of self, it makes me want to puke. I guess I'm Fell more than I am anything—or anyone—else. Just like you're more Sonja Blue than Denise Thorne."

"How did—?"

"The skull-peeping works both ways. When you were working me over at the disco I kept getting, I dunno, *flashes*. Of you and Morgan. What he did to make you . . . what you are."

A muscle twitched in Sonja's cheek as she tightened her grip on the steering wheel. "I see. But you're right, I don't really think of myself as Denise anymore. She's more someone I used to know."

"Do you like her?"

She reflected on that for a moment before answering. "Yeah, I guess I do."

"I like Tim, too. Now that it's too late to do him any good."

"What do you *mean* you can't find him?" Morgan bellowed, hurling an antique ivory music box at the cowering renfield.

The renfield dodged at the last moment, wincing as the music box smashed against the teak paneling next to his head.

"J-just that, milord. The doctor is not in his laboratory, nor is he in his room."

"Are you saying he's managed to escape?"

"No. Not exactly. He's . . . he's somewhere in the house."

"How astute! Then if he's still in the house, *why* haven't you brought him before me?"

"He's not in the *nucleus*, milord. He's . . . somewhere in the *outer* house. He's in the Ghost Trap." Having delivered this news, the renfield pulled his neck in between his shoulders like a turtle.

"*Damn* him! Damn his junkie soul to a thousand drug-free hells!" Morgan shrieked, knocking books and rare antiques from a nearby bookshelf with an angry sweep of his arm. "He did this to me! He *deliberately* set out to ruin my plans!" The vampire spun back around to face the trembling renfield, pointing a finger at the whey-faced psychic.

"You! I want the outer house searched, is that clear? Take the others with you!"

"But—but, milord!"

"Do it!"

The renfield fled the library, leaving Morgan to fume in silence.

He should never have trusted Howell. Never! The scientist had been unstable long before the drugs became a factor. But Howell's erratic behavior was what had allowed Morgan access to him to begin with. As much as it galled the vampire lord to admit it, the mistake was his own. He'd been intimidated by the scientist's facility with technology, allowing him far more autonomy than was prudent. And now Morgan was paying the price for not keeping his pet biogeneticist on a tighter leash.

If news of his humiliation at the hands of a mere *human* ever got out, he'd be the laughingstock of the Nobility! Worse, he would be perceived as weak, and *that* would endanger his alliances and encourage another round of brood wars against him. He might even be forced to surrender his title of Lord! It would no doubt please snapping jackals like Pangloss and Verité to see him brought low.

This was what his reliance on technology and science, humankind's sorcery, had brought him to. He should never have relied so heavily on something of human manufacture! These things were always confusing and somewhat frightening to Pretenders, and Morgan was no different. Yet its inherent power had been too lucrative to leave to mere humans to exploit.

While Howell might be a necromancer of unparalleled power in his postnuclear wizard's workshop, it would do him little good once he was strapped to a chair. Morgan had all kinds of interesting things planned for the good Dr. Howell. Depriving him of his precious white powder was only the first of many cruelties to be inflicted on the thankless swine. Perhaps a few judiciously applied medical probes would make him more appreciative of his betters. Of course, the good doctor would be forced to personally oversee his own flaying and subsequent vivisection. Morgan had long since evolved beyond the need to soil his hands with the blood of his victims.

But first the conniving bastard had to be caught. Morgan struck his desk with a balled fist, cracking its imported Italian marble. While Brainard Howell might be devious, vainglorious, and ungrateful, one thing he definitely was *not* was stupid.

The bastard knew that the outer layer surrounding Ghost Trap's nucleus was dangerous, especially to Pretenders and humans with psychic abilities.

While this had worked in Morgan's favor in the past, Howell's escape had turned that advantage against him.

There were *things* roaming Ghost Trap that did not like outsiders, and Morgan was in no hurry to meet them face-to-face.

"Milord?"

Morgan glanced up from his reverie and glowered at Wretched Fly. The renfield stood in the doorway to the library, the right side of his head wrapped in sterile gauze.

"Are they dead?"

"Milord—there were *difficulties*."

"Explain yourself."

"The woman, the one called Blue, uncovered our presence. My companion was killed outright. I was momentarily . . . incapacitated." He touched the bandage shrouding his right eye gingerly.

"Then what of Fell?"

"I don't know, milord. The rogue had the upper hand the last I saw her. Milord, she was *tapping* him!"

Morgan frowned. "Are you sure?"

"I'm *positive,* milord! The nimbus configuration was quite distinct. She was absorbing and metabolizing the negative energy generated by the breeder."

Morgan fell silent. He hadn't been expecting that. Perhaps it was better that his plans had collapsed, after all. His schemes had revolved around a race of vampires incapable of living on anything but blood. Feeding on emotions was something only the more advanced species were capable of. Fell had shown no signs of battening onto his terror-stricken prey for anything but plasma during the little "tests" Morgan had arranged.

"Are you certain this rogue isn't a true vampire?" he hissed.

"I am sure of it, milord. Her aural configurations were identical to those of the breeders, although much stronger."

Morgan cursed under his breath. This was *not* turning out the way he'd hoped.

"Milord—"

"What is it, Wretched Fly?"

The renfield cleared his throat. "Milord, I have failed you. And since I have done so, I offer now my life to you, for you to destroy as you see fit."

Morgan suppressed a smile. "I can do that *anytime* I want, Wretched Fly. But I appreciate the offer. No, you are too valuable to me, my friend. The eye—it is gone?"

"Yes, milord."

"Then that is payment enough for your failure."

"As you wish, milord."

Morgan watched as his maimed lieutenant left the room. It had been centuries since Morgan had last known the treachery of mortal flesh. The mere thought that he had once been restrained by the limits of bone and muscle, fearful of disease and pestilence, was enough to make his skin tighten.

✷

"Christ, I never realized how big this house was before! I mean, I knew it was *large*, but I never truly comprehended its *scale* . . ." Fell whispered in awe, tilting his head to ogle one of the ninety-nine lightning rods decorating the spires and turrets of Ghost Trap.

"Look, once we're in there I want you to stick with me, understand? The inside of this place is designed to confuse and trap the dead. It also does a good job scrambling the synapses of anything more complicated than a worm. If regular humans have a hard time dealing with it, you can imagine what it'll do to Pretenders! I still have the protective charm I used from the first time I entered the house, but I can't guarantee it'll extend itself to include you. Have I made myself clear?"

Fell swallowed hard and nodded. Sonja surprised herself by giving the boy a brief hug. Shit, the kid was brave. Fell's cheeks reddened.

"Uh, Sonja . . ."

"Later, kid. We'll talk about it later." With that she turned and put her fist through one of the downstairs windows, reaching inside to open the lock.

"No wonder Morgan wouldn't let us wander loose around here." Ever since they'd entered Ghost Trap's rambling confines, Fell had spoken in a low, reverential whisper, as if in church. "You could get lost and never find your way out again!"

"That's not all you have to worry about. There are *things* that walk these halls. Most people would call them ghosts. Spirits of the dead."

"But ghosts can't hurt you, can they?"

"Normally, no. But Ghost Trap is hardly what I'd call normal. Just keep an eye out for anything that looks like a little girl or a woman dressed in old-timey clothes."

"Are they ghosts?"

"No, they're fuckin' *tour hostesses!* Of course they're ghosts! What did you expect? I think I can find my way back to the fire room . . ."

"The what?"

"Never mind. Just keep your mouth shut and your eyes open, okay? I—"

She halted and tilted her head at an angle. She shot Fell a look from the corner of her eye. "You hear that?"

"What? I don't—" He stopped, his jaw dropping open. It was faint, but he could just make out the sound of someone whimpering. "Is—is it a ghost?"

"It doesn't sound like one. The dead tend to be mute." She motioned for him to follow her, moving stealthily through the shadows and dust of the empty rooms.

They found the source of the whimpering in a room lined with wallpaper that sparkled faintly in the illumination provided by a flashlight dropped on the floor. Fell touched the wall nearest him and felt the gold and crushed crystal wallpaper underneath his fingertips. It had the texture of sandpaper. Sonja picked up the flashlight and turned the feeble beam on its owner.

A middle-aged man dressed in a rumpled dark suit sat huddled in the far corner of the room, his face pressed tightly against the wall. His suit and hair were smeared with dust and cobwebs. One side of his face was bloody from where he'd been rubbing it against the wallpaper. He'd recently wet himself and the astringent ammonia smell clung to him. He twitched and whimpered like a kicked puppy.

"I recognize him," Fell whispered. "He's one of Morgan's renfields. But what's he doing here?"

"Whatever his reasons for entering this place might have been, I doubt he was looking for us," Sonja muttered. She took another step toward the man crouched in the corner. He stopped shivering and bared his teeth, foam flecking the corners of his mouth.

"Renfields aren't terribly stable to begin with. And being somewhere like this, I'm not surprised the bastard lost it totally," Sonja muttered as she moved closer. "Still, he might be of *some* use—"

The renfield shrieked and launched himself at her, his fingers clawing at her glasses. Sonja cursed and smashed the butt of the flashlight against her attacker's skull. The renfield collapsed to the floor, his head caved in. Sonja tossed the broken flashlight over her shoulder and bent down, lifting the dead renfield by his suit lapels.

"Waste not, want not," she growled, sinking her canines into his still-warm throat. After a minute or two, she withdrew, handing the corpse to Fell. "Here. Drink."

Fell's eyes widened and he took a step back. "No. I can't."

"You're no virgin! You said so yourself! Now, drink! You're gonna need it!"

"I . . ." Fell meant to protest further, but he'd already caught the scent of blood on her breath. His mouth began to water. He quickly battened onto the dead man. The blood was already below body temperature, but it was enough. He let the drained corpse drop.

"Feel better?"

"Yeah. I know this sounds horrible, but I feel like I've got my second wind now."

"Good boy!" She grinned, clapping him on the shoulder. "Now, all we have to do is—"

A loud scream broke the silence, bouncing through the rooms like a rubber ball, before being cut off in mid-note. Sonja and Fell exchanged looks and headed in the direction of the noise.

They found the second renfield in the hall Sonja had called the "fire room." The gas jets were still blazing as they entered. The renfield lay sprawled in the middle of the room, his skull smashed like an overripe pumpkin dropped from the top of a ladder.

Fell glanced about nervously while Sonja tried to find the secret panel the late Mrs. Seward had shown her. "This little girl and lady you mentioned—are they, uh, good ghosts or bad ghosts?"

"They're—ambivalent. Like most dead. But if you mean are they friend or foe—I think they're friendly. No, they're not responsible for this."

"Then who—?"

"Found it!" Sonja stood back, allowing the secret door to pivot open. "C'mon!"

Fell gave the mutilated remains a final glance over his shoulder before following Sonja into the secret passage.

The rental car was parked on the south side of the house, its hood still warm.

They're here, all right. Now all I have to do is catch up with them, Palmer mused sourly, nervously eyeing Ghost Trap's sprawl.

His own transport, a BMW he'd "borrowed" back in San Francisco, was in no shape for a return journey. Steam seeped from under its hood, while something dark and viscous dripped from the undercarriage. Probably ripped the oil pan off a mile or so back. Obviously, the car had not been designed to navigate Sonoma County back roads at high speeds.

Spying an open ground-floor window, Palmer checked to make sure his Luger was securely holstered before climbing over the sill in pursuit of his partner.

Three steps into the Ghost Trap, he realized he'd made a *big* mistake. If he'd found the exterior of Ghost Trap disorienting, it was nothing compared to the interior.

He remembered how, as a child, he'd pestered his parents into allowing him to enter the House of Horrors at the state fair. He'd promised them that it wouldn't give him nightmares—he was too old to be scared; he was a big boy now, not a little kid. Finally, they'd weakened and allowed him to go in. His self-assurance in his proclaimed maturity vanished the minute the wooden double doors swung shut behind him, cutting off all contact with the world where light, parents, and rational thought ruled.

Surrounded by dry-ice mist, black lights, and prerecorded screams and rattling chains, he'd shrieked at the sight of a department store mannequin dressed to look like Frankenstein. He'd been so scared he wet himself and was escorted outside by one of the employees, a pimply-faced teenager dressed in a hunchback costume. His father had called him a sissy, and they'd been forced to leave the fair early because of his "accident."

Now, thirty years later, the same paralyzing terror he'd experienced in the House of Horror was close to claiming him again. His scalp prickled and his bladder ached as if full of ground glass.

He trudged through the oddly designed rooms, barely noticing such oddities as doorways set three feet off the ground, windows that opened onto blank walls, and fireplaces that served as staircases.

With every room, he found it harder and harder to think straight. Why was he here? Why had he entered this horrible place? He knew he must have had a good reason. Or at least *some* kind of reason. Right? Now if he could only remember what it was . . .

Palmer staggered as the floor dropped out from under him. The walls bowed inward, as if made from rubber. He retched while leaning against a sharply canted doorway, the acid burning his throat. His dad was really going to yell at him now. He shouldn't have eaten all those corndogs before riding the Tilt-A-Whirl. Now they were going to have to leave the fair. But that didn't sound like such a bad idea. He'd already been too long at the fair. Now if he could only remember where the car was . . . parked.

Palmer collapsed onto his hands and knees as dry heaves shook his body. His forebrain throbbed fiercely, keeping time like a jazz drummer.

I'm gonna die in here. I'm gonna wander around lost inside this hell hole until it kills me. Just like Seward. Sonja . . .

He lifted his head and found himself staring at a small boy.

The child looked to be no more than three years old, dressed in a sailor's suit. The boy held a teddy bear close to his chest with his left arm because he was missing his right one. A knob of bone and bloodless flesh protruded from his mangled shoulder. Although the child's face was still round with baby fat, his eyes were solemn. Palmer dimly noticed that the child was transparent.

"Little boy . . ."

The child did not waver or disappear.

"Little boy . . . I need . . . help . . ."

A young girl clutching a china doll joined the boy, both of them watching Palmer with interest. The girl leaned toward her brother and muttered something that Palmer could not make out. Moving together, the children grasped Palmer by his shoulders and pulled him back onto his feet. He gasped and felt a strong chill run through his body at the touch of their tiny fingers on his flesh.

The children were in front of him now, motioning for him to follow. Shaken and weak, Palmer lurched after them. He had no way of knowing if these creatures were friend or foe, but anything was better than crawling around in circles in his own filth.

The children froze like fawns scenting the approach of a hunter. First the boy then his sister disincorporated, transforming themselves into fist-sized globs of light. The change was so abrupt it looked to Palmer as if the children had rolled up like window shades.

Palmer pressed his hands to his eyes, even more disoriented than before. What had happened to his tiny spirit guides? Or had he imagined the whole thing? And if not, what was it that had frightened them away?

The scream ripped through him like a bullet. As he listened, it ended abruptly, cut off in mid-shriek. The echo was so distorted it was impossible to tell if it had been a male or female voice.

"Sonja!"

Palmer weaved in the general direction the scream had come from. His brain churned and stretched inside his head, pressing against the plates of his skull. Sonja. He had to find Sonja. That's why he'd come into the House of Horrors. Now he remembered. Once he found Sonja she'd make the pounding in his head go away.

Palmer stared at the thing with the ax for several seconds before realizing he'd discovered the source of the scream.

The creature was shaped like a man, only taller. It carried a large, cruel-looking ax, which it was using to dismember what was left of a man in a dark suit. The ax-murderer made weird tittering noises while it hacked away at its prey. The victim's head had been cracked open from the top of his skull to his upper palate.

The thing halted in mid-swing and turned to look at the new intruder, and Palmer's bladder let go, just as it had in the House of Horrors back in 1961. Only this time he knew there was no way he would be escorted to safety by a sympathetic teenager tricked out in monster drag.

The ax-murderer had two heads. The head on the left was the larger of the pair, boasting a bat-like snout, a mouthful of jagged teeth, and pupil-less eyes the color of fresh blood. The head on the right was that of a man in his mid-thirties, the eyes brimming with a grief that extended beyond anything Palmer had ever known. With a start, he recognized the face of Creighton Seward, Ghost Trap's architect.

The two-headed monster stepped forward, hoisting the ax that grew out of its left wrist in place of a hand. Palmer wanted to turn and flee the abomination before him, but he remained frozen, unable to move.

Seward's lips were moving, whether praying or arguing with its grotesque twin, Palmer couldn't tell. As if in reply, the ax-murderer's head sneered and emitted more high-pitched titters. Suddenly Seward's head turned and bit its neighbor on the cheek, ripping free a wad of flesh. The ax-murderer's head gave a high-frequency shriek that made Palmer's nose bleed, and returned the attack in kind, scissoring off the ear nearest its mouth. Cowed, Seward's head did not attempt any further interference.

The ax-murderer's head leered at Palmer and lifted the ax-hand higher, until it almost brushed the ceiling. Palmer was not sure if the creature standing before him was flesh and blood or composed of ectoplasm, but it was evident the ax, at least, was solid enough to do its job. Palmer stared at the fiend advancing on him like a steer awaiting the butcher's knife.

Just as the ax was ready to fall, a bright light appeared between Palmer and the two-headed thing. The creature balked, uncertainty crossed the ax-murder's face. Steward's head seemed to take strength from the light and plunged the fingers of its right hand into the ax-murder's eyes. The beast shrieked even louder than before and Palmer felt blood seep from his ears.

The two-headed thing was gone. In its place stood a woman dressed in clothing better suited to an Ibsen play, her back to Palmer.

"Oh, thank God! Lady? Lady, I need your help . . ."

The woman turned to face Palmer, her left eye swinging loose from its socket.

Palmer screamed and ran. He had to find his way out of the House of Horrors. He'd been too long at the fair. It was time to go home. He bolted from the death-room and headed down a corridor lined with doors of varying shapes and sizes, the sound of his own shouts for help filling his ears.

Suddenly one of the doors opened outward and a golf club cut the air with a wicked slicing sound.

The last thing Palmer saw before the darkness claimed him was the word *Dunlop*.

“Home again, home again, jiggety-jig,” Sonja muttered as she stepped from the secret passage into the suite of rooms Fell had once called home.

“I never knew this corridor existed. I don’t think Morgan or the renfields did, either,” Fell marveled.

“I suspect it was left over from when the carpenters were working on the house. It’s only natural for a place like this to have secret passages. The building’s probably lousy with them.”

Fell picked up a paperback from its resting place on the table next to Anise’s old easy chair. He fanned the pages and put it back down.

“It’s hard for me to believe that she’s really gone. I can still smell her . . .”

“Fell, don’t.”

“Don’t what?”

“Torture yourself.”

He didn’t seem to hear her. Leaning his forearms against the mantelpiece, he studied the room’s reflection in the mirror that hung over the fireplace, as if trying to catch a glimpse of the past in its depths.

“Do you know what the last thing she said to me was?” he asked, nodding at the room in the looking glass. “She told me this was a *cage*. A prison. She was right, of course. I can see the bars now. But for a short while, this was the happiest place on earth. I . . .” He shook his head, refusing to look his companion in the face. “Damn you, Sonja! Why did you have to come into our lives? Why did you force this knowledge on us?”

“I wish I could say I did it because truth is freedom, and living in ignorance is the same as living in slavery. But that would be a lie. I did it because I wanted to ruin Morgan’s plans. I wanted to hurt him where he’d feel it. And I wanted you for myself.”

Fell frowned. "Me?"

"And Anise. And the baby. I—I've been alone for a long, long time, Fell. I was hungry for the company of my own kind. Sometimes loneliness makes you do things that are selfish. Forgive me."

"What's there to forgive? Besides, even if your reasons weren't altruistic, what you said about ignorance and slavery is still the truth."

"I hate to bring this up, but we can't waste any more time talking about our feelings. I know coming back here is painful for you, but we've got to dispatch Morgan as soon as possible. He's here, somewhere in the house. I can feel him."

"I can feel him, too." Fell's mouth pulled into a grimace. "I'm gonna fix that bastard but good."

Sonja placed a firm hand on his shoulder. "Kid, it's good that you hate Morgan. But be careful with your anger. Don't let it get out of control. Vampires feed on powerful emotions like hate and rage. It makes them stronger. Remember what happened at the bar? You've got to shield yourself from Morgan. I can't do it for you. It will be your will against his. You have to be strong, Fell. As strong as Morgan—if not stronger."

"I know. I may be inexperienced, but I'm not stupid."

✸

She was here. He sensed her presence in the house the way a spider monitors the strands of its web. How could he have slept, unaware, when first she walked these halls? How could he have been insensate to anything so exquisitely lethal?

At first he'd refused to believe she could be one of his by-blows. But now he knew it to be true. His hand had sown this dragon's tooth. In a perverse way, he was proud of her. Even from a distance there was no mistaking her potential strength. She was a thing of fatal beauty, to be feared and admired, like an unsheathed samurai sword. To know that he had played a role in creating such a fearsome and deadly creature was flattering. Such a pity she must be destroyed.

The breeder, Fell, was with her, his presence nearly overshadowed by the female's. Interesting. There seemed to be something added to the youth's psychic echo; a trace of will, similar to that in the rogue. But it was only a hint, nothing more. Most interesting. If the breeders and their gets harbored potential similar to the rogue's, then Howell's sabotage had, in the end, been in Morgan's favor. What was the advantage to siring a new race of vampires, only to have them destroy him along with his enemies?

Morgan rose from the ornately carved rosewood chair in his study and opened the antique chifforobe with the blacked-out mirror. If this was to be a formal confrontation, the least he could do was dress for the occasion.

"Who are you? I don't recognize you as being one of Morgan's lickspittle servitors. Answer me! I didn't hit you with the golf club *that* hard!"

Palmer opened his right eye. He tried to open the left, but it was swollen shut. His left cheek rested on rough wooden floorboards. He moaned as he struggled to sit up.

"Wh-where?"

"Never mind where you are! *Who* are you?" A wan, balding man dressed in a grimy lab technician's coat, a stethoscope looped around his neck like a pet boa constrictor, thrust his unsmiling face into Palmer's field of vision. The stranger's forehead bulged slightly, as if his forebrain was slightly too large for his skull. His eyes, amplified by coke-bottle glasses, regarded Palmer with a detached, insectile interest. There was something familiar about the stranger Palmer could not quite place.

"I'm not one of Morgan's renfields, if that's what you're thinking."

The moon-faced stranger grunted in distaste and swiftly shoved his hand inside Palmer's trench coat, removing his wallet and scanning the identification inside. His eyebrows lifted slightly at the sight of Palmer's private investigator's license.

"Hey! Whattaya think you're doing?" Palmer reached for his gun, only to find the holster empty.

"Looking for this?" The stranger extracted Palmer's Luger from one of the oversized pockets of his lab coat. "I might not be a private detective, Mr. William Calumet Palmer, but I know enough to disarm a potential enemy." He snorted and tossed the wallet into Palmer's lap.

"I'd rather you not mention the 'Calumet' part, whoever you are," Palmer sighed, cradling his bleeding head. He peered up at the smirking man leaning against the metal table littered with glass beakers and Bunsen burners. "I told you who I am, now who the fuck are *you?* And why did you smack me in the head with a golf club?"

"I am Dr. Howell, late of his diabolical majesty Lord Morgan's service." He bowed at the waist with the heel-clicking propriety of a Prussian nobleman. "Forgive me for introducing myself in such a fashion, but I had no way of knowing you weren't one of Morgan's minions."

Suddenly Palmer realized where he'd seen Howell's face before. "I saw you looking out of one of the windows the other day while I was surveying the house!"

"Interesting. And not impossible. But why are you here, Mr. Palmer? This is hardly a place for sightseeing."

"I'm trying to find someone."

"Indeed. Who might that be?"

"A friend. A woman."

Howell's smile widened as his eyes narrowed. "The same woman who entered the house earlier? Don't look so surprised—there's little that goes on in Ghost Trap I don't know about. So, you *are* a renfield!"

"Stop calling me that!" Palmer snapped. "I'm my own man, damn it! Unlike some!" He groaned as he got to his feet. Howell watched him cautiously, but did not threaten him with the gun. "Now, will you help me or—*Jesus Christ!*"

Resting next to Howell's elbow was a ten-gallon jar full of a clear liquid, in which was suspended the monster-fetus Palmer had seen Anise give birth to—and kill—earlier that same evening, its umbilical cord attached to a pulpy yolk sac. The sight of the little bastard made Palmer's leg ache.

"Ah! You've noticed my friend, have you? How do you like him, hmmm?" Howell leaned forward, eyeing the monstrosity in the glass jar with something resembling affection. "He was the prototype for a parasite I succeeded in sneaking into sweet Anise's unhallowed womb." He removed a syringe from one of his pockets and tapped the side of the jar with it. To Palmer's amazement, the fetus opened its eyes, revealing the cold, needful stare of an insect.

The sight of Howell's face, distorted by the glass and the synthetic amniotic fluids that sustained it, caused the fetus to pucker and extend its hideous tube-like mouth. Howell chuckled indulgently. "How cute! It thinks it's feeding time!"

"You're responsible for that—that *thing* Anise gave birth to?"

Howell gave Palmer a sharp glance. "You saw it?"

"We met." Palmer grimaced, rubbing his wounded calf.

"Hideous as it may be, it was my attempt to make amends for betraying my race. I bioengineered the creature from the breeders' own sperm and ovum, so there would be little chance of rejection, then implanted it in Anise during a prenatal exam. I performed the operation under Morgan's very nose!" Howell's face twisted into a rueful grimace. "He may be wise in the ways of the supernatural world, but when it comes to science and the technologies, he's no more than a potato-munching peasant, fearful of the shaman's magic!

"The parasite was supposed to devour the original and take its place. However, at my last prenatal checkup, there were still two heartbeats. If necessary, I was prepared to take care of the little Antichrist myself during its delivery." He leaned forward, eyeing Palmer intently. "You were there, weren't you? At the birth? The child *is* dead, is it not?"

"Yes. It's dead," Palmer lied.

Howell smiled grimly. "Good! Good! Should the breeders' child have thrived, mankind's future would have been seriously endangered!"

"How so?"

"The breeders can only reproduce with others of their kind, which are—mercifully—rare. But their child would have the ability to mate with normal humans and still breed true. Morgan—the preening fool—had no idea of what he was unleashing!"

"And your changeling was an improvement?"

Howell shrugged. "The creatures are designed in such a way that they have no means of eliminating wastes, once severed from the umbilical cord. The pathetic little monsters are destined to die of uremic poisoning within a day or so of their birth."

Palmer shook his head in an attempt to clear the ringing from it. He groaned as his vision swam.

Howell clucked his tongue in disapproval. "I wouldn't bother trying to get a better grip on your senses if I were you. It won't do you any good. This room—my 'secret laboratory' if you will—is located in Ghost Trap's attic, at an intersection of several architectural impossibilities. The barriers separating the space-time continuum are very thin here, weighting the probability factors for my experiments in my favor. Morgan and his loathsome renfields shun this place. I like it. It helps me think. Here I'm free to plot my vengeance against Morgan."

"Vengeance?"

Howell smiled a junkie's smile. "I mean to see the bastard stew in his own juices! I want to see him broken like Dresden china in a trash dump! I want to see the look on his face when he realizes his dreams of godhood have been ground to paste! Just as he destroyed *my* hopes and dreams so many years ago. The monster sorely misjudged me, and now he's paying for it. He and his loathsome little skull-peepers find my thoughts opaque. I confuse them by thinking in terms of formulae. And thanks to the interference generated by certain . . . inhibiting factors induced into my bloodstream, my thought processes are hard to decipher. Surrounded by a nest of telepaths, I've kept my thoughts to myself for over five years!"

"But you're working for this guy, aren't you? You helped him create Anise and Fell."

Howell frowned. "I am Dr. Brainerd Howell. Does the name mean anything to you?"

"Uh, well, I . . ."

"Well *does* it?"

"No"

"And why *should* it?! For years I've been under Morgan's thrall, locked away from my fellow scientists. Unable to communicate my discoveries. Kept incommunicado while slaving to find a way to restructure human DNA into that of a vampire's without the use of actual venom. In the little time I've succeeded in stealing for myself, I've worked *miracles!*"

He pointed to a shelf lined with glass jars similar to the one that housed the changeling. Palmer could dimly make out the forms of tiny triceratops, tyrannosaurs, and stegosaurs curled inside the jars like chicken embryos.

"And there is no one to see! No one to nominate me for a Nobel prize! No one to make sure my name goes down in the history books along with Pasteur! Einstein! Salk!"

"You left out Frankenstein, Mengele, and Benway."

Howell jabbed a finger at him. "Don't get smart, Palmer! I could stick you with a hypo full of miracle juice that would make your amino acids square dance. 'Swing your partner! Do-si-do! He's got three eyes and no more nose!' How'd you like *that*, Mr. 'I'm My Own Man'?!" The scientist's pupils contracted into pinpricks.

"Calm down, Doc! I didn't mean anything by it! Honest!" Palmer lifted his hands in deference. "But if you hate Morgan so much, how come you're working for him?"

"Human weakness—something creatures of Morgan's ilk are adept at exploiting. I was working at a minor research facility in Colorado when I first made Morgan's . . . acquaintance. I had acquired a fondness for certain . . . chemicals . . . during my post-graduate studies. I found that heroin and other opiates helped to stimulate and focus my thought processes. They enhanced my powers of concentration, much like Sherlock Holmes and his infamous seven percent solution. Genius, Mr. Palmer, has its price.

"Somehow, Morgan learned of my . . . foible. He came to me and threatened to expose my secret vice to my superiors if I didn't agree to work for him. I still had no idea of who—or what—he truly was. Even though he'd essentially blackmailed me into his employ, I did not find much to dislike about my situation. I was paid three times my previous salary and given access to the most technologically advanced—and expensive—equipment available in the field. Plus, my new employer provided a steady supply of narcotics for my personal use. What was there *not* to like?

"It wasn't until I was relocated to this place that I learned what he *really* was! That was five years ago. I have been a virtual prisoner in this house ever since. During that time I have been an unwilling participant in his plan to create a race of living vampires. It took five hundred experimental subjects before I perfected the serum used on the test group that produced Anise and Fell. Five hundred. Even then, the mortality rate was still eighty percent."

"You sound real calm about that."

"Do I?" Howell sighed, rolling up the sleeve of his coat, exposing a pale, surprisingly hairy arm. The inside of his left elbow looked like a pincushion. He took a small plastic bag of white powder from his breast pocket and mixed it with distilled water into a small beaker suspended over a flickering Bunsen burner. "Appearances can be deceiving, Mr. Palmer," he murmured, wrapping a length of rubber tubing above his elbow. "Very deceiving."

Sonja scanned the downstairs, finding no traces of renfield activity. Not that she expected any. For some reason, Morgan had effectively slaughtered his few remaining servants by commanding them into the outer house. That still left the oriental she'd seen back at the Shadow Box; the one Fell claimed was Morgan's heavy gun. High-caliber renfields weren't exactly easy to come by, and Morgan sure as hell wouldn't waste one by marching it into a meat grinder like the Ghost Trap.

Fell drifted after her, gazing in fascination at the sections of the house he'd never been permitted to enter. Besides the three rooms that had served as Anise and Fell's suite, the downstairs consisted of a retrofitted country kitchen, several large, disused parlors full of dusty Victorian love seats and moth-eaten, mounted fox heads, and what had once been a conservatory before the panes had been bricked in.

They paused at the foot of the staircase that led to the second and third floors, Sonja leaning on the banister. "What's upstairs?"

"Dr. Howell's laboratory and Morgan's library study. I'm not sure what else. The renfields' quarters are on the third floor. I—" He frowned and fell silent, as if listening to distant music. "Did you hear that?"

"What?"

"Someone called my name. It sounded like— There it goes again!"

Sonja scowled. "Kid, I don't hear a damned thing."

Fell trembled like a foal trying out its legs for the first time. "Oh my God, it's her! It's Anise!"

Sonja grabbed Fell's elbow, shaking him in time to her words. "Fell! Listen me to me! It's a *trick!* Anise is dead! This is Morgan's doing!"

Fell's face twisted into a grimace as he jerked his arm free of her grip. "How do you know she's dead? Were you there? Did you see her die?"

"No, but—"

"Then how can you be so *sure* she's dead?" He peered into the darkness at the top of the stairs. "Anise? Is that you, darling?" He smiled and turned to his companion, pointing toward the second-story landing. "You heard her that time, didn't you? She's alive, Sonja! Alive!" He began sprinting up the stairs three at a time.

"Fell, no! Don't!" Sonja grabbed his wrist, trying her best to hold him back without resorting to force. "It's not Anise! It *can't* be!"

Fell spun about, his fangs bared and eyes glinting red, and punched her squarely on the jaw. Sonja hadn't been expecting it and there was nothing to do but roll with the blow. She counted ten risers before the back of her head made contact with the flagstones at the foot of the stairs, then things went black.

"Anise? Anise, where are you, sweetheart?"

I'm upstairs, dearest. Waiting for you.

"Are you all right? Sonja said you were dead. So did Morgan."

I'm fine, sweet one. I've missed you so! I'm sorry about all those nasty things I said the last time we were together! I just wasn't myself. That evil woman filled my head with all kinds of horrid nonsense. I was such a naughty girl to believe her!

"Where are you, darling?" Fell stood at the top of the second-floor stairs, trying to catch a glimpse of her.

In the library, silly. Where else?

As he heard the words inside his head, the door to Morgan's study swung open.

"But what about Morgan?"

He's gone, Fell. Gone for good. We'll never have to worry about him again.

Fell didn't bother to question his luck; it was enough that his lover had returned to him and his enemy had fled. He hurried into the darkened library.

"Anise?"

She was standing in front of the marble mantelpiece that adorned the library's huge fireplace, watching him with a coy, teasing smile on her lips. Her figure had returned to the trim proportions it had possessed before the pregnancy. She was beautiful and sexy and, best of all, she was *alive*. Anise held out her arms to him and Fell threw himself into her embrace.

"Anise! Oh thank God, it wasn't true! You're alive! You're *alive!*"

"Fell, you're squeezing me."

He stepped back to feast his eyes on her precious face, only to see Wretched Fly, the right half of his head swaddled in fresh bandages, returning his gaze. Fell backed away from the renfield, shaking his head in denial.

"No! She's alive! I *heard* her! I heard her call my name!"

"You heard what you wanted to hear, my dear boy. You are still human in *that* regard!"

Fell stared at the figure dressed in immaculate evening wear seated behind the massive marble top desk. Morgan leaned forward and rested his chin on his steepled fingers, smiling affably at his erstwhile patient.

"Ah, the prodigal son returns!"

"Fuck you, Morgan!"

The vampire lifted an elegantly arched eyebrow. "It seems you've been exposed to the same corrosive influence as your poor sister. Tsk-tsk! One night away from home and you're already falling in with a bad crowd."

Fell's anger was quickly eating away at his caution. "You *used* me, Morgan! Or is it Caron? I came to you for help and you fuckin' used me as a guinea pig!" He jabbed an accusatory finger at the other. "You looked inside me and took out things that had no right being outside my head, and twisted them around so I'd be *happy* playing out your Dracula *über alles* ego trip!"

Morgan tilted back in his chair, studying Fell with a detached interest Fell recognized from Tim Sorrell's therapy sessions. Sonja had warned him about going up alone against the vampire lord, but who was this leech that *he* should be afraid of him?

Fell's hate swelled inside him like a storm, invigorating as an amphetamine cocktail with a speedball chaser. He felt like he could kick Morgan's butt to the moon and back. He was immortal and invulnerable, a child of the night to be feared by all that dared cross his path.

Fell planted his palms on Morgan's desk top and leaned forward, thrusting out his lower jaw in defiance. "You fucked with me! And worse, you fucked with someone I *loved*, asshole! I mean to get satisfaction. I'm going to flay you alive and grill your nuts on a hibachi!"

"Indeed." The vampire smiled. "Then why don't you take your best shot?" Morgan stood and stepped out from behind the desk in one smooth, seamless motion, his arms held away from his sides. "Go ahead. Be my guest."

Fell snatched up an obsidian letter opener from the desk's blotter and moved forward, ready to plunge the knife into one of the vampire's eyes. As he lifted the blade, his eyes met Morgan's and the room began to spin around as if it had suddenly been transformed into a centrifuge. He cried out in pain as an unseen hand forced his fingers back from the letter opener's hilt. The obsidian knife dropped to the carpet at Fell's feet.

Morgan watched his protégé's agony with undisguised amusement. "What's the matter, Fell? Got a cramp?"

Fell growled and looked away from Morgan's taunting smirk.

"Look at me when I speak to you, boy!" the vampire lord snapped.

Fell continued to glower at the floor.

"I said *look* at me, *boy!*" Morgan's words echoed in Fell's skull like thunder.

The youth cried out as invisible fingers yanked at the muscles in his neck, forcing him to meet Morgan's wine-dark gaze.

"Good. Now show me who's boss."

Fell collapsed to the floor, groveling at Morgan's feet like a dog desperate to ingratiate itself. He lay on his back, belly exposed, like a cub submitting to the dominant male in a wolf pack. A thin, nasal whine escaped his constricted throat, increasing in intensity as he pissed himself.

Morgan gazed down at Fell with cold disdain. "Ah, the recklessness of youth!" He knelt beside the writhing young man and caressed Fell's cheek with the ball of his thumb as he spoke. "Ready to snap the leash and bound, unhindered, into the world, as spry and eager as a pup at play! Is that what you want, child? Freedom?"

Fell tried to speak, but all that came from his mouth was a bubble of bloody froth.

"You don't have to answer me—I can see it in your eyes. You're still human enough to believe in such garbage, I fear. And it's contaminated you beyond redemption." Morgan shook his head sadly. "What is freedom but a chance to starve to death? To die at the hands of those who fear you? If you went to the zoo and threw open the doors of the tiger's cage, would it leap free of its prison and run wild in the streets, snacking on infants snatched from their perambulators before catching a policeman's bullet between its eyes? Or would it simply yawn and go back to sleep, the concept of freedom—indeed, of life beyond the confines of its cage—completely without meaning?"

Morgan kissed Fell's sweaty brow gently, like a father bidding his young son good night. "You should have stayed in the cage, Fell," he murmured. "You are now no longer of use to me. Pity. You showed such promise in therapy."

Morgan picked up the letter opener Fell had dropped, turning it about between his agile fingers. He ran his thumb down the length of the obsidian blade, watching his blood boil forth like brackish water. His thumb sealed itself before the thick, foul-smelling liquid had time to stain the carpet.

"Give me your hand."

The command was quiet, almost gentle. Fell gritted his teeth and tried to keep his right arm from unfolding. Although his muscles groaned like rotten mooring ropes, there was no escaping the vampire lord's will.

Morgan placed the letter opener in Fell's rigid, trembling hand, wrapping the youth's fingers around the hilt.

"You know what to do," whispered Morgan as he stood, his eyes fixed on the boy stretched out at his feet.

Fell ground his teeth together even harder, heedless of the blood filling his mouth as his fangs shredded what was left of his lower lip. He tried to twist his head away from the slowly approaching knife point, but it was no use. His body was no longer his to control. He ordered his left hand to claw at his right hand, to try and knock the letter opener from its grasp, but it remained paralyzed. He screamed, but all that escaped his constricted larynx was a tight, dog-like whine.

When the point of the blade punctured his right eye like an overripe grape, he managed a short, muffled shout of pain. Then, to his horror, his left hand rose of its own volition and took the obsidian letter opener from his bloodstained right hand. The left hand was faster than the right piercing his remaining eye within a few seconds.

The darkness was total, the pain beyond anything Fell had ever known in any life. Then he felt the sharp edge of the blade as his left hand began rhythmically sawing away at his neck. He continued trying to scream long after he'd severed his own larynx.

Anise, I failed you. I failed Sonja. I failed Lethe. Forgive me, please. Forgive—

"What is this! There is a child?"

In his agony, Fell had forgotten that Morgan was in his mind as well as his body.

Morgan straddled the dying man's body, slapping the letter opener from Fell's grip. Morgan grabbed Fell by his bloodied shirt front, making sure not to shake him so hard his head would fall off.

"It was a trick, wasn't it? The child *didn't* die! It's still alive, somewhere! Tell me where, breeder! Tell me!"

Fell opened his mouth, but all that came out was a large, black bubble of blood. His head tilted to the right at a sharp angle, the spinal cord nearly severed. He could feel Morgan rooting inside his dying brain, searching for the memories concerning Lethe's whereabouts. Blind and partially paralyzed, it was like being alone in a dark house with a rabid, hungry animal.

"Tell me where it is, breeder, and I'll kill you fast!"

Fell raised his right hand, the fingers closing on his long, blonde hair. He'd fucked up big time, and now he was paying for being a stupid jerk. He'd waltzed into Morgan's trap like the world's biggest fool. He'd gotten a taste of being superhuman and it had made him foolhardy. He was dying, but he'd be doubly damned if he'd betray his own daughter to this monster. But Morgan was stronger, both physically and mentally, and accustomed to getting what he wanted.

"*Tell me*, breeder!"

Fell wanted to say "fuck you," but since his larynx was severed, the best he could do was grab a fistful of his own hair and give it one good, final yank.

Morgan yowled in rage as Fell's head dropped to the floor, coming to rest on the stained Persian carpet. He let go of the body, kicking it a few times in frustration. The sound of ribs snapping did little to assuage his anger. Wretched Fly watched his master nervously.

"Send the pyrotic after Howell. Unplug its television and tell it there will be no more *Gilligan's Island* or *S.W.A.T.* until it brings the good doctor back to me! When I'm through, it can use his corpse for a host."

"Very well, milord. And the rogue?"

"She's mine."

Sonja sat up, rubbing the back of her head. Her fingers came away sticky with blood. She grunted and wiped her hand on her jacket. The kid was stronger than she'd suspected.

She got to her feet, leaning heavily on the banister. Blue-black fireworks bouquets exploded behind her eyelids. Had she been human, the fall she'd taken would have killed her. As it was, she'd suffered an insult to the brain that was far from problematic. But that could wait. She had to find Fell. Make sure he was all right. What did the young fool think he was doing, running off like that?

"Fell!" Her voice sounded weak in her ears, like that of an old woman. "Fell, where *are* you?"

Her answer came in the form of a footfall at the top of the landing.

"Fell? Kid, are you okay?"

Fell lurched into sight, his tread heavy and unsteady.

Sonja shook her head, as if somehow denying what stood before her would change it.

Fell's clothes were so black with blood they looked like someone had doused him with a five-gallon can of paint at point-blank range. The corpse lifted its stiffening right arm to display Fell's head, dangling by its long, yellow hair. The eyes had been gouged out and the nose sliced off.

Dead fingers spasmed as the body went limp, collapsing on the landing. The head bounced and rolled its way to the foot of the stairs, staring up at Sonja with its ruined sockets.

Her grief was so deep, so painful, it numbed her. Alone again. After so many years of loneliness, she'd finally found others to share her life, her knowledge with, only to have them snatched away from her within the span of a day. It wasn't fair.

From the darkness on the second floor came the sound of laughter.

She knew that laugh. She'd last heard it in London, over twenty years ago.

"I'm coming for you, bastard!" she whispered under her breath, her fingers closing on the folded switchblade in her pocket. "And I'm gonna make you pay!"

She comes. And my hands shake in anticipation. Her aura precedes her, lighting her way like fox fire. Did I create this magnificent creature? That I could have succeeded by accident where my carefully laid plans failed so horribly is both fascinating and humbling.

I must destroy her. Her very existence is a threat to my continuance. Yet I can not help but stand in awe of her—worship her.

She comes. And my hands burn when I think of her blood.

Palmer pressed his hand to his forehead, shielding his eyes from the things eeling in and out of his field of vision. They looked something like centipedes, except that they were transparent and swam about in mid-air. If Howell saw them, he didn't seem to mind; he was too busy checking his syringe for air bubbles to worry about extra-dimensional hell-creatures in the rafters.

"Uh, look, Doc—If you're worried about getting away from Morgan, I'm sure Sonja will be more than happy to help you in that area . . ."

"My dear Mr. Palmer," Howell sighed, slapping the inside of his elbow with his index and middle fingers as he tried to raise a vein. "I have spent over five years in the grip of one vampire. What makes you think I'd want to hand myself over to yet another one?"

"Sonja's not like Morgan."

"And rattlesnakes are nothing like Gila monsters." Howell deftly jabbed the loaded hypo into his arm.

Watching Howell shoot up made Palmer want a cigarette. He winced and averted his gaze.

Howell smiled wryly. "Go ahead and look away. I don't mind. Mainlining isn't a pretty sight, not even to junkies. You could jump me right now. Why don't you?"

Palmer shrugged. "I don't know." It was the truth.

Howell quickly untied the rubber tubing and flexed his elbow a few times. He turned to face Palmer, his eyes dilating as the heroin rushed through his bloodstream. It suddenly occurred to Palmer that, despite his appearance, Howell was only a couple of years older than himself.

Howell removed the Luger from his pocket. Palmer tensed. The guy was a loon and, as if that wasn't enough, a junkie to boot. There was no telling what he might decide to do.

"I'm not proud of the things I have done in Morgan's service. But it's too late to pretend they didn't happen or that I had no choice in the matter. I must admit that the work challenged me, unlike anything else I've ever done in the private sector." Howell handed the Luger back to Palmer, butt first. The detective muttered his thanks and quickly returned it to his shoulder holster.

"I dug my grave years ago, Mr. Palmer. I am a dead man. The only question is when my heart will stop beating. I do not expect to live terribly much longer. In fact, I'd be surprised if I survive to see the dawn. But I warn you, do not trust your champion simply because she is a woman. The females are even worse than the males."

"Sonja's different—she's not like the others." He frowned as he listened to himself. What he was saying sounded stupid, even deluded, but it was the truth. How could he explain it to someone like Howell?

"You love her." The scientist's voice was flat, almost dead sounding, reminding Palmer of Chaz's equally lifeless pronouncement.

"Yes. Yes, I do." He was surprised to hear himself admitting it out loud.

"They always love their masters. That's what makes them so loyal." Howell paused, sniffing the air. "Is it my imagination, or do I smell barbecue?"

Sonja followed the trail of blood to the library, where Morgan was waiting for her. She felt him as a Siamese twin senses its sibling's moods and health. It was a dreadful, unwanted intimacy, and it made her want to retch.

"*My child.*"

The library door opened of its own volition and a strange, flickering light the color of a ripe bruise spilled into the hallway.

"*Come forward, child. So I may look at you.*"

The voice was familiar, although it lacked the upper-class British accent it had possessed when she'd first heard it in 1969.

She took a hesitant step into the purple-black light, shielding herself as best as she could from the siren song of his personality.

Morgan stood in front of a mammoth fireplace, dressed in a neatly tailored dinner jacket and matching pants. His hair was bound in a ponytail by a black velvet cord. His smile was brilliant as he studied her over the top of his aviator glasses.

The Other's voice hissed a warning from its place inside her head: *Don't be fooled by the surface. You're no longer a sixteen-year-old debutante. Look beyond the illusion. See him for what he truly is!*

Sonja's vision flickered as she shifted spectrums and Morgan's image warped and twisted like a piece of cellophane held too close to a light bulb. His flesh lost its sun worshipper's glow, fading until it resembled a mushroom coated with tallow. His fingernails were long and curled, like those of a Mandarin, and his features bloated by the gases of cellular decay. The smell that emanated from him reminded her of the dead mouse she'd once found lodged in an old sofa bed. The very thought of this putrescent monstrosity thrusting its rancid member into her was enough to make her gorge rise, twenty years after the fact.

The Other thought that it would be a really good idea to pluck Morgan's eyes out and use his head for a bowling ball. Sonja agreed, but continued to fight the rage boiling inside her. She hated the leering monster who'd raped and tortured her so many years ago—in truth, she'd cultivated that hate in order to face her day-to-day existence—but this was not the time to indulge her loathing.

Sonja knew the immensity of her hate, knew what it could do once unleashed. She had sworn she'd never allow herself to lose control again. Not like last year. She could never forget the lives she'd destroyed and the souls she'd shattered that night.

"Should I say 'so, we meet at last,' and get the clichés out of the way?" suggested Morgan, his handsome, debonair visage once more securely in place.

"Do you know who I am?" She had to fight to keep the tremor from her voice.

"I know that you call yourself Sonja Blue. Or perhaps you mean, do I recognize you?" Morgan's lips curled into a cruel smile. "Do you have any idea how many hapless, silly human girls I have seduced in the last six hundred years, my dear? And you expect me to remember *one* out of that multitude?"

"My . . . *her* name was Denise Thorne. London, 1969."

The vampire nodded, as if this answered something. "Ah, yes! The heiress! You were actually missed. Careless of me. Even more careless that I didn't make sure you were truly dead when I disposed of you. I blame the sixties *zeitgeist* for that. It was such a happy-go-lucky, irresponsible era! I found it quite contagious. Didn't you?"

"Cut the routine, dead boy! You know why I'm here."

Morgan sighed and studied his fingernails. "I know! I know! You're here to kill me. How tedious. Tell me, child, what exactly would my demise prove?"

"That I'm not like you."

"Indeed? If you are not like me, how have you survived these past few decades, little one? How have you kept yourself fed?"

"I—I have my ways."

"Caches of bottled plasma, no doubt. But that is hardly enough, is it? You can't lie to me, child. I know how *bland* prepackaged blood can be. Have you killed, my pet?"

"I—"

"Answer me true, child."

"Yes."

Morgan smiled a slow, sly smile. Sonja fought the urge to rip it off his face. "How many have you taken down? Dozens? Scores? Hundreds? *Thousands?*"

"It doesn't matter."

"Ha!" Morgan laughed, the smile widening into a smirk. "And you say you aren't like me!"

"I am not one of your kind!"

"That is true. You aren't like us. Nor are you, in many ways, like your dear, departed siblings. If only Fell and Anise had turned out half as well as yourself. But perhaps that's what I get for choosing flawed templates. Still, it's a shame to destroy something so . . . unique. You remind me of something I once saw in a vision, fifty years ago—"

"—in a Gestapo torture-house in occupied Amsterdam."

Morgan's look of smug self-assurance faltered. "How do you know of that?"

Sonja smiled mockingly, pleased by the look of confusion on his face. "There are places where the future and the past blur—provided one has the eyes to see. The window worked both ways, Morgan. I saw you, dressed in your SS colonel's uniform. And you saw your death, separated from you by time and space."

He was inside her head, fast as a striking cobra. Sonja tensed as Morgan's will crashed against her own, like a wave breaking against a high cliff. As the pressure inside her skull increased, she was dimly aware of something warm and sticky flowing from her nostrils. Impressed by her show of strength, Morgan withdrew with a low, bemused chuckle. He tilted his head to one side, studying her closely from behind his aviator shades

"Why are we fighting, child? Is this how father and daughter greet one another?"

Sonja wiped at the blood oozing from her nose and mouth. "You're *not* my father!" she spat.

"I *Made* you, child! You are shaped in my image! We are bonded! There is no denying me! We are much alike, you and I. You have more in common with me than you ever did with Anise and Fell. They were weak. Flawed. Unworthy vessels. They could not surrender the illusion of humanity."

He held up his left hand, dragging the nail of his right thumb across his palm. A black, polluted liquid gushed forth. "Honor thy father, Sonja! Look into yourself and you'll find me there—it's in the blood!"

She felt it then; the relentless pressure of his will, bearing down on her like a leaden weight. It was as if she'd been suddenly transported to the bottom of the ocean floor. The temptation to capitulate was intense. It would be so easy to surrender and allow him to fill the void inside her. She dropped to her knees, her arms wrapped around her abdomen. Blackish-purple solar systems went nova behind her eyes.

Breathe! Breathe, damn you! shrieked the Other.

Morgan moved closer, smiling down at her like a punishing parent. "You are beautiful. I like beautiful things." His handsome, male model features shivered, ran, turned into a worm-eaten ruin. "You are also very, very dangerous. I like that, too. In you I see elements of my younger self—angry, volatile, scheming, defiant. I find this similarity . . . arousing." He gestured with one corpse-like hand to the knot in his pants.

"Humans are always prattling on about love. I know nothing of that. I *do* know of hunger, need, *want*. You have awakened a hunger in me, my beauty. The hunger of a moth for a flame, the mongoose for the cobra. I have spent centuries exploiting the weaknesses of others, only to discover a frailty in myself. I cannot allow this. It imperils my continuance. But, still, I can not help but be fascinated . . ."

The vampire lifted a hand smelling of graveyard mold and touched her cheek. His skin was dead and cold against her own. Sonja closed her eyes and saw a young girl, naked and bleeding, struggling to wriggle free of the red-eyed demon pinning her to the back seat of the car. She heard her screams as he emptied burning semen into her battered womb. She heard him laugh as the girl's pulse fluttered and dimmed under his cold, cold hands.

The Other's sibilant voice snarled in her inner ear:

Twenty years! You've been hunting this bastard for twenty years, living just to kill him! To pay him back for what he did to you! And what are you doing? You're cringing like a damned whipped dog offering up its throat! You came all this way to die at his hands? Let me out! Let me out, woman, before he kills us all!

"You're trembling . . ." His voice was a husky whisper, close to her ear. His breath billowed out in a mildewed cloud.

"Don't *touch* me!" The switchblade was in her hand as she struck him, slicing air and decayed flesh in a single, powerful arc.

Morgan shrieked and recoiled from her, clutching the left side of his face. A thick, yellowish fluid welled from between his fingers. "Silver! *Silver!*" His voice cracked, climbing the register. "You hurt me!" He sounded like a petulant toddler.

The sight of her enemy's pain was good. Very good. "I'm not one of your pedigreed lap dogs, Morgan! I was born in the gutter and raised on the street! And I *like* raw meat!"

There was a hysterical gleam in Morgan's remaining eye. How long? How long had it been since he'd known pain? Not the temporary discomfort of snapped limbs and ruptured tissue, but *real* pain? The kind only immortal flesh is heir to. The realization that he'd been badly—and permanently—scarred both angered and thrilled him.

"I *was* going to let you live, changeling!" he hissed. "Maimed and lobotomized, true. But still alive. Not now, bitch!" His voice dropped, becoming an inhuman growl. "Not now!"

Morgan threw wide his arms and his remaining eye rolled back in its socket. Although she'd never battled a Noble before, Sonja recognized the ritual stance used in psychic combat. She followed suit, falling inside herself in time to meet Morgan on a field of battle known only as the Place Between Places.

There was darkness and light, and at the same time, neither. There was up and down in all directions. Morgan's imago hung suspended in mid-air, its features unmarred, dressed in the flowing silks and samite of a medieval Florentine prince. His eyes burned like polished garnet and flames licked from between his lips. His hands were turned palm-upward, each cupping a ball of black energy that smoldered like malignant St. Elmo's Fire.

"Is that the best you can do, prodigal?" he sneered contemptuously, motioning to his opponent's self-image.

Sonja looked down at herself. Except for her leather jacket looking brand-new, there was no appreciable difference between her imago and her physical self. "What matter does it make? We're all naked inside our heads."

As if in reply, a tiger with three heads and the tail of a scorpion jumped out of Morgan's chest. Sparks flew from its myriad sets of gnashing teeth as it roared in unison. It pounced, knocking Sonja onto her back.

As the chimera's fangs closed on its victim's face, the Other began to laugh.

Howell and Palmer watched as the lock on laboratory door began to glow, becoming white-hot within a heartbeat. The odor of roasting pork was strong enough to make Palmer's gut growl.

"Is there another way out of here?" he snapped at Howell.

The scientist nodded, unable to take his eyes from the door. "There's a trapdoor that leads to the nucleus." He motioned to the dissection table pushed against the wall.

"Then what are we waiting on?" Palmer grabbed Howell's arm. "If that's what I think it is, you don't want to be here to tell it hello!"

Howell pulled away from Palmer, shaking his head. "No! Like I told you, I'm a dead man. Better for me to die facing one of Morgan's servants than to end up in his hands."

Before Palmer could argue any further, the door flew open, its lock and handle reduced to warm taffy. The pyrotic stepped into the room, sizzling in its own fat. Although it had the same boiled lobster complexion and dead white eyes as the elemental he'd confronted in San Francisco, Palmer doubted it was the same body. The one guarding Morgan's Pacific Heights residence would have been a puddle by now.

"So, the renfields sent you in their stead, eh?" Howell picked up a large, wickedly curved knife from the tray of instruments next to the dissecting table. "It'll do him no good! I'm not going back! You're going to have to kill me!"

The pyrotic did not seem to hear, much less understand, Howell's statement. It moved closer, smoke issuing from its ears and nostrils like party streamers.

Palmer didn't waste any more words. If the scientist wanted to purge his sins in a one-sided battle with the pyrotic, that was his business. Palmer dove under the dissection table and peered down the trapdoor; all he could see was a rickety ladder disappearing into the darkness below. Hardly the stairway to heaven, but it would do.

"No! No, stay away from that, you idiot! It's not a television! I said, *no*!" There was the sound of glass breaking and Howell screamed something unintelligible.

The changeling fetus lay on the floor, surrounded by shards of splintered glass. Its skin was the same bright, blistered pink of a boiled shrimp. The changeling emitted a plaintive mewling sound as it flopped helplessly about on the floorboards like a landed baby shark.

Palmer looked up in time to see Dr. Howell, shouting curses at the top of his voice, drive his blade into the pyrotic's stomach, slitting it from crotch to throat as easily as he would carve a holiday turkey. The pyrotic opened its mouth to scream, but all that came out was the hiss of live steam. Napalm spilled from the pyrotic's wound, splashing Howell.

The hapless scientist screeched as he was consumed by a column of flame, trampling the dying changeling under his heels. Howell's screams grew as he waved his blazing arms over his head like a small boy beset by angry hornets.

A sinuous serpent-shape made of smoke and fire, like the bearded dragons wrapped about Chinatown's luck gate, uncoiled from the pyrotic's slit gullet, twining its way through the air in search of another host.

Palmer slammed the trapdoor shut behind him and quickly descended the ladder. Whatever dangers Ghost Trap might hold below, they were preferable to being turned into a human cherries jubilee.

Sonja calmly studied the chimera squatting atop her chest, with its poison-laden stinger and triple set of jaws. The chimera thrashed, roaring its confusion, as it began to sink into its erstwhile victim's chest. She got to her feet, the chimera's oversized scorpion's tail still whipping madly about in the middle of her stomach. Her eyelids fluttered as she was transfixed by a surge of intense pleasure.

Morgan's unmarked face began to drip pearls of blood as something that looked like an ape with long, spidery arms, pulled itself free of his torso. The ape-thing had fungus-gray fur, compound eyes, and a red, lamprey-like maw. With a high-pitched squeal, the avatar launched itself at its master's foe, sinking a claw into her face.

The ape-thing emitted an ultrasonic shriek as first its wrist, then its elbow, was absorbed. The avatar jettisoned its right arm and leapt free, screeching like a bat. Clutching the stump of its right shoulder, the beast loped back to Morgan and cowered at his feet. Scowling, the vampire quickly gathered the avatar back into himself

"You surprise me, changeling! I knew you were powerful, but I had not dreamed you possessed such will! It's been a long time since I've been challenged this way! It's almost enough to make me doubt my superiority. Almost."

A tentacle burst from Morgan's chest, whipping about his head like a lariat. Two more emerged from his sides, quickly wrapping themselves around Sonja's waist, arms, and legs. She hissed as the coils tightened, the hiss becoming a yowl as thousands of tiny needle-filled mouths began working at her dream-flesh.

And she was back in the physical world, curled into a fetal ball on the library floor. Or was she? She was still aware of herself, trapped in the Place Between Places, but at the same time she could feel the nap of the rug against her check. Morgan's shell squatted over her, hunched forward like a gargoyle perched on the cornice of a cathedral. His remaining eye was rolled so far back in his head it looked like a marble.

Damn it, don't just lay there snorting dust bunnies! Kill him! Kill him before he realizes he's only trapped part of us! The Other's voice sounded weaker, somehow.

Part of us? What did it mean by 'part of us'?

Stop worrying about the duality of nature and stab the motherfucker.

Sonja's fingers were numb as she fumbled in her pockets for her switchblade. Where was it? Where?

✷

Morgan tightened his grip on his enemy's imago, grinding the illusion of bone and flesh together to generate very real pain.

"Do you know what happens to a body once its imago is destroyed, little one? It's not unlike performing a lobotomy on one's soul."

The Other spat a streamer of blood into Morgan's face.

"Choke on it!"

She spied the switchblade lying where she'd dropped it during her first seizure. Morgan's control over her body had lessened, but her arms still felt as if the marrow in her bones had been replaced with lead. She forced her right fist to unclench and slowly, painfully, inch its way toward the open switchblade.

Pain the color of an exploding sun filled the Other's eyes and ears. The more it struggled, the tighter the coils became, but the Other refused to lie still. It was not in its nature to surrender.

Morgan drew his appendages in, tilting his captive so that she dangled inches from his reconstituted face. In the real world, the jagged knife wound she had dealt him earlier would permanently render his smile into a joker's leer. But here, in the Place Between Places, such inconveniences could be ignored.

"You are beautiful, and oh, so sweetly lethal, my dear! It has been amusing, and I will bear a reminder of your murderous affliction for centuries to come." He touched his cheek as if savoring a parting kiss. "I really must end our little affair . . . but not before you tell me where you've hidden the breeder's get."

"Get bent."

✸

It was no good. She couldn't uncramp her fingers enough to reach the blade. They were going to die. So close. She'd come so *close*.

Something the size of a man's hand separated itself from the shadows and scuttled toward the switchblade lying just outside of Sonja's reach. As it drew nearer, she realized it *was* a man's hand, albeit six fingered.

"That's funny, I don't remember you falling out of my pocket . . ." Sonja murmured.

The Hand of Glory nudged the switchblade with its fingers, pushing it in the direction of her own outstretched hand.

"Good girl, Lassie!"

"Tell me where the child is, changeling! Tell me!"

Blood gouted from the Other's nostrils, tear ducts, mouth, and eardrums. The tentacles knotted themselves even tighter, grinding its internal organs into paste.

"I don't know." It wasn't exactly a lie.

"Come now, prodigal daughter! You can do better than that!"

"Why do you want the baby?"

"Why do you want the baby?"

"Because it is mine. It was my idea to create the thing—a man is entitled to the fruit of his endeavor. I intend to use the breeders' young to build a new society of living vampires."

The Other laughed, spraying Morgan's face with blood. "You stupid fuck! You don't even know what you created!"

"What do you mean by that?"

"The baby isn't a vampire, you dolt! It's *seraphim*!"

"You lie!"

The Other started laughing again, only harder. "You should have gotten a load of your face when I said that! What's the matter, dead boy? You soil your pants?"

"Shut up! Shut up, damn you! Stop laughing at me!"

"Make me!"

"Damn your eyes, Sonja Blue! I was willing to show you mercy, but now I won't be sated until you're flayed to the bone!"

The Other's blood-smeared face split into a sharp white grin. "What makes you think I'm Sonja?"

Wretched Fly dashed into the library, wringing his hands in agitation. "Milord! *Milord!*"

Lord Morgan remained hunched, immobile and silent, over the rogue's body. Wretched Fly reached out and shook his master's shoulder. Morgan's right eye rolled back down, fixing Wretched Fly with a hard, angry stare.

"What *is* it? Can't you see I'm busy?"

"Milord, the pyrotic's disincorported! It's set the house afire!"

"What?!"

"It's spreading everywhere! The south wing's sixth and fifth floors have already collapsed! Milord, the sun's rising! We *have* to abandon the premises before the entire building goes up!"

"What about Howell?"

"I can only assume the doctor and the others are dead, milord. I can not find any trace of them on wide scan."

"Very well, go and prepare the Rolls. I'll be there momentarily, after I tend to my . . . daughter."

"Like hell you will, dead boy," Sonja spat, thrusting her weapon's silver blade into Morgan's unprotected chest.

Morgan screamed like an old woman as he leapt to his feet, tearing at his expensive clothes. The edges of his wound were already turning black and withering away from contact with the silver. "Poison! Poison. You horrible,

Morgan wept as he ripped the rotting tissue from his chest with his bare hands, desperately trying to keep the taint from spreading to the rest of his body.

"Unclean! Unclean!"

Sonja staggered to her feet, her muscles shrieking as circulation was restored. She made another swipe at Morgan, but her aim was blurred by the smoke filling the room. Wretched Fly grabbed his master and hurried him from the room.

Sonja tried to follow him, but her head was hurting real bad. She took a few steps and dropped to her knees, gagging on smoke. Morgan was escaping. She had to stop him. Kill him. Get it over with, once and for all. If she died under tons of flaming timber, what difference did it make? Who would be left to mourn—or even notice—her passing?

As her body was wracked by a coughing fit, it suddenly occurred to her how *quiet* it was inside her head. The Other's needling voice, her constant companion for nearly two decades, was strangely silent.

She moved cautiously, searching for signs of the Other as if probing a sore tooth with her tongue. Could it be that Morgan had somehow managed to kill it, while sparing her?

You're not rid of me, yet.

No, the Other was not dead. But it *was* hurt. It seemed weaker than it'd been in over a decade.

You owe me one.

She was back in the burning house, struggling to pull oxygen from the smoke-filled room. She glimpsed the Hand of Glory laying on its back, fingers curled in on themselves like the legs of a dead spider. The hand suddenly twitched and righted itself, scurrying across the antique Persian carpet and out the door into the hall.

Sonja dragged herself to her feet, coughing violently as she inhaled a lung full of dense white smoke. She staggered into the hallway, now almost obscured by billowing smoke. She could hear the not-so-distant roar of fire and the laughter of children.

The house shook as Ghost Trap's west wing collapsed into its cellar, knocking Sonja to the floor. She lay there, dazed, and wondered whether she was going to suffocate or burn to death first. The sound of laughing children grew louder.

A boy and girl, dressed in clothing fashionable before Mary Pickford was America's sweetheart, emerged from the swirling smoke. Sonja recognized the little girl as the ghost-child she'd met earlier. The children grabbed her hands and lifted her from the floor. Sonja decided she was too weak to fight them; besides, they seemed to know where they were going.

The Seward children led her through smoke-obscured rooms into a dark passage. Sonja heard their long-dead, insectile voices buzzing in her ear, but could not make out what they were saying. Soon they were back within the tortured architecture of Ghost Trap's outer house. As the Seward children continued to escort her, Sonja dimly realized her feet were no longer touching the floor.

Suddenly there was a desperate banshee wail, and their way was blocked by a hulking grotesque with two heads. The ghost-children deftly yanked their dazed charge out of the path of the large, blood-spattered ax the two-headed apparition swung in their direction. Sonja tried to break free of the dead children's grasp, but they refused to let go.

The gibbering, two-headed ax-murderer wrenched its weapon free from the splintered floorboards and prepared to lift it a second time. Then came the sound of a woman's laughter—light, merry, free—echoing through the empty rooms.

The creature paused to listen, its twisted, bat-snouted face grimacing.

Mrs. Seward's ghost materialized beside that of her killer. She suddenly grabbed her husband's head by its hair and began to *pull*. The ax-murderer squealed like a frightened piglet and flailed ineffectively at Mrs. Seward with its ax-hand. There was a muffled sucking sound, like someone pulling their foot free of thick mud, and the shoulders and torso of the late Creighton Seward emerged from the ax-murderer's leprous skin.

The ax-murderer shrieked even louder than before, its clawed feet drumming against the bare boards like those of a petulant child throwing a tantrum, but Mrs. Seward was not to be denied the reclamation of her husband. With a final, mighty tug, she freed Seward's naked body of its demonic twin. Robbed of its unwilling symbiote the demon collapsed like a gutted scarecrow, its corpus returning to formless ectoplasm.

The dead man shivered like a newborn foal and threw his arms around his murdered wife, his face pressed against her bosom. Sonja stared dully at the embracing couple, reunited for the first time since that horrible night in 1907, when Creighton Seward, in a moment of weakness, made an unwise bargain in a bid for artistic genius.

Mrs. Seward, her face no longer mutilated, leaned forward and brushed her translucent lips against Sonja's cheek.

Sonja found herself lifted into the air, hurtling through room after room as if shot from a cannon, the rumble of walls crashing and floors collapsing echoing in her ears. She saw the window a split second before she was catapulted through it into the tangled, thorny embrace of an overgrown rosebush.

Sonja dragged herself a few yards before collapsing. She dimly registered the sound of yet another of one of Ghost Trap's chimneys tumbling down in a thunderclap of bricks and mortar. She knew she was in extreme danger of the exterior wall collapsing on her, but somehow it didn't seem to matter.

He had escaped. After all those years spent tracking him through the cities of the civilized world, she'd had him, felt his blood, felt his pain . . . only to have him escape. She'd been so close . . .

"Sonja! Thank God I found you!"

She squinted up at the figure kneeling over her. "Palmer?"

He looked like he'd been whacked with a golf club; his face was smeared with soot, he reeked of smoke, and he was the most beautiful thing she'd ever seen.

"It ain't the Easter Bunny, baby!" He kissed her blood-smeared brow and helped her to her feet. After they were safely away from the house, they turned to watch its death throes. Ghost Trap glowed like the rising sun.

"Look," whispered Palmer, pointing at the smoke and sparks drifting heavenward.

Sonja watched as the pellucid outlines of the Seward family ascended the currents, accompanied by an equally pale and familiar figure with long, flowing hair and the shade of a moon-faced man in a flapping white coat, a deformed infant cradled in his arms. Within seconds of her sighting them, they were gone, lost amongst the smoke and soot and lightening sky.

"I'm not going to ask why you're not on a plane to Yucatan. I'm glad you're here, Palmer." She leaned her forehead on his shoulder. "You up to driving? I've got the keys . . ."

"It doesn't matter, Sonja. The rental's buried under a couple tons of fireplace. It looks like we're going to have to hoof it into town and catch the bus into San Francisco."

She groaned and took his hand. "I guess we better start walkin', huh?"

As they made their way to the county road, Palmer heard the crunch of tires behind them. He turned in time to see a vintage Rolls with heavily tinted windows bearing down on them, an oriental man, his head swaddled in sooty bandages, behind the wheel. Without thinking, he grabbed Sonja and dove into a nearby ditch. The Rolls rocketed by, spewing gravel in its wake.

Palmer and Sonja clambered back onto the shoulder and watched the limousine's taillights disappear in the early morning mist.

Morgan lay on the floor of the Rolls, wrapped in blankets and curled in a fetal position. His chest still burned, but he was certain he'd removed every trace of the silver-tainted tissue before the toxin had a chance to infiltrate his central nervous system. His chest would heal. It might not even scar. The same could not be said of his face, however.

Morgan touched his left cheek and moaned. Wounds dealt by silver weapons never truly healed, and they always left ugly scars. But that was not the worst part. The mutilation of his flesh was a minor thing, compared to what that bitch had done to him.

Lord Morgan moaned again and huddled even deeper into his blankets. Broken bones would mend, damaged organs regenerate, even severed limbs regrow, in time. But there would be no healing for the wounds she'd inflicted on his psyche, only a gradual spread of infection.

Lord Morgan, late of the Inquisition and the Gestapo, lay on the floor of his car and contemplated the dreadful sickness that humans called Love.

EPILOGUE: MÉRIDA, YUCATAN

A man's mind, stretched by new ideas, can never go back to its original dimensions.
—Oliver Wendell Holmes

Palmer was hammering together a wooden crate on the porch of his hacienda when the mailman blew his whistle.

"Tweet, Daddy! Tweet!" squealed Lethe, rounding the corner of the house as fast as her baggy diapers would allow. Her Babar the Elephant play-shirt was smeared with mud, and, judging from the dirty tablespoon she was waving, she'd been digging up the back patio again.

"Whoa, droopy drawers!" Palmer laughed, catching the toddler in his outstretched arms, flipping her upside down. Lethe giggled and wriggled in his grip like a puppy. Not bad for a nine-month-old. "You know you're not supposed to go near the road!"

Palmer deposited the child in the macramé hammock he kept strung on the porch and trotted down to the mailbox at the foot of the hill. He made a mental note to take the Landrover into the city and buy some fencing material. Lethe was advanced for her age, but he still had problems with her wanting to run out onto the road every time the mailman made his rounds. Lethe loved getting mail.

A dark, ragged form emerged from the *hacienda* and joined Lethe in the hammock. The little girl's giggles were soon joined by the peals of crystal chimes and the yattering of dolphins.

Palmer sorted through the letters as he walked back up the path to the house. Two were from boutiques in California and New York, ordering three more crates apiece of Day of the Dead tableaux, stuffed toad Mariachi bands, and hand painted papier mâché carnival masks. There was also a package addressed to Lethe with a fistful of Asian stamps plastered across it and a postcard from Sonja.

"Look, honey! Aunt Boo sent you a present!" Palmer handed the package to Lethe, still curled in the seraphim's lap. Within seconds, the porch was littered with tatters of brown paper and Lethe was playing with a rag doll dressed in a tiny blue cotton kimono, its dyed corn silk hair pulled into an elaborate geisha's coiffure.

Palmer glanced at the front of the picture postcard a panoramic view of downtown Tokyo at night—then flipped it over to read the message. There was no salutation or signature. There never were.

Still no sign of M. But I'm getting closer The chimera is very excited. It smells its old master. The scar makes it harder for M to change identities. There are rumors of atrocities in Mainland. M? Hope to be home for Xmas. Miss you.

Palmer looked up from the card to find the *seraph* staring at him with its pupil-less golden eyes.

"No news, Fido. Same old things." The *seraph* nodded, although Palmer had his doubts as to how much the creature understood. "Lethe, sweetie, why don't you go play with Fido on the patio? I've got work to do."

Lethe nodded her tiny dark head, her golden eyes flashing in the afternoon light, and hopped out of the hammock, leading the grizzled *seraph* by the hand. Palmer smiled as the unlikely twosome, nut-brown nature-child and bedraggled street-person, disappeared around the corner of the house—Fido shambling after Lethe like a trained bear.

Even after all these months, he still had a hard time accepting it all. A year ago he'd been looking a twenty-to-life sentence in the face. Now he was living the life of an expatriate yanqui, making a decent living selling Mexican and Central American folk art to painfully chic boutiques and galleries north of the border. He'd also discovered, to his surprise, he was a damn good father. Yeah, a lot of things can change in the space of a year, he mused, fingering his jade ear plug.

Lethe had reappeared a couple of weeks after he and Sonja had set up housekeeping in Yucatan. One minute the patio had been empty, the next Lethe and the *seraph* were there. Although the baby was not yet a month old, she was already crawling and babbling.

When it became evident the *seraph* was not going to leave, Sonja decided it was time for her to continue on her hunt. Palmer knew the *seraph* made her nervous. It had taken him a few weeks to get used to the creature's presence, himself. But after he started calling it Fido, he began to relax. Somehow "Fido" seemed an appropriate moniker.

Every so often Sonja would appear on the doorstep, unannounced but always welcome, loaded down with exotic toys for her "niece." Although she adored Lethe, Sonja could not tolerate being around Fido for more than a few days.

During her brief visits, she and Palmer lay curled together in the hammock and listened to the night birds call. In its own strange way, their relationship was idyllic.

The last time Sonja had come home she'd been amused to discover the ritual tattoo on his chest.

"What's this? Have you decided to go modern primitive on me?" She giggled, running her hands over the raised markings covering his pectorals.

"I—I decided to get a tattoo to hide the scar from my surgery."

"Really?"

"Kind of. Besides, it matches the scars you leave on my back."

She was silent for a few minutes. "Do you still have the dreams?"

"Sometimes. They've gotten stronger since the hand came back."

"The hand?"

"Yeah, I know it sounds crazy, but a couple weeks ago something tapping at the window screen woke me up. At first I thought it might have been a bird. Then I saw it, squatting on the ledge outside the window. It was the hand Li Lijing gave you, scratching to be let in!"

"What'd you do?"

"I let it in."

"Weren't you scared?"

Palmer shrugged. "I've heard stories about dogs traveling cross-country to rejoin their families, so why not a six-fingered hand? Besides, it doesn't do anything except hide under the couch. My mom used to have a Chihuahua like that. And if I had to make a choice, I'd rather have an animated, amputated hand than a Chihuahua."

"Can't argue with you there. So what is this tattoo supposed to represent?"

"The old Mayan guy who did it says it used to be the seal of the *Chan Balam*, the Jaguar Lords."

However, he hadn't bothered to tell her that while his Spanish remained hopelessly retarded, he could now speak fluent Lancondoan, the tongue of the children of Quetzalcoatl, and that he'd stopped smoking his precious Shermans in favor of the burrito-sized hallucinogenic cigars favored by the Mayans. That had been three months ago. He wondered what she'd have to say about his earrings.

Palmer resumed his work on the packing crate, pausing every now and again to sip from a pitcher of lemonade. He noticed a campesino trudging his way along the unpaved road that ran past the house, headed in the direction of the paved highway three miles away where a rattle-trap bus carried locals into the city.

Palmer stiffened at the sight of the stooped, unwashed man dressed in the traditional loose-fitting white cotton pants and tunic, a machete hanging from his belt. He scanned the campesino, briefly sampling his thoughts and measuring his aura for traces of Pretender taint.

Luckily for the campesino, he was exactly what he looked like—a peasant on his way to town. He would live to ride the bus to Mérida. Palmer allowed himself a sigh of relief. He disliked killing, even Pretenders. But he knew he could not allow his vigilance to slacken, even for a moment. For as every good parent knows, the jungle is full of jaguars hungry for the blood of children.

Paint It Black

AUTHOR'S NOTE:

Portions of this novel, in a slightly different form, first appeared in the chapbook COLD TURKEY, published in 1992 by Crossroads Press.

DEDICATION

This book is dedicated to the memory of my good friend Dave Ryan (1953-1992).

Smoke 'em if you got 'em, dude.

PRELUDE

Particularly
When something like a dog is barking
When something like a goose is born a freak
When something like a fox is luminous
When something like a tortoise crystallizes
When something like a wolf slides by
All these things are harmful to the health of man.

— Hagiwara Sakataro, "Harmful Animals"

It's a beautiful world.

I look out across the pre-dawn rooftops. Most of the buildings are still dark, except for scattered windows that mark early risers and insomniacs. The moon is down and the sun has yet to make its appearance, leaving the city to a darkness that is deeper than midnight. Now is the time for the changing of the guard.

I look down on the streets from my perch and watch the night-things begin their retreat. I don't mean prostitutes and drunkards and other so-called "night owls." I refer to creatures that are genuinely nocturnal. Things that shrink from the first touch of the sun's rays for fear of burning.

A succubus wearing the outer appearance of a crack-whore barters with a drunken older man. The succubus lifts its head, nostrils flaring as it scents the coming dawn, and speeds up the transaction. The older man seems pleased that he is getting such a good deal on pussy as they stagger into a darkened alley. I doubt he'll think it's such a bargain when, in the middle of his five-dollar fuck, the whore's body starts revealing razored mouths in places he never dreamed of.

I spot a pack of *vargr* making their way down a connecting street. The early hour and the accompanying darkness have made them bold, and they run in their skins. They are young, at least by werewolf standards, and still given to such acts of rebellion. They lope along, two abreast and three deep, almost on all fours. They snap and growl and bark at the shadows. Any human unlucky enough to encounter them might, at first glance, mistake them for a pack of feral dogs — household pets gone wild. But once they stood up on their hind legs, baying to signal an attack, the illusion would be torn asunder and the truth revealed. For all the good it would do their victim.
The werewolves pass by quickly, headed in the direction of the abandoned warehouses lining the riverfront where they make their den.

Not long after the *vargr* run past, a homeless man emerges from a piss-soaked doorway. He is dressed in rags, his feet encased in busted-out boots stuffed full of newspaper. I study him a bit closer, thinking he might be a *seraph* in disguise. But no, he is a genuine vagrant. He is probably old, but it is hard to tell for sure because of the grime caking his hands and face. He might be black, maybe not. He is clutching an empty pint of vodka in one hand and muttering aloud to himself. He tilts back the bottle, tonguing the neck for one last drop. His brow furrows when he realizes it's empty and, in a sudden burst of rage, he shrieks an obscenity and hurls the bottle to the curb. The sound it makes as it breaks is impressively loud in the pre-dawn silence.

The bum seems to find a certain pleasure in making noise and continues to do so. He rants at the top of his lungs, his ravings bouncing off the surrounding buildings like a handball. He finds a garbage can to knock over and kick. A bottle or two to dash against the curb. Just as he seems to be losing steam, there is the sound of leathery wings against air and he is gone.

I look up just in time to spot a large black shape silhouetted against the dark sky. It looks to be carrying something almost as large as itself in its talons. No doubt a diligent gargoyle matriarch out hunting for prey to feed her hungry chicks.

As the sky slowly lightens, I spot my own prey. It moves swiftly, clinging to the shadows as it hurries to its nest. Its pallid features and blood-red eyes make me want to puke. I hate these creatures more than all the other Pretending races combined. The very sight of them makes my palms itch and my gut tighten. All I want to do is drive my silver switchblade deep into their worm-fed hearts. Fucking lousy bloodsuckers.

I do not want to lose the vampire's trail, so I abandon my perch. I grin in anticipation of the slaughter that is to follow; the morning breeze is chill against my exposed fangs. Without further delay, I crawl headfirst down the side of the four-story building I've been using as my observation tower and hurry after my victim.

It's a beautiful world.

— *from the diaries of Sonja Blue*

When the Dead Love

Thou who, abruptly as a knife,
Didst come into my heart; thou who,
A demon horde into my life
Didst enter, wildly dancing, through
The doorways of my sense unlatched
To make my spirit thy domain.

— Baudelaire, "The Vampire"

I see the world through ancient eyes.

They are not the eyes of an old man, dimmed by age and clouded by cataracts. And while my mind is filled with memories, I never find myself lost in the tangle of interconnecting association or the fog of recollection.

My time on earth has been tenfold that of the oldest human. I am ancient. But I am not old. I stand outside the time-stream that ages mortal flesh, makes bones brittle as glass, teeth crack like chalk. I need never fear that my world will telescope downward to what little light and sound can be strained through failing sensory apparatus.

I look upon some of the aged creatures I have personally known and sported with in years past and marvel at their irretrievable descent into decay. A breast that was once as succulent and firm as a fresh melon is now a withered dug, hanging flat and wrinkled. A penis, once proud and full of the malt of life, is now good only for the elimination of waste.

This is mankind's heritage. Its destiny. All of humanity's triumphs and advances — its art, science, technology, and philosophy — reduced to a lump of sweating flesh straining on a nameless bed. Being mortal as individuals, humans seek to embrace eternity as a species. And while I consider such attempts at "immortality" laughable, through their relentless breeding humans have succeeded in maintaining a certain continuity throughout the centuries.

I have kept a journal for seven hundred years. There are literally thousands of volumes, stored in a hundred different hiding places scattered over three continents. I have no genuine memories of my life as a human, except for those preserved in faded ink on these crumbling pages. The sentiments, dreams and fears expressed in those earliest entries belong to a creature forever beyond my ken, thanks be to the forces that Made me.

Still, humans have their uses. Of course they provide my kind with sustenance: that deep red vintage that is so much sweeter when stolen from its host. That much goes without saying. But there are other, more subtle, more...*rarefied* pleasures, to be had at their expense.

Allow me to elaborate....

There are several nightclubs in this city that cater to those humans whose personal tastes, like those of my own kind, have nothing to do with procreation. There is one club in particular — The Ossuary — I enjoy frequenting.

It's located in the meat-packing district. In fact, I was just there the night before. The exterior of The Ossuary is very unprepossessing — no different from the rest of the drab warehouses lining the street. But the interior is — by human standards — quite inspired. The walls are painted matte black and festooned with the bones of the various beasts who have met their fate at the hands of the neighbors. The boiled, peeled and bleached skulls of creatures bovine, porcine, caprine, and equine stare blankly at the prancing hairless primates responsible for their destruction, bearing mute witness to the rituals of orchestrated pain and degradation played out before their empty sockets.

Entry to The Ossuary's dank pleasure-rooms is expensive — membership in the club runs in the low four figures. One-time "tickets of passage" for curious visitors can cost upward of fifty dollars apiece, and there's always a line to get in.

Tonight is no exception. As I move to the head of the line, the bouncer nods his head in recognition and steps aside to allow me passage. They know me here, as I am known in dozens of similar establishments throughout the rest of the Americas, Europe and Asia.

I breeze past the combination dressing-undressing room, where the club's regulars change into their preferred costumes for the evening's entertainment. I have no need for such theatrics. The thump of the disco and the smell of dry ice make me smile, ever so slightly, in anticipation of the night's hunt.

The cavernous main room is filled with people — some well-dressed, others naked — milling about under the strobing lights. Beautiful fashion models, made trim and perfect by strict diets and surgery, move among tattooed and creatively pierced grotesques.

A stylishly dressed businessman, looking as if he's just vacated a Wall Street brokerage house, his power tie loosed slightly at the collar, leans against the bar. He simultaneously watches vintage Times Square porno loops on the massive video screen suspended from the ceiling, gropes the tightly trussed rear of a transvestite, and sips draft beer.

Studding the main room are several tableaux areas: a rack; a man-sized doghouse, complete with food bowl; a mirrored jail cell; manacles and stocks of every description. Some of the equipment is available for use by patrons, for a nominal fee. The snap and crack of whips, rods, and paddles on wriggling backsides fill the air.

I scan the assemblage for potential prey. I spot a beautifully coiffured blonde sitting on a barstool, staring imperiously into space as a drudge licks her boots clean. A second slave kneels before her, sucking her fingers one by one. I contemplate the dominatrix for a moment, then pass on. While taking her would no doubt prove amusing, I seek a different diversion for my night's pleasure.

I watch dispassionately as a young girl dressed only in leather boots and a blindfold is strung up by her hands. As she balances precariously on tiptoe, her partner dribbles hot wax onto her exposed buttocks. She whimpers and wiggles her bottom most becomingly. The master puts aside his candle and produces a whip, the head of which he inserts into his compliant slave, lifting her off her feet. She shrieks and moans at this violation, her hips bucking to the beat of a Cure song.

A naked man with a junior executive's paunch stands off to the sidelines, watching the couple. He pulls on his semi-hard penis with his right hand, but elevation remains elusive. Bored, he turns his voyeur's gaze — as empty as those of the animals mounted on the walls — to a fat, heavily tattooed man kneeling before a tiny Oriental woman armed with a cat-o'-nine-tails. The tattooed man's penis is clamped in the jaws of a household mousetrap.

A man dressed in unconvincing drag emerges from the dry-ice smoke of the dance floor, his wig askew, funeral crepe wrapped about his exposed penis, lead fishing lures hanging from his testicles. He smiles at me; his eyes are unfocused and unreadable, even to me.

I find what I'm looking for in a young couple dressed in leather bondage gear. The female wears a brassiere with holes cut in the cups that allow her pierced nipples to protrude, and a peaked cap reminiscent of those once favored by the Gestapo. The male wears a spike-studded halter that displays his tattoos to their best advantage. A leather bondage mask hangs from his belt. Both wear tight-fitting leather chaps that expose their pale ass cheeks. With their blond hair, tanned good looks and complementing body-work, they could be easily mistaken for fraternal twins. Perhaps they are.

The male seems a bit dubious at first, appraising my ruined eye and the scar that twists the right side of my face into a perpetual sneer. But while I might not be physically attractive enough to suit his tastes, I appear to have the necessary wealth. In the end they prove pathetically easy to snare — all it takes is the promise of free drugs and a night of excess at a fashionable address. As we leave, I probe their minds, expertly tweaking their pleasure centers while dampening their sense of self-preservation. Humans who frequent these clubs are far from cautious by the normal standards of the herd, but I find it prudent to lull them into a false sense of security all the same.

It is early morning, and as the club prepares to seal its doors against the coming dawn, the city's butchers can be seen starting their day's work, unloading freshly slain sides of beef and pork from refrigerated vans. High-pressure hoses sluice the blood from the loading docks into the gutters, where it mixes with the vomit, urine, and used condoms from the night before, filling the air with the fragrant aroma of spent meat. I find it most invigorating.

The leather couple oohs and aahs appreciatively at the sight of my vintage Rolls and the uniformed driver who awaits my return. We climb inside and I offer my new playthings cocaine and champagne in copious quantities as we roll through the streets.

They indulge themselves to excess, giggling and snorting and groping one another as I watch, smiling quietly.

The male fixes me with a questioning gaze, his eyes made hot and wet by drugs and my manipulation of his brain chemistry. "So — what's your particular kink, buddy?" He smiles slowly, knowingly. "You like to watch? Is that it?"

He slides his gloved hand between the female's thighs, massaging her *mons veneris*.

I return the drunken idiot's clueless grin. "Yes. I like to watch."

The leather couple is duly impressed when we arrive at our destination: a stylish loft apartment that utilizes the entire top floor of what was once a furrier's warehouse. The interior is an austere variant of Art Deco, all shining chrome and black marble decorated here and there by expensive Persian carpets, atmospherically lit by cunningly arranged track lighting.

I shrug out of my coat and smile comfortingly at my playthings. I take my place in an overpadded leather easychair, light a French cigarette, and cross my legs. I gesture to a corner of the room — an area of exposed brick walls, bare metal pipes and a stained concrete floor. Handcuffs are attached to one of the radiator pipes, leg manacles are set into the wall, and a metal trapeze hangs suspended at eye level from the rafters. An array of punishment devices hangs from a row of pegs.

"Why don't you show me what you do best?"

The leather couple exchange glances and shrug. As far as they are concerned, I am a jaded, somewhat physically repugnant jet-setter with too much time and money on his hands.

The male removes his bondage mask from his belt and slips it on. With its zippered mouth and eye holes, it resembles a leather scarecrow's face. The male grabs the female by the hair and drags her over to the pipe, where he handcuffs her with her arms over her head, her buttocks pointed in my direction. The male selects a cat-o'-nine-tails and, after a couple of experimental snaps, brings it down on his partner's ass.

The female squeals and wriggles as the male rains blow after blow onto her upturned derriere, leaving angry red welts across the creamy expanse of her jiggling cheeks. I yawn.

This seems to aggravate the male, although it's hard to tell with the bondage mask on.

"What's the matter? Isn't this good enough for you, scarface?" he snaps, turning from his trussed partner to glower at me.

I pretend to let his insult go unnoticed. "You haven't even broken the skin!" I sniff. "I want the Real Thing, not this candy-coated pretense!"

The male mutters something to himself and returns his attention to his slave, smacking her unprotected backside with even greater ferocity. The female shudders and weeps, struggling against her restraints as blood fills the paper-thin cuts striping her ass.

After a few minutes of this, the male stops to change hands, shaking the blood from the cat. He turns to fix me with a challenging stare from behind the safety of his mask.

"Is *this* real enough for you, you one-eyed bastard?" he snarls, slapping his partner's blood-smeared flank with the flat of his hand.

"You're not even close," I smile. "Here: allow me to show you how it's done."

He stands aside, hands on his hips, expecting me to get up and take the whip from him. Instead, I simply force my mind into his skull.

The male's body twitches as I penetrate him between the eyes; his limbs convulse involuntarily as I seize control of his nervous system. As far as he is concerned, he has been suddenly, inexplicably struck blind, deaf, and dumb. I am the only one who can hear him screaming inside his head.

I give him back his eyes and ears, but I don't allow him to open his mouth. Screaming is not allowed. Not yet.

The female turns to look at what she believes is still her partner, her eyes confused. "Frankie?"

The male grabs a handful of the female's long, flowing blond hair. I pause long enough to savor its silkiness against borrowed fingertips, then proceed to pound the captive woman's head repeatedly against the steam pipe.

At first she's too startled to respond. By the second blow she begins to struggle and swear. The punishment my surrogate is meting out is not the kind she craves.

"Frankie! Stop it, you fucker! You're hurt*ing* me, dammit!"

I have my plaything slam her head into the pipe a third time. A fourth. One of her retinas detaches. Blood streams from her nostrils, making the bottom of her face look like a clown's mouth. The female goes limp by the sixth blow, cranial fluid leaking from her ears and the corners of her eyes.

Humans have so many foolish preconceptions concerning my kind: that we cannot walk in the light of day; that we burn at the touch of religious icons; that we survive on a diet of human blood. That last bit is true, in part. Yes, blood is indeed the life. But to feed on blood alone — do humans subsist on nothing but bread and water? Of course not. And neither do we.

For those of us with more refined palates, there is the gourmet delight found in human suffering. It is to blood what crack is to table wine.

However, it is not the female's pain that thrills me, delightful though it may be. It is the anguished horror of her partner, as I force his body to batter his lover's skull into an oozing mess of matted hair and bone fragments. There are no words in the mortal lexicon to describe the exhilaration and gratification I receive from such raw, unfiltered emotions.

The female is dead, or so close to death it doesn't really matter. I have the male release her and stand before a mirror mounted on the wall. As he watches, locked within his own flesh, more helpless than the day he was born, I command his hands to snap the nostril holes of his mask shut. Then I zipper the mouth shut.

I feel panic swell within him as he realizes what I plan to do. The screaming inside his skull doubles in intensity as I seal first the right eye, then the left, leaving him to darkness.

Even after everything is sealed, the mask is far from airtight. It takes the male over half an hour to suffocate. I sit in my chair and watch, savoring the alternating surges of fear, terror, rage and despair, as the dying human first realizes and then rejects his fate. His last cogent thought is that the police will kick open the door and rescue him in the nick of time, just like on TV. Then he dies.

I frown at the dead man's body, then at the battered corpse of the female, still tethered to the radiator pipe. I had hoped this would be enough, but it is not. I close my eyes, trying to block her image from my mind, but to no avail.

I can still see her. Something in my chest aches, reminding me of my emptiness.

✷

Dawn is close at hand, but I do not fear the intrusion of its rosy fingers, here in the mirrored security of my Rolls. I am not a lowly revenant, scuttling from the sun's rays for fear of being reduced to a pile of oozing sores. I evolved past such worries decades before the invention of the steam engine.

My powers are somewhat diminished during the daylight hours, that is true. And, like all of my kind, I find it necessary to lapse into a deathlike "sleep" in order to restore my vitality and heal wounds dealt me in combat. But I am far from helpless, as the legends would have humans believe.

My driver cruises the streets of the Lower East Side. He asks me if I have a destination in mind — I almost give him an address of a low dive in Five Points, then I remember that the neighborhood was demolished close to a century ago. Too bad. A brothel in that area, operated for and by children, often provided me with great amusement in the past. Instead, I direct him to Allen Street.

The whores who ply their trade along this particular boulevard are, at best, careworn. Most of them are crack addicts or junkies, the ravages of their addictions obvious even to the most obtuse of human gazes. Even if I were prone to the human sexual urge, I would never dream of mating with one of these horrors. They are rarely beautiful, and often they aren't even women. But they are expendable and when one disappears no one notices. That is what I find the most attractive about them.

I see what I need and I order the driver to stop the car. A small knot of whores stand in a doorway, fidgeting expectantly as they eye the Rolls. The night must have been slow — or their drug consumption immense — if they are still loitering on the streets this close to daybreak. One of them, a bottle redhead dressed in a polyester miniskirt that reveals her unwashed legs almost to her crotch, saunters forward as I power down the window.

"Lookin' for someone, mister?" she coos, her breath redolent of gum disease, as she bends down to look into the interior of the car. When she smiles, I see that she is missing most of her lower teeth.

I say nothing, stabbing a finger over her shoulder to one of the girls standing behind her. She is tall, with dark hair and high, vaguely Indian cheekbones. She is too thin and too dirty, dressed in high-cut denim shorts and a halter top, but she will do for now.

The redheaded whore swears and moves out of the way to let the other girl by. I open the door and she hops in with an excited squeal that could almost pass for delight. The Rolls is already pulling away before the door closes, but not before I have reached inside the tiny, crabbed minds of my victim's compatriots, erasing any memories they might hold of either me or the car.

"My name's Cheryl," the whore says, rubbing the front of my pants with all the finesse and speed of a Girl Scout trying to make a fire without the aid of matches. When I look at her I can see the virus gestating within her, eating away at the T-cells in her blood.

I slap her hands away and I see a flare of fear spark in her eyes as she gets her first good look at my face. I reach inside my jacket and produce a roll of twenty-dollar bills the size of an infant's doubled fist. The whore's eyes widen and she licks her lower lip.

"Do you want this?"

"Yeah. 'Course I want it. What I gotta do t'get it?"

"Nothing much. All you have to do is come home with me and play a little game."

"What kinda game?" She bites her lower lip but does not move her eyes away from the money.

"Dress-up."

✷

My renfields have the costume laid out in anticipation of our return. I lead the whore into a large room, empty except for a marble table lit from below by a mauve light.

The whore frowns down at the leather jacket, stained t-shirt, ripped jeans, and scuffed engineer boots, obviously perplexed. She had, no doubt, been expecting something far more exotic.

"Is this it? Is this what you want me to wear?"

I say nothing, but simply smile. She shrugs and peels out of her working clothes. The room is cold and I watch with detached interest as her flesh creeps and her nipples harden. She is awkward and it takes her a few minutes to complete the change. Finally she shrugs into the leather jacket, which creaks with her every movement.

"So, do I look okay? Is there anything else?" she asks, holding her arms up and out, modeling the costume for me

"Just two things. You'll find them in the interior breast pocket of the jacket."

The whore sticks her hand inside the jacket and removes the items, looking puzzled. "A pair of mirrored sunglasses and a switchblade—?"

"Put them on. Put them on now." The excitement is starting to stir within me, and the words come out as a breathy whisper.

The whore is confused, perhaps even a little bit frightened, but she is unwilling to forfeit the money I promised her. She puts on the glasses.

She is dirty and smells of rank jism and vaginal secretions. Her hair is too long and oily. Her motions lack grace and suppleness But there is a resemblance, tenuous as it may be, and that is enough. She is not the one I want, but she will do for now.

I move closer to the whore, my arousal growing acute as the image of the one I want shimmers behind my eyes.

"Show me the knife." It is all I can do to keep the shiver out of my voice.

"What?"

"The knife! Show me the blade!"

"Huh?"

"Just do it!" I snap, grabbing the girl by her shoulders. Not too tightly, but roughly enough to reawaken the fear.

The blade leaps from its hilt like a minnow darting through shallow water. The whore holds the knife cautiously, but not without some familiarity, I notice. Perhaps she and the object of my desire are not so disparate after all.

"Now what?"

"Stab me."

"What? Are you fuckin' *crazy*?" The fear recedes, replaced by indignation. This is kinkier than she had bargained for. She'd figured me for some deformed pervert, one who wanted to be pissed on or made to roll around in her shit. But this was too much. Even Allen Street whores, apparently, have their limits.

"Stab me!"

I have lost all patience with this trollop. If she will not give me what I want, then I shall use force. I grab her by the throat and her eyes bug out as she realizes I mean business.

She raises her hand. I catch a glimpse of metal as her fist smashes into my chest. There is a cold sharpness as the blade enters me. I continue to squeeze her throat. Again she stabs me. And again. Blood spurts from my wound, spattering both her face and mine. I close my eyes in order to savor the illusion that it is not she, but my beloved who is ramming the knife into my heart again and again. The fear that radiates from her as I slowly choke the life from her is among the best I have experienced in recent years. I groan in ecstasy as I hold her death-cry in the palm of my hand.

I open my eyes, half expecting to see my love's face before me, contorted in death. Instead, all there is is a dead whore, her blackened, swollen tongue protruding lewdly between painted lips. The sunglasses have come loose during her struggle, dangling by one ear. The dead whore's eyes — filled with burst blood vessels — start from their sockets like those of a grotesque insect. Disgusted, I let the corpse drop.

I realize that the switchblade is still lodged in my chest. I stare down at the hilt protruding between my ribs. My white silk shirt is now the color of port wine. Chuckling to myself, I pull the knife free.

I close my eyes again and see my love moving like a panther tracking its prey, her eyes burning in the darkness. She wants me. Passion radiates from her like a dark halo. But what she lusts after is not my touch, my kiss, my seed. No, what she desires is my death.

When I look into her mirrored eyes I know fear and joy.

So beautiful. So deadly.

I stand in awe of her: my lovely, lethal masterpiece.

Is this how Pygmalion felt when his Galatea stepped from her pedestal? Granted, he did not have to worry about his creation chasing him about the studio, armed with a hammer and chisel, bent on his murder. And she came close, so very close, to killing me the last time we were together. I have suffered countless mutilations during my seven centuries of existence, including amputation, but I shall carry the wounds she dealt me forever.

She split my face open with a silver knife. And I loved it.

I touch the scar that pulls the right side of my face into a rictus and think of my fatal beauty. I close my remaining eye and see her standing there, naked except for the mantle of power that crackles about her like foxfire, and the scar over my heart puckers.

Gods of the Outer Dark: help me.

I love her.

And that is why I must destroy her. Again. And again. And again. Until I am certain I can bring myself to do the deed for real.

— *from the journals of Sir Morgan, Lord of the Morning Star*

William Palmer woke the same way a swimmer emerges from the sea: gasping for air.

He lay flat on the bed, staring up at the cracked plaster ceiling for a long moment before really seeing it, while the last vestiges of the dream bled away from the corners of his eyes.

Dream. Thank God. Just a dream.

He'd being dreaming of the house again. The house called Ghost Trap.

It had been built earlier in the century by a gifted, if demented, architect who had designed it to keep him safe from the vengeful spirits of his slaughtered family. The mansion was a crazed conglomeration of rooms without windows, blind stairways, secret passageways and other mad fancies, built according to non-Euclidean geometric principles that confused and disoriented both the dead and the living. For someone such as Palmer, possessing psionic abilities beyond those of normal humans, Ghost Trap was the psychic equivalent of the LaBrea Tar Pits.

Nearly three years ago, Palmer had found himself lost in Ghost Trap, at the mercy of the dead that roamed its halls. He'd entered in search of his friend and lover, Sonja Blue: the woman who had helped him learn to deal with his psychic powers — and who had dragged him into her battle with the master vampire, Morgan.

He'd survived that night in Ghost Trap — but just barely. He'd lived to see the horror-house consumed by flames, releasing its damned occupants once and for all. Ghost Trap was no more. Yet it still lived within his mind, playing host to his nightmares.

Palmer stared up at the ceiling fan mounted over the bed, watching the rotors beat the heavy, humid air in near silence. No doubt the stickiness and heat had contributed to his bad dream. It was too uncomfortable to be sleeping inside, really, but the mosquitoes were too fierce this season for him to try using the hammock on the front porch.

He sat up, pushing aside the sweat-drenched sheets. He wasn't going to get back to sleep — at least not for awhile, anyway. He swung his feet onto the floor and stood up with a groan, catching a glimpse of himself in the mirror opposite the bed. He ran one hand across the ritual tattoo that covered his entire chest. It was of Mayan design, as were the jade plugs that stretched his earlobes. It depicted the symbol of the House of the Jaguar Lords.

Palmer didn't believe in past-life regression therapy, channeling, Space Brothers, or any of that other New Age crap. It just happened that he was the reincarnation of a pre-Columbian Mayan. In a previous life, he had been one of the six-fingered wizard-kings of the *Chan Balam*, who saw their deformity as a sign of godhood. He was also an ex-private investigator, a pardoned felon, a telepath, and the proprietor of a successful specialty export business.

Palmer moved toward the hallway, only to freeze when something the size and shape of a large tarantula skittered out from behind the door. He let out a sigh of relief when he saw what it really was — a mummified six-fingered hand, amputated at the wrist.

"Dammit, Lefty! You nearly gave me a heart attack!" Palmer chided, nudging the thing with his foot. He'd grown fond of the gruesome relic over the months. It really wasn't so surprising that he should develop an attachment to it. After all, it had once belonged to his previous incarnation.

Palmer padded down the hallway, naked except for a pair of boxers, Lefty skittering after him like a faithful pet. He paused at the nursery, quietly opening the door so as not to wake Lethe.

I really should stop calling it the nursery, he thought to himself, not for the first time. *She's really too old for that.*

It took him a second or two to locate her amid all the stuffed animals and dolls she had in bed with her, but then he spotted her hair — as dark and sleek as a sable's pelt — poking out from between a Raggedy Ann and a Paddington Bear. As he watched, she mumbled something in her sleep.

He was going to have to get her some new clothes pretty soon. She'd already outgrown the ones he'd bought less than a month ago, having shot up another three inches literally overnight. Palmer's eyes wandered to the closet door he used as Lethe's official growth chart, scanning the series of overlapping pencil marks and their accompanying notations as to date and age. As of her last measuring, Lethe stood close to five foot one. Not bad for a child who had yet to reach her third birthday.

One of the shadows near the foot of Lethe's bed detached itself and moved toward Palmer. Two points of golden light, set about the height of a man's eyes, suddenly blinked on.

"Don't worry, Fido. Nothing's wrong. I was just checkin' in," Palmer whispered.

The hulking apparition, which resembled a mound of dirty laundry sculpted into the form of a human being, nodded dumbly and returned to its silent vigil. During the two-and-a-half years Palmer had spent in the company of the *seraph*, he still had no idea what the creature thought — or if it thought at all. While it was obviously appointed to guard Lethe, it had never once attempted to communicate with him — at least on a level that he could understand.

Satisfied everything was under control, Palmer continued his nocturnal perimeter check. He paused at the door that led to the patio, with its expensive Spanish tile and a small three-tiered fountain that constantly burbled to itself.

Palmer stepped outside; the humid Yucatan night was no relief. It felt as if the world's largest dog were breathing on him. Palmer wiped at the sweat on his brow and upper lip as he peered up at the moonlit sky.

Where are you? his mind whispered into the night.

The sound of a radio scanning through a thousand different competing signals filled his head. Some were fairly strong, others weak. Some were in languages he understood; most were not. Some were angry, some were sad, some were happy — but most were confused. The signals blurred and clashed, waxed and waned.

Where are you? He boosted his own signal, hoping to cut through the drift of muted voices that filled the ether. This time he was rewarded with a response — a voice made faint and blurry by distance, but still recognizable.

I'm here. In New Orleans.

He smiled at the sound of her voice in his head; even though she was not there to see it, he knew she felt it.

When are you coming home?

Soon. But I still have work to attend to here.

I miss you.

I miss you, too. She smiled then. He could feel it.

Any luck?

No sign of him yet, but I have a few hunches as to where he might be hiding. How is Lethe?

Fine. I guess.

Glad to hear everything's okay. I have to go now —

Sonja—? Sonja, we need to talk…Sonja?

There was no reply, only the squawk and squelch of the minds of a million strangers babbling into the void.

I have to give the dead boy credit; he has the trick of appearing human nailed down tight. He's learned just what gestures and vocal inflections hide the fact that his surface glitz isn't there to disguise basic shallowness, but an utter lack of humanity.

I've seen enough of the kind he imitates: pallid, self-important intellectuals who pride themselves on their sophistication and knowledge of what's "hip," sharpening their wit at the expense of others. Like the vampiric mimic in their midst, they produce nothing while thriving on the vitality of others. The only difference is that the vampire is more honest about it.

I work my way to the bar, careful to keep myself shielded from the dead boy's view, both physically and psychically. It wouldn't do for my quarry to catch scent of me just yet. I hear the vampire's nasal intonations as it holds forth on the merits of various artists.

"Frankly, I consider his use of photo-montage to be inexcusably banal — I've seen better at Olan Mills!"

From whom did the vampire steal that particular drollery, I wonder. A dead boy of his wattage doesn't come up with *bon mots* and witty remarks spontaneously. When you have to spend a lot of conscious energy remembering to breathe and blink, there is no such thing as top-of-your-head snappy patter. It is all protective coloration, right down to the last double entendre and Monty Python impersonation.

It will be another decade or two before the vampire dressed in black silk and leather with the stainless-steel ankh dangling from one ear and the crystal embedded in his left nostril can divert his energies to something besides the full-time task of ensuring his continuance. And I doubt this dead boy has much of a chance of realizing that future.

I wave down the bartender and order a beer. As I await its arrival, I catch a glimpse of myself in the mirror backing the bar. To the casual observer I appear to be no more than twenty-five. Tricked out in a battered leather jacket, a stained Circle Jerks T-shirt, patched jeans, mirrored sunglasses, and with dark hair twisted into a tortured cockatoo's crest, I look like just another member of Generation X checking out the scene. No one would ever guess I'm actually forty years old.

I suck the cold suds down, participating in my own form of protective coloration. I can drink a case or three of the stuff without effect. Beer doesn't do it for me anymore. Neither does hard liquor. Or cocaine. Or heroin. Or crack. I've tried them all, in dosages that would put the U.S. Olympic Team in the morgue; but no luck. Only one drug plunks my magic twanger nowadays. Only one thing can get me off.

And that drug is blood.

Yeah, the dead boy is good enough to have fooled another vampire. But didn't.

I study my prey speculatively. I doubt I'll have any trouble taking the sucker down. I rarely do, these days. Least not the lesser undead that still lack major psionic muscle. Sure, they might have enough mesmeric ability to gull the humans in their vicinity, but little else. Compared to my own psychic abilities, the art-fag vampire might as well be packing a pea-shooter. Still, it isn't smart to get cocky. Lord Morgan dismissed me in such a high-handed manner, and now he's missing half his face. That's what you get for being smug.

I shift my vision from the human to the Pretender spectrum, studying the vampire's true appearance. I wonder if the black-garbed art aficionados clustered about their Mandarin, their heads bobbing like puppets, would still consider his pronouncements worthy if they knew his skin is the color and texture of rotten sailcloth. Or that his lips are black and shriveled, revealing oversized fangs set in a perpetual death's-head grimace. No doubt they'd drop their little plastic cups of cheap blush and back away in horror, their surface glaze of urbanite sophistication and studied ennui replaced by honest, old-fashioned monkey-brain terror.

Humans need masks in order to live their day-to-day lives, even among their own kind. Little do they know that their dependence on artifice and pretense provides the perfect hiding place for predators. Predators like the vampire pretending to be an art-fag. Predators such as me.

I tighten my grip on the switchblade in the pocket of my leather jacket. Midnight! Time to drop your masks!

"Uh, excuse me?"

I jerk around a little too fast, startling the young man at my elbow. I was so focused on my prey I was unaware of his approach. Sloppy. Really sloppy.

"Yeah, what is it?"

The young man blinks, slightly taken aback by the brusqueness in my voice. "I, uh, was wondering if I might, uh, buy you a drink?"

I automatically scan him for signs of Pretender taint, but he comes up clean. One hundred percent USDA human. He is taller than me by a couple of inches; his blond hair is pulled back into a ponytail. There are three rings in his right ear and one in his left nostril. Despite the metalwork festooning his nose, he is quite handsome.

I am at a loss for words. I'm not used to being approached by normal people. I tend to generate a low-level psychic energy field that most humans find unnerving, if not antagonistic. In layman's terms: I tend to either scare people or piss them off.

"I — I—"

I shoot my prey a glance out of the corner of my eye. Shit! The bastard is starting to make his move, hustling one of the more entranced hangers-on.

"I realize this is going to sound like a really dumb come-on," he says, shooting me an embarrassed smile. "But I saw you from across the room — and I just had to meet you. Please let me buy you a drink."

"I, uh, I—"

The vampire is escorting its prey outside, smiling widely as it continues to discourse on Post-Modern art.

"There's something I have to take care of — I'll be right back! I promise! Don't go away!" I blurt, and dash off in pursuit of my target for the night.

✷

I scan the parking lot, checking for signs of the vampire's passage. I pray I'm not too late. Once a vamp isolates and seduces a human from the herd, he tends to move quickly. I know that from my own experience at the hands of Sir Morgan, the undead bastard responsible for my own transformation.

The vampire and its prey are sitting in the back seat of a silver BMW with heavily tinted windows; their blurred silhouettes move like shadows reflected in an aquarium. There is no time to waste. I'll have to risk being spotted.

The imitation art-fag looks genuinely surprised when my fist punches through the back window, sending tinted safety glass flying into the car. He hisses a challenge, exposing his fangs, as he whips about to face me. His victim sits beside him, motionless as a mannequin, eyes unfocused and fly open. The human's erect penis juts forward, vibrating like a tuning fork.

I grab the vampire by the collar of his black silk shirt and pull him, kicking and screaming, through the busted back windshield. The human doesn't even blink.

"Quit yer bitchin'!" I snap as I hurl the snarling vampire onto the parking lot gravel. "Let's get this over with, dead boy! I've got a hot date!"

The vampire launches himself at me, talons hooked and fangs extended. I move to meet the attack, flicking open my switchblade with a snap of my wrist. The silver blade sinks into the vampire's chest, causing him to shriek in pain. The vampire collapses around my fist, spasming as his system reacts to the silver's toxin.

I kneel and swiftly remove the vampire's head from his shoulders. The body is already starting to putrefy by the time I locate the BMW's keys. I unlock the trunk and toss the vampire's rapidly decomposing remains inside, making sure the keys are left in his pants pocket.

I look around, but, remarkably, there are no witnesses to be seen in the darkened lot. I move around to the passenger side and open the door, tugging the still-entranced human out of the car.

He stands propped against the bumper like a drunkard, his eyes swimming and his face slack. His penis dangles from his pants like a deflated party balloon. I take his chin between thumb and forefinger and turn his head so that his eyes meet mine.

"This never happened. You do not remember leaving the bar with anyone. Is that clear?"

"N-nothing h-happened."

"Excellent! Now go back in the bar and have a good time. Oh, and stick that thing back in your pants! You don't want to get busted for indecent exposure, do you?"

✸

I'm buzzing as I reenter the bar. I like to think of it as my apres-combat high. The adrenaline from the battle is still sluicing around inside me, juicing my perceptions and making me feel as if I'm made of lightning and spun glass. It isn't as intense as the boost I get from blood, but it's good.

Someone jostles me, and I look down at a drab, mousy-haired woman, her face set into a scowl. I pause, studying the schizophrenia that radiates from the other woman like a martyr's halo. She is thinking of returning home and repeatedly stabbing her elderly parents as they lie in their separate beds, then setting the house ablaze. This is not a new thought. The scowling woman suddenly blushes, draws her shoulders in, ducks her chin, and hurries away, as if she has suddenly awakened to discover herself sleepwalking in the nude. I shrug and continue scanning the bar for the young man who spoke to me earlier.

Give it up — he's forgotten you and found another bimbo for the evening.

I fight to keep from cringing at the sound of the Other's voice inside my head. I had managed to go almost all night without having to endure its commentary.

I find him waiting for me at the bar. I make a last minute spot-check for any blood or telltale ichor that might be clinging to me, then move forward.

"You still interested in buying me that drink?"

The young man's smile is genuinely relieved. "You came back!"

"I said I'd be back, didn't I?"

"Yeah. You did." He smiles again and offers his hand. "I guess I ought to introduce myself. I'm Judd."

I take his hand and smile without parting my lips. "Pleased to meet you, Judd. I'm Sonja."

"What the hell's going on here?!?"

Judd's smile falters as his gaze fixes itself on something just behind my right shoulder. I turn and find myself almost nose-to-nose with a young woman dressed in a skintight black sheath, fishnet stockings, and way too much makeup. The woman's psychosis covers her face like the caul found on a newborn infant, pulsing indentations marking her eyes, nose and mouth.

Judd closes his eyes and sighs. "Kitty, look, it's over! Get a life of your own and let go of mine, alright?"

"Oh, is that how you see it? Funny, I remember you saying something different! Like how you'd *always* love me! Guess I was stupid to believe that, huh?"

Kitty's rage turns the caul covering her face an interesting shade of magenta, swirling and pulsing like a lava lamp.

"You're not getting away *that* easy, asshole! And who's this — your new slut?"

Kitty slaps the flat of her hand against my shoulder, as if to push me away from Judd. I grab Kitty's wrist, being careful not to break it in front of Judd.

C'mon, snap the crazy bitch's arm off, purrs the Other. *She deserves it!*

"Don't touch me." My voice is flat and blunt, like the side of a sword.

Kitty tries to yank herself free of my grip. "I'll fucking touch you anytime I want! Just you stay away from my boyfriend, bitch! Now let me go!" She tries to rake my face with her free hand, only to have that one grabbed as well, forcing her to look directly into my face. Kitty's features grow pale and she stops struggling. I know the other woman is seeing me — *truly* seeing me

— for what I am. Only three kinds of human can perceive the Real World and the things that dwell within it: psychics, drunken poets, and lunatics. And Kitty definitely qualifies for the last category.

I release the girl, who massages her wrists, her gaze still fixed on me. She opens her mouth as if to say something, then turns and hurries away, nearly tripping over her own high heels as she flees.

Judd looks uncomfortable. "I'm sorry you had to see that. Kitty's a weird girl. We lived together for a few months, but she was incredibly jealous. It got to the point where I couldn't take any more of it, so I moved out. She's been dogging my tracks ever since. She scared off my last two girlfriends."

I shrug. "I don't scare easy."

✸

He isn't afraid of me. Nor do I detect the self-destructive tendencies that usually attract humans to my kind. Judd is not an entranced moth drawn to my dark flame, nor is he a renfield in search of a master. He is simply a good-natured young man who finds me physically attractive. The novelty of his normalcy intrigues me.

He buys me several drinks, all of which I down without any effect. But I *do* feel giddy, almost lightheaded, while in his company. To be mistaken for a desirable, human woman is actually quite flattering. Especially since I stopped thinking of myself in those terms some time back.

We end up dancing, adding our bodies to the surging crowd that fills the mosh pit. At one point I am amazed to find myself laughing, genuinely laug*hing*, one arm wrapped about Judd's waist. And then Judd leans in and kisses me.

I barely have time to retract my fangs before his tongue finds mine. I slide my other arm around his waist and pull him into me, grinding myself against him. He responds eagerly, his erection rubbing against my hip like a friendly tomcat. And I find myself wondering how his blood will taste.

I push him away so hard he staggers backward a couple of steps, almost falling on his ass. I shake my head as if trying to dislodge something in my ear, a guttural moan rising from my chest.

"Sonja?" There is a confused, hurt look on his face.

I can *see* his blood beckoning to me from just beneath the surface of his skin: the veins traced in blue, the arteries pulsing purple. I turn my back on him and run, head lowered, from the bar. I shoulder my way through a knot of dancers, sending them flying like duckpins. Some of the bar's patrons hurl insults in my direction, a couple even spit at me, but I am deaf to their anger, blind to their contempt.

I put a couple of blocks between me and the bar before I stop. I slump into a darkened doorway, staring at my shaking hands as if they belong to someone else.

"I liked him. I honestly liked him and I was going to — going to—" The thought is enough to make my throat tighten in a gag reflex.

Like. Hate. What's the difference? Blood is the life, wherever it comes from.

"Not like that. I never feed off of anyone who doesn't deserve it. *Never.*"

Aren't we special?

"Shut up, bitch."

"Sonja?"

I have him pinned to the wall, one forearm clamped against his windpipe, before I recognize him. Judd claws at my arm, his eyes bulging from their sockets.

"I'm…sorry…." he gasps out.

I let him go. "No, I'm the one who should be sorry. More than you realize."

Judd regards me apprehensively as he massages his throat, but there is still no fear in his eyes. "Look, I don't know what it was I said or did back there at the bar that put you off…."

"The problem isn't with you, Judd. Believe me." I turn and begin walking away, but he hurries after me.

"I know an all-night coffeehouse near here. Maybe we could go and talk things out there?"

"Judd, just leave me alone, okay? You'd be a lot better off if you just forgot you ever met me."

"How could I forget someone like you?"

"Easier than you realize."

He keeps pace alongside me, desperately trying to make eye contact. "C'mon, Sonja! Give it a chance! I — dammit, would you just look at me?"

I stop in midstep to face him, hoping my expression is unreadable behind my mirrored sunglasses. "That's the *last* thing you want me to do."

Judd sighs and fishes a pen and piece of paper out of his pocket. "You're one strange lady, that's for sure! But I *like* you, don't ask me why." He scribbles something on the scrap of paper and shoves it into my hand. "Look, here's my phone number. *Call* me, okay?"

I close my fist around the paper. "Judd—"

He holds his hands out, palms facing up. "No strings attached, I promise. Just call me."

I'm surprised to find myself smiling. "Okay. I'll call you. Now will you leave me alone?"

✸

When I revive the next evening I find Judd's phone number tucked away in one of the pockets of my leather jacket. I sit cross-legged on the coarse cotton futon that serves as my bed and stare at it for a long time.

I was careful to make sure Judd didn't follow me the night before. My current nest is a drafty loft apartment in the attic of an old warehouse in the district just beyond the French Quarter. Except for my sleeping pallet, an antique cedar wardrobe, a couple of Salvation Army-issue chairs, a refrigerator, a cordless telephone, and the scattered packing crates containing the esoteric curios I use for barter among information- and magic-brokers, the huge space is practically empty. Other than on those occasions when the Dead come to visit. Such as tonight.

At first I don't recognize the ghost. He's lost his sense of self in the time since his death, blurring his spectral image somewhat. He swirls up through the floorboards like a gust of blue smoke, gradually taking shape before my eyes. It is only when the phantom produces a smoldering cigarette from his own ectoplasm that I recognize him.

"Hello, Chaz."

The ghost of my former lover makes a noise that sounds like a cat being drowned. The Dead cannot speak clearly — even to Pretenders — except on three days of the year: Fat Tuesday, Halloween, and the vernal equinox.

"Come to see how your murderer is getting on, I take it?"

Chaz makes a sound like a church bell played at half-speed.

"Sorry I don't have a Ouija board, or we could have a proper conversation. Is there a special occasion for tonight's haunting, or are things just boring over on your side?"

Chaz frowns and points at the scrap of paper I hold in my hand. The ghost-light radiating from him is the only illumination in the room.

"What? You don't want me to call this number?"

Chaz nods his head, nearly sending it floating from his shoulders.

"You tried warning Palmer away from me last Mardi Gras. Didn't work — but I suppose you know that already. He's living in Yucatan right now. We're very happy."

The ghost's laughter sounds like fingers raking a chalkboard.

"Yeah, big laugh, dead boy. And I'll tell you one thing, Chaz: Palmer's a damn sight better in bed than you ever were!"

Chaz makes an obscene gesture that is rendered pointless since he no longer has a body from the waist down. I laugh and clap my hands, rocking back and forth on my haunches.

"I *knew* that'd burn your ass, dead or not! Now piss off! I've got better things to do than play charades with a defunct hustler!"

Chaz yowls like a baby dropped in a vat of boiling oil and disappears in a swirl of dust and ectoplasm, leaving me alone with Judd's phone number still clenched in one fist.

Hell, I think as I reach for the cordless phone beside the futon, *if Chaz didn't want me to call the guy, then it must be the right thing to do....*

✸

The place where we rendezvous is a twenty-four-hour establishment in the French Quarter that has, over the course of the last fifty years, been a bank, a showbar, and a porno shop before becoming a coffeehouse. We sit at a small table in the back and sip iced coffee.

Judd's hair is freshly washed and he smells of aftershave, but those are the only concessions he's made to the mating ritual. He still wears his ear- and nose-rings and a Bongwater T-shirt that's been laundered so often the silk-screened image is starting to flake off.

Judd pokes at his iced coffee with a straw. "If I'm not getting too personal — what was last night all about?"

I study my hands as I speak. "Look, Judd. There's a lot about me you don't know — and I'd like to keep it that way. If you insist on poking into my past, I'm afraid I'll have to leave. It's not that I don't like you — I *do* — but I'm a very private person. And it's for a good reason."

"Is — is there someone else?"

"Yes. Yes, there is."

"A husband?"

I have to think about that one for a few seconds before answering. "In some ways. But, no; I'm not legally married."

Judd nods as if this explains something. It is obvious that some of what I've said bothers him, but he tries to play it cool. I wonder what it is like, living a life where the worst things you have to deal with are jealous lovers and hurt feelings. It seems almost idyllic from where I am.

After we finish our iced coffees, we hit the Quarter. It is after midnight, and the lower sector of Decatur Street, the portion located in the French Market, is starting to wake up. The streets outside the bars are decorated with clots of young people dressed in black leather, sequins, and recycled '70s rags. The hipsters mill about, flashing their tattoos and bumming cigarettes off one another, as they wait for something to happen.

Someone calls Judd's name and he swerves across the street toward a knot of youths lounging outside a dance bar called the Crystal Blue Persuasion. I hesitate before following him.

A young man dressed in a black duster, his shoulder-length hair braided into three pigtails and held in place by ivory beads carved in the shapes of skulls, moves forward to greet Judd.

Out of habit, I scan his face for Pretender taint. Human. While the two speak, I casually examine the rest of the group loitering outside the club. Human. Human. Human. Hu—

I freeze.

The smell of *vargr* is strong, like the stink of a wet dog. It radiates from a young man with a shaved forehead like that of an ancient samurai. The hair at the back of his head is extremely long and held in a loose ponytail, making him look like a punker Mandarin. He wears a leather jacket, the sleeves of which look as if they've been chewed off at the shoulder, trailing streamers of mangled leather and lining like gristle. He has one arm draped over the shoulder of a little goth chick, her face made deathly pale by powder.

The *vargr* meets my gaze and holds it, grinning his contempt. Without realizing it, my hand closes around the switchblade.

"I'd like you to meet a friend of mine—"

Judd's hand is on my elbow, drawing my attention away from the teenage werewolf. I struggle to keep the disorientation of having my focus broken from showing in my temper.

"Huh?"

"Sonja, I'd like you to meet Arlo, he's an old buddy of mine… "

Arlo frowns at me as if I've just emerged from under a rock, but offers his hand in deference to his friend. "Pleased to meet you," he mumbles.

"Yeah. Sure."

I shoot a sidewise glance at the *vargr* twelve feet away. He is murmuring something into the goth girl's ear. She giggles and nods her head, and the two break away from the rest of the group, sauntering down the street in the direction of the river. The *vargr* pauses to give me one last look over his shoulder, his grin too wide and his teeth too big, before disappearing into the shadows with his victim.

That's right. Pretend you didn't see it. Pretend you don't know what that grinning hell-hound's going to do with that girl. You can't offend loverboy here by running off to do hand-to-hand combat with a werewolf, can you?

"Shut the fuck up, damn you," I mutter under my breath.

"You say something, Sonja?"

"Just talking to myself."

After leaving Arlo and his friends, we head farther down Decatur. This is a part of the French Quarter that few tourists wander into after dark, populated by gay bars and less wholesome establishments.

As we pass the Monastery, a seedy bar that caters to the late-night hardcore alcoholic trade, someone's mind calls my name.

A black man, his hair plaited into dreadlocks, steps from the doorway of the Monastery. He wears a black turtleneck sweater and immaculate designer jeans; a golden peace sign the size of a hood ornament dangles from a chain around his neck.

"Long time no see, Blue."

"Hello, Mal."

The demon Malfeis smiles, exposing teeth that belong in the mouth of a shark. "No hard feelings, I hope? I didn't want to sell you out like that, girlchick, but I was under orders from Below Stairs."

"We'll talk about it later, Mal...."

Just then the demon notices Judd. "Got yourself a new renfield, I see."

"Shut up!" I hiss, my aura crackling like an electric halo.

Mal lifts his hands, palms outward. "Whoa! Didn't mean to hit a sore spot there, girly-girl."

"Sonja? Is this guy bothering you?" Judd is hovering at my elbow. He gives Mal a suspicious glare, blind to the demon's true appearance.

"No. Everything's cool." I turn my back on the grinning demon and try to block the sound of his laughter echoing in my mind.

"Who was that guy?"

"Judd—"

"I know! I promised I wouldn't pry into your past. But you can't expect me to just stand by and not say something—?"

"Mal is a — business associate of mine. That's all you need to know about him, except that, no matter what, *never* ask him a question. *Never*."

We walk on in silence for a few more minutes, then Judd takes my hand in his and squeezes it. We stop at the corner and he pulls me into his arms. His kiss is warm and probing and I feel myself begin to relax. Then he reaches for my sunglasses.

I bat his hand away, fighting the urge to snarl. "Don't do that!"

"I just want to see your eyes."

"*No*." I pull away from him, my body rigid.

"I'm sorry—"

"I better leave. I had a nice time, Judd. I really did. But I have to go."

"You'll call me, won't you?"

"I'm afraid so."

✸

Why don't you fuck him? He wants it bad. So do you. You can't hide that from me.

The Other's voice is a nettle wedged into the folds of my brain, impossible to dislodge or ignore. I open the refrigerator and take out a bottle of whole blood, cracking its seal open as I would a beer.

Not that bottled crap again! I hate this shit! You might as well go back to drinking cats! Wouldn't you rather have something nice and fresh? Say, a good B negative mugger or an O positive rapist? There's still plenty of time to go trawling before the sun comes up.... Or you could always pay a visit to loverboy.

"Shut up! I've had a bellyful of you tonight already!"

My-my! Aren't we being the touchy one? Tell me, how long do you think you can keep up the pretense of being normal? You've almost forgotten what it's like to be human yourself. Why torture yourself by pretending you're something you're not simply to win the favor of a piece of beefsteak?

"He likes me, dammit. He actually likes me."

And what, exactly, are you?

"I'm not in the mood for your fuckin' mind-games!"

Welcome to the fold, my dear. You're finally one of us. You're a Pretender.

I shriek and hurl the half-finished bottle of blood into the sink. I pick up the card table and smash it to the floor, jumping up and down on the scattered pieces. It's a stupid, pointless gesture, but it makes me feel better.

✷

I keep calling him. I know it's stupid, even dangerous, to socialize with humans, but I can't help myself. Something about him keeps drawing me back, despite my better judgment. The only other time I've known such compulsion is when the Thirst is on me. Is this love? Or is it simply another form of hunger?

Our relationship, while charged with an undercurrent of eroticism, is essentially sexless. I want him so badly I dare not do more than kiss or hold hands. If I should lose control, there is no telling what might happen

Judd, unlike Palmer, is not a sensitive. He is a human, blind and dumb to the miracles and terrors of the Real World, just like poor, doomed Claude Hagerty was. Rapid exposure to the world I inhabit could inflict immense damage.

To his credit, Judd has not pressed the sex issue overmuch. He is not happy with the arrangement, but honors my request that we "take it slow."

This, however, does not sit well with the Other. It constantly taunts me, goading me with obscene fantasies and suggestions concerning Judd. Or, failing to elicit a response using those tactics, it chastises me for being untrue to

Palmer. I try to ignore its jibes as best I can, but I know that something, somewhere is bound to snap.

— *from the diaries of Sonja Blue*

✸

Kitty wiped at the tears oozing from the corner of her eye, smearing mascara all over her cheek and the back of her hand. It made the words on the paper swim and crawl like insects, but she didn't care.

She loved him. She really, truly loved him. And maybe now, after she did what she had to do to save him, he'd finally believe her. Proof. He needed proof of her love. And what better proof than to rescue him from the clutches of a monster?

Dearest Judd,

I tried to warn you about That Woman. But you are blind to what she Really Is. She is Evil Itself, a demon sent from Hell to claim your Soul! I knew her for what she truly is the moment I first saw her, and she knew I knew! Her hands and mouth drip blood! Her eyes burn with the fires of Hell! She is surrounded by a cloud of red energy. Red as blood. She means to drag you to Hell, Judd. But I won't let her. I love you too much to let that happen. I'll take care of this horrible monster, don't you worry. I've been talking to God a lot lately, and He told me how to deal with demons like her. I Love you so very, very much. I want you to Love me too. I'm doing this all for you. Please Love Me.

Kitty

✸

Judd woke up at two in the afternoon, as usual. He worked six-to-midnight four days out of the week and had long since shifted over to a nocturnal lifestyle. After he got off work he normally headed down to the Quarter to chill with his buddies or, more recently, hang out with Sonja until four or five in the morning.

He yawned as he dumped a couple of heaping scoops of Guatemalan into the hopper of his Mr. Coffee machine. Sonja. Now there was a weird chick. Weird, but not in a schizzy, death-obsessed, art-school-freshman way like Kitty. Her strangeness issued from something far deeper than bourgeois neurosis. Sonja was genuinely *out there*, wherever that might be. Something about the way she moved, the way she handled herself, suggested she was plugged into something Real. And as frustrating as her fits of mood might be, he could not bring himself to turn his back on her and walk away.

Still, it bothered him that none of his friends — not even Arlo, whom he'd known since high school — liked her. In fact, some even seemed to be *scared* of her. Funny. How could anyone be *frightened* of Sonja?

As he shuffled in the direction of the bathroom, he noticed an envelope shoved under his front door. He retrieved it, scowling at the all-too-familiar handwriting.

Kitty.

Probably another one of her damn fool love letters, alternately threatening him with castration and begging him to take her back. Lately she'd taken to leaving rambling, wigged-out messages on his answering machine, ranting about Sonja being some kind of vampire out to steal his soul. Crazy bitch. Sonja was crazy, too, but hardly predictable.

Judd tossed the envelope, unopened, into the trash can and staggered off to take a shower.

✸

I greet the night from atop the roof of the warehouse where I make my nest. I stretch my arms wide as if to embrace the rising moon, listening with half an ear to the sound of the baying dogs along the riverbanks. Some, I know, are not dogs.

But the *vargr* are not my concern. I've tangled with a few over the years, but I prefer hunting my own kind. I find it vastly more satisfying.

The warehouse's exterior fire escape is badly rusted and groans noisily with the slightest movement, so I avoid it altogether. I crawl, headfirst, down the side of the building, moving like a lizard on a garden wall. Once I reach the bottom I routinely pat-check my jacket and pockets to make sure nothing has fallen out during my descent.

There is a sudden hissing sound in my head, as if someone has abruptly pumped up the volume on a radio tuned to a dead channel, and something heavy catches me between the shoulder blades, lifting me off my feet and knocking me into a row of garbage cans.

I barely have time to roll out of the way before something big and silvery smashes down where my head was a second before. I cough and black blood flies from my lips; a rib has broken off and pierced my lungs.

Kitty stands over me, clutching a three-foot-long silver crucifix as if it were a baseball bat. While her madness gives her strength, it is obvious the damn thing is still *heavy*. I wonder which church she managed to steal it from.

The dead channel-crackling in my head grows louder. It is the sound of homicidal rage. Shrieking incoherently, Kitty swings at me a third time. While crosses and crucifixes have no effect on me — or any vampire, for that matter

— if Kitty succeeds in landing a lucky blow and snaps my spine or cracks open my skull, I'm dead no matter what.

I roll clear and get to my feet in one swift, fluid motion. Kitty swings at me again, but this time I step inside her reach and grab the crucifix, wresting it from her. The crucifix is at least three inches thick, the cross beams as wide as a man's hand. At its center hangs a miniature Christ fashioned of gold and platinum. Kitty staggers back, staring in disbelief as I heft the heavy silver cross. She waits for my hands to burst into flames.

"What the hell did you think you were going to solve, clobbering me with this piece of junk?" I snarl.

Kitty's eyes are huge, the pupils swimming in madness. "You can't have him! I won't let you take his soul!"

"Who said anything about me stealing—"

"Monster!" Kitty launches herself at me, her fingers clawing at my face. "Monster!"

I hit her with the crucifix.

Kitty drops to the alley floor, the top of her skull resting on her left shoulder. The muscles of her neck are the only things still holding her head onto her body.

Way to go, kiddo! You just killed loverboy's bug-shit ex-girlfriend! You're batting a thousand!

"Damn."

I toss the crucifix aside and squat next to the body. No need to check for vital signs. The girl is d-e-a-d.

What to do? I can't just toss the corpse in a dumpster. Someone is bound to find it, and once the body is identified, New Orleans Homicide will no doubt bring Judd in for questioning. Which means they'll be looking for *me*, sooner or later. And I can't have *that*.

I've got an idea, croons the Other. *Just let me handle it*.

✸

Stealing the car is easy. It's a '76 Ford LTD with a muffler held in place with baling wire, sporting a *Duke for Governor* sticker on the sagging rear bumper. Just the thing to unobtrusively dispose of a murder victim in New Orleans' outlying bayous during the dead of night.

I take an exit off the interstate leading out of New Orleans East. Originally it was to have connected a cookie-cutter housing development, built on the very fringes of the marshlands, to the rest of the world. The contractors got as far as pouring the concrete slab foundations before the recession hit. The condos were never built, but the access road remains, although there is nothing at its end but an overgrown tangle of briars and vines that has become a breeding ground for snakes and alligators.

I drive without lights. Not that I need them. I can see just fine in the dark. Having reached my destination, I cut the engine and roll to a stop. Except for the chirring of frogs and the grunting of gators, everything is quiet.

I climb out of the car and open the trunk with a length of bent coat hanger. I stand for a second, silently inventorying the collection of plastic trash bags. There are six: one for the head, one for the torso, and one apiece for each limb. I've already burned Kitty's clothing in the warehouse's furnace and disposed of her jewelry and teeth by tossing them into the river.

I gather up the bags and leave the road, heading in the direction of the bayou. I can hear things splashing in the water, some of them quite large.

I pause for a second on the bank of the bayou. Something nearby hisses. I toss the bag containing Kitty's head into the murky water.

"Come and get it!"

The assembled gators splash and wrestle among themselves for the tender morsels, like ducks fighting for scraps of stale bread.

I am tired. Very tired. After this is over I still have to drive the stolen car to a suitably disreputable urban area and set it on fire. I look down at my hands. They are streaked with blood. I absentmindedly lick them clean.

When I am finished, the Other looks through my eyes and smiles.

The Other isn't tired. Not in the least.

— *from the diaries of Sonja Blue*

✷

It hadn't been a very good night, as far as Judd was concerned. He'd been chewed out concerning his attitude at work; Arlo and the others treated him like he had a championship case of halitosis; and, to cap the evening, Sonja pulled a no-show. Time to pack it in.

It was four in the morning by the time he got home. He was in such a piss-poor mood he didn't even bother to turn on the lights.

His answering machine, for once, didn't have one of Kitty's bizarro messages on it. Nothing from Sonja, either. He grunted as he removed his shirt. Was she mad at him? Did he say or do something the last time they were together that ticked her off? It was hard to figure out her moods, since she refused to take off those damn mirrored sunglasses.

Judd wondered, not for the first time, how she could navigate in the dark so well while wearing those fuckers.

Something moved at the corner of his eye. It was the curtain covering the window that faced the alley. Judd frowned as he moved to close the window. Funny, he didn't remember leaving the window open....

She stepped out of the shadows, greeting him with a smile, displaying teeth that were much too sharp. She could smell the adrenaline coursing through him as his system jerked itself into overdrive. He was about to yell for help; then he recognized her. Or thought he did.

"S-Sonja?"

"Did I scare you?" She sounded like Pain given voice. She sniffed the air, and her smile grew even sharper. "Yes. Yes, I *did* scare you, didn't I?" She moved toward him, her hands making slow, hypnotic passes as she spoke. "I *love* the smell of fear in the morning."

"Sonja, what's wrong with your voice?"

"Wrong?" She chuckled as she unzipped her leather jacket. "I always sound like this!"

She was on him so fast he didn't even see her move, lifting him by his belt buckle and flinging him onto the bed so hard he bounced. She grabbed his jaw in one hand, angling it back so the jugular was exposed. Judd heard the *snikt!* of a switchblade and felt a cold, sharp pressure against his throat.

"*Sonja—?*"

"Do not struggle. Do not cry out. Do as I command, and maybe I'll let you live. Maybe."

"What do you want?"

"Why, my dear, I just want to get to know you better." She removed the sunglasses protecting her eyes. "And vice versa."

Judd had often begged Sonja to let him look at her eyes. Were they almond-shaped or round? Blue or brown or green? No doubt he'd always imagined them as looking human, though. Certainly he'd never pictured them as blood-red with pupils so hugely dilated they resembled shoe buttons.

She smirked, savoring the look of disgust on Judd's face. She pressed her lips against his, thrusting his teeth apart with her tongue, and penetrated his will with one quick shove of her mind.

Judd's limbs twitched convulsively as she took control of his nervous system, then went still. She disengaged, physically, and stared down at him. He did not move. She had made sure of that. His body was locked into partial paralysis. Satisfied her control was secure, she moved the switchblade away from Judd's throat.

"I can see why she finds you attractive. You're a pretty thing...*very* pretty." She reached out and pinched one of his nipples. Judd didn't flinch. Of course not. She did not give him permission to.

"But she's much too old-fashioned when it comes to sex, don't you agree? She's afraid to let herself go and walk the wild side. She's *so* repressed." She shrugged out of her leather jacket, allowing it to fall to the floor.

"I will explain this to you once, and once only. I *own* you. If you do as I tell you, and you please me, then you shall be rewarded. Like *this*."

She reached into his cortex and tweaked its pleasure center. Judd shuddered as the wave of ecstasy swept over him, his hips involuntarily humping empty air.

"But if you fight me, or displease me in *any* way — then I will punish you. Like *so*."

Judd emitted a strangled cry of pain as he was speared through the pain receptor in his head. It felt as if the top of his skull had been removed and someone had dumped the contents of an ant farm on his exposed brain. His back arched until the muscles creaked. Then the pain stopped as if it had never been there at all.

"Hold me."

Judd did as he was told, dragging himself upright and wrapping his arms around her waist. She knotted her fingers in his hair, pulling his head back so she could look into his eyes. There was fear there. Fear — and something more. She liked that.

"Am I hurting you? Say yes."

"Yes."

She smiled, exposing her fangs, and he realized then that it was just beginning. The fear in Judd's eyes gave way to terror. And she liked that even more.

✸

They fucked for three solid hours. She skillfully manipulated Judd's pleasure centers so he remained perpetually erect despite exhaustion. She randomly induced orgasms, often one right after another, until they numbered in the dozens. After the seventh or eighth orgasm, Judd was shooting air. She enjoyed how he wailed in pain each time he spasmed.

As dawn began to make its way into the room, she severed her control of Judd's body. He fell away from her in midthrust, his eyes rolled back behind flickering lids. She dressed quickly, her attention fixed on the rising sun. Judd lay curled in a fetal position on the soiled and tangled bedclothes, his naked body shuddering and jerking as his nervous system reasserted its control.

"Parting is such sweet sorrow," she purred, caressing his shivering flank. Judd gasped at her touch but did not pull away.

"You pleased me. This time. So I will let you live. This time."

She lowered her head, brushing his jugular lightly with her lips. Judd squeezed his eyes shut in anticipation of the bite. But all she did was whisper,

"Get used to it, loverboy."

When he opened his eyes again, she was gone.

✸

The Other takes a great deal of pleasure in telling me what it did to Judd, making sure not to leave out a single, nasty detail as it reruns the morning's exploits inside my skull.

My response to the news is to scream and run headfirst into the nearest wall. Then to continue pounding my skull against the floorboards until my glasses shatter and blood streams down my face and mats my hair. I succeed in breaking my nose and shattering both cheekbones before collapsing.

It's not enough.

✸

"Girly-girl! Long time no see! What brings you into my little den of iniquity this time?"

The demon Malfeis sports the exterior of a flabby white male in late middle age, dressed in a loud plaid polyester leisure suit with white buck loafers. A collection of gold medallions dangles under his chins, and he holds a racing form in one hand.

I slide into the booth opposite the demon. "I need magic, Mal."

"Don't we all? Say, what's with the face? You can reconstruct better than that!"

I shrug, one hand straying to my swollen left cheek. The bone squelches under my fingertips and slides slightly askew. Heavy-duty facial reconstruction requires feeding in order for it to be done right, and I deliberately skipped my waking meal.

"You tangle with an ogre? One of those *vargr* punks?"

"Leave it be, Mal."

Malfeis shrugs. "Just trying to be friendly, that's all. Now, what kind of magic are you in the market for?"

"Binding and containment."

The demon grunts and fishes out a pocket calculator. "What are you looking to bind? Ghost? Elemental? Demon? Muse? There's a difference in the prices, you know...."

"Myself."

"Huh?" Mal halts in midcomputation, his exterior flickering for a moment to reveal a hulking creature that resembles an orangutan with a boar's snout.

“You heard me. I wish to have myself bound and contained.”

“Sonja…”

“Name your price, damn you.”

“Don’t be redundant, girlchick.”

I sigh and heft a knapsack onto the tabletop. “I brought some of my finest acquisitions. I’ve got hair shaved from Ted Bundy’s head just before he went to the chair, dried blood scraped from the walls of the LaBianca home, a spent rifle casing from the grassy knoll, and a cedar cigar box with what’s left of Rasputin’s penis in it. Quality shit. I swear by its authenticity. And it’s all yours, if you do this for me.”

Malfeis fidgets, drumming his talons against the table. Such close proximity to so much human suffering and evil is bringing on a jones. “Okay. I’ll do it. But I’m not going to take responsibility for anything that happens to you.”

“Did I ask you to?”

✱

“Are you sure you want to go through with this, Sonja?”

“Your concern touches me, Mal. It really does.”

The demon shakes his head in disbelief. “You really mean to go through with this, don’t you?”

“I’ve already said so, haven’t I?”

“Sonja, you realize once you’re in there, there’s no way you’ll be able to get out, unless someone breaks the seal.”

“Maybe.”

“There’s no *maybe* to it!” he retorts.

“The spell you’re using is for the binding and containing of vampiric energies, right?”

“Of course. You’re a vampire.”

I shrug. “Part of me is. And I’m not letting it out to hurt anyone ever again. I’m going to kill it or die trying.”

“You’re going to *starve* in there!”

“That’s the whole point.”

“Whatever you say, girly-girl.”

I hug myself as I stare into the open doorway of the meat locker. It is cold and dark inside, just like my heart. “Let’s get this show on the road.”

Malfeis nods and produces a number of candles, bottles of oil, pieces of black chalk, and vials of white powder from the black gladstone bag he carries.

I swallow and step inside the meat locker, drawing the heavy door closed behind me with a muffled thump.

— *from the diaries of Sonja Blue*

✸

Malfeis lit the candles and began to chant in a deep, sonorous voice, scrawling elaborate chalk designs on the outer walls of the locker. As the chanting grew faster and more impassioned, he smeared oil on the hinges and handle of the door. There was an electric crackle and the door glowed with blue fire.

Malfeis's incantation lost all semblance of human speech as it reached its climax. He carefully poured a line of white powder, made from equal parts salt, sand, and the crushed bones of unbaptized babies, across the threshold. Then he stepped back to assess his handiwork.

To human eyes it looked as if someone had scrawled graffiti all over the face of the stainless-steel locker, nothing more. But to Pretender eyes, eyes adjusted to the Real World, the door to the locker was barred shut by a tangle of darkly pulsing *vévé*, the semisentient protective symbols of the *voudou* powers. So long as the tableau remained undisturbed, the entity known as Sonja Blue would remain trapped within the chill darkness of the meat locker.

Malfeis replaced the tools of his trade in his gladstone bag. He paused as he left the warehouse, glancing over his shoulder.

"Goodbye, girly-girl. It was nice knowing you."

✸

"I'm looking for Mal."

The bartender looked up from his racing form and frowned at Judd. After taking in his unwashed hair and four-day growth of beard, he nodded in the direction of the back booth.

Judd had never been inside the Monastery before. It had a reputation as being one of the more sleazy — and unsavory — French Quarter dives, and he could see why. The booths lining the wall had once been church pews. Plaster saints in various stages of decay were scattered about on display. A madonna with skin blackened and made leprous by age regarded him from above the bar, staring with flat, faded blue eyes. In her arms lay an equally scabrous Baby Jesus, its uplifted, chubby arms ending in misshapen stumps. Hardly a place to party down big time.

He walked to the back of the bar and looked into the last booth. All he saw was a paunchy, middle-aged man dressed in a bad suit, smoking a cigar and reading a racing form.

"Excuse me…?"

The man in the bad suit looked up at him, arching a bushy, upswept eyebrow.

"Uh, excuse me — but I'm looking for Mal."

"You found him."

Judd blinked, confused. "No, I'm afraid there's been some kind of mistake. The guy I'm looking for is black, with dreadlocks…."

The man in the bad suit smiled. It was not a pleasant sight. "Sit down, kid. He'll be with you in just a moment."

Still uncertain of what he was getting himself into, Judd slid into the opposite pew.

The older man lowered his head, exposing a balding pate, and hunched his shoulders. His fingers and arms began to vibrate, and his skin grew darker, as if his entire body had become suddenly bruised. There was the sound of dry grass rustling under a high wind, and thick, black dreadlocks emerged from his scalp, whipping about like a nest of snakes. Judd was too shocked by the transformation to do anything but stare.

Mal lifted his head and grinned at Judd, tugging at the collar of his turtleneck. "Ah, yes. I remember you now. Sonja's renfield."

"M-my name's not Renfield."

Mal shrugged his indifference. "So, what brings you here, boychick?"

"I'm looking for Sonja. I can't find her."

"She doesn't want to be found."

"I *have* to find her! I just *have* to! Before she does something stupid. Kills herself, maybe!"

Mal regarded the young human for a long moment. "Tell me more."

"Something — happened between us. She feels responsible for hurting me. She sent me this letter a few days ago." Judd fished a folded envelope out of his back pocket and held it out to Mal. "Here — you read it."

The demon plucked the letter out of its envelope like a gourmet removing an escargot from its shell. He unfolded the paper, noting the lack of signature and the smears of blood on its edges.

Judd,

I can never be forgiven for what was done to you. I was not the one who did those things to you. Please believe that. It was her. She is the one that makes me kill and hurt people. Hurt you. I promise I'll never let her hurt anyone, ever again. Especially you. I'm going to do something I should have tried years ago, before she became so strong. So dangerous. So uncontrollable. She's sated right now. Asleep in my head. By the time she becomes aware of what I'm planning to do, it'll be too late. I'm going to kill her. I might end up killing myself in the bargain, but that's a chance I'm willing to take. I won't let her hurt anyone again, damn her. I love you, Judd. Please believe that. Don't try to find me. Escape while you can.

"She doesn't understand." Judd was now close to tears. "I do forgive her. I *love* her, damn it! I can't let her *die*!"

"You know what she is." It wasn't a question.

Judd nodded. "And I don't *care*."

"And why have you come to me?"

"You know where she is, don't you?"

Malfeis shifted in his seat, his eyes developing reptilian slits. "Are you asking me a question?"

Judd hesitated, recalling Sonja's warning that he should *never*, under any circumstances, ask Mal a question.

"Uh, yeah."

Mal smiled, displaying shark's teeth. "Before I respond to any questions put to me, you must pay the price of the answer. Is that understood, boychick?"

Judd swallowed and nodded.

"Very well. Tell me your name. All of it."

"Michael Judd Rieser. Is that it? That's all you want? My name?"

"To know a thing's name gives one power over that thing, my sweet. Didn't they teach you that in school? Come to think of it, I guess not."

"What about my question? Do you know where Sonja is?"

"Yes, I *do* know." The demon scrawled an address on the back of the letter Judd had given him. "You'll find her here. She's inside the meat locker on the ground floor."

"Meat locker?"

"I wouldn't open it if I were you."

Judd snatched up the address and slid out of the pew. "But I'm *not* you!"

As Malfeis watched Judd hurry out of the bar, an amused grin bisected his face. "That's what *you* think, boychick." He leaned back and closed his eyes. When he reopened them, he had shoulder-length hair pulled up in a ponytail, a ring in his nose, and a four-day growth of beard.

✸

It is cold. So very, very cold.

I huddle in the far corner of the meat locker, knees drawn up to my chest. My breath drifts from my mouth and nostrils in wispy fumes before condensing and turning to frost on my face.

How long? How many days have I been in here? Three? Four? Twenty? A hundred? There is no way of telling. I no longer sleep. The Other's screams and curses keep me awake.

Let me out! Let me out of this hellhole! I've got to feed! I'm starving!

"Good."

You stupid cunt! If I starve to death, you go with me! I'm not a damned tapeworm!

"Couldn't prove it by me."

I'm getting out of here! I don't care what you say!

I do not fight the Other as it asserts its ascendancy over my body. The Other forces stiffened limbs to bend, levering me onto my feet. My joints crack like rotten timber as I move. The Other staggers in the direction of the door. In my weakened condition I have difficulty seeing in the pitch-black meat locker. I abandoned the sunglasses days ago, but as my condition worsened, so did my night vision.

The Other's groping hands close on the door's interior handle. There is a sharp crackle and a flash of blue light as the Other is thrown halfway across the locker. It screams and writhes like a cat hit by a car, holding its blistered, smoking hands away from its body. This was the twentieth time it's tried to open the door, and several fingers are on the verge of gangrene.

"You're not going anywhere. Not now. Not ever!"

Fuck you! Fuck you! I'll get you for this, you human-loving cow!

"What? Are you gonna *kill* me?"

I crawl back to my place in the corner. The effort starts me coughing again, bringing up black, clotted blood. I wipe at my mouth with the sleeve of my jacket, nearly dislocating my jaw in the process.

You're falling apart. You're too weak to regenerate properly....

"If you hadn't pounded your head against the fuckin' wall trying to get out in the *first* place—"

You're the one who got us locked up in here! Don't blame me!

"I *am* blaming you. But not for that."

It's that fucking stupid human again! You think you can punish me for that? I didn't do anything that you hadn't already fantasized about!

"You *raped* him, damn you! You almost killed him!"

I didn't, though. I could have. But I didn't.

"I *love* him!" My voice cracks, becomes a sob.

You don't love him. You love being mistaken for human. That's what you're mad about: not that I molested your precious loverboy, but that I ruined your little game of Let's Pretend!

"Shut up."

Make me.

— *from the diaries of Sonja Blue*

✸

Judd checked the street number of the warehouse against the address that Mal had given him. It was one of the few remaining warehouses in the district that had not been turned into trendy yuppie condo-apartments. There was a small sign posted on the front door that read "Indigo Imports," but nothing else. A heavy chain and double padlock secured the entrance, and all the ground-floor windows had burglar bars. But there had to be *some* way of getting in and out. He rounded the side of the building and spotted the loading dock. After a few minutes of determined tugging, he succeeded in wrenching one of the sliding corrugated metal doors sufficiently ajar to slip through.

The inside of the warehouse was lit by the midafternoon sunlight slanting through the barred windows. The whole place smelled of dust and rat piss.

The meat locker was on the ground floor, just where Mal had said it would be. Its metal walls and door were covered in swirls of spray-painted graffiti. What looked like a huge line of coke marked the locker's threshold. Judd grabbed the door's handle and yanked it open. There was a faint crackling sound, like that of static electricity, and a rush of cold, foul air. He squinted into the darkness, covering his nose and breathing through his mouth to try to offset the stench.

"Sonja?"

Something moved in the deepest shadows of the freezer.

✸

"J-Judd? Is that you?"

"It's me, baby. I've come to get you out of here."

"Go away, Judd. You don't know what you're doing."

Judd steps into the locker, his eyes adjusting to the gloom. He sees me now, crouching in the far corner with my knees drawn against my chest, my face turned to the wall.

"No, you're wrong, Sonja. I know *exactly* what I'm doing."

"I let her hurt you, Judd. I could have stopped her, but I didn't. I let her

— let her—" My voice grows tight and my shoulders begin to shake. "Go away, Judd. Go away before I hurt you again!"

Judd kneels beside me. I smell like a side of beef gone bad. My hands are covered with blisters and oozing sores. Some of the fingers jut at odd angles, because they healed without being properly set. I pull away at his touch, pressing myself against the wall as if I can squeeze between the cracks if I try hard enough.

"Don't look at me."

"Sonja, you don't understand. I love you. I know what you are, what you're capable of — and I love you *anyway*."

"Even if I hurt you?"

"*Especially* when you hurt me."

I turn my head in his direction. My face looks as if it has been smashed, then reassembled by a well-meaning, but inept, plastic surgeon who had only a blurry photograph to go by. My eyes glow like those of an animal pinned in the headlights of an oncoming car.

"What?"

Judd leans closer, his eyes reflecting a hunger I know all too well. "When you did those things to me, at first I was scared. Then, after awhile, I realized I wasn't frightened anymore. I was actually getting into it. It was like the barriers between pain and pleasure, animal and human, ecstasy and horror, had been removed! I've never known anything like it before! I love you, Sonja! *All* of you!"

I reach out and caress his face with one of my charred hands. A renfield. The Other turned him into a renfield. And he doesn't even know it, the poor sap. In the space of just a few hours he was transformed into a junkie, and now I'm his fix.

"I love you, too, Judd. Kiss me."

I want to think I am being merciful.

✷

I sit behind the wheel of the car for a long time, staring out into the darkness on the other side of the windshield. Nothing has changed since the last time I was out here, disposing of Kitty.

I press my fingertips against my right cheek, and this time it holds. My fingers are healed and straight again. I readjust my shades and open the car door and slide out from behind the wheel of the Caddy I bought off the lot, cash in hand, earlier that evening.

Judd is in the trunk, divvied up into six garbage bags, just like Kitty. At least it was fast. My hunger was so intense that I drained him within seconds.

He didn't try to fight when I buried my fangs in his throat, even though I didn't have the strength to trance him. Maybe part of him knew I was doing him a favor.

I drag the bags out of the trunk and head in the direction of the alligator calls. I have to leave New Orleans, maybe for good this time. Kitty might not have been missed, but Judd is another story. Arlo is sure to mention the missing Judd's weirdo new girlfriend to the authorities.

It is time to blow town and head for Merida. Time to go and pay Palmer a visit and check on how he and the baby are making out.

Palmer.

Funny how I'd forgotten about him. Of all my human companions, he is the only one I've come close to loving. Before Judd.

I hurl the sacks containing Judd's remains into the water and return to the car. I try not to hear the noise the gators make as they fight among themselves.

I climb back into the car and slam a cassette into the Caddy's tapedeck. Lard's "The Last Temptation of Reid" thunders through the speakers, causing the steering wheel to vibrate under my hands. I wonder when the emptiness will go away. Or at least be replaced by pain. Anything would be preferable to the nothing inside me.

I don't see why you had to go and kill him like that. We could have used a renfield. They do come in handy, now and then. Besides, he was kind of cute....

"Shut up and drive."

—from the diaries of Sonja Blue

It was late afternoon, sliding toward evening, and Palmer was out in the courtyard, hammering together a shipping crate for a collection of hand-painted Dio de los Muertos masks. The masks — made of papier-mâché and painted in primary colors so bright you could still see them when you closed your eyes — were piled in a small heap nearby, grimacing blindly at the failing sun.

Palmer dropped his hammer and straightened up, massaging his lower back. He pulled a bandanna from his pocket and mopped his brow. God, he hated this part of the business. Building the crates for shipping was a relatively minor hassle. Loading up the Land Rover and taking it into the city were the real ball-busters. Still, the pay was pretty good, and money went a lot farther in Yucatan than it did back in the U.S.

He looked down, and his gaze fell across the masks in their nest of excelsior. He'd bought them as part of a larger job lot from a family of artisans who'd been producing carnival decorations for over four generations. Until now, he hadn't paid that much attention to them. He sifted through the collection, studying the workmanship. Most of the masks were small, designed to cover the face of a child. All of the traditional carnival personas were represented: there were skeletons, their teeth bared in aggressive, lipless grins; what were supposed to be tigers, judging by the stripes, but looked more like jaguars, broom-straw whiskers bristling from their snarling muzzles; blood-red devils with grease-pencil mustaches and shoe-polish goatees, licorice-black horns jutting from their foreheads; grinning clowns whose noses and chins met, like the Punchinello puppets of medieval Europe.

Yet there were less typical false-faces scattered throughout: a sheep's head, the wool cunningly made from balls of cotton; a wolf, fangs bared in a predatory snarl; a rooster caught in midcrow, its beak open and throat sac extended. Palmer chuckled to himself as he sifted through the empty masks, remembering Halloweens spent dressed as pirates, cowboys, hoboes and other exotica.

Then he found the black mask.

It was at the very bottom of the pile. He frowned and picked it up, turning it over in his hands. Like the others, it was papier-mâché. Unlike the others, it was adult-sized. And, except for the eye holes, it was without features of any kind. There were no overly exaggerated human or animal characteristics, merely an oval painted black and coated with several layers of varnish, so that it shone like a scarab's carapace. There was something oddly compelling about the mask — something that made him set it aside from the others as he prepared to load them into their crate.

It was dusk by the time he finished driving the last nail into place. He tossed the hammer back into the toolbox and stepped back to appraise his handiwork.

A bootheel scraped behind him. Palmer spun, his mind bristling. A figure stood in the door leading to the front of the house. Whatever had breached the security of his home could not be human, or else he would have heard — or at least felt — its thoughts long before it reached the front door.

Before Palmer could launch his psionic strike, the figure laughed dryly and stepped from the shadows.

"Hello, Bill. Did you miss me?"

"Sonja!"

She stood there looking tired, her leather jacket powdered with road dust, her mirrored shades equally grimy. In one hand she held a battered black nylon duffel bag, in the other a neatly wrapped present bound with colored twine. She smiled tightly, as if the corners of her mouth concealed fishhooks. Her head was surrounded by a blackish-red halo that strobed and pulsated like a lava lamp. The Other was very active tonight, it seemed. Palmer tried not to let his dismay taint his own aura.

He hugged her, savoring the smell of her as he pressed his face into her hair. For a moment her shoulders seemed to quiver, as if struggling to shrug off an invisible burden.

"Auntie Blue! Auntie Blue!"

Palmer and Sonja stepped apart as Lethe bounded onto the patio, grinning broadly. Dressed in a Teenage Mutant Ninja Turtle t-shirt and a pair of bright yellow stirrup pants, she could have passed for a normal child — except for her golden, pupil-less eyes. Shambling in her wake, Fido paused at the sight of Sonja. Although Palmer could rarely "read" the *seraph*'s aura, he knew that it, too, was disturbed by evidence of the Other's activity.

Sonja smiled and the stress drained from her face at the sight of her godchild. She dropped down on one knee, opening her arms wide. "C'mere and give me a hug, sweetie!"

Lethe shot into Sonja's arms like an arrow, clinging to her tightly. "Are you staying this time, Auntie? Are you really staying for good?"

"Maybe not for good — but at least for a couple of months. Here, let me get a look at you.... You've grown, child! Hasn't she, Bill?"

"Eighteen inches in the last six months."

"Did you bring me something, Auntie Blue?"

Sonja laughed and ruffled Lethe's dark hair. "Here you go, darling. I just hope you haven't gotten too big for dolls...."

"I'll never be too big for dolls! They're my babies!"

Palmer stepped forward, gently nudging Lethe in the direction of the house. "Lethe, why don't you and Fido go play with your new doll? Auntie Blue and I have some things to talk about. And tell her thank you for the gift."

"Okay, Daddy. Thank you, Auntie!"

Sonja watched as Lethe skipped away, Fido lumbering after her like a demented pull-toy. "She's big, Bill. Too big for thirty months."

"You're telling me? That's why I've been trying to get you to come home — we need to figure out what to do with her."

✷

Several hours passed before they could be alone. First Palmer had to prepare dinner for those members of the household who actually ate food, then they had to go through the process of readying Lethe for bed. After baths and bedtime stories, it was close to midnight before he could join Sonja on the front porch. He found her curled up in the hammock, watching the night sky. She was still wearing her sunglasses.

"I brought some refreshments," he said, holding up a bottle of tequila. "Any room there for me?"

"Maybe," Sonja smiled, moving so he could join her.

Palmer cracked the seal on the bottle and took a hefty swig before placing it on the floorboards of the porch. He lifted his arm and Sonja flowed into its hollow like a shadow, one cheek pressing against his breastbone. They lay there for a long moment, Palmer idly stroking her hair.

"Things are getting weird, Sonja."

She lifted her head from his chest and gave him a quizzical look. "'Getting'? I thought they'd been there for some time now!"

"You know what I mean. This stuff with Lethe is getting out of hand — I don't know what to expect from one day to the next! Hell, this time last year she looked like she was ready for kindergarten! Now she looks like she should be in the fourth grade!"

"Is she giving you problems?"

"No — far from it. She's an angel. A little rambunctious at times, but she's no real trouble. But she's starting to want to go with me on my trips to the city. She's becoming curious about the outside world. We can't keep her hidden away forever, Sonja."

"We can't risk anyone finding out about her. You know that as well as I do. If Morgan finds out where she is, there's no telling what he'd do to her. Or with her. I promised her parents I'd never let Lethe fall into that bastard's hands. Besides, the locals would probably not look kindly on a child as — unique — as Lethe."

"I realize that, Sonja. It's just that — well, it's not natural for her to be alone like this! All she has in the way of playmates are Fido, Lefty and me. That's hardly what I'd call a 'well-rounded' play atmosphere."

"What do you expect me to do? I know as much about Lethe's true nature as you do. Hell, you probably know more, since you're the one who actually takes care of her. As far as I can tell, she's a healthy little girl who just happens to be somewhat — advanced — for her age. There's nothing either of us can do except try to take care of her and wait to see what will happen. And as to her having playmates...well, Fido and Lefty will have to do for the time being. At least she isn't being raised by the lousy TV set!"

The subject was closed. Palmer knew enough not to reopen it. At least not now. He took another hit from the tequila bottle, offering it to Sonja. She shook her head.

"So...how was New Orleans?"

Her body tensed, like a cat preparing to leap. "Fine. Why do you ask?"

"No reason. Just curious, that's all. That's where we first met, after all. Remember?"

"Yeah. I remember."

"Hey, what's wrong? You're really tense, you know that? I feel like I'm cuddling an ironing board!"

"Sorry," she muttered, pulling away from him. "I guess I'm not ready to relax yet. It's just that I—" She let the sentence trail off.

"Just what? Did something happen in New Orleans?"

She turned her mirrored gaze away from him. "I had some trouble with the Other. Bad stuff."

"Want to tell me about it?"

Silence.

Palmer took another hit from the tequila and began to climb free of the hammock. "I better go check on Lethe…."

Sonja touched his arm. "No, you stay here. Let me do it."

Palmer shrugged and settled back. "Whatever. Bring me back a couple of beers, won't you?"

"Sure thing." As Sonja entered the house she paused on the threshold, fixing Palmer with her unreadable eyes. "Do you love me?"

Palmer looked up, slightly taken aback by the question. She rarely spoke the word "love" with her mouth — only her mind. "Of course I love you!" He gave a short laugh to show how silly a question it was.

She paused, as if weighing his response. "Why?"

Palmer blinked, his smile slowly dissolving into a frown. "I just love you, that's all."

"Oh." Again the pause. "I'll be back with your beer in a few minutes."

Palmer sat in the hammock under the starlit sky, listening to the calls of the night birds, and wondered what the hell had gone down in New Orleans.

✷

The door to Lethe's bedroom was slightly ajar, allowing light from the hall to filter in, so Lethe wouldn't wake up in the middle of the night and be scared to find herself alone in the dark. Sonja was uncertain whether Lethe was actually scared of the dark or not, but it seemed the proper thing to do.

She stuck her head inside the door, her eyes automatically adjusting to the dim light. Lethe lay on her side, her back to the door, surrounded by a multitude of dolls. She had kicked off her bedclothes. Sonja stepped inside the room, quiet as a shadow, and stooped to retrieve the discarded covers. As she straightened up, there was a motion at the corner of her eye.

Fido had moved from its sentinel position at the foot of the bed, its eyes glowing like molten ore. Although she knew the *seraph* meant her no harm, Sonja felt the hair on her scalp prickle and a low, guttural growl begin deep inside her chest.

Lethe rolled over and opened her eyes, smiling beatifically. "Don't be afraid, Auntie Blue. Fido's just protectin' me, that's all."

"Why should he have to protect you from me? I'd never hurt you, sweetie."

"I know, Auntie. But the Other would. It wants to hurt me right now, doesn't it?"

Smart little fucker, isn't she?

"I would never let the Other harm you, Lethe. You know that."

"I know, Auntie Blue. But Fido isn't so sure."

✸

Palmer started from a light doze as a Tecate, still dripping ice from the cooler, was pressed into his hand. He jerked awake like a science-lab frog zapped by a dry-cell battery.

"Uhn! Oh — thanks." He tilted back the bottle for a quick chug. Sonja straddled him as he lay in the hammock. Except for her sunglasses, she was naked.

She perched atop his crotch, the moonlight outlining her body in silver and shadow. Her breasts were still as full, her stomach and thighs just as taut as he remembered. Palmer set aside his beer and reached up with one damp hand to tweak her nipples. They were cool and hard between his fingers, like smooth little stones.

She reached down with one hand and yanked open his denim shirt as if it were made of newspaper, sending buttons flying in every direction. Lowering herself atop him, she slid her legs down his, wrapping her arms around his neck. Palmer caressed her naked hips and she moved to fill his hand, like a cat eager to be stroked. A heady rush of arousal and fear surged through him, as it always did before their lovemaking.

On a deep, instinctual level, Palmer knew the beautiful creature that fondled him was death personified — yet, on an intellectual level, he trusted her not to kill him. His physical excitement came from the knowledge that his lover could, at any given moment, tear him apart like fresh bread.

The moment his fly was open, Palmer's penis leapt free. He closed his eyes as Sonja took him into her mouth, exhaling a long sigh as the curvature of her fangs glided against the head of his penis. A sane man would go limp knowing razor-sharp teeth encircled his cock. But Palmer hadn't been sane in a long while. Trembling, he pulled her head away from his crotch, gasping between his teeth as he fought to regain control.

She moved quickly, lowering herself onto him before he could protest. Palmer reached up to cup her breasts and, with a firm upward thrust of his hips, penetrated both her body and her mind. To tell the truth, he missed the mental bonding more than he missed the physical aspects of sex. He could always jerk off when she was gone, but there was no such thing as masturbatory telepathy. And without further effort, he surrendered all thought and self; all barriers dissolved before the bond.

✸

Once again Palmer found himself in the other-place he and Sonja shared during their trysts. As he moved through a gray space that was neither air nor water, he was uncertain whether he was flying or swimming. It was warm and comforting, like he imagined the womb must be.

Sonja emerged from the gray, as swift and sure as a shark in its element; her features were blurred by speed, her arms and legs impossibly long and tapered. Her hair was a dark blur, trailing behind her like jet exhaust. She looked more like a nude painted by an Impressionist than a flesh-and-blood woman.

She wrapped herself around Palmer, and he wrapped his own limbs about her, pulling her into himself. Thoughts, feelings, perceptions jittered between them like static electricity. Their inner voices grew alternately louder and softer as they merged. This sharing of self and experience, more than anything else, was how they managed to 'catch up' with one another after so many months apart. Sonja's face floated inside his mind's eye, the features softened by release as she flowed into him and he into her.

(missed you…)

(need you…)

(love you…)

(worried…)

(gone so long…)

(love you…)

(judd…)

(?judd?)

Sonja's eyes went hard and cold and suddenly Palmer was no longer in the warm gray place, but falling, plummeting through space as if he had stepped from the edge of a cliff into the deepest, darkest pit in the Carlsbad Cavern. It felt as if he were spiraling down, down, down into the mouth of Hell itself. The transition was so sudden that he didn't even have the time or breath to scream for his life.

He hit hard, but because he was not a physical thing, there were no broken bones. He groaned and got to his feet, surveying his new surroundings. The first thing he felt was the wind, cutting into him like a flaying knife. He was in the middle of a vast arctic ice field; a dark, moon-haunted sky stretched over his head. In the far distance he could make out the humps of vast glacier-bound mountains. As he turned around, shuddering in the frigid mind-winds, he marveled at the frozen desolation surrounding him. Nothing could be seen but an empty tract of ice, gleaming blackly in the moonlight. As far as he could tell, he was the only living thing for thousands of miles in any direction.

(sonja?)

There was no answer to his mind-call as it echoed across the frozen sea.

(SONJA!)

Nothing moved or waved or responded to his cry.

Exasperated, and starting to get a little scared, Palmer struck off in the direction of the full moon on the horizon. He didn't know why — it simply seemed like the thing to do. He had never gotten lost inside anyone before — at least he assumed the icebound tundra was Sonja's mental construct, not his own. But he was certain he would have to rely on his instincts if he wanted to get out of this mess.

The ice was smooth beneath his feet, at least ten feet thick, but he didn't have any trouble moving across the glasslike surface. He had gone a mile, possibly more, before he realized he was being followed by something below the ice.

It appeared to be a shadow — black and amorphous beneath the thick layer of ice. For a moment Palmer experienced a surge of blind fear, recalling a nature documentary he'd once seen on PBS where a killer whale stalked a seal sunning itself on a floe, smashing its way through several feet of ice to snatch the hapless beast and drag it to its death.

Struggling to remain calm, he reminded himself that he was nowhere near the Arctic Circle and that whatever might be lurking beneath the ice, it certainly wasn't a killer whale. Marshaling his courage, he dropped to his knees, wiping with numbed hands at the fine layer of dry snow covering the ice, peering intently at the thing beneath. It was probably Sonja, no doubt trying to find him.

(sonja?)

Twin fires ignited underneath the ice, glowing like embers from hell's furnace. Only then did Palmer realize what he'd stumbled across. He opened his mouth to scream for help, but it was too late. The Other knew he was there. And unprotected.

Arms burst through the ice floe, the skin cold and hard and blue. The hands were those of a crone, with hooked, cracked nails. They flailed about blindly, seeking purchase on the slippery surface. The Other pulled itself out of its frozen grave, like a woman wriggling free of a girdle. The head emerged after the arms, the hair transformed into a dark sunburst by rapidly forming icicles. The eyes burned with anger, and the lips seemed obscenely full, like freshly fed leeches. They pulled back into a predator's grin of anticipation, revealing shriveled black gums and the teeth of a killing thing. Yet as demonic as the Other's features were, there was a horrible familiarity to them — like those of a loved one's picture torn to shreds and pasted back together by inexpert hands.

(Look who's come to pay me a visit!)

The Other's mind-voice sounded like a clotted kitchen sink trying to approximate human speech. It made Palmer ill to feel its cold, hateful venom leaking into his consciousness.

(give me a kiss, loverboy!)

He smashed his fist into its face as hard as he could. Blood the color and consistency of transmission fluid flew from the Other's nostrils. It laughed — a sound that resembled a cross between a lion roaring and a toilet backing up. The Other's laugh made him hit it harder — and harder — but all it did was laugh and laugh and laugh.

Suddenly Palmer was back in his own body. He landed two more blows before he realized he was hitting Sonja.

Somehow he had gotten astride her and pinned her throat with his left hand while his right rose and fell, rose and fell. She lay underneath him, her face smeared with something sticky. Her sunglasses had fallen off, revealing eyes the color of a dying sun. In the dark, the pale ichor that passed for blood among her kind looked almost normal. Palmer stared at his lover's bruised and swollen face — the damage already righting itself before his stunned eyes — then at his right hand. It was still clenched in a fist. He slowly opened it, as if expecting a stinging insect to fly out.

"Oh, God. God. I'm sorry Sonja — I don't know what happened. I was — I thought I was fighting — I must have flipped out. I didn't mean to hurt you—"

She smiled then — the slow, lazy smile of satiation — and placed a finger on his trembling lips, halting his babbled apology.

"Hush."

"But—"

"I said hush." She pulled him down to her, pressing his face between her breasts. He could not have escaped her embrace even if he tried.

They lay together for a long time until Palmer finally fell asleep. In his dreams he heard the groan of approaching glaciers and the echo of inhuman laughter.

They had sex every night after that — sometimes more than once. But the telepathic communion they had once shared was now strained, bordering on the nonexistent. Sonja was always guarded during their trysts, her psionic defenses at ready. It was as if she did not dare allow herself to relax, even during the most intimate of moments. Palmer was uncertain whether she was afraid of the Other getting out or him getting in.

She became a blank wall as far as he was concerned — unreadable and impenetrable, shrugging off his attempts at psychic rapport. While her mental frigidity bothered him, Palmer never pressed the issue. Whatever secrets Sonja kept locked inside herself were hers and hers alone.

As the telepathic aspect of their relationship dwindled, the sadistic side grew. The first time she came to him with the whip, he threw it down. He yelled his defiance. He did not want to play that game. He refused to hurt her. Then she took off her sunglasses and looked at him with those terrible eyes mutated beyond tears, and something within him broke.

He beat her until the blood flew, stippling the walls and spotting the bare lightbulb hanging over the bed. He beat her until his arm ached and the whip fell from numbed fingers. All to meet her need. She *needed* his blows. Needed them as much as his caresses. Maybe more. Palmer did not know what sins she hoped to expiate with stinging leather kisses and roses fashioned of swollen flesh and splattered blood, nor did he want to. Some things are sacred. Even to monsters.

✸

About a week after her arrival home, Palmer awoke to find the bed empty. His first thought was of Lethe, and his heart leapt in fear. He hurried to the child's bedroom, but Lethe was sound asleep. He felt a surge of shame. Sonja would no more harm Lethe than he would. He looked out the window at the nearby forest. No doubt she was out hunting. After all, she *was* nocturnal.

He returned to his room to find her crawling in through the window. She was completely nude, her mouth and belly smeared with fresh blood.

"Sonja?"

She turned like a startled cat, hissing a warning. The hairs on his testicles stood on end as he realized he was looking into the face of the Other.

The Other spoke in a gravelly, slurred baritone, sounding like a cleverly remixed version of Sonja's normal voice. "So — loverboy's still up! Why does she keep you around, Palmer? It can't be the way you fuck!"

The Other laughed as Palmer flinched. She licked the blood smearing the back of her hand, as if she were a cat cleaning itself.

"I want to talk to Sonja."

"Tough titty, asshole," the Other growled, dropping onto the bed. "She ain't here."

"Then I'll wait until she gets back," Palmer said, folding his arms.

"Back off, renfield!" the Other snapped, baring her fangs in ritual display. "I'm not in the mood!"

There was a sound from the direction of the door, and the Other fell silent, something resembling fear flickering across its face. Palmer glanced over his shoulder and saw Fido standing on the threshold, his eyes glowing in the dark. When Palmer turned his attention back to the Other, Sonja was sitting there, looking puzzled. Fido turned and lumbered back toward Lethe's room.

"Bill?" She frowned at the blood drying on her belly. She swiped her finger along the smear and tasted it, grimacing slightly. "Don't worry, it's not human—" She glanced back up at him. "Why are you looking at me that way?"

"You went out hunting and the Other came back."

She shifted uncomfortably. "Did — did it say anything?"

"About what?"

Her eyes flashed angrily and for a heart-stopping moment Palmer was afraid the Other had returned. "Did it talk?"

"Yeah, but it didn't say much. Told me I was a lousy lay, if that's what you mean."

"That's not true, you know that."

"Do I?" Palmer knelt beside her on the bed, taking her hands into his.

"Sonja — what's wrong? What happened in New Orleans that you're not telling me—?"

She looked at him, her dark-adapted pupils so dilated they filled her eyes. The sadness inside her pressed against him, wrapping him in stifling grayness. Her depression filled his lungs, crushing the breath from him. His heart seemed first to swell, then to wither as the misery inside her sought to pull him down into its depths. Palmer knew that if he succumbed to the vortex, he would be lost. Marshaling all his strength, both physical and mental, he drew back and punched her as hard as he could, right in the face.

He told himself it wasn't cruelty. It was self-preservation. The gray pain had retreated from his mind. In its place was a red-hot coal of anger, betrayal — arousal.

He hit her again.

And again.

And again.

His orgasm took him by surprise. He looked down, blinking in confusion, at his wilting penis. He hadn't even touched himself. Sonja lay, face down, on the bed, her body twisted in sheets smeared with her blood and sweat and Palmer's spent seed. She didn't seem to be moving.

"Sonja?"

No response. His fists ached from the pounding they'd administered. His body trembled like a plucked guitar string.

"Sonja?"

He rolled her over. Her body was so heavy, so limp. Her face was a mess of blood, pulped cartilage and shattered bone. The walls looked as if someone had tried to clean a dirty paintbrush by flicking it dry. Her brain sounded like a radio tuned to an empty channel.

Bile rising in his throat, Palmer lurched to his feet and headed for the bathroom. He locked the door behind him and splashed water on his face. When he looked up, he found himself — haggard and drawn — staring out from the mirror. There was a mad gleam in the eyes — one he recognized. He'd seen its like in the eyes of the humans in the service of the vampires Pangloss and Morgan. Renfields. They called them renfields.

The Other had called him renfield.

Palmer placed his bruised and bleeding hands against his eyes. The screech and squall of the world-mind pressed against his head, threatening to breach his barriers and inundate him with others' fears, hopes, dreams, secrets and sins until his individuality, his consciousness was erased.

"Stop it!" he yelled at an old lady in Poughkeepsie, who couldn't decide whether or not to put down her cancer-ridden poodle. "Get out of my head!"

he screeched at an aging businessman in Taipei, who was worried about his waning potency. "Leave me alone!" he bellowed at a Nazi war criminal in Paraguay, who was certain he was being followed by an Israeli task force.

"Bill?"

He jerked open the bathroom door. Sonja was standing on the other side, her cheekbones already restructuring themselves, her lips deflating, the bruises covering her eyes fading from black to blue to yellow.

"You alright in there?"

He had failed her. He would always fail her. She was insatiable. How could he hope to satisfy a woman who healed within minutes? Palmer wondered if he would ever be able to fuck a woman again without trying to kill her.

As he lay beside her on the bloodstained bed, watching the dawn chase the shadows across the walls of their room, he wondered what was worse: thinking that he'd killed her, or being disappointed she was alive.

✸

Later that day, while Palmer was building yet another shipping crate — this time for obscene pull-toys: terra-cotta figurines sporting enormous penises with wheels affixed to the glans — Lethe came out onto the patio to watch him. She was carrying the black mask he'd kept from the previous shipment.

"Where's Auntie Blue?"

"Auntie Blue's sleeping. You know she sleeps during the day, Lethe."

"Not all the time."

"You're right — sometimes she's awake during the day. But only under special circumstances."

Lethe held up the mask so that it covered her face. Her eyes, golden and pupil-less, shone in the empty sockets. For some reason it made Palmer's flesh creep.

"Put that thing away!"

Lethe flinched at the sharpness in his voice, and Palmer inwardly cursed himself. His problems with Sonja were beginning to reflect in his attitude toward others. He opened his mouth to tell Lethe he was sorry — that he hadn't meant to bark at her like that — but she was already back inside the house.

Lefty crawled out from under a pile of excelsior and began playing with one of the pull-toys, rolling it back and forth on its wobbly hand-carved wheels. Palmer set aside his tools and massaged the back of his neck, grimacing down at his former incarnation's left hand.

"Well, I screwed the pooch that time, didn't I, Lefty? Just like last night. I should have toughed it out — ridden out the depression until I got to the heart of what's been bugging Sonja, but I was weak. I freaked and took the easy way out, because I was afraid of being alone with the Other again. It's not that I don't want to help her, it's just that she's making it so damned hard...." Palmer shook his head and grimaced in disgust. "Jesus! I must be crazier than I thought! I'm telling a disembodied hand about my woman trouble!"

✸

Lethe stood in the house and looked out the window facing the courtyard. Daddy was squatting down, talking to Lefty and looking sad. Lethe knew Daddy didn't want to be mean to her. She knew he was having problems — something to do with Auntie Blue. Still, Lethe's feelings were hurt. She looked down at the black mask she held in her hands. It was turned toward her, the empty eyes and mouth staring up at her, as if awaiting an answer.

Sighing to herself, Lethe placed the mask on her stepfather's work table, where she'd first found it. She wondered what she would do to pass the day. She was tired of playing by herself and she'd read all her books so many times she'd lost interest in them. Daddy tried hard to keep up with her needs, but at thirty months she'd long outgrown Laura Ingalls Wilder, Frank L. Baum, and Robert Louis Stevenson. Even David Copperfield and Huckleberry Finn were no longer challenging.

She wished Daddy would let her go into town with him. She really wanted to see other children, other people, other places. There was the video player and its monitor, but seeing pictures of things wasn't the same as experiencing them. All her life — for as far back as she could remember — she had been kept away from what Daddy called "normal people."

Daddy and Auntie Blue agreed that "normal people" would not understand her. She was different — and "normal people" don't like things that are different. They would look at her eyes and get scared. They'd want to take her away from Daddy and Auntie Blue and put her in some horrible place where they would experiment on her. The other reason Daddy refused to take her anywhere was fear of the Bad Man finding her. Lethe knew the Bad Man's real name was Morgan, and that he'd done something to hurt Auntie Blue a long time ago. She also knew that he was, somehow, related to her. Like a grandfather. Auntie Blue said the Bad Man killed Lethe's real mommy and daddy, back when Lethe was a little baby.

Lethe couldn't remember much of what happened back then. What memories she did have were of being hungry or cold or wet — baby stuff. If she thought about it really hard, she could dredge up a memory of someone warm and dark, who smelled like milk. When Lethe told Auntie Blue about it, she told her she was remembering her real mother, Anise. When Lethe asked if Anise was Auntie Blue's sister, she said they'd had the same father. So did Lethe's real daddy, Fell. Lethe couldn't remember *him* at all. The first time she'd been told that Daddy wasn't really her flesh-and-blood father, she'd burst into tears and clutched his pants legs, terrified that she was going to be taken away. But that was back when she was a little kid and didn't know any better — twenty months ago.

Now she was growing up — faster than Daddy — or even Auntie Blue — could possibly realize. The only one who knew that her childhood was nearing its end was Fido. Fido talked to her at night while she was asleep. Well, he didn't really *talk*. Not with his mouth, anyway. But he didn't talk with his head, the way Daddy and Auntie Blue did at times, either. It was more like he *felt* things to her.

Fido was as important a part of her life as Daddy, even though he never did things like fix her peanut-butter-and-banana sandwiches or buy her toys or read Dr. Seuss to her before going to bed. Fido made sure she was safe. It was his presence, more than anything else, that ensured that the Bad Man would never be able to find her. It was his job — or "destiny," as he called it — to make sure she grew up, so she could fulfill *her* destiny. (Fido used destiny a lot whenever he talked to her.)

Even now, as she thought of him, Fido lumbered into view. He was big and bulky and shaggy, like a Saint Bernard given human form, wrapped in filthy castoff sweaters with newspapers stuffed in his boots. Daddy said Fido looked like a homeless person, which confused Lethe somewhat, because Fido had always lived in their house. She knew it took a lot of energy for Fido to maintain his physical form, and that he would be a lot happier if he could go around without his body slowing him down, but it was important for him to remain manifested on the physical plane, at least for as long as she required protecting. Which wouldn't be much longer. Fido was kind of excited about the prospect of being able to rejoin his brother-sisters, but part of him was sad, too, because this meant Lethe was growing up and wouldn't need him anymore. Lethe tried to cheer him up and told him she'd *always* need him, but they both knew it wasn't true.

Growing up was scary, but then everything really important is kind of scary, once you think about it. Soon she wouldn't be able to turn to Daddy for help, or rely on Fido for protection. Her success or failure would be totally up to her and nobody else. Part of her cringed at the thought of so much responsibility. But, at the same time, growing up meant she would finally be free to see the world and everything in it firsthand. She could go to town, if she wanted — or anywhere else on the face of the planet. Thinking about growing up made her scared and excited all at once, mixing her up inside.

Lethe padded down the hall to the bedroom Daddy shared with Auntie Blue whenever she was home. The door was shut but not locked, so Lethe was able to get in. The room was very dark and stiflingly hot. No human could possibly sleep in such a sweatbox, but Auntie Blue lay on the bed, covered by a sheet.

Lethe moved to the bed while Fido hung back. Auntie Blue didn't like Fido. She said he made her nervous. What she meant was that the Other was scared of him. Lethe sent Fido to go and scare the Other away the other night because she could tell it wanted to hurt Daddy. Lethe knew Auntie Blue loved Daddy, but she sometimes had a hard time controlling the Other.

Auntie Blue lay cold, white and silent on the bed. She wasn't wearing any clothes under the sheet. She wasn't breathing and she wasn't sweating, although the room's temperature must have been over ninety degrees There was what looked like blood smeared on the pillowcases and sheets, and the room smelled like stinky socks. Lethe looked back at Fido, who shuffled back and forth at the threshold.

"It's okay, Fido. The Other's asleep, too."

Lethe gently brushed aside a lock of dark hair from her stepmother's forehead and kissed her brow. Sonja's skin was cool and dry under her lips.

"Bye, Auntie Blue," she whispered. "Thanks for helping me get born."

✷

Palmer decided to fix Lethe's favorite meal as a peace offering and went to her room to tell her to wash up.

"Lethe? Time for dinner! I made pigs-in-a-blanket — how does that sound? Lethe—?"

Fido looked up from his guardpost at the foot of Lethe's bed, his eyes unreadable as ever. There was no sign of Lethe amongst the jumble of dolls and stuffed animals. In the space where she normally slept was what looked like a sleeping bag made of translucent yellow plastic.

"What the—?" Palmer stepped forward, frowning. Maybe it was something Sonja had brought back for Lethe from New Orleans....

As he got closer, he could tell that whatever it was, it sure as hell wasn't a sleeping bag. Almost four feet long and two feet around, the thing seemed to pulse and glow from within. And even though he could not see enough of her to make a positive identification, he knew whose small, slender body hung suspended in its amber core.

"Lethe!"

Palmer lunged at the cocoon to tear it open and yank his daughter free. The moment his fingers brushed the outer casing, a surge of psychic energy shot up his arms and into his brain, hurling him backward as if he'd tried to scale an electric fence.

As he shook his head to clear it, Fido moved to stand between him and the bed. The *seraph*'s arms were outspread, its chin lowered in what Palmer recognized as a protective stance.

Palmer's legs were wobblier than a newborn colt's and his nose was dripping blood, but otherwise he was unharmed. "Damn you! Stand aside!" he snapped as he got to his feet.

Fido did not move.

"She's hurt! I've got to help her!"

Fido's arms wavered for a second, then lowered.

Palmer stepped forward.

The second blast kicked him into the hall. His goatee and hair were singed. Without using his hands, Fido closed the door to Lethe's bedroom.

It took Palmer a few seconds, but he somehow managed to get to his feet. His nose was still bleeding and his ears rang as if he'd been sitting on top of an air-raid siren. He staggered down the hall, propping his shoulder against the wall to keep from falling.

Sonja was still asleep. Her skin felt strangely dry and cool under his hands, like that of a reptile.

"Sonja!"

She moved sluggishly, brushing at him with her left hand as if he were a bothersome insect intruding on her sleep. She mumbled something under her breath, then rolled over, pulling the sheet over her head. Trying not to let panic overwhelm him, Palmer took a deep breath and stepped back from the bed, focusing himself long enough to fashion a heavy-wattage thought-bolt. Then he threw it at her head.

(Sonja!)

The thought-bolt arced Sonja's body upward as if she'd been juiced with a car battery. Her eyes flew open and she sat up like a knife blade. The hair on her head stood on end and crackled like static on a radio. When he reached out to grab her naked shoulder, she drew back and hissed at him.

"Sonja! Sonja — it's me! Something's happened!"

Sonja blinked and lifted a hand to her brow. "Something's happened to Lethe—?"

"How'd you know that?"

Sonja slid out of the bed and began pulling on her clothes. "I had a dream she told me good-bye."

She followed Palmer back up the hall, listening to him recount what had happened earlier. The door to Lethe's room was still closed. Sonja tried the doorknob; it wasn't locked.

"It's probably safe to go in. Fido would never let anything hurt Lethe, so whatever you were planning to do was probably interpreted as dangerous to her...."

"I was going to get her out of that — that *thing*!"

Sonja gave Palmer a hard look. "Bill, just shut up and let me handle this, okay?"

The door opened effortlessly. Sonja stepped inside, Palmer following her. Fido still stood at guard point, shuffling from one foot to another, watching them vigilantly with his golden eyes.

Sonja held her hands palms-outward, smiling nervously. Being in such close proximity to the *seraph* was actively unpleasant — it felt as if she'd been dipped in honey and placed on top of an anthill.

"We don't want to hurt Lethe, Fido. We know you won't allow that. We're not going to touch her, Fido—"

"Like hell we aren't!"

"Shut up, Bill! Don't mind him, Fido. He's just scared. He thinks something bad has happened, and he just wants to help Lethe...."

The *seraph* continued rocking back and forth, its head wavering like a Parkinson's outpatient.

Sonja turned back to Palmer and grabbed his arm above the elbow, squeezing it until he grimaced. "Bill, I want you to promise me that you won't do anything stupid, like try and touch Lethe. You got off lucky the first two times — but if you try it again, Fido will no doubt burn your brain like bacon in the pan! Do you understand me?"

"Yeah," Palmer muttered sullenly.

Sonja turned back to Fido. "We just want to look at her, that's all...."

Slowly, the *seraph* moved aside, allowing them an unimpeded view of what lay on Lethe's bed. Sonja could see how Palmer could have first mistaken it for a sleeping bag, since it resembled one of the mummy-case models. It was close to five feet long and three feet around, and seemed to be made from amber. It was translucent in spots and filled with a thick fluid that gave off a diffuse light, like that of a glowworm. Deep within the fluid she glimpsed what appeared to be the outline of a child.

"It's grown," Palmer muttered. "It wasn't this big when I first found it...whatever it is."

"By the looks of it, I'd say it's a cocoon."

"What the hell is she doing in a fuckin' *cocoon*?"

"Undergoing some sort of metamorphosis — that's what cocoons are for."

"For the love of God, Sonja — aren't you going to *do* something? That's our little girl in there!" Palmer shouted, lunging for the bed.

Fido moved to block his path. A sound resembling dynamos gearing up filled the room, the vibrations causing Sonja's fangs to ache. Swearing under her breath, she grabbed Palmer and tossed him over her shoulders in a fireman's carry, slamming the door shut behind her.

She stomped into the kitchen and dropped him unceremoniously into one of the chairs. Palmer was livid, his anger so fierce he was choking on his words. It didn't matter — she could hear what he was thinking.

"You can think I'm a cold-blooded bitch all you want, William Palmer," Sonja snapped. "But I just saved you from having your brains scrambled in your skull! If Fido had let you have it, you'd be shitting in diapers and eating through tubes for the rest of your natural days!"

Palmer's face lost some of its blood. "I — I realize that, Sonja. I'm sorry I thought those things about you — but, surely you can't expect me to stand by and do nothing!"

"That's *exactly* what I expect you do — and that's what you're *going* to do! Bill, you've known all along that Lethe isn't a human child — hell, you were there when she was born."

"Don't remind me," he mumbled, massaging his calf. "I still have scars from where that mutant hell-twin of hers tried to chew off my leg."

"Lethe was born of two human vampires — creatures such as myself. But she's obviously not a vampire. I used to think she was some kind of *seraph*, but now I'm not so sure. But whatever she might be, the *seraphim* consider her important enough to be placed under their protection. And for all we know, this cocoon stage is perfectly natural. The fact Fido won't let us touch her suggests that interfering with this — I dunno, call it a larval stage — would be dangerous to Lethe."

Palmer shook his head and got up to retrieve the bottle of tequila he kept in the pantry. Sonja was surprised by how old he looked. The psychokinetic pummeling he'd taken certainly didn't help matters; his face was puffy, and bruises were slowly blossoming under his eyes, as if he'd been struck by the world's biggest air hammer.

They had first met more than two years ago, when Pangloss had hired him to track her down. Not even three years, and already he was starting to age. His once-dark hair and goatee were now liberally shot with gray, and his nose was beginning to dominate his face. Palmer had changed dramatically during their time together — what with his obsession with Mayan body modification — and now he was starting to grow old. Funny how she hadn't noticed that before. Was this how it was between vampires and their human lovers? One day they're handsome youths, the next they're old and withered? She had to struggle to remember his age — forty-three? Forty-four? How old was that in human years?

And, without realizing it, she began to think of Judd. About his youth and his innocence and his humanity —

"Sonja?"

She reined in her thoughts, slamming them behind a protective wall. "Yes, Bill?"

Palmer was sitting there at the table, the tequila bottle at his elbow. He watched her with eyes as distant and unreadable as a dead man's.

"Nothing. Nothing at all."

✷

Sonja woke up just as the sun went down. She showered immediately, making sure to wash away the previous evening's blood and semen. Then, wrapping herself in a kimono she had picked up in Tokyo, she went to check on Lethe's cocoon. She soon discovered that it was no longer resting on the child's bed but out on the patio, with Fido still standing guard.

Palmer was in the kitchen, drinking tequila. In the three days since Lethe had retreated into her golden cocoon, Sonja had yet to see Palmer do anything but drink. Maybe he ate while she was asleep, but she doubted it.

"What's the deal? Why's the cocoon on the patio?"

"Dunno," Palmer slurred, lifting the bottle to his lips. He wasn't even bothering with the rituals of salt and lime. "Mebbe it got too big for the bed. Fucker's almost six feet long now."

Sonja glanced out the window facing the courtyard. Palmer was right. The cocoon had grown at least another foot in length.

"All I know is that when I woke up today, it was sittin' out on the patio. Guess laughing boy there moved it while I wasn't looking." Palmer set aside the bottle and began pawing through the pile of mail and invoices on the kitchen table. "By the way, you got a letter...."

Sonja stiffened. "A letter? Addressed to me?"

"That's what I said — here." Palmer retrieved a business-length envelope from the pile and handed it to her. "There's no return address, but it was mailed from the States. There's a New York City postmark."

She took the letter, smiling grimly. He was still the private detective, even pickled in tequila. Or perhaps being this drunk made him feel more like the old Palmer, the one that had existed before he learned the truth about the things in the shadows.

The envelope was nondescript, addressed to "Sonja Blue c/o Indigo Imports." The address was typed, not handwritten. There was no way to tell who — or what — had tracked her down. Was it a friend or foe? Apprehensively, she opened the envelope.

Inside was a single sheet of paper. Sonja carefully unfolded it, frowning to herself. It was a photocopy of a news clipping from a national paper. The headline read: *Wife of Millionaire Industrialist Suffers Stroke.*

"What's it say?" Palmer asked, one eye fixed on Sonja as he tilted back the tequila bottle.

"My mother's in the hospital."

✷

"You're not really going, are you?"

Palmer watches me from the door of our bedroom as I busy myself with packing my bag. He's drunk. Sloppily so. His sense of betrayal wraps itself around me like a damp towel left to mildew in a gym locker for a few weeks. I know it should make me feel bad, but I'm getting angry with him instead. I always get mad when people try to make me feel guilty.

"Of course I'm going! What the hell does it look like?" I snap, shoving a pair of leopardskin bikini briefs, a black lace camisole, and a Revolting Cocks t-shirt into my flight bag.

I go to the wall safe and retrieve the special strongbox in which I keep my various passports and credit cards. I dump them onto the bed, rummaging through them for an appropriate alias for my trip to North America. I decide to use Anya Cyan and pocket the corresponding identification.

"But what about Lethe? You just can't get up and leave her like this!"

"Bill, I can't do anything for her while she's like this! What the hell difference does it make if I'm here or not?"

"Sonja — please. Don't go. I need you to stay. Please…"

I turn to look at him and I'm shocked to see how quickly he's fallen apart. He hasn't shaved since Lethe went into the cocoon, nor has he bathed — or changed his clothes, for that matter. With his earplugs, tattoos and nose piercings, he looks like a demented Humphrey Bogart from *The Treasure of the Sierra Madres*. Weakness radiates from him like carbon monoxide fumes from a busted muffler, and I turn away for fear he will sense the disgust welling inside me. I know, then, I cannot stay in that house another hour; it is in the vampire's nature to exploit — even destroy — those weaker than it.

Palmer raises a trembling hand to his face, brushing drunkenly at his tears. "Jesus, Sonja — what's happening to us?"

Part of me hears the sorrow and confusion in his voice and wants to reach out and hold him — to pull him into my arms and comfort him as best I can. But another, darker, part sees his tears and wants to smash him in the face and grind my boot into his groin. I stuff the last of my gear into the flight bag and zip it shut, all the while refusing to look him in the eye.

"I doubt if anything is happening, Bill."

*

And I leave them behind, just like that.

I'm not proud of what I'm doing. I realize I'm using my mother's illness to escape an uncomfortable situation at home. Things have changed between us, and there is no use in trying to get back what we had. I've been trying to figure a way out of the situation since the day I got back. Lethe's metamorphosis merely accelerated the process, that's all. Over the years, I've developed the ability to cut myself off from people I care about. Or thought I cared about. It's a survival mechanism — one I've been forced to evolve over the last twenty years. I don't think it's a side effect of my being a vampire. I'd like to be able to blame it on that, but I know better. Monsters don't have a lock on cruelty.

I catch the first flight for the States, flying first-class, as usual. I always fly first-class — it guarantees a certain amount of privacy, and if the stewardesses notice I don't seem to breathe while I sleep, they keep it to themselves.

I spend most of the flight from Yucatan trying to remember my mother. That's not entirely true. Shirley Thorne was never my mother — she was Denise's.

As I sit and watch the clouds slide by my window, I try to find a memory from the life before my own. I reach back…back…back before Palmer…back before Chaz…back before Ghilardi and Pangloss…before Morgan and his horrible, blood-red kisses….

I am sitting *on a picnic bench — where? Where? Backyard? Which house? The one in Connecticut? There are lots of balloons and brightly colored crepe-paper streamers and other children running around dressed in party clothes. I'm wearing a pink dress with lots of ruffles and petticoats. I don't like the petticoats because they're itchy and make it hard for me to put my arms down to my sides. There's a man dressed like a clown walking around making wiener dogs and bunnies out of balloons for all the children. Another man is leading a pony around in a big circle. Some of the older kids cling to its mane and wave to their moms. Or maybe they're their stepmoms. Or nannies. Everybody's wearing silly cardboard hats and carrying party-favor noisemakers. How old am I? Four? Five? And suddenly everyone's smiling and pointing behind me and I turn around and look. There is my mother, standing in the doorway that leads from the house to the backyard and she's holding a big cake with lots of pink icing and big roses made out of white marzipan. She's smiling and she looks so happy and beautiful and everyone starts singing "Happy Birthday" and gathering around the picnic table. Someone says "make a wish, Denise" and I have to stand up on the seat to blow out the candles. I don't remember whether I made a wish or if it came true....*

"Ma'am — are you all right? Did you hurt yourself?"

I look up at my stewardess, still too stunned by the weight of the memory I've unearthed to do more than grunt. "What—?"

"Ma'am — your hand."

I glance down at my left hand. One of the perks of first-class service is that your drinks are served in actual glassware, as opposed to crappy plastic cocktail cups. My fist is full of shattered glass, melting ice, and Seagrams V.O.

All I can say is "Oh."

"Are you hurt?" the stewardess asks again, and I can tell she's trying to figure out if I'm drunk, stoned or stupid. She can't see past the sunglasses and it's making her uneasy. I don't want her watching me the rest of the trip, so I reach into her skull and plant an explanation.

"There must have been a flaw in the glass. What with the cabin pressure changes and everything — I'm just lucky I didn't get cut."

"You're really lucky, ma'am," she clucks, her head bobbing in agreement as she takes what's left of my drink out of my hand. "You could have gotten a bad cut."

"Yeah, I'm really lucky," I mutter, moving my hand so she does not spot the gaping, bloodless slice across my palm.

— *from the diaries of Sonja Blue*

✸

It was daylight by the time she reached her destination. Her bones ached from spending close to forty-eight hours in a cramped sitting position. The flight from Yucatan took six hours, then she'd spent six hours in Los Angeles, waiting for the proper domestic carrier. She could stay active during the day, but it took its toll. It made her slower — more vulnerable to the tricks and pitfalls that might come her way. Although her body might crave its sleep — rather, the regenerative coma necessary to repair any physical damage suffered over the course of the night — at least she didn't have to worry about contracting immediate and lethal skin cancer from being exposed to the sun's rays. Not yet, anyway.

She rented a car at the airport and drove into the town that, until 1969, Denise Thorne had called home. Although her first instinct was to unlock the trunk and crawl inside, she climbed in behind the wheel instead. As she drove through the suburbs into the city, she passed the Thorne Industrial Complex. It was even bigger than she — that is, Denise — remembered. She had to hand it to the old man — he always knew how to make a buck and a half.

Light poured into the car, making Sonja's skin prickle a little bit. She told herself that she wasn't used to direct sun anymore, although she kept eyeing her hands, looking for signs of quick-blooming melanoma. She'd seen a couple of vampires die of sunlight poisoning — not a pretty sight. Their skin burned and was quickly covered in blisters that swelled and swelled until they exploded. Then the vampires simply withered away, like earthworms on a hot sidewalk. It only took a couple of minutes — five, tops — for a dead boy to bust 'n' bake.

Yep, not a pretty sight.

The clipping had said Shirley Thorne was staying at St. Mary's Hospital, over on the Upper East Side. It was the same hospital where Denise had been born. Sonja parked in the public garage attached to the hospital and made her way to the information desk. An aged nun wearing bifocals looked up at her, frowning quizzically.

"May I be of some assistance, young lady?"

"Yes, sister. I'm looking for a relative's room — Thorne? Shirley Thorne?"

The nun scribbled down the name on a slip of paper and turned to consult a computer terminal. She clucked her tongue and shook her head and turned back to face Sonja, her bifocals making her eyes look strangely warped. "I'm so sorry, dear — but I'm afraid Mrs. Thorne isn't with us anymore."

"She's been released?"

"She died yesterday afternoon, according to the computer."

Sonja stared at the terminal, at the name highlighted in amber against a black screen. The cursor blinked like a stuttering firefly.

"I — Is there any notation on where to send memorials?"

"It says flowers should be sent to the Bester-Williamson Funeral Home." The nun pursed her lips and offered Sonja a sympathetic smile. "I'm dreadfully sorry, dear — was she a close relative?"

"No. Not really."

✸

Sonja called the funeral home from the lobby of the hospital. The receptionist informed her that the loved one's services were scheduled for the next day, during the late afternoon. The graveside services were to be held at Rolling Lawns Cemetery. Sonja didn't have to ask where that was — it was the same graveyard Claude Hagerty was buried in. And Chaz.

After finding out all she needed to know concerning her mother's funeral, Sonja drove the rental car out to a suburban shopping mall and crawled inside the trunk to sleep away the remaining hours of daylight.

✸

She wasn't certain that what went on inside her head when she was not awake qualified as "dreaming." She saw things. But were they dreams, or shadows of things that had happened before or of things to come? Sometimes she found herself inside other people's dreams — or their nightmares. Or their madness.

She was walking through a dreamscape made of dripping moss and rotten lace. Sitting on a canopy bed adorned with mildewed satin draperies was a woman dressed in a white bridal gown. She seemed to be adjusting her dress. As Sonja drew closer, the bride looked up, like a fawn surprised while drinking at a stream. Her face was almost obscured by the heavy veil. She spoke without opening her mouth. It was the voice of a five-year-old girl.

He made me dirty.

She looked down at the woman's lap, expecting to see a bouquet. Instead she saw the woman's hands — they were those of an aged crone, with long, crooked nails. She clawed at her crotch with hideous witch-fingers. The material of the gown tore away, exposing her withered thighs and her gray and wrinkled sex. It was all bloody because she'd scratched away her labia and clitoris.

✸

When she woke up, she knew something had happened while she was asleep, because the car was in motion. She pressed her ear to the dividing wall that separated the back seat from the trunk and heard the heavy, rhythmic thump of rap music and, above that, laughter.

Males. Two of them. Adolescent from the sound of their voices and taste in music. Two kids on a joyride? She concentrated harder, tuning out the intrusive music and background noise, focusing on their conversation.

"—The Chopper will pay five, mebbe six bills for this baby—"

"What about The Red? He ships cars over to the Russian black market...."

"He only takes Japanese and Euro shit. This thing's American."

"Fuck!"

"Shit, there's no point in lettin' Chopper get *everything*. Maybe there's something in the trunk we can take over to King Fence for a quick buck or two, huh?"

The car slid off pavement onto gravel. She bounced around for a few minutes more until everything came to a stop. As she thought about it, she realized she was pretty damn hungry. She hadn't eaten in almost seventy-two hours and she was beginning to grow irritable. The car doors slammed and shoes crunched on gravel, heading back for the trunk.

"Think there's anything back there?"

"Maybe just a spare tire and some jumper cables. Then again, mebbe some cunt left her bags from Nordstrom's."

There was a scraping sound as one of the car thieves worked at the lock with a screwdriver. Probably the same one he'd used to force the door, open the ignition cowl and start the car. The lock gave with a loud pop and the trunk swung open — and Sonja was on them in six seconds flat.

They were young. Their surprise and fear made them seem even younger. They were suburban white boys with bad haircuts, dressed in clothes four sizes too big for them. One of them had a gun stuck in the waistband of his pants. She grabbed him first, taking him to the ground hard enough to break his back. He screamed like a little girl — high and pure — as she tore into his throat.

His companion shouted something and tried to drive a six-inch screwdriver into her back. The leather jacket deflected the blow — but it was enough to make her look up from her feeding. She grinned at him, displaying her fangs, and hissed in disapproval. The kid dropped his weapon and wet himself. It took less than a second to snap his neck. Sonja finished draining the first youth, then took as much as she could handle from the second. She then kicked their emptied bodies into a nearby ditch. How thoughtful of them to pick such a nice, secluded spot for their own disposal.

✸

The ignition was hanging from its socket, so she had to hot-wire the car to get it started. No doubt the rental company would not be pleased. Like she cared.

It was still early, by her standards — just after midnight. She decided to cruise the old hometown, to see if anything triggered a memory from what was left of Denise Thorne. It worried Sonja, at times, that she felt so little of her previous self's pain. Denise used to be more a part of her personality, decades ago, but over the last few years her voice had grown gradually weaker until it had been drowned out by the increasingly strident Other. Maybe a visual cue would spark something inside her — generate an emotion that corresponded to the memories in her head. Because without those flashes of sentiment, all Sonja had were dry and flavorless souvenirs of another's life; shadows of the dead rendered meaningless to her — like watching someone else's jerky, disintegrating home movies without the benefit of sound or reference to the players.

She drove around and around, but so much had changed in the twenty years since Denise Thorne walked those streets. Nothing seemed familiar. Suddenly the gates were in front of the headlights, casting striated shadows. Sonja blinked and looked around, uncertain as to how she'd gotten there. Had she deliberately steered the car in this direction? Or was something besides her subconscious behind her arrival? The gate was rusty and the twelve-foot brick walls that screened the estate from the road were overgrown with creeping ivy and covered with graffiti. A heavy chain coiled around the gate like a chrome python, secured by a padlock the size of a baby's head. A metal sign read: *No Trespassing. Violators Will Be Prosecuted to the Full Extent of the Law.*

Sonja killed the headlights and slid out from behind the wheel of the car. She held the lock in her right hand, judging its heft; it was a beauty, all right. It would even give a New York bicycle thief reason to pause. Sonja yanked on it twice and it came away in her hand, the chain unspooling at her feet. The gates to the Wheele estate swung inward with a rusty squeal.

She walked in the direction of where the main house once stood, her bootheels crunching on the overgrown drive. Weeds and small trees poked their way through the slowly dissolving layer of bleached shells.

She scanned the area for signs of derelict habitation or teenage lovers and came up empty. This surprised her. The abandoned five-acre estate was perfect for suburban youths to hide from the apathy of their parents and practice their drinking and sex, but she couldn't pick up the faintest trace of such activity. Instead, as she neared the blackened remains of the Wheele mansion, she began to receive psychic signals similar to those she'd experienced at Ghost Trap. The place was haunted. Big time.

Sonja wrinkled her nose. Even though the place burned to the ground five years ago, it still smelled scorched. There wasn't a lot left of the house — she'd made sure of that when she set it on fire. She'd also killed everyone in it beforehand. And a lot of people in the surrounding area, for that matter. Sonja still felt kind of bad about that part of the massacre. But it wasn't really her fault — the Wheele bitch was the one who'd kidnapped her and kept her in that shithole of an insane asylum for six months. Wheele was the one who'd started it. But she had finished it, by damn. Besides, the psychic shockwave she'd released that night only affected those with true darkness in their souls. At least, that's what she liked to tell herself.

A light moved among the ruins. It was a cold, unnatural luminescence, glowing greenish-white against the darkness. At first it was formless — a glob of pulsating light hovering amid the collapsed timbers and fallen masonry of the destroyed house. The will o' the wisp fluttered for a few seconds, then began to change, taking on shape and substance. It was a woman — or something that had once been a woman.

It had no eyes, no ears, no tongue — its skin hung from its phantom bones like an empty sack. Although it had arms and an upper torso, its legs ended in glowing tatters. Even though it had no eyes in its sockets, Sonja knew that it could see her. And that it recognized her.

"Hello, Catherine. It's been a long time, girlfriend."

The ghost of Catherine Wheele, erstwhile televangelist and faith healer, raised its glowing arms and howled like a damned soul. Which was only natural, since that was what it was.

"Can the spook routine, sister. It might work on teenagers looking for a place to screw and bums out for a midnight tipple, but it doesn't cut any mustard with me."

The ghost shrieked like an owl with its tail caught in a blender and swooped toward her, fingers crooked into claws. Sonja held up her right hand, and a burst of electric-blue light flew from her palm, catching the ghost in its reconstituted midsection. Catherine Wheele rolled up like a window shade, reverting to the form of the pulsating ball of light.

"You're as ignorant dead as you were when you were alive," Sonja sighed. "The Dead cannot physically interface with the mortal plane except on Mardi Gras, the vernal equinox, and All Hallow's Eve. And just because you're dead doesn't mean I can't kick your butt, lady."

Catherine Wheele reassembled herself, scowling at Sonja from across the Divide. Smaller, feebler lights began to appear, floating through the night air like fireflies. One of the ghostly balls unraveled itself, taking on the appearance of Dr. Wexler, the corrupt psychiatrist who first steered Shirley Thorne in Catherine Wheele's direction, then arranged to keep Sonja locked up in his sanitarium. Sonja was glad to see he was being forced to spend his afterlife in the company of his former lover. The other, lesser lights took on human forms as well, turning into the Wheelers, Catherine's private cadre: a mixture of religious fanatics, hired muscle and studmuffins. Sonja had killed each and every one of them.

"It's nice to see you're not lonely," she smirked, carefully searching the wanly glowing faces in search of one in particular. When she did not find it, she heaved a small sigh of relief and turned to go. But she couldn't resist one last jab. "Y'know, they called it "Jonestown in America." All the stuff about your parents dying under mysterious circumstances, your late husband's fraud convictions, the graft and corruption in your church — all of that got into the papers. But now the Wheeles of God Ministry is gone — *kaput*. All your worshippers jumped ship for other, less controversial preachers. And since Waco went down, you're old news. You're trivia for atrocity buffs, nothing more. Just thought you'd like to know."

The ghost of Catherine Wheele threw her mouth open so wide it struck her breastbone and issued an agonized shriek that told Sonja she'd better watch her ass come Halloween.

Sonja chuckled to herself as she sauntered back to the car. Who says you have to be nice to people simply because they're dead?

✸

Rolling Lawn Cemetery unlocked its gates at dawn. By that time, Sonja had been inside the grounds for a couple of hours. But before crashing in a suitable tomb, she had a couple of visits to make.

She did Chaz first.

She wasn't sorry she killed him. She'd felt a little guilty about it, at first, but she never really felt sorry. Chaz had been a deep-down, dyed-in-the-wool bastard. He'd betrayed her — sold her out for a suitcase of money. Not that it did him any good, in the end. Instead of running off to South America, like he'd always dreamed of, the idiot hung around town, frittering his fortune away on hard drugs and rough boys. It was like he'd been waiting for her to find him.

Just like he was waiting for her now, perched atop his gravestone.

"Hello, Chaz. You're looking well."

Truth to tell, he looked like shit. Composed of a grayish-purple fog, his features were beginning to soften, the eyes turning into empty smudges, the nose a hint of shadow. If she hadn't known him already, it would have been difficult for her to identify him. He was still smoking, though. He remembered enough about his former life to cling to its habits, at least.

"Judd's dead. I guess you already know that, though." She expected some sign of malevolent glee on his part, but he gestured dismissively with one hand, leaving trails of ectoplasm in its wake. He remained as ambivalent in death as he had in life.

"Why haven't you moved on? What holds you to this plane? Is it me?"

Something flickered in the smudges that were once his eyes. As Sonja looked at the tattered shadow, memories rose inside her. Memories of when they had been friends — times when they had been lovers. She closed her eyes to ease their stinging, but she still couldn't find it in her to feel sorry.

When she opened her eyes again, Chaz was gone.

*

Claude was nowhere to be found near his grave. For that she was relieved. His death had been an unpleasant one, and often such traumas keep the Dead tethered to the mortal plane for years — even decades — after their deaths. But it seemed Claude Hagerty had managed to move on to whatever it is that awaits humans when they die. The same could not be said of all of Rolling Lawn's internees, whose after-selves flickered amid the tombstones and vaults like phantom fireflies.

The sun would be rising soon. She went to the tomb she'd chosen as her crash space. Since the last occupant had been laid to rest two decades before, she knew she could sleep without having to worry about being discovered by a grieving family member. The memorial sconces were empty and cobwebs hung from the ceiling in delicate tatters. It smelled pleasantly of graveyard mold and dead leaves. She curled up in the darkest corner, setting her watch alarm for four o'clock. As she drifted off into what passed for sleep among her kind, she marveled over how little she'd thought about either Palmer or Lethe. That probably meant they were okay.

Palmer couldn't remember the last time he'd taken a sober breath.

He couldn't remember the last time he'd shaved or changed his clothes, either. He was certain he'd been sitting at the kitchen table, naked except for a pair of khaki safari shorts, for several days, but he wasn't sure just how long.

He staggered over to the calendar hanging next to the stove and squinted at it. He'd gotten it from a *pharmacia* in Medina. The calendar showed a handsomely muscled Aztec warrior, garbed in brilliantly colored feathers and a skimpy loincloth, shooting a bow at the coming twilight while at his sandaled feet sprawled a voluptuous Aztec maiden, wrapped in a diaphanous robe and looking more like a Vargas model than a virgin priestess. Palmer was unfamiliar with the myth the picture was supposed to represent — was the warrior defending the fallen priestess, or was he the one responsible for her death? And what the hell was he shooting at, anyway?

Thinking about the picture on the calendar made his head hurt. Palmer wobbled back to the kitchen table and sat down with an explosive sigh. It took him a few seconds to realize he'd forgotten to count how many days it'd been since Lethe disappeared into the cocoon and his life went into the crapper.

He wasn't sure how long Sonja had been gone, either. He was too drunk to cast his mind for her, but something told him he would not have been able to reach her, even if he were straight. Besides, the possibility of accidentally locking minds with the Other again — no matter how distant — was enough to keep him from trying.

Palmer's gaze fell on the black mask sitting atop a pile of unpaid bills and unfiled invoices. The empty eyes stared up at him, the lips parted as if anticipating a kiss — or a bite. His head continued to hurt, so he rested it on the table.

When he opened his eyes again, it was dark.

Palmer grunted and jerked upright in his chair, knocking the half-empty tequila bottle onto the floor. It shattered, spraying his bare feet and legs with liquid gold. The color of the tequila made him think of Lethe's eyes. And the cocoon.

The cocoon. Time to check the cocoon.

Palmer lurched to his feet and turned to face the patio door. He always checked the cocoon at night. During the day it didn't seem necessary — but night was different. Strange things happened at night. Plus, he had to admit the cocoon was pretty once the sun went down. The weird glow that suffused it grew more intense, making it look like a piece of amber held in front of a flashlight. Sometimes he could see something moving inside the cocoon — as if someone was swimming around in there.

Palmer opened the door and stepped out onto the patio, expecting to be greeted by the cocoon's mellow glow. Instead, there was only darkness. The second thing he noticed was that its guardian was nowhere to be seen.

"Fido?"

He stepped forward hesitantly, looking around for some sign of the *seraph*'s bulky figure. Had it taken Lethe's cocoon someplace else? To a more secure hiding place? Then, as his eyes became more accustomed to the dark, he saw something lying on the bricks of the patio.

At first it looked like a big, deflated balloon, the kind used by weather services. It lay there, limp and forlorn, like an octopus cast upon a shore after a storm. As he moved closer, he could make out a faint, yellowish fluorescence. He knelt and poked at the empty chrysalis. It felt like a cross between a freshly shed snakeskin and a wet blanket.

Palmer's head swiveled around drunkenly. "Lethe? Lethe — where are you, darlin'?" He struggled to get to his feet, trying his best not to black out. The adrenaline in his system was now battling the tequila for mastery, but he was too far gone to sober up fast.

"Lethe?"

The light came from above, pouring down on him as if someone had switched on a tiny sun right over his head. Palmer cringed and lifted a hand to shield his eyes. His first thought was that someone was hovering over the house in a helicopter, pointing a surveillance light down at him, like they do in Los Angeles. Then he realized that what he thought was the sound of rotors chopping the air was his own pulse hammering away inside his ears. And then the light spoke.

(Daddy.)

The light lowered its wattage, became a steady glow, and Palmer saw the thing at its heart. Its form was that of a young woman — no older than sixteen or seventeen. Her hair was long enough to braid into a rope, floating free like a mantle buffeted by gentle winds. Her skin was dusky, her eyes golden without pupil or iris. Her breasts were full, her hips wide, drawing his eye to the dark triangle of hair between her thighs. She was beautiful. She was woman. She was all women. Unbidden, Palmer felt his penis stir and grow heavy at the sight of the lovely, naked woman suspended above him like a vision of Venus. Or the Madonna.

"L-lethe?"

The glowing woman smiled and when she spoke her lips did not move. Her voice was smooth as velvet, as comforting as a cool hand on a fevered brow.

(My childhood is over. It is time for me to begin my work. I owe you much for keeping me safe — for giving me love and treating me as your own — for showing me what it is like to be human. I owe you all this — and that is why I shall make you the First.)

"First? First what?"

(Father of the coming race.)

Before Palmer could ask her what *that* meant, Lethe swooped down, catching him up in her arms. He was too drunk and surprised to protest, until he looked down and saw the tops of trees skimming by below his feet.

"Lethe! What the hell do you think you're—?"

He didn't finish the sentence, because Lethe placed her mouth over his, her tongue darting inside his mouth. For a moment Palmer felt himself begin to respond; then he retched and tried to push her away.

"Lethe! Stop that! I'm your father—!"

(My father was a vampire named Fell.)

"You know very well what I mean! Stop this foolishness and put me down on solid ground right this minute, young lady!"

Lethe's face filled his vision, her eyes becoming huge twin harvest moons. Palmer wanted to scream, but there was no breath inside him. The child he had raised for the better part of three years was nowhere to be found in this strange, glowing woman.

(You are the First of my Bridegrooms. The First to engage in the wedding flight. Do not fear me, William Palmer. This is your reward for your years of nurturing. You are being honored.)

Palmer shuddered as he felt his penis stiffen, responding to hormonal cues older than upright posture. He kept telling himself that it wasn't happening; that he wasn't being ravaged against his will by a glowing woman as they sped across the night sky, that he was really passed out in a pool of his own piss in the kitchen. Even as orgasm seized his body and wadded it up like a piece of old newspaper, he kept telling himself it was just a dream, nothing more.

When he woke up, it was to find himself lying in an orchard. He was naked, his safari shorts lost somewhere along the way. His head throbbed with a monstrous hangover and his crotch was sticky and smelled of sex. Palmer rolled onto his stomach and began to sob, tearing at the grass with clawing hands. Then he threw up.

There was the sound of a twig snapping, and Palmer began looking around for something to cover himself. He froze at the sight of the young native girl, a basket of fruit balanced atop her head, staring down at him. He could tell by her diminutive stature and the shape of her eyes and cheekbones that she was one of the Lancondoan — the purebred descendants of the ancient Mayan kings who had ruled the land before the arrival of the *conquistadors*. The girl regarded him curiously, but did not seem to be afraid or alarmed by his nakedness.

"Are you well, *señor*?" she asked.

Palmer began to laugh, which made the girl look at him even more oddly. "No. I am not well at all." This made him laugh even harder. Then he threw up some more.

She overslept somewhat and nearly missed the funeral. She made it just in time to see Shirley Thorne's casket lowered to its final rest. It was made of mahogany and shone like a burnished shield in the dying sun. A large floral tribute rested atop the coffin, clutching it like a spider. After each of the mourners tossed the traditional handful of sod into the grave, the group broke up and wandered toward the phalanxes of black limos, BMWs, and Rolls-Royces.

Sonja stood at a distance, screened from view by a weeping angel. She scanned the milling crowd, trying to spot the faces of family and friends, but to no avail. The only person she recognized was Jacob Thorne.

He looked considerably older than the last time she'd seen him, five years ago. The iron will and steely resolve that had made him a millionaire several times over had succumbed to rust. Jacob Thorne — once the mightiest industrialist this side of Howard Hughes — had become an old man. When the last mourners shook his hand and muttered their sympathies, Thorne did not move to join them in leaving the cemetery. Instead, Denise's father stood by his wife's open grave, hands clasped before him, peering down into the hole as if he could see the future in its depths. No doubt he did.

Sonja moved from her hiding place, gliding between the headstones as if maneuvering across a dance floor. She knew he was not her father. At least not the "her" that called itself Sonja. She opened her mouth to call his name, to say "Mr. Thorne"; but what came out was:

"Daddy—?"

Jacob Thorne looked up from his wife's grave. He did not looked surprised to see her. But neither did he looked pleased. His brow furrowed and his scowl deepened.

"Somehow I knew you'd be here."

"Mr. Thorne—? Is everything all right?" Thorne's chauffeur made his way toward the gravesite. He was a big man with an obvious holster bulge inside his jacket.

Thorne dismissed his bodyguard with a wave of his hand. Sonja could see it was covered with liver spots. "It's okay, Carl. I know the young lady."

She joined Thorne at the lip of the grave. It was very dark down there. And lonely.

"I — I'm sorry. Did she — did she suffer?"

Thorne shrugged, his shoulders looking thin and narrow in his suit. "In her way. But that was always Shirley's prerogative — suffering. She was designed for martyrdom. Agonizing over Denise was the one thing that kept her going." He looked at her, his eyes hard. "You killed her, you know that? Whatever it was you did to her mind that night — the night she finally accepted Denise's death — that was the beginning of the end for her. She just gave up living after that."

"Please believe me when I tell you I meant only to help her — to free her from her madness. I never intended to harm her. She — she was my mother."

Thorne's pale features suddenly grew red and he began to tremble. He pulled a handkerchief out of his breast pocket and used it to blot his face. "The hell she was! I don't know who — or what — you are, but you are not Denise!"

"No. I am not Denise anymore. But once — a long time ago. A lifetime ago..." Sonja bent and gathered a handful of dirt. It felt damp and rich between her fingers. It struck the lid of her mother's casket with a dull thud. "Mr. Thorne, I did not ask to come into this world. Nor did Denise ask to leave it. I did not choose to be what I am."

Thorne looked at her again, the hardness leaking from his eyes. "No. I guess you didn't."

"I — I have memories now and again. Some are dim. Others are quite vivid. There is one of a birthday party — there were other children, a clown, a man giving pony rides...."

Thorne barked a laugh, sounding both surprised and pleased by the memory. "You couldn't possibly remember that! You were only two years—" He cut himself short, his hands fisting the handkerchief into a ball. "I mean, Denise was only two years old at the time."

"Your wife was wearing a dress with a Peter Pan collar and a big skirt — she was so pretty. And happy. And the birthday cake was vanilla with pink icing—"

"Why are you telling me this?" Thorne's eyes gleamed with anger and tears. His voice was tight, wavering on the verge of breakdown. "Isn't it enough I've lost my wife? Do you have to make me relive the loss of my daughter as well?"

"Mr. Thorne — there is another place beyond this world. Several, actually. Every man, woman and child holds the keys to heaven and hell within them. There are as many different paradises as there are living things. Just as there are infinite varieties of damnation. I just want you to know that your wife is happy now."

"That's what the minister said," Thorne sniffed contemptuously. "'She's in a better place, Jacob. She's beyond the pain of this world.' Hmph!"

"Mr. Thorne, would you say that I might be something of an authority on the supernatural?" Thorne looked at her oddly, as if it had never occurred to him that a vampire might actually be evidence of the existence of something beyond the worm and the tomb and the winding sheet. "Mr. Thorne, your wife is at peace. You see, heaven means different things to everyone. And for your wife — heaven was an afternoon in 1955, celebrating the birthday of her only child."

Thorne nodded his head. "Yes — yes, I can see where it would be. I — I — Oh, God—"

Tears began to run down his cheeks. No doubt they were the first real ones he'd shed since his wife died. His shoulders shook so violently he looked as if he were about to topple headlong into the open grave. "Dear God — Denise—"

He reached for her with his trembling, old-man's hand, but she was already gone.

By the time she got back, everything had turned to shit. She could smell a psychic taint the moment she got off the plane in Cozumel. The closer she drew to Merida, the more powerful the reek became. She had no idea what had happened during her absence, but, obviously, it had not been good.

She arrived to find the front door unlocked. She walked in, scanning for signs of life, and came up empty. The kitchen table was covered with unpaid bills, unopened mail and empty tequila bottles. Lots of tequila bottles. Sonja went out onto the patio, searching for signs of Lethe's cocoon — but all she found was something that looked like pieces of snake molt, made brittle and black from exposure to the sun.

"Lethe?" Sonja called out, looking around, half expecting her stepdaughter to come rushing from some hiding place, giggling in delight at having tricked her. There was no answer.

"Lethe?"

Silence.

She went back into the house and headed for the nursery. She stared at the plush stuffed animals and coyly smiling rag dolls that lined the shelves and filled every corner of the room. Something behind her eyes began to pulse and ache. She could hear Shirley Thorne's voice singing "Happy Birthday To You."

Sonja waded into the sea of stuffed toys, tossing them aside as she searched for Lethe. Panic and confusion and self-loathing rose in her gut. How could she have been so stupid? How could she have walked off and left the child? Was this how Shirley Thorne felt when she'd received the news that her daughter had disappeared? No wonder the poor woman had retreated into madness.

"Lethe, this isn't funny anymore! Come out where I can see you!" Failing to get any response with her voice, Sonja called with her mind.

(Lethe!)

"Lethe doesn't live here anymore."

Palmer stood slumped in the doorway, arms folded across his chest, watching her with unreadable eyes. He looked rough, but he was wearing clean clothes and was freshly shaven. Nor was he drunk. The odor of dead love came off him in waves.

He'd come up behind her without Sonja picking him up on radar. Which meant either she'd been really out of it — or he was screening himself. Probably both.

(Bill—?)

She stepped toward him and he drew back, hugging his elbows as if afraid she was going to try and touch him.

"Talk with your mouth," he rasped. "I don't want you in my head."

"What do you mean she doesn't live here anymore? Where the hell is she?"

Palmer laughed, only it sounded more like a hiccup. He hugged himself tighter. "I don't know where she is. Nor do I want to."

"What th—? Bill, we're talking about Lethe here! She's only three years old! Where the hell could she go?"

Palmer shrugged and laughed that weird laugh again.

"Palmer — dammit, what's wrong with you? Where's Lethe? She couldn't have just flown away!"

Palmer's laughter now had an edge of hysteria to it. He guffawed until he couldn't catch his breath and dropped to his knees, doubling over to cradle his heaving stomach. Sonja reached down to touch him, but he recoiled from her, shaking his head frantically as he forced himself to speak between bursts of giggling.

"Don't — touch — me—"

"Palmer, what the fuck is going on—? For the love of God, straighten up, man!" She grabbed his elbow, helping him back to his feet. He snarled and lashed out at her with his mind. Had she been a normal human, he might have crippled her, but Sonja was far from human. Palmer's attack was the same as that of an angry child, hammering at the legs of his mother with chubby fists. And Mother had had enough of it.

She pinned him to the floor with her mind as easily as she might mount a butterfly on a piece of velvet. He lay at her feet, his muscles twitching and jerking as he tried, in vain, to regain control of his body.

"I don't want to play rough, Palmer, but you're leaving me no choice. Now stand up."

Palmer's arms and legs moved jerkily as he obeyed her commands. The look in his eyes was black and ugly. Sonja looked away, but there was no way she could shield herself from his hate. It was thick and viscous and burned like boiling tar.

She led Palmer's body out of Lethe's bedroom into his own, where she made him sit on the bed. She positioned herself opposite him and withdrew her control. Palmer's shoulders sagged and for a moment Sonja was afraid he was going to pass out on her, but then he straightened his back and took a deep breath.

"Okay — tell me what happened here."

Palmer glared at her, then glanced in the direction of the patio. "She — she came out."

"When?"

He shrugged. "I — I don't know. A couple of days after you left. I was too drunk to remember exactly when."

"What happened when Lethe came out of the cocoon? What did she look like?"

Palmer's eyes suddenly went distant, as if he were seeing something inside himself. "Beautiful. She was beautiful. She was older than when she went in — she was maybe sixteen or seventeen. But she was beautiful. And she — and she — she was on fire."

"On fire? Like the pyrotics?"

Palmer shook his head violently. "No! Not like burning on fire — she was glowing, you know? Like the pictures of the Virgin Mary..."

"Palmer, what did Lethe say to you? What did she do?"

Palmer took a deep breath and his gaze fell to his hands, which were battling with one another like dueling tarantulas. "She — she thanked me for taking care of her — for protecting her when she needed it — and she said I was — I was going to be the first."

"The first? The first what?"

"Bridegroom." Palmer's lower lip began to tremble and he looked up at Sonja. Anger and confusion and hurt filled his eyes, and for a moment she was once again standing by her mother's grave, staring into the face of her father.

"Bridegroom—? Palmer, what did she mean by that?"

"I don't know. All I know is that she — she made me do it. I wouldn't have done it on my own — you know that, don't you? You know I would never have done something like that—"

"Done what? What did Lethe make you do, Palmer?"

"Fuck her."

Sonja sat there for a moment, letting what Palmer said sink in. She didn't know if she was shocked or not. After all, Palmer hadn't actually sired Lethe.

But, then again, what difference did that make? He'd been a daddy to her in every other way. As much as he'd professed to detest children, Palmer had proved himself a championship father.

God, no wonder he was in such a state. The human animal came with a lot of behavioral hard-wiring — some of it biological, some of it societal. The incest taboo was one of the few that might be both.

Sonja walked over to the window and stared out at the jungle-covered hills.

Forget Palmer. He's meat. Look at him, if you don't believe me: his circuits are blown, whispered the Other. *You knew it'd come someday, sooner or later. It happens to all renfields, eventually.*

Sonja closed her eyes and dug her fingernails into her palms until the blood came.

"Palmer — what happened then? After — after Lethe fucked you?"

"She flew away."

She sighed and turned back to face Palmer. He was still seated on the corner of the bed, staring down at his hands as his fingers battled with one another. What had she gotten herself into? She had come home in an attempt to patch up her family, only to find her stepchild has raped its father and flown off to who knows where, leaving behind a severely traumatized victim of incest.

"Bill—?"

"Yes, Sonja?"

"You're going to go to sleep for a little while. When you wake up, you won't remember anything about Lethe. You won't remember her living with us. You won't remember taking care of her. You won't remember anything. It will be as if she never existed."

"But—"

"Go to sleep, Bill."

✷

When he woke up she was out hunting, tracking a wild pig through the dense jungle undergrowth. She brought it down with her bare hands. It squealed angrily and tried to slash her with its tusks. It struggled hard, like all things do when they know their lives are at stake.

Just before she sank her fangs into its jugular, the pig released twin streams of shit and piss in a last-ditch bid for freedom. Or maybe it was simply that scared.

It was well past midnight by the time she returned to the house. She climbed in through the bedroom window, expecting to find Palmer where she'd left him: sprawled, fully clothed, across the bed. Instead, the bed was empty, Palmer gone. She searched the other rooms. Palmer was nowhere to be found in the house.

She stepped outside and cast her mind into the dark, searching for the hum and buzz of thought that had become so familiar to her in the last three years. At first she picked up nothing — then, as she intensified her scan, she found traces of him. He had constructed an elaborate system of telepathic baffles in order to shield himself. But why? She had edited Lethe from his mind. His trauma should have vanished along with his memories. So why was he still trying to keep her from speaking to him mind-to-mind?

Sonja found a path at the bottom of the property, leading into the jungle. She recognized it as the trail that led to a Mayan ruin on a nearby hill. She'd only been there once, but she knew Palmer visited it often. Quite often, if the condition of the path was anything to go by.

She followed the trail to the top of the hill, where a vine-covered jumble of stone that had once been an ancient observatory sat lumped against the night sky. Palmer was seated on a mammoth block carved to resemble a snarling jaguar. He was not alone.

The woman with him was young — little more than a girl. She was from one of the native tribes — the ones Palmer called the Lancondoan. She was short, with long black hair that hung down between her shoulder like a curtain. They sat side by side, turned toward one another. Palmer held her hand in his and they spoke in a language she did not recognize. Not that she needed to recognize the words to know what they were saying. It was perfectly clear they spoke as lovers.

See? See what your precious little loverboy is doing? The Other's voice was sharp, sweet and nasty, like honeyed razor blades. *This is what happens when you let your renfields run free. It happened with Chaz; now it's happening with Palmer. In they end, they betray you. They'll always betray you.*

Palmer lowered his head, bringing his face close to the girl's. Sonja could imagine the heat of his breath on the girl's cheek, the smell of him filling her senses, the taste of his lips. She clenched her fists and ground her teeth together. The anger building inside her was thick and hot, like boiling wax. Her head ached and her forebrain felt as if it had been stung by a swarm of wasps. The Other's voice was loud, giggling like a harpy.

You have to put them on a short leash. That's how to keep them in line. That's how Pangloss and Morgan and all the others keep their renfields loyal. You've got to scrape every vestige of free will out of them, hollow them out like a fuckin' jack o'lantern. You have to turn them into slaves. Believe me, that's the only way. And they deserve it. They even like it.

"How cozy."

Palmer jumped up at the sound of her voice, automatically shielding the girl with his body. Sonja felt first a twinge of pain, then anger, at seeing this.

"Sonja!"

She emerged from the darkness like blood rising from a wound, the jungle moonlight dappling her leather jacket. She paused, leaning against the pockmarked limestone of the ruin like a tough lounging under a streetlamp. The girl gasped and crossed herself. Obviously Palmer had told her about his live-in girlfriend.

"So, this is your back-door woman, huh?" She jerked her head at the cowering girl. "Does she know you're fresh from my bed? Can she smell me on you — like I can smell *her*?" The last few words came out as a growl as she showed her fangs. The girl cried out and her nails bit into Palmer's naked upper arm.

"Leave her be, Sonja. Concha's innocent. If you've got to punish someone, punish me."

"You love her." It wasn't a question.

Palmer glanced down into Concha's dark-brown eyes, now bright with fear, and nodded. "Yes, I do."

When Sonja finally spoke, her voice was very still. She could tell this scared Palmer more than anything else.

"I could kill her, you know. I could kill her and make it so you wouldn't even know she had ever existed. It would be as easy for me as wiping a chalkboard clean. Easier."

"Don't you think I know that?"

"Do you?" she laughed, taking a step forward. It would be so easy for her to reach into his head and flip the switch, releasing the memories she had hidden from him only hours before. Part of her wanted to see the look on his girlfriend's face when the memories came back, washing over him like a tidal wave, smashing his ego into kindling. That would be fun. She could do it over and over again, wiping his memories of Lethe and then restoring them, so that every time he experienced the pain it would be fresh and raw, like it had never happened before. Maybe she would do that with his girlfriend's murder. Make him forget her, then force him to relive her death over and over....

Sonja halted, swaying slightly like a drunkard brought up short. Her gaze was fixed on Concha, who returned her stare like a sparrow entranced by a snake.

"Don't do it, Sonja. Don't make me try to kill you."

Her laughter was as hollow as old bone. "Try is all you *could* do. You're no match for me, Palmer."

"I know that. There's no way I could hope to defeat you. But I'd try."

She grunted and came closer, peering down at the cowering girl pressed tightly to Palmer's side. Palmer was watching her face, trying to decide if he was dealing with Sonja or the Other. Concha moaned slightly and gripped Palmer even tighter than before.

"Why this one? What's so special about this particular female?" Sonja sniffed.

"Concha found me naked and sick in the jungle miles from here…I don't know how I got there, or why I was there, but she nursed me back to health. She helped me get home. She was there for me when I needed someone."

"But she's not like you!"

"She's human. I need human, Sonja."

"You know what I mean! She's not a sensitive. You can never commune with her on the same plane that you and I do…."

"We don't have that anymore, Sonja. You know that as well as I do. You shut yourself away from me the moment you got back from New Orleans. I tried to reach out to you — to understand whatever it was you were going through — but it was no use. It's as if you can't be satisfied unless I'm as miserable as you are."

"Palmer — Bill — you don't understand! I didn't want you to be hurt, that's all. I didn't want you to see me as a monster—"

"It's a little late for that, don't you think?"

"Don't do this to me, Bill. Don't make me beg. I need you."

"You don't need me. You don't need anyone."

"That's not true."

"Is it? Sonja, if I stay with you, I'm in danger of losing my soul. I'll end up just like one of Morgan's renfields. Is that what you want for me? Is it?"

Don't *bother answering the jerk, just reach into his head and snap his will off at the faucet*, hissed the Other. *By the way, I liked the bit about killing his girlfriend and making him forget her, then relive her death whenever you feel like a chuckle. Not bad. Not bad at all. You're getting the hang of this stuff, girlfriend.*

Sonja balled her fists and looked down at her boots. "No. Of course not." The Other hissed and spat obscenities no one else could hear.

"Then give me my freedom."

She jerked her head up, moonlight flaring across the mirrored lenses of her glasses. "You've always had it!"

"Have I?"

Sonja opened her mouth as if to answer, then turned her back on Palmer and his lover.

"Go."

Her voice felt tight and sharp, like a piano-string garrote had been slipped around her throat. She could hear Palmer shift his weight, trying to decide whether to stay or flee.

"Sonja—" There was a hesitancy in his voice.

"I said go! Before I change my mind!"

Palmer grabbed Concha by the hand and hurried from the ruins into the surrounding jungle. Just before he disappeared into the tangled shadows, he turned and called out to her with his mind one last time.

(I did love you.)

Then he was gone.

Sonja tossed back her head and shrieked like a cornered jaguar. Yowling obscenities, she kicked and pummeled the ancient limestone ruins, obliterating friezes depicting the rule of Mayan wizard-kings a thousand years dead. With a yell that swelled her throat like a bull ape's, she bashed her shoulder against the remaining wall until it collapsed in an explosion of yellowish-white powder.

When it was over, she stood in the middle of her handiwork, trembling like a winded stallion, her face and clothes limned with the dust of centuries.

I loved you too, she thought.

But there was no one to hear her.

✸

When she got back to the house, Sonja was too tired to hate or even feel sorry for herself. The house seemed horribly empty. Lethe was gone. Now Palmer was, too. Within the span of a few days, the little nest she'd built for her family had turned into a tomb.

A featureless black papier-mâché mask sat atop a small pile of mail heaped on the kitchen table. As she picked up the mask, a thick business envelope slid off the heap and fell onto the floor. She noticed, with a rush of excitement, that it was addressed to Sonja Blue.

Inside the envelope were several clippings from the New York City/Triborough papers, the oldest dating back six months, the most recent clipping dated two weeks previous. Most of them were brief, taciturn accounts of the deaths of nameless prostitutes, none of the columns garnering more than an inch. As she placed them on the table where she could read them, she immediately noticed the one item that linked them: "*the deceased was found dressed in a black leather jacket, wearing mirrored sunglasses.*"

Sonja picked up the envelope and searched for a letter. Nothing. The post mark told her it had been mailed in New York City from the Cooper Postal Station. The West Village. Already the gears were engaged, the wheels in her head turning.

Palmer and Lethe might no longer be a part of her life.

But there was still Morgan.

London, England

Mavis Bannister was a charwoman. Oh, they had a fancy name for it nowadays — "maintenance engineer," she thought it was. Just like they had a fancy name for the women's toilet: "the ladies lounge." But, in essence, her job was to swab down the loos at Farquier & Sons. Farquier & Sons was one of the more prestigious department stores in London. It had started out catering to the carriage trade over a century ago. The store's reputation rested on a royal commission it had landed during the Edwardian era and had yet to update — something involving spats. In any case, its clientele included movie stars and rock musicians, not to mention stockbrokers and MPs. Still, if anyone were to ask Mavis, she would tell them that the rich and famous treat public lavatories just like the *hoi polloi*. You'd be surprised how many couldn't bother to flush.

Nonetheless, mopping the jakes of the overprivileged had its definite perks. Like the time she found a pair of mink-lined gloves left next to the sink. Or the time she found close to twenty quid lying on the floor next to the second stall — no doubt it fell out of some rich twit's pocketbook. Most of them were so well-off they'd never notice it was gone — or, if they did, would assume they'd dropped it while getting in or out of the taxi, not while they were taking a squat in a public bog.

Mavis wasn't really thinking about much of anything that day except whether to warm up a tin of stew or pop for some takeout vindaloo as she wheeled her mop and bucket into the ladies lounge. It was toward the end of the business day and time for the third of the four scheduled daily cleanings. Farquier & Sons prided itself on the cleanliness of its "lounges."

At first she thought she was hearing things. It sounded like a baby crying, only muffled. No doubt she was hearing a child crying out on the floor. Then she realized that the sound was coming from the litter bin next to the sinks.

Mavis flipped back the little metal hood and stared down into the cylinder. There, nestled amid wadded-up brown paper towels and discarded tampons, was a newborn infant, wrapped in a swaddling of newspaper, just like an order of fish and chips. The baby stopped crying and looked up at Mavis with eyes the color of marigolds and smiled at her.

"Merciful God!" Mavis gasped. "You poor thing!" She set aside her mop and bucket and removed the top of the litter bin, reaching in to retrieve the child. There was a sound from behind her as the Home Secretary's wife entered the ladies lounge.

"Go get the floor-walker!" Mavis barked.

The Home Secretary's wife looked first startled, then indignant. "I beg your pardon—?" she began to huff.

"I said, go fetch the floor-walker! Someone's gone an' left a baby in the bleedin' litter bin!"

The Home Secretary's wife blinked, her face going blank for a moment. "Oh. Oh dear. Of course. I'll go find him."

Mavis chuckled to herself, taking a moment's pleasure in the role reversal, then looked down at the baby she held cradled in her arms. It had been a long time since she'd held a child that small. The baby's dark hair was still damp with birth fluids and his skin was smeared with tacky blood. It was a boy and apparently healthy, although the umbilical cord looked as if it had been chewed off. Whoever the mother was, she must have given birth in one of the stalls. Mavis opened each door, looking for signs of blood and placenta. To her surprise, the toilets and the floors were spotless. But that was impossible....

The floor-walker, an elderly man with a neatly clipped salt-and-pepper mustache, opened the door to the ladies lounge and peered in, mustache twitching. "What's all this nonsense about there being a baby left in here? And have you gone mad — that was the Home Secretary's wife you yelled at!"

Mavis held up the baby, still wrapped in its receiving blanket of newsprint. "You call this nonsense, sir?"

The floor-walker's eyes widened at the sight of the child. "Good Lord!"

"Did you see a pregnant woman come in here in the last ten, fifteen minutes? The poor thing can't be more than five minutes old himself!"

The floor-walker looked genuinely perplexed. "I don't understand! There hasn't been a woman in such a condition on this floor since noon! I could swear it! I'm sure I would have noticed...."

"So where'd this poor tad come from, eh?" Mavis sighed, running her work-roughened hand against the baby's cheek. "His mum must have been in the store. Surely the fairies didn't leave him. Too bad he can't tell us who he belongs to."

The nameless son of William Palmer yawned, waved his chubby little fists in the air, and smacked his toothless gums, wondering all the while when he was going to be fed.

✷

Heilongjiang Province, The People's Republic of China

The madman's name was Sun Wang Zuocai, and he had spent the last thirty-three of his seventy-seven years locked away in a private sanitarium in the frozen climes of Heilongjiang Province. There are many such sanitariums scattered throughout Communist China where those considered bent on "criminal insanity against the State" and deemed impossible to reeducate have been banished. What made this particular sanitarium different from the others was that Sun Wang Zuocai was its only inmate.

None of the six staff members assigned to watch over the old man could understand what was so important — or dangerous — about him that he had to be kept in isolated confinement and dosed with the most potent of psychoactive drugs.

Thin to the point of emaciation, his arms and legs withered from decades spent strapped into a straitjacket and manacled to his bed, with a long beard and mustaches the color of fresh snow, and a piercing gaze that seemed to look through both time and space, Sun Wang Zuocai appeared more like a crazed wizard from the Beijing opera than a senile mental patient. And that, more or less, was the truth. Although no one except a select handful of Party leaders knew of his existence, at one time Sun Wang Zuocai had served as mystic advisor to Chairman Mao.

Wang Zuocai was born in 1917 in Zhejiang Province, a place renowned for its scenic beauty. His father was a wealthy man, heir to a sizable tea plantation and silkworm concern that stretched back three centuries. His mother, however, was of even nobler stock. Her family was descended from a long line of sorcerers who had advised the emperors since the days of the Ch'in Dynasty. By the time Wang Zuocai was five years old, his talent as an oracle was already making itself known. But then the Japanese came and things became bad for his family. His parents hoped that he would someday become a member of General Chiang Kai-shek's retinue, but Wang Zuocai's second sight told him that the future lay with Mao Zedong. So, at the age of eighteen, he joined the Chinese Communist Party and found himself on the Long March.

During those hard, torturous years — on the run from both the Nationalists and the occupying Japanese — Wang Zuocai became one of Mao's most trusted — and secret — personal advisers. At first his precognitive abilities were limited to a few minutes and those who were physically present, but as time progressed, so did his power to see into the future.

Mao relied on Wang Zuocai's talents a great deal, but he had to be exceptionally careful in concealing the exact nature of his confidant's ability. If his Soviet advisers got wind of Wang Zuocai, they would either dismiss Mao as a fool — or try to steal Wang for their own uses. It would not help matters among Mao's fellow workers if it was discovered he was using the services of an oracle, a habit associated with the Imperial dynasties. Thus, although Sun Wang Zuocai was one of the most powerful and influential members of the CCP, no one knew who he was. And so it went for twenty-two years.

Until 1958.

Before 1958, there had been the First Five-Year Plan, which emphasized rapid industrial development and expansion. Iron and steel, electric power, heavy engineering, and other sophisticated, highly capital-intensive plants were developed at the expense of agriculture, which, up until then, had occupied more that eighty percent of the population.

Now Mao proposed the introduction of the Second Five-Year Plan — which he called the Great Leap Forward. The Great Leap Forward called for the abolition of private plots and the formation of communes, and the increase of agricultural output through greater cooperation and physical effort. The Chairman called his oracle to him, told him of his plans, and asked what great future Wang Zuocai foresaw for China.

What Wang Zuocai saw was crop failure and famine, leading to the starvation of millions and, eventually, to the dissolution of diplomatic ties between China and the Russians and Mao's forced retirement as Chairman of the republic. Mao, already growing accustomed to being worshipped as the wisest of men, took exception with Wang Zuocai's prophecy and denounced him as a reactionary. The very next day, Wang Zuocai was arrested as he left his house and taken to a "reeducation facility" in Jiangxi Province.

He spent most of his time in solitary confinement. Endless tape loops quoting the wisdom of the Chairman harangued him from hidden speakers day and night. The only times he saw other people were when the guards came in to beat him. Malnourished and forced to sleep on lice-ridden straw, denied anything to read except the writings of the Chairman, Wang Zuocai's talent began feeding on itself, growing stronger and wilder. Soon he was able to predict the guards' arrival within the minute of the hour of the day, even though he had no way of keeping time.

One time, as he was being beaten, he looked up into the face of one of his guards and said: "Your wife is being untrue behind your back. She takes the village Party official into her bed the moment you leave the house. He is with her now." The guard called him a liar and struck him with his rifle, breaking Wang's jaw. Two days later, the guard caught his wife in bed with the village Party official and shot them both, then turned the rifle on himself. Wang Zuocai saw that part, too, which is why he'd told the guard in the first place.

By 1961 the Great Leap Forward had proved itself to be a disaster. Uncounted millions had starved to death in the outlying provinces, and the Soviets had left in disgust, taking their blueprints with them. Mao, chastised, retired as Chairman of the republic, if not the party. Not long after his resignation, Mao ordered Wang Zuocai's release from prison and had his old advisor brought back to the Forbidden City. But he quickly discovered that the Sun Wang Zuocai who stood before him was not the man he used to know.

Although Wang Zuocai was only forty-four, his ordeal had turned his hair white and cost him most of his teeth. But what Mao found most discomforting were his eyes — they seemed to see into a disturbing distance. Occasionally Wang Zuocai would grimace or shake his head or smirk at something only he could see. After offering his former confidant some rice wine, Mao asked him what it was he saw. Wang Zuocai said he saw many things, but at that moment he was watching the assassination of the Americans' most recent president.

He then went on to forecast, in no real order, the fall of Saigon, the death of a black musician, and Nixon standing on the Great Wall.

Mao did not know if the oracle was, indeed, seeing the future or if he'd gone mad. When Wang Zuocai veered from forecasting the future and began espousing the existence of nonhuman races dwelling unseen among humanity — even going so far as to accuse Mao's own wife, Jiang Qing, of having the head of a she-fox — Mao decided Wang Zuocai was indeed insane. As much as it saddened him to realize that he had been instrumental in destroying his friend's mind, part of him couldn't help but sigh in relief. That bit about Nixon and the Great Wall really had him worried for a moment....

So Sun Wang Zuocai was bundled off to the frozen frontiers of Heilongjiang Province, to be tended for the rest of his natural life by nurses and doctors better suited to the treating of farm animals. (Though Wang Zuocai's natural life proved considerably longer than Mao's.) In the years since his initial commitment, he'd had only one visitor — Deng Xiaoping. He'd come in and asked Wang Zuocai two questions, then never returned. However, Deng did order that Wang be kept in a straitjacket round the clock from that day forward. Now, after fifteen years, he was to receive his second — and final — visitor.

She poured herself through the reinforced window, her skin glowing like light shining through a glass of plum wine. Wang Zuocai watched silently as she moved toward his bed, her feet skimming the cold tiles. Everything in Heilongjiang was cold. The winters were fierce and harsh, lasting up to eight months. For someone such as Wang Zuocai, born and bred in the warmer southern climes, nothing was ever warm enough. But that was about to change.

The glowing woman smiled down at him, radiating a heat that sank through his wrinkled skin and into his ancient bones. How long had it been since he'd last known a woman? Thirty-six years? It had been the better part of a decade since he'd been able to masturbate.

The woman gestured with her hands, and the canvas straitjacket that had been Wang Zuocai's one article of clothing since 1979 disintegrated as if made from tissue paper. Freed at last, Wang Zuocai's member rose to greet its liberator. Smiling demurely, the woman climbed onto the bed and straddled the old oracle.

Sun Wang Zuocai had foreseen this night's encounter the day he went before Mao and spoke of the American president and of Lady Mao being of the *kitsune*. He knew that Mao would dismiss him as mad, but that was the only way to ensure that he would survive the coming years of turmoil, with its Cultural Revolution and Gang of Four and Ti'animin Square. It was the only way to make sure that he somehow managed to live to see the arrival of the beautiful glowing woman, who would make him the father of a new and wondrous race.

It didn't take him long. After all the planning, all the waiting, everything was happening so fast. As his celestial lover pulled herself off him, Sun Wang Zuocai felt something in his chest fold in on itself. Fast. Everything was happening so fast — first the mating, now his death. Even as his seed quickened in her womb, Wang Zuocai's life came to its end. Of course, he had already known it was going to happen.

✸

WHEN THE DEAD DIE

Death is not the greatest of evils; it is worse to want to die, and not be able to.

— Sophocles, *Electra*

The fever called 'Living'
Is conquered at last.

— Edgar Allan Poe, "For Annie"

As Sonja stepped out of the limo in front of the Chelsea Hotel, the first thing she saw was a homeless person pissing in a doorway. She smiled and tossed the driver an extra twenty.

Hell, it's New York.

The limo pulled back into traffic and she shouldered her one piece of luggage — a black nylon duffel bag — and strode toward the entrance of the hotel, just in case she was being watched. She did a turn in the revolving door and was back on the streets within seconds, her hair five inches longer and the color of raw honey.

She kept a nest in Tribeca, a stone's throw from City Hall. There were a couple of holding companies and realty agencies involved in collecting rents and maintaining the property, but essentially she owned the building. She'd bought it several years ago with some of the proceeds from Ghilardi's estate.

She dodged into the subway entrance on Eighth Avenue, dropping her vision into the Pretender spectrum, scanning for signs of the inhuman among the commuting hordes. In any major city there were numerous shadow races hidden amongst the bread-and-butter featherless bipeds, and New York was certainly no exception.

It was five-thirty — well into rush hour — and the subway platform swarmed with the Pretending Kind of a dozen different cultures, each having followed its traditional prey group to the New World in search of a better life. A *naga* wearing the skin of an elderly Pakistani gentleman flared his cobra's hood at her in ritual warning, then resumed perusing his newspaper. A *garuda*, cloaked in the disguise of a lowly busboy, clattered its bill nervously as it fed itself unshelled sunflower seeds. It and the *naga* kept exchanging glances at one another. Their respective species were ancestral enemies, but having to maintain the illusion of humanity — and catch a train — forced the necessity of coexistence. At least for the moment.

An ogre, its misshapen limbs hidden by homeboy fashion, slouched against one of the support beams. A succubus, dressed in the body of a young woman, smiled seductively at an older man wearing a London Fog raincoat and carrying a briefcase, who was fumbling for a light for her cigarette. Sonja doubted he could see the succubus' cyclopean eye or the mane of living, writhing worms she sported in place of hair.

Suddenly the smells of ozone and filth announced the A Train's arrival. It screeched to a halt and the doors opened. Stepping inside, Sonja found a vargr dressed as an investment banker, and a thick-set, clay-eyed *golem* serving as an escort for an extremely old Hasidic man who, according to her peripheral mind-scan, was carrying a fortune in diamonds on his person.

She rode the train to the World Trade Center, then made her way to the surface. The first thing she saw as she exited the glass-and-steel megalith was the seventeenth-century churchyard across the street. Twilight had mellowed into dusk while she was underground, and — amazing as it might seem for such an urban landscape — a handful of fireflies danced among the leaning tombstones.

Her nest was located on Chambers Street, off West Broadway. The building was six stories tall, identical to those flanking it. The first three floors housed various businesses — a karate school, a photographer's studio, an accounting firm — while the top two floors stayed vacant.

It was after six o'clock and all of the businesses were closed for the day. The elevator was old, with a collapsible gate and a control switch that looked like something from an old-fashioned ocean liner. Sonja stopped the elevator on the fifth floor and rolled back the protective gate so she could unlock the outer barrier. She made a mental note to be careful not to trigger the booby-traps she'd installed.

The entrance barrier rolled back with a rusty squeal, and she squeezed her eyes shut and grimaced, but nothing happened. She stepped out of the elevator and into the foyer. A double-barreled shotgun and a loaded crossbow rigged with fishing line and lead counterweights, were pointed at the elevator.

She unlocked the door to the fifth-floor loft and was swallowed by total darkness. Not that it mattered; she could read the *New York Times* in the deepest pit in Carlsbad Cavern without straining her eyes. The loft had the dusty, close smell that sealed rooms often get. As it was, her nest was actually on the sixth floor. The fifth was empty of anything except booby-traps. She liked keeping as much space as possible between herself and whatever might be looking for her.

One of the first things she'd had the renovators do when she bought the building a decade ago was alter the interior staircases. The original staircases had been sealed and a second staircase had been installed that bypassed the fifth and sixth floors on its way to the roof, thus ensuring her privacy. But this was New York City, after all, so she placed a few booby-traps in her private stairwell just to be on the safe side.

She unlocked the door that led to the roof, after disabling the speargun aimed at gut level. The moment she opened the door, she knew that one of the traps had been sprung.

She found what was left of the would-be burglar on the landing between the roof and the sixth floor. He'd triggered the deadfall, sending a cinderblock into the middle of his face. He had probably been young, although it was hard to tell with most of his features pulped. He'd been lying there at least a month or two, and he'd decayed to the point where she couldn't tell if he was black, white, Latino, or Asian. In any case, he was dead.

Sonja dragged the body down to the sixth floor and unlocked the door to the loft, careful not to trigger the bayonet-studded box-spring mattress hinged to the ceiling just inside the threshold. The sixth floor was sectioned into three large areas centered around a long hallway. The area closest to the entrance was a fully outfitted workroom, containing a carpenter's bench, a huge array of power-tools, and a large, glass-lined metal tub.

With the help of a few well-chosen power tools, it took her less than ten minutes to reduce her unwanted guest into component parts. She tossed the limbs and viscera into the glass-lined tub and opened one of the industrial-sized hydrochloric acid bottles she kept in a special cabinet. The solution was meant to process metal, but it was also handy in turning troublesome dead bodies into soup.

Satisfied that her erstwhile intruder was liquefying nicely, Sonja shucked her protective gloves and apron and headed down the hall to the room set aside as living space. At a thousand square feet, it was larger than most New York apartments. A kitchenette, complete with microwave, dishwasher, gas range, refrigerator, and breakfast bar, took up one corner. There was an inch or more of dust on every surface and a shriveled orange the size of a walnut in the fridge. What had once been a walk-in closet was now a bathroom, complete with shower and toilet, and a loft bed occupied the exposed brick wall. Thick Persian carpets covered the floor, and the ceiling was decorated in drooping falls of mosquito netting, giving the space the feel of a Bedouin's tent. A couple of starkly chic halogen lamps, a free-standing antique wardrobe, and a oversized leather chair set in front of a projection television screen were the only other pieces of furniture.

Sonja opened the wardrobe, and the smell of cedar filled the room. Inside hung several expensive silk suits sealed in protective plastic wrappers, along with a half-dozen matching black silk shirts. Four pairs of Italian shoes littered the floor of the wardrobe. Chaz's stuff. He'd had a taste for the expensive things in life. Not necessarily good, mind you, just expensive. She bundled the suits together and dumped them in the tub with the melting burglar, then went back into the living area and stripped naked.

She didn't realize she was still a blonde until she looked down at her crotch in the shower. She closed her eyes and concentrated. When she reopened them, the last of the yellow was being replaced by black. Her hair was still long, though. Since it was impossible for her to shorten her hair the same way she forced its growth, she elected to jettison it. She ran her fingers through her hair and all twelve inches dropped to the floor of the shower. By the time she stepped out to towel herself dry, her scalp was already bristling with fresh growth.

✷

If I am going to find a clue to Morgan's whereabouts, it will be in the traditional hunting grounds of the urban vampire — the nightclub. I hit the first one around midnight. The interior is designed to resemble a church, with stained-glass windows and a disc jockey spinning CDs in the pulpit. The waitresses are dressed as nuns, except that they wear miniskirts, high heels and fishnet stockings. There are a lot of lasers and loud music, but the faces that stare back at me through the dance-floor fog are painfully human. I leave before one o'clock.

The second club is a cavernous space filled with taxidermy exhibits liberated from defunct roadside attractions. A cougar, frozen in midleap, reaches out for a startled mountain goat. A grizzly bear, its fur somewhat moth-eaten, towers over the main bar, as if warding off imprudent drinkers. The head of a gigantic water buffalo — its nose worn down by club patrons stroking it for luck — peers off into space, no doubt eyeing the ghost of the Great White Hunter who plugged it decades ago.

As I wind my way through the clubgoers, I get the distinct feeling I'm being watched — and not just by the glass eyes of the dead animals on the wall. I duck through a beaded curtain into one of the orgy alcoves off the main floor. The walls are painted with fluorescent paint and lit by black-light tubes. A king-sized mattress on a carpeted dais dominates the middle of the room. A couple of queens tricked out in Mary Tyler Moore drag, wearing six-inch platform shoes, are sitting on the bed, smoking a joint. They look at me quizzically, then return to their previous conversation.

"So what did you tell Donny?"

"Just that she should go ahead and get big ones. I mean, if she's planning on dancing to pay for the operation, she ought to give them what they want...."

I grab my shadow before he even clears the curtain, slamming him against the wall. I place my forearm against his windpipe and my switchblade a millimeter from his right eye.

"Tell me why you're following me, or I'll put it out," I hiss.

The drag queens gather up their purses and exit the alcove as quickly as their platform heels can carry them.

My shadow smiles slow and wide, opening his hands to show me they are empty. "No need to get hostile, milady. I mean you no harm."

I step back and let him go, but I do not put away the knife. My shadow is a man of slight build, about five foot seven. His hair, which he wears in a medusa's coil of tightly woven dreads, is gray, but it is hard to guess his age. Ceramic beads, pieces of metal, and what look like knucklebones are braided into his locks. He wears a loose-fitting black overcoat that reaches almost to his ankles, tight-fitting black leather pants, a black velvet dress shirt with a ruffled dickey, and Doc Martens that lace up to his knees. Although his hands are finely manicured, he sports pimp spoons on both ring fingers — nails so long they curl inward. He smiles easily at me, but his pale blue eyes watch me intently, like a cat trying to calculate the best way to evade the jaws of a dog.

"Why were you following me?"

"It's my job to follow — those such as you." His right hand dips into the breast pocket of his overcoat and retrieves a printed invitation. "My — employers — are discreet and very...discriminating...as to whom they allow in their establishment. Their clientele is most select, indeed." He hands me the card with a flourish. "Tell them Jen sent you, milady." And with that he slips from the alcove, pausing only long enough to look over his shoulder to make sure I'm not about to plunge my switchblade into his back.

I study the invitation, frowning slightly. In appearance it looks no different from any of the thousands of invitations and announcements handed out on the New York party circuit every night. The picture on the front is of a naked female torso. The nipples are pierced and connected by a fine filigreed chain, the labia infibulated. A surgical steel ring winks from the model's navel. On the back is printed, in Gothic script, *The Black Grotto at No Exit: W.14th @ 10th Avenue. Open to the Trade.*

There is something odd about the texture of the ink used to print the card — and something familiar about it, as well. I sniff it, then taste it with the tip of my tongue. Human blood has been mixed with the ink. Quite a bit of it, too.

I step out of the alcove just as the two drag queens are coming back with the bouncer. I slip into the murk of the dance floor and I'm out the door in seconds. No matter. I already know what nightclub I'm going to hit next.

✷

The doorman at No Exit is dressed in black leather chaps, a suede jockstrap, and a leather-and-chrome-studded slave harness. He scowls at me and lifts his hand to block my path.

"Seventy-five dollars t'get in."

"Jen sent me," I reply, holding up my invitation so he can see it.

The doorman jerks back his hand as if I'd scalded him, eyes widening. "I'm sorry, milady! I — I didn't realize…! Welcome to No Exit! You'll want the second door on the right after the ladies room, in the back of the main hall."

I breeze past him into a cinderblock antechamber filled with gym lockers. I pass through a doorway hung with black velvet curtains and find myself headed down a concrete corridor lit by lurid red spots that make everything seem awash in blood. Fifty feet later there is a heavy vault door. I turn the handle and the door hisses open on pneumatic pistons. The sound of Sonic Youth amplified beyond human endurance pours into the confines of the corridor.

The main hall of No Exit is large enough to park a jet in. The cinderblock-and-poured-concrete floor motif continues, accompanied by the standard disco fog and laser light displays. A long bar made from cinderblocks and glass bricks occupies most of the west wall, with a handful of tables and booths nearby. An elevated stage juts from the north wall, with a set of stocks, a flogging post, and a rack of whips and chains.

Close to a hundred people, all in various stages of dress or undress, wander the floor. Some have black leather masks over their heads; some wear harnesses; and one patron walks around with a chrome bit in his mouth, the attached reins held by a pudgy woman stuffed into a merry widow corset. All of them, to my surprise, are human.

I make my way to the back of the club. The ladies room is a toilet placed in the middle of a waist-high corral of cinderblocks. The door I was instructed to find is guarded by a monstrously huge specimen wearing leather pants, a muscle shirt, and a zippered leather face mask. Try as it might, the hood cannot conceal the fact that the bouncer is an ogre.

"Jen sent me," I say, flashing the invitation.

The ogre grunts something and stands aside, swiping a magnetic key through the computer lock that secures the door. I glimpse a stairway leading to the basement. Once I'm inside, the ogre closes the door behind me, leaving me to whatever fate I've walked into.

I hear music — not disco or techno or rave, but the strains of Mozart — as I climb down the stairs. At the bottom is yet another secured door, this one guarded by an ogre too misshapen ever to be mistaken for human, with or without a bondage mask. His single brow furrows and he rubs his lower left tusk as he studies the invitation I hand him. In his huge, gnarled hand it looks like a playing card.

"Jen sent me," I explain.

The ogre makes a snorting noise like that of a warthog and unlocks the final door with a key the size of a tire iron. "Have good night," it oinks.

The interior of the club is dark, lit by low-wattage, rose-colored bulbs so the human attendants don't trip and fall as they work the room. There is a lot of black velvet drapery, antique statuary and Victorian furniture in evidence. But the first things that catch my notice upon entering are the people hanging from the ceiling. Some are men, some are women, some are children. Almost every major ethnic group seems to be represented. They are all naked and suspended by piano wire from hooks fixed in their flesh. Some are wrapped in barbed wire. Some have been flayed, peeled to expose the muscles beneath their skin. All of them are alive.

Something warm and wet strikes my hand. It's blood. I look up to see a partially skinned young man suspended directly overhead. The skin on his legs and feet has been carefully pared away, leaving only the bone. He smiles down at me like a medieval martyr, his eyes flickering in and out of focus as he speaks.

"Welcome to the Black Grotto, milady."

The other human chandeliers echo his greeting, their voices slurred and dreamy.

This is my kind of place.... purrs the Other.

I'm too distracted by the chorus of flayed cherubs to try to squash the

Other's voice, so I lick the blood from my hand and move on. A woman encased completely in black latex except for her throat, her arms stuffed into a single glove and bound behind her back, walks up to me, accompanied by the whir of a chain being played out. I notice her dog collar is attached to a spool of stainless-steel chain set into the wall. Her exposed jugular is outfitted with a phlebotomist's shunt.

A slender young man dressed in lollypop panties and a starched pinafore steps forward, holding a solid gold serving tray. On the tray are a syringe and a Baccarat crystal wine glass.

I stare at the syringe, then back at the shunt set in the woman's neck. I cannot see her face — it is obscured by a leather bondage mask, the mouth zippered shut from the outside. Her eyes are wet and gleam like a trapped animal's.

I shake my head and turn away, both disgusted and excited by the display around me. In one corner of the room, a string quartet plays Mozart's "Symphony No. 40 in G Minor." Upon closer examination I can see that the musicians' eyelids are sewn shut and their mouths are filled with ball gags.

There is a scream from elsewhere in the room and a naked boy no older than ten runs out from a curtained booth, blood streaming from the wound in his neck. A vampire dressed in the cassock and collar of a priest darts after him, hissing angrily. One of the attendants grabs the frightened boy by the hair and slams him against the wall, dazing the child. As I move forward to intervene, the priest-vampire slaps the attendant so hard the blow snaps his neck. The naked, bleeding boy, sniffling and knuckling his teary eyes, runs forward to embrace the vampire. The priest coos endearments and strokes the boy's hair, all the while leading him back to the curtained booth. The string ensemble switches from Mozart to the Kronos Quartet's arrangement of "Purple Haze." An ogre shambles out of the shadows and picks up the body of the dead attendant as if it weighs no more than a suitcase, tossing it over one stooped shoulder.

"I see you decided to come check out the scene."

Jen is standing off to one side, watching me with a twist of smile on his lips. He has his left arm draped over the narrow shoulders of a naked girl-child who looks to be about six or seven. The girl's eyes are heavily painted, like those of an Egyptian priestess, and her hairless pubes are sewn shut.

Jen's smile disappears and he jerks his head in the direction of one of the curtained alcoves. "My employers would speak with you, milady."

"Your employers? And who might they be?"

Jen lifts the heavy velvet curtain at the mouth of the alcove and gestures for me to enter. "Their most Serene Majesties Baron Luxor and Lady Nuit."

The names sound familiar, although I cannot place them. They are

Nobles, that much is certain. In the twenty years I've spent in search of Morgan, I've only come across one other vampire of power — Pangloss, Morgan's own vampiric sire. Most of the bloodsuckers I've dealt with are exceptionally minor-league — many no more than brain-dead revenants. Now I'm being brought before not one, but two, Nobles. I make sure my switchblade is ready before entering.

Inside the audience chamber is an antique love seat on which reclines a male vampire, naked except for a black leather pouch, garter belt, black silk stockings and matching patent leather pumps. His hair, shaped to resemble a shaggy Beatles cut, frames a long face that has neither eyebrows nor lashes. The vampire's flesh is so pale it seems translucent, like that of a finely polished opal. A human male wrapped in a full bodysuit of latex lies curled at the vampire's feet like an adoring hound. I shift my vision into the Pretender spectrum in order to gauge the vampire lord's aura. It is a powerful one, surging and bubbling around his head like boiling sugar.

"You are the Baron Luxor?"

The Noble's lips pull up in an approximation of a smile. "And you are the Blue Woman?"

"I am Sonja Blue, if that's what you mean."

Luxor sits up slowly, his eyes never leaving me. No doubt he's assessing me as well. "We ordered Jen to keep an eye out for you. The old man told us you'd be coming sooner or later."

"The old man?"

"Pangloss." Luxor stands up, wobbling slightly on four-inch heels. "He was the one who told us about you — that you were the one who marked Morgan, the one who devoured his chimera...."

"You keep saying "we," but I only see one of you. Where is this Lady Nuit Jen mentioned?"

Luxor smiles and turns to face me, flashing a brief glimpse of fang. "Oh, she is here. She is always here."

Suddenly Luxor's opalescent flesh twitches and ripples, as the muscles underneath begin to dance. The vampire lord's waist seems to draw in on itself, as if being cinched by an invisible hand. The muscles lining his chest ripen and swell, blossoming into small but serviceable breasts. The leather pouch covering Luxor's sex deflates as he retracts his testes. The bones in his face squelch and groan as they mold themselves into softer, more feminine aspects. A tight nest of coppery curls sprouts from his scalp, spilling down to cover his shoulders. I have to admit I'm impressed. Such tightly controlled shapeshifting is not easy, even among Nobles.

Lady Nuit claps her hands and the latex-coated slave jumps up and scurries off into the shadows, returning a moment later with a silk kimono decorated with butterflies. She stands there, arms outstretched, and allows him to dress her.

"Why were you looking for me?"

"We were told you were a creature of great power. A creature of...purpose. And that you would see the Lord of the Morning Star dead."

"What's that got to do with you?"

Lady Nuit produces a syringe and sticks it into a shunt that juts out of the latex-slave's elbow. As she speaks, she draws a quarter-pint of blood and decants it into a champagne flute. "Morgan has been our enemy for centuries — our broodlings have clashed and struggled with one another since the days of the Bourbon Kings. Countless renfields have died in our service, protecting us from his attacks on our person. We would see him dead forever."

"So?"

Lady Nuit pauses to sniff the blood she's just drained, then sips it. She smiles appreciatively and motions for me to help myself. "Exquisite! Please do try some. It's from my private stock, as you can see."

It has been a couple of days since I last fed — and on animal blood, not human. I can feel my palms begin to sweat and itch as I eye the latex-slave. "N-no thank you."

Lady Nuit studies me, rolling the champagne flute between her palms thoughtfully. "Ah, yes...Pangloss told us you had a peculiar attachment to humans. But you have tasted their blood, have you not?"

"Yes."

"Then why do you hesitate? All the humans you have seen here tonight came here of their own free will. They begged us to use them in such a fashion. The world is full of those who seek their own destruction. They are drawn to our kind, like moths to the flame. You know that, my dear."

"Even the children?"

"Runaways, each and every one of them — fleeing parents and guardians far more inhumane than ourselves. They asked us for refuge, and we provide it."

"I don't believe you." I focus my attention on the latex-slave crouched at Nuit's feet. There are control threads the color of raw veins sprouting from his cowled head, leading back to Nuit/Luxor. With a single swipe of my mind, I sever the leash binding master to slave.

The latex-slave jumps to his feet and begins screaming. He pulls off the mask shrouding his head, revealing himself to be an older man with gray hair and the look of a prosperous banker. Still shrieking, he claws at the shunt stuck in the crook of his arm, his eyes bulging out of their sockets like ping-pong balls.

"How dare you!" shrieks Lady Nuit, her bone-white cheeks blotched with unbecoming raspberry blotches. She must be *really* pissed to get that much blood pushed into one area. "How dare you break my leash?!?"

The latex-slave's body snaps like a whip as Nuit shoves her will back into him. He collapses onto the floor, lips foaming and limbs twitching spasmodically. There is a ripe, unpleasantly organic smell as he shits his suit.

Nuit spins to face me, eyes flashing red, fangs bared. She is so flustered she's lost control of her physical nature and her features are sliding back toward those of Luxor's. I briefly glimpse the vampire for what it truly is — a walking cadaver with skin the color of tallow, its withered flesh stretched taut over desiccated muscle — then the illusion is once more in place.

"I'll take your heart for that, stripling," Luxor/Nuit snarls, reaching for me with fingers capped by six-inch long talons.

"I don't think so," I reply, the blade of my switchblade leaping out from my fist.

Luxor's eyes flare with fear at the sight of the silver blade and he draws back his hand as if he realized he was about to stick it in a hornet's nest. "Put it away! Put that horrid thing away!" he hisses.

"What's the matter, your ladyship? Didn't Pangloss tell you about my little toy? The one I used to mark both Morgan and him?"

Luxor doesn't take his eyes away from the blade. He stares at it the way a cobra follows the motions of a fakir's flute. "Silver," he mumbles. "*S-s-silver.*"

I start backing away from Luxor and out of the alcove, every fiber of my being ready to fight my way out if need be. "So — you hate Morgan and want me to get him out of your way, is that it? Funny, Pangloss came to me with a similar proposal three years ago. Since you two — or should I say three? — are such good friends, I'm surprised he didn't tell you. You fuckin' Nobles are all the same — too afraid to get your own hands dirty! I could care less about how you feel about Morgan. Oh, I'm going to kill him. But I'm going to do it for me, not some gender-bending bloodsucker! Oh, and Luxor—? Once I've done him, I'm coming back for you. *Both* of you."

✷

I know I'm being followed. I felt my "fan club" stalking me long before I left the West Village. And, from what I can sense of his mind, he isn't human. One of Luxor's by-blows, no doubt, sent to keep an eye on me and find out where I'm dossing down. Well, he's going to discover that I don't like being watched — the hard way.

I pretend I don't notice him, making sure to screen my thoughts just in case the dead boy on my tail actually has some esper muscle. I saunter along the streets, leading him in the direction of Alphabet City, my hands stuffed in the pockets of my leather jacket, whistling a tune between my teeth. I stop in front of a store on First Avenue and study an artfully arranged display of Day of the Dead figurines. A papier-mâché-and-pipe-cleaner skeleton dressed as a surgeon opens up a skeleton patient; a skeleton groom marries a skeleton bride; a skeleton beautician washes the bare skull of a skeleton patron. I smile, charmed by such naive, and practical, interpretations of the After.

Even though it is going on four A.M., there are still people on the streets. I pass a handful of partygoers standing outside one of the Korean delis, clutching thirty-ouncers to their chests as they try to decide where to head to next. A severely drunken man with a Jersey accent is bellowing into a nearby pay phone at the top of his lungs.

"Fuck you! Fuck-fuck-fuck!"

He tries to slam the receiver into the cradle, but misses. This makes him so angry he uses the receiver to beat the pay phone's protective metal shell.

"Fuck!fuck!fuck!"

The partygoers back away, uncertain how to handle their companion's slide into alcoholic rage. The pay-phone abuser then tries to throw the receiver at a passing cab, but it doesn't go very far. However, the momentum of his swing spins him into me as I walk by. The sound he makes as I casually slam him back into the phone is meaty — like that of a dog struck by a speeding car. He stops shouting "fuck." The partygoers, their eyes suddenly wide and sober, clear the sidewalk as I pass.

I feel my shadow hesitate. The unconscious drunk is tempting, especially since his companions for the evening have abruptly abandoned him to whatever fate might come his way. I don't want what's following me to think I'm paying attention, so I keep walking toward First and Houston.

The entrance to the F Train stop is in the middle of an asphalt wasteland that claims to be a recreation area. A narrow strip sandwiched between Houston and First Street, it boasts a neglected swingset, a tiny handball court, a couple of fiberglass chickens set on oversized springs for toddlers to ride to nowhere, and a basketball court without a net. Or a backboard. The rest of the area is painfully bare — except for when the homeless and street hustlers set up their pathetic thieves' market on the weekends. But it is way too late for anyone to be interested in playing b-ball or picking over other people's rubbish. The early morning emptiness gives the area genuine urban menace.

I head down the stairs leading to the subway, switching from low to high gear. When I mingle with humans on their level, I often feel as if I'm moving underwater, like a thoroughbred horse racing with a handicap. But every so often — when no one is looking — I shed all pretense and move between the doors of human perception.

I flit past the token booth, pausing for a fraction of a heartbeat, staring into the bulletproof cage at the bored Transit Authority worker inside. To my eyes she is moving even slower than in real-time, if that's possible; her index finger is frozen as she pages through a copy of *People*. If she senses me at all, it is as a brief shudder of gooseflesh, nothing more.

No alarm is raised as I vault over the turnstiles and dash toward the uptown platform. I glide down the stairs, keeping to the shadows between the thick red columns that hold the crumbling roof aloft.

A bare concrete platform runs the length of Houston from First to Second Avenue, broken only by a single wooden bench and a central post inlaid with red and white tile. The platform is empty except for a bum, who is forced to sleep upright on the bench because of the wooden dividers that split the bench into individual seats. There's a puddle of vomit between the bum's busted-out army boots. If I were a human, I would no doubt be nervous about waiting for a train in such a station.

I climb up one of the red columns and squat among the cross beams, surprising a rat in its nest. It squeals at me and shows its teeth. I grab the animal and snap its neck in one clean motion, silencing its complaints. Satisfied, I peer down between my boots for my shadow's arrival. I don't have long to wait.

It is a male. Looks to be thirtysomething. Dressed very nondescriptly, but respectably. A banker, maybe. Perhaps some variety of accountant. Something very unobtrusive, but not worthy of contempt. That is what vampires strive for in their camouflage — at least that's true of the majority. Only the older and more powerful ones flaunt their differences and risk drawing attention to themselves.

The vampire, like myself, is operating on high gear, which means he's practically invisible to the human eye. If the bum comes to or another passenger comes onto the platform, all that person will see is a blur at the corner of his eye. Perhaps, if he is particularly astute, he might feel anxious and hurry to leave.

I watch, amused, as my shadow flits back and forth along the platform, snarling in frustration at my apparent disappearance. It seems Luxor has sent one of his duller drones. I wait until the vampire is almost directly under me before dropping down. I tap him on the shoulder as I land, causing him to spin around in confusion. I'm pleased by the fear and surprise on his face. It's been a long time since anything last got the drop on him.

"Lookin' for me, dead boy?"

I catch him with a left to the jaw and the corpse just *takes* it! His lower jaw swings free like a busted gate as I plow into him, punching his gut hard enough to lift him off the ground a foot or two.

The edge is off the surprise, however, and the dead boy shrieks and claws at me, catching the side of my face and slicing it open to the bone. The mask of Marvin Milquetoast, Boy Executive, crumbles and I find myself tangling with a gaunt, red-eyed, noseless ghoul with three-inch fingernails and breath that could knock a buzzard off a shit wagon at ten paces. It isn't the first time I've found myself in such a predicament.

We hit the ground, spitting and clawing at one another like a couple of wildcats in heat. Luxor's drone is strong — I'll give it that — but it lacks stamina. It's used to battening on hapless commuters and frightened street people, nothing more. It sure as hell isn't used to having a real fight on its hands.

I straddle the dead boy's chest, wrap my hands around its milk-white throat, and begin to hammer its skull repeatedly into the concrete. I know I should take out my switchblade and do the deed and leave the rotting excuse for a bloodsucker's head on his master's doorstep as a warning, but I stay my hand. I want to kill the wretched piece of shit — but I want to do it *slowly*.

"Freeze, punk!"

A gun presses against the side of my head. I look up and find myself staring into the business end of a Glock, held by the bum that had, until a moment or two before, been unconscious on the bench. The bum, dressed in reeking rags stuffed full of newspaper, holds up a badge in a battered leather wallet. Great, just my luck! I was so preoccupied with the vampire that I didn't bother to check to see if the bum was real, too.

I let go of the dead boy and stand up slowly. The muzzle of the Glock is barely an inch from my head. I could probably take the cop, but I don't want to chance it. A bullet in the head's fatal, vampire or not.

The cop grabs me by the scruff of my jacket and throws me up against the nearest column. "Okay, you! Hands up where I can see 'em! Keep those fingers spread out or I'll fuckin' break 'em, unnerstand!?"

Keeping one hand on my shoulder, he turns back to look at my opponent. "Are you all right, sir? I've got backup on the way — do you need an ambulance?"

I hear the approaching sirens already echoing in the subway tunnels, like the screams of banshees rushing to a feast. So can the dead boy, and it's making him nervous. His assignment has turned out bad. Bad enough that his master will no doubt do something very unpleasant to him. Something worse than being dead.

"Sir — can you answer me? Do you need assistance?"

The dead boy moves toward him and the undercover cop gets his first good look at the so-called "victim." The sight of the vampire's dislocated lower jaw and gore-smeared skull makes the cop shift his weight uncomfortably.

"Uh — sir?"

The vampire's on him in less time than it takes to swallow. The cop screams as the dead boy sinks his fangs into his throat, somehow managing to squeeze off a couple of rounds into his attacker's midsection. The Glock punches huge, ugly wounds in the vampire's front and out his back, but they don't seem to faze him.

I grab the bloodsucker by the top of his head, peeling him off his victim like a leech. The undercover cop's lost a substantial amount of blood, but he's far from drained. He clutches his wounded throat, horror and confusion in his eyes, as I hold the vampire in a hammerlock. The beast spits and screams and claws at the air like a bobcat with a hot wire up its ass.

"Get the hell outta here!" I snarl. "Now!"

The cop doesn't wait to be told twice.

The sirens are almost on top of us. I've long since grown weary of the game. It's time to play hardball

"Shut the fuck up!" I hiss at the struggling vampire. When he refuses to quiet down, I slam his head into the nearest column hard enough to make something squirt out his ears.

"I *was* going to kick your ass and send you whimpering back to your liege like a whipped dog. But then you had to go and get cute and try and wipe the cop! That was stupid, dead boy! Very, *very* stupid!" I emphasize just *how* stupid by repeatedly banging his head against the column.

There's a sudden rumbling and the platform begins to vibrate below my feet. The tunnel fills with a hot, gritty wind that smells of piss and electricity. I grin in anticipation. A noise from the upper level draws my attention away from the approaching F train.

A couple of uniformed Transit Authority cops thunder down the stairs to the platform, guns drawn, eyes bugging with adrenaline and fear. The one in front nearly steps on the wounded undercover officer, who got as far as the foot of the stairs before collapsing from blood loss.

The second uniformed T.A., a painfully young Hispanic who looks more afraid than an armed man should, moves toward me.

The train drowns out his words, but it's not hard to read his lips: *"Transit Police! Halt or I'll shoot!"*

So I hurl the vampire in front of the F Train.

I see the conductor's face in the little window at the front of the train. I see the look of horror in his eyes as he realizes what is happening. The train's going very, very fast, even for late at night. No doubt he's already been alerted to the trouble on the Second Avenue platform and has been ordered not to stop. The Other finds his anguish quite amusing. And appetizing.

The train keeps going, rumbling by like a great steel dragon. The wind from its passing musses my hair and forces me to step back in deference to its blind, automotive power.

Clack-clack-rumble — brief glimpses of bleary, frightened faces peering out from the safety of the individual cars — and the F train's gone, headed for the Broadway/Lafayette stop four blocks away.

The young Transit Authority cop, momentarily frozen by the passing of the train, still has his gun leveled at me. I stand at the edge of the platform, hands upraised, smiling pleasantly. The cop's partner, an older Oriental man, circles me from the side, his gun pointed directly at my head. I smell the fear radiating from them. It's thick and pungent, like that of a pot roast ready to come out of the oven. The Other's growing agitated. It wants to feed.

"Morning, officer."

"You fuckin' crazy bitch!"

"I beg your pardon?"

"You threw him off the platform! You killed that man in cold blood!"

"I beg to differ on both counts, officer. I didn't kill him — and he wasn't a man."

"What?"

"Look for yourself."

Without really wanting to, the younger cop glances down onto the track — and what he sees causes him to scream.

"Jesus, Diaz!" snaps the older cop. He's patting me down while trying to keep one eye on his partner. "You seen suicides chewed up by trains before! Get a hold of yourself!"

The younger cop doesn't seem to hear him. Instead, he begins to empty his gun at something below the level of the platform.

The older cop loses what little patience he started out with. "Diaz! Cut the crap!" He has his cuffs out and is securing one of the bracelets to my left wrist. "We don't have time for bullshit like this!"

"Neither do I," I sigh, slipping free of the older cop's hold and ramming my elbow into the middle of his face. He falls like a bag of suet.

The younger cop's exhausted his clip, but he keeps on firing anyway. His face is rigid with terror as he backs away from the platform. The vampire — or what's left of it — has finally succeeded in dragging itself off the tracks.

The train cut him in two as neatly as a magician's saw, chopping him off at the waist. The viscera dangling from his ruined torso look like party streamers dipped in transmission fluid. Eyes glowing with an inhuman hate, he lifts his truncated torso on his arms, using clawed hands as feet.

I relieve the unconscious cop of his gun, shaking my head in amazement. "Buddy, you just don't know when to call it quits, do you?"

The vampire swings his right arm forward, then his left, dragging a length of intestine behind him like a gory bridal train.

"Any last words, butt-munch?"

The vampire bares his fangs at me and hisses.

The policeman's gun takes off the top of his head, dropping the vampire as effectively as it would any garden-variety criminal. The younger cop stares at me for a second, his face the color of new cheese. I smile at him. His eyes get even bigger and he runs for the stairs.

There are more sirens up top. Flashing lights from arriving cop cars and ambulances leak through the cracks in the ceiling. I hear the thunder of city-issued shoe leather on pavement. Within seconds the platform will be swarming with police. It's time for me to kiss this scene goodbye.

I toss the cop's gun off the platform like I would a spent wad of chewing gum and shift back into high gear. I speed up the platform, in the direction of the Second Avenue exits, away from the arriving cops. Because the Second Avenue exits are near the Sara Delano Roosevelt Park, a favorite spot for the neighborhood derelicts, the gateways are kept chained shut from nine in the evening until six in the morning. Not that I care. I push against the gates and the chain shatters, sending the lock flying.

I ghost up the stairs on the Chrystie Street side of the intersection, gliding over an elderly black man sitting in a pool of his own waste, a bottle of malt liquor clutched to his chest like a beloved child. He starts awake, flailing at the air with a grimy claw.

"Awgeddofmutherfuckerdontocuhmahshitsparequatah?"

His voice joins the inchoate roar of the city, and it echoes in my ears as I race through the shadows, along with the screams of police sirens fading into the coming dawn.

Anhwei Province, The People's Republic of China

Qi You Wu and his wife, Mei Li, were simple workers who lived in a two-room house on the outskirts of the town of Pang-pu. Both Qi You and Mei Li liked to think of themselves as "modern." They had married out of love, not family obligation, having met while working side-by-side on the assembly line at the tractor factory. Being modern young workers, Qi You and Mei Li understood the importance of population control to their country and the Party. When Mei Li became pregnant earlier that year, they signed a document declaring that upon the birth of their child they would both undergo sterilization procedures. They would be rewarded for their selflessness by being given special consideration for promotions at work and recognition by the local Party officials as dedicated workers.

Mei Li had been a little apprehensive at first — what if their baby was a girl? Even though she was modern, it was hard to ignore centuries of ingrained Chinese culture. Boy children had always been far more valuable than girl children. To have many sons is the definition of Chinese luck and happiness. She worried and worried about what might happen if the baby was a daughter. However, when she was finally brought to the midwife's station, she delivered a boy, whom the couple named Qui En. Three days later, Mei Li and her husband underwent the sterilization procedures they'd agreed to. But now, two weeks later, Mei Li was beginning to wonder if they had not made the biggest mistake of their lives.

The Wu house was a concrete box with a red tile roof, identical to the hundreds of other low-ranking industrial workers' homes lining Pang-pu's streets. The two rooms comprised a combination kitchen/living area and a smaller sleeping room. The house was drafty in the winter and hot in the summer, and the Wus shared a communal toilet with the household next door. Mei Li and Qi You dreamed of someday making good and moving to more spacious and pleasant surroundings. But for now, Mei Li was forced to keep the baby's cradle next to the oil stove that provided the family with heat and food. It was close to midnight and Mei Li was still sitting next to the stove, watching her baby and worrying.

"Mei Li — when are you coming to bed?" Qi You was standing in the door to their bedroom, his hair tousled and eyes puffy. "You have to be at work at the factory the same time as I do — how can you make your quota if you don't get any sleep? The line supervisor is sure to notice—"

"Something is wrong with Qui En. He wouldn't take his bottle."

"It's probably just a cold. All the babies at the creche have colds."

Mei Li frowned and leaned forward, fussing with the blanket around the baby's feet. "I should not have placed him in the creche so soon. He's so little...."

"Mei Li, we've already discussed this. We agreed that leaving Qui En at the daycare center was the only logical answer. Your mother lives too far away and we cannot afford for you to stay home with the baby...."

"You are right, Qi You. I know you're speaking the truth. But I still can't help but worry. He's our only child. The only one we'll ever have."

Qi You smiled despite his weariness and kissed the top of his wife's head. "It is good that you worry for your son. It means you are a good mother. I worry, too. But I will be even more worried if I do not get my promotion."

Mei Li held her husband's hand tightly for a long moment, her eyes never leaving the cradle. "Go and get some sleep. I'll join you in a little while. I won't be up much longer — I promise."

Qi You sighed and went back to bed alone, while Mei Li remained perched on a stool beside the stove, rocking her son's cradle and singing lullabies. She could hear her husband snoring in the other room. The sound reminded her just how tired she was. Suddenly her eyelids grew heavy and her head began to nod. Ten minutes after his mother fell asleep, Qui En stopped breathing.

A golden light filled the front windows of the Wu house, and the door opened inward as if unlatched by a phantom hand. Standing on the threshold was a naked woman with long hair that fluttered about as if blown by gentle winds. In her arms was a baby boy with dark hair and Oriental eyes. The stranger hovered beside the sleeping woman for a moment, then took the body of little Qui En from the cradle, leaving the living baby in its place. Then, as quickly and silently as she arrived, the glowing woman floated out the door.

Mei Li awoke with a start, blinking in confusion. She must have fallen asleep. She looked into the cradle to check on Qui En and was both surprised and relieved to find that whatever had been bothering her son had passed. Qui En gurgled happily at her, waving his little hands at her as if in greeting.

New York City

Two voices on a telephone line:

"She's here."

"Are you sure it's her?"

"I'm positive. It's her, of that you can be certain."

"Good. I knew she'd come once she got the clippings. But be careful. She's deadlier by far than any other you've ever crossed, my boy."

"I know. That's why she fascinates me so."

✹

Something's in the room.

It wasn't even a thought. More a feeling. A sensation picked up by slumbering sensory apparatus and fed into an unconscious mind. Is it the real thing or merely a dream of intrusion?

Wake up, you stupid bitch! the Other shrieked, answering the reality-dream issue once and for all. *We've got company!*

Sonja came off the loft bed in three seconds flat, fangs extended, hair bristling like a cat's back. There was no time for her to wonder how they managed to find her. No time to try and figure out how they got past the booby-traps. She hit the ground in a low crouch, hissing a warning at the intruder seated in the leather easy chair.

"No need for such theatrics, milady," Jen purred. There was no fear in his eyes. Caution, yes — but no fear. "I intend you no harm."

"If that's the case, what are you doing here?"

"My employers wanted to know where you're keeping your nest. They told me to assign a shadow to you. I'm sure you remember him. However, you needn't fear me. I won't tell them I know where you spend your daylight hours."

"What are you getting at, renfield?"

Jen's spine stiffened and indignation flickered in his eyes. "I am not a renfield."

"You couldn't prove it by me. You're a human working for vampires — that makes you a renfield in *my* book. Theirs, too, I'd say."

This seemed to make him bridle even more. "I am my own man, damn you! I work for Luxor and Nuit because it suits my needs, not because they've got a slave collar snapped around my mind!"

"All the more reason for me not to trust you. At least renfields don't have much control over what they do. After all, they're addicts. You — you on the other hand — you're one of their bellwethers. You lure your fellow humans to their doom to benefit your vampiric partners and line your own pockets!"

The pale blue of Jen's eyes seemed to intensify as he glowered at Sonja. "I am not a renfield, nor am I a bellwether. I am like you."

"You are *nothing* like me!"

"Perhaps. Perhaps not. But you're wrong about my species. I am not human — I am *dhampire*."

Sonja turned to stare at him. "*Dhampire*? I've heard rumors of such things — the supposed byproducts of vampire-human matings."

Jen smoothed his braided coils like Medusa calming her snakes. "There are very few of my kind in this world. As I said, I am *dhampire*. My mother was human...."

"And your father a vampire? Impossible! Vampires are dead things — their sperm inert. They may very well be capable of erection — even ejaculation — but they are incapable of reproduction."

"I am very well aware of the procreative failings of the living dead," Jen sniffed. "If you will allow me to continue, I'll explain. My biological father was human enough, although I have no clue as to his identity. Not that it matters. My mother was a streetwalker. Whitechapel, in fact. No doubt my father was a drunken sot with tuppence in his pocket and a hard-on in his pants. She was only fourteen when she had me, mind you. However, shortly after becoming pregnant, my mother fell in with a certain gentleman of Noble mien, if you understand me.

"She was his favorite for a couple of months — until she began to show her condition. Such things are anathema to vampires — they are forever frozen in time, changeless and unchanging. The withering and dying of their human consorts is one thing — entropy, after all, is the vampire's handmaiden — but the creation of new life! Ah, that reminds them that they are, indeed, outside the chain of Nature. They pretend to have disdain for how humans reproduce, but they are secretly envious and jealous to the point of mania.

"As I said, my mother's lover may have cast her aside, but it was too late. I was already affected by the venom he released into her each time he fed. When I was born my mother placed me in a foundling home and went in search of similar lovers. I was always — strange. My life was made a living hell by my warders and fellow inmates. Then, when I was eight years old, my mother reappeared and took me to live with her.

"Over the years my mother had developed into a courtesan for those of Noble make. She'd become quite wealthy and bought a fashionable house in London, which she turned into a salon of sorts where she entertained her clients. She even had a few lovers outside the vampire race — the occasional *vargr* prince, *kitsune* diplomat, or ogre businessman. Compared to the brutality and indifference of the foundling home, it seemed perfectly normal to me.

"It wasn't until I was twelve years old that I realized that I was far from human. While I lay curled deep within my mother's womb, her lover's tainted seed had worked its way into my system. I was hardly a vampire, but I could walk the streets of London and actually see the Pretenders for what they were. I also benefited from heightened senses and an intuition for what those around me truly desired. In no time I was serving as my mother's pimp, searching the streets and back alleys for eager clients.

"But, by far, my surrogate father's most lasting contribution was in the realm of longevity. How old do you think I am?"

"I don't know," Sonja shrugged. "Forty? Forty-five?"

"I'll be one hundred and twenty-seven come next June!" Jen cackled, clapping his hands. "Bet you didn't guess *that*, milady!"

"You're right on that account. But it still doesn't answer why you're here — and why I shouldn't kill you where you sit."

Jen held up one hand, begging her indulgence. "My employers are just that — employers. They are not my liege and lady. I came of age in the very breast of monstrosity, if you will. I feel no kinship for humans — yet I do not consider myself a vampire. I am a nation unto myself. A member of a solitary race. I serve many masters — yet I am slave to none. And I am not here to see Luxor's petty vendetta carried out. I am here on behalf of one known to you — one who considers himself more friend than foe."

"Pangloss."

Jen grunted as he pushed himself out of the easy chair. "Most astute. He sent me instead of one of his personal servitors because of your predilection for slaying vampires on sight. I am to bring you to him."

Sonja shook her head and folded her arms over her chest. "I have no interest in seeing Pangloss again. I've had my fill of his mind games and trickery. You can tell him what I told Luxor — if he wants Morgan dead, tough. I don't subcontract."

"You misunderstand — Pangloss doesn't give a rat's ass about Morgan. Not anymore, that is. He wants to see you for other, more personal reasons."

"Such as?"

"He's dying."

✹

Pangloss's lair was located in the top three floors of a tony apartment building in Gramercy Park. The doorman scowled at Sonja when she first entered the building. When he saw Jen, however, his eyes glazed and his face went slack.

"Pangloss has him conditioned," Jen stage-whispered into her ear as they hurried into the elevators. "Whenever he sees me or one of the servants, he goes into a fugue-state. Doesn't remember who came in or when. Otherwise, he's a tough doorman to sneak by unannounced."

The elevator let them out at the penthouse. A renfield dressed in pale green surgeon's scrubs, his hair under a sterile disposable paper cap, greeted them.

"Thank goodness you brought her! We were afraid you weren't going to make it in time! He's getting worse!"

"The old bastard's managed to continue for over fifteen hundred years," Jen sneered. "I'm sure he can hold out for another hour or two."

The renfield's eyes hardened and Sonja could tell he wanted to say — or do — something to Jen, but was afraid to. If Pangloss was indeed dying, his renfields would soon find themselves stuck for a fix — and protection.

Jen watched the indignant servant storm off, then whispered behind his hand. "Renfields! They're all such drama queens!"

Sonja was led into a large, handsomely appointed living room. A sliding glass door opened onto a patio that boasted a panoramic view of the city. The Chrysler Building glowed in the night like an Art Deco syringe. An old man sat in a wheelchair in front of a large television, watching a program with the volume turned off. The old man turned his head toward the pair and smiled, revealing blackened gums and fangs the color of antique ivory.

"Hello, my child. So good of you to come."

Sonja was shocked by Pangloss's debilitation. The last time she'd seen him — three years ago — he'd looked as he had in 1975 when she first met him. He'd seemed a healthy, vigorous and virile man in his early fifties, with only a touch of gray in his hair. The creature that sat in the wheelchair, however, looked more like late-era Howard Hughes than classic Cary Grant.

Although he was rapidly going bald, what little hair Pangloss still possessed was the color of a soiled sheet and hung almost to the middle of his back. His frame was wasted and his limbs twisted and infirm. She noticed he had the persistent wobble of a Parkinson's patient. His hands and feet were wrinkled and looked more like the claws of a vulture. He was swaddled in a white terrycloth bathrobe and an adult diaper. When Luxor had referred to Pangloss as "the old man" she'd been puzzled by his choice of words. Now she understood.

"How have the mighty fallen, eh?" gasped the old vampire. "I can tell you're surprised — I don't need to use telepathy to know that."

"Jen said you were dying — but I really didn't believe him." Sonja moved closer, circling the thing in the wheelchair, trying to find the flaw in the disguise that would tell her it was all a trick. She couldn't find one.

Pangloss smirked and nodded his head. Sonja couldn't tell if it was in understanding or from a body tremor. 'Jen is a terrible liar. And he always tells the truth. You'd be wise to remember that, my dear." He fixed his eyes on the *dhampire* and for a fleeting second some of the old, self-assured Pangloss came back. "You've done what was asked of you, boy. My renfields have your pay voucher ready. Go now. I would speak with my granddaughter alone."

Jen sauntered out of the room, pausing long enough to give Sonja a wink before closing the door.

"You must forgive the boy," Pangloss wheezed. "His mother indulged him overmuch, out of guilt for placing him among strangers the first few years of his life. He fancies himself a *dhampire*. He is more than a little mad because of it — but is better at handling it than are the renfields. He rents himself out to humans as well as vampires, did he tell you that? His pain threshold is immense, and he can withstand tremendous amounts of physical punishment without undue side effects. He allows himself to be abused by humans with a taste for others' pain."

"I've been there," Sonja muttered.

"But enough about my half-bastard," Pangloss grimaced. "Oh, yes — I am the one responsible for his condition. Did he not tell you? The two of you are related, as our kind understand such things. I suspect you want to know why I sent you those news clippings."

"I know why you sent them — you wanted me to know where Morgan is so I can kill him and you can claim the glory and come off looking big with your bloodsuckin' buddies."

Pangloss's laughter was somewhere between a chuckle and a choke, and it made him double over. For a second Sonja was afraid he was going to cough up a lung. Resuming composure, Pangloss said, "My dear child, you have every reason to be suspicious of me — I've certainly done nothing to earn your trust in the past. But I am a changed man — or should I say vampire? The Pangloss you see before you is as different on the inside as he is on the outside."

He motioned feebly with one hand in the direction of the window. "Could you do me a favor, my dear? Could you push me over to the window? I would look at the night one last time."

Sonja grasped the handles of the wheelchair and pushed Pangloss toward the sliding glass door. She was surprised at how little he weighed.

"I know this is going to sound stupid," she said. "But how can you be dying? I mean — you're already dead."

"A good question. And not at all foolish. There are those who think that vampires — we who were first known as the *enkidu* — are immortal things. And, by human lights, we are. There are vampires who have continued for thousands of years. I myself have walked this earth since the fifth century A.D., before Clovis embraced the Christian god. But all things have their spans, even the living dead.

"Oh, the dead can be destroyed — of that you're well aware. We can be killed by damage to our brains or spinal cords — we can be burned to death — decapitated — or die from exposure to the sun or silver. However, we are impervious to the host of illnesses that thin the human herds, and age no longer affects us once we are resurrected. Indeed, we are immune to all diseases except one — the Ennui."

"You mean you're dying from *boredom?*"

"Wretched, isn't it? But this is the fate that awaits all vampires, once they have amassed the power and knowledge to transcend the nightly concerns of keeping themselves fed. What are brood wars but games of chess using animated pawns? Why do we tamper in human affairs, if not to keep things interesting? Once we have indulged our appetites, what is left for us? We have spent so much time and energy maintaining the semblance of life, we are loathe to admit that there is no reason behind any of it, beyond our inborn need to continue our existence.

"In each vampire's span there comes a time when ceaseless scheming, plotting, and manipulation lose their attraction. When that happens, we begin to question our motives — we begin to doubt whether our needs truly are as important as we once imagined them to be. That is when the Ennui sets in and we begin to die. That is what happened to me. I can trace the beginning of my fall to Rome, when you marked me with your knife. The wound you dealt me never truly healed...."

He opened his robe and pointed to the long, jagged scar in the middle of his chest. There were dozens, even hundreds, of pale, nearly invisible scars covering his body, ghostly souvenirs of past battles. Although Sonja knew the wound to which he pointed was nearly twenty years old, it still looked fresh. It was also the only part of him that looked genuinely alive.

"I have suffered far more grievous injuries in my existence. However, unlike those others, this one has refused to be dismissed. When I look at it I am reminded of how close I came to dying at your hand — and for what? I found myself musing over mortality and what, if anything, I have done in fifteen hundred years of walking this planet.

"I have known great men, both in the field of power and in the arts. I sat in the court of Charlemagne and watched it fall apart upon his death. I counseled popes and bishops and cardinals of every stripe. I watched the plagues sweep through the cities of Europe. I saw London burn three times. I have seen religions born, countries rise, kings fall. Da Vinci, Botticelli, Bosch, Voltaire, DaFoe, Moliere — they all knew me, in my various guises. Yet I had no real hand in anything that happened. I can claim no influence, except for when I used my manipulative powers to destroy a marriage or weaken a friendship. My role has never been that of a creator — only that of a parasite, feeding off human society's veins."

Pangloss's head was trembling so violently she was afraid it was going to snap off and land in his lap. "They dismiss me, you know. The other Nobles. They always have. Because I never took a title like 'baron' or 'count' or 'duke.' I called myself 'doctor.' I knew better than to lay claim to royalty. Once you do, they're on you like leeches, trying to bring you down. I didn't continue for fifteen hundred years out of dumb luck. They also think me a fool for not feeding on the stronger emotions — I preferred the petty jealousies and intrigues of art clichés and intellectual movements to the horror of concentration camps and reeducation centers.

"That idiot, Luxor, even had the audacity to insult me last time we met! No doubt he hoped to provoke me into declaring a brood war. Luxor is such a coward! And Nuit's no better! I've grown so weary of it all, Sonja — what is the point of continuing if I must spend the remainder of my nights dealing with jackanapes such as Luxor? I am so tired of it all…so very tired."

"But I still don't understand — if you have, as you say, lost interest in playing the game, then why did you send for me?"

Pangloss's lower lip trembled and Sonja was shocked to realize how much, at that moment, he reminded her of Jacob Thorne.

"Because I'm scared, Sonja. I'm scared of dying by myself. I want you to be with me when it happens."

*

She didn't know why she did it, but Sonja agreed to escort Pangloss to the necropolis.

There were several necropoli scattered throughout the great cities — and several of the once-great. They were sacred ground to all Pretenders, no matter their breed. Sonja knew New York possessed one such place, although she had no idea where it was located.

"It's accessible only through tunnels adjacent to the old subway system," Pangloss explained. "There is an access point in the basement of this apartment building. We can start from there."

It was clear from the way Pangloss' servants behaved that none of them liked the idea of their master heading for the Elephant's Graveyard. They were all very agitated and kept talking among themselves, eyeing Sonja cautiously. Sonja had never liked renfields. While they served a purpose, she'd never understood why vampires elected to surround themselves with servants who were nothing more than junkies. Renfields were addicted to vampires. They had an uncanny knack for tracking down the undead. Not to mention a taste for their own destruction. Almost all of them were sensitives of one sort or another, and all were heavily dependent on their masters for whatever it was that kept them going, be it drugs, sex, pain — or the semblance of sanity.

But now, watching them flutter about their dying master like moths around a fading light, Sonja finally began to understand. Vampires spent their existences doing nothing but taking from others — be it blood or the psychic energies of the living. Vampires are needful things. With their renfields they could experience, in a flawed fashion, what it was like to be needed.

"Please, master, I beg you to rethink what you're about to do," whispered the renfield who had greeted Sonja and Jen when they first exited the elevator. His voice was hoarse with unshed tears.

"There's no putting it off," Pangloss replied, levering himself out of his wheelchair. "I've gone too far to turn back now." He took a feeble step forward and nearly fell. Sonja reached out and grabbed his elbow, steadying him as best she could.

"But master — what of us? What will become of us once you're gone?"

"You'll be free to make your own ways in the world — just as you have all along," Pangloss sighed. "Come, Sonja — it's time to go."

There were two basements to the apartment building. The first one was clean and well lit and had recycling bins and a set of coin-operated washer-dryers for the tenants. The second basement was dark and damp and smelled of age and rat piss and could only be reached by a special elevator in the penthouse.

Sonja held Pangloss's elbow, helping him along as they wound their way through stacks of moldering newspapers and steamer trunks dating from the last century. He pointed at a narrow, low-set iron door. There were strange runes chiseled into the lintel, written in the brain-twisting script of the Pretender tongue. Pangloss produced a key from the pocket of his robe and handed it to her.

Sonja fit the key into the door and gave it a turn. The door swung open with a squeal, displacing enough cobwebs to rig a schooner. Sonja smelled old earth and stale water; in the distance she heard the rumble of subway cars. Pangloss's long, unkempt nails bit into the flesh of her upper arm, but he said nothing.

The tunnel that connected Pangloss's basement to the city's underground labyrinth of service tunnels and subway tracks was indeed old. It was shored with rotting timbers and lined with mammoth slabs of natural stone, Sonja was reminded of how the men who'd laid the foundations for the Brooklyn Bridge had labored hundreds of feet underwater, in little more than crude airlocks. To whoever had dug these tunnels, such working conditions would no doubt have seemed idyllic.

The entire tunnel suddenly shuddered, sending dirt and loose mortar drifting down from the decaying ceiling onto their heads. By Sonja's reckoning, they were directly under the Number Six line. Pangloss pointed at a set of stone steps, worn from the tread of countless feet, that led upward. The staircase was so tight and steep Sonja had to place Pangloss ahead of her and walk immediately behind him, her hands bracing his back and hips in case he lost his balance and fell. It was a slow, torturous climb, but finally they came to another old-fashioned iron door. Pangloss opened it, and they stepped out into the main lobby of Grand Central Station.

No one seemed to notice them leaving what looked to be a locked janitor's closet. Pangloss shuffled across the main concourse, leaning on Sonja for support. In the time since they had left his lair, he'd aged even more. His back was now completely bowed, his head dropped between his shoulders like a turtle's. Sonja was sure someone would notice them — no doubt one of the depot's employees would insist on providing a wheelchair for such an infirm old man. Then she realized that although people were looking right at them, no one saw them; they were walking between the cracks in human perception. Without her being aware of it, Pangloss had cast a glamour about them. The old vampire's body might be decaying, but it seemed his psychic abilities were as strong — if not stronger — than ever.

As they made their way onto one of the lower platforms, Pangloss suddenly teetered and collapsed onto one knee. No one seemed to notice. Sonja helped Pangloss back onto his feet, but she could tell his kneecap had dissolved.

"I'm afraid — you'll have to carry me — from here on —" he rasped. "I wanted to go to my death on my own two feet — but I fear I've left it too late—"

Sonja scooped him up into her arms. He weighed about as much as a bag of dead leaves. She was afraid to tighten her grip on him, for fear he would crumble in her hands like chalk.

Pangloss pointed to one of the tunnels and Sonja stepped off the platform onto the tracks below. The interior of the tunnel was lit by the occasional industrial-strength lightbulb set into the brake-man alcoves that lined the walls. The vaulted brick roof was black from decades of soot, and graffiti smeared the walls. There was rumbling from behind her and Sonja quickly sidestepped into one of the alcoves, watching the Amtrak train's lighted windows flash past. An old woman with cat's eye glasses gaped at them for a quarter of a heartbeat, then was gone.

After a few more yards, they came to what looked like a service tunnel. Pangloss motioned for Sonja to enter. Spent rubbers, broken syringes and empty Thunderbird bottles littered the ground. Pangloss reached out and pressed a brick in the wall. Sonja heard the sound of stone grating on stone, and then the side of the wall opened.

"Hurry," Pangloss whispered. "These tunnels are rife with homeless humans and other such detritus. They must not see the entrance — and live to tell of it."

Sonja slipped through the opening and the door pivoted back into place. They stood at the head of yet another set of ancient stone stairs corkscrewing into the earth. There was no light in the antechamber, nor was there evidence of there ever having been any. Still, Sonja's dark-adapted eyes could see perfectly well in the inky blackness. Unperturbed, she descended the stairs.

Pangloss plucked at his robe with long, yellowed talons, his voice as thin and fragile as a cobweb. "Did — did I ever tell you how much I loved him?"

"Loved who?"

"Morgan."

Sonja tensed at the mention of her Maker's name, the muscles going rigid in her arms. "I believe you mentioned it, the last time we met."

"I loved him so very, very much — more than any of the others. I'd had scores of lovers before him, and hundreds since — but he was the only one I loved as an equal. The only one I loved enough to make like myself. So we could be together forever. But he betrayed me, in the end. He left me to go off on his own. He said I was not an ambitious enough partner for his tastes. He planned great things for himself. He dreamt of raising a vampire army, loyal only to him, so that he might be the first of our kind to step from the shadows and rule the world of Man." Pangloss giggled, his body shivering with the effort. "Well, we know where his 'great plans' got him, don't we, my dear?

That's what he gets for trying to use science to meet his ends. Science is a human thing. Whenever the Pretending Kind try to use it, it turns in our hands, like an angry serpent. We are things outside nature, beyond reason — perhaps it senses we are not its true master."

"Science isn't a force unto itself, like the weather or magic," Sonja countered. "It's just — well, it's just science."

"That is what you think. But you're wrong. There are a lot of things that are wrong." Pangloss's voice had taken on the vague, querulous tone of the senile. "Did I tell you I loved him? Loved him better than any of the rest?"

"Yes. Yes, you did."

"I forgive him. I forgive him for leaving me. For betraying me. I hated him for a long, long time — longer than I loved him, actually. I hated him for at least five centuries. I've never hated anything or anyone that long. But I forgive him now. It's easier to forgive than hate. It doesn't use up quite so much energy. You should learn from that, child."

"I'm not the forgiving kind."

"Why are you carrying me, then?" Pangloss's eyes were no longer cloudy but clear and sharp, waiting for her reply. Just as quickly his gaze grew vague and his voice resumed its old man's timbre. "Whatever happened to that nice Palmer fellow? Are you two still together?"

"No. No, we split up."

"That's a shame. You looked so nice together."

Finally, after what seemed like a small eternity, they reached the bottom of the stairs.

Spanning outward, as far as the eye could see in every direction, was a mammoth underground labyrinth, the walls of the maze carved from the living rock itself. At the mouth of the necropolis was a huge iron gate. A pair of ogres, their flesh the same translucent white as cave-born lizards, guarded the portal. As Sonja moved forward, the bigger of the two — he stood nearly twelve feet tall — swiveled his wide, flat head in her direction. His eyes were blind lumps of jelly the color of oatmeal, but his hearing and sense of smell were evidently quite keen.

"Who go there?" it rumbled.

"I am Pangloss of the *enkidu*. I have come here to die."

The ogre sniffed the air and frowned. "You not alone. Who woman?"

"She is Sonja Blue, also of the *enkidu*. She is my companion."

The ogre held a brief conference with his fellow guard — a mere stripling at seven feet — then unlocked the gate, swinging it open as easily as a screen door. "Very well. Good journey, *enkidu*."

"Thank you, friend ogre," Pangloss replied.

The interior of the necropolis reminded Sonja of the catacombs of Rome, with their narrow stone corridors and burial niches. However, some of the niches in the labyrinth were large enough to accommodate giants, while others were no bigger than a child. All of the niches closest to the entrance were occupied. As they trudged through the maze, she stared at the collection of dead ogres, *nagas*, *kitsune*, *larvae* and other Pretender species.

Pangloss motioned for her to stop as they walked by the corpse of what had once been a woman, dressed in the rotting remains of Edwardian finery. Her face was that of an unwrapped mummy, the hair long since dissolved into dust. Pangloss stared at the dead vampiress for a long moment before speaking. His voice was dry and rasped in his throat.

"I always wondered what had become of her. It never occurred to me that she was dead."

"Did you know her?"

"In her time."

After wandering the labyrinth for what felt like a day and a night, they finally found an empty niche. Sonja carefully eased Pangloss into his final resting place, not terribly sure what to do next. The elder vampire stretched out on the narrow stone ledge. He sighed and smiled as if he were resting on the softest mattress in the world.

"This will do just fine," he said.

"Are you sure you're comfortable?"

"I am. But you don't seem to be."

"I guess I'm just not used to the idea of natural death. Not only for vampires, but for *anyone*. It's not something I've experienced that much of."

"Does it frighten you?"

"Not really. I just feel — awkward, I guess. What does dying feel like to you? Does it hurt?"

"Of course there is pain. But I have known much greater pain than this. No, what I feel isn't physical — it comes from somewhere besides the body. I feel — both empty and ready to explode. It's as if, after century upon century of taking the life-force of others, without ever giving in return, I am full to the brim. That's the funny thing about all this — even as my body wastes away from the Ennui, my psychic energies have yet to weaken. I simply have no interest in using them. It's as if I am feeding on myself, just as I once fed on others."

Pangloss reached out and took Sonja's hand in his own. His skin felt dry and flaky, like that of a snake shedding its skin. There was fear in his eyes, and sadness. "I'm afraid of what it will be like, Sonja. I'm afraid of what's beyond. I know what it's like to be dead. But what is there beyond unlife?

What happens when the dead die? I know that humans seem to have all kinds of options as to what happens to them in the After — but what about us? Do we go to heaven? Or do we go to hell? Or do we simply not go anywhere at all?"

"I don't know, Pangloss. I honestly don't."

Pangloss tightened his grip on her hand and motioned for Sonja to draw closer. "You have done me a great service, Sonja. Greater than I deserve. As payment for your kindness, I will tell you something of great value." Pangloss smiled at Sonja; his eyes were rolled up so far in his head that all she could see were bloodless veins. "He loves you, did you know that? He loves you like the moth loves the flame, like the mongoose adores the cobra. He—" Pangloss's voice trembled, then broke. "I'm so sorry, so sorry. It's all been for nothing, hasn't it? All the pain, all the death, all the intrigue — it means nothing."

To Sonja's amazement, actual tears leaked from the corner of Pangloss's eyes. The old vampire reached up and touched the wetness running down his face, looking confused. "What — what's this?"

"They're tears," Sonja whispered. "You're crying, Pangloss. You're actually crying."

"At last," Pangloss rasped. Then he died.

Within seconds, Pangloss's body seemed to cave in upon itself, as if someone had deflated a balloon. A burst of light the color of raw electricity shot out of the niche, zipping past Sonja's right ear and making the hair on her scalp tighten. She was so startled she stumbled backward and landed on her ass. A ball of St. Elmo's fire bounced back and forth among the walls of the labyrinth like a demented pinball; then, with a crackle of static, it shot straight up and disappeared.

It took her a minute to realize she was still holding Pangloss's hand, although it had snapped off at the wrist. Before she could react, it crumbled into chalk.

✸

Sonja resurfaced in Central Park. Dawn was creeping over the skyscrapers. She felt like she'd been pulled feetfirst through a knothole. She still wasn't sure what it all meant. As she strode through the park, she spied a homeless person rummaging through one of the garbage cans, in search of half-eaten pretzels and aluminum cans. It looked like every other homeless person on the streets of the city, dressed in castoffs scavenged from a dozen dumpsters, its shoes stuffed full of newspapers, a dirty stocking cap pulled over hair that hadn't seen washing in weeks, if not months. However, as Sonja drew closer, it looked up from what it was doing and transfixed her with pupil-less eyes the color of gold. *Seraph.*

Sonja paused and returned its stare. There was something familiar about this particular specimen, although she couldn't put her finger on it. It couldn't be its appearance, since they all looked generally alike. No, the sense of recognition was on a far more intangible level. Then she noticed how the *seraph's* head seemed to bob like a balloon on a string.

Pangloss.

Of course.

So *that's* where they came from! She should have figured it out for herself when Morgan's tampering with the vampire life-cycle produced a baby *seraph* instead of an infant bloodsucker!

After centuries of feeding on the misery of others, those vampires who could no longer bring themselves to feed on the living became *seraphim.* It kind of balanced out, once she thought about it.

After all, what is an angel but a demon yet to fall?

The Victoria Desert, Australia

It was a toss-up as to which was hotter — the sun under which he walked or the ground on which he walked. His skin hung in peeling tatters from his bare shoulders, pinker than boiled shrimp. His back felt as if he'd laid down on a white-hot barby grill, producing blisters the size of walnuts. How long had he been on walkabout? Three days? Four? How long could a man walk naked in the Northern Territory of Australia before dying of exposure and thirst? Two days? Three?

A month ago his name was Charlie Gower. He worked as a commercial artist in Canberra, designing logos for tinned meat and flavored chips. Then the advertising firm he worked for landed a state-sponsored job. Charlie wasn't too sure what the campaign was about — some kind of anniversary or something — but he was supposed to draw on ancient aboriginal designs for the campaign. So he found himself checking out books on *tjurunga*, the sacred object art of the aborigines. Charlie had never paid too much attention to native art before — being Australian, he spent most of his time in art school studying the Old Masters of Europe and the painters of English landscapes out of national insecurity. But the minute he laid eyes on the sinuous primitivism of the ancient Koori, as the aborigines called themselves before there were Englishmen to tell them otherwise, something changed inside Charlie Gower.

Fascinated by the artwork of these primitive nomadic tribes, Charlie began to look into the history of the peoples themselves — something rarely, if ever, mentioned in his schooling. And, to his surprise, he discovered he had aborigine blood in him.

His great-great grandfather, Jebediah Gower of London, had been arrested for stealing a coat and sent to Australia to serve his country and queen as convict labor. He'd been fifteen years old at the time of his arrest. He worked his way to freedom by the age of twenty-one and took an aborigine girl to wife. All Charlie could find out about her was that she had been of the Wurunjerri and Jebediah had renamed her Hannah. When he asked his Grandfather Gower about Jebediah and Hannah, the old man had been scandalized by the suggestion that his ancestors had been anything but good, upstanding white folk.

"Where'd you get this rubbish about your Great-Great bein' a convict and marryin' an abo?" Grandfather Gower demanded, all but spitting out his false teeth in disgust. "Jebediah Gower came over as a guard! And Hannah was white as you an' me!"

"I found it in the public record, Grandfather — they've got it all on microfiche now."

"Rubbish! Absolute rubbish!"

Charlie really didn't know what he'd expected to hear from his grandpa. Grandfather Gower's generation had been raised to be ashamed of its convict and aborigine heritage, and his parents weren't much better. His mother, a devout Christian, was exceptionally concerned over his interest in pagan art, fearing for his immortal soul. As far as Charlie was concerned, they were all overreacting. He had simply discovered a new hobby — one that allowed him a freedom of expression denied him by the commercial strictures of his job.

Charlie read of how the Koori called the time before the birth of Man the Dreamtime. At the dawn of time, beings of great power shaped the land and filled it with all the plants and animals that would ever be. After the beings of power died, they transformed their physical bodies into the stars and the rainbow and the mountains, and their spirits withdrew from the earth into the spiritual realm, where they Dreamed the world. However, the Dreaming Things retained their power over the physical realm, which they would continue to release as long as humans followed the Great and Secret Plan. But it was only through dreams that the living could commune with the spiritual realm of the Making Gods and gain strength from them. All of this was well and good, if you were an anthropology major, but Charlie didn't really think that much about it. Until one night, when he found himself in the Dreaming.

In his dream he was walking naked through a strange and hostile land, both beautiful and frightening in its inhospitality to man. As he walked under the beating sun he saw the Great Snakes Ungunel, Wanambi, and Aranda rise from their watery hiding places and stretch themselves until they filled the sky with their writhing, endless bodies. Mudungkala, the old blind woman who was mother to all mankind, crawled from the middle of the earth, clutching to her withered breasts the three babies that were the first human beings, and scolded him for being so slow.

"You best hurry up, Djabo, if you would be father to the new race."

"My name isn't Djabo — it's Charlie. Charlie Gower."

"Maybe that is the name you wear in the land of the white men," Mudungkala told him. "But in the Dreaming you are Djabo. And it's best not to keep your bride waiting, no matter what your name." The old woman pointed in the direction of the horizon. Charlie saw a beautiful woman in place of the sun, shining like she held a thousand stars in her belly. The Dream Woman opened her eyes and pinned Charlie with their golden stare. Then she spoke his name:

(Djabo.)

Her voice echoed in his head for several days as he tried to focus his attention on an advert for a beer company. He was supposed to be drawing a kangaroo with a six-pack of lager in its pouch in place of a joey. After he'd finished drawing the kangaroo, the clients told him they wanted the kangaroo to be wearing a bush hat because that would, somehow, "masculinize" the kangaroo and then no one could accuse them of encouraging pregnant mothers to drink beer. As the client's PR representative droned on about kangaroos with hats being more masculine than kangaroos without hats, Charlie Gower heard somebody call his name. Not his white name. His Dreaming name.

(Djabo.)

Charlie's eyes widened as they darted around the conference room, but he couldn't see anyone besides the usual suspects.

(Djabo. It's time to go walkabout.) the Dreamtime voice said.

And it was right. It *was* time to go walkabout.

Without saying a word, Charlie stood up from his chair and began taking off his tie. Everyone in the room fell silent and stared at him as if he'd just sawed off his right leg.

"Gower! What's the meaning of this—?" his boss blustered.

Charlie did not respond; instead he marched out of the conference room and headed for the elevator. He left his jacket lying on the street outside the office building he had worked in since graduating from university.

That was what? Three? Four days ago?

He'd walked along the highways until they turned into roads. Then he'd walked along the roads until they began trails. Then he'd walked along the trails until they became paths. And now he was climbing Ayers Rock, one of the biggest bloody rocks on the face of the earth. Not that he'd done it all on his own.

He'd had some help along the way, such as the elderly full-blooded Bindubi who had let him ride in the back of his beat-up old Land Rover for a hundred miles, or the shapeshifting *mura-mura* who, upon seeing how close to starvation and death from dehydration Charlie was, came dancing out of the shimmering heat with a length of cooked 'roo tail and an emu egg full of water. Sometimes the *mura-mura* looked like aborigines, sometimes they looked like kangaroo-headed humans, other times they had dingo heads. In any case, they'd proved fairly friendly.

He clawed his way up Ayers Rock like an insect, scraping the tips of his fingers away on its rough, red surface. All conscious thought, all identity besides that of Djabo continued to flake away with his burnt and peeling hide. And finally, after struggling for the better part of a day and a night, he finally made the summit and lay on his back, his face turned toward the sun, his arms and legs splayed to embrace the universe.

As he stared up at the punishing sky with the last of his scorched vision, he saw a piece of the sun break off and fall from the heavens. As the piece of sun got closer, he could make out arms and legs and a head. He smiled then, for he recognized the Dream Woman and knew he was not dreaming. The Dream Woman scooped him up in her golden arms and bore him into the sky, where she wrapped his scorched flesh in soft clouds and coaxed the honey of life from his loins with only the slightest movement of her own.

When Charlie Gower woke up, he found himself being tended to by a tribe of Ngaanatjara, several hundred miles south of the Ayers Rock. His skin was darker than a beetlenut, and there was what looked like tribal scarification on his face and belly. He wasn't sure if he'd done that to himself or if the Dream Woman was responsible. The first day he was in the Ngaanatjara camp he wondered how he was going to get back home to Canberra. On the second day he wondered if he still had a job, or if someone else was drawing hats on beer-packing kangaroos. On the third day he said to hell with it and declared Charlie Gower dead. From now on there was only Djabo, picture-maker and sorcerer to the Ngaanatjara. And that's who he remained for the rest of his life.

She's here.

Lords of the Outer Dark preserve me, she's here.

One of my operatives saw her the other day, prowling the streets of Chinatown, asking questions about Wretched Fly. Clever girl. Very clever. Seek out the master by tracing his servant. It will only be a matter of a day or two — if not hours — before she connects Wretched Fly with Kepa Hudei. Then my years of rehearsal will be behind me, and I will find myself faced with the real thing.

The question is: Am I ready? Am I ready to cast aside my proxies and step inside the tiger's cage? Why do I even ask myself such a question? Am I not Morgan, Lord of the Morning Star? In the past I would no more ponder such things than I would walk unprotected in daylight. But that was before our last meeting. She did more than permanently mark me — that alone was insult enough — but she took something from me as well. As we battled on the psychic combat field, in the Place Between Places, she absorbed a part of me shaped in the form of a chimera. By doing that, she gained a certain control over me. She made me love her.

It is not fair that I should find love now. I have prided myself on loving no one and nothing in seven hundred and fifty-three years. Love makes fools of even the shrewdest player — witness how it led Pangloss to the tragic mistake of making me his equal. I certainly never loved the loathsome old pervert, either as a human or a vampire. I tolerated his attentions for fear I would undergo the gelder's knife and sing *castrati* in Celestine IV's papal choir.

I have heard from reliable sources that Pangloss is dead — or close enough to it. The old fool finally succumbed to the Ennui. Good enough for him.

I have walked throughout my existence without fear of wounds, or capture, or slavery — for I have worn death as my armor. Nothing living could move my heart or stir me to more than the basest appetite. But now I find myself gazing into the eyes of Medusa, reflected back at me by my own shield, and I find myself smitten. It is not fair that I have found love, for I do not want it and it would destroy me if I give it half a chance.

She's here. She's finally, really here.

I can hardly wait.

— *from the journals of Sir Morgan, Lord of the Morning Star*

✹

Chinatown had proved a hard nut to crack, even for Sonja. All Asian communities are fiercely cliquish, but none moreso than New York's. *Low faan*, be they Anglo, black, or Hispanic, stick out like sore thumbs in its overcrowded streets. She could use her telepathic abilities only so far — most human minds were not designed to withstand intrusive scans. If she wasn't careful, their psyches could very well crumble like elaborate sugar confections, rendering them useless, both to her and themselves. Still, there were those who would always provide information — for a price.

There was nothing to distinguish the front of the Yankee-China Drugstore from any of the others on the block. The windows of the old herb pharmacy were so dusty that most passersby would automatically assume it was no longer in business. They would be wrong.

A little bell over the threshold rang as she entered the shop. Inside was dark and dusty, although she could make out the original fixtures from the middle of the last century. A twenty-foot-long gilded screen of chrysanthemums and grinning lions blocked the view into the back of the store. A couple of faded paper lanterns hung from the pressed tin ceiling. A long wooden counter with glass windows displayed mass-produced ceramic Buddhas and mah-jongg sets and even cheaper tea sets with poorly woven wicker handles. Everything was coated by a fine patina of dust.

A young Chinese man dressed in gray sweats stepped out from behind the screen that blocked access to the rest of the store. He looked hesitant, obviously unprepared for a *low faan* entering the establishment.

"I'm looking for Hu Tong of the *Junren Mao*."

The young man shook his head vigorously. "No here. No one that name here. You got wrong place maybe yes."

"Don't hand me that crap," Sonja snapped back in Cantonese. "Hu Tong has been operating out of this store for one hundred and thirty years, give or take a decade. Now go tell him he's got a customer!"

“Go back to work, Pei Lu” purred a deep masculine voice from behind the screen. “I shall see to our customer myself.”

Hu Tong, chieftain of the *Junren Mao*, stepped out from behind the gilded screen and fixed Sonja with his eyes of lambent green. It was hard to decide what was more impressive: his formal Mandarin dress, complete with elaborately embroidered dragon robe and peacock feather tassel; or the fact that he had the head of a tiger.

“Greetings, Hu Tong. It has been a long time since last we met.”

Hu Tong bowed his head slightly, his hands remaining tucked inside the sleeves of his *p'u-fu* jacket. “As humans estimate such things, it has indeed been many years. Six, is it not?”

“I am in dire need of information, Hu Tong.”

“Of course. Why else would you come to the chieftain of the Cat Soldiers? Certainly not to drink tea and gossip.”

“I'm looking for a man. A Chinese human. Late forties. He's missing his right eye. His name is Wretched Fly. He's a psychic — and a powerful one at that. He is a renfield in the service of a vampire called Morgan.”

Hu Tong removed his hands from his sleeves and picked up an abacus from behind the counter. His nails were over four inches long and tipped by protective gold sheaths that kept them from growing crooked. “I see. And how do you propose paying for such information — provided it is mine to give?”

Sonja produced a bundle wrapped in plain brown paper and twine. A wax seal the color of old blood, bearing the imperial mark of the Ch'ing Dynasty, was affixed to the top of the package. Hu Tong's ears moved toward the front of his head.

“This is the *yen hop* of Fu-Lin, first of the Manchurian emperors. It is yours.”

Hu Tong's claws tore through the paper and twine as easily as they would tissue paper, exposing a black lacquer box whose lid was inset with mother-of-pearl and fine jade in the shape of a peacock. With trembling fingers, he carefully placed the opium box's contents on the counter. The pipe was made of ivory with silver filigree and a golden mouthpiece. The bowl for the opium was made of gold, as were the dipping needle and the scissors for cutting the bricks into pills. Hu Tong regained his composure and bowed to show his appreciation.

“You honor me greatly, my friend. I am not certain, but I believe that the man you seek is of the Bot Fun Guey, the White Powder Ghosts. The Ghosts are a gang that deal largely in heroin and human cargo. Until recently, they were relatively small and inconsequential compared to the On Leong and Hip Sing tongs. But in the last year they've suddenly grown quite powerful in

Chinatown. They've branched out into smuggling humans into this country and gambling. They are known to be quite vicious in their dealings with others; furthermore, their leader, Kepa Hudei, is said to be a sorcerer. He is missing his right eye and wears a patch embroidered with a luck dragon."

Sonja smiled and returned Hu Tong's bow. "I thank you, Hu Tong. Perhaps someday soon we can sit and drink tea and gossip. But as of now I have much to do."

"Be careful, Sonja. The White Powder Ghosts are indeed fierce enemies."

"So am I."

✸

Wretched Fly sat with his back to a wall full of sharks and sipped a cup of fragrant tea. He chose the Black Lotus Restaurant as his headquarters because of the wall-length saltwater fish tank filled with dog sharks, blowfish, rays, jellyfish and other colorful, if far from pleasant, denizens of the deep. It helped his reputation as a *kiu ling*, a tong bigshot, to be seen in such impressive surroundings.

In the last year he'd turned the White Powder Ghosts from a gang of scruffy drug runners into a force to be reckoned with in Chinatown — and soon Taipei and Hong Kong.

Wretched Fly caught a glimpse of his reflection in the tank's glassy wall. Dressed in an exquisitely tailored sharkskin suit, equally expensive Italian shoes, his dark hair slicked back and his right eye covered by an embroidered black velvet patch, he looked like a boss right out of a Hong Kong gangster flick, an impression he worked hard to maintain. He also worked to continue the belief — spoken underground, never to his face or even aloud — that he was a black sorcerer.

Oh, that part was true enough, in its way. Wretched Fly — or Kepa Hudei, as he was known to the citizens of Chinatown — possessed powers beyond those of most men. He was descended from a long line of psychics born, so family legend had it, of a tryst between a peasant girl and a Shaolin master. His family had served the Chinese emperors from the days of Chu I-Chun of the Ming Dynasty until the death of the Dowager Empress at the turn of the twentieth century. Wretched Fly's forefathers had deliberately interbred, cultivating some of the finest psionic talents to be found in human stock. Unlike most sensitives, those of Wretched Fly's house were known for their comparative emotional and mental stability. Whether this had to do with genetics or the rigorous physical and mental training based on the teachings of that long-ago monk, not even Wretched Fly himself could say.

In any case, the minds of his fellow men were as transparent to him as the shark-wall of the Black Lotus — and filled with similar beasts. He could look at a man and know his hopes, his dreams, his plans, his schemes — even his deepest fears and darkest sins. And, if he did not like what he saw within the heads of those around him, he could reach out and crush them without lifting a finger. He'd done it twice — first to his thuggish predecessor, then again to a lieutenant he'd discovered working a deal with the Chinese Freemasons to overthrow him. Each time his victim collapsed to the floor, hemorrhaging from the eyes, ears and nose.

Of course, no one knew the truth behind the fiction of Kepa Hudei, not even the sweet-faced little wife he'd taken earlier that month. No one knew his true name — or that the feared crimelord served a master far more powerful than the Triad bosses in Hong Kong. Wretched Fly had set himself up as a bigshot in the underworld of Chinatown on orders from his one true master — Sir Morgan, Lord of the Morning Star.

Wretched Fly had been a servant of the vampire Noble for fifteen years, ever since Morgan had won him from his previous owner, a Mandarin vampire by the name Shou Xi. Wretched Fly was completely and utterly devoted to his master. There was nothing he would not do for him — nothing he had *not* done. He had even lost his eye in the service of his liege. If his master decreed that he should take control of a struggling gang and turn it into one of the most feared and powerful crime cartels in the city, then he would do that thing.

His master relished the combination of emotions generated by the smuggling of human cargo into the United States. On one hand there was the excitement and anticipation of arriving in the fabled "land of gold" — only to have it replaced by disillusionment once the new arrivals realized they were indentured to their smugglers for thirty thousand dollars and destined to be used as slave labor in restaurants and sweatshops. Their despair at ever earning their freedom was compounded by a paralyzing fear of the tongs. Morgan found this emotional melange — especially the curdled hope — quite exquisite. After all, vampires did not exist off blood alone. The more sophisticated ones, such as Morgan, required a psychic buffet to sate themselves.

Wretched Fly eyed the main dining room of the Black Lotus, automatically scanning everyone present as he did so. It was early evening, but the restaurant had yet to see any business. Not that it mattered. Wretched Fly paid the owner a handsome sum to keep the place open, thus satisfying his near-daily craving for steamed mussels in oyster sauce. The restaurant occupied the top floor of a business tower on the edge of Chinatown, not a stone's throw from the Tombs, and the only way in or out was via the elevator that faced the main dining room. Wretched Fly always made sure he faced the elevator.

This afternoon the only people in the restaurant besides the owner, his wife and the kitchen staff were Wretched Fly's bodyguards, Bing Yan and Zhong Ming. Both were young, energetic, stupid, and sadistic. No doubt they would go far in the gang. Out of habit, Wretched Fly scanned the minds of those around him. No one was thinking anything dangerous to him. And some, such as his bodyguards, were not even thinking at all. Good. That suited Wretched Fly just fine.

Then the elevator doors pinged open and a cloud of hate as thick as a swarm of angry hornets boiled into the room.

Sonja Blue stepped out of the elevator into the main dining room of the Black Lotus Restaurant. Despite the intense hatred radiating from her, her physical manner was quite nonchalant — almost insulting. Her hands were in the pockets of her leather jacket, her shoulders slumped. The owner of the restaurant, dressed in a suit and bowtie, stepped forward, smiling nervously and clutching a menu as if it were a shield.

"Yes? One for dinner? Smoking?"

Sonja shook her head and pointed at Wretched Fly. "No thanks. I'm here to see that man sitting over there."

The owner's smile faltered and his eyes flickered in the direction of Wretched Fly. "That not possible."

Sonja slid past the owner as if he didn't exist. Bing Yan and Zhong Ming moved to block her path. They were dressed in cheaper, less fashionable versions of their headman's suit, which did little to disguise the bulges made by their shoulder holsters. Bing Yan wore wrap-around sunglasses, while Zhong Ming chewed an ivory toothpick.

"You go now. This not your place," said Bing Yan, who was the more proficient in English. "You stay, you get hurt maybe yes."

Sonja stroked her chin and nodded to herself, as if weighing the wisdom of the thug's words. "You know — you've got a point there, buddy." She began to turn, as if she'd thought better of her actions. Bing Yan and Zhong Ming exchanged knowing smirks.

Sonja's fist caught Zhong Ming in the side of the head, sending the ivory toothpick in his mouth flying across the room, accompanied by a shower of teeth and blood. Bing Yan caught a spray of his friend's blood in the face and cried out in alarm and disgust, wiping at his eyes with one hand while going for his gun with the other. To his surprise, his holster was empty. Then he saw his gun in the hand of the strange woman.

"Lost something, laughing boy?" Sonja asked as she slammed the butt of the gun directly between Bing Yan's eyebrows, dropping him like an ox.

The owner's wife came out from behind the register, screaming hoarsely into her hands, her eyes starting from her head. The owner held her by the shoulders, his eyes fixed on Sonja. He was too frightened to be anything but concerned for his wife.

"Get out of here!" she told them. They stared at her, their English destroyed by their terror. She repeated herself, this time in Cantonese, and they bolted into the kitchen.

Zhong Ming was still crawling on the floor, spitting up pieces of molar and bicuspid like they were mah jongg tiles. As Sonja moved toward Wretched Fly's table he clawed frantically at his shoulder holster. The steel tip of Sonja's right boot caught him in the side, lifting him off the carpet and filling his lungs with broken ribs.

Wretched Fly did not stand to greet her, but nodded his head in acknowledgment. "So. We meet again, halfling."

"I see you remember me."

"One does not forget being maimed," he said, lifting a hand to caress the velvet of his eyepatch.

"You know why I'm here, Wretched Fly."

"I will not tell you where he is — even if he demanded it himself. But please, be seated, Ms. Blue—" He gestured to the chair opposite him.

Sonja sat down, never taking her eyes off him. "You would disobey him? You have changed, haven't you?"

"My loyalty is without end. It is because of this that I would keep you from him."

"You must not have much faith in your master's power if you fear a 'halfling' such as myself."

Wretched Fly's remaining eye flashed angrily. "You wounded my master. You ruined that which was without flaw. But I must share the blame — for if I had succeeded in killing you that night in San Francisco, my master would never have been harmed. My punishment for failing was being blinded."

"Let's get to it, then."

Wretched Fly placed his hands, palms downward, against the table. Sonja did the same. And the battle began.

✷

She was standing in the middle of a Chinese watercolor, the kind found on calendars. In the distance were hazy mountains, green blobs against a pale blue sky. There was the suggestion of a waterfall, the artful representation of bamboo — but none of it was real. It was a clever approximation of place — nothing more than stage dressing. Sonja knew that they were in the no-man's-land known as the Place Between Places — the limbo where all psychic battles were fought.

There was the sound of silk banners snapping in a high wind, and something hurtled down out of the painted sky, knocking her to her knees. A bolt of pain shot through her right arm, and Sonja stared at the hole ripped in the right sleeve of her leather jacket. Blood welled up from deep scratches scoring her flesh. Although she was not physically harmed, she knew all too well that wounds dealt and suffered during psychic combat were all too real, in their own way.

She looked up and saw her attacker framed against the sun, fluttering like a kite. An Oriental storm-dragon grinned down at her. Thunder clouds poured from its flared nostrils, giving the illusion that it was wearing mustaches. Its razor-sharp talons glistened with her blood.

The storm-dragon spoke to her, and its voice was that of Wretched Fly.

(You are strong, halfling. I give you that. But you lack finesse. You are like a child, destroying what it does not like. In this world, I am the one who is to be feared — not you!)

As if to prove the point, the storm-dragon went into a power dive, extending its claws like landing gear. Sonja tried to run, but it was no use — the dragon was too fast. It caught her from behind, snatching her up like a hawk would a rabbit. Wretched Fly's *imago* tightened its grip, sending talons deep into her belly and back. Sonja kicked and hammered her fists against the dragon's claws, coughing blood as she cursed Wretched Fly at the top of her lungs.

(It ends now. You have caused my master much trouble, halfling. With you dead, Morgan will be as he once was. His love will be mine, and mine alone, as is my right.)

Sonja opened her mouth and Wretched Fly wondered if she thought to beg for mercy. He hoped so. He would like it if she begged. But as her mouth continued to stretch, growing wider than it ever could in the world of flesh, he glimpsed three pairs of eyes staring at him from inside her. A three-headed tiger with the tail of a scorpion leapt from the vampire's mouth, roaring in angry chorus.

While Wretched Fly was expecting trickery, he was unprepared for the horrible rush of recognition that came when he saw the chimera. Although it had been vomited up by the halfling, the beast was Morgan's. It was more than a familiar of the vampire lord — it was an actual piece of him. And Wretched Fly had been conditioned from birth never to raise his hand against his master — no matter what the situation.

Sparks flew from the chimera's multiple mouths and its roar was that of swords striking shields. Wretched Fly screamed as the chimera's venomous tail delivered several stings to his dragon-body in rapid succession. The storm-dragon flickered, became transparent, revealing Wretched Fly coiled within its belly. The chimera pounced on the cowering psychic, sinking its fangs deep into his neck and worrying him as a farm cat would a field mouse

When it was finished, the chimera returned to Sonja and rubbed its left head against her thigh, purring like a bus left in low gear. Sonja stroked its middle head and wiped the blood from the right head's muzzle.

"Good kitties."

✸

When she opened her eyes she found Wretched Fly lying face down on the table, blood seeping from his ears, nose, and remaining eye. Wretched Fly had been a worthy opponent. She couldn't deny him that. And he had, indeed, proved himself loyal to his master. She still had no clue as to Morgan's whereabouts in the city. Abstractedly, she noticed that all the fish in the wall tank were dead or dying as well. She watched a two-foot-long dogfish thrash out its final agonies, then go still, drifting in the captive current. She pushed back her chair and stood on wobbly feet, scanning the room.

The owner stood framed in the door of the kitchen, watching her the way she imagined the first mammals must have watched the tyrannosaurs as they thundered by. He eased out from behind the swinging door that led to the kitchen, staring in horrified silence at the bodies littering his dining room. When he turned to look at Sonja, she fixed his mind in place as neatly as she would a butterfly with a hat pin.

"The On Leong did this," she told him in Cantonese. "Retaliation against the Bot Fun Guey for muscling in on their territory."

The owner nodded his head, his voice sounding as if it were coming from miles away. "Tong war. Such things happen all the time."

The owner blinked and shook his head to clear it. Horrible. So horrible. He hurried back into the kitchen to check on his wife and his cooks, who were hiding near the freezer unit. He needed to call 911 and report what had happened, but first he had to calm down his wife, who was babbling about a demon-woman with mirrors for eyes. His wife was not yet accustomed to the ways of the Americans. It wouldn't do to have her babbling about demons while the police were investigating a gang hit.

Jen sat astride one of the lions guarding the central branch of the New York Public Library on Fifth Avenue, grinning like a demented bareback rider. It was close to midnight and the library had long since closed its doors.

"I got your message, Jen. What do you want?"

"I heard about Wretched Fly. Impressive, milady. Truly impressive."

"So?"

Jen mock-pouted and leaned forward, resting his chin atop the lion's chiseled mane. "My, you *are* unsociable. You really must brush up on your small talk, milady. A little chit-chat now and again never hurts. Besides, I meant what I said. I'm genuinely impressed. I always found Wretched Fly a particularly loathsome specimen — always pretending he was better than the other renfields because he could control his telepathy without the benefit of drugs."

"Is there some point to this? Or did you summon me here simply to praise my disposal of a one-eyed psychic?"

Jen sighed, reached into his overcoat and pulled out a single, long-stemmed black rose and a sealed envelope, which he tossed at her feet. "I was told to deliver these to you."

"Is this Luxor's doing?"

"I have more than one employer — when it suits my needs," Jen replied, and without further comment jumped off the back of the lion and vanished into the surrounding night.

Sonja bent down and retrieved the rose and envelope. On closer inspection, she saw that the stem of the rose was made from braided strands of barbed wire and that the petals were fashioned of black velvet. The wax seal on the envelope bore the symbol of Fenris swallowing the Moon. Inside was a folded piece of parchment on which was written in a spidery hand: *Meet me at the Cherub Room.*

✷

The Cherub Room was a trendy nightspot just off Columbus Circle. It catered to the bridge-and-tunnel crowd that poured into the city each weekend in hopes of rubbing elbows with the rich and famous or, failing that, experiencing what would pass for decadence in Hackensack. The overall decor was that of leopardskin, pink vinyl, gold paint and winged babies. And lots of 'em. Pudgy little dead babies were everywhere: shouldering cornucopias with speakers hidden inside them, cuddling bunnies, holding aloft mirrors, peeing champagne into silver basins. Gilded baby dolls outfitted with cardboard wings hung from the ceiling. The overall feeling was not unlike being sealed alive inside a box of Valentine's Day chocolates.

The club was crowded and the music cranked up loud enough to render normal conversation impossible. Suspended over the dance floor were a couple of dancer cages, where young women and men dressed in silver lamé thongs and tinfoil halos gyrated to the techno beat.

Sonja was uncertain why Morgan would have chosen this place, of all the clubs in Manhattan, for their rendezvous. Maybe, she pondered, he was afraid of what she might do to him without witnesses.

She felt him the minute he entered the room. It was a strange sensation, as if someone had thrown a switch and completed a current, bringing long-dormant machinery humming to life. The hairs on the back of her neck prickled and her lungs felt suddenly heavy, as if the oxygen in the room had been miraculously transformed into mercury. The space between them ignited with the energy that exists between Maker and Made, Creator and Creation. It was as if they were two powerful magnets — both pulling and pushing against one another. Sonja scanned the room and saw him standing in the far corner, beside an oversized papier-mâché Cupid armed with an actual bow and arrow.

Although she knew she had marked him during their last confrontation, her mental image of Morgan was still that of the smiling, debonair *bon vivant* who had first swept Denise Thorne off her feet twenty-five years earlier. She was shocked to see the full extent of his wounding. The left side of his face was pulled into a permanent sneer, and the eye was as gray and sightless as a baked fish's. Where once his hair had been dark, now a shock of white sprouted from his left temple. He still wore an expensive and exquisitely tailored suit, which somehow glamorized his scars, turning mutilation into a fashion statement.

She waited for the expected surge of hate to fill her, but in its place was something else. She had hurt him. Humbled him. The snip of a girl he had tossed away like so much trash had left her mark on him, repaying him for dismissing her so callously. There was no rage inside her — only a grim sense of satisfaction and something that felt almost like — pity?

The thumping of the disco, the flashing of the lights, and the smell of sickly sweet mixed drinks reminded her of the night she'd first met him. The night a naive young heiress made the mistake of getting a little too drunk and allowing herself to be separated from her friends, then made the mistake of getting into a car with a strange man. She'd gone to the bar for a taste of the forbidden fruit of adulthood, only to find herself swept away on the wings of storybook romance.

She'd known the clumsy kisses of school friends, but Morgan was something else entirely. What he promised was true romance — the kind every woman dreams of. She was the ashpail princess and he the noble knight. When Morgan looked at her she felt so beautiful, so special.... And it had nothing to do with her daddy's millions, since he was rich himself. He loved her. Just her, and nothing else.

When he promised to treat her to a night unlike any other, she eagerly accompanied him into the back of his chauffeured Rolls. Where he raped her and drank her blood and threw her, naked and dying, onto the streets of London.

Sonja began moving in his direction, wondering with each step when the hate that had been her constant companion would boil forth, filling her guts with its familiar heat.

Morgan stiffened as she drew near, his leer belying the caution in his remaining eye. He nodded slightly, acknowledging her presence.

"I'm glad you're here."

Sonja sensed the chimera — the part of Morgan's self she had absorbed years ago — shift inside her head. It sensed its old master. She felt as if thousands of ants were crawling over her skin. She had to fight to keep from twitching and shaking like a junkie in need of a fix. Being so close to Morgan made her muscles vibrate like the cables on a suspension bridge in a high wind.

As if in response, the hate finally made its appearance, circling her brow like a crown of thorns, the weight of it digging through her skull and into her brain.

Kill him, whispered the Other, its voice urgent. *Kill him now and get it over with*. Sonja was amazed to feel fear surging through her vampiric half. She wiped at the cold sweat beading her upper lip. "I'm going to kill you, Morgan."

"You'll try. But not here." He gestured to the dance floor. "It's far too crowded to be discreet."

Screw discreet, nail him now. Nail him before he tries to call the chimera back.

"Why do you insist on fighting me, child?" Morgan's voice was mellifluous, the tone as soothing as a cool hand on a fevered brow.

"You know damn well why."

"You still consider your condition a curse? I gave you immortality — freedom from the ravages of old age and disease!"

"I didn't ask to be made into one of you. I didn't ask for any of this—"

Morgan arched an upswept brow. "Didn't you? There are those humans our kind hunt down as prey — and there are those who seek us out. You know that as well as I do, child. You responded eagerly to my seduction. I used no beguilement, no mind control."

"You can't blame me! You can't blame me for what happened!" she hissed.

Morgan's smile tried to be charming, but the scars twisted it into something else. "I'm not blaming *you*, child. After all, you are not the girl who followed me into the London night, are you? You are not Denise Thorne — but a creature of my seed, shaped in my image, born within her dead flesh."

"She never died."

"Then where is she now?"

Sonja blinked, uncertain of how to answer.

Stop playing word games and kill him! The Other's voice was close to hysteria. *He's playing with you — trying to lull you off guard! He's trying to throw a glamour over you!*

Morgan reached into his breast pocket and produced a small jeweler's case. "I realize now that what I did was wrong, horribly wrong. I don't mean turning you. That I do not regret. However I was a fool to throw away such an exquisite thing as you. I must have been deluded indeed to not recognize you for what you are—" He held the case out to her, flicking it open with his thumb. Lying on the red velvet interior was a crucifix made of sterling silver, fashioned to look like entwined thorns. "Please, I want you to take this as token of my shame — of my idiocy. What I did in London was a cruel and thoughtless thing. I was your sire and I turned my back on you. You have every right to hate me for bringing you into a world without pity. But I want to try to change that, my child."

Sonja stared at the crucifix and the length of black velvet ribbon that held it. Morgan's voice was thick and sweet in her ears, like honey dripping from the comb.

"What happened between Denise Thorne and me does not concern us, my pet. Let us begin our time together anew. You have avenged your outrage by marking me. Our scores are settled, wouldn't you agree?"

Sonja reached out as if in a trance. Her fingertips brushed the outside of the case.

Don't take it! Don't take anything he offers you!

She blinked rapidly, as if coming out of a trance, and drew back her hand. There was a look of displeasure on Morgan's face that he could not hide.

"What are you trying to pull?"

"Pull? I don't understand what you're getting at—" Morgan's good eye suddenly ceased its pretense at congeniality and began darting about. His shoulders tensed and he stood a little straighter, his body language that of a man who has suddenly realized he's in trouble.

"We have company, I fear."

Sonja followed his stare, scanning the room as she did. To her surprise, she spotted a half-dozen undead gradually making their way across the dance floor toward them. To the eyes of the humans nightclubbing it up, the intruders looked perfectly normal. No one seemed to notice their rotting flesh and decaying features, in any case.

"They're Luxor's brats," Morgan snarled. "That accursed half-bastard of Pangloss's must have told him I'd be here — but I never thought the hermaphrodite so bold!"

Sonja found herself standing shoulder to shoulder with Morgan, facing the approaching vampires. Part of her still wanted to slay Morgan and get it over with, but this sudden change in her game plan was forcing her to rethink her priorities.

"Maybe he thinks we've formed a truce — that we're teaming up against him?" she muttered.

Morgan nodded. "That makes sense. Luxor is nothing if not insecure."

The assembled vampires seemed to shudder, as if the air surrounding them had winked. They were shifting into overdrive. Sonja shifted as well, preparing to meet her attackers on their level. Fighting in high gear used up a lot of energy, but it was the only way she could hope to get out of the situation with her head still attached to her shoulders.

The frantically dancing clubgoers seemed to freeze in midstep, like the images on a videotape placed on still-frame. The strobes ceased their stutter, becoming spotlights, and the thumping bass of the disco transformed into a muffled heartbeat.

Luxor's brood surged forward, yowling like banshees. Sonja met the first one head-on, driving her switchblade into its chest. She glimpsed a moment of pain and confusion in the vampire's features before it folded around her fist like a punctured pool toy. Before she could pull the blade free, a vampiress dressed in '70s retro bell-bottoms and a macramé tube-top slammed into her, knocking her off her feet. Sonja rammed her palm into the vampiress's chin as she lunged to rip out Sonja's throat, snapping her lower jaw like a piece of celery. The vampiress shrieked her displeasure and tried to plunge a hooked thumbnail into Sonja's right eye. Sonja dodged the attack, biting off the vampiress's thumb and spitting it back into her face.

A vampire dressed in black leather pants joined the fray, kicking Sonja in the side of the head with a steel-toed Doc Marten. As he drew back his foot to deliver a second blow, Sonja snagged his bootlaces and yanked, jerking his feet out from under him. She scrambled back up, driving her elbow into the vampiress's gut. She snatched the hilt of the switchblade from the first vampire's rapidly decomposing chest, and it came away with a sucking sound. The retro-vampiress landed on Sonja's back, clawing at her face with three-inch long fingernails. Swearing under her breath, Sonja reversed her grip on the knife, ramming it into the creature's left eye. She yowled once and let go, dropping onto the floor to spasm like a hooked fish at her enemy's feet.

Morgan seemed to be holding his own ground with a lot less sweat. As Sonja watched, he plucked one of his attackers out of midair and, with a practiced turn of his hand, twisted the vampire's head completely around, so that it stared at Sonja from between its shoulders. The vampire's eyes blinked, more surprised than pained, then went gray. Morgan tossed the dead thing aside as casually as he would discard a broken toy.

Before Sonja could decide whether to aid him or join with his attackers, the leather-pants vampire was back on his feet, slamming his head into her gut like a billy goat. The force of his blow drove her into the wall, cracking the plaster. Sonja rammed the silver blade into the back of his neck, between the third and forth vertebrae. The vampire dropped, his body twitching and jerking as the silver toxins swept through his central nervous system.

Sonja looked up in time to see Morgan twist the head off the final member of Luxor's suicide party and hurl it in the direction of the packed dance floor. Despite everything, she really had to admire the guy's style.

Kill him.

She was tired. The battle had taken a lot out of her; it was becoming more and more of a struggle to remain in high gear. Assessing her condition, she could tell she'd sustained a skull fracture and four broken ribs — possibly a ruptured spleen. Nothing she couldn't handle, really. But there was no way she could possibly take down a vampire of Morgan's power right now. Part of her was even relieved that she would not be forced to act on what had, only minutes before, seemed the only sane thing to do.

Kill him.

She stood there, nursing her splintered ribs, and it suddenly occurred to her that it was the Other's voice, and not her own — or that of the vanished Denise — that was the most strident when it came to her obsession with Morgan. At first the three voices had been united — equally strong in their hatred, in their desire for revenge. But over the years Denise's voice had flagged, and now she discovered her own passion fading as well, leaving only the Other's disembodied voice.

Kill him or die, the Other growled. *Kill him or we're all doomed.*

"Shut up," she whispered. "I'll do it when I'm good and ready."

When she looked up again, Morgan was gone — but the jeweler's case he'd presented to her was lying on the ground at her feet, the thorny crucifix glinting up at her.

Silver. It was really silver. Considering the horror in which most vampires held the metal, it must have taken a great deal of courage on his part even to touch the case, much less carry it on his person. She found herself oddly touched by this show of bravery. She bent down and picked up the crucifix. He might be a murdering inhuman monster, but at least the guy had taste.

She grimaced as something deep inside her (the spleen?) began hemorrhaging. She had to get out of the club and drop back into human time if she wanted to keep out of the morgue. She would hate to wake up and find some coroner splitting her open like a Christmas goose.

She waited until she was out of the fire exit before slipping out of overdrive. Behind her rang a chorus of shrill screams as the vampire's head landed amid the dancers. The owners of the Cherub Room would no doubt have a hard time explaining to the cops what the hell six horribly mutilated — not to mention inexplicably decayed — corpses were doing in their club. Screw 'em. That's what they get for letting just anyone in.

✹

Why didn't I kill him?

He was standing right there. I could have killed him. It wouldn't have been easy — it wouldn't have been clean — but I could have done it. I could have at least *tried.*

But I didn't. And the funny thing is, I didn't even *want* to.

This wasn't like the first time I saw him after my transformation. Back then I'd wanted to kill his ass but good. But something in me short-circuited. There is a dominant-submissive switch that gets thrown whenever a broodling wants to destroy its sire. But it's not infallible. It takes willpower and determination to overcome it, but it can be done. But that's not what happened to me tonight. It's not like I couldn't move against him. I just looked at him and whatever was eating my belly simply disappeared.

Maybe it's because he doesn't *look* like Morgan anymore. He doesn't look like the Morgan of my nightmares. He doesn't look like the Morgan who killed my friends. He's — changed. I never believed such a thing was possible for vampires, but seeing Pangloss in his final hours has made me unsure. There's so much I still *don't* know about my kind — about the world in which we exist—

The only part of me that seems to be certain about Morgan is the Other. It wants him dead with lilies on his chest. But I can't figure out why. Morgan is a vampire. The Other is his creation. So why does it want to kill him? The Other is the part always eager to wreak havoc on those weaker than itself. The part that revels in hurting people. So why does it want to destroy Morgan, a creature that shares the same interests? I've spent my existence fighting the Other, trying to ignore its needs and desires. What should I do now?

Perhaps Morgan is right — perhaps it's time for me to put my vendetta aside. It no longer really concerns me. Do I want to turn into a pathetic, vengeful moron like Luxor? For immortals, the Nobles seem to be a particularly petty group, constantly warring with one another over perceived slights.

With everything that's happened lately — Judd, Palmer, Lethe, Pangloss — maybe I need to take some time out and reassess what's going on. I—

Shut up. Shut up.

I'm not going soft. I'm *not*. It's just that I'm tired. I'm so damn *tired*.

I need to think. Need to sort out what I'm feeling. What's important to me.

Bullshit!

I'm *not* falling in love with him! That's bullshit and you fucking well know — what do you mean it's *her* doing?

Denise is dead.

— *from the diaries of Sonja Blue*

✸

All in all, it went quite well. I could have done without Luxor's kamikaze squad, but in the end it worked to my advantage. It seems to have weakened her resolve against me. Good. It will make the seduction easier.

I have seduced thousands upon thousands of women over the centuries. Casanova was a rank amateur compared to me. There is little genius in coercing a woman to surrender her virtue. I, on the other hand, rob them of far more than their maidenheads. Oh, yes, they bleed — but in a far grander style. Yes, I have lured a legion of fair women to their dooms, but none were so deadly and so dangerous as my precious Sonja.

I must be careful that she does not scent the truth behind my motivations. She must believe that my affections are sincere. And, in part, that is the truth. I do love her.

I must confess I was proud of her tonight. The way she handled Luxor's dog soldiers was poetry in motion! She is indeed a prodigy. To think she's only twenty-five years old—! Most vampires don't attain such skill and self-possession until they're well into their first century! She is strong — like a samurai blade tempered in the forge of a master smith. No wonder Luxor feared that she and I might team up against him!

Together, no Noble would dare stand against us. She has never scuttled under rocks or into dumpsters to hide from the sun. But neither has she submitted to the will of another. That is why she must die.

If only there were another way. The thought of destroying her pains me, but not so much as loving her does. I can only hope my dress rehearsals have been successful in preparing me for what I must do.

This will not be easy for me. In fact, it may very well prove to be the hardest thing I've done since I broke free of Pangloss's fealty, five hundred years ago. Nor will I take pleasure in what I must do. Although she is the one who ruined my face, forcing me to walk the earth for the rest of my days as a sneering one-eyed freak, I will not rejoice when she is no more. She is the only thing I have ever loved, and I must kill her. I *have* to kill her. There can be no other end to this. I am Morgan, Lord of the Morning Star. I will be slave to nothing living or dead.

Not even love.

— *from the journals of Sir Morgan, Lord of the Morning Star*

✸

There was another barbed-wire rose, along with a parchment note, tacked to the refrigerator when she woke up. No doubt Jen's work again. However, judging by the bloodstains on the carpet and the crimson fingerprints on the wall, he hadn't been entirely lucky in dodging the booby-traps this time.

Sonja removed the note and read it, deciphering the spidery script that resembled both calligraphy and spirograph drawing — the secret language of the Pretenders.

Morgan wanted her to meet him on the top of the Empire State Building.

How romantic.

✸

The observation deck of the Empire State Building, the most famous once-tallest skyscraper in the world, was officially closed to the public. But nothing is off limits to creatures who can step between the cracks of perceived reality.

On street level the wind had not been particularly noteworthy, but one hundred and two stories above the sidewalk was a different matter. It grabbed at Sonja's clothes, tugging on them like a persistent child, while her hair fluttered about her skull. Even with the windbreaks and protective barriers designed to keep suicides from plummeting down onto Fifth Avenue, the strength of the elements could not be denied.

Morgan was waiting for her, balanced on one of the railings, his hands clasped behind his back, looking out over the city lights that lay spread before them like stars reflected in a still pond. The wind made his opera coat flap and snap like a banner. He spoke to her without bothering to look over his shoulder to see if she was there.

"I knew you would come. Do you still wish to kill me?"

"What else is there to do? I don't play cards."

Morgan laughed and turned to look at her, his twisted smile growing wider. "You *do* have a sense of humor, then?"

"About some things. You're not one of them, though."

He pointed at the thorny crucifix hanging from her neck. "You honor me. I take it you liked my little token of affection?"

Sonja shrugged. "I'm wearing it, aren't I?"

Morgan nodded and returned his gaze to the city. "It's beautiful, is it not?" he asked, gesturing with a sweeping movement of his left hand. "The city, I mean. It's alive, you know. Not like a human is alive. More like a simple one-celled organism or a sponge. Hundreds upon thousands upon millions of humans eating and drinking and shitting and fucking and dying in such a small physical space — their minds and life-forces united on a subconscious level, connecting them on a wavelength unacknowledged but not unfelt. Then again, perhaps a better metaphor might be that of a herd of cattle. Have you ever seen a stampede?"

"Only in the movies."

"It is a fearsome thing, even for creatures such as we. It is nothing more than Nature stripped bare, naked and unreasoning. The smallest thing can trigger a stampede — sometimes nothing at all. If the cattle are edgy, the slightest shift in air pressure can turn them from docile, cud-chewing cows into mindless, raging beasts. The effects can be as devastating as a tornado or an earthquake — and just as sudden. This city is like that. It is constantly on the brink of a stampede."

"You're not telling me anything I don't know."

"Am I? I'm sorry, I don't mean to be pedantic." Morgan pointed in the direction of the Lower East Side. "Right now a drunken stepfather, enraged by his wife's refusal to give him sex, is strangling her three-year-old son. He's going to put the boy's body in the incinerator chute of his housing block to avoid detection."

Morgan hopped down from his observation point and trotted to the opposite side of the deck, waving a hand in the direction of Central Park. "Police are still searching for the body of an eighteen-month-old child of tourists from Iowa, reported snatched from his stroller by a wild-eyed negro. In truth, the child was beaten to death three days ago by his parents and buried in a shallow grave in their backyard."

Spinning on his heel like a demented weather vane, Morgan dashed toward the southwest corner. "A balding closet queen of some political clout is chatting up a surlily handsome young man in a discreet piano bar in the West Village. The surly-looking young man has raped and killed eight older gay men over the last three years, chopping up their bodies and wrapping them in plastic garbage bags before tossing them out on lonely upstate highways."

Morgan swerved again, like a compass needle being drawn to magnetic north. "In Harlem there is a dark, stinking one-room apartment with no electricity, no running water, no heat, no furniture, no food. There are eight children, ranging from nine months to seven years old, locked in the apartment while their respective mothers and fathers sell themselves or each other for crack." He grabbed one of the pay telescopes mounted on the edge of the railing and swung from it like a child on a monkey bar, the delight in his face rendering his scars momentarily invisible. "God, I *love* this town."

Kill him, you stupid bitch! Don't stand there staring at him like a lovestruck cow — slit his throat from ear to ear!

Sonja bit her lip until the blood came. The Other's voice stung her like scorpions and whips, but she refused to act. She had spent so many years fighting its influence that resistance to its demands had become automatic.

"You seem troubled, my child — is something wrong?"

Morgan had levered himself back to the deck and was watching her. His good eye seemed concerned, but its damaged twin was what drew her attention. It had been a long time since she'd had to rely on simple physical cues to decipher another's thoughts and emotional state. There was no way she could easily tap into his mind — Morgan's skill at psionic cloaking was equal to her own.

"Why did you ask me to meet you here?"

"Because I wish to continue our conversation from last night, my dear. And this time I doubt we'll be interrupted quite so rudely."

"Nothing has changed between us, Morgan. I'm going to kill you, no matter what."

"If that's the case, why aren't you killing me now?"

"I-I just don't feel like it right now."

Morgan clucked his tongue at her. "Come now, child — don't insult me by telling me such a wretched lie. You may be an angry girl — but you're not *stupid*. You possess a rational brain, of that I've no doubt. Perhaps you've stayed your hand because you've realized that there is no longer any point to your vendetta?"

Sonja fixed him with an angry glare, but the sight of his dead eye made her look away. "What makes you think you know what's going through my head?"

"A parent knows its child — even a prodigal such as yourself. A current exists between us — do you not feel it? You and I are simpatico, far more than any get I've spawned. We are left hand and right hand, the tide and the shore, *yin* and *yang*. We are the same, you and I."

"I'm nothing like you!"

"Do you drink the blood of living things?"

"Yes."

"Have you ever taken pleasure from the pain and sufferings of others?"

"I—"

"Be truthful!"

"Yes, but they deserved—"

"Do you find humans blind and ignorant sheep, dragging the rest of creation with them on their mad dash to extinction?"

"Not all of them—"

"You are exactly like me! The one difference is that you still cling to the ghost of your humanity! You've somehow gotten it into your head that humans are to be pitied and envied instead of used. Why should you hold yourself to ideals that the vast majority of humans have discarded? Our kind do not create Evil. Humanity does that all on its own. We of the *enkidu* — and others of the Pretending races — merely manipulate human misdeeds to suit our needs. We did not invent the Nazi concentration camps, or the Russian gulags, or the Khmer Rouge killing fields, or the Serbian rape camps — but we would be fools to turn our backs on such fertile sources of — nourishment."

"I've never had anything to do with anything like that—"

"Haven't you? Then why do you prefer to spend your time in the inner city? It's not just a matter of camouflage. Don't you feel a high every time you prowl a ghetto neighborhood — the more crime-ridden the better? Does it make you feel more *alive* — more *alert* — to trawl for prey in the most hopeless sectors of town? Oh, I'm sure you tell yourself you're stalking those neighborhoods because that's where your prey is most likely to be. But there's more to it than that, isn't there? A lot more."

He was right. She'd never been willing to admit it to herself before, but now there was no denying it. It was like he knew her — knew her in a way no other had before. The intimacy was both disturbing and compelling.

"Do you know what it's like to be lonely, Sonja?" Morgan's voice was quiet but intensely personal, as if they were standing by a country lake inside of high atop a skyscraper. "Do you know what it's like to be surrounded by people but remain painfully, horribly *alone*? Do you fear that you might someday disappear into the emptiness that once held your heart?"

"Yes." Her voice was so small she wasn't even certain she'd actually said the word aloud. Perhaps she hadn't.

"You know nothing of loneliness," Morgan hissed, his voice suddenly growing hard and rusty. "You won't even have an *inkling* of what it's like for another century or two! To stand outside the flow of time and watch those you once called friends, confidants, and lovers wither away and die like leaves on a tree — knowing that no matter how many servants and consorts you surround yourself with, in the end you will always be alone. And the most horrible thing of all is that you will come to realize that you have no equal. No one will ever truly fulfill your needs, challenge your expectations, or understand what drives you.

"The humans who are drawn to our kind are far from worthy companions. They're attracted to our inhumanity — our monstrosity, if you will. They love us for what we are not, not for what we are. Even the brightest and most loyal renfield is little more than a pet. One that you will outlive and, in time, forget. How could it be otherwise?

"As the years bleed into decades, the decades lengthen into centuries — your attention span will become so vast you'll be bored by everything and everyone. Nothing will be new. No sight will be unseen. No act undone. Without diversions and stimulation, the Ennui will eventually claim you. Meddling in the affairs of humans provides us with a certain amount of stimulation, but even that wearies after awhile. That was why I spent so much time and energy trying to create my own breed of vampire. A desire to have my progeny rule the earth was a motivating factor, I'll admit to that. But mostly it was an attempt to keep myself — *involved;* to provide myself with new challenges.

"Of course, it failed horribly — largely because of your interference. I've realized in the years since then that my plans were foolish — perhaps even dangerous. Anise and Fell were made of weaker stuff than yourself — but they proved themselves stronger than I had imagined possible. And *that* is what prompted me to thinking — -that I have been surrounding myself with inferiors. All vampires do — we naturally fear those as strong as ourselves. In vampire society there are only two positions — slave and master. Not to be one is to be the other. We tend to ensure that our get will be subservient. We rarely infect those who show signs of the inner strength, intelligence and ambition that, in time, will result in Nobles. For a vampire to assert its will and claim its place in the hierarchy, it must break free of its Maker. And few of us are willing to pay for companionship with our very existence."

"You didn't kill Pangloss."

Morgan fell silent for a moment, his face unreadable. "Pangloss — did not need to be killed. When the time came, he recognized me as his better. He surrendered his control over me in exchange for his continued existence. As I said — ours is a society of masters and slaves. That is why, in the five hundred years since I threw off his yoke of obedience, Pangloss was never able to do me genuine harm."

"Perhaps it was because he loved you."

Morgan barked a humorless laugh.

"His last words were of you."

Morgan did not look surprised, but instead seemed to take it as his cue

"He's dead, then?"

"The Pangloss you knew no longer exists."

Morgan shrugged. "He no longer concerns me. What concerns me is you. I have found in you a strength unparalleled in others of my kind. You possess a freshness — a vitality — I find most invigorating. Perhaps it is your extreme youth, as the *enkidu* measure such things, that inspires me. But when I look at you, when I am with you, I feel as if the world has been remade anew and that I am its conqueror."

"What are you saying?"

"Only that I have had numerous brides in my past — but I have yet to take a queen." Morgan gestured to the winking lights that stretched as far as the eye could see. "We could rule the vampire and human worlds alike, you and I. With your immunity to silver and ability to travel during the daylight hours, we will be invincible. Every Noble would be forced to swear allegiance to us and submit to our will. We will be unstoppable. We will be *forever*."

"What makes you think I'll go along with it?"

"I don't. But what else have you to do? "

"I could kill you."

"And then what? Will you marry? Raise children? Prepare for retirement? Will killing me turn you back into Denise Thorne? Once I'm gone, what then will provide you with a reason for your existence? Will you continue mindlessly killing vampires simply because you have grown accustomed to it? Or will you succumb to the Ennui, as did Pangloss?

"You must cast aside your childish understanding of how the world works. *All* Nobles have blood vendettas against one another — but none of us truly wish the other's demise. Otherwise we would soon grow tired of the game and find ourselves withering away from boredom. You, on the other hand, are a genuine psychopath — killing the very thing that provides your reason for continuing.

"I blame myself, in part, for your madness — after all, if I had been there for you, schooling you in the nuances of Noble society, you wouldn't be as confused as you are now. Child, you have been acting on instinct out of ignorance and self-loathing — doing what comes naturally to our kind but without understanding the whys and wherefores of it all.

"Tell me the truth, Sonja — don't you grow weary of constantly battling with yourself? Don't you long to surrender the burden of conscience? Don't you grow weary of forever being on guard against losing control?"

Sonja's eyes seemed to look somewhere far away. "Yes," she whispered.

"Then cast away your hatred! Put aside your weapon! Embrace me as a queen would her king, and the struggle will be over! We were meant to be together, Sonja. Ignorance and fear have kept us apart for these many years

— but no longer! Do it, Sonja. Just do it."

His words were so soft. So sweet. So soothing. Some of what he said made no sense, but a lot of it hit home. Sonja felt something within her soften and begin to give way. She suddenly felt so tired. So very, very tired. All she wanted was to curl up and fall into a deep sleep.

The Other dug its fingers into her forebrain, shrieking and spitting like an enraged mountain lion. The pain that filled her head was so huge there was no way she could even scream.

Stupid cunt! He's reeling you in like a fish! Morgan's an expert at finding vulnerable spots and manipulating them to his advantage! All this sweet talk about 'queens' and 'equals' is nothing but bullshit! Vampires are either master or slaves! He said so himself! He's setting you up, girlfriend — and you're falling for it like the proverbial ton of bricks! Wake up, damn you! Wake up and kill him — kill him now!

Sonja staggered backward, away from Morgan, as another bolt of agony ripped through her gray matter. Purple-black stars exploded behind her eyelids.

Why are you doing this? Is it Palmer? Is it Lethe? Is this how you're trying to punish us for killing Judd? By letting Morgan turn you into one of his fuckin' get? If you think I'm gonna sit on the sidelines and let you do that, sister, you've got another thing coming!

Morgan struggled to hide his smile as Sonja spun away from his grasp, clawing at her temples and snarling like a wounded thing. A quick check of her aura revealed a spiky nimbus pulsing about her skull, alternating pulses of red and black. Morgan was reminded of sea snails battling one another. The only thing he'd ever seen like it was back in old Bedlam, when the gentry paid the Master of Lunacy to watch the madmen "at play." In any case, his little game had paid off. He'd succeeded in pitting the divided elements of Sonja's unstable personality against themselves.

Sonja doubled over and vomited a gout of brackish blood onto her boots. Morgan wrinkled his nose in distaste. The bottled stuff.

✹

Inside Sonja's head the scene was quite different from what was going on outside it. Sonja found herself floating in a great blue-black void. Although she was in her own mind, her *imago* — her self-image — was that of her physical body in every detail. She hung in midair, uncertain which was up or down. Not that it mattered. The blue-black nothingness folded in on itself, like a piece of paper being wadded up by a child, and just as rapidly *unfolded*.

She was standing on a vast, empty ice field. The wind howled like an angry thing in her ears. A huge, pockmarked moon climbed the starless sky, barely clearing the glaciers on the horizon. The ice gleamed darkly, like the carapace of an insect.

(Where are you, dammit?) she thought, honing her mind until it was a tight, hot beam, scouring the ice floe's surface like a laser sight. *(Answer me — where are you? You can't hide from me!)*

Suddenly the ice beneath her feet pushed *upward* and *outward*, sending her flying. She stared in amazement as the Other climbed forth. Although they had shared the same body, the same consciousness, for twenty-five years, Sonja had no idea what her vampiric self looked like. She hadn't *wanted* to know.

The Other looked like one of the hag-queens medieval parents had used to frighten their children into good behavior. Her skin was blue and her breasts hung flat and empty against her ribs. Her hands were like the grasping feet of a bird of prey, and her talons were as long and sharp as knives. Although her overall appearance was corpselike, her lips were obscenely full and seemed to writhe with a life of their own, exposing blackened gums and teeth better suited to an attack dog. She moved like an ape, her red eyes burning with an endless rage.

(I'm here.)

Sonja got to her feet and pressed the eye of her switchblade. The silver blade leapt out, glinting in the moonlight.

(Then let's dance, bitch.)

The Other dropped onto all fours and scuttled forward like a great scorpion, her joints bending at impossible angles. Sonja tracked as she circled her, shifting to keep the Other in front of her at all times. Part of her wondered if this was what the few humans capable of perceiving the Real World saw whenever they looked at her, and she shuddered in revulsion.

The Other used this momentary distraction to launch itself, its claws tearing at her midsection as its fangs strained for her throat. And then all conscious thought dissolved and there was only the need for survival.

✷

Morgan stepped back as Sonja dropped onto the floor of the observation deck, spasming in the grip of what looked to be a *grand mal* seizure. Foam flecked her lips and her limbs twitched as if someone were running powerful bursts of electric current through them. Morgan did not dare get any closer because she still held her switchblade tightly in one fist — and the blade was exposed.

The surges of psychic energy he'd seen earlier were stronger than before. Now there was sound as well as a light show. Squeals of psionic static ripped through his head like the scream of a dentist's drill. Morgan grimaced and placed his hands over his ears, even though he knew it would do no good.

He had almost decided against killing her, but this was definitely changing his mind. Anything capable of such anarchic energy release was far too dangerous for him to allow its continuance. He glanced up at the two hundred and twenty-two-foot television tower that jutted from the very top of the Empire State, stabbing the sky like a hypodermic needle. The very air around its tip was beginning to boil. Morgan licked his lips in anticipation. This was going to be good.

✷

The psychic membrane that bound the eight million minds that compose New York City shuddered and flexed in response to the psionic disturbance, triggering minor ripples in the gestalt. Or to follow Morgan's metaphor, the herd looked up and saw the lightning tearing holes in the sky and began to grow agitated without really knowing why. Something bad was coming.

Times Square

Ernest Tremouille paced his tiny studio apartment overlooking Times Square. He chewed his left thumbnail to the quick and continued gnawing until the blood came.

Lenox Avenue

The baby wouldn't stop crying. Normally it didn't bother Yolanda that much, but tonight it was really getting on her nerves. She wished her mother would come home from work soon so she could go out and hang with her friends. She thought having the baby would make her happy. She liked the idea of having something that had no choice but to love her. But now she wished she were still back in the eighth grade and able to go out when she felt like it. Little Rodrigo stood in his playpen and screamed as he rattled its bars. Yolanda turned the TV up as loud as it could go and pulled the kitchen chair so close her nose almost touched the tube. She put her hands over her ears and tried to shut out the sound of Rodrigo's angry, demanding cries.

Irving Place

Normally, Sam was fun to be around. More than fun. He was Cindy's one true love. They'd met at a friend's wedding nine months ago. She was the bridesmaid and he was working the bar. One thing led to another, and now they were sharing an apartment on the Upper East Side. All their friends envied their relationship.

"You two are so perfect for one another."

"We've never seen a couple so happy together."

Even strangers commented on the perfection of their romance. Sam was usually understanding and supportive and affectionate toward her. But tonight was proving to be a major exception. He was in a really foul mood for no reason, sitting in front of the TV and slamming down beers and not talking to her at all except to make hurtful comments about her weight and her taste in friends and clothes and her intelligence. Once or twice she caught him staring at her with this really weird look on his face. And as she stood in front of the kitchen sink, washing the dishes, she began to think about their relationship. Sam was a struggling actor. She worked for an investment firm. She was seven years older than Sam. They actually lived on her salary, since Sam waited tables in order to keep himself free for any work that might come in from his agent. Although they both worked eight-hour days, somehow she seemed to be the one to find the time to wash the dishes, handle the laundry, and clean the apartment. The more Cindy thought about it, the more unfair it seemed. The more *deliberate* it became. She wondered if he wasn't planning on dumping her for some cute young thing the moment he got a serious break in his career. She was fuming hard enough to blow smoke out her ears as she dumped the silverware into the soapy water.

The Church of Our Father the Redeemer

Father Ignatius closed his eyes and prayed for the visions to go away. Holy men are supposed to have visions, or so the Bible claims. But the visions that afflicted Father Ignatius were far from spiritual.

In his vision his mother is sitting in her chair near the window, fanning herself and looking down through the chintz curtains at the street below where they once lived in Hell's Kitchen. She's sweating and fanning. Sweating and fanning. Her dress is open, exposing her massive breasts. Sweating and fanning. Sweating and fanning. She stares out the window like he's not in the room. His mother hitches up her skirt over her hips and, without taking her eyes off the street outside her window, begins massaging the thing between her legs. The room smells of animals. She twitches a bit and moans, as if she's hurt herself. Then she looks directly at Father Ignatius and smiles, exposing bare gums. She's missing her upper plate. His mother is seventy-two years old.

✷

Sonja was straddling the Other, hammering its head into the black ice. The wind that blew across the frozen void shrieked wordlessly in her ears. She had never been so happy before in her life. Never before had she truly been able to let go of herself, to fight without restraint. It felt *good*, the same way a long-distance runner felt good once her body transcended simple exhaustion. It was a feeling of freedom, of being severed from time and place and identity. There was only the now of the act.

The Other snarled and slashed at her with its razored claws, ripping Sonja open from throat to crotch. It chuckled darkly as Sonja scrambled to shove her intestines back into her body.

(He's *planning to kill you. You realize that, don't you?)*

✷

Sonja's body bowed upward, the muscles straining until she was balanced on the top of her skull and the heels of her boots. The psychic feedback grew louder, causing Morgan to grit his teeth in pain. He had not expected such a dramatic reaction to his tampering. With a squeal of psionic reverb, dark energy leapt from Sonja's midsection, hitting the television aerial like a reverse lightning strike. The wound in the sky began to swell even further, as if filling with pus.

The wind was picking up, growing even stronger than before. Morgan moved closer to Sonja's prostrate form. As he reached out for her throat, there was a loud crackle, the smell of ozone, and a burst of black electricity. He drew back his hand, snarling in pain. The fingers of his right hand smelled like roasted pork. He'd forgotten about the damned silver crucifix he'd given her! He cursed under his breath and pulled the gun from the interior pocket of his opera cape. Normally he had no use for such crude weapons of destruction. He either killed with his mind or with the hands of others. But Sonja was a very special case.

He sighted down the barrel, aiming at her head.

Too bad it had to be this way. She might have provided him with centuries — perhaps millennia — of interesting duels. But she was too dangerous. He'd told her so himself. She refused to play by the rules. To her, vengeance was more than a game to while away the decades. She was sworn to destroy him and, sooner or later, she would do just that. But, worst of all, she tempted him. Tempted him to love. And to love is to be weak and to be weak is to be a slave. And that was something Morgan could never allow to happen. Ever.

"Farewell, my perfect love," he whispered, and pulled the trigger.

✷

Sonja reeled her guts back in and snapped her body cavity closed behind them, careful not to cut off her spleen or her liver. She kicked the Other squarely in the mouth, sending teeth flying like Chiclets.

(I've had all of you I can stand! I'm sick of hearing your fuckin' voice screeching inside my ear every damn day! You've ruined everything for me! Everything! And now it's time you paid!)

The Other wiped the blood from her mouth and grinned crookedly. *(You're a real ass, you know that? How about me — you think I've enjoyed being cooped up with a fuckin' goody two-shoes all this time? Always rolling around in self-pity, feeling sorry for yourself because you're a big bad monster? Go ahead — beat on me all you want! Kick me! Punch me! It won't make a damn bit of difference! You've already tried starving me out, but that didn't work either, did it? Face it, sweetmeat — I'm here and there's nothing you can do to get rid of me!)*

The entire ice field shuddered, as if shaken by a massive earthquake. Both Sonja and the Other looked at one another.

(Did you do that?)

(Fuck no!)

There was a cracking sound, as if the world's largest piece of celery were being snapped in two, and a fissure opened up between them. There was a roaring sound and the moon overhead shattered into a thousand silvery fragments. There was another, larger shudder and the chasm widened ever further, hurling the Other into darkness.

✷

The sky directly above the Empire State Building looked strange even to casual passersby. The clouds churning about its tip resembled blossoms of ink jetted forth by a frightened octopus. However, none of the nearby weather services had picked up signs of a disturbance on their radar screens. So everyone was at a loss to explain the thundercrack that shook every window in the city at ten minutes after midnight. But the mysterious thunder did far more than rattle windowpanes. It split the thin membrane of sanity that kept New York from chewing off its own leg like a coyote in a trap. And then, to put it politely, all hell broke loose.

✷

Cindy came out of the kitchen, trailing soapy water behind her. In one hand she clutched a carving knife. Sam was still watching the TV, his back to her. The nape of his neck was the only thing she could see. It was as if the rest of him didn't even exist. If she squinted her eyes a little, she could see the dotted line marked across it.

Ernest Tremouille heard the screams coming from outside his window and went to look. Screaming on the streets surrounding Times Square wasn't particularly rare, but the sheer volume and the sounds of crunching bumpers and smashing glass hinted at something besides the usual territorial dispute between hookers. Even as he leaned out his window, a cab jumped the curb and plowed into the pedestrians on the sidewalk. The driver was hunched over his steering wheel and grinning like a fiend as the cab scattered drug dealers, hookers, drag queens and tourists in every direction. A second cab slammed into a car with Jersey plates. The drivers got out and begin kicking and punching each other in the head and groin, shrieking like wild animals. A crowd gathered, their eyes too wide and their faces too empty to be human. The cabby grabbed the guy from Jersey and rammed his head through the windshield. As the cabby staggered back, blood and busted safety glass dripping from his hands, a Molotov cocktail sailed through the air, smashing against the front of the Papaya King stand across the street, spraying the crowd with burning gasoline. The air filled with screams and shouts of anger and the smell of burning hair and roasting flesh.

Ernest Tremouille had seen enough. He went to the closet where he kept his rifle. The End Times had arrived. The Tribulations had begun. And it was time for the Chosen to make their stand. He started out by sniping at the drag queens. They were the ones who disturbed him the most. He tracked one in particular with his scope — the one he gave twenty dollars to let him suck its dick a couple of months ago. Ernest had regretted the act the moment it was done. And it especially bothered him that the drag queen recognized him and called his name whenever he walked by. He screamed as he shot the drag queen. He screamed as he shot each and every one. He didn't know why. He was killing sinners, but it felt like he was shooting part of himself. When there were no more drag queens, he started in on the blacks.

Rodrigo wasn't crying anymore. The TV was still turned up real loud, but Yolanda didn't hear it. There was a lot of noise next door — sounded like a domestic argument. A real knock-down drag-out. Not that such things were rare. Yolanda decided it was time to take the garbage to the dumpster. She tossed an empty can of Ravioli-O's and a dirty diaper into the bag. She rammed her foot down on the refuse to make some more room. Rodrigo's hand popped up, the fingers already starting to stiffen. Yolanda told herself it was just a doll. Just a doll.

Father Ignatius counted his rosary and thanked God for taking away the visions. However, his prayer beads were wrapped around the neck of an elderly parishioner who reminded him of his mother. The smell of animals filled the confessional.

The streets of the city seethed with madness long contained and left to fester for years, even generations. Pedestrians knocked paper coffee cups from the hands of beggars, kicking them in the kidneys as they scrambled on their hands and knees to recover their scattered change. Firemen armed with axes battled any who tried to put out the blazing fire stations.

Policemen fired tear gas canisters point-blank at the heads of the rioters filling the street, while other officers waded into the crowd with nightsticks and drawn guns. After a few minutes the line between rioter and police dissolved, as the baton-wielding policemen began beating each other as well as the unruly populace.

The carriage horses at Central Park screamed and reared back on their hind legs, desperate to jump their traces, as swarms of hungry people boiled from the park's surrounding greenery, armed with rocks and sticks and appetite.

Windows smashed as looters climbed into Fifth Avenue storefronts to liberate merchandise. Waiters and busboys doused the patrons of five-star restaurants with alcohol and flame, turning them into living cherries jubilee and banana fosters. Nurses in neonatal wards went from incubator to incubator, disconnecting the life-support systems. Wild-eyed Hasidic men and women cried out to Mosiach and hurled cinderblocks from the roofs of their housing developments. Thousands of undocumented immigrants poured into the narrow streets of Chinatown, torching the sweatshops.

Gunfire crackled everywhere. Burning buildings dotted the city like candles on a cake. The screams of the hunted and the hunters filled the night. Manhattan and its surrounding boroughs tore at themselves, locked in a blind, claustrophobic frenzy, like the berserkers of old who whirled themselves into a killing rage by slashing themselves with their own knives. Those unaffected by the insanity huddled in fear and wondered if it was the end of the world — or just the end of New York? For some, there was no difference.

✸

Sonja struggled to regain her feet. The ice field was bucking and shaking like a wild animal, sending pillars of ice shooting upward. The sky overhead had changed from perpetual night to a pulsing aurora borealis. She had to get out of this rapidly disintegrating limbo and back into her physical body. Whatever was happening to her material self was obviously pretty major. But every time she tried to concentrate and take herself back into the material world, another shelf of ice shot upward, blocking her path.

She had to get a hold of herself. None of this was *real*. Not in the physical sense, anyway. She was inside her head, not trapped on an arctic glacier. All she had to do was open her eyes and she'd be free—

There was a sound like a cannon going off and the ground beneath her exploded in a shower of ice. Stunned, Sonja stared in mute horror as the Other emerged from its icy womb. It was huge — its head and shoulders blocking out the sky. The Other smiled and reached for her with a claw the size of a Buick.

Sis-s-ster, it growled. *We can never be safe until he who Made us is destroyed. So long as he exists, we will be weak. Join us, sister. Join us so that we might be reborn yet again.*

Morgan's ears were still ringing as he picked himself off the floor of the observation deck. There had been a flash and something like a clap of thunder the second after he fired the gun. He was lucky the force of the concussion hadn't sent him flying over the edge of the deck.

He got to his feet and staggered over to where Sonja's body lay sprawled. Curls of steam rose from her like a turkey fresh from the oven. He wanted to rejoice over the fall of an enemy who had cost him so dearly, but the laughter refused to come.

Then Sonja sat up.

Curse the instruments of Man's dominion! His aim had not been true! Instead of blowing her skull apart like an overripe cantaloupe, the bullet had grazed the right side of her head.

Although she was missing her right ear and a fist-sized patch of her skull now gleamed wetly for all to see, she was still very much alive.

"Morgan?"

He quickly returned the gun to his pocket and knelt beside her.

"I'm here, child. Are you all right? You fell into a seizure—?"

Sonja seemed dazed, as if waking from a drugged sleep. "You were right, milord," she whispered. The lenses of her sunglasses were cracked and she removed them with trembling hands. "I have allowed myself to be led astray by misplaced hatred. Your enemies have worked to turn me against you for their own ends. I would see them suffer in your name."

As Morgan helped her to her feet, she allowed her forehead to drop against his shoulder. Morgan struggled to keep his face from pulling into a triumphant sneer. All was not lost. If he could actually break her to his will, her death could still be avoided. But if the fire in her belly was extinguished, if she became just another of his adoring brides, then there would be no reason to love her. What provoked his passion was her deadliness, her ferocity, her *threat*. Part of him found the prospect of crushing her will and keeping the physical shell as a reminder of his victory rather appealing. Yet another side of him still hesitated.

Sonja's arms slid about his waist, pulling him closer. She looked up into his scarred face with eyes the color of blood. Eyes so very much like his own. "Hold me," she sighed. "I'm so very tired, milord. Please hold me."

"I will do so gladly — but only after you put aside your weapon."

Sonja glanced down at the switchblade she still clutched in her hand. Her fingernails had dug so deeply into the flesh of her palm that blood dripped from her finger. Her face contorting in disgust, Sonja hurled the silver knife away from her, sending it sailing over the edge of the observation deck into the night.

Morgan tightened his grip on her. She felt so soft, so vulnerable — it would be so easy to slide into her mind and crack open her ego like a rotten nut. He lowered his face and their lips brushed. She reached out hungrily for him, pulling him into a full embrace, her tongue searching for and finding his. And their minds met and were one.

✸

They were standing beside a meditation pool in a Japanese rock garden. Dappled *koi* swam just below the jade green surface, mouthing crumbs of bread. Morgan's *imago* wore the costume of a *shogun* of the Edo period. Sonja's *imago* was dressed as Sonja always was. Her black leather jacket creaked as she pinched off another handful of bread crumbs and tossed it into the pool.

Sonja looked up at Morgan and smiled. Her eyes were once more hidden behind slivers of mirrored glass, only now the lenses seemed to grow directly from her brow ridge and merge into her cheekbones. "Are you going to try to kill me now? Is that why you picked such a comforting mindscape? So I would be lulled into trusting you?"

Morgan shifted uncomfortably, the corner of his mouth jerking fitfully. The features belonging to his *imago* were whole, but he had grown accustomed to smiling with only half his face. "I don't know what you mean, my love. You are my queen — why should I kill you?"

Sonja shrugged and resumed feeding the goldfish. "I dunno. Because I'm dangerous? Because I'm a threat to your continuance? Because I trashed your plans for world domination? Because I fucked up your face? Because I killed your most trustworthy servant? Because I scare you? How about just because?"

“What if I tried to kill you? What would you do to stop me?”

“Nothing.”

“I don’t believe you.”

Sonja shrugged again. The piece of bread in her hands had yet to dwindle. “Believe what you like. But I won’t stop you. I’ll even give back your chimera. Assuming you still want it, that is.”

“Are you serious?”

“I’m not laughing, am I?” Sonja unzipped her jacket and reached inside the breast pocket, removing a small ivory statue. She dropped it onto the ground and the statue began to twitch and writhe, growing larger. Within seconds the three-headed tiger with the scorpion tail was standing beside her, lashing its barbed tail and growling.

Morgan reached out with one hand and the chimera began to melt and warp, like a chalk drawing caught in the rain, becoming a *yakuza*-style tattoo on his bare chest.

“There. You have your chimera back. I hope you’re happy. You can kill me now, if you like. I won’t stop you.”

He could tell she wasn’t lying. He stepped back and drew his samurai sword from its scabbard. Instead of being forged from steel, the blade was made of black volcanic glass. He drew back the sword as if he were readying to tee off. Sonja watched him placidly for a moment, then resumed feeding the fish.

The sword cut through her neck as easily as it did the air, sending her severed head arcing into the meditation pond. The body stood for a few seconds more, blood gouting from the stump like a fountain, before collapsing.

Morgan wiped her blood from the blade, marveling at the ease of it all, yet concerned by her failure to defend herself. After all, this was the woman who had wrested a part of his very self from him in combat and made it her own. He had expected *something* resembling a fight.

There was a thick, bubbling sound from the direction of the pool. Morgan glanced up in time to see the waters first turn red as blood, then black as ink. The *koi* bobbed to the surface, their gill slits straining as they gasped their last. The middle of the pool was aboil, as if an underwater geyser were about to erupt.

A female figure emerged from the heart of the pool, rising on the befouled water like Aphrodite from the foam. Her skin was black as polished night, her dark hair thick and wild, like the mane of a lion. Her teeth were white as pearl and curved into fearsome fangs, and her tongue was long and narrow, like that of a cat. She had four arms and in each hand she gripped an instrument of destruction: a shield, a sword, a noose, and a submachine gun. Around her neck was a garland of skulls and about her hips she wore a girdle of severed hands. When she turned her head, Morgan could see three faces: one was that of a virgin, the second that of a blue-skinned hag, and the third was Sonja's.

The black-skinned she-demon nodded to Morgan as if acknowledging a debt. When she spoke, all of her mouths moves in unison. "I thank you, father, for once more creating me anew. Before I was separate and unequal. Now I am whole."

Morgan wasn't sure what to make of the black-skinned demon-goddess that stood before him. Was she one of Sonja's tricks?

"Who are you? What are you doing with Sonja's face?"

As if in answer, the black-skinned demon-goddess brought her blade against the shield, making it ring like a gong. Morgan cried out and clutched his ears.

"Don't you know me, father? I am your death."

The demoness laughed then, her multitude of voices filling Morgan's skull. He watched, awestruck, as she began to grow, until she towered over him like a building.

"I am the Dark One! I am the Queen of Nightmares made flesh! And you made me, sweet father, as all children are made: out of ignorance and appetite. I am your daughter, Lord of the Morning Star, and your executioner."

Panicking, Morgan's *imago* cast aside its human form in favor of something more suitable for battle. His skin became mottled and scaly as his head widened and flattened itself. His arms and legs were rapidly absorbed by his torso as his body first doubled, then quadrupled in size and length, until he was the size of a city bus. Hissing his defiance, Morgan flared his hood and rose to challenge his enemy.

The demon-goddess laughed and began to dance, her four arms weaving in rhythmic patterns. Morgan reared back and spat a stream of venom at her eyes, but she blocked it with her shield.

"There is no denying me, sweet father, " she chided. "I am the Slayer of the Dead."

Morgan struck again, hoping to plunge his fangs into the she-demon's naked thigh, but she moved too fast, slipping her noose about his neck and yanking it tight. Morgan hissed and flailed, his body lashing back and forth like a bullwhip.

"I have been a long time being born, sweet father," the voices chorused. "And birthing is hungry work. I would feed now."

The she-demon carefully laid aside her weapons while keeping a firm grip on the head of the giant cobra. Morgan shrieked and hissed and struggled with all his might, but there was no escaping the noose. The dark-skinned destroyer licked her lips with her long red tongue, her eyes gleaming like polished skulls, and sank her fangs into the back of her captive's neck with a satisfying crunch.

✷

Any who might have seen them then would have mistaken them for lovers, locked in a passionate embrace. And, on some level, that would have been the truth. But if they looked closer, they would have seen the crackling sheath of purple-black energy that pulsed around the couple like St. Elmo's fire, and how the aura surrounding Morgan was beginning to stutter and pale, while Sonja's pulsed like a drum.

Sonja opened her eyes and found herself staring into the face of a dead thing. The illusion of life that Morgan had maintained for so many centuries had finally failed him. His skin was the color and texture of parchment. His once-dark hair was now white and patchy, like a dog with mange. His flesh had melted from his bones, leaving him little more than a dry husk, a pitiful scarecrow outfitted with fangs. Although he looked like an ancient mummy, his eyes still burned with stolen life.

"Enough," he wheezed. "Please—"

"No," she answered, her voice that of the black-skinned demon-goddess. "More. I need more. Give me the chimera. Give me your love."

Morgan raised a sticklike arm in a feeble attempt to stay her, but it did no good. Undeterred, Sonja sank her fangs into what was left of his throat. The vampire lord shrieked and dark fire burst from his eyes and ears as his brain spontaneously combusted. Sonja continued to feed, oblivious to how Morgan's limbs continued to wither and draw in on themselves, disappearing into sleeves and pantslegs. Only when there was no more to drain did she let him drop.

What was left of Morgan lay at her feet, surrounded by a mound of clothes. It looked something like a cross between a pickled monkey and a petrified fetus, the discolored skin pulled tight over brittle bones. Even though she had drained it of seven hundred and fifty-three years of stolen energy, the creature still clung to the pretense of life. It lifted its oversized head on its feeble stalk of a neck and looked around with blind eyes, its dry bones rattling like the limbs of a marionette.

"Forgive me," it piped.

She brought her bootheel down on its skull, shattering it like a lightbulb, and stepped over the pathetic remains of the thing that had created her and climbed onto the ledge of the observation deck. Her hands seethed with a black fire laced with tongues of crimson. The energy she had stolen from

Morgan coursed through her veins, filling her with euphoria.

Her body vibrated like a tuning fork, juiced on the ultimate high — the life-force stolen from the undead. Morgan's power surged through her body, amplified by the negative energy that hung over the city like a pall of smoke. She reached out and recalled the madness that had shaken the city. The wind was so strong now that the television tower groaned to itself like an old man. She grinned and stretched her arms upward, as if to embrace the stars. And she stepped off the ledge into empty air.

She called the winds to her and they came, bearing her aloft as if she were a leaf. She giggled in delight, like a child on a rollercoaster, and opened her arms wide, spiraling high into the night sky. She sped along, oblivious to the dazed and frightened populace trembling naked and bleeding in the streets below her. Those forced from their homes by fire found themselves gathering in the open parks, awaiting the arrival of the sun. Those who dared look up saw the silhouette of a woman streak across the sky, then quickly looked away.

Sonja shot upward, higher than the tallest buildings, like a skydiver in reverse. She was so jazzed on the energy pulsing through her she didn't care where she was going or who saw her. After years of ignorance and fear, she now knew the truth. She knew who she was. What she was. Tonight the last step in her creation had been reached. Her evolution was complete. She was the Angry One. The Shatterer. She Who Cannot Be Turned Aside. She was the Ultimate Predator: the vampire who feeds on vampires.

The Nightmare Queen began to sing her victory song, banging her sword against her shield as she danced on the body of her defeated foe. The faster she danced, the more intense the black fire surrounding Sonja's flesh became. Her ears were filled with the sound of drums and the clashing of swords and the ringing of bells. Flushed with victory and the exhilaration of birth, the newborn Destroyer touched down atop the World Trade Center and roared a challenge to the world.

✸

Deep within the bowels of the Black Grotto, Lady Nuit froze. The scalpel she'd been using to flay a stock analyst from Connecticut fell from her fingers and stuck, point-first, into the floor. The human chandeliers began to moan again.

"Shut those damned fools up!" Nuit snarled, her voice dipping lower as Luxor's features and testes slid from their hiding places. "I just got them to quiet down! I've had enough of their complaining tonight!"

"Yes, milord," said Jen, smiling behind his hand. "I'll see to it immediately."

✸

The buzz wore off while she was out over the Atlantic Ocean. One minute she was filled with enough energy to pulverize continents, the next she was riding on fumes. The first thought that ran through her mind was: *Wow, wotta rush!*

The second was: *What the fuck—? I can't fly!*

She plummeted from the sky like Wile E. Coyote suddenly realizing he'd run out of cliff, falling a hundred feet before hitting the water. She couldn't even see the land.

Six hours later, a beachcomber on Coney Island stared in amazement as a woman clothed in a leather jacket, jeans, and boots staggered out of the surf, a length of seaweed wrapped around her neck like a Hawaiian *lei*. Before he could react to the strange sight, a man appeared from out of nowhere and threw a blanket over her, hurrying her off the beach.

WHEN THE DEAD RETURN

"From fairyland she must have come
Or else she is a mermaiden,"
Some said she was a ghoul, and some
A heathen goddess born again.
— John Davidson, "A Ballad of a Nun"

It didn't take the jungle long to reclaim the house.

The porch is alive with creepers and other blooming vines. The hammock I once shared with Palmer is now a mildewed, tattered mess, hanging from the hooks in the rafters like a monstrous spiderweb. A couple of empty Tecate bottles lying on their side amid the litter wink at me darkly in the afternoon sunlight.

The front door is unlocked but the frame is badly warped from the heat and humidity, making it somewhat difficult to open. I inadvertently yank it off its hinges when I try to open it. Inside the house smells of mold, rising damp, and rotten garbage. Small lizards skitter out from underfoot as I go from room to room. Some of the windows are broken, allowing leaves and other detritus access to the house, but it looks as if no one has set foot in it since I left, months before. I'm not really surprised. The locals are exceptionally superstitious about matters dealing with *Señorita Azul.*

I step out into the courtyard. It looks desolate, with dead leaves collecting in the corners and weeds poking their rough heads among the tiles. The fountain no longer burbles to itself and the stagnant water has grown a scum of algae.

The back of the house is even more overgrown than the front. The rapidly encroaching jungle has swallowed Lethe's old swingset and monkey bars. A wild she-boar and her piglets burst from cover at my approach, fleeing in the direction of the forest. I follow them, but not with the intention of hunting.

The pig-path is still there, of course. It's been there for several hundred years, and it will be there for several hundred more. I climb to the top of the neighboring hill, where the ruins of the ancient Mayan observatory once stood. I dust off one of the tumbled limestone blocks and sit on it, lotus-fashion, and cast my mind into the jungle.

Hours later, as the sun begins to sink, I receive an answer to my summons in the form of a man emerging from the jungle.

He wears a jaguar skin draped over one shoulder and an unbleached linen loincloth. Jade earplugs stretch his lobes almost to his shoulders, and his lower lip boasts a similar ornament. Tattoos of Mayan sky-serpents and jaguar-gods swarm his naked torso and arms. His graying hair is pulled up into a warrior's topknot, adorned with the feathers of brightly colored parrots. In one hand he carries a machete, and across his back is slung an AK-47.

"Hello, Bill."

"I don't go by that name anymore," he replies. "I'm called *Chan Balam* now. Lord of Jaguars."

As he moves closer, I see that a disembodied hand rides his shoulder. It waggles two of its six fingers in my direction like antennae.

"I see you've still got Lefty with you."

Palmer allows himself to smile. "It would be hard to do without him. He's my good right hand. So to speak." The smile disappears as quickly as water on a hot griddle. "Why are you here, Sonja? Why did you come back?"

"Don't worry, I'm not here to try and force your return to my service, if that's what you're thinking. I just wanted to see you one last time, that's all. I wanted to tell you that everything's okay. I — I'm not the woman I once was."

Palmer frowns and squints at me, looking for things only he might see. He nods, and some of the tension drains from his face. "You are different. You're more — I don't know — *together*. It's as if the Other no longer exists."

"Oh, she's still here," I laugh, thumping my chest. "Just as Denise is still here. I guess you could say we've reached an understanding. Hard as it might be to believe, the Other actually saved my ass. Kept me from doing something really stupid. We no longer war among ourselves. What about you? Are you happy with your new life?"

"I've founded a guerrilla group, of sorts, composed largely of *campesinos* of Mayan descent. The government ridicules us in the media, but they're scared. They hunt us like animals, but they've yet to catch us. We keep our supplies and weapons hidden in the sacred *cenotes*. I guess you could say it's a back-to-Queztalcoatl movement." He shakes his head and I glimpse some of the old Palmer, the one I used to know. "I'm a pragmatic man. A reasonable man. You know that. But I had a dream not too long ago, and in it I saw the world change. It was fierce and frightening, but not hopeless. It was as if the world was being reborn, not destroyed. All I want is for my people to prepare themselves for that day, away from the madness and ugliness of the world that now exists. Sonja — am I crazy?"

"No. Just prescient."

There is a movement in the trees behind Palmer, but he does not seem alarmed. He glances over his shoulder and nods, then turns back to me.

"I must go. Farewell, Sonja. Please don't misunderstand me when I tell you this — but I hope we never meet again."

As Palmer slips back among the trees, I glimpse the figure that waits for him in their shadows. It is the girl, Concha. As she turns to go, I can see her belly is swollen with life.

✷

It is almost dark by the time I get back to the empty house. I pause for a second, then reenter the building. *One last walk through,* I tell herself. *Just for old times' sake.*

The bedroom I shared with Palmer smells like old jock straps. The sheets on the bed boast large blossoms of fungi. Rats and mice have chewed their way through Lethe's collection of stuffed animals. The kitchen reeks of rotten garbage and whatever was left in the refrigerator when Palmer moved out. Unopened invoices and bills of lading still sit atop the kitchen table. So does the black mask.

I pick up the mask and hold it so its impassive features are level with my own. Even though it has been left untouched for months, its surface still shines like a piece of polished onyx. I feel her presence before I see it, much the same way I'd been able to sense Morgan before he came into a room. Suddenly the darkened kitchen is filled with a golden light that pours in through the windows facing the courtyard.

(*Auntie Blue.*)

The voice in my head is Lethe's, but it isn't the voice of a child. Still holding the mask in one hand, I step out onto the patio, shielding my eyes against her brilliance with an upraised arm.

The light fades as if someone hit a dimmer switch, revealing a female figure at its heart. The woman is not the teenage beauty Palmer described to me, but a very, very old woman — her breasts hanging loose, her thighs and sex withered and wrinkled. I can hardly believe that this ancient crone is my three-year-old stepdaughter.

"Lethe?"

(Yes. I was Lethe.)

"What the hell happened to you?"

(I underwent a sea-change. As did yourself.)

"You know about—?"

(We are agents of change, you and I. True, we are fashioned for completely different tasks, but our goals are the same. You are the Destroyer, I am the Maker. You're the sickle, I am the seed.)

"That still doesn't explain why you're—"

(An old woman?)

"I wasn't going to be that blunt about it, but — well, yeah."

(Everything is creation and destruction. Death and rebirth. It has always been so. Such was the case before the rise of Man, before the reign of the great lizards and the Unnamed Ones before them. Things are built, things prosper, things are destroyed. And the time has come for things to change again.

(The last such change occurred several hundreds of thousands of years ago, when a particularly clever species of ape was given a boost up the evolutionary ladder. However, mankind was lead into a blind alley. You see, in the beginning all humans possessed what is called "sixth sense." Over the millennia, they have lost their awareness of the Real World, since it was in the interest of the enkidu and the vargr and other Pretending Ones to manipulate the breeding stock to ensure that they would remain in control. But by doing this, the scales of Nature were thrown horribly awry.

(Once stripped of its awareness, Mankind became more of a danger than any Pretender ever dreamed. At first Mankind flourished. Then it metastasized. It grew like a cancer, stripping the earth for its needs, stoking the very fires of destruction. Born blind and deaf, it cannot see the damage it does, the harm it inflicts. And, with every generation, it waltzes closer and closer to the brink of extinction — and with it, the destruction of the Real World. The time has come for the game to be set aright.

(For too long the enkidu have preyed upon the hearts and minds of Man. It is time for the playing field to be leveled. It is fitting, in its way, that by tampering with a system already out of balance, Morgan's dream of shaping a race in his own image would result in my creation.

(The universe is Positive and Negative. Give and Take. Chaos and Order. If there is too much of one element, then the center can no longer hold. The Natural and Supernatural Worlds spawned us — the first of our kind — in an attempt to set things right. You are the Destroyer, the one who must prepare the way by slaying the demons that would challenge the race to come. You are the midwife to the rebirth, making sure the way will be clear. And I am the Creatrix, the Madonna, the Magna Mater — mother to the new flesh.

(I have mated with twenty-five men, all of whom possessed the ability to see beyond. And I have borne twenty-five sons. Unlike myself, they shall live a normal mortal span. Each shall have the inner sight, to varying degrees. Some will be powerful psychics, others will merely have a knack for finding other people's car keys. All of them, however, will be aware. And, thanks to genetics and charisma, all twenty-five shall be highly attractive — at least as far as the females of the species are concerned. Should all twenty-five of my sons succeed in spawning four times each — and I doubt that will be a problem for them — and their descendants do likewise, within ten generations there will be twenty-six million of them. By the thirteenth there will be over one billion. By the fifteenth generation Homo Sapiens will be no more — there will only be Homo Mirablis.)

"Twenty-five? And Palmer—?"

(His was the first of my sons. The child has been adopted by the British Home Secretary and shall grow up in the seat of power.)

"You damn near broke Palmer's mind, using him for stud like that."

The old woman that had once been Lethe stares at me with flat, golden eyes as if I'd commented on the weather.

(His seed was needed.)

"Yeah, well, whatever."

(My time here is short. My corporeal self is deteriorating. Soon I will be without form, reduced to energy alone. I merely wished to see you—)

"For old times' sake?"

The old woman smiles, and for a second I glimpse my stepdaughter's face hidden within the sagging flesh and wrinkled skin. The light emanating from her begins to intensify, until she glows like a tiny star.

(They will need you to make them safe, as you made me safe. You are their midwife, as you were my own. Watch over my children, Sonja.)

"Like they were my own."

✹

Jen yawns and stretches behind the wheel of the Land Rover as I climb back inside. "About bloody time! I thought you'd never get back!"

"I ran into some old friends."

"Anyone I might know, milady?"

"No. And stop calling me 'milady.' My name's Sonja."

"As you wish, milady." Jen points to the mask I'm still holding in one hand. "What's that?"

I glanced down at the thing in my hands. The empty eyes stare up at me. I lift it to my face. The world I perceive from inside it is limited in its view and claustrophobic. I remove it and hurl it out the window.

"It's a mask. Something to hide behind and scare others with."

Jen turns the key in the ignition and the engine comes to life. "Where to next?"

I shrug and kick back in the passenger seat, resting my feet on the dash. "It's a big world out there, Jen. Surprise me."

"As you wish, milady."

—*from the diaries of Sonja Blue*

NANCY A. COLLINS BIO

Nancy A. Collins was born in 1959 and raised in rural Arkansas, where she lived until 1982, when she moved to New Orleans. In 1988 she sold her first novel, SUNGLASSES AFTER DARK. Her novels include TEMPTER (1990), IN THE BLOOD (1992), and WILD BLOOD (1993). She wrote for DC Comics' SWAMP THING series from 1991 to 1993. She has won the Horror Writers of America's Bram Stoker Award for First Novel, and the British Fantasy Society's Icarus Award. Her historical weird fantasy, WALKING WOLF, and the first installment of the comics adaptation of SUNGLASSES AFTER DARK are scheduled for early 1995. She is also serving as coeditor on two anthologies: FORBIDDEN ACTS and BLOOD LUST. Collins is a former member of the Horror Writers of America, the Science Fiction Writers of America, and the Girl Scouts of America. She remains a SubGenius hierarch of Hidden Rank and currently lives in New York City with her husband, underground filmmaker & anti-artiste Joe Christ. She is presumed to be armed and highly dangerous.